LAND OF THE AFTERNOON SUN

OTHER BOOKS *by* BARBARA WOOD

Rainbows on the Moon

The Serpent and the Staff

The Divining

Virgins of Paradise

The Dreaming

Green City in the Sun

This Golden Land

Soul Flame

Vital Signs

Domina

The Watch Gods

Childsong

Night Trains

Yesterday's Child

Curse This House

Hounds and Jackals

BOOKS *by* KATHRYN HARVEY

Butterfly

Stars

Private Entrance

LAND

of the

AFTERNOON SUN

A NOVEL

Barbara Wood

TURNER

Turner Publishing Company
Nashville, Tennessee
New York, New York

www.turnerpublishing.com

Land of the Afternoon Sun, A Novel

This is a work of fiction. All the characters and events portrayed in this book are
either products of the author's imagination or are used fictitiously.

Cover design: Maddie Cothren
Book design: Glen Edelstein

Library of Congress Cataloging-in-Publication Data

Names: Wood, Barbara, 1947- author.
Title: Land of the afternoon sun / by Barbara Wood.
Description: Nashville, Tennessee : Turner Publishing Company, [2016]
Identifiers: LCCN 2015044729| ISBN 9781681623887 (softcover) | ISBN
  9781681623849 (hardcover)
Subjects: LCSH: Married people--Fiction. | Self-realization in
  women--Fiction. | Palm Springs (Calif.)--Fiction. | GSAFD: Romantic
  suspense fiction.
Classification: LCC PS3573.O5877 L36 2016 | DDC 813/.54--dc23
LC record available at http://lccn.loc.gov/2015044729

[9781681623849]

Printed in the United States of America
15 14 13 12 11 10 9 8 7 6 5 4 3 2 1

For my husband Walt,
with all my love.

LAND OF THE AFTERNOON SUN

PROLOGUE

Palm Springs, California
The time of the snowmelt, 1920

FAR UP MESQUITE CANYON, beyond the pools of mists and rainbows, deep in the shadows of towering fan palms and cottonwood trees and along a rushing creek where Indians had drawn sweet water for thousands of years, a lone woman worked at her labors.

She was what her people called a *pul*, a shaman, and she was a member of the Cahuilla tribe in the Coachella Valley of Southern California. The white men had told her she was born in the year 1860, before the railroad tore the valley in half. Her Indian name was Nesha, which in the Cahuilla language meant "woman of mystery." Not that she herself was mysterious. Luisa knew they had named her Nesha because she would spend her life interpreting mysteries. But when she was little, the Catholic priests came out from the San Gabriel Mission in Los Angeles to baptize her. They changed her name to Luisa. When she was fifteen, she married José Padilla, and she gave him many children, some of whom survived.

José was no longer alive. He got killed when he fell from the top of a very tall palm tree while stealing dates.

Today she was harvesting reeds her people called *pa'ul*, but which the white man called bulrushes. She prayed as she gathered the tall green stems and tied them together in a bundle to carry on her back. She asked the spirits of the plants to bless her hands and her work—it was going to be a sacred basket, and she had yet to determine its pattern.

Luisa chanted softly as she harvested the rushes. "*Meyáwicheqa núkatmi pálpiyik me chéngeneqa, núkatmi; ívim pen metétewangeqa, pen mekwákwaniqa' men me' í'isneqa ívim.*" It was the story of how, when people and animals were first brought into the world, the moon goddess gathered all the Created Ones and took them to the water where she painted them. This was why birds and snakes and lizards and wild cats and insects were so brightly colored and covered in eye-pleasing patterns. Everything in the desert had a design that was painted on it by the moon goddess, which was why the desert was the most beautiful place on earth.

As she moved along the creek, she came upon a wild almond tree that she had not known was there. Ever since white men brought this nut tree to the valley, the seeds had been carried by wind and birds, to grow here and there in special, hidden places. Luisa smiled. The tree was covered entirely with pink flowers, which meant it produced sweet almonds; those trees with flowers that were almost white at the tip of the petals and were red at the base produced bitter almonds. The green nuts, she saw, were nearly ripe. She would return with a basket and harvest them. Then she would crush the nuts and store them in a warm container to allow the oil to rise.

Her people made many uses of almond oil, but Luisa had a particular one in mind. The oil created a lubricant for lovemaking. In her own experience, no man could resist a woman who had bathed her soft *t'pili* in sweet almond oil. Nice for the woman, too, when her husband's stiff *húyal* was slippery with oil.

When she heard a bird chirping on a nearby bush, she paused to listen. Luisa was her clan's spirit-reader, receiving messages from the spirit world in times of danger and strife. She most often received spirit-messages when she was working, for that was when her mind was clearest and she was most receptive to communications from the other world.

The bird was telling her about a sunrise. Luisa saw clearly in her mind the eastern horizon, the golden cresting of the sun, while overhead and in the west, stars still shone. The sharper the message, the more important it was. Luisa had learned this over the years. Clear messages came to her when the spirits were anxious. It was their way of shouting. And so, because of its clarity, its depth of color and detail, she knew that the vision of the sunrise was important. Perhaps urgent.

Something was going to happen at a sunrise.

"Is it going to happen soon?" she said to the small brown-and-yellow bird.

She listened to his voice. He was repeating his message. So, a very important message.

Cautiously, she stepped closer. When she heard a hissing sound, she stopped and looked around. There, amid a clump of flowering cactus, lay Mésax, the red diamond rattlesnake. She watched him. Listened. The wind whispered past her ears and spoke in the palm fronds overhead. She looked up. The tips of the green fronds caught sparks of sunlight. Beyond, the sky was deep and blue and stretched to eternity.

Luisa looked at the snake. He was big, a grandfather, with a pattern of red diamonds on his fat back. He was not coiled to strike. His black, beady eye was fixed on her.

She listened.

A storm is coming . . .

"Aii, Mukat," she whispered. "From which direction?" she asked.

From the East. The storm comes by train . . .

She clutched the long reeds against her bosom. White people were coming. Dangerous white people.

"Is the white man coming at sunrise?"

No . . .

"What is happening at sunrise?"

Not the white man, not the storm . . .

Luisa frowned, and then she realized that she had received two separate messages.

"Aii!" she said out loud. Rarely did the spirits confuse her this way; rarely did they compete for her attention. But now two spirits had spoken, two had portended events to come, and Luisa only understood the second. The meaning of the first message was lost to her.

"What must I do?"

The new white people will walk on the sacred places. They will walk on the forbidden places. They must be stopped. Hurry back to the village and warn your clan. The snake blinked his dark, beady eye and then uncoiled his long, fat body and slowly slithered away.

"But what will happen at sunrise?" She looked for the brown-and-yellow bird. But it was gone.

Quickly gathering up her bundles of pa'ul, Luisa started back down the ancient trail that led to her home at the base of the canyon. Her heart raced with fear. But she was thankful to Mésax for his warning. She would weave her new basket in his honor; she would weave the red diamond rattlesnake pattern.

A storm! Her clan always worried about storms. Clouds remained hidden behind the mountain, wreaking havoc on the summits, unseen by people below. And then the rumbling would come, and a great churning wall of water that would sweep away their village and any people who did not scramble to higher ground.

That was why Luisa's position of spirit-reader was so important to the tribe. Her job as a spirit shaman literally meant life or death.

And now she had received the message that evil was coming to the valley. It was coming by train . . .

PART ONE
1920

CHAPTER ONE

Stullwood Hall, Derbyshire, England

1920

THE STALLION RACED ACROSS the emerald green grounds of Stullwood Estate, great thundering hooves kicking up dirt clods and clumps of grass.

The horse was a bright bay whose name was Blaze because a white blaze covered the whole bridge of his nose, from forehead to the nostrils. His rider, wearing boots, jodhpurs, and a tweed riding jacket, was the heir to Stullwood. Twenty-four-year-old Nigel Barnstable, famously handsome and athletic, was soon to be one of the richest men in Britain.

As he rode his horse furiously, in a lather of high excitement, Nigel's skin felt tight, as if he were too big for his body. He remembered feeling this way as a boy growing up, that he was too big for his skin. He remembered exploring Stullwood Hall as if he were an adventurer in Africa, finding room after room filled with treasure and his mother asking his father where the boy's energy came from. Nigel Barnstable had been born restless. He had even come into the world three weeks early, squirming and waving his fists and eager to get on with things, and he hadn't stopped squirming and waving his fists over two decades later as his horse ran flat out, its wind holding. The stallion was used to its master's whims, his speeds, his need to get somewhere else before he had even passed somewhere here. Mount and rider were perfectly matched, the horse being high spirited even in its stall, where it pranced and snorted impatiently. Neither could keep still. Impatience was their shared trait.

But this time, for once, Nigel really was in a hurry. The solicitor was due to arrive at any moment and then the will would be read, and Nigel would officially move up to become the ninth Baron Stullwood. Every single one of these one thousand acres, with its farms and tenants and holdings, and even the village of Stullwood, plus the house that was like a palace, and the horses and hundreds of people who worked the estate, and the millions in the bank—it would all be his.

Upon receiving news of his father's death, while Nigel had respectfully mourned the old man's passing, he had felt new ambitions begin to bubble inside him, effervescing like good champagne. When his older brother died at the Front, fighting in the war, Nigel had still thought the old man would come home. It seemed nothing was going to cut the indomitable Baron down, not even a war meant to end all wars. And so Nigel had not thought of himself as being the next Baron Stullwood quite so soon, not for years in fact, as the old man was vigorous, robust, and given to healthy living.

But then his father had been shipped back to England with severe wounds, to be laid up in a military hospital in the touch-and-go world that hovered between life and death. Even then, when he had gone down to London to visit the old man, Nigel had thought he was going to pull through.

But the Spanish flu that had claimed millions of lives around the world took the old Baron, and Nigel suddenly found himself with the most splendid inheritance on his hands.

Which was why he had spent the morning inspecting the estate's deer park—an enclosed wooded area bounded by a ditch and a stone wall. Deer "leaps," composed of external ramps and inner ditches, had been constructed long ago, allowing deer to enter the park but preventing them from leaving. Unfortunately, because of the war, the deer park had fallen into neglect, which Nigel intended to rectify as soon as possible.

As he neared the stables, he saw that the solicitor had not yet arrived. He reined the horse and jumped down. "Give him a good rub down, Mac," he said as he handed Blaze over to the groom.

"Aye, Your Lordship."

Knocking the mud off his boots, Nigel entered the house and pulled at his gloves, dropping them on a mirrored table in the hall. A maid appeared to take his tweed riding jacket, leaving Nigel in jodhpurs and a white tailored silk shirt. She dropped him a quick curtsy, a shy smile, and hurried away. Nigel caught the rose blush in her cheeks. He was aware of his handsomeness; aware of his effect on women. But he wasn't conceited about it. Good looks were something he had simply been born with, along with abundantly thick, wavy hair and a smile that both dazzled and invited.

He strode into the salon where Grandmother and his younger brother, Rupert, were waiting. The weather chose to break at that moment, and rain began to pelt the centuries-old mullioned windows. "It's starting to come down," he said as he strode to the drinks cart and poured himself a small whiskey. "I hope Radcliffe doesn't get caught out in that." Radcliffe, the solicitor, bringing the old man's will. Nigel downed the drink in one swallow. He couldn't wait to get started on the changes around Stullwood.

When the lights flickered, Her Ladyship the Dowager Baroness, Nigel's and Rupert's grandmother, tugged a bell pull and presently a footman appeared—a young man in a black tailcoat with a starched white shirt over a black waistcoat.

"Yes, Your Ladyship?"

"Please see to it that oil lamps are placed in all the rooms, along with matches, in case the electric generators go out."

"Very good, Your Ladyship."

The Dowager Baroness thought that the modern age wasn't all as convenient as it was cracked up to be. Stullwood Hall even had a telephone and, while making some aspects of life easier, she found that it curtailed communications that would otherwise have occurred face-to-face. We shall soon be a nation of telephone-talkers, she thought, and never see one another again.

She clasped her hands tightly as she sat stiff and straight-backed in a Queen Anne chair. She dreaded the reading of her son's will. It placed a finality on his death that she couldn't face. In the span of three years, she had lost her only son and her eldest grandson—in a war that made no sense, no matter how many times it had been explained to her. But despite her dread of this inevitable moment, she wanted the solicitor to arrive and get on with it.

Mr. Radcliffe arrived at last and was brought to the salon, a small and neat little man, who immediately arranged his papers on an ornate antique desk, clearing his throat so many times that Her Ladyship quietly asked the footman to bring a glass of water. Nigel took a seat and said to his younger brother, "Don't worry, old boy, I'll allow you to continue to live here for as long as you wish. Bring your bride, too, should you ever decide you fancy women."

Rupert didn't respond. He wished Nigel wouldn't take on such a cavalier attitude at such a somber moment. He didn't seem to take anything seriously. No doubt he had gone down to that old deer park again to conjure up expensive plans for its revival.

Mr. Radcliffe cleared his throat and began to read. The first pages were filled with legalese that the others barely listened to. Their attention sharpened when he came to individual bequests. The butler and housekeeper were remembered, as was the late Baron's faithful valet, who had followed him into the army and survived the war. The masters of his stables and hounds also received gifts.

Finally, what the remaining three Barnstables had been waiting for: "My mother shall continue to live at Stullwood Hall for as long as she desires and will continue to receive the allowance that has been paid to her all these years, with cost of living adjustments. To my son, Nigel, I leave the sum of one hundred thousand pounds. The rest of my estate, all its lands and titles and various incomes, as well as the family fortune, I leave to my youngest son, Rupert."

As rain washed down the windows and fire crackled on the grate, three faces stared stonily at Mr. Radcliffe, who looked elsewhere.

Finally Her Ladyship said, "Surely you have transposed the names, my good man. It is Rupert who is to receive the settlement while Nigel inherits the estate."

The solicitor cleared his throat and got a look on his face that said this was the part he had been dreading and that he would actually rather be anywhere else in the world than here. "I made no mistakes, Your Ladyship. You may examine the document yourself if you like."

"I'd like to take a look at it," Nigel said, striding to the desk and snatching the papers out of Radcliffe's hands.

A quick read and then Nigel laughed in a scoffing way. "This is a joke of some kind!"

"It is not, Your Lordship."

"But . . . but . . ." Nigel sputtered in a way that was completely out of character. Nigel Barnstable never sputtered. "This can't be legal!"

Mr. Radcliffe ran his fingers along the edges of the papers that lay before him, making sure they were perfectly aligned and giving him an excuse not to meet Nigel's eyes. "I assure you, Your Lordship, it is all quite legal."

Nigel made a dismissive sound. "Toward the end, Father was in a lot of pain and feverish from so many infections. Plus the influenza. He wasn't sound of mind."

Radcliffe cleared his throat again, making the others in the room wonder if it was an affliction brought on from years of reading bad wills. "Your Lordship, this will was drawn up before the late Baron enlisted in the army."

He gave them a moment to digest this nasty bit of suet, and they did so in a frown-filled silence, grandmother and two grandsons, then he said, "There is one more document. A letter."

The three looked sharply at Radcliffe. A letter! The Dowager Baroness felt her heart leap. Her son's last words. It was almost as if Harold had briefly come back to her. It gave her, for a quick moment, a strange kind of joy.

"It is addressed to you, sir," he said, finally looking at Nigel, and the Dowager's heart dropped. As her joy had been brief, she now experienced a brief stab of resentment against the grandson she loved. It was a queer mix that momentarily unbalanced her, loving Nigel and yet begrudging him the thing she herself wanted most—her son's final words.

When Nigel held out his hand to receive the letter, Radcliffe went a little pale, with the look of a man who was considering changing professions, which he had in fact considered on occasions such as this. But he would never change professions; he liked what he did. The pay was excellent, and for the most part he was the bearer of good news, in which case he was treated very well in these big-moneyed houses.

"I have been instructed to read the letter out loud," he said, avoiding eye contact with Nigel. "To all three of you." He waited until the tall and imposing Barnstable slowly backed away and returned to his chair where he was less of a physical threat.

Radcliffe cleared his throat two more times, trying not to look at the clock, trying not to let his discomfort show, then read: "Dear Nigel, it pains me to have had to do what I did. I love you, son. I'm proud of your many qualities. You are intelligent and clever, and you put people at ease. In a word, son, you are a charmer. But you are also impulsive, and when you don't get your way you tend to act irrationally and without thinking. These are the traits I worry about and must keep in mind as I consider the welfare of Stullwood Hall and the family name.

"But more worrying, Nigel, is you are ambitious. You were ambitious as a boy and grew to be an overly ambitious man. With this fierce ambition comes impatience and poor planning. Impatience leads to failure. While I feel you have the intelligence and skills for running the estate, I fear that your ambitions will only lead to its ruin. Stullwood must remain unchanged. I cannot allow you to tear up the land for fanciful dreams. I know Rupert to be level-headed and possessing a true devotion to tradition. I am confident that Rupert will see to it that Stullwood carries on as it has for centuries. But you, my son, will be the ninth Baron Stullwood. Carry the title with honor and grace. It is my sincerest wish, Nigel, that you contain your ambitions someday and learn to settle down to your duties as a Barnstable and a gentleman, and as the Lord to our people on the estate. I have every confidence that in this endeavor you will do us all proud."

Radcliffe set the letter down and gave his audience of three a chance to absorb it.

The Baroness wasn't so much concerned with her son being so critical of Nigel as that he had addressed not a word to her or about her. Rupert was thinking along the same lines, thinking what an odd and unexpected letter it had been, trying to fit it into the frame of his new life. And with the significance of what Barnstable Senior had said, Rupert realized in shock and then deep disappointment that Father had not so much given the estate to Rupert as he had taken it from Nigel. Any feelings of reward or personal credit that Rupert had felt in the receiving of the estate died at once, and for unfathomable reasons, he was suddenly miserable.

Nigel's thoughts marched along a different path.

He couldn't believe it. His father had essentially given him a dressing down in front of his grandmother, his brother, and this solicitor. Why had the letter needed to be read out loud? Was humiliation his father's intent? No, Nigel knew his father better than that. The old boy had never been one to purposely humiliate anyone. Then it must be that the old boy had thought that having his words spoken out loud, broadcast into the air through a human voice, would have more impact, and help drive his point home all the harder. And to give Grandmother ammunition in the future to remind Nigel of what his father had said, basically making her and Rupert the keepers of Nigel's personality and ambitions.

Radcliffe, who had read many wills for many wealthy people, was a keen forecaster of bad tempers. The air in the salon was so charged that he expected lightning to start forking down from the ceiling. Avoiding the thunderous expression on the oldest son's face—Nigel looked fit to kill, and Radcliffe had seen that look before, too—he hastily scraped his papers together and said, "I will leave the letter here, but I must hurry if I'm to make the London train." A cowardly retreat, he knew, but he also knew he was going to be the target of a rage that could be felt building up in the air.

"We'd be happy to put you up," the Dowager said graciously, trying to hide her utter shock from the solicitor, "until the storm has passed."

"I've business in the city. But thank you, Your Ladyship. I appreciate the offer." And he hurried out.

Radcliffe's exit brought a whole new silence to the salon as the three sat in such astonishment that none could for the moment speak. Then Nigel, almost too breathless to talk, breathless with a rage that was starting to churn in his soul, said, "Grandmother, did you know about this?"

She had gone chalk-white. Her son's final words, the last she was ever to hear, had not been addressed to her. "No, I did not. But Harold had his reasons, and he had a head on his shoulders."

Nigel got up and went to the desk, where the letter lay. He looked down at it and saw at once the familiar handwriting, impressed boldly upon the page with no evidence of the shaky hand his father had had in his final days. The solicitor spoke the truth. The old boy had written this before enlisting in the army.

Nigel couldn't remember receiving such a shock, not even when his mother died and his father said she was never coming home, and seven-year-old Nigel had sat by the window for weeks, waiting for the carriage that was bringing her, he so staunchly refused to believe the truth. He felt that way now, that Radcliffe was going to re-appear any moment and say it had all been a prank. But Radcliffe, like his mother, didn't return. "So that's it then?" he said finally. "That's all I'm to receive? My title and a settlement?"

Neither of Nigel's companions responded. The silence in the parlor was so heavy, Nigel thought, that it was almost deafening. A ponderous silence brought on by the combined shock of three people who had just received unexpected news.

"Sorry, old boy," Rupert finally said, rising to stand for a moment, only to sit again as if just the decision of whether to stand or sit were too much. "I had no idea Father was going to do this. But . . ." Rupert inspected his fingernails in the annoying way he always had when searching for pleasant words to deliver unpleasant news. "I rather agree with him. You're not good at collecting the rents, Nigel, or seeing to repairs. When tenants need a dispute settled, you go off to London to meet with an architect. Instead of inspecting the farms, you're out marking off where golf greens and fairways are to go. Stullwood needs a good business head." He wanted to add, and yes, when things don't go your way, you turn into a spoiled brat. But Rupert knew when to shut up.

Nigel stared at his brother as if Rupert were a rhinoceros that had just wandered in. Then he got up and went to the window to look out. The rain was abating. The sky seemed to have let loose its water only for the reading of the will and now had moved on to rain on someone else's bad day. Nigel thought wooden thoughts: My younger brother gets the family fortune while I, Father's legal heir, will receive a . . . check.

Nigel turned and looked at them both, the elderly woman and the young man twenty-two going on fifty. In that instant, he despised them. He had never really cared for the domineering old matriarch who Nigel sometimes thought believed herself to be Queen Victoria reincarnated, the way she dressed in black and wore her corset so trussed that her big bosom nearly reached her chin. And Rupert, the baby brother who couldn't even spell the word *ambition*, let alone possess any.

"This is ridiculous," he muttered, as he turned on his heel and stormed out of the salon, leaving the two startled.

"Nigel, wait," Rupert said.

"Nigel, where are you going?" his grandmother called.

He grabbed his riding crop from the table in the hall and marched over puddled gravel toward the stables. "Fetch Blaze," he said to the groom. "Saddle him up."

"I've only just got him dry, Your Lordship."

"Just do it!"

Nigel paced among the damp stalls, slapping his thigh with the leather riding crop that had been a gift from the Earl of Shrewsbury on his eighteenth birthday. Meant to be used as a reminder to a horse who was in charge and how the horse was expected to move, Nigel now used the short, stiff whip as a device of self-flagellation, stinging his thigh so sharply that it could be felt through the fabric of his riding breeches. Outside, a light drizzle lingered and a cold wind came up.

Nigel had left his jacket back at the house. But he didn't feel the cold. All he felt was anger and it was like a thick, heavy coat weighing him down.

A title—that is all he left me. A title with no substance behind it. He has reduced me to a figurehead. People will laugh and wink behind my back. I will be a tenant in my own home, in a domain I am meant to rule. He castrated me and left me impotent.

When Nigel mounted the horse, the anger was joined by other weights—bitterness, feelings of betrayal, even a good measure of sulk—so that when he put spurs to the horse, he gave Blaze free rein until they were riding flat out across the parkland. That morning, his brain had bubbled with ambitions and goals, like sparkling wine, but now it boiled with hot, dark emotions like a lake of volcanic lava.

He rode back to the deer park as if he had left something there and needed to find it. And perhaps he had. Earlier he had ridden through the forest a very rich and well landed man, heir to the Stullwood Estate and its millions. Now he returned as simply heir to an empty title and a mere hundred thousand pounds. A laughingstock! People will ask: Why did the old Baron do it? What's wrong with the oldest son that he wasn't given the estate?

Nigel rode Blaze hard and mercilessly, bringing the crop down again and again, into the rain so that both horse's mane and Nigel's thick hair streamed with water. He wanted to shout. He wanted to bellow his indignation to the sky. He wanted to kill Rupert. The horse galloped and lathered up, and the crop came down again and again, harder, Nigel venting his fury and resentment on a creature that didn't know what it had done wrong but was afraid to disobey.

After a long, hard gallop, he slowed his mount to a trot and then to a lope to let his scattered and strung-out thoughts catch up to him. He rode through the deer park where deer wandered in but couldn't get out, living a trapped existence until bullets ended it.

Taking the stallion down to a walk, Nigel realized he had outrun his anger and other turbulent emotions, and they weren't catching up. Instead, a cold fog enshrouded his mind, the chilling mists of England that he sometimes felt in his blood.

I am John Lackland, he thought in a strange detachment. A noble without lands—a powerless man.

He started to feel ashamed, and yet he had done nothing wrong. I committed the sin of being born with ambition. The need to change things, to grow and expand, to take what is and turn it into something that should be.

Like that much maligned king of long ago who had lost his lands and had launched armies to get them back, Nigel was not going to take this defeat lying down, for defeat it was, in his eyes at least, as most surely it would be seen among his peers. Nigel felt a fight start to rise in him, a rebellion against an injustice.

As the stallion, panting and snorting, hoofed the wet ground, Nigel felt a curious peace settle over him, just briefly, not a surrender but a shifting of thoughts and viewpoints.

John Lackland, King of England, he thought again. *Johan sanz Terre,* in Norman French. I lack land. I am without land . . .

He sat his restless mount as the fog in his mind, the cool calmness, started to swirl and lift in the light drizzle in the silent deer park where the only sounds to disturb his thoughts were the jingling of the stallion's bit, the creak of the saddle, raindrops spattering leaves.

And then, strangely, Nigel felt excitement begin to steal over him. A high excitement, suddenly. Rising up from deep within himself. An unexpected lifting of his spirits. High excitement, higher than his first blooding when, as a child, he had been initiated as a new follower of the fox hunt. Ten-year-old Nigel had been giddy with pride as the master huntsman had smeared the blood of the captured fox on his cheeks and forehead. An excitement higher than that—what did it mean?

He looked across the rolling green acres where fingers of white creeping ground fog swirled around the bases of stately, spreading oak trees—he looked at the massive, blocky house that rose from the emerald lawns, majestic and imposing against the gray sky, and the strangest thing happened. Nigel felt as if he were looking at his home for the first time, as if someone had plucked his eyes out of their sockets and replaced them with someone else's.

Smack dab in the center of a thousand acres of perfect parkland stood a blocky old manse, three stories tall with fortress-like crenellations along the roof, a Greek-like dome with a flag on top. It boasted ninety rooms and as many drafts and leaks. It wasn't Stullwood at all, not to his new stranger's eyes. Familiar and yet not. He blinked. He rubbed his eyes. As the sun moved swiftly in and out of the protection of dark rain clouds, Nigel thought his eyes were playing tricks on him. When you're born in a house and grow up in it and call it home and it's the only residence you've ever known, you get rather familiar with it. So why was Stullwood Hall looking now unfamiliar and out of place?

It isn't the house that has changed, he speculated. And once that thought entered his sphere of notice, he sat on it for a minute, to turn it around, analyze it, chew on it a bit and see what it meant.

If the house hasn't changed, he asked the trees in the deer park, then what has? Because that boxy old thing constructed of homely yellow bricks no longer looked familiar to him.

"You have too much ambition," his father had said. But what was a man if he didn't have ambition? Ambition was what made the blood pulse through a man's veins. And ambition gave rise to dreams, which gave rise to energy. A man shouldn't have dreams handed to him on a silver platter—he had to create them, pursue them, work for them, otherwise they didn't give him energy.

Barnstable men, with the exception of Nigel, were notoriously without ambition. Maybe he wasn't a Barnstable. Now there was a thought. Maybe Mother entertained an ambitious visitor one day twenty-five years ago when Father was in London on business. It wasn't true, of course. Nigel's resemblance to the eighth Baron Stullwood put an end to that. Still, it was a pleasant fantasy for a few minutes—to think that some giant of a man, a Titan with ambition, had come to the Hall and Mother had given in and Nigel was the result. Because Nigel now fully embraced that ambition, since it was what he had been born for.

He started to laugh. John Lackland, he thought again. It was a sign. A turning point. One of those pivotal moments in a man's life when he knew destiny had stepped in and was calling. What he had seen just an hour before as a bitter defeat, a slap across the face, he saw now as an opportunity, shining and golden. I lack land, he thought, as he spurred his mount and headed back to the house, but that is only so that I can go on to acquire land.

As Stullwood Hall drew near, old and stately and uninspiring, Nigel held a mental dialogue with his father. "Impatience leads to poor planning, which leads to failure," the old baron said. To which Nigel retorted: "Impatience gets things done, which leads to success."

Grandmother and Rupert were still in the salon, in their chairs, as if they had been caught in a pocket of frozen time, as if they needed Nigel's presence to animate them again.

Without a word, Nigel strode straight to the desk and, to the others' shock, picked up his father's letter and tossed it onto the fire. As it caught flame and burned and curled into black ash, he turned to face them, as if expecting them to challenge his right to destroy a letter addressed to him.

"I'm really sorry, old boy," Rupert said after a moment, with little conviction.

Nigel stared at his younger brother and experienced another trick of the eye. Just as he had looked across the green lawns to an unfamiliar manse, he now looked at a total stranger. If asked to identify the man in the chair, Nigel could have said, "That's my brother, Rupert." But at a deeper level, on some primal, instinctive plane, he had no idea who that fellow was. Looking at him for the first time, as he had just a while ago looked at Stullwood Hall for the first time, Nigel now realized that while young Rupert possessed some fine Barnstable features—a straight nose and square jaw, Rupert was short. He also had a receding hairline, at twenty-two! And he sat with soft hands and the flaccid expression of an easily vanquishable foe.

Thinking of Rupert's personality traits suddenly riled Nigel— Rupert's casual manner, his almost indifferent attitude toward life. It was a lazy sense of entitlement, what some called the "idle rich," that had snuffed any backbone out of him, any germ of ambition that might have blossomed had Rupert been given a chance. Instead he had been given a life of money and ease.

But so had I, Nigel thought in a moment of curiosity about what force of nature could create two such opposite brothers. Nigel had been raised in money and ease, he had never had to work, he had never even had to go off to war (although Nigel had wanted to enlist as soon as he turned eighteen, his father had insisted he stay at Stullwood while he and his eldest went off to the war). And yet he was gifted with ambition and drive. Why was that? he wondered.

"You're not sorry, Rupert," Nigel said in a queer mix of anger and calm. Perhaps mostly what he felt was annoyance. "You got the whole lot. Well, old boy, I hope you enjoy it because you will have it all to yourself."

The Dowager Baroness snapped herself up, when he had thought she couldn't possibly sit any straighter. "Nigel, what are you talking about?"

"I'm leaving, Grandmother," he said, and as the words left his mouth, he realized he was enjoying himself, eliciting two shocked looks on faces that were normally complacent. Yes, he was relishing this! "I'm leaving Stullwood and England."

She gasped and sputtered, and he could hear the stays of her corset creaking. "What! Preposterous. You can't leave. You're the lord of the estate. Your duty is to Stullwood." She looked at Rupert. She looked at the portraits hanging on the walls. Searching for someone to back her up. "Don't be ridiculous. For one thing, where on earth would you go? This is your home. We're your family. Your father left you a nice settlement, but it won't last forever, not if you go out on your own. You can live here at Stullwood quite comfortably."

But Nigel didn't want to be comfortable. Why couldn't they see that? He looked at the two, grandmother and grandson, like museum pieces stuck in this house. He resented them, and it suddenly amused him to think that they would never know where he was, if he was alive or dead, if he had a son. Rupert would never know when the title passed to him, if it ever did.

Suddenly the Dowager Baroness was frightened and her spine went slack. It was a slicing, icy fear that she couldn't recall ever having experienced before. In fact, she couldn't recall when she had last been this afraid. When father and son had sailed off to war in their uniforms— she had been afraid then, but it was for them, for their safety and their lives. This sudden terrible fear encompassed something much bigger than two men dying. It was as if the war had done more than kill soldiers. It had wounded the very fabric of society. Young men had died and their deaths had triggered the unraveling of a way of life that had been entrenched in English society for hundreds of years. She imagined Samson pulling down the pillars of the temple of the Philistines. She saw England resting on pillars that were crumbling. She closed her eyes and thought, My son, by bequeathing the estate to Rupert, you have done Stullwood no service at all! Your plan to save the estate and its traditions has had the opposite effect. You have crippled us by driving Nigel away.

She opened her eyes and looked at her handsome grandson. Stubborn, ambitious, impatient. Yes, those were his weaknesses. Yes, he would not manage Stullwood well. Other houses had been driven to ruin by reckless men who thought only of their own ambitions.

But fear kept her from voicing this to Nigel. Instead, she was amazed to hear herself say in a confident tone, "If you do leave, Nigel, you won't be gone for long. England is in your blood. You cannot turn your back on ancestry and birthright. Stullwood will always beckon." A fine speech, she thought bitterly, but she didn't believe it herself.

No matter how homesick Nigel became for Stullwood, he would stay away out of stubbornness.

By coincidence, her grandson was thinking the same thing. "You've sealed it, Grandmother, with your very own words," Nigel said. "Now that you predict I will come back, you must know that once I go away, I will stay away."

"Really, Nigel," Rupert said, suddenly agitated, conflicted by feelings of happiness over his unexpected windfall along with guilt and a sense of not deserving it. Such feelings spawned resentment against the brother who was making him feel guilty and undeserving. Rupert dearly hoped Nigel would leave Stullwood and stand true to his promise never to return. With Nigel gone for good, Rupert was confident that in time his guilt would fade and he would come to realize that, yes, he did deserve this inheritance after all.

"Really, Rupert," Nigel mimicked. "I don't know what plan Father had in mind for me when he stole my birthright and gave it to you, brother, but I have plans of my own now."

A footman came in just then carrying a silver tray with tea service. As he watched Grandmother in her black, tightly corseted gown lift the silver teapot and pour, just the way she had every afternoon since Nigel could remember, it struck him now how entrenched this house and its family were in tradition. Her son's will had been read, her middle grandson had been dealt a shocking blow, yet she went on with her afternoon tea.

He looked at her with disdain. Suddenly, the mansion felt small, despite its enormity. It was the minds within it that made the manor house small. A man is put upon this earth to achieve something, he thought as he watched her trembling hands add sugar to her tea. A man has to leave his mark, otherwise what's the point to it all? Rupert will see to it that Stullwood trundles on with tradition, he will make sure the cycle of seasons continues—pheasant shooting, fox hunting, horse racing, and sculling on the river. Idle pastimes that would leave no man's mark. Rupert will grow old within these walls and leave the estate to the next bored and entitled Barnstable and the cycle of tradition will continue on unbroken.

But I have been set free from this cycle. I am no longer a slave to this house and its traditions.

"Will you please have some tea, Nigel, and talk things over with us?" Grandmother asked in time to catch a look in his eye that made her suddenly feel defensive. He had always been a restless one, Nigel, and now he was more restless than ever, now that he had lost Stullwood. He seemed to resent the tea service and the lumps of sugar for some reason. What had he expected her to do? Run around screaming? She had just heard her only son's final words, read from a piece of paper by a London solicitor who cleared his throat too many times. She needed to think about it, about what Harold had said and done. She needed an anchor for a while or maybe she would go running around screaming. Afternoon tea had always been afternoon tea, it marked a passage in the day; it was a ritual that connected her back through the years to her own mother and grandmother before that. How could Nigel begrudge her this small solace while she thought about hearing her only son's final words?

She fought back the tears. She didn't want him to leave, but it wasn't in her character to beg, to expose vulnerable emotions. The raw truth was that, of her three grandsons, Nigel bore the closest resemblance to their father. Even his voice was the same. It was a little like having her beloved Harold around. If Nigel left, her son would die all over again.

Nigel met her eyes. She doesn't believe me. She and Rupert don't think I'm serious. But I have never been more serious.

Suddenly, renovating old deer parks held no allure, and a nine-hole golf course could satisfy ambition to only a small extent. With those two matters laid aside, Nigel shifted his attention to the next piece of business: Where would he go?

Perhaps East Africa. That's where the savvy chaps are going. Buy up land in the Kenya Highlands and grow coffee. Valentine Treverton took his family there. Might join them.

But there was the thing of all those blacks. Nigel didn't fancy being in the middle of a bunch of savages. He thought of India. That was a warm place. But old. And full of heathens that worshipped idols. Where was there a place of sunshine and wide spaces and room for a man to pursue his dreams? Untouched and unspoiled. That was what Nigel wanted. Surely, somewhere in the world, a man of his refinements and money could find land and set himself up and build his own empire. A place that wasn't tied down with so many rules and laws and traditions.

He espied the folded newspaper on the polished round table—*The London Times*, freshly ironed and ready for Grandmother to read with her tea. A headline above the fold: "United States Senate Passes Women's Suffrage Bill."

He blinked. Something was occurring to him, or perhaps it had been occurring all day, just waiting for the right moment to take a bow. The theme of his day had been "old"—realizing how old Stullwood Hall was, how governed it was by old tradition, how old Grandmother was, and even Rupert, at twenty-two, already old and stodgy in his ways.

Maybe it was time to bring the word "new" into his life. His eyes settled, like butterflies on a flower, on the words United States. Our bastard cousins, he thought. A mongrel race of ingrates that thumbed its nose at Mother England and went its own merry way without so much as a thank-you for giving them language, culture, and history.

The more he thought of that wide continent with its varied climes, from snowy pine forests to blazing deserts, the more it occurred to him that America was just the place for a man of his ambitions. America. The New World. Where he had heard they did not have aristocratic titles, where a man who called himself "Lord" could distinguish himself.

I will have land. I will have power.

He had entered this room expecting to be handed the keys to a kingdom—a kingdom that was rightfully his—and now he was to walk out of it a pauper. One hundred thousand might seem a fortune to a lesser man, but it was nothing to a man who was to have been one of the richest men in England. But in America, he had heard, a man with only two pennies in his pocket could make himself a millionaire as long as he had the drive, imagination, and ambition. And Nigel Barnstable, newly seated ninth Baron Stullwood, possessed those in plenty.

"You'll come back," Rupert said with a conceited sniff, suddenly feeling superior to the brother he had felt inferior to for twenty-two years. "You won't stay away for long."

"Victor Hugo said that perseverance is the secret of all triumphs," Nigel replied. "I will be triumphant, dear brother, while you will remain a settle-for man all your life. In fact, Rupert, when you die, you will die without having ever been alive."

"You'll miss us," Rupert said, ignoring his brother's invectives. "You mark my words. You will miss this house, and you will miss us."

Nigel thought about that, thinking back over the years, examining his heart and his feelings. No, he decided. He wouldn't miss the house or them. But there was one thing he would miss. He would miss Blaze, his horse, who always ran exactly as Nigel wanted him to.

CHAPTER TWO

RMS *Mauretania*

April 1920

"I AM ADAMANT ON this, Lizzie," Mr. Van Linden said to his nineteen-year-old daughter. "You cannot be allowed the management of your trust fund. Women simply haven't the mental capabilities for managing money."

Elizabeth tilted her head. "And yet Congress has granted us the right to vote."

"By God, it's a travesty, letting women vote! All it means is that married men now have two votes. And don't change the subject. Whomever you marry will be the custodian of your trust fund, and that is all there is to it."

"But then that means I have to marry."

He stared at her as if she had just spoken Chinese. "Well, of course you have to marry. What else would you do?"

To this Elizabeth had no reply. She had no idea what else she would do, only that she lived with a vague sense that she was meant to do *something*.

She and her parents were seated at a small table in the Verandah Café, situated on the *Mauretania's* boat deck, protected by screens from the inclement Atlantic weather. It was cold and everyone was bundled up. When they saw, out on the gray, choppy water, large, flat ice floes drifting by, foremost in everyone's mind was the *Titanic*, which had gone down only eight years prior.

"Really, Elizabeth," Mrs. Van Linden said, "must you bring Button to the table?"

Button was a brown miniature poodle Elizabeth had had since she was fourteen. He went with her everywhere; he even shared her bed at night. "I hate leaving him alone in the stateroom, Mother."

"Do sit up. You're slouching. And while we're at it, I don't think mauve is the color for you. What ever was I thinking when I selected the fabric for that dress? I shall go for warmer colors this year."

Elizabeth sighed. She had hated the mauve, but her mother had insisted. Elizabeth never got to pick out the fabrics for her clothes, never got to choose the color of her bedroom's décor, had to have Mother's approval in everything, including her friends. Elizabeth suspected her mother would have apoplexy if she knew that her newest friend, Libby, was the daughter of a progressive woman—a feminist! It was one of the few secrets Elizabeth kept from her parents.

"How about Ostermond?" Mr. Van Linden said, stroking his black walrus moustache. "He's a decent fellow. Well educated. Got a head on his shoulders. I thought you liked him."

"I do. I like him very much. But I don't know how he feels about me."

"Well, give it time, my dear," her mother interjected. Mrs. Van Linden was wrapped in an elegant sable coat, the egret feathers on her hat quivering in the ocean air. "Be amenable, Elizabeth. Don't talk too much. Don't try to sound smart. Flatter him. And above all, agree with everything he says."

If Mrs. Van Linden came across as nagging, it was not her intention. Her heart was in the right place. In fact, when it came to her only child, her heart was all over the place, worrying, doting, fawning, guiding, correcting. But loving, always loving. When it came to her precious daughter, Mrs. Van Linden was a bundle of maternal imperatives: to see that Elizabeth was happy, safe, taken care of, without worry, lacking for nothing, protected, and above all, well placed in marriage.

Nineteen years ago, it had been the nannies, and Mrs. Van Linden had so over-managed her baby's nannies that they had left, one by one, because the lady of the house wouldn't let them do their jobs. Then it was the governesses who could barely breathe, Mrs. Van Linden hovered and fretted so. School teachers had then learned to expect weekly visits from Elizabeth's doting mother, and piano instructors, and men who gave horseback riding lessons, and the parade of tutors Mrs. Van Linden hired to see to it that Elizabeth was brought to perfection so that now, at this crucial husband stage, Mrs. Van Linden could tell herself she had done a good job of producing a daughter every mother in the world would wish were hers.

But she could not rest on her laurels. While nannies and governesses and teachers and tutors had been vitally important in the forming of this girl, none came anywhere near to the astronomical importance of the next step—choosing Elizabeth's husband. It could not be just any man. The Van Lindens of New York moved in such a wealthy, exclusive, socially restricted world that Elizabeth's husband could only be drawn from an equally wealthy, exclusive, and socially restricted world.

Elizabeth's grandfather, Josiah Van der Linden (they had since dropped the "der" to sound less foreign) had come to America a nearly penniless youth, but he had worked hard, saved his money, gone hungry, lived in alleys, educated himself, had even stolen and cheated when he had to, finally investing wisely to gradually make a fortune in steel, textiles, and railroads. The result was that the Van Lindens lived on Park Avenue, along a stretch called Marble Row—a string of mansions built by industrial billionaires in the late nineteenth century, men with names like Vanderbilt, Rockefeller, and Carnegie. Their seventy-five-room mansion took up half a city block. It was said that Mrs. Astor had twenty servants; therefore, Mrs. Van Linden had twenty-one.

Being their only child, Elizabeth was the center of the Van Lindens' universe. Now it was time to see that she was properly married, her fortune safely in the hands of a level-headed man.

When her grandfather died, he had left a generous trust fund for his only grandchild. Unfortunately, the bequest came with conditions. Believing that women didn't have a head for finances, Josiah stipulated that the trust fund was to be managed by Elizabeth's husband when she married. If she remained unmarried, the money was to be handled by her father. While Van Linden continued to enlighten his daughter on women's innate weaknesses ("They can't help it; it's how God made them."), Elizabeth's eyes drifted to the man standing alone at the ship's railing.

He was there every day, his coat collar turned up as if he were blocking out the world. Such a small barrier, Elizabeth thought, a piece of black velvet standing up against his ears. Yet it seemed to work. He looked out over the rolling ocean as if he were searching for something—as if, long ago, the wind blew his hat off and he'd been looking for it ever since. She saw how the cold Atlantic wind roughed up his hair, standing it on end, as if he were in permanent fright.

He was tall and broad shouldered. There was the hint of an athletic physique under the long coat.

During these past days at sea, Elizabeth had noticed that he always dined alone, at a small table protected by a potted palm. Afterward, he stepped into one of the elevators next to the grand staircase and disappeared—to his stateroom, she supposed, as he was never seen in any of the social salons, smoking rooms, libraries, or ballroom.

He was terribly good looking. She wondered if he was married.

*   *   *

Nigel could feel her eyes on him, devouring him as if he were an éclair. He had seen her about the ship over the last few days, always accompanied by that steam engine of a mother. Blond, slender, and quite pretty, she had intrigued him from the moment he first glimpsed her, as they walked up the first class gangway when they boarded the ship. Nigel had gotten to work gathering information on the family.

Nigel had seen their type before. They believed themselves to be "old money," the closest to an American aristocracy as there could be. Old money in England went back centuries, two thousand years even. They thought their blood was blue. It was water compared to the bloodlines of Britain. But none of this mattered in his new plan. Nigel might have a hundred thousand pounds for now, but he knew it wouldn't last forever. And he needed cash, great amounts of it, to build his empire. Which was why he had chosen Miss Elizabeth Van Linden to be the next Baroness.

But he had to come up with a strategy. The days of American girls greedily seeking English lords as husbands were over. American millionaire fathers, after six decades of paying off the huge debts of their wastrel "Sir" and "Lord" son-in-laws, finally got fed up and said, "The money stays in America." And anyway, the glamour of being married to a Baron or an Earl had worn off. It had been a jolly competition for many years, but then they began to see their husbands for what they were—not medieval knights in shining armor but simply men who had foibles and weaknesses like any other. And the tide turned. Suddenly it was passé and even vulgar to marry an English Lord.

Therefore, Nigel had to play another card, and there was one card that always played successfully, no matter what generation: charm the mother to get to the daughter.

He watched them for a moment as they talked and ate and pampered the dog. Nigel sensed that Miss Van Linden didn't belong to her mother's repressed generation. He could see it in her eyes, the way she licked her lips, the pulse that throbbed at her throat—a girl of the new, free generation—or wishing to be. Not yet a "flapper"—that new breed so named because they resembled baby birds trying to escape from the nest, flapping their arms on the dance floor in dresses that rose shockingly above the ankle. But he sensed Miss Van Linden yearned for that same freedom.

Stepping away from the railing, he approached them. "I say, I do hope you'll pardon my forwardness. The steward told me you are the Van Lindens, and if I may intrude for but a moment, Mrs. Van Linden, I must say you bear a most astonishing resemblance to Princess Helena. In her younger years, of course! She was a famous beauty in her day and, forgive me, but I think you outshine even her flame."

The three sat in startled silence, until Nigel broke it by saying, "I am Nigel Barnstable, on my way to New York and traveling alone. Well, then, I shall be on my way. Sorry for the intrusion."

"Um, wait a moment," Mrs. Van Linden said, looking up at the handsome young man with a charming smile. "How do you know the Princess?"

"I am Baron Stullwood and enjoy the acquaintance of the royal family. Now I've intruded long enough."

"Please, Lord Stullwood," Mrs. Van Linden said hastily, sizing up the good looks, thinking of family fortunes, trying to recall what she knew of the Barnstables and Stullwood—the allure of an English Lord not yet so passé for Gertrude Van Linden. "Won't you join us? I believe I've seen you in the dining salon. You always look so lonely."

He didn't look at the daughter, made a point of not looking at her, but he knew she was watching him as he took a seat at the small table that groaned with tea service, cakes, strawberries, sugar, and cream.

"Are you traveling to America on business, Your Lordship?" Mrs. Van Linden asked. Two of her cousins had gone across the Atlantic to marry English Lords and so she easily fell into the proper form of address.

"Not exactly," he said, adding nothing more.

"We had to attend three funerals in Essex," Mrs. Van Linden said. "My cousin, Lady Monford, and her two children succumbed to the Spanish flu."

Nigel averted his face and said, "The plague claimed my father as well."

She pressed a hand to her bosom. "My condolences, Lord Stullwood."

The four fell silent then, the Van Lindens sipping their tea in the bracing air while waiters hurried here and there to serve other passengers as the *Mauretania* cleaved the choppy gray waters of the Atlantic like a leviathan. Elizabeth studied their guest out of the corner of her eye. He was very tall, with lovely dark hair and a brooding air about him. In her social circle, young men loved to talk about themselves. In fact, it seemed to be a favorite pastime, and with some it was almost a competition, to see which of them could say the most impressive thing to gain a girl's attention. The untalkative Lord Stullwood was a refreshing, and intriguing, change.

"Your Lordship," Elizabeth said impulsively, "would you do us the honor of joining us at dinner this evening?"

Mrs. Van Linden shot her daughter a corrective look. Sometimes the girl was too bold for her own good. And then Mrs. Van Linden thought, No! It's the perfect gambit. Of late, mother and daughter had been locking horns over who got control of the daughter, Elizabeth starting to stand up to her mother more and more. Mrs. Van Linden realized that if she herself had made the invitation to Lord Stullwood, Elizabeth would have later scolded her mother out of contrariness. Mrs. Van Linden suppressed a smile. It was an interesting game, the contest between mother and adult daughter, although at times exasperating.

"Oh, yes, Lord Stullwood," Mrs. Van Linden said. "We would love for you to join us."

Nigel hesitated, to appear to think it over, purposely leaving them on the brink of anticipation, although the dinner invitation was exactly what he had been hoping for. "Let me ring my stateroom and inform my valet that I will be dining in company tonight." There was no valet, of course. Nigel had to be sparing with his money, and the stateroom was the cheapest cabin first class had to offer.

Without saying anything further, Nigel took his leave, promising to join them that evening.

*   *   *

Nigel's stateroom may have been small with no portholes or sunlight or fresh air, but the ship itself was a floating palace.

The *Mauretania* was the very definition of luxury, fitted out with twenty-eight different types of wood in the public rooms, along with marble, tapestries, and grand furnishings. Skylights brought filtered daylight into the interior of the ship, adding elegance to dining areas, libraries, and lounges.

And the multi-level first class dining salon, where Nigel now made his entrance, had been inspired by mid-sixteenth-century French châteaux. Above its oak splendor rose a domed ceiling decorated with the signs of the zodiac.

Nigel, dressed in elegant dinner attire, paused to scan the equally elegantly attired crowd moving among the tables, finding their places, greeting one another while the orchestra played "A Pretty Girl Is Like A Melody," and waiters glided about like automatons.

When Nigel saw the Van Lindens, he paused. Mother and daughter wore off-shoulder gowns of black silk and satin, as befitting their mourning state. But the décolletage was cut low on both—attractive on the daughter, but Nigel thought the mother too old and heavy for the look. Both sported delicate egret plumes in their elaborately upswept hair. Glittering diamonds, rubies, and emeralds completed the ostentatious picture.

They were not alone. Besides the prosperous-looking Van Linden, whose large stomach was festooned with a gold watch chain, a distinguished-looking gentleman in his thirties, with slicked-back blond hair, was also at their table. A few generous tips to waiters and cabin stewards, and Nigel knew the names and backgrounds of anyone of importance on board the ship. He recognized the man as Richard Ostermond, a young doctor currently making a name for himself at Harvard Medical School, and he was returning from Britain where he had presented a paper at a medical and scientific conference. Ambitious, Nigel had heard, and seen of late in the company of Miss Elizabeth Van Linden and her mother.

So, Nigel had competition.

When he arrived at their table, Dr. Ostermond rose and held out his hand. "I understand you are to join us tonight, Your Lordship," he said affably while Nigel shook his hand.

"I'm so glad you chose to join us, Lord Stullwood," Mrs. Van Linden said, diamonds glittering at her throat. "We were just discussing *The Decameron* by that old Italian author."

"We were trying to discuss it," Elizabeth said with a smile. "Mother won't hear a word of it."

Mrs. Van Linden arched her right eyebrow. "From what I understand, the book is immoral and irreverent. I don't think it's proper dinner table talk."

"Have you read it, sir?" Dr. Ostermond said to Nigel, who had taken a seat.

"I have," Nigel said as he unfolded his linen napkin. "It has its good points and its weak points. But in my opinion," he said, directing his words at Elizabeth, "a book is neither moral nor immoral. Books are either well written or badly written and that is the extent of it." He held up a finger before the others could reply. "However, I believe Mrs. Van Linden is justified in this case. And I agree with her on the choice of dinner table topics."

Mrs. Van Linden offered him an appreciative nod of her feathered head.

He turned his smile to the young man sitting next to her. "So you are a doctor, sir. What specialty may I ask?"

"I am conducting research in antibiosis, a way of synthesizing compounds to fight such infections as the recent Spanish flu. I believe it is possible to create chemicals that would kill bacteria without harming the human host."

While the orchestra switched to "I'm Forever Blowing Bubbles," and a waiter discreetly placed a plate of dinner rolls and pats of butter shaped like seashells on the table, Ostermond continued to hold the Van Lindens in thrall.

"Think of what a discovery like that could mean to the human race! The influenza epidemic that recently swept the world killed an estimated fifty million people. How many lives could have been saved," Ostermond said, "had we had an antibiotic for such a disease, delivered in the form of a preventative vaccine?"

"A flu vaccine! Can it be done?" Van Linden said, muttering something about looking into pharmaceutical investing, while Mrs. Van Linden and Elizabeth were watching Richard Ostermond with keen interest.

"There is very good evidence that—" Ostermond began.

"I say, Mrs. Van Linden," Nigel said, leaning forward to give the lady one of his most irresistible smiles. "Do you enjoy riddles?"

She looked at him and their eyes met briefly in a kind of challenge. If she were younger and single, she would have thought he was flirting with her. "If they are clever enough," she replied with a smile.

With Ostermond and Van Linden and the Van Linden daughter paying attention, Nigel said, "What falls but doesn't break, and what breaks but doesn't fall?"

Van Linden frowned, Ostermond rubbed his cheek, Elizabeth kept her eyes on Nigel, and Mrs. Van Linden widened her eyes and said, "I have no idea. What is it?"

Nigel looked at the others. "Any guesses? Very well then, what falls but doesn't break, and what breaks but doesn't fall are night and day."

As his companions digested this bit of word play, each arriving at the conclusion that it was a clever riddle, Nigel smiled to himself. He had them now.

But then, to his astonishment, Mrs. Van Linden's attention snapped like a whip back to Ostermond, asking him another question about himself. Nigel was briefly nonplussed. His charm and wit never failed to capture and hold an audience. Yet here were the Van Lindens, eating Ostermond up with a spoon, Van Linden showing keen interest in the man's medical research, saying he wanted to hear more about it, and Mrs. Van Linden inviting Ostermond to visit them in New York. When Ostermond declared he would love to, as he was from the Midwest and had had little occasion to venture beyond Boston, Elizabeth quickly said, "I should be happy to show you around New York City," and Nigel saw the sparkle in her eyes.

This gave him pause. Nigel wasn't used to competition. It startled him and then irritated him. And then a thought occurred to him— that Elizabeth was going to be the target of every fortune hunter that came within sniffing range, now that she was of marrying age, with the mother hen and bulldog father giving every hopeful suitor the beady eye, judging, weighing, perhaps finding more merit in a noble crusader selflessly working to save humanity from calamitous epidemics than an English baron who seemed to be doing nothing at all.

So it was true what his friends had been saying, that a title and money were no longer an automatic ticket to the easy life, especially in America where competition seemed to be a national pastime. No longer to the lord did the spoils de facto go, by right and privilege. Nigel would now have to enter the ranks of the competitors. And it seemed he would need more than a title and an ancestral fortune to fight with (although, he didn't really have the fortune, he just gave the illusion of having it, but his competitors didn't know that).

He found himself looking at Richard Ostermond in a new, calcu- lating way.

Under other circumstances, Nigel might have welcomed the challenge and looked upon the competition for Elizabeth as a game.

But he was in a hurry without the luxury of time. This could be no leisurely seduction as his funds were limited with no prospects in the future. Ostermond had to be eliminated from the competition.

*   *   *

The next day, everyone in first class was wondering where Richard Ostermond was.

"It's quite the mystery, Your Lordship," Mrs. Van Linden said at lunch. "The captain has the entire crew searching from top to bottom.

"Really?" Nigel said as he cut into his filet mignon. "I ran into Dr. Ostermond in the passage last night. He said someone was sick down in second class, and he was going to see if he could help. Rather decent of the fellow, I say."

"Henry," she said, nudging her husband whose mouth was full of mashed potatoes. "Go and tell the captain. They are searching in the wrong places!"

But a full day's search, from first class to steerage, turned up no missing doctor. Speculation was that he had met somehow with misadventure, although exactly what, no one could guess.

A movie was being shown in the main ballroom that evening, but the Van Lindens were too upset over poor Dr. Ostermond and what might have become of him to attend. But Nigel went, and attendance was otherwise good. Nothing like a rousing cowboy adventure to help one get over a shock.

The movie had a simple plot. Outlaws were terrorizing a rancher and his family. A lone cowboy in a white hat rode into town, got rid of the outlaws, and rode off into the sunset with the rancher's pretty daughter.

The audience clapped and voiced their appreciation of a good show, but Nigel Barnstable, ninth Baron Stullwood, was absolutely mesmerized. He had never seen a cowboy movie before. He was positively seized by the sunlight. The wide-open spaces. The far horizon and vast sky. As he watched horses gallop along dusty trails, as he saw braided Indians jump up from behind tumbleweeds and cacti, as the camera captured the immensity of the sky with hawks circling, Nigel felt a subtle reshaping of his mind—no, his vision. The intertitles said the place was called Arizona, and it was out in the West. Nigel knew little of the American continent, only that it was vast. But now this film, hypnotic in its rushing images, showed the true immensity of that continent. The camera could not find the horizon. The wide and flat desert scenes made the sky look as if it were simply an upward continuation of the earth. There was no horizon.

That's because it's too far to see.

Nigel felt a familiar high excitement steal over him, the same excitement he had experienced when riding Blaze across Stullwood's grassy parkland and the budding thought had made itself known that he was not meant to stay there, that he was destined for more important places. And then, in the Hall with Rupert and Grandmother, the notion of the New World had come to him, appealed immensely to him, and he had known that was where he must go. But beyond that, the vague concept of America, he had formed no further specific destination.

And now here it was.

Forgetting that he was sitting in a chair with a crowd of people in a dark theater, and that beneath him rolled a mighty ship, Nigel Barnstable was up there on that screen, riding Blaze as they chased outlaws and Indians—but more than that, they galloped across acres too numerous to count because there was no horizon to stop them.

A place where a man could own a "spread" running hundreds of head of cattle and be the big man in the nearby town.

Just like Stullwood.

Now he knew exactly where he was going. Not only to America, but the American West, where he was going to build an empire.

With Elizabeth Van Linden's fortune.

CHAPTER THREE

Tombstone, Arizona

May 1920

CODY MCNEAL, DRESSED ALL in black, rode slowly into town, looking to the right and the left until he came abreast of the saloon. Dismounting, he tethered his mare to the hitching post, between another horse and a Model T Ford. His boots made the boards of the wooden sidewalk creak, and his spurs jingled as he strode with purpose toward the saloon's double doors, where he paused to look inside.

Just a few men playing cards and a bartender wiping down the bar. Sawdust on the floor, brass spittoons here and there. Like any other saloon in the West. Except this one had a few light bulbs burning. So, electricity had come to Tombstone. Cody would wager there was a telephone in this town, too. Although the population had greatly shrunk since the nearby silver mines dried up, he had noticed a movie theater down the street—that doubled as the local church on Sundays—with a marquee advertising a Clara Bow film. Cody had seen a movie or two, up north, but he didn't care for them.

He felt the heat of the day penetrate the cloth of his long black duster. Under his wide-brimmed black Stetson, his hair was damp. He yearned to go north. He longed for the big skies of Montana. The Colorado Rockies. The land of the Sioux and Shoshone. But a desperate need drew him southward, into deserts and hot sun. He was not his own man but a prisoner of destiny.

He had traveled many miles for many years, always on the move. Always one step ahead of the dark devils that nipped at his heels.

He was searching for a man and couldn't rest until he had found him.

Looking down the quiet street, he saw Indians sitting on a bench in front of the General Store. Apaches, he assumed, from the nearby reservation. Peaceful now, but once a warrior tribe. Thirty-four years ago the capture of Geronimo ended the Indian wars and took the fight out of his people.

That was before Cody McNeal's time. He was twenty-eight years old, born on a Montana ranch where he had grown up among cattle, riding, roping, and branding, a cowboy in the literal sense of the word. But that life lay far behind him now because of a destiny that had made a drifter of him.

Cody turned his eyes to the west. That way lay California, the land of opportunity, the last frontier.

A sign in the saloon window said, "Abiding by the new federal law of Prohibition, this establishment absolutely does not sell alcohol or spirits of any kind. We offer a fine selection of imported teas."

He stepped through the swinging doors. It was dark and quiet inside, with a few cowboys playing poker. "What'll it be, friend?" the bartender asked.

"Tea, strong," Cody said, keeping his head down and pulling the wide brim of his black Stetson lower on his forehead.

The bartender decanted brown liquid from an unlabeled bottle into a shot glass. "Oolong," he said with a wink. "From China."

Cody tipped the bracing liquor back and felt it go smoothly down his throat. Bourbon.

"I like your hat," the bartender said, a comment that Cody heard wherever he went. It was the unique hatband, created out of a rattle-snake. The snake's head had been posed in a striking position by a master taxidermist, and it sat on the wide brim as if protecting the hat. The snake's skin was wrapped around the crown, and a working rattle stood up behind the head.

"I'll give you twenty bucks for it."

The Tombstone bartender wasn't the first to make such an offer. But Cody would never sell. "The snake killed my dog," he said, "so I killed the snake."

Daylight briefly flooded the establishment as the swinging doors opened and a customer came in. Cody saw the star on the man's chest as he ordered "some of that imported Darjeeling."

The sheriff looked at Cody. Their eyes met in the way strangers' eyes met in saloons all over the West. A brief sizing up, wondering at a fella's occupation, his business in town, his intentions, whether he could be friend or foe. Finally the sheriff said, "I know what you're thinkin', son. That a lawman oughta be upholdin' the law. But if I arrested every man in these parts who was making moonshine—hell, son, I'd be arrestin' my next-door neighbors, my brothers, my uncles, my two sons, the mayor, the blacksmith, and the preacher! Ain't got a jail big enough. It's a foolish law, you ask me. Gonna cause more trouble than it was intended to stop."

The sheriff took his drink and joined the cowboys at the card table.

When the bartender refilled his glass, Cody said, "Any chance of finding work around here?"

Cody's wanderings had taken him from Montana on a winding trail through the Black Hills of South Dakota, through Cheyenne, Wyoming, Denver, and Colorado Springs. Then east to Amarillo, Texas, to meander back westward through El Paso, and finally to Tombstone, a near-ghost town of about five hundred souls and a lot of abandoned, dilapidated buildings. Thirty years ago, this was a booming mining town, making men millionaires overnight. But the veins of silver ran dry and the miners left.

Cody's had been a long trek of long rides across the prairie, sleeping under the stars, cooking at his solitary campfire but also receiving the hospitality of Indians living peacefully on their reservations, and the hospitality, too, of farmers and ranchers who offered a meal and a cot in exchange for an honest day's work. Cody was a good horseman. He knew cattle, too, and there wasn't a job on a ranch or farm that he couldn't do—wrangling, roping, branding, shoeing, hay baling. Everywhere he went, there was always the need for an extra hand. Sometimes it was a dangerous life, but he wore a six-shooter on his hip. He never drew it except to kill his evening supper. But if it came to it, he would use it to defend himself.

"You won't find any work in this town, friend," the bartender said. "Most cowhands, after the ranches shrank to nothing with all that over-grazing, they went to California, to Hollywood, where I hear the studios are willing to pay a man five dollars a day plus a box lunch for riding and roping. You might say Hollywood is kind of a last trail town. My brother went. He could lasso a bull with the best of them, and he knows how to use his fists. But he says most of it's sitting around a horse barn on Sunset Boulevard waiting for some studio to send a truck to pick up riders. Still, the pay's better than any they'd got on a ranch and, ironically, they're paid to fall off the horses instead of staying on!"

But Cody wasn't interested in the movies. He loved the West, but not the way it was being portrayed on film. But that was none of his concern. He just needed to find the next town, the next place where he could hide in numb anonymity until the dark devils came over him again, forcing him to move on once more in search of a man named Peachy.

Cody paid for his drinks and left.

Before leaving town he stopped at Boot Hill cemetery and looked at headstones that sported names familiar to Cody: Clanton and McLaury. Victims of the last shoot-out in Tombstone. Dead at the hand of a man named Wyatt Earp.

The man responsible, in part, for the dark devils that pursued him relentlessly in his search for someone. Earp, a name Cody had grown up hearing from his father's bitter lips. In a way, the Earp family was responsible for all the bad luck and misfortune in Cody's life.

Looking westward, something deep in his bones told him that his journey might be coming to an end. Something in the way the wide blue sky beckoned and the sun baked into the black cloth of his long coat, maybe even the way his spurs sounded as he strode back to his mare. Something spoke to Cody McNeal, and he prayed as he saddled up that somewhere in the desert of Southern California he would find a man named Peachy and finally be free of the dark devils that had chased him for ten years.

CHAPTER FOUR

New York City

June 1920

"YOU'RE SPENDING RATHER A lot of time with my daughter, young man. What are your intentions?"

"I find her company delightful and charming," Nigel said. "I confess, I am rather taken with her."

Sitting at his enormous desk in his spacious den that looked out over Central Park, Van Linden chewed his cigar and gave Nigel a beady-eyed stare. "I'll be frank, Barnstable. I have retained the services of an international private investigation agency to look into your family and your background."

"I expect you would," Nigel said as he folded his lanky frame into an antique chair, a slow, careless gesture intended to show lack of concern. Truth was, he was getting impatient.

When the *Mauretania* docked in New York two months ago, the Van Lindens had invited him to stay for a few days at their house in the city, but he had graciously turned them down, saying he preferred hotels. He couldn't risk them finding out he not only hadn't a valet, but that he possessed only a few pieces of luggage and was living on a budget in order to conserve his money. They thought he had a suite at the Plaza Hotel, but he was in fact staying in a cheaper place on 42nd Street.

In his campaign to gain control of the girl's fortune, Nigel was working to win the parents over. Amazingly, despite his wealth, Van Linden went to an office every morning to conduct business. And so Nigel had subtly let it be known that he was interested in dabbling in finance of some kind, perhaps finding an occupation in the stock market. "Being idle is unhealthy," he had told Van Linden more than once. "And just because the Stullwood Estate has left me extremely well off and in no need of employment, a man must put his mind to good use. I appreciate the value of hard-earned money. It seems to me these days that people know the price of everything and the value of nothing."

To the mother he had spoken of his desire to remain in America—planting the idea that, in case of marriage between Elizabeth and a certain Baron Stullwood, Mrs. Van Linden wouldn't have to cross an ocean to see her daughter and possible future grandchildren.

Groundwork laid, Nigel's seeds had been planted, and now they were beginning to sprout with promise. He needed to proceed next with caution and care, and with all the meticulous planning of a precision military campaign.

"I would be surprised if you didn't run a check on me," he said now, "considering Elizabeth is your only child. Let me facilitate your effort by saying that my ancestral home is Stullwood Hall in Derbyshire. Your agent can pay a visit to my grandmother, the Dowager Baroness. She will inform him of everything you need to know."

Nigel wasn't worried. He knew that Grandmother was more concerned about family honor than the truth. She would do anything to protect the family name. What a scandal it would be—a peer of the realm walking away from his ancestral home. To explain Nigel's absence, Grandmother would have immediately started disseminating a story of her grandson's thirst to see the world and how he had started off by following his friend, Lord Treverton, to visit the highlands of East Africa.

* * *

The Capitol Theater on Broadway was a veritable palace that seated four thousand people and resembled a Renaissance palazzo with gilded statuary, gaudily carved walls, and red velvet everywhere. The musical soundtrack was pumped from an ornate Mighty Wurlitzer pipe organ.

They were watching *The Fall of Babylon* by D. W. Griffith. Elizabeth was entranced by the film's heroine, a plucky tomboyish mountain girl who, in the last days of ancient Babylon, was fighting for her beloved king while the city was being attacked. What was it like to have a cause? Elizabeth wondered as the action played out on the giant screen, with dialogue appearing on intertitles between scenes. Something to believe in and fight for. To wake up in the morning and face a day of goals and challenges, and go to bed at night with a sense of success and accomplishment.

She thought of the brave women who had given up their comfortable lives to train as nurses to take care of the wounded during the war. Others, who had chained themselves to the White House fence, demanding the right to vote. What must it feel like to join with like-minded women in a united cause?

After graduating from high school, Elizabeth had spent a year at an upstate finishing school for young ladies, where the emphasis was on social skills and etiquette. But she hadn't wanted her academic education to end. She had suggested to her mother that she attend college, perhaps a co-educational university, and her mother had said, "What for?"

Elizabeth couldn't put a name to it. During the war, women had been forced to learn to drive automobiles; they had taken up occupations left vacant by men who had gone off to the trenches. And now that it was peacetime, women felt they could be more useful to society. But Elizabeth didn't feel the calling to work in an office or a hospital. Surely there was a place for her somewhere.

She kept these thoughts to herself. She knew that no one would understand her need to find out where she belonged. She had been born into wealth and privilege, had never wanted for anything, and would never want for anything. So why would she want to be someplace else?

The music changed as the organist at the Mighty Wurlitzer switched to a sweet romantic theme while, on the screen, the heroine declared her love to King Belshazzar, who took her into his arms and thanked her for saving the city. He rewarded her with a kiss that had many women in the audience sighing deeply.

Elizabeth looked at Nigel, his handsome profile. It was exciting, sitting with him in the dark. To feel so intimately alone with him while at the same time surrounded by thousands of people. But their attention was on the movie, not on Nigel and Elizabeth, and it caused an unexpected and delightful stirring in her abdomen. She had sat in theaters with boys before, but never with a man.

The past eight weeks had been breathlessly exciting, going out on the town with her handsome English Lord, dancing at the best clubs, riding in Central Park, attending Broadway shows, going to parties. Her mother had expressed the worry that the relationship was moving too rapidly. If this was indeed a courtship, it needed to be scaled back to a more respectable pace. In her mother's day, young men came courting with flowers and manners, and sat in the parlor drinking lemonade. But Elizabeth and her friends didn't want slowness. They needed speed. Her mother and father had courted in a horse and buggy. Nigel took Elizabeth out on the town in his rented Stutz sports car.

Nigel suddenly turned and looked at her, as if he read her thoughts. Their eyes met in the darkness. Elizabeth's heart jumped. His expression was unreadable, but his eyes held a challenge, as if daring her to take a bold step—or so it seemed to Elizabeth, who felt the breath catch in her chest and her heart begin to race. While the Wurlitzer lifted the screen lovers to ecstatic heights, Elizabeth felt herself become aroused—by the booming music of the pipe organ, by Nigel's piercing gaze.

When he reached for her hand, she felt a jolt go through her. He inclined is head and she leaned into him, her breathing rapid now and shallow. She licked her lips in readiness for the kiss, but before they could meet, the audience exploded in applause and the house lights came on. Nigel and Elizabeth broke apart, laughing breathlessly.

They walked home from the Capitol Theater under the bright lights of Broadway. Elizabeth loved strolling beneath the electric signs outside the theaters. Colored bulbs had originally been used, but they burned out too quickly and so white lights had been installed, bestowing upon Broadway the nickname "The Great White Way."

As they walked with other pedestrians, Nigel said, "I came to America to make something of myself, Elizabeth. I can't be content to sit in my ancestral home like some baron of old. I want to make my mark. I want to make a difference. My brother, Rupert, is more suited to managing the Stullwood Estates."

Elizabeth laughed, enjoying the freedom of walking hand in hand with a beau and no chaperone to come between them.

When they reached her home, Nigel turned to her on the sidewalk and said, "I'm leaving New York soon, Elizabeth."

"What? Why?" she cried, the romance of the evening suddenly shattered. She knew she shouldn't be surprised. He had spoken of this from the start. But the past few weeks had been so wonderful, and Elizabeth had started to feel secure with Nigel, in a way that she hadn't with ordinary boys. A sureness with him that this would never end. "Where are you going?"

"I'm going west, Elizabeth. They say there is no longer a frontier out there, but they're wrong. A man faces many possible futures in the West. He can stretch his legs and set his sights as far as he can see." Taking her by the shoulders, Nigel said with heat, "I want to live, Elizabeth! Do you understand that? And I want you to do the same. Promise me, after I have gone, that you will live the wonderful life that is in you! Let nothing pass you by. Seize upon new sensations. Seek adventure! Be afraid of nothing, Elizabeth, and be a blazing new comet in the sky."

Swept up in his enthusiasm, she could barely breathe. She wanted to shout, Yes! Yes! Instead, all she could do was think: The West. A land that was so wild and far away, in her mind, that it might as well be on the moon.

But the panic inside her was quelled and replaced instead by a new excitement. A vision. The West, she thought with a racing heart. The West with Nigel . . .

*   *   *

"You're going out without a corset?" Mrs. Van Linden said in a shocked tone.

"I am wearing a girdle, Mother," Elizabeth replied as a maid did up the many buttons at the back of her dress. "They're all the rage. Girls don't wear corsets anymore. You should try it, Mother. Girdles feel quite liberating. We have so much more freedom of movement." Truth to tell, the tight elasticized fabric encasing her hips, buttocks, and abdomen gave Elizabeth a slight feeling of arousal. But she could never tell her mother this.

Mrs. Van Linden wasn't certain she liked the new fashions coming out of Europe—dresses that hung in straight lines with no waistline, no bust, no derrière—no curves at all. But she did like the fabrics, soft and floaty chiffons and crêpe de Chine.

"And who exactly is going to be at this party tonight?" she asked as she sat and watched as her daughter was being dressed, occasionally giving the maid an instruction or two.

"Just Libby and a few of her friends."

"College boys?" Mrs. Van Linden asked, suspicious of young people's parties these days, which she was certain were nothing like the polite and proper parties of her day.

"A few, I guess." Elizabeth daren't tell her mother it was going to be a "petting party"—couples pairing off to engage in heavy necking. It was all the rage. Elizabeth had only been to two, and the boys she had experimented with hadn't set off fireworks. But her stomach was in knots in anticipation of what Nigel might do tonight.

"And I assume Nigel Barnstable will be escorting you again?"

Elizabeth smiled at herself in the full-length looking glass. Oh, yes, Nigel Barnstable was escorting her again. And she could barely contain her excitement, thinking that tonight she might find herself in a passionate embrace with him. They had yet to kiss, and she was growing impatient. Everyone was kissing these days.

"This exclusivity is highly improper," her mother said as she went through her daughter's purse to make sure Elizabeth had money and a handkerchief. "Unless he makes his intentions known. People are going to talk, Elizabeth."

Let them talk, Elizabeth thought as she draped a fox fur stole, complete with head, paws, and tail, around her shoulders. She had never been the subject of society gossip. The idea of it now quite appealed to her.

Mrs. Van Linden watched her daughter inspect herself in the mirror—flawless as always, the proud mother thought—and wondered if a wedding was in the near future. She wouldn't mind Elizabeth marrying an English Lord. Nigel was a handsome young man, charming and polite. But she wished she could meet his family. Henry was checking on his background and so far all he'd learned was that the Barnstables of Stullwood were a very old and wealthy family.

As they left the bedroom, Mrs. Van Linden laid a hand on her daughter's arm and said, "If there's to be a wedding, I need to start planning it now."

"Oh, Mother," Elizabeth said impatiently. "I want to enjoy my evening with Nigel. Don't spoil it with your scheming."

Mrs. Van Linden watched her go, a trifle hurt at the rebuke. It isn't scheming, she wanted to say, if it's just a mother watching out for her precious child. And then she was suddenly gripped by a fresh and unexpected fear. From the moment a baby girl had been placed in her arms, Gertrude Van Linden had planned and imagined and fantasized about her daughter's wedding. But now, out of the blue, she was terrified of her daughter actually getting married. It was strange, she thought now as she went down to dinner, which was to be alone with

Henry, that something could be both bad and good, could make a person both sad and happy. On the surface, it was just a wedding. But the hard reality was that marriage would make Elizabeth no longer her little girl but a woman in her own right, and Mrs. Van Linden wasn't sure she was quite ready to accept that.

Elizabeth's friend Libby lived with her mother in a tenth floor apartment in Manhattan. Elizabeth and Nigel joined others in an elevator and when they arrived at the tenth floor, found the party already underway and spilling into the hall. Music spilled out too—"My Island of Golden Dreams"—from the gramophone.

Elizabeth handed her coat to a Negro maid and looked around for familiar faces. While young men shed their jackets, girls who arrived wearing foundation garments, forced on them by their mothers, stopped in the bathroom first to "park their girdles" to allow for more freedom when dancing. And, according to some girls, girdles discouraged boys from getting fresh.

"Help yourself to drinks and something to eat," Elizabeth said to Nigel. "I have to find Libby. I so want her to meet you."

Nigel roamed the room. He felt edgy. Tonight was crucial. He needed to make the next move in his pursuit of Elizabeth without appearing impatient. He checked his appearance in a mirror. Good. Stylish. Not like the fraternity boys around him, slouching in baggy pants and raccoon coats, throwing out the latest slang, calling each other "the real McCoy." He accepted a drink and waited patiently.

Elizabeth found her friend Libby by the French doors leading to the balcony. She was standing with a knot of girls, showing them something while they had their heads together over it. They all wore shapeless dresses that stopped at their calves. They wore their hair long in imitation of "America's Sweetheart," movie star Mary Pickford. But Libby had daringly bobbed her hair, shocking her friends by marching into a barbershop to sit with men while the barber chopped her hair off.

"I found this next to my mother's bed," Libby said, her eyes flashing. It was a pamphlet called *Birth Control Review*. She had it open to a baffling illustration. The caption described it as being "a diaphragm."

"What's that?" asked one of the girls.

"It prevents babies," Libby said in a knowing tone. "It's also called a Dutch cap because they come from Holland, but they're illegal in this country."

Elizabeth tried to picture how it worked but couldn't. "Where does it go?" one of the other girls asked, and the rest giggled.

Libby said, "My mother told me all about Mrs. Sanger. Four years ago, she opened a family planning clinic—"

"A what?"

"It's a place where you learn about birth control. It was the only one in America, and they handed out contraceptives. But it's against the law to give women information on contraception, so right after the clinic opened, Mrs. Sanger was arrested. She went to trial and was convicted because the judge said that women did not have the right to copulate when they are sure there would be no resulting conception."

She paused to let her friends digest this very risqué information while the gramophone belted out the voice of popular singer Billy Murray as he sang "Are You From Dixie?"

Libby resumed her informed discourse, enjoying being the one in the know, because of her progressive mother. "Mrs. Sanger has started a birth control movement—my mother is a member—and because it is growing in popularity, and because of mounting public interest, the law has been amended to allow medical doctors to prescribe contraceptive information, so long as it's for medical reasons."

One of the other girls said, "I wonder if that's what happened to Phoebe Hogan. If she, you know, needed this birth control."

"What are you talking about?"

"Didn't you hear? Phoebe eloped with John DeGuy!"

"No!"

"Where did they go?"

"Up to Canada. Just across the border there are Gretna Green towns where they don't make you wait. All you need is your birth certificate and it's all legal. She said her father wouldn't give her permission to marry John, so they ran off."

"Surely her father will disinherit her."

Libby shrugged. "John DeGuy is filthy rich."

"And terribly good looking!"

Drifting away from her friends, Elizabeth searched the smoke-filled room for Nigel.

While someone kept fox-trots going on the gramophone, the party progressed and couples paired off to get themselves in clinches around the room, on the stairs, the sofa, on overstuffed chairs, girls in boys' laps, arms entwined, mouths glued together like limpets. The girls making sure their knees and garters showed. Elizabeth knew they never carried it further, never followed their dates up to a bedroom.

It was all show. Girls wanting to appear "hot" for shock value. All of them thinking, what would Mummy and Daddy think?

She sighed restlessly. Normally she loved being with her friends. But tonight . . . something was different. As she listened to the girls exchange gossip and the boys voice cynicism, she thought: What are they going to do with their lives?

She found Nigel across the smoky room. He was leaning in a doorway, flicking his gold cigarette lighter on and off, staring at the flame. He looked so sophisticated and debonair, so out of place among these kids. He looked up. Their eyes met and his words from several nights ago rang again in her ears: "I want to make something of myself. I'm going west, Elizabeth. They say there is no longer a frontier out there, but they're wrong. A man faces many possible futures in the West."

And suddenly these boys and girls with their pretensions and posturings seemed shallow. None of them spoke of dreams and goals. None of them had ambitions. They didn't seem, in fact, interested in anything at all except how daring and shocking they could be.

But Nigel . . . he was a visionary. She knew he was going to realize his dream. She envied him. Men had the freedom to do whatever they wanted, to brave a new frontier and make a change in the world. Women were restricted, they had to do what they were told, and Elizabeth, who had been obedient all her life, suddenly no longer wanted to do what she was told.

She went up to him and drew him aside. "I'm bored," she said. "Take me somewhere exciting."

He raised his eyebrows. "Now?"

"Right now."

He grinned. "I know just the place."

They rode in the sports car he had rented for his stay in New York, and Elizabeth loved the openness of it, the feel of the wind against her face. Nigel wouldn't tell her where they were going. When she asked, he would just send her a mysterious smile and a wink.

In the thick of Saturday night traffic, they headed up Fifth Avenue toward Uptown, and when they crossed 96th Street, she realized they were heading into forbidden territory. They arrived at the corner of 142nd Street and Lenox Avenue to stop in front of a brightly lit place called the Ebony Club. Elizabeth sucked in her breath. They were deep in Harlem, where New York's black people lived.

Kids loitered out front, and Nigel offered them a dollar to watch his car. Then they went inside and Elizabeth received a further shock.

She knew from her more progressive friends that there were Afro-American clubs in Harlem owned and operated by blacks, with all-black entertainers, but the audience was exclusively whites. Other clubs, owned and operated by Negroes, catered to a black audience and few white people ventured through those doors. It was to one of the latter establishments that Nigel had brought her.

Elizabeth trembled with excitement as they were met by a smiling maître d'. The club was brilliantly lit and beautifully decorated with potted palm trees, the tables covered in white cloths, a glittering ball revolving over the dance floor. As they were taken to a table, Elizabeth looked around at all the black people, spotting only a couple of other white faces in the crowd, and she wondered in excitement laced with fear what deliciously sinful delights she was going to taste tonight.

Nigel ordered two glasses of tonic with lime—like the other patrons, he had brought a gin flask with him.

The band finished playing a ragtime number and launched into something new called "jazz." The soaring sounds of brass trumpets and trombones accompanied the amazing piano of a young jazz musician from New Orleans named Jelly Roll Morton. The white people in the audience thought themselves very trendy and sophisticated, not knowing that the pianist's real name was Ferdinand Lamothe and that his adopted nickname, "Jelly Roll," was Negro slang for female genitalia.

Next came a solo trumpeter who played a toe-tapping Dixieland piece that was followed by a young black woman who belted out a gut-wrenching song called "The Blues." The song was both sad and spiritual, the lyrics about a tragic romance but sounding also like a gospel hymn. And then a black man came out and sang a song called "Swanee," written by a young composer named Gershwin, and the audience went wild.

Elizabeth was mesmerized. She had never heard such sounds before, had never been moved by such rhythm. She felt "fast" and "racy." The music was hot; it throbbed under her skin. Black couples danced in a wild, uninhibited way. The dance had come from a city in the South—Charleston—and the women flailed their bare arms and spread their legs in immodest abandon.

A young black woman in a red satin chemise and long strands of pearls caught Elizabeth's eye and motioned her to come out onto the floor. Elizabeth jumped at the challenge.

"Let the music move you, sister," the young woman said. "You don't do the dancing, the music does the dancing for you. Now follow me. Right foot forward, now back. Left foot forward, now back. That's right! Stand with your feet apart, like this, bend your knees and put your hands on them. Bring your knees together and cross your hands over."

Elizabeth laughed as she fumbled and stumbled and tried to move to the beat. She saw Nigel at the table, watching her, smiling. As the other dancers encouraged her, Elizabeth threw herself into the music and began to feel it run hotly in her veins. With each flail of her arms she felt invisible bonds break, as if she were casting off chains. With each stomp of her foot on the parquet floor, she felt as if she were stamping out the old ways of thinking and looking at the world.

Our mothers wore whalebone corsets and hobble skirts that bound their ankles together so that they walked with mincing steps and could barely climb into a taxi.

This was what she wanted! *This* was freedom!

The music changed, Elizabeth thanked the dancers, and when she returned to the table, fanning herself and dabbing her perspiring forehead with a napkin, Nigel stood up and took her back out onto the dance floor. But this time they swayed to a slow, bluesy song, holding on to each other. Elizabeth closed her eyes and lost herself in Nigel's masculine embrace, felt his body against hers, his firm guidance as they stepped and turned. She wanted to stay like that forever.

He slowly guided Elizabeth across the floor, away from tables and people, to stop behind a lush potted plant where he took her by the shoulders, looked into her eyes and said, "Oh, Elizabeth, you've gotten under my skin. When I came to New York I hadn't planned on falling in love. But you cast some sort of spell over me. I wish I could stay, but I have my eye on a certain property in California, and I can't let someone else grab it."

While he spoke, and someone sang, "I did more for you, baby, than the good Lord ever done," Elizabeth let herself get lost in his intense gaze, felt his dark pupils reach down for her soul and draw it out to join his. She couldn't breathe. She felt herself change, as if something in her drink were metamorphosing her into a brand-new creature. And as this miraculous transformation was under way, she began to feel a thought grow in her mind, from germ to embryo, gaining shape, solidifying until it was complete, perfect, frightening.

She knew that her mother had her only daughter's wedding all planned, that it was one of Mrs. Van Linden's favorite pastimes. It would be the society wedding of the season, a huge affair with hundreds of guests.

And Elizabeth would have no say in any of it.

"Take me with you," she said impulsively. "Take me west."

"What?" He laughed. "What are you talking about?"

"I want to go west with you, Nigel. I want to be with you. And I need my freedom."

He chuckled, shook his head. "Your parents would never allow it!"

"If we get married they'd have no say-so."

He stared at her. "Of course I want to marry you. It's all I've thought about these past weeks. But I can't wait that long, Elizabeth. Your mother would insist on at least a twelve-month engagement."

"We'll elope. We can go to Canada." Yes! To the Gretna Green towns Phoebe and John DeGuy had daringly run off to.

He laughed, and then grew serious. "Your parents wouldn't be happy about that."

"I'm almost twenty years old. In another year I shall be able to vote. I know my own mind, and I want to be free to choose."

Elizabeth knew that, more than anything, *she* wanted to choose her own clothing, *she* wanted to decide what to order from a menu, *she* wanted to govern her own life and be free of her mother's suffocating control. "Nigel, I have to make my way in the world. I don't know yet what I will do, but I know I am not cut out for parlors and corsets. I want to be a frontier woman with challenges and dreams." And as soon as she said "frontier," it felt right and perfect in her mind, as if it had been there all along, waiting for her to find it. "I want to discover the West, Nigel, with you."

"My God, Elizabeth," he said, taking her face between his hands, speaking with passion. "I must be dreaming, for I am the luckiest man alive. I love you."

He drew her to him and, holding her tight, pressed his lips to hers in a long, deep kiss. As Elizabeth snaked her arms around his neck and squirmed against him, as the band started up another Charleston number and the club was filled with the thunder of shoes stomping on the dance floor, Nigel thought he was truly lucky indeed. He had not expected his seduction to come so easily and quickly. She had played into his hands far better than he had anticipated. And the elopement was an added bonus, as it eliminated the need to explain to the Van Lindens why none of his family was going to come across the Atlantic to attend his wedding.

*   *   *

In the lobby of his hotel, Nigel entered the phone booth and, undoing his tie, placed a phone call.

When it went through, he spoke into the instrument. "Baron Stullwood here, Mr. Franklin. You recall that last week we discussed my interest in purchasing land out west. Specifically Southern California. You said that I needed to secure the financing first. Well, I am happy to inform you that limitless financing is soon to be available to me. Money will be no object."

He listened. "Tomorrow will be fine. I shall be there first thing." He listened again. "How much land do I wish? Why, my good fellow, as much land as you can possibly find for me, of course."

CHAPTER FIVE

Palm Springs, California

June 1920

AS LUISA CROSSED THE stream to the other side of the canyon, she reminded herself that she was no longer on Indian land.

But how could that be?

Luisa Padilla puzzled over the mystery as she made her way up the narrow canyon, a basket on her back.

For generations, her people had lived here. And then pale-skinned men came and drew lines in the earth. They said, "This is Indian land, this is white man's land. You live there." They called it a reservation. That was where Luisa lived.

But how could this not be Indian land when the mother of her people came here long ago, to drink water and rest after her long journey?

Luisa was a proud woman. She cherished her dignity. Although age sixty, she stood straight and tall, refusing to bend with the years. She wore a long skirt made of calico, and a white, long-sleeved blouse that was tucked into her belt. Before the white men came to the valley, the women of Luisa's tribe wore short skirts made of grass, and walked bare-breasted beneath the sun. And then the white men said they had to cover up. Luisa still did not know why.

She wore her long white hair in two neat braids, the way the Spanish priests had taught her people. They didn't like to see women's hair hanging loose and flying in the wind. It made the priests nervous.

Luisa and her people had seen mountain men come through this dry valley, trackers and trailblazers, white men with mules and wagons on their way to "better" places like San Diego and Los Angeles. Then came Mormons and stagecoaches, and men with paints and drawing

pads, and men with instruments to measure the desert's many unquan-
tifiable natures. Then came the railroad, and the stagecoaches vanished.

Luisa's people welcomed them all with food and water and shade.
The priests who came from Spain changed her people's names and
called them "Mission Indians." Then came the Mexicans who taught
the Indians how to build houses out of adobe. Then the white man
came with another language and many different ways to worship Jesus.
And a white man in a faraway place called Congress said he was giving
land to the Indians and called it "reservation." But how could he give
them what they already owned?

There were not many white people here when Luisa was young.
An Indian agent, a railroad agent, a few scattered settlers. Now they
were coming in more numbers, buying land, and staying. Calling this
place theirs.

And new ones, now, she thought, recalling what the spirit of the
red diamond rattlesnake had told her while she was gathering reeds
for her basket. Different white men, who were going to bring evil.

She trudged up the gradual slope, her sandals stepping over
rocks and boulders worn smooth from centuries of flash floods that
periodically raged through this wide ravine. Luisa followed a stream
that sparkled and gurgled and fed the many majestic palm trees that
marched in a line up the canyon. The trees were very old and sacred
to Luisa's people. The white man named them Washingtonia, after a
man Luisa had never heard of.

She stopped to harvest ripe elderberries growing near the stream.

Forty years ago, men who were called the Federal Government sent
agents to come and take care of Luisa's people. Why do we need agents,
she wondered, when we have been taking care of ourselves since the
dawn when Mukat created us and instructed us how to live?

She shook her head as her brown hands worked. White men had
called her people "blanket Christians" because they thought the Indians
had converted to Jesus so that the priests would give them blankets.
That wasn't so. There was plenty of room for gods, what was one more?

Luisa was a Christian. Once a week Father Vega came from Banning
to set up an altar on the back of his buckboard wagon. Luisa and her
people knelt and crossed themselves and said, "Our Father" and "Hail
Mary." They accepted the Sunday wafer but not the wine. Only the
priest got the wine. He led a prayer for the repose of the soul of one

of their departed. He spoke the deceased's name but Luisa and her people did not. It was bad luck to speak the names of the dead. And souls did not repose. The spirits of the dead stayed among the living. No one ever really went away.

She paused when she heard the train whistle. Shading her eyes, she saw across the valley the locomotive ten miles in the distance, shooting like a black arrow across the flat desert. She wondered if the new white people that she had been warned about would be getting off at the small way station where the engine took on wood and water.

She remembered the day when she was seventeen and the new railroad came through. As the white man reckoned, the year was 1877, and great sledges drawn by oxen carried timber and iron to the desert and many workers laid a curious "road." She remembered when the first noisy, steam-belching engine roared down from Banning Pass to race across the flat desert like a hungry beast determined to devour all in its path. Luisa and her people had stood in silent attendance to witness what they knew was the end of the old ways. The railroad would bring more white people. From that day on, Luisa had known that there would be no stopping them.

Luisa was called by a name that came from a country she had never seen, India. The real names of her people were buried in the sand of their desert. They would never know those names. The white men said Luisa's people were a band of Indians in the Cahuilla tribe. But her people had never been to India. And Cahuilla was not a word in her language. They call us Morongo and Cabazon and Agua Caliente, she thought, all words from Spain. And I have never been there either.

She waited and watched. This time, the train did not stop. It spewed out its steam and raced on by, to streak up the valley to a place called Yuma, Arizona.

Luisa sighed. The white men she had been warned about were not coming today. She picked up her basket of blackberries that would be used to make a medicinal drink, or sun-dried to be stored and eaten later. She said a prayer of thanks to the spirit of the bush who had just relinquished its berries, and then she went back down the canyon, a lone Indian woman, with too many things on her mind.

At the mouth of the canyon, where the terrain flattened and the streams fanned out to sink into the sand, she saw a stranger riding toward her on a black mare.

He dismounted. "Greetings, Mother," he said, pulling on the brim of his Stetson where Luisa saw a rattlesnake frozen in a strike. She wondered if it was his clan's totem.

She was wary of him. Was he one of the evil ones that had been foretold? She looked at the snake on his hat again, thought about it, then decided that it was a sign that he was a man she could trust because she herself was weaving a red diamond rattlesnake pattern into a sacred basket. So she knew the spirits wanted her to speak with this man. They told her she could trust him.

"Señor," she said.

"Do you speak English?"

"I do."

"May I drink from your stream?"

"You may."

Cody McNeal had ridden four hundred miles from Tombstone. He had taken back roads and trails by day and slept under the stars at night. He couldn't travel by main roads and highways because the occasional automobile spooked his horse.

As he approached her, Luisa saw that he walked with a spirit at his side, but he didn't know it. The spirit told her that the stranger came from a land of tall pine trees and snow. There were Indians there, of a tribe not familiar to Luisa. His heart was filled with sorrow and anger and regret.

And he was alone in the world.

Spirits were not the only ones who spoke to Luisa. Signs were all around and she kept herself alert at all times to catch them. The way the stranger's spurs sounded like bells when he walked. There was meaning there. The swish of his long, black duster coat. It, too, was saying something. But she needed to think upon these signs to interpret their message.

Thirst slaked, Cody rose to his feet and said, "I'm looking for a settlement called Palm Springs. I was told I could find it at the base of this mountain."

She lifted her arm and pointed to the east. "In the next canyon. White men live there."

Cody squinted eastward, following the jagged base of the foothills as they jutted in and out of the flat, yellow desert. In Banning he had been told that there were some settlers here, farmers, a general store, a church, a school. He wondered if electricity had arrived there, and the telephone, and automobiles.

He looked up at the stark mountain, rocky halfway up, and then the timberline started. He looked across the flat, yellow valley to lavender mountains in the distance. His eyes took in sand dunes and cacti, palm trees and creosote bushes. A barren, desolate land but possessing a haunting beauty.

A place where a man could rest his weary mind and pray that the dark devils didn't catch up to him.

"Thank you for the water, Mother," he said and reached into his vest pocket. She accepted the coin graciously. *Water is not free. We Indians own the water. The Great Father in Washington said so.*

She smiled. He was respectful. Most white men called her "Ma'am," or "Lady." Some didn't address her politely at all. This one knew the way of Indians. Up north, she thought, other tribes. He lived among them.

When she was a young woman, a white man came to the village and asked questions. He wanted to know her age. She said she was born in the Year Of the Second Famine. This did not satisfy him. He asked more questions until he said, "You were born in 1860." He seemed happy with himself as he wrote things in a little book and then left. Other men like him came through the Valley, strangers with little books and pencils, who asked questions and seemed pleased with themselves. Luisa learned that they were called anthropologists and that they were "studying" Indians. They told her she was Cahuilla, even though she told them she was Iviatim, and they said her tribe was the western division of the Shoshone people. She had never heard of these people. They said her language was in the Uto-Aztecan family. She had never heard of this family. For all their studying, Luisa thought, they knew very little about Indians.

But this white man, dressed like a cowboy, he knew Indians.

A man of many words but who spoke little. *People think he has nothing to say. They are wrong.*

She watched the stranger mount his horse and ride off. The man from the land of snow and pine trees hasn't come for land or money, she thought. *He is looking for something. He will find it, but it will not be what he wants.*

CHAPTER SIX

New York City

July 1920

"THE TOWN IS CALLED Palm Springs, Mr. Barnstable. Well, it's more of a village really. There is a church and schoolhouse. But no electricity. However, telephone and telegraph services are available at the general store."

Nigel was sitting in the office of Wallace Property Sales & Management, located on the tenth floor of the Fuller Building on Fifth and Broadway, a skyscraper lovingly nicknamed the "Flatiron."

Nigel and Elizabeth had spent the past three weeks secretly preparing for their elopement, which was to happen tonight. They had drawn Libby into their drama, who was only too eager to help. She was going to pick Elizabeth up from her home with the story that the two friends were going upstate to visit Libby's cousin. But in truth, Elizabeth would be taken to Grand Central Station where Nigel would be waiting for her.

In the meantime, Nigel had been looking at various available properties in Southern California and had found something desirable in Riverside County. To push the more pricy properties, the land agent had gone to the expense of getting the photographs hand-colored.

"Palm Springs is technically only a village right now, but the potential for investment and growth is limitless," the agent continued. "It might interest you to know that date palms were imported into the Coachella Valley from Arabia nearly forty years ago and have proven to flourish with very little care. One can make a good living cultivating and harvesting dates."

As the agent brought out photographs and spread them on his desk, Nigel's thoughts seized upon this new idea and began to run with it. Arabian dates, he thought. He had known he wanted to found his empire on a particular enterprise, but he had not yet decided on cattle or sheep, or possibly the citrus industry. But dates now sounded exotic and new and challenging.

"This horse property was built by a family in Seattle," the agent said, showing Nigel the hand-colored pictures. "They named it La Alma del Desierto, which means the soul or spirit of the desert, and they used it as their winter home. But the head of the family died and his widow didn't want to make the twice-a-year journey, so she has put it up for sale. The house sits on a hundred acres, with stables, a carriage house, servants' quarters, and a bunkhouse for ranch hands, should you wish to keep the horses."

There was no question that Nigel was going to keep the horses. He wished he could have brought Blaze out from England. But he had no doubt that he would find a good replacement.

"The house itself boasts fifteen rooms, all spacious and airy with tiled floors throughout, high ceilings and tall windows with spectacular views of the desert and mountains. The property lies a mere six miles from a railroad that connects Palm Springs with Los Angeles and cities north, and eastward with Phoenix and all the way to the East Coast."

As Nigel looked at the expanse of land with clusters of palm trees, flowering cacti, and creosote bushes, he saw possibilities.

"Palm Springs might be a little out of the way," the agent continued, eager to make the sale as he had had it on the books for two years, and the big house was expensive to keep up, "but it is an oasis—and Eden, if you will—of palm trees, natural waterfalls, and mineral hot springs that purportedly cure all ailments and restore youth and virility. And again, although the area is a desert, I assure you that you needn't worry about fresh water sources. The Coachella Valley sits on an enormous aquifer. In some places, fresh water lies at depths between fifty and two hundred feet. Engineers have dug gushers that will provide water for hundreds of years to come."

He waited anxiously. This was usually the point where the sale fell through. No matter how many times he mentioned water, no matter how much he pushed the waterfalls and springs and ponds, it all boiled down to the fact that the property was in the desert. And not a lot of people wanted to live in a desert.

However, to his immense relief, Nigel Barnstable said, "Yes. I want this property." It surprised the agent, as he hadn't thought an Englishman would gravitate to so hot and dry a climate. And then he thought, actually, the fellow might be looking for a complete change, in which case you couldn't get more changed than England to the desert.

But Nigel wasn't going to be satisfied with just a hundred acres. He had been told that he couldn't buy all the land he wanted because some of it was Indian land and no one could purchase that. But no one was going to tell Baron Stullwood what he could or could not do. The British were buying up thousands of acres in East Africa and Australia, creating small kingdoms for themselves. Why should America be different? He certainly wasn't going to let a few Indians stand in his way.

*   *   *

Elizabeth sat at the vanity in her hotel room, staring at her reflection as she brushed out her silky blond hair. She looked for signs of change. She was a married woman now, and yet her face looked the same.

The change will come later, after tonight.

She had read *The Sheik* by Edith Maude Hull, a sensational romance novel that was making American women sigh in their sleep, and while Elizabeth wasn't sure what "ravishment" entailed, she hoped it would be as thrilling with Nigel as it was between Lady Diana and Sheik Ahmed. Ironically, while Edith Hull's book was highly sexually charged, it was woefully lacking in informative details. Somehow the author had been able to insinuate what was going on inside the tent without illuminating the reader—that Ahmed forced himself on his unwilling prisoner every night until she fell in love with him.

When Elizabeth was younger she had asked her mother about sex, but all Mrs. Van Linden would say was, "Women don't enjoy the act. We draw our pleasure from our children. So while he's doing it, just close your eyes and think of children."

And now she waited for Nigel to join her. The adventure had been a heady whirlwind of excitement, glamour, and romance straight out of a fairy tale. Libby had taken them to Grand Central Station where she had seen them off with rice and a bouquet of flowers for Elizabeth. The train ride up the Hudson Valley. The excitement of finding an out-of-the-way hotel. Speaking vows before the justice of the peace. A romantic dinner. And now . . .

Nigel emerged from the bathroom wearing a red velvet dressing gown over white silk pajamas. He knelt before Elizabeth and took her hands in his. "You have made me the happiest man alive. Why did God smile on me so? What did I do to deserve such a beautiful angel?"

Tears filled her eyes. "It is I who is the lucky one, my dearest." She touched his cheek, and her fingers trembled.

Nigel reached into the pocket of his dressing gown and brought out a large envelope. "Here is my wedding gift to you."

She laughed. "What ever is it?" She excitedly opened the envelope and drew out the photograph of an exotic looking house. "A picture?"

"The house, my darling. It's yours! I bought it for you. It's in California, an elegant Spanish-style house built for a true lady."

She looked at the picture and then at Nigel. "You've already bought a house?"

His smile fell. "Don't you like it?"

"Yes," she said quickly. "It's wonderful. I had just thought we would pick our home together."

"My dearest," he said, smiling again. "You are the love of my life, and I want to set you up with your own kingdom. You are a Baroness now and entitled to rule over your own domain."

He rose and drew her to her feet. "My sweet angel, you will have the freedom of the wide-open spaces. We will have horses and gardens, and we will know only the best people. We will be the Baron and Baroness of a splendid property that will be unlike anything seen in the West."

She returned her gaze to the hand-tinted photograph. She could not argue that it was an enchanting scene. The arches and columns of cream-colored stucco, the deep veranda with purple shade, the blue-tiled fountain and red-tiled roof. But what captivated her more was the backdrop: towering green palm trees with a snow-capped mountain rising behind them beneath a clear, azure sky. How curious. Tropical trees and snow. She hadn't known such a place existed.

He kissed her then, and said, "Now come. It's our wedding night. Let me worship your body. Let me show you how truly and deeply I love you."

It wasn't at all as her mother had warned about. If Elizabeth closed her eyes, it wasn't to think of children but to experience Nigel's embrace more sharply, to think of the two of them as the only people on earth. She had not known a man's hands could be so exciting, to find places on her body that set her on fire. He took his time, was gentle yet intense. His kisses burned her lips. He made her moan and then weep with happiness.

Later, as Elizabeth drifted off to sleep, dreaming of their new life in the West, Nigel smoked a cigarette and thought about their new home. A hundred acres wouldn't do. Not by a long shot.

* * *

"You did *what!*" Van Linden shouted so loudly that Button jumped off Elizabeth's lap and ran to hide under the sofa.

"We got married, Daddy," Elizabeth said calmly. She and Nigel sat side by side in a Louis Quinze love seat upholstered in damask. They were holding hands and showing a united front. "I'm sorry we deceived you, but I didn't want a big wedding."

His eyes burned with fury. "People will raise eyebrows. They'll wonder why you were in such a hurry. They'll think you had to get married!"

"They can think what they want," Elizabeth said quietly, "but I didn't want to wait through a traditional year-long engagement simply because that was the way it was done before the war. Engagements have gotten shorter. It's a different age."

"So people keep telling me," Van Linden growled. He looked at his wife who had so far said nothing. "Gertrude?" She didn't reply. The shock of the news was so great that her body had gone limp. She stared at her daughter and tried to breathe. She felt as if the floor, the entire planet, had been knocked out from under her. After all she had done for her daughter, this was how the girl repaid her? Gertrude realized that her thoughts were selfish, that she was thinking only of her own happiness at the moment, but then wasn't it about time? After nineteen years of doting on Elizabeth, of making sure she was happy, Mrs. Van Linden felt she was owed a little something in return. A big wedding. Had it truly been too much to ask for?

"Nigel and I are so very happy, Mother."

"I promise to take good care of your daughter, Mrs. Van Linden."

"I had so looked forward to a big wedding," she finally managed to say. It sounded feeble, and she hated sounding feeble, or looking feeble. Of all the shocks in the world that she had thought she was prepared for—someday, someone coming to her door to say that Henry had had a heart attack at his office—none of that preparation had prepared her for this.

"But it was my wedding," Elizabeth said gently.

"Weddings aren't just for the bride and groom," Mrs. Van Linden said fretfully, and she hated sounding fretful more than she hated sounding feeble so she decided she wasn't going to say another word.

Van Linden glared at his errant daughter with a thunderous expression. He didn't care about weddings but what he had expected was Nigel's formal request to marry his daughter. He knew what was going on here—Van Linden was not a stranger to power struggles. He'd engaged in enough in his time. Young Turk showing the old man who was really in charge here—when it came to Elizabeth, at any rate.

It was nothing less than a hostile takeover. Van Linden had used such tactics in the past in his own business dealings, acquiring a company whose management was resisting by going directly to the shareholders. He had to grudgingly hand it to the boy, it was a brilliant move.

And as it was obvious his daughter was happy, he supposed that was all that counted when it came down to it. He loved his baby girl but these new times baffled him. Van Linden didn't know if he could have handled a headstrong young woman under his roof, driving him to worry every time she stepped out with her wild friends. Now she was under Barnstable's firm hand, she was his responsibility, and good luck to him for that.

"There's something else," Elizabeth said.

"Good Lord, how could there be something else?"

"We're moving to California."

Mrs. Van Linden gave a cry, and Elizabeth immediately went to her side.

"California!" Van Linden shouted.

Nigel spoke quickly. "It's a land of countless opportunities, where a man with vision and courage can really make his mark in the world. There are empires to be built, fortunes to be made. I tell you, my good man, before long you will be hearing the name Nigel Barnstable spoken in financial circles."

Van Linden eyed his new son-in-law. This was certainly unexpected. Nigel's desire to move west and make something of himself. Now that was something they had in common—the pioneering spirit. Hadn't Van Linden himself blazed a few trails in industry, adapting to new technology when other companies fell behind? He always said that progress was Henry Van Linden's middle name. So Barnstable wasn't going to expect his father-in-law to give him a leg up in the world after all. Making a go of it on his own. Suddenly he was looking at his new son-in-law in a different, vastly improved light.

"California, eh? You've bought how many acres? Horses, is it? A ranch," Van Linden said, his mind filling with illustrations he had seen in *Harper's Weekly*, Western stories he had read as a boy, reproductions of famous paintings done by Remington and Russell—vistas of plains and buffalo and hardy pioneers settling a wild land.

Of course, the West was tame now, but the wide-open spaces were still there, and as the boy said, countless opportunities for a man to make something of himself. Oh well, the pragmatic industrialist thought, nothing to be done about it now. Water under the bridge, and all that. The adaptable businessman was the successful one. And the boy showed spirit. Fine. He would arrange to take Barnstable to the family attorney in the morning and work out the details of Elizabeth's trust fund.

Elizabeth patted her mother's hand. "Nigel has bought the most beautiful house. You will have to come and visit."

But Gertrude Van Linden couldn't speak. Two lethal blows in one afternoon, the second far more devastating than the first—Elizabeth moving away. In all her years of planning and maneuvering, in all her scheming and machinations, in all her fantasies about the future, all the times she had tried to peer ahead through the years—the fact of Elizabeth leaving the Van Linden mansion had never come up. It had always been assumed that after their daughter married, the newlyweds would be given an apartment in the big house, with servants and a private entrance of their own.

You have hurt me beyond words, Elizabeth, she thought, retrieving her hand. But she didn't voice this out loud, because there were in fact no words.

"There's a telephone in town and we can keep in touch through letters," Elizabeth said anxiously, wanting reassurance from the mother who had always reassured her. "I'm sorry I shocked you, Mother. This was something I had to do. I had made up my mind to marry Nigel, and I wanted it to be on my own terms."

"Just promise us," Van Linden said, "that you won't shock us like that again. I don't know that your mother's heart could take it.

"I promise," Elizabeth said with a smile. "Besides, I will be blissfully happy with Nigel. What could I possibly do to shock you again?"

* * *

"I don't like that man," Mrs. Van Linden said.

"Why ever not? He seems quite the gentleman."

Gertrude Van Linden held onto the bedpost to steady herself as her lady's maid unlaced her corset. "He robbed me of a wedding and now he's taking my only child three thousand miles away."

When the corset came off, Mrs. Van Linden released a heavy sigh. While Fiona Wilson helped her into a satin peignoir, she said, "Elizabeth says I should stop wearing corsets and switch to girdles. But I'm fifty-four years old, Wilson. At my age, I would feel naked without a corset."

As she took a seat before her vanity table so that Wilson could take down her hair, she pressed her hand to her breastbone and winced.

"Are you all right, Madam?"

"The doctor has me on a new medication. It gives me heartburn."

"I really think you ought to tell Miss Elizabeth about your condition," Fiona said as she removed hairpins from her mistress's elaborate coiffure.

"No, she has enough to deal with right now. And I don't want to worry her." The truth was, Gertrude hadn't the strength to tell her daughter how terribly hurt she was. When Gertrude had realized that she had both looked forward to and yet feared her daughter getting married, that was nothing compared to this. She supposed that all mothers were divided on the issue of daughters getting married—it was both a celebration and a loss of sorts. But this had not even entered Gertrude Van Linden's field of vision. That Elizabeth should move away. Three thousand miles . . .

"Have you solved the domestic staff problem?" Fiona asked.

"I have, thank God." Four servants, willing to go west.

She glanced at the reflection of the woman standing behind her, a somewhat pretty woman in her forties, plainly dressed with her hair in a bun. Gertrude Van Linden weighed her next words. "That just leaves Elizabeth's lady's maid. Wilson, I have a tremendous favor to ask of you . . ."

Fiona's hands froze in the air, hairpins in one, comb in the other. She felt her heart skip a beat. "Yes, Madam?"

"I want you to go to California and take care of Elizabeth."

Fiona's heart skipped another beat and then it sank. California!

"I . . . hardly know what to say, Madam." Fiona was dedicated to her mistress and would be forever grateful to Mrs. Van Linden for rescuing her from a terrible situation. Her previous employer, a countess in Sussex, had accused her of stealing. Not only had Fiona, thirty-three years old at the time and a faithful servant, gotten sacked, the countess had said she would not give a good reference and, if asked, would tell prospective employers that Wilson was a thief. Serendipitously, Americans were staying at the home where Fiona's sister was the housekeeper. The sister had told her mistress, and therefore the Americans, what had happened, and Fiona had gotten hired by Mrs. Van Linden.

Their eyes met now in the mirror as Mrs. Van Linden recalled the day she was visiting her cousin who had married a duke thirty years ago. They were enjoying tea when her cousin noticed that the house-keeper was distracted. "What is it, Mrs. Anderson? Please do tell."

And she had told a story of her sister getting wrongfully accused of theft and subsequently losing her job. "Now she's got nowhere to go. Her little bit of savings won't last, and I haven't much to offer. She didn't do it, Madam. My sister Fiona is the most honest woman on earth."

Mrs. Van Linden's cousin had said, "I know the countess. She is known for losing things and blaming the servants. I'll see if I can find her a position."

But in that moment Mrs. Van Linden had thought it would be nice to have a proper English lady's maid and had spoken up for Fiona on the spot.

She knew, as they looked at each other in the glass, that Fiona was remembering the same thing. She also knew that Fiona did not want to go west.

"I know it's a tremendous thing to ask of you, Wilson, but I am worried about Elizabeth. I need to know that she has a kind and familiar body with her in that wild place."

Fiona compressed her lips to keep her chin from trembling. Mrs. Van Linden didn't know about Lawrence, Fiona's one chance at marriage and happiness before getting locked into spinsterhood and a dismal future.

At forty-three and being a domestic servant, her prospects of meeting a man and getting married were slim to none. And she had been resigned to this when she had been taking her usual Sunday walk through Central Park one blustery day and a bowler hat had tumbled across her path. "Hoy there!" came a voice on the wind, and she saw a hatless man running toward her. Immediately Fiona broke into a run, and the pair of them chased the hat down a paved path, much to the amusement of onlookers, until Fiona snagged it with her foot and picked it up. The flustered man thanked her profusely, and they took a bench to catch their breath.

He was an accountant for an advertising firm—"a growth industry with opportunities for advancement" he had said—and although she had known that admitting one was a domestic servant was the kiss of death for romance, Fiona couldn't lie. "A lady's maid," he had said with a smile that crinkled the skin at his eyes. "How very important sounding."

They had taken up meeting on Sunday afternoons after that, and while it wasn't the flaming passion she had dreamed of as a girl, Lawrence had a stable job, lived by himself in his own apartment, was in his forties and decent looking. They were comfortable together, and Fiona yearned for a retirement from domestic service with a man who could provide for her and make her laugh.

They had been seeing each other for eight months, and she suspected he was getting close to asking her to marry him. She would say she needed to think about it, but she already knew her answer. And say good-bye to domestic service.

"We can make it temporary," Mrs. Van Linden added. "A year. And I'll pay you to go."

Fiona saw the fear and pleading in her mistress's eyes. But more than that, she remembered the cold, hollow feeling when she had been discharged from the countess's employ, with nowhere to go, not a penny to her name, and no prospects of employment.

"The doctor says my heart is under a severe strain due to my imminent separation from my only child. I believe the strain can be eased if I know you are there taking care of my Elizabeth."

"Of course, I'll go, madam," Fiona said, wondering how she was going to break it to Lawrence, because it was for certain he would not follow her out west.

"Promise me, Wilson, that no matter what, you'll never leave Elizabeth."

Forgetting about her mistress's hair, forgetting everything except the worry that Lawrence might not wait a year for her, Fiona wanted to throw down the hairbrush and rage against the injustices of a world where rich people ruled the lives of the poor and helpless. *I will lose*

Lawrence because of you! Just as I almost went to the poorhouse because of the countess.

In all her forty-three years, Fiona had never realized how helpless and manipulated domestic servants were, at the whim and mercies of a sometimes selfish and arrogant class. She had always counted herself a grateful and faithful servant, but now just the word *servant* felt vile on her tongue.

Nonetheless, Mrs. Van Linden was awaiting an answer, and so Fiona, deflated and disappointed, seeing her future happiness in ruins, said, "I promise I will never leave Elizabeth."

*   *   *

Grand Central Station was like a giant, crowded cathedral, filled with noise, energy, and life. The perfect jumping off point to a new life.

As a wedding present, Mr. Van Linden reserved three private railroad cars for his daughter and her new husband. The first was lavishly appointed with velvet drapes, deeply upholstered furniture, Turkish carpet, a large bed at one end, a private commode at the other, and a mahogany dining table alongside one row of windows so that the passengers could watch the passing scenery as they dined.

The second car, for the servants, was a standard Pullman, with passenger seats on one side, curtained berths on the other. At the end was a small kitchen in which Mrs. Flannigan was to cook meals for the Baron and Her Ladyship. The third car was for all their luggage and extras, such as Elizabeth's English sidesaddle and Nigel's newly acquired rifle and gun collection.

These cars were to be coupled and uncoupled at various bifurcations along the route as the Barnstable party traveled from New York, down the East Coast, to run west where they would join the Southern Pacific's *Sunset Limited* in New Orleans for a straight shot to Southern California.

Mrs. Van Linden's wedding gift to her daughter was the domestic staff that was to accompany them and set up house in the West. Mr. and Mrs. Norrington, husband and wife butler and housekeeper pair. She had found them through a domestic agency, and they had assured her that, both being sixty years of age and seeing retirement in ten to fifteen years, they found tremendous appeal in retiring in a land of sunshine and palm trees. Norrington had said he would be pleased to act as Nigel's valet. The housemaid was Ethel, a marriage-minded girl in her twenties, eager to go west and find a husband. And Mrs. Flannigan, the Irish cook, who had been with the Van Lindens for fifteen years and wasn't keen on picking up and going to a "land of savages," as she put it. But Mrs. Van Linden threw in a generous bonus, and Mrs. Flannigan reluctantly took the bribe.

The conductor on the platform called, "All aboard!"

Tears rose in Van Linden's eyes as he hugged his daughter. Then he took her hands and said, "I want you to have a wonderful life, pumpkin. I want you to be happy. Love life, pumpkin. Dive into it. Give life all that you've got and take from life all that you can. If you achieve only this, then I've done my job here on earth, and I can die a happy man." He kissed Elizabeth on the cheek and whispered, "Give your mother a grandson. It's the one thing she wants in this world."

Mrs. Van Linden was less sentimental. Burying her pain over the loss of her daughter, she summoned up the strength to sound pragmatic. "We're counting on you to represent the Van Linden name in the way it always has been, with honor and pride. Show people what a lady you are. Set an example to the common people in the village. Show them how the upper class lives. They will look up to you. Teach them the social graces. Make us proud."

While the Van Lindens were saying good-bye and the servants were boarding their special car, Fiona Wilson twisted the handle of her handbag, nervously looking around.

There he was! Lawrence, pushing through the crowd. She noticed that he was wearing his Sunday suit. As he handed her a tin of biscuits for the train ride, he said, "I'll wait for you." But his eyes said something else. With a good job and nice looks, he knew he had his pick of women, and he wasn't getting younger.

"Good-bye," he said, and there was such a tone of finality in it that she knew she was never going to see him again. And she thought of her promise to Mrs. Van Linden, a much-regretted promise, but spoken all the same and if Fiona had few personal rules in life, one of them was that a woman must always keep her word. Especially a woman who had no family, no money, no status in life—her word was all she had and it was a precious commodity.

"All aboard!" the conductor called one last time. And the remaining passengers fell into each other's arms, all up and down the platform, with tears of sadness and joy, promises to write and telephone.

The Van Lindens embraced their daughter and son-in-law one last time while the servants climbed into their rail car, saying good-bye to friends and relatives who had come to see them off.

As the train gave out a great whistle and the iron wheels began to turn, Elizabeth went to the window in their private car and watched her parents slowly glide away from her. Coming up from behind, Nigel wrapped an arm around her waist and murmured, "It is just you and me now. You and me and the great, golden American West."

Yes! Elizabeth thought in a mixture of sadness (saying good-bye) and excitement (setting off for a new future), wondering what she was going to find there, or if something was going to find *her*.

CHAPTER SEVEN

Palm Springs, California

October 1920

LUISA SAT IN THE shade of a cottonwood tree and chanted as she wove her sacred basket, making coils of the dyed bulrushes, sewing them together using a bone needle. The pattern was the red diamond rattlesnake to honor the spirit that had warned her and her clan about the coming of new white men to the valley.

There already were white men in the Coachella Valley. They had been coming here for as long as Luisa could remember. Some just passed through, some stayed. Some she had even become friends with, like the people who ran the green grocery and the general store, on the rare occasions when the Indians had money to spend.

But the new white men coming to the valley were bringing bad magic, red diamond rattlesnake had said. And so for the past seven days she had walked to the depot, five miles away, to wait for the train. For seven days it had sped by with a friendly blow of the whistle. But now she knew.

The white people were arriving today.

Setting aside her basket and drawing a shawl over her shoulders, the Cahuilla spirit-reader struck off down the dirt road.

* * *

The train slowed to a stop with a great hissing of the brakes. A conductor jumped down and unfolded the metal steps at the ends of only two train cars—no other passengers were disembarking at this deserted station.

Nigel stepped down to the platform first, then held up a hand to assist Elizabeth.

He was dressed in jodhpurs, riding boots, and a tweed hunting jacket over a stiff white shirt with a red silk ascot tucked into his collar. He was dressed for the outdoors, and they had certainly arrived at the outdoors.

Nigel scanned the landscape that he had come to dominate and tame. He looked out and thought, movies and photographs don't do this place justice. It made England look so . . . small. And in England a man, rich or poor, had no choice but to walk where countless others had already tread. There a man, rich or poor, was shackled by tradition. But here on this vast, sandy, boulder-strewn plain a man planted his feet on virgin soil.

He smiled. He was going to turn that yellow-gray wilderness into a sea of dense green palms. When Nigel was done, God was going to be jealous.

Farther along, the domestic help stepped out into the fresh desert air and sunshine. The Barnstables' servants wore coats designed for fall in New York, but the October morning in the Coachella Valley was already warming up. They each carried a satchel or carpetbag, and Mrs. Flannigan the cook also carried an umbrella. But the sky was crystal blue with not a cloud from horizon to horizon, unblemished except for a lone hawk riding the thermals overhead.

The men in the baggage car unloaded their boxes and crates and trunks, heaping them in a mountain on the wooden platform. Then the train gave out a great, steaming hoot, the wheels turned, and the giant iron beast lumbered on, leaving seven people to stand in the desert silence.

The Palm Springs train station was nothing like the stops they had visited during the trip, getting out to stretch their legs and maybe buy some nuts and a soda pop. There was nothing here but a platform and a shack. No station master. No ticket window. No concession stand for snacks and magazines. Not even any benches to sit on. As they looked around at the expanse that spread away to distant mountains, utter bewilderment stood on their faces.

But what struck all seven of the newcomers most of all was the silence. They had never heard such silence.

A flat sea of gray-yellow sand stretched in all directions, with stunted scrub brush here and there, the occasional wretched tree, while an ancient wind seemed to blow. They had to hold on to their hats as they looked this way and that, the Baron and his lady, and the servants, standing wide-eyed at the utter isolation of their journey's end.

Where was everyone?

Mrs. Flannigan and Ethel, the housemaid, stared at the godfor-saken landscape with dubious expressions, as did Fiona Wilson and Mr. and Mrs. Norrington.

In the distance, at the foot of majestic mountains, Nigel thought he could see structures. That must be the town, he thought. But it was too far away and the buildings were obscured by dense walls of trees.

"I thought Mr. Lardner was meeting us," Elizabeth said, wondering if they had gotten off at the wrong place.

"His last wire said he would be here on this day at this time. I shouldn't think he has forgotten. I'm certainly paying him well enough."

Elizabeth chewed her lip as she scanned the desert, looking for any sign of life. There were no horses or wagons at the depot, no automo-biles. No people. What if Mr. Lardner had forgotten? What if no one came for them?

And then Elizabeth did see someone, and it so startled her that she could not for the moment speak. In a thicket of palm trees that grew a hundred feet from the railroad track, a lone woman stood, her eyes fast on the newcomers. She wore her long white hair in braids and was wrapped in a colorful shawl. By the copper tone of her skin, the high cheekbones and prominent nose, there was no doubt she was Indian. But the way she stood staring, unmoving, without coming forward to say something, gave Elizabeth a sudden chill.

Mr. Lardner had assured them that the local Indians were friendly. "No wars with the Army in this region," he had written after Nigel had hired the man to be his agent in Palm Springs. "None of the bloody battles that took place up north on the Plains. Southern California Indians were pacified by the Spanish a hundred years ago."

But Elizabeth was not so sure. The look in the Indian woman's eyes was far from friendly or peaceful. Elizabeth doubted the woman would help them.

She does not want us here.

Unlike his companions, Nigel was undaunted. Where others saw desolation, he saw a challenge. The more impossible the task, the greater the success.

"I'm going to grow medjool dates, Elizabeth," he said now, breaking her thoughts, distracting her from the disturbing Indian woman, "which are the best in the world." Nigel had planned on calling his new property Stullwood Farm. But now, as he looked out toward infinity— he had never seen so much untouched land—he thought: No, it won't be a mere farm. It will be a plantation.

"Did you know, Elizabeth, that the *Phoenix dactylifera*, can grow more than a hundred feet and live more than two hundred years?" Nigel continued while the domestic staff shifted nervously and wondered who was coming to get them. "Palm Springs has the perfect conditions for growing dates because the temperature, the sandy soil, and the surroundings as similar to those where the date palm flourished in Africa for thousands of years."

"Will the grove be near our home?" she asked, continuing to scan the distance for approaching motor cars.

"There is an alluvial plain at the base of the canyon. Perfect for planting. And right next to the house. That's where the offshoots will go."

Besides the books and scientific monographs he had studied, Nigel had engaged in correspondence with the Bureau of Plant Industry in Washington, DC, and in particular, gaining insight from a pomologist who worked for the federal Department of Agriculture.

Elizabeth wondered when Mr. Lardner was going to arrive. The depot was miles from Palm Springs and she was eager to get into her new home. Along with the luggage and trunks piled on the platform, there were wooden crates stamped Fortnum & Mason and Harrods, crates packed with top shelf scotch, champagne, brandies.

Unconcerned about the absent Mr. Lardner, Nigel strode to the edge of the wooden platform to look across the desert. He stood with his hands on his hips, his feet apart, as if challenging the distant mountain, called San Jacinto. "Think of it, Elizabeth! This valley boasts an average of 330 days of sunshine in a year! No more cold mists of England. No more Atlantic rain. A place where oranges grow year-round! Yes," he said, "I'm going to do something with this land." His eyes blazed as the wind whipped his hair and cut through his shirt. He had a wild, challenging look, as if daring the desert to defeat him. Elizabeth sensed something barely harnessed within her husband, an energy only just under control. It was a strange power that drove him, she knew, a force that had propelled him out of dull, old, law-burdened England and into this untamed land. She didn't know from what deep, troubled well this energy sprang. She had never asked Nigel, but she speculated it had to do with his father's untimely death, a reminder to Nigel of the brevity of life and the need to realize his dreams before it was too late. When thinking about him, it reminded her of a quote from *The Rubaiyat of Omar Khayyam*: "Ah, fill the Cup—what boots it to repeat, How time is slipping underneath our feet."

Nigel's hands curled into fists as if he were readying himself for a fight. He would make this land truly his own, not like back home, where obsequious cap-lifting peasants lived on mediocre farms and looked up at the big house as if it were a Christmas pudding. Derbyshire was a pale place with tradition and done things and eternal sameness, where men's imaginations stretched no further than teatime. He suddenly felt alive. He looked around himself and saw what he had to do, where he belonged.

Elizabeth could only guess what he was thinking, but he looked so terribly handsome and warrior-like that she had never loved him more than in that moment. Nor had she ever been so excited. They couldn't see the small town from here, but the wide expanse, the vastness of the sky, the wind whistling across dunes caused her soul to reach out and wish to fly to the sun. So this was the desert. In all the films she had seen, all the novels she had read, she had never known it could be like this: pure, clean, primeval. Just as God created it millennia ago.

She thought of London and New York, crowded and noisy cities that felt like a whalebone corset, where one could hardly breathe and spread her arms. And then the *Sunset Limited* had left the cities and streaked across the lush green countryside of Southern cotton farms to finally enter Texas cattle country that was the flattest, most wide-open land she had ever seen. As she and Nigel had enjoyed tea and toast, she had watched the sun crest the eastern horizon and paint the deserts in pinks and oranges that one never saw in the gray cities in the East. She just knew she would make something of herself here, away from the confines of concrete and her parents. The West, where opportunities abounded, where a woman had options and choices.

Nigel and I will leave our stamp here. We will create something new that wasn't here before. No old English manor houses, no Park Avenue mansions for us. We will start a new dynasty here, children to carry on our names and our work, like the pioneers of yesteryear. We will build from scratch, work hard and produce, and at the end of it all, leave this valley a better place than when we arrived.

Her thoughts were interrupted by a shout. Turning, she saw two rather crude wagons being pulled up to the platform.

She blinked. When the management company had said they would be met at the depot by some local men to convey them, their serving staff and their luggage to their new home, she had pictured large motor cars. Not rattling old wagons with bent boards being drawn by tired, spavined horses.

"Howdy, folks!" the driver of the first wagon called. "Hope you haven't been waiting long!"

Nigel strode forward. "Not at all, my good fellow! You must be Lardner."

"I guess I must be," the man said as he jumped down from the wagon and climbed the steps to the platform. Augie Lardner was a large man with a big head, closely set eyes, and a heavy jaw. Almost ugly, Elizabeth thought, until he smiled and the rather apish face was transformed. He wore a plaid shirt tucked into the waistband of khaki trousers, and a shapeless khaki hat stood on the back of his head.

Three months ago, the agent for Wallace Properties Management had put Nigel in touch with Mr. Lardner, who was the postmaster in Palm Springs. He also operated the only telephone, the telegraph, and ran the general store. Mr. Lardner was the man everyone went to when they needed something. Nigel had been in communication with Mr. Lardner over the past few weeks, getting things ready for the launch of the new Stullwood Plantation.

He removed his hat and scratched his head. "Who are all these people?"

Nigel gave him a look. "They are our servants."

"There's a lot of them."

And then Lardner looked at the boxes and trunks in a pile. Standing upright and packed in thick wadding was clearly a grandfather clock. And an enormous wrought iron birdcage with intricate filigree work. "Is all this yours? I'm afraid I'll have to send wagons back for it all."

"Can't we take it?"

"Haven't the room."

"Then leave your man to watch it." Among the wedding gifts they'd received from the Van Lindens' friends was a priceless Ming Dynasty vase, not to mention all the silver service.

"You don't have to worry about anyone snatching it, Mr. Barnstable. We don't steal around here. We don't even lock our doors at night. Shall we get going then?" Lardner said, and he gestured to the man in the second wagon to fold down seats in the flatbed for the additional passengers.

The wagons rolled away from the depot with Nigel and Elizabeth riding next to Lardner in the first wagon. In the second wagon, five silent men and women—a butler, a housekeeper, a cook, a housemaid, and a lady's maid—rode on two benches, their heads filled with thoughts, emotions, misgivings, and excitement.

Lardner said, "Your house abuts the Indian reservation, Mr. Barnstable. You'll have to make sure you don't overstep boundaries. Chief Diego guards his land like a hawk. He's mighty powerful in these parts, has a lot of influence among the Cahuilla bands, with a few of the whites as well. You'd do to get on his good side."

"I hope you have the labor lined up," Nigel said, leaning forward, elbows on his knees, as if urging the horses to go faster. "I'm going to plant my offshoots as soon as possible." Nigel had decided against growing trees from seed, having learned that the fruit from seed-grown palms was not as good as that grown from offshoots—growths that spring from the trunk of the mature palm tree.

"I'm afraid we've run into a bit of an obstacle as far as workers, Mr. Barnstable. I spoke with the Chief of the local band. He won't let any of his people work for you."

"Why not?"

"He's opposed to your choice of location for the orchard. Says it interferes with the sky or something. They're highly superstitious. Plus, he's most likely worried you'll steal his water. Keep in mind, Mr. Barnstable, that despite the fact that the date palm is a desert plant, it is a very thirsty one. As we say, they thrive with their feet in the water and their heads in the sun. They need plenty of high heat, arid weather, and plenty of water to produce fruit. Your trees will need to be flooded every seven to ten days to ensure their root system will be kept wet."

"If the local Indians won't work for me, where will we find the labor?"

"From the other bands," Mr. Lardner said. "We'll find good workers from the Soboba, Cabazon, Santa Rosa, and Morongo bands. They always need money."

At the mention of Indians, Elizabeth turned in her seat and looked back at the cluster of palm trees beside the depot. The Indian woman was gone.

CHAPTER EIGHT

"WHAT'S GOING ON?" NIGEL said, leaning forward on the wagon seat. "Who are all those men?"

"The sheriff's getting up a posse," Augie Lardner explained. "A local Indian boy shot and killed a white man in Banning, and there's a reward to bring him in alive. The Sheriff needs volunteers for the search."

"He can count me in!" Nigel couldn't believe the perfect timing. The local town folk plus the Sheriff all in one place. He couldn't have asked for a better welcome and a way to establish right at the start his authority in his new community.

But Elizabeth wasn't interested in the mob of men. Like her husband, she leaned forward on her seat—a flat board that had no springs as a defense against the badly rutted dirt road—to stare at the mountains directly ahead, rising dramatically up to the clear sky. Elizabeth could hardly breathe, she was so excited. They were arriving at their new home—her home, of which she would be the sole mistress. She couldn't wait to release Button from his carrier and let him run free.

Palm Springs, she saw now as they drew near to the base of the mountains, was a small collection of buildings baking in the sun. The town seemed to straddle a single main street, dusty and without asphalt or sidewalks, and in the center of that street, a man standing on a box, shouting at a large group of people gathered around him. The Sheriff putting together his posse.

She searched for their new house. Wallace Property Sales and Management had assured her that they had hired people to open the house, air it out, and make it ready for the new owners. She prayed they had done a good job. Elizabeth yearned for a hot bath and a bed that did not rock like a train car. But she couldn't see the house, just dense clusters of tall palm trees and the commotion in the middle of the street. The men, she noticed, seemed highly agitated.

*   *   *

Doc Perry, a resident of Palm Springs, watched the wagons trundling along the road as they entered the town. He thought the timing of their arrival rather unfortunate. They might have arrived in time to witness a lynching.

As the newcomers drew near, Doc Perry eyed them. The whole valley had been talking about the Lord and Lady who had purchased La Alma del Desierto. Doc counted five people in the second wagon. Family members? The Lord was young, a tall, good-looking fellow, Doc Perry thought. His wife was a looker, with hair the color of dandelions piled on top of her head Gibson Girl fashion. In their spotless clothes and pale complexions, they looked exotic to him.

"Now listen up!" the Sheriff shouted to quiet the crowd that was eager to start the hunt. "I'll make a grid on a map and assign groups to different sections. Johnny Pinto's been on the run for three days. No telling where he is by now. He's armed and dangerous—"

"Hell, Sheriff," one of the men shouted. "Everyone knows ain't nothin' more dangerous 'n an Injun with a gun!"

The crowd erupted in a roar mixed with laughter and angry calls. Their blood was running high. Doc Perry wouldn't wager a wooden nickel on Johnny Pinto's life right now.

Look at 'em, he thought, as he stood in the shade of Lardner's General Store. Like kids waiting for a candy store to open. All hopped up and raring to go. A few looked as if they'd dusted off their old six-shooters and strapped them around their middle-aged waists. Most wore bowler or derby hats, but a few wore cowboy hats as if movie cameras were aimed at them. That's what comes of watching too many Tom Mix movies.

Although, Perry thought, as his eyes shifted to one man in particular. A newcomer to Palm Springs. Rode into town a few weeks ago. A stranger who kept to himself and didn't let his name be known. No one knew his business here—he kept camp up the canyon instead of lodging at the local boardinghouse—but he looked like a real cowboy, the sort of Western drifter Doc Perry had known back in the days when he had traveled through cow towns selling snake oil and Kickapoo Indian cures from the back of his colorful gypsy wagon. The stranger, dressed all in black, with a curious rattlesnake hatband, stood separate from the feverish mob, watching the scene with a calculating eye. Perry would bet that the six-shooter on his hip had known some genuine gunfights.

He wondered if the stranger was going to join the hunt. Doc Perry wasn't going to. He figured that with all those loose guns and feverish thirst for Indian blood, he'd best stay here and be prepared to dig bullets out of men.

"Hey, Sheriff, what about the local reservation? Could Pinto be hiding there?"

"My deputies and I already did a thorough search. Chief Diego isn't harboring Johnny. Now before we all go running like rabbits, we're going to establish a central command post where we keep updated on the hunt, receive orders, and rest between searches. Any suggestions where we can set this up?"

Doc Perry looked around. A few of the town citizens shifted on their feet. They lived and worked here, in small houses and at modest businesses. Perry himself had a quiet medical practice out of his home. But no one was equipped to host a "central command."

On the other side of the street, standing under a cottonwood tree, Cody McNeal was thinking the same thing. The residences of Palm Springs were spread far apart, the businesses were scattered along the main road with large empty lots in between. He reckoned this wasn't the Sheriff's first manhunt. He'd figure something out. As for Cody himself, he didn't want to get involved with local events, but he felt compelled to join the search for Pinto. He had experience in this. It wasn't Cody's first manhunt. He was an ace tracker, taught by a Lakota Sioux when he was young. But more than anything, it was because he wanted to make sure the Indian got a fair shake. He'd seen this before, when fevers and passions ran high. He saw it in these men's eyes now.

He also watched the two wagons come into town, a young couple riding with Augie Lardner, the second wagon carrying five others.

As Cody McNeal and Doc Perry watched the wagons roll to a halt, Nigel suddenly stood up in the wagon and said in a commanding tone, "I am Baron Stullwood, and it has always been my family's duty and responsibility to assist local authorities in matters such as this. I offer my house as the command center."

To Augie Lardner, he said, "Let's go," and the wagons turned off the main road.

"Okay, boys, you heard him," the Sheriff said. "Follow the gentleman!"

Doc Perry joined the parade to the big house hidden behind trees, and Cody McNeal fell in behind.

The Spanish-style house had been built when people with chest ailments discovered the healing properties of desert air and mineral springs. La Alma del Desierto, Soul of the Desert, stood against a low foothill on the flat desert floor. Behind it, palm trees and stony plateaus rose up to join the mountain slope of the San Jacintos. The driveway from the dirt road was paved with flagstones, as was the parking area in front of the house—beautiful inlaid flagstones of desert colors. The driveway itself was guarded by a tall, wrought iron gate with La Alma del Desierto written boldly on top in wrought iron. Palm trees and flowering bougainvillea shrubs flanked the gate, creating an imposing entrance fit for the ninth Baron Stullwood and his bride.

When they pulled up, Elizabeth caught only an impression of adobe walls covered in cream-colored stucco, windows framed in dark wood, roof tiles the color of sunsets. There were plants everywhere, in pots and boxes or put straight into the ground. She hadn't time to pause and take it all in as the mob of men came huffing up the drive to disrupt her brief moment of tranquility and a chance to think. We are home. Instead she felt suddenly confused and slightly lost. This was not how she had imagined her arrival at her new home to be.

Nigel went ahead, up the flagstone path to the entrance, which consisted of two large double doors of dark wood, carved with intricate designs and curved at the top to fit the stone archway. Mr. Lardner handed him the keys and Nigel ceremoniously unlocked the doors, and pushed in to the cool interior. Elizabeth went in next.

And then the Sheriff's unruly posse.

Already familiar with the home's floor plan, Nigel led them through to the dining room so that Elizabeth was afforded only an impression of dark Spanish wood, black wrought iron, tiled floors, and a cool interior because the rowdy posse suddenly filled the air with their noise. They came to a polished dining room table that could seat fourteen, and in the center, a large vase of desert flowers had been placed there. No doubt a welcome present from Wallace Property Management.

The Sheriff picked up the vase and, without asking permission, set it on the floor. "Okay men!" he barked. "Gather round." He spread a huge map out on the table while the mob clustered around, elbowing, pushing, trying to see, and Elizabeth stood to the side, watching in bafflement as she held Button's carrier. Outside, Mrs. Norrington the housekeeper took charge of the staff, leading them around the side of the house in search of a service entrance.

In the dining room, Nigel went up to Elizabeth, touched her elbow, and said quietly, "Welcome to our new home, darling."

Then he joined the Sheriff and, while they drew lines and assigned groups to grid points, Elizabeth stood in indecision, wondering what she should do, unaware that, across the room, a stranger watched her. He was dressed in a long, black duster coat with a black Stetson on his head, a snake for a hatband.

Cody had heard that an English lord and lady were coming to live at La Alma. But he had not been prepared for the couple that had arrived. For some reason, he had expected someone much older, more staid and conservative. Not an energetic young man with a slender wife who, Cody thought, possessed a stylish beauty. In the midst of these rough men, she seemed unreal, almost strange.

He also thought manhunts weren't for ladies and saw that the Baroness thought so, too, as after a moment of hesitation, she backed away from the mob and found her way to the kitchen. He watched her go through the doors that swung shut behind her, then he stepped up to the dining room table to hear the plans for the hunt for Johnny Pinto.

*   *   *

"All right then," Mrs. Flannigan the cook said in a sharp voice as the group arrived at the back door. "Let's find the stairs."

They looked around the small entry where hat and coat hooks were affixed to the wall, along with brooms and mops. "I don't see any stairs," Ethel the housemaid said and in the next instant gave out a cry. "Here's the kitchen!"

"What?" Mrs. Flannigan pushed her hefty bulk through, and her eyes bulged at the sight. The kitchen was large and cavernous with a high ceiling and three stoves, an enormous stone oven, and two sinks. In the center, a blocky table with chairs. "Jesus, Joseph, and Mary! The kitchen is on *this* level!"

The door opposite stood open, and they saw the gathering of men in the dining room, the sheriff's deep voice rising above the din.

"Good heavens," Mrs. Norrington said as she rushed to close the door. "The kitchen is right next to the dining room."

"Are you sure there's no basement?" the cook said.

"None that I can discern," Norrington the butler said. "Nor does there appear to be an attic."

The Norringtons were sixty years old, married for thirty years, with no children. Mrs. Norrington was short in stature, which she made up for by wearing specially built-up shoes in the belief that servants followed orders more readily from a tall person than a short one. She had been pretty once but was now faded.

Mr. Norrington was tall and walked with his chest out, his chin pulled in, as he had been trained to do long ago at a school for domestic help. In order to hide his bald spot, he let one side of his hair grow out in order to comb it over and which he kept in place with pomade. With a big nose and bushy brow, he wasn't what one would call handsome, and he had cultivated the stern expression of a man used to having his orders followed. In the privacy of their quarters, both eased their bearings, laughed, and showed affection.

"Who ever heard of a house this size all on one level?" Mrs. Norrington said. "We'll be walking miles."

"I rather like not having to traipse up and down stairs," said Mrs. Flannigan, the cook. "What do you think, Ethel?"

But the young maid was at the kitchen sink, looking out at the garden, her gaze shooting straight across the paved patio, across paddocks and corrals, to men leaning on a fence and pointing at the house. They were slender, brown-skinned, with very white teeth, and they wore cowboy hats.

The cook joined her at the sink. "My goodness," she said. "Those would be Indians and Mexicans, wouldn't they?"

When Elizabeth came into the kitchen, the servants fell silent. "What now, Milady?" asked Mrs. Flannigan.

"What now," Elizabeth said with a thread of confidence as she placed Button's carrier on the table, "is we get to work and put this house together." She opened the carrier and the miniature poodle jumped out and into her arms.

"His Lordship will be shortly going out to the hunt," she said to the five awaiting instruction, "and when he returns this evening, he'll want his bath, a change of clothes, and a proper dinner in the dining room. That means you'll all need to be changed into uniforms and ready to do your jobs."

As they began removing their coats and exploring the kitchen, making comments, Mrs. Norrington quietly said, "I don't see how we'll pull it all together by then, Your Ladyship. We don't even have the china and linens."

"Mr. Lardner has promised to go straight back to the depot and bring our things to the house."

"Begging your pardon, Your Ladyship," Mrs. Flannigan said, unpinning her hat and giving her surroundings a dubious look. "Are those men coming back here tonight and am I supposed to be feeding them?" She nodded toward the door that led to the dining room, and the way she said "those men" divulged a mixture of distaste and fear. The ride from the train depot had thoroughly shaken her. Knowing that one was transferring to the desert was quite a different state of mind than actually arriving there.

"I'll find out, Mrs. Flannigan. In the meantime, we'd better take stock of what we have."

Voices drifted in from the dining room, mostly the Sheriff's booming baritone: "Ed's group, you go up Tahquitz Canyon. Jim, you take your men to Andreas Canyon."

"You think Pinto will head for Idyllwild, Sheriff?"

"Pray that he doesn't 'cause we'll lose him in that forest for sure. He could hold out there for years in those caves and never get found. Mike, I want you and your men to get up to Big Horn Valley."

"That's more than a day's climb, Sheriff!"

"I know, but do what you can. He might head for the sacred caves. We all meet back here at sundown. No way we can track Pinto at night."

"What if we tell him to freeze and he keeps running?"

"Disable him. I want that boy taken alive. Mr. Barnstable, you're new to this area. Go with Ed's group here. Mr. McNeal, I understand you're new to Palm Springs also. You can join—"

"I've been here long enough to acquaint myself with the area. I'm going alone."

Elizabeth then heard Nigel speak up. "I say, Sheriff, which group am I to lead?"

"You ain't leading no group, friend, since you're brand spanking new to this area. In fact, I'm not sure it's a good idea to have you along. Safer for you to stay here with your Missus."

"He can ride with me, Sheriff."

"Suit y'self, Mr. McNeal. That's it, men," the Sheriff announced. "You have your assignments. Get to it. And remember, we want Johnny Pinto alive."

The men hollered and whooped, as though they were going to a carnival, and dashed out with their rifles and guns. Nigel came into the kitchen, causing the servants to fall silent and turn back to their separate tasks. Taking Elizabeth's hands into his, he said quietly, "Are you all right, darling? I'm so sorry to be dropping all this on you, but I can't ignore the manhunt. It's important that I establish my status in this town. They need to look upon me as a leader."

"I understand."

He smiled. "We'll be home by dark."

And then he was gone.

The servants stared after him, and then they started talking at once. But they were silenced a second time by a voice calling out, "Yoo hoo!" A strange woman came through the back door and into the kitchen, saying, "Hello there! I'm Lois Lardner, your new neighbor."

No one said a word as she smiled all around. Plump, in her forties, Augie Lardner's wife wore a print dress that reached her ankles and her hair tucked into a bun. Elizabeth's staff didn't know what to make of her. She had just pushed her way in without being invited. And if she had come on a formal call, why wasn't she wearing a hat and gloves?

Lois Lardner looked around with intense joy. She had heard that La Alma's new owners would be arriving with servants, but she hadn't expected so many! All these new mouths to feed were going to greatly profit the town. Mr. Allenby, the green grocer, was about to enter into a business boom, while Lois herself and her husband, who owned the only general store in miles, were going to be doing a rip roaring business with so many newcomers needing sundries, canned goods, shoes, aspirin, soap, handkerchiefs, and needles and thread. Not to mention men's removable collars, hooks for buttoning shoes, pots and pans, matches, and ribbons.

"I've come to tell you that the ladies in town are going to help out with the posse. We've got beans and stews going, and Mrs. Allenby will provide any salad you'll need. I'll bring the plates and cutlery. Cups, too. Augie's gone to the depot to get your stuff."

"It's very kind of you," Elizabeth said. "I'm Mrs. Barnstable, Lady Stullwood."

Mrs. Lardner patted Elizabeth's arm and five pairs of eyebrows shot up. "It must be confusing for you to have that mob of men on your first day here. And you have your own house to get in order." She looked around the kitchen, smiled at the people who stared at her and who did not smile back, as she wondered who they all were, then said to Elizabeth, "Anyway, I just wanted to introduce myself and let you know that my friends and I will be taking care of the members of the posse."

After Mrs. Lardner left, with Mr. Norrington muttering something about Americans being pushy but that this was over the top for even them, Elizabeth said, "I guess our first business is to inspect the house. Mrs. Flannigan, His Lordship and I will expect a formal dinner tonight. You have the menu. Norrington, once the luggage arrives, please unpack the silver and make sure it is polished. And His Lordship will want hot water for his bath tonight."

To Mrs. Norrington she said, "I am relying on you and the others to bring order to this . . . anthill that has been kicked over."

"We shall do our best, Your Ladyship."

While the high-ceilinged kitchen roared with the noise of chaos, Elizabeth looked through the garden window and saw Nigel by the stables, talking to one of the ranch hands. His voice drifted on the morning breeze. He was trying to explain to the man that he wanted one of the horses saddled. But the man seemed to speak Spanish with very little English, and she heard frustration in Nigel's tone. Then the cowboy dressed in black appeared, leading his horse. There was a brief exchange and the ranch hand seemed to understand.

As if sensing he was being watched, the stranger turned and looked directly at the kitchen window. For a startled moment, she thought he was looking directly at *her*. His face was in shadow. He looked like an illustration out of *Leslie's Weekly*, one of their stories about the Wild West.

Nigel appeared a moment later, atop a chestnut mare with a rifle across his saddle, and looking every inch the lord of the manor. One would think he was off to shoot pheasant instead of hunting for a man. As Elizabeth watched her husband and the stranger in black ride away, Mrs. Norrington came up and said, "Begging your pardon, My Lady, but we've conducted a thorough search, and we have found not the slightest trace of what could be taken for servants' quarters. I was wondering, where are we all to be staying tonight?"

CHAPTER NINE

WHILE THE WHITE MEN went riding off to hunt for Johnny Pinto, Luisa hurried through the village toward Chief Diego's house.

This was not the time to be modest or to show proper feminine decorum by walking slowly so as not to draw attention to herself. Men could run, women could not. But the news was dire. She had to get it to Chief Diego at once.

Red diamond rattlesnake had spoken to her again. And the message was even worse than his last.

After watching the posse ride off, Luisa had returned to the place of the bulrushes to go in search of the yellow and brown warbler who had warned her of a disastrous sunrise. She needed to hear the rest of his message.

Because the world was frightening and unpredictable, Luisa's people had long ago devised a system for bringing order and control into their lives—the shaman system, in which special tribal members were endowed with unique gifts for helping the clan. Luisa's gift was the ability to receive prophetic messages from the spirit world. Like Luisa, Chief Diego was a pul, a holy person, and his special power was his observance of the night sky. As the clan's star-reader, he was able to tell the Cahuilla when to plant, when to harvest, when to hunt, and when to gather.

Chief Diego was in front of the ceremonial hut, which was his home as he was the clan's chief, weaving a net for catching quail. He sat on a stool while, cross-legged on the ground, a small boy listened as the chief spoke. The boy was the clan's future star-watcher shaman, and Diego was teaching him.

Luisa slowed her pace.

Not only was she bringing bad news, her heart was filled with disappointment.

When Luisa had heard that the big house named La Alma had been bought and was going to be occupied again, she had grown optimistic. The family that had lived there before, even though they didn't stay all year, had hired the women in Luisa's village to work as maids and laundresses, and so the band's income had increased, enabling her people to buy things. But then those people had said they didn't want to come back and Luisa began to worry. Her village was poor. They had little money. Many of the children had no shoes. Although they received the monthly food ration and goods from the Great Father in Washington, it was not enough. And it seemed that, every year, the allotment was smaller. She remembered when the Great Father allowed them five pounds of meat per week per person. But now it was down to one pound of meat per week per person. The deer were scarce, and the antelope gone. Now the women had to go farther afield to catch rabbits and quail so that her people had enough to eat.

But with new white people coming to the big house, there had been the hope that Luisa and her people could earn real money and go into the local shops and buy food for the children.

And then she had walked from the train depot to follow the wagons. So many white people had come to live in the big house! When she had heard that someone had bought the property, it was that two people were coming, a man and his wife. The property agent had explained that while the ranch hands would be kept on, the man and wife would not be hiring any Indian women to work in the house. Luisa now saw why. It was a large family that was moving in and so they would all share the work.

She had seen the many boxes and trunks piled on the train station platform. She wondered what they contained. Things that made the white people happy, she supposed.

Her house in the village was not like the white man's. It was small, rectangular, and made of stout posts driven into the ground, the walls and roof covered in palm fronds and daubed with adobe to keep wind and rain out. Inside, there was a pit for a cooking fire, with a hole in the roof to let the smoke escape. Luisa's few dresses and shawls hung on pegs nailed to the support posts. Her bed was a pile of blankets on the earth floor. Clay jars filled with water or seeds and berries, her metate where she ground corn and nuts, a spare pair of sandals, and a plaster statue of Jesus given to her by a priest made up the rest of her belongings.

She thought now that not even her entire house, with its roof and walls, would fill one of the white lady's big trunks.

"Now I will tell you the story of the New Stars," Chief Diego was saying to the boy who sat at his feet. Diego had the round, fleshy face of a man of advanced years, dark brown skin contrasting the snow-white hair that was cropped at the shoulders with a red bandana tied around his head. Like most of the men of his tribe, he wore a white, long-sleeved shirt tucked into the waistband of his baggy white trousers—clothes the Cahuilla had been taught to wear when the Franciscan priests came to Coachella Valley to Christianize the Indians.

While he told the boy a story, Diego wove a quail net made of plant fibers, his coarse, aged fingers rapidly interweaving, twining, and knotting the palm fibers. Toward sunset, he and other men too old for the deer hunt would go into the bushes and trap quail.

Luisa waited a moment before clearing her throat, loudly enough to make her meaning known. He looked up at her with displeasure at the rude interruption, his sharp eyes glinting within folds of wrinkled copper skin. It was within his right to scold her, but she stood her ground. The message had to be heard.

That the white man's trees would someday block Diego's view of the stars.

"Go now," he said to the boy. "And remember what I taught you today." Then he rose to stand and face Luisa.

She was stunned to see such naked grief on his face. Johnny Pinto was his grandson. Cahuilla men were proud of their stoicism and believed that emotional displays were the purview of women. Luisa could not remember when she had last seen emotions on his face. But his grandson had been accused of murder.

He is in pain.

"You have news?" he said in a tight voice. "Of my grandson?"

Her heart softened. She reached him in three strides and drew the old man in her arms. Her tribe frowned upon displaying affection in public, and there were villagers all around them. But Luisa didn't care. She had known Diego all her life. And he was her husband.

She embraced him for a long moment and Diego, despite his fierce, masculine pride, allowed himself to be held, then she stepped back. "No news of your grandson. But the white men have begun searching for him."

"Will they find him?" Diego's eyes flashed with tears.

"He is well hidden. I come on another errand. Diego, the red diamond rattlesnake spoke to me again."

In truth, she had sought out the snake only to confirm what she had overheard at the train depot when the white man had stood on the platform and talked about planting trees. The white man himself had delivered the frightening prophecy, but the rattlesnake in the bulrushes had confirmed what she had heard. She told this now to her husband, whose expression shot from sadness to one of alarm. "Aii!" he whispered. "He will plant the offshoots on the plain at the base of the canyon?"

"Yes."

The trees would grow quickly, and in a few years, when Chief Diego came out of the ceremonial house to observe the stars, his view would be blocked. He would not be able to discern when a season was starting, when to plant or harvest. To block out the stars would be to starve his people.

He tried to think, tried to gather together his panicked thoughts as if they were stampeding horses. If those trees grew, then what would he do? In all his years, and the years of his people going back to the ancestors, the stars had never been blocked.

Should I move? he asked himself. Should I find another place for star reading?

But Diego had always read the stars from the same place, with the same vantage point of the sky. To climb higher to another point would be to view the stars differently. But there was more to it than that. It had to do with the encroaching white man.

Diego remembered, as a boy, traveling to all the villages in the valley with his father. Walking side by side, with spare water and tortillas, to stop and visit with the many families to whom they were related. And then the white man laid down the iron road and the trains cut off the visiting trails so that Diego's people had to find other ways to travel in the valley. And then white men came to build ditches and divert water from Indian land, so the Indians were told to move. And then more white men came and put up tents and houses and told the Indians to move once more.

We are always moving, Diego thought, as a hardness stole into his heart. We are always making room for the white man. They do not move for us. They do not say, this time, we will be the ones to make room.

Diego saw this new white man's trees as a sign—more white men were coming, the Indians would have to move again. If Diego changed his star-reading place to please this new white man and his trees, then other white men would see that the Indians were weak and permitted themselves to be moved here and there like furniture. He could not allow that.

No, Diego thought with a hardening of his spirit. I will move no more. Here we make a stand. I will continue to read the stars from the same place I have always read them. No white man is going to make me change it. It is he who has to change. He cannot plant his trees here. And then future white men will know that our people no longer make room for them.

Diego knew something about date growing. "In the night, after the planting," he told his wife now, "we will dig up the offshoots and chop them to bits. The white man will plant again, and we will dig up again. Like other white men who have come to this valley to get rich, he will give up and go home. Only the Indian will endure because we grew out of this desert. We are a part of it. The white man is not.

"So we will wait and watch for the small offshoots to arrive, small clumps of fronds no taller than a child. And we will destroy them."

But Luisa secretly wondered if it was going to be so simple.

CHAPTER TEN

ONCE THE HOUSE WAS empty of intruders and the hunt for Johnny Pinto was under way, Elizabeth was eager to explore her new home—and little Button was eager to follow, his nails tapping on the tile floors.

Asking Fiona Wilson and Mrs. Norrington to accompany her, Elizabeth left Mrs. Flannigan and the maid to sort out the kitchen until Augie Lardner arrived with luggage and crates.

As promised by the realtor, the residence was fully furnished. Indian rugs covered the tiled floors. Wicker screens could be placed to block wind and sun, or to open up a room to light and breezes. The furniture in the living room was upholstered in pale yellow linen and piped with black. Some of the rooms had been wired for electricity, but the generator needed to be refueled before she could turn them on. The rest all had chandeliers, wall sconces, and tall iron candle holders.

The furniture was custom crafted—ornate replicas of eighteenth-century Spanish Colonial—massive cabinets, armoires, buffets, tables, chairs, and benches intricately carved from heavy wood by skilled artisans in Toledo, Spain. Every fireplace had a screen made of hand-forged bronze in complex yet attractive patterns. The cabinetry throughout was made of polished mahogany and marvelously carved. The Old World elegance of the interior made Elizabeth think she was visiting Queen Isabella.

The layout of the house was simple, two wings stretched away from the central large living area, with a dining room just off that, and the kitchen behind that. The north wing seemed to be for the family of the house, with a library, an office, a solarium, two small bedrooms, and a grand master bedroom at the end. The south wing contained six bedrooms with adjoining baths in between. These would be for guests.

By the time they had completed their inspection, with Mrs. Norrington making a list of what was in each room, what Elizabeth wanted to get rid of, what needed to be added, Augie Lardner had delivered their trunks and crates.

All that was left was the problem of where the staff was going to sleep.

In the meantime Mrs. Flannigan had familiarized herself with the kitchen and cupboards, delighted to find fresh steaks and salad greens in the electric refrigerator that ran off an outdoor generator. She had found a well-stocked pantry, plenty of pots and pans, and cooking tools. Thank goodness there was sufficient wood for the stove. There was no power in the valley, she had been told, neither gas nor electric, except for what the house could provide through generators, so she was thrown back to the Stone Age, to Mrs. Flannigan's way of thinking. But she was old enough to remember the days of coal and wood and made good use of what was at hand.

When the trunks arrived, Mr. and Mrs. Norrington got down to the business of unpacking. Norrington took care with his master's wine collection and finding a place to store it; Fiona Wilson got to work sorting out Elizabeth's wardrobe, finding spacious cupboards to hold it all, and Ethel was put to work helping Mrs. Flannigan with the cooking, making the beds, stocking wood at all the fireplaces, and seeing to it that all the bathrooms sparkled.

Once His Lordship's dinner menu and evening clothes were settled on, the problem of the servants' quarters could be addressed. With Mrs. Norrington accompanying her, Elizabeth made a wider inspection of the property, finding horse stables, corrals, a bunkhouse for the ranch hands, tool sheds, and tack rooms, but no sign of the servants' quarters promised by Wallace Management. As the house had no attic or basement, that left only the guest bedrooms.

These would be for the staff, Elizabeth decided as she and Mrs. Norrington inspected the nicely furnished bedrooms that were certainly better than anything the staff had stayed in before. Each room, Elizabeth discovered, not only had the door to the hall but opposite, glass-paneled doors that opened onto the patio garden. It was going to be practically luxury living for Ethel, Wilson, Mrs. Flannigan, and the Norringtons. She left it to Mrs. Norrington to assign quarters, which boiled down to Ethel and Mrs. Flannigan sharing a room, Mr. and Mrs. Norrington in another, with Fiona Wilson by herself in the third.

As a great flurry was under way to get the dining table set with polished silver and gleaming china and crystal, Elizabeth collected flowers from the garden and made several arrangements of yellow and red chrysanthemums, goldenrod, and marigolds, with sprigs of red and pink bougainvillea. The previous owners of La Alma had planted a wonderful garden well suited to the climate.

She checked the time. It was getting late. The sun was setting. "Norrington, please see to it that plenty of hot water is on the boil for our baths."

Norrington, who was to serve also as His Lordship's valet, and Fiona Wilson had assessed their employers' situation: the master bedroom had no separate sitting rooms for the Baron and Her Ladyship, nowhere for them to dress or get ready to retire. Apparently, the previous owners of the house had had little in the way of domestic staff. They had made their fortune on Northwest timber and so Fiona imagined a family descended from rugged pioneer stock who made do for themselves. She and the butler/valet were forced to improvise. One of the Barnstables would have to make do with the bedroom to get ready for dinner; the other would use the spare bedroom across the hall. Not an ideal situation, but it was their first night in a very unexpected house.

Elizabeth decided to go out onto the patio and watch for Nigel and the posse, who should be returning shortly. As she went around the side of the house, she was not prepared for an astonishing sight that met her eyes.

The mountains across the valley, fifteen miles away, were undergoing a mysterious transformation. She was facing east, and as the sun slipped behind the San Jacintos behind her and across the gray-yellow desert, while inky shadows crept snakelike over sand and dunes, suddenly—

Elizabeth gasped. Her lips parted. She couldn't close her mouth; the sight was so stupendous.

Suddenly an entire mountain range went from pink to orange to reddish orange. And then, in a wink, the mountains were red. The ragged peaks and barren slopes blazed crimson, and she thought the whole mountain range would burst into flame.

The light behind her faded as the last rays from the sun were blocked by the two-mile-high Jacintos. Across the valley, the crimson faded back to orange, pink, lavender, purple. Soon, the sawtooth silhouette stood black against the twilight.

For a long moment she couldn't move. It hadn't just been a beautiful sight, a view to behold with wonder; it had felt strangely spiritual—in a way Elizabeth had never felt before. No artist could do it justice, no camera could catch such majesty. One had to witness the phenomenon with the naked eye, to stand silent and with held breath as the desert mountains underwent a metamorphosis in the final blazing light of the setting sun.

Hearing Nigel behind her, calling out for a wrangler to take his horse, Elizabeth stirred herself. Behind him, other riders came in, and men on foot. She heard automobiles out on the drive, brakes squealing, doors slamming, and above it all, the noise of men who apparently had had a jolly good time. It reminded her of weekend hunts in England, at the cousin's house in Sussex. Except that this hunt had been for a man.

Nigel's face was flushed, his hair disheveled, and he had an overall rumpled look about him. But he was electrified with energy. "You should see this country, Elizabeth!" he shouted. "There are wonders to be seen out there!"

I know, she said silently, the scarlet sunset-mountains still burned in her brain. "Tell me all about it at dinner," she said, taking him by the arm and leading him from the kitchen where Mrs. Flannigan and Ethel stood in dismayed silence. Why hadn't His Lordship used the front entrance?

Elizabeth used the bath first, luxuriating in her first good soak in days. Nigel, in the meantime, went into the den where Norrington had placed His Lordship's valise and locked boxes of important papers.

Wilson helped Elizabeth dress, doing up the buttons of her long white evening gown and then fixing her hair as she sat before the vanity mirror. "How was your first day, Wilson?"

"Bewildering, Your Ladyship."

Elizabeth looked at Fiona's reflection in the glass. There were dark smudges under her eyes. Even though Wilson insisted she had volunteered for this grand adventure, there was an air of sadness about her.

After fixing gold combs into Elizabeth's upswept blond hair and fastening a necklace around her neck, Fiona handed her mistress the long, white satin evening gloves she was to wear. When she was done,

Fiona thought Lady Elizabeth looked elegant enough to be presented to the King.

In the room across the hall, Norrington dressed His Lordship, fixing his bow tie, snapping on his cuff links, helping him into a white dinner jacket and giving it a sweep with the coat brush.

Nigel met Elizabeth in the enormous living room, where Ethel served champagne. Nigel strode about, touching things, pausing to look at paintings, seemingly to inspect his new home, but Elizabeth sensed he was distracted. The outlaw Indian was on his mind, perhaps? Or medjool dates. Nigel's lively mind, she had discovered, could race along several tracks at once.

Norrington came in to announce in a baritone, "Dinner is served, Your Lordship."

Elizabeth and Nigel sat at one end of the long table and Norrington began serving, with Ethel's help. The table was beautifully set with white linen, sparkling china and crystal, candelabras giving off a soft, flickering glow. Elizabeth could almost believe she was back at home on Park Avenue, especially once she and Nigel helped themselves from a tureen of clear consommé, offered at their left by Norrington.

And then, through thick adobe walls and an open window, they were serenaded by a harmonica and a banjo in the impromptu camp out back, men's voices, laughter. As promised, Mrs. Lardner and other ladies had arrived at sunset with pots of stew and baskets of bread, handing plates around while the members of the posse, exhausted but still stirred up, found places to sit around La Alma's patio, gardens, and paddocks. Reminded that she was not on Park Avenue after all, Elizabeth wanted to go through the kitchen and look out. She yearned for her first glimpse of the true West.

Suddenly, in the distance, Elizabeth heard another sound that rose and fell as a backdrop to Western banjo, a strange wailing that sounded sad and haunting.

"So how did the hunt go, Nigel, darling?" she asked as a salad was brought out and Norrington served His Lordship first, and then Elizabeth, offering vinaigrette dressing.

"We'll find him," Nigel said as he took a sip of wine. "The hue and cry are out, no one is going to let an Indian get away with killing a white man."

The kitchen door swung open again as another course was brought out. It was disconcerting to Elizabeth to see into the kitchen, to see the staff at work, to find herself so close to all that labor.

"Nigel, I haven't had a chance to tell you. The house is beautiful. More than I imagined. When you bought it simply based on a photograph—"

"We have a hundred acres," he said as he took another sip of red wine. "But it isn't nearly enough, not for what I have planned. The Indians next door are sitting on *thirty thousand acres* and they won't sell any of it. Can you believe that?"

Elizabeth searched for a response. She wasn't sure exactly what Nigel's plans were beyond planting date palm offshoots. In the silence she became aware of the sound of their forks on their plates while Norrington stood at watchful attention with a bottle of wine in his gloved hands.

"I think we'll have the house in order in a few days," she said as she speared a buttered asparagus tip. "We have a few eccentricities to iron out."

Nigel said, "Hm," and cut a large piece of steak.

He was preoccupied. She wondered with what. The hunt? The new plantation? The coming night? Elizabeth was looking forward to their first night together in their own bed.

And then the door swung open again, and two men marched into the dining room, uninvited, unannounced, spurs jangling, long duster coats giving off a smell of leather and horses and dust. "Begging your pardon, Mr. Barnstable," the gray-haired Sheriff said, a barrel-chested man who did not so much speak as shout. "We've got a problem that needs your help."

Nigel froze with his spoon halfway to his mouth. Elizabeth looked up, startled. The stranger with the curious snake hatband was with the Sheriff and he, too, had stopped to stare.

Mrs. Norrington came hurrying out of the kitchen. "I am so sorry, Your Lordship, I told them you were at dinner but they insisted."

"It's all right, Mrs. Norrington," Nigel said, recovering from his brief shock. They were, after all, in the middle of an emergency situation. "What can I do for you, Sheriff?"

But the two men kept staring, at the table, at Norrington, at Nigel and Elizabeth. As if they had stumbled upon something they could not recognize.

Elizabeth realized that the cowboy accompanying the Sheriff was staring at her place setting, particularly her spoons, knives, and forks. She supposed that, for him, dining was a simpler affair. He made her feel suddenly self-conscious.

"My good fellow," Nigel said, "you wish to see me about something?" Neither man, he noticed, had the good manners to remove his hat.

"Ten new men just arrived," the Sheriff said, remembering himself. "They came in cars. We don't have enough horses. Mr. McNeal here took a look in your stables. He says you have a few fine mounts. I'd like to requisition them for the new men."

Nigel's eyes flickered to the cowboy, rested on the Stetson, long duster, and six-shooter for an instant, then he speared a new potato and said, "Of course. Any stock you need. I'm told I have a foreman. I haven't had a chance to acquaint myself with my outdoor staff yet. I'm sure you can find him."

When the Sheriff and Cody started to leave, Elizabeth said, "Sheriff, what is that strange wailing we hear far off?"

"It's coming from the reservation."

"What does it mean?"

"Beats me," he said.

Cody spoke up. "They're singing. Whenever someone is about to die, the Cahuilla sing a death song asking the spirits to escort the deceased's soul to a peaceful afterlife."

"Who is about to die?"

"Johnny Pinto. They believe that the white men are going to kill him when they find him."

"I am sorry about that, Your Lordship," Norrington said after the two men left and he stepped forward to refill their wine glasses.

"I suppose things are different on American ranches," Elizabeth said.

"By the way, Elizabeth," Nigel said. "I have a big surprise for you."

"Whatever is it?"

"You'll see," he said with a secretive grin.

After dinner they retired to the living room where a fire roared behind a bronze screen. Nigel had a brandy while he told Elizabeth about the wonders of their new countryside, and she sipped coffee as she listened with interest and Button lay curled in her lap. She was surprised how exhausted she was. Only that morning they had been entering the Coachella Valley after rushing through the Arizona desert.

Now they were in their new home.

She tried to block out the sounds of the servants in the kitchen, cleaning up, washing dishes and pots, speaking in shrill tones, and then themselves sitting down to their own supper, right there at the table where Mrs. Flannigan had rolled pastry and cut vegetables. She wasn't used to hearing the servants or being so aware of their presence.

And then it was time for bed.

Elizabeth left Button with the kitchen staff, where he was to sleep in a spacious pen, to be let out in the morning by the first person in the kitchen.

Wilson and Norrington had devised a plan for helping His Lordship and his wife retire for the night. As there were no adjoining sitting rooms, they decided to use the bedroom across the hall for this purpose. First, Fiona undressed her mistress and brushed out Elizabeth's hair to twist it into a long braid. Elizabeth then went to bed in the master bedroom, with Fiona retiring for the night. Norrington and His Lordship then made use of the spare bedroom, the butler secretly thinking it a horrendous arrangement but for the moment would have to do. In his pajamas and dressing gown, saying good night to Norrington, Nigel stepped across the hall to where his bride was waiting.

But his thoughts were not on Elizabeth. He was thinking of the surprise he had for her—for everyone, really. It had come to him during the search for Johnny Pinto—his first day in the desert, his first day discovering what he was truly up against. The desert was a mighty challenge; it needed a mighty man to face it head on.

Yes, a big surprise indeed. For everyone.

He slipped between the sheets and took her into his arms. "Oh, Nigel," she breathed. "It's all so magical and wonderful. I'm the happiest woman on earth."

He silenced her with a kiss and then he was soon transporting her to that special realm they had created together, starting with their wedding night, unfolding during their honeymoon as they learned each other's rhythm and special places, with more discoveries during the train ride in their private car under stars that stretched from mountains to deserts to prairies.

When they were done, and Nigel was snoozing, Elizabeth continued to lie awake in the delicious afterglow. Lovemaking was always so heavenly with Nigel. She was full of joy and anticipation. She couldn't wait for tomorrow. Couldn't wait for their new life to begin.

*   *   *

In the servants' wing of the house, the Norringtons were getting ready for bed. "We're going to have to adjust to a house on all one level," the housekeeper said as she exchanged her black bombazine dress for a long white nightgown. "Apparently in these wide-open spaces, people do not build *up*, they build *out*."

"And we shall have to have whistles and bells installed, else how are they to call us?"

But despite it being a rough place that needed getting into shape, Mr. Norrington was quite pleased with the arrangement as they were so far away from anyone who might be looking for him, and certainly no one would think to look for him in this godforsaken place. As his wife had promised, his secret was safe.

In the next room, young Ethel and middle-aged Mrs. Flannigan were likewise assessing their new place of employment. "Doesn't look like there's any brass to polish," Ethel said.

"Small favors!" the cook said as, already in her nightgown, she turned back the sheets and blankets of a bed that was a good sight better than the narrow one she had been used to back on Park Avenue.

"Do you suppose those Indians are the scalping kind?"

"What about the boy they're hunting for? They said he's an Indian."

"I heard them call him Johnny Pinto."

"It sounds so romantic. I'll bet he's an outlaw."

"What if he sneaks back around and takes one of us hostage? I've heard that Indians like to do things to white women."

Blowing out their lamps, they lay in the dark, Ethel thinking about the dark-skinned men on the other side of the horse corrals, Mrs. Flannigan not at all pleased with having to work with a wood stove.

Lastly, Fiona had a nice wide bed all to herself. But it was a lonely reminder of her dream of marrying Lawrence and sharing a bed with him. She doubted now that was ever going to happen.

*   *   *

Outside, under the stars, stretched out on his bedroll with his head on his saddle, Cody thought about barging in on the Barnstables' dinner. It was so formal, you'd think they were expecting the president of the United States. Maybe that was how it was with wealthy New York folk. He'd never met anyone of their stripe. Or maybe it was being English.

And then he thought of her, in the long white gown. With her hair swept up the way it was, it had given him a view of a pale, graceful neck. She reminded him of his days in Colorado, ten years ago, when he was eighteen and mining for gold. A theatrical troupe had come through to entertain the miners, setting up a stage in a saloon. They had performed acrobatics, pantomimes, juggling acts, comedy acts, and musical numbers. There had been a singer—a beautiful young woman with golden hair and an equally golden voice. Hers was the only act the rowdy miners remained politely silent through. She had enchanted them with her songs, her angelic looks. Every man in the saloon had wanted her.

And then he put Elizabeth Barnstable from his thoughts as it was no use thinking about someone that had absolutely nothing to do with him. And anyway, Cody was going to be on the move again, and soon.

*   *   *

Across the alluvial plain, a thousand yards from the Barnstables' property, Luisa Padilla lay beside her husband, Chief Diego. He was her third husband, she his second wife. They had no children together. The relationship was not a romantic one but based on mutual respect and a desire for companionship. Menil, the moon goddess, had not wanted her children to be lonely, so when she had danced in the early days, and painted patterns and designs on the new creatures in the world, she had told people that they should come together and keep each other company and safe from harm.

Although Chief Diego's main residence was the ceremonial house, where sacred medicine bundles were kept, at night he came to his wife's house made of wood and palm fronds and found warmth and affection in her arms. But tonight he could not sleep. The newcomers greatly troubled him. He feared that bad magic had come to the valley.

At his side beneath the blanket, Luisa also could not sleep. Something terrible was going to happen at sunrise, and the brown-and-yellow bird would not tell her what.

CHAPTER ELEVEN

"PEOPLE ARE SAYING THAT having an English lord and his lady living in Palm Springs has brought some class to our humble village," Doc Perry said as he savored the cup of tea Mrs. Flannigan had given him. He was sitting at the cluttered kitchen table while sounds from the yards drifted through an open window. He wondered if he might coax some of that sizzling bacon from the cook.

"Actually, Dr. Perry," Fiona Wilson said as she finished ironing a blouse for her mistress, "it's only His Lordship who's English. Lady Elizabeth is American."

"Is she indeed? But you are English, I believe?"

Fiona smiled and excused herself. It was time to get Her Ladyship dressed.

Doc Perry watched her go. He had started coming by the big house to be on hand for injured posse members. But now it was to catch Miss Wilson's fetching smile.

It was the morning of the eighth day of the hunt for Johnny Pinto, and the camp outside was breaking up, the men getting ready to receive new orders from the Sheriff. As each grid was cleared and crossed off his map, the Sheriff drew out new squares, assigning men to each one. The search was widening, and the posse was now composed of a hundred men. The manhunt had attained national attention, as reporters and photographers, and even film crews for newsreels, were camped in front of La Alma, wiring daily updates to their newspapers.

Tension was also building between the Indians and the whites. The Sheriff sent men onto the reservation every day to make sure Johnny Pinto hadn't snuck back. They went into every shack and dwelling, even brazenly entering Chief Diego's ceremonial house, guns drawn. He had protested to the Indian agent in Banning, but the man had said there was nothing he could do.

The servants at La Alma were filled with anxiety as each day the posse returned empty-handed. Ethel had taken to sliding a chair against the patio door to her bedroom, worried that an uprising was going to erupt at any moment. Mrs. Flannigan carried a rolling pin with her everywhere for protection.

"Do you think there will be a battle, Dr. Perry?" she asked, her normally ruddy complexion now pale with fear. "Will we be scalped?"

"You don't have to worry, Mrs. Flannigan. These Indians are peaceful."

Because injuries were brought directly here, Doc Perry had taken to arriving every morning with his medical supplies as he had been called upon to tend to injuries that ranged from climbing accidents to wild shootings. Some nasty cases of poison sumac had also been brought to him by men who had poked around where they shouldn't. Perry reckoned it was only a matter of time before he was called upon to treat a rattlesnake bite or a gunshot wound.

Doc Perry was in his fifties, a handsome, robust man with a cheerful smile and manner. He wore an old-fashioned tailcoat and a shiny satin vest. On his head, a stovepipe hat with a feather in the hatband—his costume from the old days when he drove around the West selling cure-alls to gullible farmers and townsfolk. Now he was settled in Palm Springs, a lifelong bachelor, and everyone in this remote town liked and appreciated him for his healing skills and homemade medicines.

Doc Perry had an eye for the ladies, which was why he had never settled down. And the ladies liked him in return. He had known at an early age that he was attractive and had learned that the handsomer the man, the more success he made as a quack. He often joked to fellow hucksters that men who were not so blessed in the looks department were forced to go to medical school and become real doctors.

He had been without a lady friend for a while, but now, with the newcomers in town, here was the fetching lady's maid. He judged she was in her forties, but possessed a pale, dewy complexion. Slender as a whip. He loved the way the hem of her skirt fluttered around her calves. Hard to believe she was a maid. She looked more like a lady. Leland looked forward to courting her.

*   *   *

Button was on the bed, chewing on a crust of toast while Elizabeth used her breakfast tray to write another letter to her mother. She was alone. Nigel had gotten up over an hour ago to bathe and dress and join the men camped in the back.

Elizabeth thought what a strange week it had been, her property being used as a bivouac for an army of sorts. A curious introduction, she had written to her mother, to her new life in the West.

For the past few nights, after dinner, Elizabeth had stood on the rear patio where, in shadow cast by lanterns, she surveyed the great horde of tired and hungry men. They were a strange bunch, sitting on their haunches around small fires, shoveling food into their mouths from fine China plates—Elizabeth thought it was the least she could do for them, being their hostess. They weren't at all like Eastern men. They all wore boots, many with spurs. Blue jeans, plaid shirts, and cowboy hats. They politely called her "Ma'am" and few removed their hats in her presence.

Many spat tobacco juice.

She noticed that the cowboy who had barged in during dinner with the Sheriff sat off by himself with his back against a mesquite tree as he ate in thoughtful meditation. Once in a while, she looked over at him and caught him staring at her. She had learned that his name was Cody McNeal.

Elizabeth had taken to watching the men in the mornings, when they came in for the day's orders, and she had gotten a closer look at Mr. McNeal. She noticed his hands were callused and scarred. Hands that wrangled cattle and horses, roped and branded, she thought. The hands of a true cowboy, a reminder that there were parts of the West that were still wild and untamed, that perhaps Palm Springs itself was a remnant of the frontier and that people in this rugged country needed to be tough and strong. The six-shooter holstered on his hip, and the belt of bullets slung around his waist, reminded her also that she wasn't in New York anymore.

During dinner Nigel would speak excitedly of his day on horseback, traveling with expert trackers over trails and boulders, in a landscape filled with cactus plants, rattlesnakes, and the occasional coyote.

Elizabeth had used the opportunity to try making friends with the local women who came to help. But they were standoffish, as if they didn't know where to put the newcomer in their lives.

Fiona came into the bedroom. "The men are starting to arrive, Your Ladyship."

Elizabeth shooed Button from the bed and then planted her feet on the floor. "Let us pray, Wilson, that the fugitive is found today."

*   *   *

Out at the corrals, the men were saddling up, checking firearms, receiving orders, and reviewing maps. Nerves were strained, and tempers were wearing thin. Some had left the posse to go home, while new men had joined. All were frustrated, especially as they knew they were in the national spotlight now that newspapers and wire services were running the story.

Cody McNeal was saddling his black mare when he looked across the noisy camp and saw her there again, the old Indian woman who had given him water the day he had arrived at Palm Springs. He had learned that her name was Luisa Padilla, and she had come to La Alma every day since the hunt first began, to stand at the edge of the crowd, silent and watchful. After the men rode off, she would disappear, to return at sundown, and stand again like a silent statue, watching, listening.

Cody thought it was very brave of her. He had heard that the local tribe was frightened and terrified of leaving the reservation. With hot-headed white men thirsty for blood, running around with guns and shooting at anything that moved, the Indians stayed huddled in their houses for safety. Luisa did a courageous thing, Cody thought, venturing so near to a vigilante mob.

He suspected she was collecting intelligence. She would listen with a solemn face, and then disappear, no doubt to report to Chief Diego on the progress of the manhunt. It made Cody wonder if she also reported the information to Johnny Pinto himself, that perhaps she was a relative of Pinto's, that perhaps it was Luisa who was keeping Pinto one step ahead of his trackers.

Cody knew that the Sheriff was acting on the theory that Johnny Pinto would want to get as far away as possible. But in Cody's mind, if these natives were anything like the tribes in the north, Pinto would not want to be separated from his people. He would go to them for help.

As the men now started to mount their horses, Cody watched the old woman turn and walk away. And he wondered if she had been leading the posse in circles. Cody mounted his horse and, instead of riding off with his assigned group, decided to follow Luisa.

On the eastern boundary of the Barnstable property lay the wide expanse of sand, grass, shrubs, and palm trees that made up the "mouth" of Mesquite Canyon. This broad alluvial fan plain was where the stream, tumbling from the great heights of Mount San Jacinto, branched out and drained into the soil. On the other side of this flat, fertile plain lay the Indian reservation.

He hung back as Luisa stepped over the smaller, branching streams, through clusters of palm trees, over lush grass and desert sand, and into her village.

No fences or signs marked the reservation's borders. The sprawling group of huts, dwellings, and granaries were all centered around a larger structure, made of adobe with a dome-shaped roof covered in dried palm fronds, which Cody knew was the ceremonial house, the heart of the village. The Chief would live there, and all-important rituals would be held there. Spreading out from this long structure, like wheel spokes, were well-trodden paths leading to family homes, storage huts, and open-air arbors where the Indians worked at their various crafts. Dogs and chickens roamed about freely, children ran and played, women sat in front of their houses weaving baskets and gossiping.

Like many other Indian villages Cody had visited.

He watched Luisa walk among the low, square dwellings, past the arbors that were little more than four posts supporting a grass roof, and into a house with a wooden door and windows and a grass roof. She came out carrying a cloth bundle. She continued on through the village to where it abutted the foothills. Here, cliffs rose up to begin the ascent to the heights of the San Jacintos.

She reached the mouth of the great ravine known as Mesquite Canyon, one side of which belonged to the Barnstables, the other side of which was owned by the Indians. The stream down the center was the dividing line.

Luisa started up the canyon. Tethering his horse, Cody followed on foot, staying behind, hidden. The slope was gentle and gradual as Luisa followed the bubbling stream, walking in the shade of towering palm trees with great shaggy heads. Cody held back, moving only when he was sure she was out of earshot, then he crept along the trail. The silence was broken only by the whisper of a breeze that blew down the mountain, rattling the branches and leaves of mountain oak and mesquite trees, and the cry of a red-tailed hawk that rode the thermals high above. Cody kept an eye out for rattlesnakes as he silently tracked the old woman slowly up the mountain.

When he lost sight of her, and she could have taken one of three trails that branched off into ravines, he squatted over some footprints—a few old, others recent, of different sizes, barefoot and shod. He studied them, examined the soil around them and determined by the degree of dryness to the soil which footprints were the freshest. The old woman would not go barefoot and these impressions had been made by sandals, with shallow depressions, indicating the wearer was not very heavy. The old woman was continuing on ahead.

He followed the footprints until he came to another branching of the trail, each branch disappearing left or right into trees and boulders and mountain slopes. He inspected the vegetation and saw a fresh break on a bush of red berries he could not identify. A broken branch exposing moist sapwood indicated a break so recent it was in the last few minutes. The old woman was staying to the main trail.

Finally he caught sight of her. He stopped behind a cluster of short, dwarf palms before continuing on, staying behind, hidden, tracking her following indicators along the trail as an Oglala Sioux named Spotted Eagle had once taught him. The air grew cool. The stream widened and was now full of fish. The great, shaggy palm trees continued to march up the slope, like sentinels on either side of the stream whose sparkling water gave them life.

Cody felt his ears pop. He looked back. He estimated they had gained a thousand feet in elevation, and the old woman didn't slow down.

Finally, after an hour's trek, he watched her enter a cave, to come out a few minutes later empty-handed. He waited until she disappeared into the brush before crossing the rushing stream, stepping on large stones, to get to the Indian side of the canyon. He paused to listen, then he slipped into the dark cave. Johnny Pinto was sitting there, wolfing down acorn cakes.

Cody froze. *He's just a kid.*

Pinto couldn't have been more than sixteen years old. He had shaggy hair and wore a midnight-blue shirt with white buttons, a bright yellow kerchief tied around his neck. He looked up, his eyes flying open, his cheeks bulging with food. They stared at each other. The worldly cowboy and the frightened Indian boy.

All Cody wanted was to bring the boy back, not cause him any harm, but Pinto suddenly fell to his knees, hands in the air. "Was another white man shot that rancher," he wailed, food spilling from his mouth. "I don't kill nobody, mister."

"Listen, son," Cody began.

"I did not kill that man!" the boy wailed, tears streaking his bronze-colored cheeks.

Cody released a ragged sigh. "We'll have to let a judge decide that. Come on, son, I'm not going to hurt you."

As Pinto got to his feet, sobbing and wiping his eyes with his fists, Cody McNeal was suddenly remembering another Indian boy, an Arapaho up near the Powder River in Wyoming. A local rancher had accused the boy of stealing horses, but that boy had also protested his innocence. Cody had believed him but couldn't prove it. So he had visited the boy's village on the reservation and had walked through the Arapahos' horse herd, inspecting each animal for a telltale brand. The rancher's horses weren't among them. Cody doubted the boy would have had the spirit to steal them and then sell them. So where were the horses?

Cody had ridden back to the range, only to find that the cattle herd had moved on, the rancher nowhere to be seen, but the Arapaho boy's body hung from a tree, a rope around his neck.

"Never mind," he said now in a quiet voice, "I'm not going to take you in, Johnny. Run, boy. Get as far from here as you can. I know you want to be near your people, but sooner or later, the Sheriff's going to find you. Understand?"

Johnny nodded.

"You have friends who can help you?"

Johnny nodded again.

Cody stepped to the side and said, "Go. Run as fast as you can."

"Thank you, mister, and God bless you." Then the boy took off like a shot, dashing from the cave and out into the open.

Cody went to the entrance to watch him go, a skinny, unarmed kid that was probably some white man's fall guy.

And then a loud shot exploded in the canyon, echoing off the walls. Cody saw Johnny Pinto go down like a sack of corn.

He went running, calling the boy's name. When he reached Pinto, Cody knelt down and saw that the boy was dead. He looked up to see Nigel Barnstable striding up, holding a rifle. "I saw you follow that old Indian woman," Barnstable said. "So I decided to follow as well and see what was up. I'd say I came just in time, wouldn't you?"

Cody jumped to his feet. "What the hell is the matter with you? The kid was unarmed and running for his life. A warning shot in the air would have stopped him. You didn't have to kill him!"

Nigel shrugged. He didn't have to explain himself to this man. The truth was, Nigel had spent the past week nurturing a powerful resentment.

He had said nothing about it to Elizabeth, but he had been greatly rankled that he had not been put in command of one of the search groups. Instead the Sheriff had barked orders and hadn't once conferred with the master of the house as to what his opinion might be.

Of course Nigel knew he was new to the area. The Sheriff hadn't needed to point out the obvious. Nigel hadn't intended to *lead* the men in the search, as naturally that would fall to someone familiar with the area. But putting him in a sort of honorary command would have been a gesture of acknowledging that Nigel was the highest-ranking man in this valley.

Instead he had been reduced to a member of the rabble, and he didn't like it one bit. For eight days this thought festered within him, growing with each "pal" and "friend," with each, "Mr. Barnstable, you ride with Harry's group today." Which was why, when he saw the Indian boy, he had seen it as the perfect opportunity to let it be known that no backwater lawman was going to tell a Barnstable what he could and could not do.

As he turned to go back down the canyon, they heard a new sound, a high-pitched keening sound, and they saw the Indian woman break through the trees, holding her skirts as she ran. "Aii, Mukat!" Luisa cried as she dropped next to Johnny. "No, no, no, nooooo!" She gathered him into her arms and cradled him, rocking back and forth with her husband's grandson, tears streaming down her cheeks as she wailed up to heaven.

"Dear God," Cody muttered.

They heard voices calling from down the canyon. Nigel turned and shouted, "Up here, Sheriff! I got the Indian for you!"

The Sheriff and others came up on horseback. "Well, well, looks like your hunch was right, Mr. Barnstable. I would have preferred to take him in alive, though."

Cody went to Luisa and, squatting at her side, he laid a gentle hand on her shoulder. "I'm sorry, Mother. It's not what I wanted."

The Sheriff eyed the Indian woman. It was going to be difficult to pry her apart from the boy, who apparently was kin. He felt sorry for the old thing. He looked up at the sky, listened to the wind, and thought about eight days of a hunt that ended in death. It was time to get back to the city. He'd write up his report and close the book on a white rancher's murder.

"What about the body?" one of his deputies said.

"Let the Indians bury him. It's the least we can do for them."

Cody stayed at Luisa's side as the Sheriff turned his horse and rode back down the canyon, the old woman's cries echoing off the ancient rocks and stones.

*   *   *

Back at La Alma, the crowd was breaking up. The Sheriff had sent some of his deputies to round up the other search parties. When word reached the reporters camped out on the main road, they had all taken off to interview the Sheriff and get pictures.

Elizabeth couldn't find Button. All these men and horses, the mob breaking up, no one looking where they were going, Button could get underfoot, get hurt. Calling his name as she made her way through the chaos, she ended up at the far eastern edge of their property where it abutted the flat alluvial plain at the base of the canyon. Button sometimes came out this far when chasing rabbits.

"Button!" she called, and he came dashing from dense under-brush, covered in twigs and cactus spines, wagging his tail so hard he almost fell over.

"There you are, you naughty boy," she said as she picked him up. "Let's get back to the house before you get stepped on." But as she started to turn, she saw, emerging from the dense palms at the entrance of the canyon, Mr. McNeal leading his horse. An old Indian woman walked at his side. Elizabeth recognized her as the woman at the train depot the morning they had arrived. And then Elizabeth saw the body of a young man lying across Mr. McNeal's saddle.

She watched as Indians came from the village, running to the horse, wailing and crying, reaching for their dead kin, gently taking him down and carrying him back to their homes. Tears rose in Elizabeth's eyes, and she felt something move in her chest. The Sheriff had said Pinto had been killed but had offered no further details.

She waited as Mr. McNeal led his horse along a dry creek bed, and when he was near, she said, "What happened, Mr. McNeal?"

He removed his hat and Elizabeth saw a thick head of jet-black hair. She guessed he was in his late twenties, and he was very handsome. She saw sorrow in his eyes, and something else—a grim anger.

"The boy got shot, ma'am. They just left him there."

She glanced toward the reservation where the sounds of mourning and grief had begun to rise to the sky. "It was kind of you to bring him back," she said. Elizabeth felt her chest tighten. She had never seen death before. Was he a murderer? she wondered. And the boy had looked so young.

"I'm sorry you had to see that, ma'am."

"But how much worse for those poor people! Their singing—it's so filled with pain."

Cody gave her a long look, studied and intense. Elizabeth had the feeling he wanted to ask her something, or perhaps shout at her about something. For an instant it was just the two of them, bound together by tragedy and helplessness. He had replaced his hat so that his eyes were in shadow.

"I was afraid this was going to happen," she said, sweeping an errant lock of blond hair from her face—a fluid, graceful action, Cody thought. Barnstable's wife possessed a distracting beauty. It was her forehead, he realized. Smooth and pale and high, as if noble thoughts floated behind it. It might almost give her a snobbish look were it not for the fact that, when she smiled, snobbery was the last thing that entered a man's mind.

"With all these men so bent on justice or revenge or whatever one would call it. Couldn't they have just used handcuffs and taken him to jail?" She sighed and absently stroked Button's head. "I feel so sorry for his poor family."

Cody looked at the little dog in her arms, and he reached out to stroke its head. When Button licked Mr. McNeal's hand, Elizabeth said, "I'm surprised. He normally doesn't take to strangers. He still hasn't warmed to my husband."

Another moment stretched between them, filled with noise and silence and shared emotion, an intimate moment as their eyes locked and unspoken things remained unsaid. Then Elizabeth cleared her throat. "I have to get back to the house."

Cody stepped back, touched the brim of his hat, said, "Ma'am," and continued toward the corrals.

*   *   *

Nigel watched the stranger as he collected his bedroll and gear from the stable and loaded up his horse. He then looked at the Mexican and Indian ranch hands who had come with the property, cleaning up after the mob. One of the reasons Nigel bought La Alma was because it was horse property and Nigel loved to ride. The property came with stable hands but he needed someone to run the show, a white man. Nigel wasn't keen on dealing with someone who barely spoke English.

"I say, my good fellow," he said, walking up to Cody. "I was wondering if you could use a job."

Cody paused and looked around. Then he looked at Nigel. "Are you talking to me?"

"You look like you know your way around horses. How about coming to work for me as my ranch manager?"

Cody stared at him. The man was acting as if he'd simply shot a rabid animal instead of an unarmed youth. "Thanks, but I'm not looking for a job." Cody stepped into the stirrup, mounted his horse, and rode out of the corral.

Elizabeth, standing on the patio, searching for her husband, watched Cody leave. She had heard Nigel offer him a job. She thought it a shame he was unable to take it.

The Sheriff and his posse killed Johnny Pinto and left him in the wilderness. But Cody McNeal brought him back to his people.

Elizabeth forced her thoughts away from McNeal and the tragedy of the Indians. Now that the posse was gone and order was being restored, Elizabeth wanted to devote her full attention to her new home—not just the house and staff, but the village and its citizens.

The collection of stores and scattered houses and small farms—there were even tent houses with their own gardens—seemed so like a frontier, a place of promise and growth. She had been born and raised in a city that had its beginnings three hundred years ago—a city of high-rise buildings and miles of brownstone rowhouses, a city that took up every inch of land so that the only direction for growth was up.

But here, with so much space and room . . .

She couldn't wait to meet her neighbors properly, make friends with them, get to know them, get to know their ideas and plans for their community. Now that she had had a taste of what it was like to unite with others in a cause—the energy from the posse still made her blood rush—she was eager to roll up her sleeves and get to work. And the first thing she was going to do was join the local women's service club. Mrs. Van Linden had belonged to such a club for as long as Elizabeth could remember, raising money for the public library, running milk drives for orphans. They had rolled bandages during the war for the Red Cross and had knitted socks and mittens for the soldiers in the trenches.

But now, women could do so much more. This was a new era, a progressive age in which men were not the only ones who shaped landscapes and politics. Women now had the vote and a voice, and Elizabeth wasn't going to waste a single moment getting started in her new life.

But as she turned to go back into the house, where she heard Mrs. Flannigan talking to Mrs. Norrington about whether to make blancmange or Charlotte Russe for his Lordship's dinner tonight, the image of Cody leading his horse out of the canyon, the lifeless form of Johnny Pinto draped over the black mare, came back to her mind, sharp, vivid, sickening.

As her superstitious mother, who went to fortune-tellers, would say: It was a bad omen.

CHAPTER TWELVE

THE BIG DAY AT last.

The local citizenry had turned out, as well as nearby fruit farmers and folks scattered over the valley, itinerant Mexicans and people just passing through hoping for a morning's distraction and a chance to socialize.

Elizabeth had put the word out that everyone was invited to a picnic, and soon the rear property was crowded again, as it had been during the hunt for Johnny Pinto. But while the local white folks seemed eager to enjoy themselves, everyone noticed that the Indians were nowhere to be seen. The reservation was strangely quiet. Chief Diego's people had wailed non-stop for seven days as they mourned the death of Johnny Pinto. Now they were silent.

The ranch hands had constructed long wooden trestle tables, and chairs had been brought outside from the house. The tables were covered in white sheets anchored down against the morning wind with heavy candlesticks. The day before, Mrs. Flannigan had labored over a feast, and soon the tables would groan with smoked salmon pâté, beef and cheese sandwiches, sweet corn on the cob, bean salad, potato salad, lemon squares, and jam tarts.

Mrs. Allenby, whose husband owned the green grocery, stood with Mrs. Lardner and Mrs. Henry, who was a widow. The three had been friends for over fifteen years, ever since they came out to the desert, separately, with their husbands to make new lives for themselves.

Cody McNeal was among the crowd watching the road from the east, the main road that ran through town, connecting Palm Springs with the small hamlets strung along the base of the foothills. Waiting for the arrival of fifty offshoots that were to be planted next to La Alma.

When he had ridden away from Palm Springs after the Johnny Pinto tragedy, he had explored the old mining town of Twentynine Palms in his search for a man named Peachy, and then he had tried to steer himself north, but a strange compunction had brought him back to this little town in the Coachella Valley. Just a bit more time, he told himself. Cody was filled with the curious sense of having unfinished business here. But he hadn't taken the job Barnstable offered him. He wouldn't be here that long.

Elizabeth stood on her rear patio along with everyone else, excited as she watched the road where Nigel was soon to appear. The holes had already been dug, fifty in neat rows, ready to become an orchard. No, she thought, a grove. It sounded more biblical. She had heard that the Indians were not happy about Nigel's new farm. She wondered if they were going to stage some sort of resistance or protest.

But it was all legal, what Nigel was doing. This was Barnstable property.

She had learned that most people who came to the Coachella Valley came for one of two reasons: their health, or to become a grower. Already the nearby desert was turning green with citrus, apricot, and almond orchards. Now Arabian dates would add to the verdure. In ten years, Nigel had said, they would be sitting in the shade of magnificent, towering trees.

Nigel had left the day before with two ranch hands, telling Elizabeth that he would be returning this morning with the new date plantings. The offshoots were coming from a date farm near Indio, a town that lay twenty-three miles to the east.

For the past two weeks, the eastern side of the Barnstable property had been a beehive of industry as Indians from other villages in the valley had been trucked in and given shovels (Chief Diego had forbidden his own people to work for the new white man). With Nigel overseeing the project, they had dug fifty holes, prepared and fertilized them, and now the virgin soil was ready to accept the new plantings.

Elizabeth saw Mr. McNeal standing off to the side of the main crowd, as seemed to be his habit. She had been surprised when he had returned to Palm Springs a few days after his departure, this time taking a room at Mrs. Henry's boardinghouse because the nights had gotten desert-cold.

She eyed a group of ladies—Mrs. Lardner and the others who had taken care of the men in the posse. Elizabeth desperately wanted to make their acquaintance. She was eager to get involved in local town activities. But she had been here for six weeks, and so far no one had invited her to tea.

But now this opportunity had arisen, and Elizabeth was going to seize it. As soon as Nigel arrived and the festivities were under way, she would ingratiate herself with her guests.

Fiona Wilson watched the road with little interest. It had been seven weeks since they left New York and Lawrence had seen her off at the train station. Since then, she had written him several letters but had received no replies. She found herself feeling resentful toward a woman to whom she should be extremely grateful. But she supposed that was how it was—a favor done calls for a favor in return. Mrs. Van Linden had given Fiona employment when she was out in the cold and frightened. She had every right to call in the favor.

Doc Perry was there with his medical bag. Agricultural accidents were commonplace in the valley. He had brought a good supply of sutures, antiseptics, and bandages. But his mind was less on anticipated injuries and more on the slender and wistful Miss Wilson, who seemed to him to always be far away and just on this side of sadness.

As the morning progressed and the crowd grew anxious, a red-tailed hawk swooped overhead, emitting a high-pitched cry. Elizabeth looked up, shielding her eyes from the sun.

And then a moment later she heard, far off, a faint rumbling sound. She looked around, trying to determine its origin.

Others picked it up, looked this way and that. As the sound grew, people speculated. A thunderstorm behind the mountains? Earthquake tremors?

The rumble grew to a roar. Elizabeth looked to her right, toward the rocky spur that jutted onto the desert floor from the foothills on the eastern boundary of the Indian reservation.

And then everyone was looking in that direction, frowning, murmuring, feeling uneasy. When a brown plume rose behind the rocks, someone shouted, "Fire!"

But it wasn't fire. The plume consisted of dust, not smoke.

"What is it, Your Ladyship?" Fiona said nervously.

Elizabeth's heart started to race. "I don't know . . ."

Doc Perry said, "What's that noise?"

The roar grew, the ground trembled. The dust cloud intensified. Something was coming.

And then a bright yellow beast suddenly emerged around the bend, kicking up dust as it raced toward Palm Springs. Nigel driving his brand-new Stutz Bearcat, a hundred-and-nine horsepower, four-cylinder sports car that gleamed like the sun and raced like the wind.

In the next instant, to everyone's shock, a line of tractors slowly emerged from around the bend, great machines looking like prehistoric beasts pulling enormous wheeled drays, each laden with five of the biggest trees anyone had laid eyes on. Ten tractor-drays in all, rolling steadily behind Nigel in his golden chariot, a bizarre procession that fooled the eye and upset the senses because the trees were lying down.

Massive date palms, stacked like logs, green fronds gathered up in rope and twisted like topknots, rolled toward the town, leaving a gigantic cloud of dust and sand behind, filling the air with the smell of gasoline as the motors chugged and strained with their massive hauls, belching smoke and fumes into the pristine desert air.

"My heavens," Elizabeth whispered as the enormous drays were guided off the main road and onto the plain between La Alma property and the reservation.

"There's a sight you don't see every day," Doc Perry said.

Now the Indians came out, appearing from their doorways, blinking in the daylight, materializing as if summoned by the roar of the beasts—over three hundred men, women, and children, to walk to the edge of the reservation and watch in eerie silence.

The Bearcat had hardly rolled to a stop when Nigel jumped out and came running up the dirt track to the back of La Alma. "What do you think?" he shouted. "Didn't I tell you I had a surprise for you?"

The idea had come to him during the first day of searching for Johnny Pinto, when he had been struck by the utter vastness of the desert, and its extreme age—and a sense that things moved very slowly here. He had decided then that he wasn't going to waste time watching offshoots grow. He wanted trees.

"What happened to the offshoots?" Elizabeth said breathlessly.

With his hands on his hips, Nigel proudly surveyed the careful maneuvering of the tractors and drays, axles groaning, gears grinding, men shouting directions, waving their hats to prevent collisions. Nigel was hatless so that the wind whipped his hair. "Gonzalez told me that offshoots take eight to fifteen years before they bear fruit! I can't wait that long! So I brought mature, fruit-bearing trees. We'll have our first harvest in a year."

So this was what Nigel had been busy doing the past few weeks, making telephone calls from Lardner's General Store, sending and receiving telegrams, making frequent trips to Indio. He had been arranging for this project of gargantuan proportions. "But, Nigel, how on earth will you get those monsters into the ground? I can't see how all the manpower in the world will manage it!"

He just smiled and said, "It's another surprise."

The Indians watched the white people run down to the drays and act as if they had never seen palm trees before. They laughed and opened their arms wide to measure the massive root balls, and they all congratulated the white man for his decision because he was going to have a magnificent grove in no time.

Chief Diego was not pleased. He had thought small offshoots were coming. At night, his men would sneak out and destroy them. But giant mature trees were going to be planted instead. The white man was too impatient to wait years for offshoots to grow. Diego was angry with himself. He had not reckoned for the white man's impatience.

"We cannot destroy those trees, they are too big, too strong," he said to Luisa. "But we can stop them from being planted. If we do not, we will never see the stars again."

*   *   *

The picnic was such a huge success that everyone returned the next day to watch how Mr. Barnstable expected to get the great, unwieldy trees into the ground. Wagers were made. Even the staid Norrington couldn't resist putting money down on the kitchen table, saying that His Lordship would have no trouble planting the trees, against Mrs. Flannigan's money that said he would. Fiona and Doc Perry had an amicable competition that didn't involve money, while Elizabeth worried about people getting hurt. Getting those trees upright and settled in their holes struck her as being a Pharaonic feat that rivaled the building of the Pyramids.

Nigel barely touched his breakfast of fried eggs and tomatoes and meaty bacon. And he was in such a hurry to get out to his monumental project that he had dressed himself, leaving Norrington to stand uselessly in the bedroom across the hall.

Elizabeth took her time over her breakfast tray, sharing toast with Button whom she had decided must be sequestered in the house lest he get trod upon by workmen. She pictured the raising of massive Egyptian obelisks by ten thousand slaves.

As Fiona dressed her, she said, "What do you think of His Lordship's endeavor? Can it be done?"

Fiona shook her head. "Doc Perry said he would bring extra medical supplies as there are bound to be injuries."

They all went to the edge of the property, Elizabeth and her staff, the ranch hands, neighbors, people who lived on far-flung plots around Palm Springs. On the other side of the plain, they saw the Indians gathered silently on the reservation. The tractor-drays were parked on the Barnstable's side of the fan plain, gargantuan trees waiting to be plucked up and planted like marigolds.

Elizabeth frowned. There didn't seem to be enough manpower to hoist those green monsters. Who was Nigel going to use?

And then she heard the roar of motors and presently two large trucks appeared on the road, flatbeds carrying men in work clothes, wearing straw hats, brawny men who looked eager to work. They looked like Indians. Since Chief Diego had forbidden any of his people to work for Nigel, someone must have gone around the valley and collected men from the Cabazon, Soboba, and Morongo bands. But it still didn't look like enough, Elizabeth thought. What if one of those trees fell on them? She was beginning to think Nigel's ambition had outstripped his common sense and that the project was going to fail, when another roar arose in the distance, and the ground trembled.

All heads swiveled northward, in the direction of the train depot. A behemoth was trundling across the landscape, grinding up everything in its path. "What the hell is that?" Augie Lardner said, scratching his head.

It was a strange looking conveyance, comprised of the front part of a truck, with a cab for the operator, and a flat bed housing what looked like an enormous hoist. The whole of it didn't move about on wheels but on metal treads on either side of the vehicle, rolling in a continuous loop. A long, telescoping boom was fixed to the flatbed, with the truck and crane joined together by a turntable that allowed the boom to swing in an arc. A long cable was suspended from the boom, with enormous hooks at the end. A towering, steel, gasoline-belching crane that looked as if it could lift the trees as if they were toothpicks.

It reminded Elizabeth of pictures of tanks she had seen during the war. She had seen cranes before, at the harbor and at train stations. But this one was mobile. "It's the very latest invention!" Nigel said with enthusiasm. "Mr. Gonzalez just imported it from England, and I'm having one of the first goes at it."

As Gonzalez guided the crane driver, watching where he stepped, using his arms to signal which way to turn, when to go straight, when to slow down or speed up, the monster machine approached the trays loaded with trees until Nigel shouted, "Stop! That's good!"

A wind picked up. The sheets on the picnic tables fluttered, a few things fell off. But no one moved. Everyone crowded at the rear of the La Alma property—the ranch hands, the domestic staff, townspeople, and outsiders—all watched in breathless anticipation as the crane's enormous boom was slowly guided over the first dray. They watched the cable slide down. And then Indians rushed forward to secure the giant hooks into the meaty neck of the palm just below where the fronds emerged at the crown. Others lined up along the length of the trunk in readiness for guiding the tree as it swung up from the dray and over to its planting place.

While Gonzalez and Nigel shouted instructions and everyone's eyes were riveted on the spectacle, a small procession appeared across the alluvial plain. A knot of six people—five men and one woman—slowly approached the trucks and machinery and holes in the ground. They said nothing, made no sound as they drew near. But when one of the worker Indians saw them, he froze. And then another, and another, until all the hired workers had stopped in their tracks.

"What the hell—?" Nigel turned in the direction they were all staring and frowned at the delegation stepping onto his land. "Who's that?" he said.

Gonzalez came to stand at Nigel's side. "That's Chief Diego. He's legendary in this valley. An influential leader and a powerful shaman. All the bands respect and fear him."

Nigel snorted. The old man in ill-fitting clothes with a bandana around his white hair didn't look like much. He looked as if the wind could carry him off.

The intruders didn't say a word, they just stood like statues while the men from Morongo and Cabazon slowly lowered their eyes.

"Ignore the old fart," Nigel said. "Let's get back to work."

But no one moved. "They fear him, Señor," Gonzalez said. "He can place bad magic on their families. He can bring sickness to their clan."

"But what's he doing here?"

"Chief Diego doesn't want you to plant the trees here."

"What do I care what he wants? Get to work!" Nigel shouted, shoving two of the Indians by the shoulder. But they wouldn't budge.

"I warned you, Señor."

On his own date farms, Gonzalez hired workers from the Santa Rosa band, and word had reached them that Chief Diego of Palm Springs did not want the big trees to go here. Gonzalez had tried to warn Señor Barnstable, but the Englishman wouldn't listen.

On the patio, holding Button in her arms, Elizabeth watched the curious showdown on the flat plain. She recognized the woman standing with the Chief as the one who had come down from the canyon with Mr. McNeal and Johnny Pinto's body. Considering that she walked at the Chief's side while the rest walked respectfully behind, Elizabeth assumed she was a woman of importance.

"Very well," Nigel said. "Mr. Gonzalez, if you please?" The man nodded, signaled to the driver of the other flatbed truck, climbed into the other one, and together they drove off toward the east, leaving the newly arrived Indians to look around themselves in puzzlement.

If you won't work, Nigel thought, then you can walk back to your reservations.

He looked at Chief Diego, standing smugly triumphant. So it's going to be you and me, old man, is that it? Nigel thought. I'm always up for a good fight, but I can promise you right now, I'm going to win.

Gonzalez arrived two hours later, the flatbed trucks again filled with men. These bore a resemblance to the Indians, but they were Mexican migrant workers who crossed the border near San Diego and roamed California with knapsacks and bedrolls, following crops, planting times, and harvests.

They jumped down and got to work at once.

When the first tree had been hoisted high in the air and was swinging perilously from the boom, Fiona asked as she stood next to Doc Perry, "Won't the machine tip over?"

"I reckon the crane truck weighs around thirty thousand pounds," he said, "while a tree weighs between six and ten thousand pounds. So I think it will be stable."

But at that very moment the crane started to tip as its treads began to sink in the soft soil. "Drop it!" Nigel shouted. "Drop the bloody tree!"

As the palm was lowered, the Mexicans rushed forward to pack large rocks under the truck's metal tracks to stabilize it.

They tried it again, with much grinding of gears and smoke coming out of the truck. But this time, with ten men, arms raised, reaching for the root ball, the towering tree dropped into the hole with a crash that made the ground shake, and then it swayed perilously as men dashed this way and that to stay out of its path. But the tree settled and when it did, the crowd erupted in cheers.

The Mexicans got to work filling in the dirt and packing it down—men possessing the strong, stocky build of their Aztec forebears—while Nigel stared up at the top of the tree where the fronds had been tightly bound together to form an onion-shaped topknot.

"Bring the ladder!" he shouted.

Mr. Gonzalez, the grower from Indio dressed in denim work clothes, with a wide-brimmed straw hat on his head and leather gloves on his hands, said, "Mr. Barnstable, I told you we have to leave them tied up until the trees have adjusted. The transplanting will put them in shock for a few weeks."

But Nigel was already whipping off his tweed jacket. Unclipping his cufflinks and throwing them to the ground (to Norrington's shock), he rolled up his sleeves and, grabbing a machete from the back of a truck, proceeded to scale the ladder.

"Señor!" Gonzalez shouted. "You cannot do that! You do not have the training. It is very dangerous!"

But when Nigel reached the top, everyone staring in open-mouthed astonishment, he swept his arm out in an arc and brought the machete down on the rope that bound the palm fronds. They sprang free—massive feather-shaped leaves with dangerous spines—making a whooshing sound as they fell out into their natural bouquet-like arrangement, catapulting the rope through the air with such ferocity that everyone thought for an instant Nigel was going to be decapitated.

Everyone gasped. And then the crowd cheered. They had never seen mature trees transplanted before, had never witnessed the opening of secured fronds, and the Allenbys and the Lardners, Mrs. Henry, the school teachers, and the auto mechanic, the folks from nearby farms all marveled at Nigel Barnstable's daring ingenuity and audacity to challenge nature the way he had. For the men in the crowd, the word "balls" came to mind. For the women, it was Douglas Fairbanks in *The Mark of Zorro*. And they looked at Elizabeth Barnstable with envy.

But Cody McNeal, who watched the display with a cynical eye, thought: Arrogant, reckless.

Seven more trees got put into the ground before it was too dark to plant any more. People drifted back to their homes, congratulating Nigel on an amazing feat.

Before driving back to Indio, Pedro Gonzalez paused to shake hands with Nigel. "You will do very well here, Señor. On behalf of myself and the other date growers, welcome to the valley. I look forward to seeing your farm grow."

He had an olive complexion with a gold front tooth that shone as he grinned and said, "And we would like to invite you to join our association. Although our farms are competitive, we are cooperative and have formed an association that assures stable prices and that everyone gets a share of the market. And, please, Señor, if you ever need help with your trees or your fruit, anything, just give me a call and I will come and help."

Nigel had never felt so energized. He felt as if he could go without sleep for the rest of his life. His body was charged. He felt drugged on power. He knew he was not going to stop with these fifty. He was going to plant another fifty right away, or a hundred, or five hundred. Mr. Gonzalez had said it might not be easy to procure that many, that he might have to go as far as Phoenix for more stock, but Nigel had already told him money was no object.

His empire was only just beginning.

Doc Perry picked up his medical bag and, tipping his stovepipe hat to Fiona Wilson, said he looked forward to returning tomorrow to watch the rest of the planting.

The Mexicans made camp among the newly planted trees, and Nigel paid Augie Lardner and Mr. Allenby to bring food and supplies to them.

"I wish I could expand on that side," Nigel said at dinner after he and Elizabeth had bathed and changed into evening clothes. He could barely eat. It confused Norrington, who didn't know if he should remove His Lordship's half-touched fish and have the duck brought out.

Elizabeth didn't say a word as she listened to her husband's plans to buy more land and bring in engineers to drill for wells. "Today's trees will be watered by the run off down Mesquite Canyon," he said, holding up his glass for a refill of his Riesling wine. "But if I plant on the west side of the property, I'll have to find another water source."

Elizabeth listened with a smile, pleased for his success. When Nigel fell silent and she saw his thoughts drift away from the table, she said, "How clever of you to have a back-up plan if the Indians wouldn't work."

"Gonzalez tried to get me to hire Mexicans to begin with. But I would have to feed and house them, while the Indians could leave every day and go back to their reservations. It's going to be an extra expense that I hadn't planned on."

As dinner came to an end, with the lemon trifle going untasted, Nigel rose from the table and murmured in Elizabeth's ear, "Dismiss Wilson as quickly as you can. I'm going to check on the trees and will join you in a few minutes."

Elizabeth hurriedly dressed in the peignoir she had worn on their wedding night. Wilson seemed to want to linger over her mistress's hair, slowly braiding it as she talked about how exciting it was to see the first trees planted.

"I'm tired, Wilson. It's been a long day."

Then she waited in bed for Nigel. Her body hummed in anticipation of his touch. Watching him scale that tall ladder and wield the lethal machete had been extremely arousing. She had expected that Nigel would be a more books-and-paper manager of a plantation, leaving the hard sweaty work to hired men. She had not expected him to be so . . . hands-on. She pictured again the tension in his muscles as he climbed the towering tree, the fabric of his shirt straining over his back and shoulders. It was like something out of a movie.

There was a soft knock at the door, and then it swung open and Nigel came in wearing his dressing gown. He must have undressed and washed in record time. She saw the fire in Nigel's eyes, saw the rapid breathing, and she knew he was as ready for her as she was for him.

He turned out the lights. She heard the dressing gown drop to the floor. The bed dipped and Nigel's cologne reached her an instant before his hands did. The nightgown came off and then she felt his heat against her, bare skin to bare skin, making her groan with desire. She waited for the caresses, the gentle exploration that always brought her to peak arousal. But the kisses were rough, urgent. He pressed her down onto her back and forced his knee between her legs. She wasn't ready, but he was intent upon his goal, as he had been with his trees, with a single-minded urgency to seize whatever it was he wanted.

While everyone slept, across the silent fan plain, among dark huts and another race of people slumbering in dreams, Chief Diego looked up at the stars and read the message in them. He knew what he had to do.

CHAPTER THIRTEEN

LUISA FIRST SMELLED THE smoke.

Stinging, acrid. Had she forgotten to dampen her cooking fire for the night? In a village constructed of old wood and dried palm fronds, there was always the danger of fire.

And then she opened her eyes. It was late. The village was asleep. But the smell of smoke was strong. And growing stronger.

Alarmed, she sat up and listened. Outside, silence. If a house was burning, there would be voices, shouts. Throwing off her blankets, she struggled to her feet and went to the doorway to look out. A blinding sight met her eyes. Flames leaping to the sky, hot and golden, licking the stars like devils' tongues. The heat blasted against her face. She saw ash and cinders raining down on her village, falling from the sky onto the flat alluvial plain.

The white man's new orchard was burning.

She ran toward the fire, shielding her face with her arm. As she neared, her ears filled with the roar of the conflagration, she saw her husband, Chief Diego, running through the grove with a flaming torch, setting fire to the remaining few trees so that they, too, burst into flames that rushed up the dry trunks and ignited the oil-rich fronds.

And then she saw . . .

She froze. Men came running from the white man's big house. She saw him, the Señor named Barnstable, running with a rifle in his hands. Other men, too, from the bunkhouse, running with buckets and shovels and blankets. But she knew they couldn't save the orchard.

It would burn through the night until there was nothing left and the sun would rise over black ash.

Was this what the brown-and-yellow bird had warned her about? Was this to be the terrible dawn?

When she saw the Señor stop, raise his rifle, and take aim, she shouted at Diego. But he did not see the white man and the rifle. The shot rang out in the night and Diego fell.

"No!" Luisa screamed. "Noooooo!"

Her eyes snapped open and she stared into the darkness of her raftered ceiling. A dream. But so real, so vivid. No, not a dream, a message from the spirits.

And then she felt the blankets at her side. Diego was not there.

Luisa jumped to her feet, slipped into her sandals and, wrapping a thick shawl about herself, went to the door and looked out.

There was no golden conflagration, no flames jumping up to the stars. And the wind was cold. She looked across the alluvial plain at the white man's big house, where windows stood dark and silent. To the left, where Chief Diego had once been able to see the rising stars, the dark bulky shapes of towering trees with thick trunks and wide-spreading crowns blocked out the night sky.

She listened. Something was wrong. The spirits didn't send dreams for no reason. She turned her head, cocked her ears, and then she heard it—faint, whispering. Men moving through brush.

Luisa left her house, hurried through the silent village, and entered the fan plain where wild cottonwoods grew and giant cactus slumbered. On the other side, where the white man's property began, she searched the darkness. There! Movement. Silhouettes of men moving stealthily among the new trees. And then Luisa saw the fiery torches.

And then she saw baby flames at the base of a tree.

She whipped off her shawl and ran. "Help me!" she cried, throwing her shawl on the fire. The shamans spun around, stared at her, their faces cast in flickering light, illuminating eyes filled with fear. "Put this out!" she cried, picking up the shawl covered in sparks, throwing it down again and again on the flames at the base of the new palm tree.

"No!" Diego said, running up to her, a flaming torch in his hand, a wild look in his eye. "We do not take orders from a woman."

"The spirits sent me," she shouted, bringing the shawl down on the flames. "This is *their* command."

The shamans looked at one another and then rushed forward and stamped on the flames with their sandaled feet. Luisa was a pul, a very powerful spirit-reader.

When the flames were out, she grabbed the torch from Diego's hands. "Quickly! We must hurry from here before the white man sees us."

But he stood his ground.

"You must not do this, Diego," Luisa said, stepping up to him, speaking in a level voice. "It is not the way. Think, husband! The Great Father in Washington will take away our rations. No more free beef and cheese for our people. No more free medicine and blankets. We are poor, we need these gifts from the Great Father. Your fire will only bring ruin to our people. I have seen this. The spirits have shown me."

He firmed his jaw. "I will not move for the white man. Instead, I will move his trees. I cannot see the stars, but I will not move one more time to find the stars. The Cahuilla have moved and moved for the white man, but now I plant my feet in the ground and here I stay."

She made an exasperated sound, keeping her eye on the big, silent house. "Then don't move. Here, look," she said, pointing up through the leafy crowns of the date palms at the night sky. "From here you can see the stars. Do you see? Same vantage point from the village. Closer, in fact. You just come to the white man's trees and look up to read the stars."

When she saw the stubborn set of his face, she said more gently, "Do not burn down the Señor's trees, husband. He will fight back. He will kill you as he killed your grandson." She laid a hand on his arm. "Husband, your father signed the treaty saying we would fight no more. That was the agreement with the Great Father. If you break that treaty, you dishonor your father. But Diego, there is another way to fight the white man. And it is with a weapon he does not have."

When they returned to the village, Chief Diego and the shamans went to the ceremonial house where they would chant and ask the gods for guidance. Luisa returned to her home where she struck a match and heated the coals in her cooking pit. Throwing mesquite branches onto the coals, she watched the fragrant smoke rise up to the hole in the roof.

Then she lifted a basket that was hanging on the wall. It was new; she had just finished it. The main body of the basket was the color of straw, but the intricate design was done in dark red. It was the red diamond rattlesnake design, which imbued the basket with special powers. She had begun weaving it months ago, when she had received two messages in the canyon. She had woven it in honor of the snake.

Now she was going to put it to work.

Holding the basket over the mesquite smoke, she turned it in circles, lifting it up and down, and then she sprinkled sacred chia seeds into it, shaking them around, emptying them into the hot coals. She chanted as she worked, asking the spirits to come to her husband's aid. He needed to save face. He should not have to come to the white man's trees to see the stars. As she chanted her final prayer, Luisa was satisfied that the smoke had carried her plea to the realm of the spirits and the gods, and it would be they who would decide the fate of the white man's grove.

Lastly, in the cold of the night, with a blanket wrapped around herself, she stole across the moon-lit sandy plain, crossed the boundaries, stepped between the giant trees and around to the back of the white man's big house. The windows were dark, the house silent. On the roof she heard the *hoo-hoo-hoo* of an owl. She took it as a good omen.

Placing the basket on the step by the back door, she called upon the spirit of the red diamond rattlesnake to come to the aid of his people. Then she turned and vanished back into the night, leaving the basket that was woven with red diamonds to be found by the white people and taken, with its special magic, into their house.

*　　*　　*

"This area's pretty much all mined out," the old prospector at Joshua Tree had said. "You'd do better lookin' for your friend in the high desert. Up Tylerville way, folks say there's still some gold to be found."

Tylerville was located eighteen miles east of Twentynine Palms, and eight miles north of Joshua Tree, making it an inconvenient fifty miles east-northeast of Palm Springs. The man Cody was searching for had said that if he didn't strike it rich at Horsethief Creek in Colorado, then he would keep on trying.

Peachy hadn't struck it rich in Colorado.

After six months of combing this region, exploring every abandoned gold mine and talking to old-timers, Cody decided Peachy hadn't come through this way. So he was going to say good-bye to Palm Springs and to the few folks whose acquaintance he'd made here. He wasn't sorry to be leaving. A loner by nature, Cody was used to saying good-bye.

He had passed the Indian reservation and was now riding up to the border of the Barnstable property where fifty magnificent date palms pleased the eye. His thoughts went to Elizabeth Barnstable. He wondered how she, a city woman born and bred, was adjusting to her new life. She had only been here three months. He reckoned she would need time.

The folks at Palm Springs liked to call themselves a town, but it was really just a village with thirty or so residences scattered along the few rustic roads shaded by cottonwoods and pepper trees. Some years back, surveyors came and laid a grid on this patch of fertile ground watered by San Jacinto's springs. They drew lines on a map and called them "roads" and "lanes." Enterprising land agents, wishing to attract buyers, had planted trees along these dusty, unpaved byways so that they were shaded from the desert sun. Trees that produced oranges, lemons, figs, almonds. People came, purchased lots, and built modest places of business, adobe homes, and some still lived in tents. There were few fences as this was the desert and hospitality was a number-one rule. No outdoor lighting. When neighbors went calling at night, they carried lanterns.

It was winter now and the white population, Cody knew, stood around two hundred—residents and visitors. In the summer, he had discovered, the number of white residents shrank to a dozen, and of visitors there were none. Those who could afford it summered in the mountains or as close to the ocean as they could. As for the Indians, who numbered around three hundred depending on their festival cycle, they went up into the canyons to escape the oppressive summer heat. He had seen their abandoned camps up there, and Indian relics.

As he neared the La Alma property, he saw Elizabeth Barnstable walking on a stretch of land that reached from the rear of the corral to the mouth of the canyon. She was looking down, as if searching for something. Button was following her, running off every now and then to chase a rabbit.

Cody reined in and watched her. Reaching into his shirt pocket, he pulled out a scrap of paper and a pencil. "An elegant creature stepping delicately over the rough ground, as if plucked from a painting and dropped into a savage environment. She does not belong here . . ."

He liked to watch Elizabeth Barnstable when she didn't know anyone was looking. She had said she was trying to find a spot for a vegetable garden. But that was not how it appeared to Cody. There was a kind of . . . loneliness in the way she walked, stopping occasionally to look up at the snow-capped peak of San Jacinto. What was she looking for up there? What did she hope to find?

La Alma del Desierto was the first property one encountered traveling westward from the eastern end of the valley, as Cody was. After one passed the Indian reservation on the left, with the stony foothills rising up to lofty mountain peaks, one rode across the fan-like alluvial plain—home to a variety of trees and shrubs and wildlife—and on the other side, at the base of a rocky plateau, the beautiful Spanish California home called La Alma, surrounded by corrals and outbuildings.

There, on a patch of ground covered in wild grass and weeds, Elizabeth was searching for something.

He remembered seeing her, after the first day of searching for Johnny Pinto and the posse members had returned to La Alma, standing at the side of her house, staring across the valley at the distant mountains. The sun had just set. The mountains had blazed every shade of red—blindingly, against a darkening sky, in such sharp relief that even at a distance of fifteen miles he could see the boulders on the barren slopes, the deep ravines, every jagged peak. Elizabeth had looked like a woman witnessing her first sunset. She had stood positively transfigured. Cody had seen many a blazing sunset, on prairies, deserts, the Great Plains where buffalo and Indian had once dominated but were now scarce. Beautiful, dazzling sunsets. But somehow, in his years of roaming the West, his eyes had become inured to beauty and dazzle. To him, a sunset marked the end of the day, telling him to start his campfire, catch small prey, spread his bedroll.

Elizabeth Barnstable and her mesmerized state had reminded him of a time when he, too, had stood mesmerized at a sunset.

Folding the paper and returning it along with the pencil to his pocket, Cody spurred his horse forward.

*   *   *

The bird of paradise was in bloom, pushing its orange and blue "plumage" up through dagger-shaped leaves. The flower was not native to the desert. Someone had imported them from a tropical clime, but they thrived in this valley and entertained the eye with their resemblance to an exotic bird in flight. They grew in profusion here at La Alma.

Elizabeth assumed the people who built this house had planted them.

There was snow on the mountains. Elizabeth shielded her eyes and peered up at the summit, rising two miles almost vertically from the desert floor. She didn't know why she kept looking up at the mountain, why its silent mystery seemed to beckon. She thought that, if she stood absolutely still and listened hard enough, she would hear what it was trying to tell her.

"Hello there!" a familiar voice called.

"Good day, Mr. McNeal." She shielded her eyes from the sun as she looked up at him high atop his black mare. As always at their chance encounters, he politely touched the brim of his hat.

"You seem to be looking for something,"

She laughed. "I was thinking of planting a vegetable garden. But how does one go about doing it? I've never planted anything in my life."

Cody might have offered to give gardening advice, from his years of growing up on a Montana farm, but he was leaving Palm Springs and didn't want to get involved in other people's lives. Nonetheless, he found himself suddenly curious about her. "How do you like life in the desert, Mrs. Barnstable?"

"It is an adjustment, Mr. McNeal. The desert is filled with miracles and one must adjust to coming upon miracles on a daily basis. I saw a hummingbird yesterday. Up close. It was buzzing among my bougain-villea. I have never seen such a perfect work of nature. They come through New York State in the summer, when they migrate from the Caribbean to Canada, but I have never seen one. I am told they live here year-round. The babies hatch in May."

She fell silent, suddenly self-conscious about speaking of things this man was no doubt an expert on. But she couldn't resist the compulsion to share her discovery of so extraordinary a world. "I'm glad you happened by, Mr. McNeal," she said. "We are having a party on Christmas Day. We would be honored if you joined us."

Cody saw how sunlight and wind contrived to create a halo of her hair, how the white muslin of her long skirt was blown against her legs to define their shape, how she seemed to look at him with the expectation of a "yes." He decided he would delay his departure until after Christmas.

*   *   *

As Fiona was getting ready to pay an urgent visit to Doc Perry, Mrs. Norrington was saying, "I'm telling you, we'll have to watch Ethel. She tends to be frivolous, and I've noticed that the Mexican and Indian ranch hands have been eyeing her in curiosity. It's hard enough, let me tell you, to keep maids in line when tradesmen and the like come to the back door. But this is a dangerous situation. Those boys will have farmyard morals."

"I'm sure the girl will be careful," Fiona said as she slipped her gloves onto her hands. She had been on her way out when the house-keeper had intercepted her with a complaint. The kitchen was filled with noise and industry as the cook, with Ethel's help, was preparing breads and cakes for Her Ladyship's Christmas party. Fiona noticed an Indian basket in the middle of the huge table cluttered with bowls, pans, and rolling pins. It was cream colored with a curious red diamond pattern. Fiona wondered who had bought it.

"It's not just that," Mrs. Norrington said, the key chain at her belt rattling with agitation. "It's a matter of her free time. The girl has every Sunday evening off, and one whole day a month. But what is there for her to do here? It is a risky situation, I tell you."

"I'm sure it will be all right, Mrs. Norrington. And now I really must go."

The housekeeper frowned. "You never said why you're going to visit the doctor." But Fiona was through the back door and gone.

* * *

Doc Perry's place was down the main road and set back among cottonwood trees, a modest one-story house, white stucco with a red tiled roof. There was a parlor and a kitchen, two bedrooms, a consulting office, and a treatment room.

Doc Perry was in his stockroom, chewing his lip in worry.

As he scanned the shelves, he wondered how he was going to restock his supply of medicines. He made them himself—nostrums, elixirs, tonics, potions, tinctures—using water and a variety of vegetable colorings and flavorings, but the main ingredient was alcohol. His patients never knew they weren't getting real medicines, all they knew was that after drinking his concoctions, they felt better. But what was he going to do when his supply of alcohol ran out? Only legitimate physicians had access these days, through pharmacies, to alcohol. With the new Prohibition law, there was no other source.

Born at the end of the Civil War on a hardscrabble farm in Texas, Perry never knew his father, who had run off one day and never came back. When he was five, his mother took up with a traveling salesman who showed up periodically with money and dresses and fine words. She married him when Perry was ten, and they moved to a great, noisy city called Chicago. Young Perry bided his time until he could run away, back to the wide spaces of the West, where a man could make something of himself.

He learned early on that there was salvation in books. The more knowledge a man possessed, the more advantage he had over the next fellow. So he went to the local school and read his books and did his sums and listened to the teacher.

But he got in trouble with the law in Chicago, when a gang of kids tried to rob a candy store, severely beating the owner in the process. Perry wasn't part of the gang, but the cops didn't believe he was an innocent bystander. The local coppers came by the apartment now and then, asking after him, but by then he had run away, promising his mother he would stay in touch. For a few years, as he roamed the West working at odd jobs (and always reading anything he could get his hands on), he regularly sent a letter to his mother that said, "Dear Madam, we trust that you are satisfied with the latest volume of our encyclopedia." Mrs. Perry never bought encyclopedias. It was their secret code to let her know he was all right, and the law would never catch on.

And then came the day when he was twenty that a letter came back, "Return to Sender, Addressee deceased." He wrote no letters after that.

He roamed Kansas for a while, settling a spell in a boomtown called Dodge City. Queen of the Cowtowns, Dodge was famous in its heyday for its saloons and brothels. Perry didn't want to soil his hands in the cattle business, so he drew on his first love: books. He traveled around to homesteads and farms, selling books to folks who couldn't afford them or even read. He called himself Professor Perry and offered his services to tutor boys who lived too far from a school. But after a while, he saw that there were worse afflictions than illiteracy. He sent away for mail-order medical books and taught himself the names and symptoms of every ailment known to man. He learned the Greek and Latin terms to make himself sound educated and therefore trust-worthy. He purchased scales and tubes and calipers and a new fangled instrument called a hypodermic syringe. He changed his title from Professor to Doctor and his new career was born.

He became a familiar figure in town and prospered. But as more agricultural settlers moved into western Kansas, and the cattle trail was shut down, and the cowboys, saloon keepers, gamblers, and brothel owners moved west to greener pastures, so did Doc Perry.

He acquired a colorful wagon, a bay mare named Maudie, a stethoscope, tongue depressors, a pill-making machine, empty bottles, labels, and glue and set himself up in the traveling medicine show business. For good measure, he hired an Indian (he was never sure of the tribe) to sit on the tailgate of his wagon, knees drawn up and wrapped in a Navajo blanket, silent and statue-like while Perry hawked his Indian cures.

He met a woman in Abilene and lived with her for a while. She gave him a son out of wedlock and ran off with a gambler at first chance, leaving Perry to raise the boy on his own.

Was a time, he thought now, when Doc Perry was known and loved all over the Southwest. When he rode into a town in his gypsy wagon filled with "magical cures" and "wondrous potions," people flocked around him, waving their dollar bills. He dispensed hope to the hopeless, beauty to the homely, strength to the weak, virility to the impotent. All in bottles and tins and packets.

But changing times and new laws and regulations had forced him to retire his wagon and take up in an office here in a desert valley, where he was well known and still loved. But the valley itself was now changing, and new doctors (real doctors) were bound to come. And people were always attracted to the new and novel. It was human nature. A younger man in a shinier suit was bound to offer better medicine, wasn't he? Well, Perry might not have sat in a formal classroom, but life had given him a schooling that none of those youngsters could possibly have. However, with the establishment of the new Food and Drug Administration, tighter control of medicines and stricter oversight of physicians and medical licenses, Doc Perry knew that the likes of his kind were soon to die out and never to be seen again.

And now the new Prohibition threatened to cut his livelihood in half, because Doc Perry didn't make money from patient visits but rather the cures he sold to them.

Hearing the front doorbell, he left the stockroom and went to answer it.

"Miss Wilson! Come in, come in. I trust you are not unwell?" Leland Perry's one weakness was the ladies. He had been with more women than he could count—virgins and farm wives, saloon girls and school marms. He didn't remember their names. Didn't remember which pretty face went with which town. They were a blurry parade of perfume, breasts, and thighs. But at the time, he had loved each and every one of them.

Just as he was going to "love" Miss Wilson when the time came.

Fiona looked around. There were shelves of medical books, anatomy charts on the walls, a skeleton hanging from a hook. Doc Perry always assured his patients that, although he was in his fifties, he was still learning and always kept up with the latest medical advances. His newest device stood in the corner, with a brass plate affixed to it that said, Electrical Detector Machine For the Locating and Extracting of Bullets and Other Metal Objects.

The office of a modern doctor.

What she didn't know was that Doc Perry was not a real doctor. If anyone looked closely at the diploma on his wall, handsomely framed behind glass, they would see that the word "College" was misspelled. But he hadn't had enough money at the time to pay the calligrapher to re-do it, so Perry stood a tall plant in front of it and no one was the wiser.

"I was told you're the best doctor in town," she said.

"I also happen to be the only one."

"Still," she said as she looked around. "You seem to be doing well."

He winked. "It keeps me in bacon and eggs. Now then, what can I do for you, Miss Wilson?"

"I'm afraid I've come about a rather embarrassing situation," she said.

"Then come have a seat in my treatment room."

He thought she was very pretty. He guessed she was around forty, but with her dewy complexion, unlined and blemish-free, she looked younger. "You know," he said, clearing his voice and straightening his waistcoat, "there is something I've been wanting to tell you."

"And what might that be, Dr. Perry?"

He tried not to wince. It sounded so formal and important when she said his name like that. "Doc" Perry sounded more like a nickname and therefore not as fraudulent.

"I like your accent," he said.

She looked at him. Their eyes locked for a long moment, then she said, "I like yours."

"Mine?" He placed his hand on his chest. "But I don't have an accent. I'm American!"

They laughed together, and then she grew serious. "I was out in the garden yesterday and I wasn't watching where I was going, and I seem to have bumped my leg against something rather nasty."

She reached down and lifted her skirt, revealing red bumps and inflamed skin. Doc Perry delicately lifted her leg and propped it on a stool and bent to examine it with a magnifying glass. "I see you have some swelling. Is there pain or itching?"

"Both."

"Can you describe the plant you bumped into? It will help to determine if there are spines or thorns that need to be removed."

"It's green and flat and grows in clusters. I believe it's called a prickly pear?"

"Ah, yes. Nasty things if you touch them. Some types of cactus, like the prickly pear, are covered with very fine, hair-like, barbed thorns called glochids. And glochids can become embedded at the slightest touch and are hard to see to remove."

He brought in a basin and washed the area with mild soap and water. And then he used tweezers to remove visible thorns and barbs. He was remarkably gentle. She was braced for pain when none came. For the invisible glochids, he pulled strips of cellophane tape from a roller, pressed them onto her calf and pulled them off. Fiona found the experience to be mildly erotic. Although he was a medical man and she was in a doctor's office, there was something intimate about the way he handled her leg, touched her bare skin.

As he worked, he talked to put her at ease. "So what exactly does a lady's maid do?"

"I help my mistress with her makeup, hairdressing, clothing, jewelry, and shoes. It's also my job to keep her things in good condition, removing stains, mending, and altering garments as needed. I bring Her Ladyship's breakfast to her in her room and draw her bath."

He lifted his head. "All that for just one woman?"

She saw that he wasn't criticizing or making fun. He was genuinely baffled. And for the first time, now that she was seeing it through his eyes, she could understand why those who hadn't been brought up in that world would find it excessive.

"I grew up in an industrial city in northern England," she said, wondering why she was telling this man her story, wondering if it was to justify to herself the decisions she had made in life. "We were very poor. Many nights we went to bed hungry, or supper was bread and margarine. There was a Sunday dish we always had. Broth simmering in a skillet with what few veggies mother could scrape together. And when it was really hot, she would add a thick rasher of bacon that made a loud, sizzling sound, and it got our months watering, anticipating a bite of that bacon."

She paused. Doc Perry looked up. "Please go on."

"I don't wish to bore you."

"Believe me, I am far from bored."

"When Mother couldn't afford the bacon, she simmered the broth in the skillet as usual and when it was ready, she'd take a hot poker from the stove and stick it in and it would make the same sizzling sound as the bacon. Our mouths would water and we'd rub our hands together in anticipation of a bite of that bacon. We knew there was no meat in it, just a hot poker, but the sound of it made us think we were getting bacon, and we gobbled that broth down as if we were."

"From industrial England to a lady's maid in the California desert," he said in a tone of wonder. "How did you manage that strange transition?"

"I was the eldest of eight, and when I turned fourteen my mother told me I had to leave school and go to work because she and my father couldn't afford to feed me. I hadn't any skills so I had to settle for domestic service. I started as a kitchen maid, the lowest servant in the house, little more than a slave. I worked long hours at hard labor for very little money. But I was determined to rise in the ranks," she said, adding with pride, "and I did."

When he saw how she blushed, he said with a smile, "Would I make a good butler?"

When she hesitated, he said, "I wouldn't?"

"While you are attractive, Dr. Perry, you see . . . butlers are tall."

"Tall? Why?"

"They represent the household. When visitors come calling, it wouldn't do to have a short man answer the door and escort them inside. Not that you are short," she hastened to assure. "But butlers must be imposing. And being tall is practically a requirement. In Britain, the stately houses make something of a competition of it. Norrington is over six feet tall."

Another examination with the magnifying glass told him he had gotten all the cactus fibers. Finally, he applied ointment and then wrapped the leg with gauze. "If the itching gets too bad, use a cool water compress fifteen minutes at a time. After you bathe, dry the area and apply a little petroleum jelly. Keep the bandage on for protection during the day, then you can remove it to let the rash air out at night. We will monitor the area for signs of infection. There you go, all done."

He delicately drew the hem of her dress down and lifted her leg from the stool. Then he sat back and looked at her.

A fly buzzed into the room, flew noisily about for a moment, then left. In that brief moment, Doc Perry, the huckster and flim-flam artist, suddenly wished he were the most important and educated physician in the world.

"By the way, Miss Wilson," he said, trying to sound casual, as though what he was about to say had just occurred to him, as if he hadn't been practicing it with the intention of putting the question to her the next time they met.

"Yes, Dr. Perry?" she said, wondering if she were imagining his sudden self-consciousness, wondering if she were the cause, hoping she was the cause. Although Doc Perry wasn't what one would call handsome, he had distinctive features, lovely brown eyes full of kindness and understanding. And he still cut a fine figure for a man she guessed was in his mid-fifties.

"I had occasion to visit the drugstore in Banning and found that they have installed a new soda fountain. They offer ten flavors of ice cream. I was wondering if you would care to join me some afternoon when you are free?"

"Oh," she said. And suddenly Lawrence came into her mind and their afternoons in New York when she had thought that perhaps he might ask her to marry him. Although he had seen her off at the train station and said he would miss her terribly, he had still not written back.

"Why, Dr. Perry," she said, and it was her turn to feel self-conscious. "I would be delighted to."

*   *   *

Progress was coming along on the new bunkhouse for his farm workers. Nigel was pleased with what he saw as he inspected the long structure, currently a skeleton of wooden framework. A shipment was due from a lumberyard in Riverside. By next week the exterior should be done and not long after that, his workers could move in.

Nigel wasn't planning to add much in the way of amenities. The Mexicans—up at dawn and working like drones until after dark—had few needs. Their only interest, it seemed, was earning American money and taking it back to their families in Mexico. He would have a wood-burning stove installed at one end, and a latrine at the other, with the upkeep of the whole thing left in the hands of the workers themselves.

It was his new grove that consumed all of his time and attention, as he made inspections three times a day. The trees had been removed from the ground after their dates had been harvested in Indio and therefore little care was required at the crowns, not until the first berries began to show in January. What Nigel's crew was most concerned with at this phase was trimming the fronds of their sharp thorns, which would be a danger to the workers during the pollination and harvesting phases.

As Nigel inspected the base of each tree, reaching down to feel the damp soil, he came upon a few that appeared to have some blackening at the base. In alarm—was it a tree fungus?—he bent down, ran his hand along the trunk then brought it to his nose and sniffed. It smelled like charcoal. These trees had recently been burned.

How had that happened?

Then he noticed footprints in the soil at the base of the trees, and more charred bark and grass. He looked across the flat alluvial plain at the reservation on the other side. So, the old chief thought he could burn the grove down? What had stopped him?

Nigel turned to look up Mesquite Canyon, a narrow ravine cleaving the granite mountain like a V, lush and verdant and filled with native palms and other dense growth. The property line ran down the middle of the canyon so that one side of the ravine belonged to Nigel, the other to the Indians. The stream was the demarcation line, giving both parties water rights. But Nigel wanted both sides of the canyon.

He smiled grimly. Maybe this attempted arson was a blessing in disguise. From now on, armed guards were going to patrol the perimeter of the orchard, with orders to shoot trespassers on sight. As an incentive, he was going to promise a reward for each trespasser caught.

With the Indians out of the way, Nigel could claim water rights on both sides of the canyon.

*   *   *

The whole town turned out to watch the movie being filmed, even Mrs. Flannigan and Ethel, who were up to their elbows in sugar and flour, busily making cakes and pastries for Her Ladyship's upcoming Christmas party.

In the early days of filmmaking, movies were shot in several US cities, most dominantly in and around New York on the East Coast. But weather was often inclement and indoor lighting was insufficient. When filmmakers visited Southern California, they were taken with the warm climate, almost year-round sunlight, and the varied scenery, allowing movies to be shot at an ocean, a desert, alpine forests, and even in the snow, all within a few hundred square miles. Southern California, it was soon discovered, was the ideal place for making movies, and so the filmmakers arrived in droves and could be seen all over with their troupes of actors, their trucks and wagons loaded with equipment. The desert was a particularly popular filming spot because the sunlight was unsurpassed, and also because areas such as Palm Springs, with just a few props, could pass for North Africa, Arabia, or the Middle East. And so the citizens of the Coachella Valley were used to seeing movie people coming in from nearby Hollywood to erect their facades, ranging from Moroccan Palaces to foreign legion outposts, and set up their cameras, supplemental lighting, and tents for the actors and actresses.

Every time a production company came into town, the locals came out in droves, from as far away as Indio and Hot Springs, hoping to be used in crowd scenes. Cody stood with Luisa and her granddaughters in front of Allenby's Grocery. Down the street, a fake facade had been affixed to the front of Lardner's General Store, turning it into the City Jail, where the "Sheriff" was arguing with an angry "rancher." The film's leading lady appeared, taking her place next to the angry rancher. Like all movie actresses who played romantic parts, she was young and virginal.

"Señor Cody," Luisa said as the crowd watched the movie scene being set up, "why is that man's hat so big?"

"It's his trademark. That's Tom Mix. He's very famous."

"His hat is too big."

"It's called a ten-gallon hat."

"Those men over there on horses, why do they wear so many feathers?"

"Because they're Indians."

Her eyebrows rose. "But they are white men."

"They're portraying Indians, and war bonnets tell the audience that they are Indians."

She gave Cody a dubious look. "We don't wear feathers."

"Those are supposed to be Plains Indians. They wear feathers. Although," Cody added wryly, "I doubt the Plains tribes wore socks with their moccasins."

"That man in black, he is the bad man?"

"Yes. He's the villain, and the villain always wears black."

She looked at Cody again. "You always wear black. You are not a bad man."

He laughed. "It's just the movies, Mother."

But he understood her confusion. The Old West as depicted in Hollywood movies, Cody had discovered, was a far cry from the real West, the one that had been his home for twenty-eight years. It saddened him to see this, knowing that American movies were watched all over the world, imprinting on people's minds an erroneous depiction of a way of life he so loved and cherished. And now the Old West was vanishing and in its place was a sham history. Soon, no one was going to know the true stories of the West, just these vacuous dramas that had nothing to do with the real thing.

Filming was suddenly called to a halt as a wagon was taken down the street with a large barrel pierced with holes so that water sprinkled the dirt.

"Why are they doing that?" Cody asked one of the cowboy actors standing idly by.

"The director don't like the clouds of dust that fly up when the horses gallop. Says it blurs the picture."

"But clouds of dust are a feature of frontier life. That's hardly going to be realistic."

The actor shrugged. "Who says movies are realistic?"

Cody smiled. He looked the man over. By his weathered skin, squinty eyes, and bowed legs he guessed he might be a real cowboy. "By the way, that was a neat trick you pulled back there with the horse."

"It's called the Running W. A pair of wires is attached to hobbles on the horse's front fetlocks and connected to a ring the rider holds in one hand. Those of us who are supposed to bite the dust while galloping at a fast clip simply kick our feet free of the stirrups, aim a shoulder at the ground, yank the wires to trip the horse, and hope we don't break any important bones when the animals goes down."

"Have you done a lot of this work?"

"Hell, mister, the ten years I've been busting my ass in this business, I've acted in three hundred and eighty Westerns. And I'll tell you something, every one of them is the same—the gunfight in the street, the circled wagons, the stagecoach holdup, the fight in a saloon, riding to a woman's rescue, clashing with cattle rustlers, and chasing after Indians. The story never varies. Tells you something about movie audiences, don't it?"

The water wagon having done its job, the director called everyone to their places and the actor strolled away. The director lifted the megaphone and shouted, "Awright, places everyone! One, two, three—action!"

The cameramen began hand-cranking the 35mm cameras at sixteen frames per second as the door to the City Jail suddenly flew open and the villain, recognizable by his trademark handlebar moustache, came running out. As "deputies" chased after him, he flew onto the back of his horse in an acrobatic move that made the onlookers cheer and clap.

Besides the film crew, there were photographers with tripods. Some were shooting publicity stills, others were from newspapers and magazines. A reporter from *Photoplay* magazine was there to interview the actors. Luisa's fifteen-year-old granddaughters, Isabella and Gabriela, watched in fascination. She didn't like the looks on their faces, as if they had spells cast over them. She had reminded them twice to return to their chores in the village and twice they had come back to watch the filming. It worried Luisa. She had never known them to be disobedient, but the allure of a movie production was strong. She wished these people from Hollywood would not come to her valley. Weren't there other cowboy places?

Gabriela was particularly fascinated, more so than her cousin Isabella. Every time Gabriela opened a movie magazine or saw the camera men come to town, she felt a strange yearning in her breast. She and Isabella had seen a movie in nearby Hot Springs and it had been a transformative experience for her. She couldn't stop thinking about the magic of seeing gigantic people on a screen, experiencing adventure and romance. Their mouths would move and then words would appear on the screen, saying things like, "I will love you until the day I die and beyond!" Gabriela was praying the white man with the megaphone would notice her and put her in his picture.

As it turned out, the man with the megaphone had his eye on another girl in the crowd. Not particularly pretty but with a curvaceous figure that could take him to the moon. As production halted for a break and actors dispersed to the lunch tables, the director laid aside his megaphone, hiked up his belt, and strode over to the girl who was wearing a maid or waitress outfit. "Hi. I'm Mike. I'm directing this movie."

"I know," Ethel said, giggling and turning red.

Reaching into his pocket, he brought out a business card. He leaned close as he handed it to her and said, "I think you could make it big in pictures." He glanced down at luscious breasts straining against the bib of her apron. "I can see to it that you get a screen audition."

"Really? Oh, gosh!"

"Take my card. My private number is on it. Next time you're in Hollywood, give me a call."

*   *   *

On his way to La Alma for the Christmas party, Cody stopped at Lardner's, where he purchased a single sheet of stationery and an envelope. Using the pen and ink bottle provided by Lardner for folks writing telegrams, he scratched a few lines. After the ink had dried, he folded the sheet, slipped it into the envelope, sealed it, and on the front wrote, "For Lady Elizabeth. Merry Christmas."

*   *   *

Chino Canyon, west of Palm Springs, was the widest of the San Jacinto canyons and boasted a reliable wagon road that reached the timberline. The men of Palm Springs and outlying farms and ranches got together every year to go up the slopes and cut down pine trees, to bring them back to stand in their living rooms, sparkling with decorations. At La Alma, the tall pine was strung with colorful electric lights, and decorated with sparkling globes and streaks of tinsel.

For the occasion, Nigel saw to it that the generator was monitored and kept fueled so that the whole house glowed with electric lights.

Besides the breathtaking tree, there was a buffet offering a dazzling and delicious array of food, while Ethel circulated with drinks trays, and Norrington passed hors d'oeuvres around. Few locals had made the acquaintance of the former owners and so they were thrilled to get a look inside the spacious house. They had also come for the booze, as many people's personal supplies of wine and spirits, carried over from before the signing of the new Prohibition law, had run out.

But mostly the locals, who were farmers or shopkeepers, enjoyed being the invited guests of a genuine Lord and Lady. Elizabeth watched as they clustered around Nigel in the large, sunken living room as he entertained them with his wit. Nigel was making friends easily in this desert town, whereas she was having a little harder time of it.

She had voiced this to Nigel and his common sense reply had been, "That is because they are seamstresses, shopkeepers, schoolteachers, and farm wives, whereas you, my dear, are a Baroness."

"I hope you don't mind, Mr. Barnstable," Mrs. Allenby, the grocer's wife, was saying now to Nigel, dressed in a formal dinner jacket and standing out among his more plainly dressed guests. "But we've all been talking about you."

"My dear lady," he said with a smile. "There is only one thing in the world worse than being talked about and that is *not* being talked about."

They laughed and sipped their drinks and lifted pâté crackers from Norrington's tray.

Nigel said graciously, "It's nice to be among people who have a sense of humor. I find that humanity takes itself too seriously. It is the world's original sin. If the caveman had known how to laugh, the history of the world would have gone differently."

"I couldn't agree with you more!" boomed Augie Lardner, who himself had the stature a caveman.

Elizabeth smiled. The party was a success. The wine flowed, food was enjoyed with gusto, and the Victrola played, "Look For the Silver Lining," "Prohibition Blues," and Al Jolson singing, "Swanee." She saw Cody McNeal by himself, a drink untouched in his hand. "You look melancholy," she said, joining him. "It's the time of year, isn't it? I miss my parents terribly. I was hoping they would come out, but Mother isn't up to the long train ride. Do you have family, Mr. McNeal?"

"Not anymore," he said cryptically. Elizabeth noticed that even he, like the others, wore his cowboy hat indoors. One more peculiar custom of the West.

"Are you from California?" She hoped she wasn't being too nosy. He seemed disinclined to talk about himself.

"I'm from all over, really. But I was born in Montana." He gave Elizabeth a self-conscious smile. "I might have been born in Tombstone, Arizona. But my parents left and went north." He was quiet for a moment, a dark look in his eyes. Then he looked at Elizabeth, saw the interest in her eyes, the smile that was one of anticipation. She was one of those women who were natural born listeners, and for some reason he felt like telling her the story.

"Almost forty years ago, a shoot-out took place in Tombstone between violent outlaws and lawmen. The frontier was an open range for outlaws in those days, as they were largely unopposed by law enforcement who were spread thin over vast territories. So certain lawmen decided to put an end to the reign of terror generated by those outlaws. Most of them were killed in the gunfight, and a few of the lawmen were wounded. My father was one of the witnesses to that gunfight, and he didn't want to get caught in the middle when it came to a court trial. So he packed up and left for Montana."

"Just over a gunfight?"

He thought for a long moment. He seemed to think a lot of things over, Elizabeth thought, weighing and discarding. Mr. McNeal was a careful man when it came to words. "It's what happened afterward that sent my father packing. The outlaws who survived went after two of the lawmen and killed them. Their brother, Marshal Wyatt Earp, formed a posse and went on a bloody vendetta ride. That was what my father didn't want to get caught in—Wyatt Earp's thirst for revenge. It was a bloody chapter in the history of the West, and I don't blame him for leaving."

Cody blinked, looked at the untouched drink in his hand and then, as if remembering himself, remembering that this was a Christmas party and that his hostess, dressed in a shimmering white gown, shouldn't be regaled with blood and gloom, shrugged. "It happened forty years ago at a place you haven't heard of, and I'm sure no one even remembers the O.K. Corral anymore. But one thing I do remember, the name of the man who struck terror in my father's heart. Wyatt Earp. He was the reason my parents left the good life in Arizona for a life of hardship in the north. It happened eleven years before I was born, but I grew up hearing the story many times. Funny how a name sticks with you."

Cody paused to look around the party from beneath the wide brim of his Stetson. He looked at his hostess in the white gown, and he realized she hadn't seemed to mind the story about what drove his father from Arizona, and he suddenly felt he could say a little more, that he *wanted* to say more. "I don't know if many people can look back and pinpoint the day, the hour, the very moment their lives took a turn and radically altered the course of their life forever. My father could, right back to that shoot-out. And, in fact, so can I, although I'd never realized it until now. The moment that set my father on a different course, by extension set me on my course. Isn't the son's life an extension of the father's?"

Elizabeth found herself traveling back in her mind to find a pinpoint moment in her own life and arrived directly at the day on the *Mauretania* when she and her parents had been seated at a table outside the Verandah Café, on the ship's boat deck, protected by screens from the inclement Atlantic weather. A handsome and charming stranger had approached and remarked on her mother's resemblance to Princess Helena. Elizabeth wondered if, many years from now, she would look back and still claim that one moment as the single most pivotal moment in her life. She hoped so.

Their eyes met for a moment while the Victrola played "I'll Be With You In Apple Blossom Time," and then Cody said, "I'm forgetting my manners." He reached into his shirt pocket and pulled out the envelope. "I'm afraid I don't have much money. But I wanted to give you a Christmas present for inviting me here tonight."

Elizabeth stared at the envelope as he slipped it into her hand.

"It's just a little something I wrote. You can read it later."

A sudden shout snapped their attention to the other side of the room, where Nigel had taken a seat on the sofa. They saw him shoot to his feet and wave his arms as if he were on fire. But those around him were laughing. "Oh dear," Elizabeth said, "pardon me."

Cody watched her go to her husband, and when the guests made way for her, he saw a large red wine stain covering the front of Barnstable's immaculate pleated trousers. "What happened?" Elizabeth said, retrieving a napkin and dipping it into a glass of water.

"It was that dog," Nigel sputtered. "Jumped onto my lap."

"And what a sight it was!" Augie Lardner said.

Nigel looked at the man, and when he saw the others laughing, turned red and, laughing self-deprecatingly, said, "Yes, you're right. What a sight I must have been. Pardon me while I change."

*　　*　　*

Yearning for a smoke, Cody slipped out into the rear garden where he leisurely filled a paper, sealed it, struck a match, and filled his lungs. The stars were icy-bright, the moon cold and distant. When he exhaled, he couldn't tell if it was smoke or breath coming out of his lungs. Cody always loved winter in the desert. There was something pure about it.

He wished he hadn't told Elizabeth about Tombstone and Wyatt Earp. You vocalize one painful memory and the rest come rushing out.

Horsethief Creek, Colorado. A woman named Belle. A gold miner named Peachy. The dark devils that drove Cody McNeal to travel from town to town, a man searching his past.

He eyed the new date palms, tall and imposing against the stars. That was some feat Barnstable had pulled off. And now it was rumored he had ordered a hundred more and was having them shipped from Phoenix. The Mexicans were still camped out under the stars, about a hundred yards from the property, having a party of their own, Cody guessed, according to the guitars and singing.

He heard the kitchen door open and slam shut and saw someone stealing away from the house. He recognized Nigel Barnstable, and he carried something in his arms.

Button the dog.

Lowering his cigarette, Cody watched as Nigel went into the gardener's tool shed. He listened. He heard a muffled thump and a sharp yelp. A moment later, Nigel emerged, still holding the dog. He strode to the edge of the corral, stopped and lowered the animal, holding it by a hind leg.

Button didn't make a sound and hung like a flour sack.

Drawing his arm back, Nigel swung the little dog up and behind his head, and then flung it as hard as he could. Button sailed through the air like a ghostly spirit, white and limp, to land yards away in a dense clump of creosote bushes. Brushing off his hands, Nigel turned and went back into the house.

Cody didn't move, the cigarette forgotten in his hand.

CHAPTER FOURTEEN

RIDING HIS BLACK MARE, Cody entered the hilly mining country around Tylerville. This was his first visit to the area. He was looking for one man in particular, and he had combed the rocks and hills to the west and south of the town, to find only abandoned mines. But this morning, as he had come through the narrow pass that led back to Twentynine Palms, he had seen, a few miles in the distance, a column of gray smoke rising to the sky. A small column, as if from a campfire.

Could it be the man he had been searching for at last?

He knew to approach with caution. The Tylerville area was honeycombed with abandoned mines that moonshiners had taken over to operate their illegal stills. And they guarded those stills, he had heard, with ferocity. But he had to make sure that the campfire didn't belong to the man he had been seeking for ten years. A man nicknamed Peachy, and all Cody had to go on was the fact that Peachy had gold fever and had said he wouldn't stop until he struck it rich.

Cody felt sorry for the poor devils who operated stills out here. The desert was the perfect place for making moonshine, lots of caves and canyons plus thousands of miles to police. Impossible for the authorities to find them. He wouldn't be surprised if there were a 'legger or two near Palm Springs as well. Hoping to get rich quick, they would more likely get blown up by their own equipment. The newspapers were always reporting on bootlegging operations that exploded out in the desert, killing or dismembering the moonshiners. And they had to be constantly on the lookout for federal agents or thieves who came to steal their hooch.

He neared a cluster of abandoned gold mines. Overhead, the sky was blue and deep and without a cloud, and stretched away over a desert so flat and dotted with scrub that it looked artificial. He reined his horse, sat, and listened. He heard no voices. Only the wind. The smoke from the campfire began to dissipate, but he could follow its course with his eye. He reckoned the source lay behind a pile of boulders as tall as a two-story house.

It could easily be a mine entrance on the other side, he thought. And there was definitely someone there.

Getting down from the saddle, he crept closer to the boulders. He paused, listened, then continued to follow the rocky wall, hugging it, stopping every now and then to listen. When he heard footsteps, the sound of someone whistling, pots and pans being rattled, he waited.

The sounds died down. He proceeded cautiously, but as he rounded the boulder, a shot suddenly rang out, ricocheting off rock, and a man's voice called out, "I know yer there! Get away from my property!"

"I'm looking for a man named Peachy. Would that be you?"

"You don't back off, I'll shoot ya dead!" Another shot and the bullet grazed the rock close to Cody's head. He jumped back.

"Have you maybe run into a man named Peachy?" Cody tried again.

"I'm comin' after ya, and I ain't gonna stop till yer dead. I don't care who you are! Man's got a right to defend himself!"

When the wind shifted and his nostrils were assailed by the stench of sour mash, Cody realized he wasn't dealing with a gold miner at all but a moonshiner. Jumping onto his horse, he goaded her into a trot and was galloping off as a final shot rang out in the desert air.

* * *

On the breeze through the open window, Elizabeth heard Nigel arguing with his ranch foreman. There was a lack of communication due to the language barrier. To make himself understood, Nigel shouted, as if the man were deaf.

Also drifting through the window were sounds of construction work—sawing and hammering and men calling out. She would be glad when the new bunkhouse was done and the Mexican workers had proper housing. She hoped it would be sufficient. Nigel was negotiating with Mr. Gonzalez to have a hundred more date palms shipped in, which would mean more workers.

While Wilson put the finishing touches to her hair, Elizabeth thought about home, Manhattan in the winter, ice skating in Central Park, making the rounds of friends' houses, drinking hot rum, singing carols, and exchanging gifts. It seemed a far cry from this desert oasis.

Ten minutes later, Elizabeth and Fiona were walking down the lane where a few winter flowers splashed color against the brown and gray-green of the desert. The December day was blue-skied and sunny but with a brisk breeze. Elizabeth thought of the people who lived here and what she had learned about them.

Mrs. Henry came for her husband's tuberculosis and when he died, she used their savings to build a small boardinghouse. The house had grown and now offered detached cabins. Augie Lardner had worked in a hardware store in Detroit and when it burned down, he was out of a job. Tired of the winters there and the lack of work, he and Lois came out West to start over. Starting in a tent that sold everything from tin pots to sewing needles, they now owned the main store in town and got the government contract for postal service. It was the same story for the Allenbys, the barber and his wife, the hairdresser, the local seamstress—they came from all corners of the United States, leaving disappointments behind, to start over here in this land of possibilities.

That's what this place is, Elizabeth thought with buoyant spirits, a place of fresh starts and new beginnings. No matter where you lived before, or what you did in your past, whatever mistakes or regrets you left behind, the Coachella Valley offered a clean slate. It applied to Elizabeth as well, who believed one didn't have to be penniless to want to start over. In New York, she would have followed in her mother's footsteps. She would have been initiated into the ladies' service club there and become part of her mother's circle. But out here, in this land of new beginnings, Elizabeth was going to find her own calling, perhaps even create it all by herself.

As they walked in the cool winter day beneath a deep blue sky, with a cold wind blowing down from the mountains' snow-covered peaks, Elizabeth kept her eye out for Button. After the little dog had gone missing, Nigel had had several of his workers scour the area around La Alma, but no trace of Button had been found. Elizabeth was beside herself. It worried her that he might be hurt somewhere, injured and in need of rescue. She herself had walked their acres, calling his name, frantic over the thought of a terrible fate. But Button liked to go after small animals, so she held out the hope that he had simply run off after a rabbit and gotten lost. She prayed he would find his way home, or a local farmer would find him and bring him back.

They reached the white schoolhouse, silent and empty now for the holiday week, and went around to the cottage at the back of the property, where the two teachers lived, Miss March and Miss Napier.

Miss Napier answered the door. "Oh! Mrs. Barnstable, what a surprise." Her eyes were wide.

"I hope I haven't come at an inconvenient time."

Miss Napier was a petite woman with fashionably short hair and hands that fluttered like sparrows. "Not at all. I was just . . . we were just . . ."

"Who is it, dear?" Miss March, taller, more thickly built and wearing, of all things, trousers, appeared next to her. "Oh, Mrs. Barnstable!" She looked from Elizabeth to Fiona, who held out her hand. "I'm Miss Wilson, Her Ladyship's maid. How do you do?"

An awkward moment on the threshold, and then the visitors were invited inside. "We were just about to have tea," Miss Napier said. "Would you like to join us?"

It was a very small and cramped little house. Besides the nook of a kitchen and the tidy parlor, there seemed to be only one other room, and Miss March went directly across to close the door to it, but not before Fiona Wilson glimpsed a double bed.

They took seats and Miss Napier brought out a tray with cups and a teapot. The two hostesses seemed flustered and embarrassed. "Please forgive the look of the place. The school district owns the cottage, and we can't afford to fix it up much."

"I have some concern about the Indians," Elizabeth said, getting to the point of her visit, unaware that she and Wilson were overdressed for the occasion, or that the teachers' tea set was mismatched, or that they cleared their throats as if nervous or self-conscious. "Mrs. Lardner told me that the Indians have a high rate of illiteracy," Elizabeth said. "Especially among the children."

"Unfortunately that's true. Please have a biscuit. I'm afraid they're packaged, not home baked."

"Thank you," Elizabeth said, politely selecting one and placing it on her saucer. "But surely the federal government provides for their education."

"It does indeed. We are paid for every Indian child we take in. But Chief Diego won't allow the children of his village to attend our school."

"Why ever not?"

"The government has strict guidelines when Indians attend a public school," Miss March said, adding three teaspoons of sugar to her tea. "The children are not to speak their native tongue, and they are not to be taught their people's culture or history. The purpose of attending school here is to acclimate them to the white culture. To make them less Indian, as it were. Chief Diego wants the children of his tribe to be taught native ways."

"But the cost is illiteracy."

"Sadly, yes."

Fiona tasted her tea. She suspected that tea leaves were used more than once in this modest cottage, as teachers were notoriously underpaid. "What makes Chief Diego so powerful?" she asked.

"His age," Miss March said. She seemed to do most of the talking for the two. "He is estimated to be around eighty years old and his memories are said to go back further than any other member of the clan. He has more knowledge than anyone, and the Indians know that knowledge is power. He has seen things the younger ones haven't. When the Spanish priests came here a hundred years ago, to convert the Indians to Christianity, they sometimes used ruthless methods. Their intentions were good, but . . ."

"What sort of methods?" Elizabeth said, politely sipping the tepid tea.

"Indians who had become Christianized at the missions were sent out to the villages to kidnap children and bring them back to the missions, where they were forced to learn Spanish and European culture. Chief Diego remembers when he was a child and his clan was forced to live in caves far up Mesquite Canyon, watching for the kidnappers in the valley below. They were like hunted animals finding safe places to hide their young. It is a bitter memory that he holds against the white man to this day."

"I don't blame him. But the children must be taught to read and write. What can we do?"

Two blank faces looked at her. "What do you mean?"

"Surely there is a way we can reach the children," Elizabeth said. "I had in mind a literacy program of some sort, apart from your school and government guidelines. A ladies' volunteer group, perhaps. I was also thinking that a library would benefit the settlements in the valley. I have quite a few books I can donate, and perhaps others will, too."

As the teachers had nothing to offer at the moment and needed to do some thinking, the conversation quickly ran to the weather, the hope that 1921 would bring prosperity to everyone, and then the visitors said good-bye and left.

As they walked back down the shaded road, Elizabeth said, "What do you think, Wilson? Was it a successful visit?"

Fiona replied yes, but secretly thought that the teachers did not know what to make of ladies and their maids.

*   *   *

Dressed in a long, colorful skirt and a white, long-sleeved blouse tucked into a beaded belt, Luisa Padilla thought: It is a sacred day. The spirits are out, and they are happy.

Just before dawn, three days prior, Chief Diego had gone down among the Señor's trees and, through the crowns, had seen the stars on the horizon that heralded the annual sacred winter ritual. A day of rejoicing and remembering. It was a time of visiting and trading, when people from villages all over the valley paid visits to other villages. The tribes were all connected. That was how every Cahuilla could say, "I am related everywhere."

It was also a very special day for Luisa Padilla.

Today she would be given a young apprentice. They were always revealed at the annual Mukat fiesta. She had been expecting her new apprentice for a few years, and she knew that the presentation would be today.

The members of Luisa's clan did not follow in a parent's footsteps or choose their own path in life. A person's occupation was determined by how he or she was called to it. A dream or a sign from the spirits. When Luisa was a girl, she had been gathering acorns up the slopes with her mother. She had strayed and gotten lost. A puma found her—a beautiful, sleek brown and tan mountain lion that spoke inside the child's head, telling her that she was to be the clan's next spirit-reader, after a man named Juan Rivera died. When her mother found her in the forest, Luisa told her what the puma had said. Her mother took her to Juan, and Luisa lived with him until he died, and in that time he had taught her how to listen to the spirits.

Last year, at the Mukat fiesta, a Morongo father had stepped forward to present his son to Chief Diego saying, "My boy told me he dreams about the stars every night. He is to be a star-watcher." And so now that boy sat with Chief Diego in the ceremonial house, where he received instruction in how to be the clan's next star-watcher. Other shamans, too, had apprentices that had been chosen through dreams and signs.

Today, Luisa would receive her successor.

Was it to be a Morongo girl? A Soboba boy? She must make arrangements in her house for the child to live. Unlike Chief Diego's position that must always be passed on to a male, the spirit-reader pul could be either a man or woman.

That morning, Luisa and her family had knelt before Father Vega as he placed wafers on their tongues, saying "Corpus Christi." The Indians crossed themselves and returned to their places on the ground, where they sat cross-legged for the remainder of the Mass. When it was over, Luisa had hurried home to prepare for the fiesta honoring Mukat, creator of the Cahuilla and Lord of the universe. After the sacred rite, there would be a feast of roasted quail and rabbit, a stew of mesquite beans and mushrooms, and acorn cakes with sweet cactus and berries.

The Indian way was one of hospitality and generosity. One never entered into another home without bringing gifts. And one never entertained a guest without sending them away with gifts. A centuries-old tradition that ensured the equal distribution of food and goods so that no one in the tribe had more than another, no one went hungry while others ate.

After she cleared a space and laid blankets for a bed for her new apprentice, she stepped into the afternoon sunshine and joined others along the paths that connected all houses to the ceremonial house that stood in the center of the village.

The men, women, and children filed quietly into the big house and took places along the sides in an orderly fashion. There was no room to sit, as they had to leave space for dancers. Holes in the roof admitted daylight.

As she took a place next to her granddaughters, Gabriela and Isabella, Luisa looked around the ceremonial house that was illuminated by lanterns with candles. Where was her cousin Lucinda's family? Where was Uncle Joe and Cousins Maria and Juanita? There were fewer people at the Mukat fiesta this year. Where were they? Why had they not come?

At one end of the long house stood three men—white hair contrasting their bronze skin. They wore denim pants and white shirts. Their shaggy hair was cut to their shoulders, and all three wore a cloth tied as a bandana around their heads. They stood proud and solemn as they waited for everyone to take a place.

And then the one in the center of the trio raised his arms and began to chant. Soon, the gathered company joined him, all chanting together. The Cahuilla did not write; they had no alphabet, no books. Their history was oral, passed down from generation to generation in their songs. Their laws, too, were kept in their songs. When they needed to know something, if a thing was good or taboo, the Chief and the shamans would sing the songs of the people and they found the answer. If someone broke a tribal law, they said he was "going against the song."

The chant ended and a man came out carrying a wooden drum stretched with leather. Sitting on the floor, he began to tap out a rhythm with his hands. The Chief and shamans took up another chant, with different words, different inflections. It wasn't really a melody but a mesmerizing raising and lowering of the voice. Once again the gathered company joined in and the people sang the story of how Mukat created the universe.

The chant ended and dancers came out. They wore no costumes but were in their regular attire. However, the four men and four women carried eagle feathers as they performed a line dance, stamping their feet on the earthen floor. Again the gathering lifted their voices in song, telling the story of Menil the moon maiden, who long ago instructed the people to bathe every day. She said, "In the evening when you see me in the west, you must run to the water and bathe." To be clean of the body was to be clean of the spirit. Clothes, pots, cooking utensils, and houses must be cleaned every day and in this way the people honored Menil the moon maiden, who gave them health.

More songs followed, and more dances with the rhythmic beating of the drums. A fire was lit and soon gave off fragrant smoke. The air was filled with communal passion for their past and their culture. There were smiles on their faces as they lifted and lowered their voices and repeated words and phrases over and over.

When the singing stopped, five children were brought before the three elders. Luisa grew excited. Her new apprentice would be among them.

But then she saw one of the shamans lean down and whisper something to each child. Her disappointment was sharp. This was simply a naming ceremony in which the shaman was giving the children their secret names. Before the Spanish priests changed the individual names of Luisa's people, they had their own names. But the priests could not change their secret names because they did not know about them. It was the name that only that person knew; it was his or her real name. This way, enemies could not use their names against them in evil magic.

The ritual came to an end. The dancers and musicians left, the Chief bestowed Mukat's good magic upon the gathering, and everyone filed out.

Luisa followed Chief Diego. "Was there no child brought to you who will be the next spirit-reader?"

"No child has received a sign," he said sadly.

As she returned to her house, where she had prepared a bed that would now not be slept in, she felt her heart skip in alarm. I am getting old. Not many teaching years left to me. Why have the spirits not chosen my successor?

Then she thought about Chief Diego. He almost burned down the white man's new date grove. Diego should know that this white man will not go away. He will fight us. And he is stronger. He has money. But Diego has his pride, and he holds fast to the told ways. He does not want change to come to his people. Now he goes among the new trees to read the stars and that hurts his pride. What will the white man do next, and what will Diego do in retaliation?

If a battle was coming, Luisa knew that her role was vital. The role of spirit-reader was essential to the safety and survival of the clan. The day would come when Luisa would not be here to warn of disasters, to avert tragedies, and then what? If there was no new spirit-reader, it could mean calamity for her people. Diego will do something that will anger the Great Father in Washington, and he will withhold food and blankets and medicine.

There must be, among all the Indian bands in the valley, a child who knew he was the new spirit-reader. Perhaps he had received the vision and did not understand it. Luisa could wait no longer. She must go out into the valley and find her successor.

*   *   *

The film director's business card had burned in Ethel's pocket for all of eight days, during which she bought every movie magazine Lardner's carried, devoured every story, memorized every glamorous photo—compared herself to starlets, compared her story to theirs ("Hometown girl makes good in Hollywood"). until she decided that, no doubt about it, a movie career was the only way for her to go.

"I'm giving my notice, Mrs. Norrington," Ethel said proudly. "I'm going to be a film star. And might I have my New Year's bonus in advance?" she added with uncharacteristic boldness.

* * *

Doc Perry checked his pocket watch every few minutes, and then his hair, nervously smoothing it down. Miss Fiona Wilson was due any minute to have the dressing on her leg changed. He was screwing up his courage to ask her something.

They had had a pleasant time together, going for ice cream at the drug store in Banning, and now he wanted to step it up. An evening in Riverside, he thought, a romantic dinner at the Mission Inn, followed by a movie. The problem was, should it be a Chaplin or Keaton comedy? There was a new Wallace Reid picture, *Forever*, purported to be a love story. But would that be too obvious? *The Three Musketeers* starring Douglas Fairbanks was getting rave reviews. But did he want Fiona watching the dashing Fairbanks on the screen and comparing Doc Perry to him, perhaps find him wanting? A western was always safe, with plenty of adventure and romance, but didn't they get enough of that here?

He shook his head. Who would have thought that deciding on a movie could be so taxing!

Let Fiona choose the movie, he thought. That way, he could cleverly gauge her aspirations as far as their relationship went. If she requested a comedy or a swashbuckler, his knew his chances were slim. But a drama or a romance would give him hope.

She finally arrived, and he tried not to let his nervousness show as he treated her rash and had her good as new again.

As he escorted her to the front door, he said, "My dear Miss Wilson, I was wondering if you might join me for an evening in Riverside, dinner and a movie, shall we say, and take the train?"

Only one thought flew through her mind: that Lawrence had still not written to her from New York. Not even a Christmas greeting, and yet she had sent him a card. "I should very much love to, Dr. Perry."

"I'll choose the restaurant, and you can choose the movie."

She thought for a moment, then said, "I have heard that Mary Pickford's latest, *The Love Light*, is quite romantic."

Doc Perry's heart soared to the sky.

*   *   *

The high desert, flat and desolate, was dusted with snow.

Cody shivered as he drew up the collar of his heavy sheepskin coat. He had slept many a frosty night under the stars in that coat. The feel of it, the smell of it brought back memories. *The blizzard of 1910, trapped in a Green River, Wyoming, saloon for two weeks with horse wranglers, sodbusters, gamblers, cowboys, a few sporting ladies, two salesmen from Boston, and an old Indian named Mampoo. Two weeks of drinking and playing cards and fighting and making friends, dancing with the gals and sleeping it off. When the blizzard passed, they went outside and found horses and cattle frozen where they stood, even a few bodies of local farmers caught out before they could run for shelter. Cody couldn't remember when he had been that cold, or that warm.*

He looked up at the stars, the brightest he had ever seen. He wondered why they were clearer and seemingly more numerous in the desert. The new year lay two days away. He wished he could be back at Palm Springs for the holiday. At Christmas, Elizabeth had made him feel truly welcome. But that was the problem. She was getting under his skin, and that was dangerous. Which was why she was the other reason he had taken to the back trails on his horse in search of a ghost town and a man named Peachy.

But although he had put miles between himself and Elizabeth, she was still with him. Her hair, pale gold in the desert sunlight. The way she tilted her head when she listened to him. He tried not to think about her. Cody was a man governed by personal rules and ethics. He didn't believe in getting involved with another man's wife. But his heart seemed to be forgetting those rules. His heart, which he had thought would never feel again, was coming back to life.

The Horsethief Creek gold rush of 1909. Seventeen-year-old Cody, green and gullible, and determined to save his father's Montana ranch, had joined the stampeders up through Horsethief Pass, Colorado, where he staked a claim. He found gold. He was rich. And then he met a woman . . .

His mare snorted. Cody looked up to see shooting stars streak across the black firmament. He didn't want to think about Elizabeth

Barnstable or that other woman. He wanted only to stay on the move until he left his dark devils far behind.

Finally, he saw a collection of silhouettes standing on the vast moonlit plain, square and rectangular shapes blocking out the stars and the mountains on the distant horizon. It had to be Tylerville. Folks back in Twentynine Palms had said it lay in this direction. There were no lights, no signs of life. No bootleggers to shoot at him.

In fact, Tylerville was worse than Tombstone, where at least a few hardy souls still lived. He could see, as he drew near to the town, that Tylerville was dead, the store fronts all boarded up, weeds growing up through the wooden sidewalks, doors hanging off hinges. A town that had once been alive with music and laughter and hopes and dreams now lay rotting and forgotten.

It wasn't the first abandoned town Cody had encountered in his travels. The West was dotted with settlements that had sprung up overnight because of silver or gold, only to be abandoned once the mines ran dry. They were given names like Last Chance or New Jordan; some were simply named after the first man to discover gold there, as Tylerville most likely was.

Towns like Tylerville and Horsethief Creek were replicated a hundred times in the Old West, suddenly appearing with tents and wagons and flimsy wooden shacks, the noise of hammers and saws rising to the sky as men raced to erect shops, hotels, saloons, smithies, livery stables to accommodate the burgeoning population. As the prospectors poured in from all over, another wave followed: the bootmakers, barbers, laundresses, bakers, card sharps, con men, and prostitutes. Some Western towns managed to thrive and grow. Others, like Tylerville and Horsethief Creek, burned brightly like a shooting star and then were abandoned and left to rot.

Cody reined in when he reached the center of town and his eyes began to focus on the storefronts, the faded signs that said Painless Dentist, Honest Lawyer, Saloon, Smith & Son Undertakers, Ladies for Companionship. The shoulder-high swinging doors, the red and white barber pole, the tall, lifelike Indian carved from wood.

My God, he thought as he looked around with wide eyes. It was just like Horsethief Creek. The same size and layout. Not so short-lived that it was more underdeveloped than Horsethief, not so long-lived to have outgrown Horsethief. But an exact replica.

He recalled what he had heard about this area. Gold was discovered here in 1883 and within months the town of Tylerville was in full swing. Other mines in the area began producing, and a boom was under way. But then the mines went bust a year later and everyone left. Tylerville had flourished for exactly two years. Just like Horsethief Creek.

And in an instant he was thrown back—to Belle and Peachy, when Cody's personal demons were born.

Suddenly it was eleven years ago. The memories came flooding back. About to lose the ranch in Montana, his father broke, the bank making threats, seventeen-year-old Cody hearing of a gold strike in Colorado, his father giving him an heirloom watch to grubstake a claim . . . young Cody arriving in the boomtown swarming with miners hoping to strike it rich.

Dismounting now, he led his horse down the center of the deserted street, but he saw ghost-like people in doorways, strolling on sidewalks, galloping down the street firing guns to signify a gold strike. He heard honky-tonk music pour through open doorways. He saw bare-shouldered women leaning from second story windows, showing off their wares. Respectable ladies were there, too, as cooks and seamstresses. Wherever gold was found, an enterprising population soon gathered and the high times were rolling.

Cody paused to lift his hat and run his hand through his hair. He couldn't believe his eyes. He'd passed through plenty of ghost towns in the past few years, but none had born such a strong resemblance to Horsethief Creek. It was as if that other boomtown had been plucked from the Colorado foothills and dropped here in California's high desert.

Cody suddenly felt sick.

All these ghosts. *Are Belle and Peachy here, too?*

Shrill laughter suddenly tore the night air, making the hair on the back of his neck stand up. It was terrible, eerie laughter that always froze his blood—coyotes in a frenzy over a fresh kill. His father had once said a pack of yipping coyotes sounded to him like evil little girls laughing.

Cody realized he had made a terrible mistake. After ten years of staying ahead of the dark devils that dogged his trail, Cody had come to a town he'd never heard of, only to find them waiting for him with their mocking laughter.

Cody pulled a pad of paper from an inside pocket, pulled out a pencil and, touching it to his tongue, began to write.

He was obsessive about his writing. He couldn't leave the past alone, he kept revisiting it, over and over, through his pencil and words, reliving gunfights and cattle drives, Indian dances and peace pipes, card games and dance hall girls—the Old West that was already vanishing by the time he was born but which he found here and there in his travels, pockets of timelessness in towns where the future was held at bay.

Putting the paper away, he decided it was time to move on. Find the next town, the next gold mining district that, with luck, Peachy was working and would allow Cody to finally reclaim his life.

And then he thought about Button and Elizabeth, and Nigel shooting Johnny Pinto. While Elizabeth had gone around the property calling the dog's name, Cody hadn't had the heart to tell her what had happened to her pet. He also wouldn't come between husband and wife. If Elizabeth didn't know Barnstable had killed the dog, there was a good chance she didn't know the true character of the man she had married—but Cody wasn't going to be the one to tell her.

Since his drifting days began, in towns he passed through, where he stayed long enough to start caring about the inhabitants, he would pull back and leave before getting involved. He was at that point with Elizabeth Barnstable. He had to move on now. But he couldn't leave her without a proper good-bye.

*   *   *

The moon was a bright silver dollar in the starry sky, shedding light across the silent desert.

A lone rider, casting a long shadow on the sand, cantered over dunes and sagebrush, deep in his thoughts. As Cody neared La Alma, he saw lights still on, even though the hour was late. The Barnstables enjoying a nightcap?

He was tired. He needed to think. Tylerville had had an unexpected emotional impact on him. He wished he hadn't found the place. He wished he had been able to move on. Wished he hadn't come back to Palm Springs.

Cody's mare followed the beaten trail alongside the house that led to the rear corrals, paddocks, and outbuildings. The trail went past the eastern wall of the house and then edged the vast patio in the rear. Across the way, on the eastern border of the property, fifty towering date palms stood sentry.

The patio was paved with flagstones and landscaped with potted plants. Cody was startled to see someone out there, standing among dwarf palms and dormant hibiscus bushes.

Elizabeth! Standing out in the cold night, looking up at the stars. Rather, Cody noticed as he followed her gaze, the mountain, an eerie white in the moonlight.

"Hello," he called out, reining his horse.

She turned. "Mr. McNeal! Welcome back. Did you have any success?"

He dismounted and looped the horse's rein over the garden fence. Removing his hat, he joined her in the ghostly garden. He wondered that she didn't mind the cold. It couldn't be more than forty degrees out here, and all she wore over her dress was a thin sweater.

Her hair was down. He had never seen it that way before. It fell below her shoulders. She looked ethereal, a pale apparition among the patio furniture, statuary, and plants.

"I found Tylerville. It was interesting." He didn't tell her the rest, that ghosts haunted Tylerville, his ghosts, that gave him no peace.

She looked up at him. He hadn't shaved in a few days, and his eyes bore the shadows of sleeplessness. She wondered if something had happened during his visit to the high desert. "I didn't get a chance to thank you for the Christmas present, Mr. McNeal," she said. "It's lovely."

"Glad you like it. I scribble things down and then give them away."

"So you're a writer."

He shook his head. "Not formally. Stories, not literature, is what I'm about. Something the man in the street would enjoy and women would paste in their albums. Something schoolboys would read out loud and the fellows in a saloon would quote. I belong to simple folk, and I like to please them."

"Where do you get your material?"

He shrugged. "I collect it. Wherever I go, whichever place my stars lead me to, I talk to folks, ask them about themselves, about the town or countryside they live in." He paused, scratched his chin. "I guess you could call it a compulsion. I feel the need to preserve a way of life that's vanishing. The West, as my father and grandfather knew it, so folks won't forget."

"Do you publish them?"

He just laughed and shook his head. "I'm not that good. Anyway, I just came by to let you know I've only come back for a few days. There's a place I want to explore in the high desert up near Victorville. Another ghost town. After that, I'll be moving on."

She tilted her head. "Why ghost towns, Mr. McNeal?"

Cody couldn't say, but he was inexplicably drawn to them. He would walk the deserted streets and wonder about the people who had lived there. The hopes and dreams they had brought to the ramshackle storefronts that seemed to stare at him with blank eyes and gaping maws. The tumbleweeds would roll silently along the dust, testament to failed dreams. Cody sometimes wondered if he visited ghost towns maybe in search of himself. Looking for a way to relive his past, live it differently, erase a horrendous mistake that ended up costing lives. Or maybe he was just looking for a place to live because he felt like a ghost at times, as if Belle had not only stolen his gold but his life as well.

"It's just an interest of mine," was all he said.

Elizabeth was surprised at how disappointed she was to hear that he was leaving and realized she was going to miss him. She walked him to the kitchen door, where his horse stood nibbling bougainvillea. "Will you come in for a cup of tea, Mr. McNeal? The cook has gone to bed, but she always leaves a hot kettle on the stove."

He hesitated. He wanted to reach up and tuck back an escaped tendril of blond hair. But he held back. For ten years Cody had protected his heart. In every town he had passed through, from Montana to Wyoming to New Mexico, he had withstood the temptation to fall in love. The closest he had come was with a dimple-cheeked waitress named Ginger in Odessa, Texas. But he had left in the middle of the night to go in search of the next town.

But perhaps this moment of hesitation was no longer just about himself and his need to protect his heart. The hard fact was, Elizabeth was married, she was wealthy, and she was from the East, a place of tall and crowded cities that he could only imagine. A woman totally out of his reach.

He looked at the welcoming glow of the kitchen and thought that there was nothing he would love more than to sit with this woman in that warmth and share some tea.

"You know," Elizabeth said as she reached into the pocket of her skirt and brought out the envelope with her name and Christmas greeting written on it. "Of all the gifts I received for Christmas, yours touched me the most."

She unfolded the single sheet of stationery and read for the hundredth time what Cody McNeal had written on it.

It was the last year of the Yukon rush, and my luck had run out. My gold was gone, and all I had was a heel of bread, a scrap of cheese and some jerky. It was Christmas and a blizzard caught me out in the woods. But I saw a cabin and let myself in, bringing my horse in with me. I slept and was woken by an old man who said he was hungry. I was hungry, too, but he looked starved so I gave him the last of my food. The blizzard had passed so I took my leave and thanked him for the use of his cabin. He said his name was Hollis Jones and then he handed me a bag of gold dust for the food. When I reached Dawson City, I told the men in the saloon my good luck story and they said a man named Hollis Jones had indeed lived in that cabin, but he died of starvation five years ago in the middle of a blizzard on Christmas Day, so I must have dreamt it.

But I had the gold to prove that my story was true.

Elizabeth smiled. She knew Mr. McNeal hadn't written about himself because the Yukon gold rush happened in 1898 when he would have been six or seven years old. So an old timer, perhaps, had shared his story, and Cody had passed it along to her.

"I will treasure it," she said, folding the paper back into the envelope.

As they stood in the glow from the kitchen, with icy stars overhead and the cold breath of the desert swirling around them, Cody looked past Elizabeth at the solid, arched doorway to the kitchen. He thought of Tylerville with its gaping doorways. His visit there now seemed like a dream. As if, out on the flat, black desert he had conjured up an old abandoned town for himself to walk through—hell, to make him feel sorry for himself in. He hated it when men wallowed in their emotions, when they got nostalgic and melancholy. And it seemed to him now that that was exactly what he had done up at Tylerville. He had gotten sad and he had wallowed.

Cody felt a sudden need to know what was a dream and what was real. That arched kitchen doorway was real. This woman standing with one of his stories in her hand was real. The freezing cold stars were real.

And Nigel Barnstable, throwing a little dog like it was a sack of garbage, was real.

And this sudden reality brought Cody to a decision that he would not have in a million years thought he would make. Yet here he was, opening his mouth and saying, "I did some thinking while I was up at Tylerville, and I've decided that, if the job of ranch manager here at La Alma is still open, I'll take it."

"What about the ghost town near Victorville?"

He smiled. "I don't think it's going anywhere."

"I'm sure Nigel will be thrilled. He gets very frustrated trying to talk to the Mexican foreman. I'm afraid the man doesn't speak much English and Nigel has no Spanish whatsoever."

"I'll be back tomorrow then," he said, touching a finger to the brim of his hat. He returned to his horse, mounted, and rode off in the direction of Mrs. Henry's boardinghouse.

Elizabeth watched him disappear into the night. She was very pleased that Mr. McNeal had decided to stay.

PART TWO
1921

CHAPTER FIFTEEN

ELIZABETH WONDERED IF SHE was coming down with something. A winter cold, perhaps. For the past few mornings she had woken up nauseated and was thinking now that perhaps she should pay a visit to Doc Perry.

She was sitting up in bed, awaiting her breakfast. Through a large window, she had a view of the rear garden, where the spacious flagstone patio was planted with formal shrubbery, native plants and cacti, and various flowers. She could see the mountain that towered over Palm Springs: snow-covered peaks rising behind glittering palm trees. Where else on earth did one see such a sight, she wondered? It was January. Back home, her family and friends were trudging through snow beneath gray skies.

Her eyes went past the scarlet bougainvillea, across the corrals and settled on the bunkhouse where ranch hands were quartered. Cody McNeal lived there now as the new ranch boss. He never seemed to join the wranglers and other ranch hands in the evening, as they laughed around a campfire and sang songs to harmonica and fiddle. Always off to the side, thinking. A loner, she thought, a man who did not seek the company of others. She supposed the West was full of such men; perhaps the West attracted them with its vast plains and deserts, wide skies and ever-blowing winds.

When he had said good-bye after Christmas, Elizabeth had been disappointed to see him go. Although she knew very little about him, she had enjoyed their chance encounters during his stay in Palm

Springs. But when he had returned unexpectedly, to inquire after the job Nigel had offered him, she had realized she was both happy and relieved that he had come back. Relieved because Nigel no longer had to deal with the ranch hands who spoke little English. She had to admit, Nigel's sudden temper flares startled her. He was otherwise always the gentleman. Hardworking and driven, yes, but not a taskmaster. Now that Mr. McNeal was the ranch manager, there would be fewer lost tempers at the corrals.

It was not to say that all was peaceful at La Alma. Although the new bunkhouse was finished and the Mexican workers had decent housing, they were out in the orchard from dawn until dark, filling the air with their constant shouts and laughter. A hundred more palm trees, shipped from Phoenix, Arizona, had just been planted on the western side of the property, and it seemed to Elizabeth that just as many more migrant workers had arrived.

There was a soft knock at the bedroom door and Wilson entered with Elizabeth's morning tray. "I'm afraid I'm a bit late, Your Ladyship. Mrs. Flannigan has no help in the kitchen, now that Ethel's gone."

"She has been asking me to find a replacement," Elizabeth said as she lifted the warm teapot. "I know that Norrington isn't pleased that we lack a housemaid. His duties seem to be piling up on him." She poured tea into her cup and lifted the cover from her plate to expose eggs covered in creamy hollandaise sauce nestled on slices of toast.

The toast reminded her of Button. She had always shared her breakfast with him. Augie Lardner speculated that coyotes had gotten him; it happened to domestic pets out in the desert, and it tore her up to think how his life ended.

Elizabeth set aside her tray. She suddenly had no appetite. "I'll talk to Mrs. Norrington about hiring new help. In the meantime, Wilson, could I ask you to pay a visit to Doc Perry and ask him to fix me up with a tonic?"

Fiona's heart jumped. She would gladly pay a visit to the doctor. Now that her rash had cleared up, she had no reason to stop by, and she had come to think that it would be nice to develop a relationship with him. It was time she accepted the fact that she was never going to hear from Lawrence, and why she still carried a torch for him, she couldn't say. But common sense told her that the best way to douse one torch was by striking another.

*   *   *

"Watch out there!" Nigel shouted as he ran to the end of the row where the workers were maneuvering a tall ladder up to a date palm. He had already had two men fall to the ground with serious injuries, and he couldn't afford more. It wasn't that he cared about the workers, it was that every time an accident happened, work came to a halt as the Mexicans ran to the aid of their fallen friend. A lot of these men were fathers and sons, or brothers, or they came from the same village in Mexico. He sometimes thought work would be a lot more efficient if he hired men who were total strangers to one another.

Taking hold of the unwieldy ladder on one side, he grunted and groaned with three men to get it up against the tree, the top ends sliding into the bottom rails of a steel ladder at the top. Because date palms grew one to two feet each year, the day would come when the portable ladders would not reach the fruit and so growers fixed permanent ladders to the crowns and brought the portables to them, joining them together.

Pollinating season would begin next month, in February, when workers would climb these ladders, search for new female flowers, and sprinkle male pollen on them. It was a backbreaking, labor-intensive job, and Nigel intended to be out here every day, watching the men, to make sure they earned every penny he paid them.

Lifting his straw hat to run his hand through his hair, Nigel scowled as he gazed across his property, across the plain that stood between La Alma and the Indian reservation. He had wanted to expand his first orchard, but he couldn't because it would encroach on Indian land. And so the second orchard had to be planted here, where there was no water.

It was ridiculously unbalanced. He had been told that the reservation covered over thirty thousand acres and, from what he saw, aside from a few fruit trees and cash crops of vegetables, the Indians weren't using the land. But they wouldn't sell, they wouldn't even lease a few acres to him, so he was forced to plant another orchard on the other side of his property. The problem was the water. There was no nearby source.

"You can take water from the stream," Gonzalez had said with a toothpick in his mouth, "but you only own a little bit of the water. The federal government gave the majority of it to the Indians."

Nigel squinted across the flat plain to the opening of the canyon, where wild palms grew so thickly it looked more like a jungle than a desert. He didn't care what the federal government said. Nigel wasn't going to let a few impoverished Indians stand in his way.

*   *   *

"Sorry to bother you, Doc," Cody said, "but we need liniment for the horses and the general store is all out. I'm hoping you might have some."

"I do indeed, Mr. McNeal. Come in." Doc Perry stepped aside.

Cody removed his Stetson as he entered the parlor. "Please, call me Cody. We've seen each other around for the past few months, I reckon we can consider ourselves neighbors."

Perry led Cody into his office where a tray stood on his cluttered desk, holding a glass and a frosty pitcher of pale yellow liquid. "Was just about to have some lemonade. Care to join me?" Going to a cabinet, Perry brought out another glass and as he filled them, Cody looked around.

One wall of Leland Perry's office was covered with photographs, some yellowed with age, taken in different locales, with different people. When Doc Perry was a traveling medicine man, he had clearly made friends wherever he went.

"I remember as a kid, outside of Blackwater, Montana," Cody said as he examined a photograph of Perry wearing a flashy waistcoat and an old-fashioned stovepipe hat, standing next to a colorful gypsy wagon, with a small boy on one side, a stoic Indian on the other. "I used to love it when the medicine show came into town. Did you ever get that far north, Doc?"

"Can't say as I did," Doc Perry said as he handed Cody a glass. "But I look back on those days with fondness. And a little bit of guilt."

"Why guilt?"

"Most of my medicines were fakes."

Cody scrutinized another photograph. He could make out Doc Perry's products standing on shelves: hair restorers, slimming powders, sleep aids, energy pills, moustache wax. "You know what's missing?" Cody said with a smile. "Cancer cures. Tuberculosis cures. Potions and pills guaranteed to restore a destroyed liver or a failing heart."

Perry nodded. "I drew the line at those, my friend. Others of my kind, men of less integrity, took money from folks with fatal illnesses and promised to make them well. That was something I could never do."

"You sold colored water and sugar tablets. But you know? Folks knew that. Maybe some believed those medicine hucksters actually sold cures, but most enjoyed the show—the pitch from the back of the wagon, the colorful spiel. There was always a silent Indian for some reason." Cody sipped the lemonade. It was cold, tart, and sweet.

"Of course, the alcohol helped," Perry said, a line of worry appearing between his brows.

"That it did. I knew a few teetotalers who loved their daily spoonfuls of Dr. Smith's tonic or cure-alls. I hear you make all your own medicines, Doc. Mrs. Allenby swears by your arthritis formula, and Lois Lardner can't sleep at night without your remedy for insomnia." He gave the older man a long look. Perry had an honest face, Cody thought, but very often it was that look of honesty that made a man the best huckster. "I'll bet Prohibition is having an effect on your private pharmacy."

Perry sighed. "That it is, son."

"I was up Tylerville way a few weeks ago, nosing around the mines, hoping to run into an old friend. I got shot at by a bootlegger. He didn't ask questions, just fired at me and nearly took my head off."

Perry thought about his diminishing supply in the stockroom, wondering what he was going to do when it was gone. "I reckon that in the business of making illegal liquor, they'll shoot anybody who comes within a hundred yards of their operation. And there isn't a thing the authorities can do about it because I've heard the moonshiners are shooting at the police, too. Bootlegging is profitable. They'd risk a lynching for the kind of money they're making. Besides, if a law isn't supported by the people, you'll never have enough lawmen or jails to enforce it. I doubt the authors of the Prohibition amendment had this new crime in mind when they drafted that ridiculous bill."

"With luck it will be repealed."

Not in time to save my business, Perry thought.

He had heard that moonshiners had come out this way, too, hiding in the rocks and caves near Palm Springs, brewing white lightning, protecting their operations with shotguns. They were supplying night-clubs in Los Angeles that had turned into speakeasies, and who paid good money for the illegal hooch. But the moonshiners weren't the only hazards resulting from the new law. Club owners who didn't buy from bootleggers managed to find another pipeline for their illegal liquor trade—from Canada, down the West Coast on private vessels, off-loading on Catalina Island and ferrying it to the mainland during the night. Liquor was also smuggled across the Mexican border, a mere ninety miles away, too close for Perry's comfort.

He drained his glass and set it down. "You came for liniment." He went to a cupboard and brought out a large, sealed bottle. "This is my own formula, guaranteed to relieve pain and stiffness, especially sore muscles or arthritis. I made it for humans but it will work just as well for horses."

"Thanks, Doc." Cody replaced his hat and started to leave. But he paused in this room filled with the past, a museum to an age he hated to see disappear. "Doc, I'll bet you have some stories to tell."

Their eyes met in mutual understanding. Perry's lips curved in a knowing smile. "That I do, my friend," he said softly. "And don't forget the ladies," he added with a wink. "Especially the ladies."

As he closed the door, Doc Perry thought of one lady in particular, Fiona Wilson, who had sat with him in a dark movie theater while a romance unfolded on the screen. He had boldly taken her hand, and she had allowed it.

He was looking forward to taking the courtship to the next step.

*   *   *

Elizabeth sat at the small writing desk in a sunny corner of the spacious living room, composing a letter to her mother. She was interrupted by Mrs. Flannigan the cook, who requested a moment of Her Ladyship's time. She stood stiffly before her employer, frizzy hair escaping the cap on her head, cooking stains on her apron. "I'm sorry, your Ladyship, but I'm giving me notice. I'll be leaving your employ."

Oh no, Elizabeth thought. First the maid and now the cook. "Are you unhappy here, Mrs. Flannigan?"

"The truth is, My Lady, with my skills I can earn up to three thousand dollars a year working at a restaurant."

"What are we paying you now?"

"A hundred and fifty dollars, Your Ladyship."

Elizabeth stared at her. "A *year*?"

"Yes, Your Ladyship."

"I'll see if I can raise it, Mrs. Flannigan." Nigel handled the household expenses.

"Truth to tell, Your Ladyship. I don't like it here. I would rather live in a city. It's what I'm used to. I have been looking at job offers in the newspaper, and I've found a good position in Riverside, at a posh hotel."

After Mrs. Flannigan left, Elizabeth rang for Fiona. The system of bells and whistles that worked in the big houses of Manhattan and Britain had not been installed at La Alma. But with the house being on one level, a handbell could be heard well into the kitchen.

"Yes, My Lady?" Fiona said when she came into the living room.

"I suppose you know we're losing Mrs. Flannigan. Wilson, I know nothing about the financial running of a house. May I ask what we pay you in annual salary?"

"A hundred and twenty-five dollars, My Lady. But I'm not complaining. We get room and board, don't we?"

Elizabeth didn't know what to say. The servants' private lives rarely crossed her mind. Especially how they spent their free time, what they did with their money, how they felt about their situation. But now that she thought about it, it seemed to Elizabeth to be very unfair. It had never occurred to her to wonder how some houses could afford to pay such large staffs. Nigel had told her that Stullwood Hall had a staff of fifty indoor servants and fifty outdoor. It was almost slave labor, she thought.

She would discuss it with Nigel. They still had the Norringtons, and Wilson, of course. But they couldn't afford to lose any more. We will raise their wages, she thought as she picked up her pen to apprise her mother of this latest development. And tomorrow she would go across to Lardner's and see about finding a domestic agency in Riverside.

*   *   *

Luisa feared that bad times were coming. She had found out that the reason there had been fewer people at Mukat's annual winter fiesta was because her cousins had chosen to go to a Christmas celebration instead.

Our people are being seduced, she thought as she crossed the alluvial fan and entered the grove of fifty date palms. They want white man's things. They will forget the Indian way.

She was especially worried about her two granddaughters, nearly sixteen years old, who liked to go to Lardner's store and look at magazines about film stars. They were at an age where they were easily influenced: Gabriela, third daughter of Luisa's youngest daughter, and Isabella, youngest daughter of her fourth daughter. By coincidence, the same age. Cousins who looked like sisters.

As they emerged from the grove, she stopped and looked at the big house called La Alma del Desierto. She had heard that the lady's servants had left and she needed help. That was why Luisa was here today, with her two granddaughters obediently following her.

Luisa Padilla had worked at that house for the past few years, when the previous owners came down from the north for the winter. The work was not hard and it paid good money. But now the white man in that house was the one the red diamond rattlesnake had warned her about—the man who killed Johnny Pinto. How could she work for the wife of such a man?

But they are rich and we are poor, she thought. We cannot supplement our government allotment with meat and eggs. The agent said the Great Father in Washington has cut back our rations again. And the children need shoes.

As she worried over this dilemma, Luisa looked at it from another side and realized that, by offering to help the lady at La Alma, she could help her granddaughters at the same time.

Change was coming, it was inevitable, and Luisa Padilla wanted her family to adapt and survive. It was what the Cahuilla had done for generations. The desert had thrown intense heat and freezing winters at them, had sent sandstorms and flash floods, had washed away entire villages, had sent lightning to burn their food supply and cause decimating famine. But always the Cahuilla had adapted and survived. And now the desert was bringing the white man and they must once again adapt.

If her granddaughters were doomed to learn the white man's ways, it was going to be under Luisa's watchful eye. Luisa would nurture her two girls in such a way that they adapted to the new white ways but at the same time kept her people's culture and traditions. Luisa wanted her granddaughters to be guided, not seduced.

She knocked at the back door and a woman in a long black dress answered. "We have come to help," Luisa said, standing tall and proud. Her granddaughters, Isabella and Gabriela, stood behind her. "You need help with house, we will help."

"Wait here, please." The lady went away and a moment later the lady of the house came to the door. "Mrs. Norrington said you wish to speak to me?"

"We can work for you, Señora. Every year, for the other family, my granddaughters and I come to help."

Two blue eyes stared at her. "Oh!" Elizabeth said. "Please, come in."

As they stepped inside, Luisa saw her red diamond rattlesnake basket on the big kitchen table. It was filled with snake power intended to drive away the evil that had come by train. So far, it hadn't worked.

"I understand you are familiar with this house," Elizabeth said, recalling that Mrs. Lardner had said that the prior owners never brought domestic staff, but hired local Indians. "Then we will be happy to have you," she said, adding with a smile, "all three of you."

Elizabeth suddenly put her hand to her forehead and reached for the back of a chair to steady herself.

"Are you all right, Señora?"

"I haven't been feeling well. Something isn't agreeing with me. I have woken up every day this week feeling sick."

Luisa studied her with keen, lively eyes. Years ago, a famous photographer named Edward Curtis came through this valley and took pictures of the natives. One of his subjects had been a young Luisa Padilla, and it turned out to be one of his more striking portraits as she was a handsome woman, strong-jawed, large-nosed, with intense dark eyes. Though her features had softened with time, Luisa's eyes possessed the same piercing gaze, as if she could see right through a person and examine his naked soul.

She studied Elizabeth that way now. And then, remembering that the Señor and his wife were newlyweds, she said, "Señora, when did the moon visit you last?"

Elizabeth looked at her. "I beg your pardon?"

"The moon. The woman's moon. Can you remember the last time?"

"I have no idea what you're—" Elizabeth's eyes widened. "Oh!" Then she said, more softly, "Oh . . ."

*　　*　　*

Elizabeth waited two weeks, checking her calendar to make sure, in case the Indian woman's diagnosis of her condition was erroneous. She had confided her secret in Fiona Wilson, from whom she learned about other signs of pregnancy. Although Fiona had not herself ever been married or given birth, she had been around long enough to pick up such information. Elizabeth's breasts were tender, and her fingers slightly swollen so that none of her rings would fit and her wedding ring couldn't come off. Then there was the morning sickness and unexplained weight gain.

Elizabeth hoped the baby was a girl. I will raise you to flout convention, she thought. You will be your own woman. I will not tell you what to wear, what to choose on a menu. The world will be open to you. Choose your own destiny. Just because you're a woman shouldn't mean doors are closed to you. Study law or medicine. Be an artist. Make your mark in this world.

Elizabeth marveled at how pregnancy expanded a woman's mind. Having that tiny spark of life in her body brought her out of herself. It was now time to think of another life, one that she created and which she was now obligated to watch over, nurture, protect—an endeavor she was going to embrace with utter enthusiasm as Elizabeth now understood how her mother had felt, why she was so doting and smothering. All the years of what Elizabeth had seen as nagging were just an overwhelming outpouring of love. And in realizing this, Elizabeth learned something new: the pain she had caused her mother by eloping and then coming out West.

I am so sorry, Mother. I had no idea.

But Elizabeth now had a way to make it up to her. And the thought of it made her suddenly so giddy that her knees went weak. Her mother would come out in the late stage of the pregnancy and stay afterward, to help with the baby. Elizabeth could hardly contain her excitement. What an astonishing moment! To realize in one instant that she had hurt her mother, and in the next to come up with the solution to make amends. How amazing life could be! How marvelous the world was. Elizabeth had not thought such joy was possible, and as she went looking for Nigel, her thoughts raced ahead with delicious plans— which room to put her parents in, showing them around the town and Nigel's groves and up in the canyons, how their days would be laid out. All of them together and happy.

*　　*　　*

La Alma's Spanish-style living room was sunken, with steps leading down from the dining room and front entrance. The floor was paved with orange-brown Saltillo tiles imported from Mexico, the high ceiling beamed with dark wood, the three chandeliers made of black wrought iron imported from Spain. Tall windows and glass doors admitted radiant sunlight and a view of the front patio landscaped with plants, statuary, and a fountain. Beyond, lay the main road that ran along the base of the foothills from Banning in the west to Indio in the east. On the other side of the road lay vacant property with palm trees, and beyond that, the flat desert stretched away to lavender mountains in the distance.

But Nigel was aware of none of this as he sat on the long leather sofa, studying a large map spread out on the enormous coffee table inlaid with blue and gold Spanish tile. He was drawing on the map with a pen, making notations, writing down instructions—his plan to dig earthen canals from Mesquite Creek to his date palms.

Elizabeth paused under an archway, her hand resting on a pillar made of carved cantera stone, quarried exclusively in Guadalajara, Mexico.

Nigel was so handsome! In the seven months since they had eloped, Elizabeth still couldn't believe her luck. At twenty-five, Nigel was tall, attractive, poised, and polished. An accomplished horseman, an expert marksman, and now, master of a new plantation. If he were a film star, the critics would describe him as "dashing."

It was the servants' day off. The Norringtons and Fiona Wilson had taken the train to Banning for some shopping, leaving only Luisa and the two granddaughters in the house. As they were working in the kitchen, Elizabeth knew she and Nigel had privacy. "Nigel, may I have a word?"

When he didn't reply, she repeated her question.

"Not now," he said, keeping his eyes on the map as his hands moved energetically over the topographic features, sketching long, curving lines from the canyon to his two date palm groves. He frowned as he worked. The eastern grove would have adequate irrigation. But the western one was a challenge. Would the canals be sufficient?

"Nigel, I have something to tell you. Can you let that go for a minute?"

He didn't respond.

She went around and stood at the edge of the table.

"You're blocking the light," he said. Elizabeth had seen him this way before, whenever he was embroiled in plantation plans. She recognized the tone. His mind was on a singular course and would not be moved. Previously, when he let it be known he wasn't to be disturbed, she had left, waiting to talk to him when he said he was available. But this news couldn't wait.

"Nigel, there is something I need to tell you."

He looked up with a frown. "For God's sake, Elizabeth. I have a headache and I'm going to be late for an appointment with a hydro-engineer in Indio. Surely whatever it is can wait."

"No," she said with a smile, knowing he would quickly change his mood once he heard her announcement. "This cannot wait. Not for water or date palms or hydro-engineers. Nigel, darling," she said. "I'm afraid that, very soon, we won't be having this house entirely to ourselves."

He waited. She saw impatience throb in a vein at his throat.

She laughed. "Actually, it will only be one person, and a very small one at that. Nigel, I'm going to have a baby."

He stared up at her as sounds from outside drifted through an open window. Although it was the dead of winter, the day had a touch of warmth and the breeze was almost spring-like. The air was filled with the noise of trucks and men's voices and, beyond, wranglers in the corrals exercising the horses.

"Aren't you going to say something?" she said, her excitement bubbling, a dream every young wife held dear, informing her husband of the coming arrival of their first child.

Nigel's frown deepened. He seemed distracted. Returning his gaze to the map he said, "Yes, yes, it was to be expected, wasn't it? But it's nothing we need to talk about right now."

She stared down at him, at his thick black hair and broad shoulders, his hand once again flying this way and that over a map that, for some reason, was more important to him than what should be more important to him. Maybe he hadn't heard right. "I'm pregnant," she said, thinking that other words would reach him. "We're having a baby, Nigel."

His hand had a mind of its own, drawing, outlining, scratching out until he made a sound of exasperation—a sound familiar to Elizabeth in that she had heard it many times in the past weeks, a sound that meant it was best if she retreated and approached him at a better time. But she stood her ground. For once, the plantation was coming second.

"The child should be born around the beginning of September." She paused, waited, felt her own impatience start to bud. "Aren't you going to say something?"

He glanced at his wristwatch, muttered, "Christ, I'm late," and rose to his feet. Elizabeth knew that Nigel hated tardiness, that he hated it in others but loathed it most in himself. It was a weakness, he always said, and he did not tolerate weakness in others or himself. But she thought that surely an exception could be made in this case. It wasn't every day a man was told he was soon to become a father.

As Nigel strode across the room to the entry hall where coats and hats were hung, Elizabeth pressed down her disappointment at his reaction, or lack of one, telling herself that maybe men didn't get as excited over these issues as women did, and said, "I'm going to write to Mother and ask her to come out and stay with us while I'm pregnant, and for a while after the baby is born."

He stopped and turned. "Your mother? Here?"

"Oh, Nigel, it will be so wonderful to see my parents again. And perhaps we can persuade Daddy to stay on, too."

He waved a dismissive hand. "That's not possible. I have a great deal on my mind right now, and I can't have distractions."

"But they won't be a distraction. If anything, they'll be a help. You won't have to worry about me all the time. I'll have my parents with me and that will free you to focus on the plantation."

"No. I've said no, Elizabeth, and that's that." He started for the hallway again, climbing the three tiled steps up from the sunken living room. Following him up the steps, Elizabeth reached out for his arm. "Nigel, I want to talk about this. I have to have my mother here, at least my mother."

"I said not now," he said, jerking away from her, striding toward the coats. His car was a convertible. He would need something warm when he made the drive back in the evening.

She reached for him again and seized his arm. The moment was spoiled. What she had thought would be a celebration had turned upside down. And now he was walking away as if she had simply announced a burned roast. In their seven months of marriage, Nigel had always had the final say, and Elizabeth had been fine with that until now. But this was *her* moment, *her* special business, and it was only fair that for once she had the final say. "You can change your appointment, Nigel. You can see the engineer tomorrow. I need to talk about this now."

He spun around, startling her. "Don't you dare use that tone of voice with me!" he snapped. "I have said no and that's final. Your parents are not coming here."

She stared at him in shock. He had never spoken to her that way before. It sparked something inside her, a defiance that had come out in a few of her rows with Daddy when he was being stubborn and impossible. "And I say that my parents *are* coming here!"

His hand shot out so fast she did not see it coming. When his palm connected with her face, in such a startling, painful slap, she staggered back, nearly slipping on the tiles. "There," he said, "did that finally get my point across? We will discuss the baby when I say we will. And don't you ever, *ever*," he thrust an index finger in her face, "contradict me again."

Something inside her snapped. Slapping his hand and his pointing finger away, she shouted, "I have a right to say what I want, and I should think our baby is more important than your damn plantation!"

The second slap caught her in the eye. The force of it spun her around so that she fell down the three steps into the living room and landed hard against a chair. It was a big, heavy chair and carved from dark, smoky wood, with arms that ended in lion's claws. The back of the chair was ornate and throne-like, with the top carved into a row of leaves and flowers culminating in a rising cluster of flowers in the center. Because Elizabeth stumbled from the top step down into the sunken living room, the chair was below her. And when she collided with it, the skillfully carved flowers and leaves in the hard wood met her square in the abdomen.

"That's the last I want to hear from you on the subject!" Nigel boomed. "We'll talk about it when I bring it up and not a moment before."

She gasped and doubled over, clutching the chair. She heard the front door open and slam shut. And then she sank to the tiles.

A roaring sound reached her ears and she realized it was Nigel's car, driving off. As she lay on the cold tiles, stunned, unable to grasp what had happened, she felt her soul leave her body, riding a wave of pain—pain that was beyond excruciating. It was her body coming apart inside her, loosening, tearing, bleeding. It was carrying her up, up to the ceiling, the sky, the universe. There weren't enough knives in the world to combine together and create such pain. She knew that it was the pain of losing life. Of losing a child. She couldn't hold onto it. Her body was betraying her. The one she had been entrusted to protect was slipping away, and she was powerless to save it.

"Señora! Aii, Señora!" Luisa came running in. "Señora, dios mio, are you all right?"

Elizabeth couldn't speak. Her face was scarlet and twisted in a grimace. Luisa tried to help her to her feet. Choking sounds came from Elizabeth's throat. She wheezed and coughed and when she finally had breath, managed to whisper, "I need help. Something is wrong. I'm in pain . . ."

Luisa ran into the kitchen and flung the back door open. "Isabella, go find Señor Cody! Tell him to fetch the doctor! The Señora has had an accident. Hurry!"

Cody was in the bunkhouse, taking a noon break with a cup of coffee, a pencil, and a notebook. "Señor," Isabella said breathlessly as she knocked on the frame of his open door. "Something is wrong with the Señora. We need the doctor."

In the living room, Luisa was unable to lift Elizabeth to her feet. "Let me help you to the bedroom, Señora."

But Elizabeth couldn't move. She cried out in pain. Her knees gave way. And then Luisa saw the red stain spreading on Elizabeth's white skirt.

"Aii, Mukat!" she cried.

"What is it?" Cody said, running into the living room. When he saw Elizabeth, he ran to her, reached down, and lifted her up, slipping one arm under her back and the other under her legs. He hurried to the master bedroom where he gently laid her on the bed. "What happened?" he said to Luisa.

But the Indian woman didn't respond. With a grim look on her face, she went into the bathroom and emerged with towels. "Please fetch Doctor Perry," she said, and Cody left at once.

As she removed Elizabeth's skirt and undergarments, Luisa thought: There is bad magic in this house.

Doc Perry arrived ten minutes later with his medical bag. Leaving Isabella and Gabriela to assist him, Luisa and Cody stepped out. "Mrs. Padilla, what happened?" Cody said. He was still dressed only in shirt-sleeves, and hatless with his hair uncombed. He had run all the way to Doc Perry's place.

Luisa drew herself tall and straight, her hands clasped at her waist. She needed to think. The red diamond rattlesnake had warned her of the coming evil. She had thought the Señora was part of that evil, as she was the wife of Johnny Pinto's killer. But in the two weeks that Luisa and her granddaughters had worked at La Alma, she had sensed no evil in the Señora.

And now she knew. The Señora was as much a victim of the evil white man as Johnny Pinto had been.

Luisa suspected that the Señora might not want anyone to know the truth, that pride would make her protect her husband—just as some prideful women in Luisa's tribe did. But the Señora herself needed to be protected. And so Luisa would confide in just one person. "Señor Cody," Luisa said finally, in a low tone so that no one could hear. "The Señora would not want me to tell you this, but you must know.

I heard an argument. They were fighting. And then I heard a sound like a slap. I think he slapped her. She fell. I do not know. I think he slapped her again and then he left. He has gone away in his car."

Cody stared at her. "Someone *hit* her? But who—"

Their eyes met. A man who would shoot an unarmed Indian boy and kill an innocent dog.

Rage flared up in Cody McNeal, hot and dangerous, the impulse to get on his horse and ride after the monster in the yellow car, drag him to the dirt, and beat him to death.

"Do not say anything, I beg you, Señor. Let us wait and see."

They waited half an hour, Cody pacing back and forth, ramming his fist into his hand, Mrs. Padilla standing silent and stoic by the bedroom door. Finally Doc Perry came out, rolling his sleeves down and buttoning his cuffs. One of Luisa's granddaughters followed, carrying his coat, hat, and medical bag, while the other remained at the bedside. "I'm afraid Mrs. Barnstable has lost the baby," he said.

"Baby!" Cody looked at Luisa. "Elizabeth was pregnant?"

Luisa closed her eyes and crossed herself, sending a silent prayer to the Blessed Virgin and to Mukat, creator of all things.

"She will need plenty of bed rest and nourishing food, Mrs. Padilla," Perry said. "Plenty of green vegetables to build up her strength. Red wine as she can tolerate it. The whole event should be over in a few days. In the meantime, does anyone know where the husband is? He needs to be informed." Perry searched the housekeeper's face and then Cody's. His question had been a formality, a way of preserving Mrs. Barnstable's dignity. Doc Perry suspected that the lady had been the victim of marital abuse—the large, round bruise on her cheek and the swollen eye had not come from a simple fall. But it wasn't his place to interfere between a husband and wife.

"I have an idea where he is," Cody said. *And I'll do more than inform him . . .*

But Luisa laid a hand on Cody's arm, staying him, and said, "The Señor will be home at sundown, doctor. That is when he always comes home. For his dinner."

"When you see him," Doc Perry said, putting his jacket on and settling the stovepipe hat on his head, "tell him that when Mrs. Barnstable is better, he might see to it that she visits a specialist in Riverside. I can't say for certain, but there is a danger that she might never be able to conceive again, or that if she does, it could be detrimental to her health. Possibly even life threatening."

While Luisa escorted Doc Perry out to the driveway, Cody knocked on the bedroom door. Gabriela opened it. "I'd like to see Mrs. Barnstable for a moment. I won't stay long."

Cody pulled up a chair and sat at the bedside. Elizabeth was shockingly pale, her eyes closed, hands at her sides. Lying beneath a satin counterpane, her blond hair fanned out on the white pillow, she looked angelic, he thought. She also looked fragile and vulnerable.

Her eyes fluttered open. Cody leaned forward. "How do you feel?" he said.

"I fell," she whispered. "I tripped and fell. I hit the back of a chair."

His eyes met hers. He saw the silent message in them. "Yes," he said. He laid his hand on hers and gave it a reassuring squeeze.

Cody wanted to kill Nigel Barnstable. He would settle for threatening the man. But in the end, Cody knew that whatever he did or said would only endanger Elizabeth all the more. So he would keep her secret and would respect her privacy. But Cody was going to keep a close eye on Nigel Barnstable from now on.

He had hoped to leave Palm Springs soon. But now everything had changed.

CHAPTER SIXTEEN

ELIZABETH DRIFTED IN AND out of consciousness, from dream-state to a reality in which she sensed people gathered around her, looking down, worrying, whispering. She was aware of pain and sadness, both being physical conditions, although how sadness became physical she didn't know.

At one point she heard, somewhere in the house, voices raised in anger. No, just one voice in anger, the other raised in defensiveness. She recognized Doc Perry's baritone, Luisa's broken English, Cody McNeal at one point, even-toned, and Nigel, shouting as if guiding giant trees into excavated holes. A consortium of voices arguing, debating, accusing, defending.

They are fighting about me . . .

She rolled her head on the pillow. She saw light streaming through the windows. Bright yellow jasmine hugged the glass panes, little ruby-throated hummingbirds flitting among the blossoms.

But it's winter, Elizabeth thought distantly. The sky should be gray, the shrubs flowerless, the birds back in their home in the tropics.

She was weak. How long had she been lying here? She tried to think back. There had been an argument. Nigel had slapped her.

The baby . . .

Under the covers, she laid her hand on her abdomen. Someone had dressed her in a nightgown. She had no recollection of that. Beneath her hand that rested in the valley between her two pelvic crests, she felt a dull ache. Yesterday, or whenever it had happened, it had been the sharpest pain she could imagine, where she had impaled herself on a chair. But now there was just an ache there. And an emptiness, too, as if someone had scooped out her organs.

She's lost the baby. Someone had said that over her and, funnily, it made Elizabeth picture a baby in a little tub, being bathed, and she turned away for a moment, to get the soap or a sponge, and when she turned back, he was gone. That was how you lost a baby. Not by falling against a chair.

She suddenly felt very lonely. Alone and lonely, and tears pricked her eyes. Where was Nigel? *I want him here. I need him to comfort me. We'll cry together. Our first argument as a married couple and look how it ended! We'll mark the event and then vow never to fight again.*

I shouldn't have pressed the issue of my parents coming here. Nigel has a lot on his mind. Why did I push it? Why couldn't I have simply said, "All right, we'll talk about this later, whenever you wish." But the small rebellion that had risen up in her then rose up now: No, this is important, and it is what I want to talk about, and I say we talk about it now.

But the whole issue was moot now because there was no baby and therefore nothing to talk about.

She wished Nigel would come. She was anxious about the moment. She wanted them to cry together and forgive each other and both say they were sorry and vow never to let it happen again. But, in her foggy state—had she been drugged?—she tried to define "it." If they weren't going to let "it" happen again, she needed to know what "it" was.

He slapped me. So hard that I fell. He slapped me twice, and then he got in his car and drove off.

That was the bare bones of what had happened. Elizabeth couldn't deny it. And she hated the bare bones of what had happened because they revealed a frightening truth about the man she had married that she hadn't known was there—that, if he didn't get his way, he was capable of hitting a pregnant woman, twice, and so hard that she fell against a piece of hard furniture. And then he had walked out.

Voices sounded in the hallway beyond the closed door. Another round of anger and defensiveness. Nigel and Wilson. And then the door flew open and Elizabeth saw, through a haze, her husband standing there, a look of fury on his face. Behind him, Fiona Wilson wrung her hands.

He paused in the doorway, and from beneath barely raised eyelids, Elizabeth saw a look on his face she had never seen before—hatred and disgust.

She blinked. She looked again and the strange face was gone to be replaced by Nigel's familiar frown—the one he presented to date palms and Indians and anything that eluded his control. He strode to the bed and towered over her. "You lost the baby," he said bluntly, and Elizabeth thought she heard a note of accusation in his voice, but surely she had imagined it.

"How," she began with a dry mouth. "How long . . . ?"

"You've been in bed for three days. Doc Perry gave you something to sleep. But now it's time to wake up." He looked over his shoulder and said to the worried Fiona, "Close the door, please." When they were alone, he said, "Sit up, Elizabeth, we need to talk."

She struggled to push herself up in the bed, nudging her pillow up behind her back, while Nigel watched. When she was upright and propped against the pillow, weak and drained, he sat on the edge of the bed and reached out to touch her swollen cheek. She flinched. He touched it again, harder.

"I was very angry at first," he said. "When I came home and was told what you had done. I want an heir, Elizabeth. You know that. You could have been carrying my son. But you went and lost it."

Elizabeth decided that whatever Doc Perry had given her, it contained ingredients that caused hallucinations, distorted the senses, created another reality. Because what she was hearing couldn't be real. She saw Nigel's stony expression. He was waiting for her to say something. She tried to arrange her jumbled thoughts. The argument about her mother, the slap across the face that had sent her tumbling—surely false memories conjured up by Doc Perry's potent elixir. Nigel couldn't have done that.

And yet, as she looked at him now in a room filled with bright winter sunlight while hummingbirds sipped nectar from yellow jasmine, Elizabeth saw something new in Nigel's eyes. A patina of coldness that she had never seen before.

But wait . . . if memory served, she *had* seen that look, in brief glimpses that lasted for less than a second so that she dismissed them as tricks of light or tricks of her own imagination. Christmas, when Button caused the wine spill on his trousers. Before Nigel laughed with everyone else, Elizabeth had caught a quick flash of cold anger to be immediately covered up by a self-deprecating smile.

But Nigel Barnstable is not a self-deprecating man, she thought now in something that felt like an insight, or the brink of an epiphany. But Elizabeth was too weak, her mind too muddled to bring the revelation into fullness, so she said the first thing that came into her mind. "You hit me." It hurt to talk, with her bruised face.

"And whose fault was that?" Nigel's voice was cold and harsh. "I should be very angry with you, Elizabeth. I don't know that I can ever completely forgive you for losing our child. But I have to take into account your age and inexperience. You think you are still living with your parents whom you have twisted around your finger, especially your father. I imagine you whined and argued with them interminably to get your way. But that won't happen with me, Elizabeth, so you are going to have to forget your old habits."

He sighed with annoyance. "I had such a high regard for you. But to go on and on the way you did, pressing to talk about something when I said it had to wait. Well, I thought you were smarter than that. Look what you made me do. A man can be pushed only so far until he is provoked."

It wasn't just being provoked, Nigel thought, as he looked at her in disgust. She wasn't quite so pretty with a bruised and swollen face. Sometimes a man just had to act. Like shooting an Indian to prove who was the real authority in these parts—certainly not a man wearing a tin badge. Or destroying a dog that had made him a laughingstock at a party. And now Elizabeth with her sudden disrespect, contradicting him, arguing, determined to get her own way.

He reached for her hand. She looked down and saw the strong, sunburned fingers curl around hers. Possessively. "I shouldn't forgive you," he said, "but I do. Anyone can make a mistake the first time. It's the second time that can't be forgiven." His fingers tightened around hers. "Do you understand, Elizabeth?"

She understood his words but not what was happening. What had Doc Perry given her to distort everything so?

Something was wrong. She looked at the window. The winter jasmine and hummingbirds were there. All normal. She swept her gaze around the spacious sun-lit bedroom and saw the handsome furniture imported from Spain, the wrought iron chandeliers and wall sconces. Everything as it should be. But when she came back to Nigel, he wasn't quite right. *He* was what was wrong. He was Nigel and yet he wasn't.

And then she thought that perhaps it wasn't Nigel who had changed but rather her perception of him. Did Doc Perry's medicine somehow magically make a person see others differently? I must ask him, Elizabeth thought, making a mental note to ask Doc Perry about a medicine that enabled a person to look at someone and see different sides to him that weren't visible otherwise.

"I should fire Wilson," Nigel said, "and the Norringtons for allowing this to happen. I've a good mind to, but unfortunately we need them to run the house."

It's not their fault, Elizabeth said. They didn't slap me so hard that I fell against a chair that stabbed me in the abdomen. They didn't slap me twice after I had just announced I was pregnant. Why can't you see that? Answer me!

And then she realized she wasn't talking out loud.

Running her tongue over her lips, she tasted sweetness and a memory came back: Doc Perry spooning something sweet into her mouth, saying, "This will help with the pain, Mrs. Barnstable. Swallow it now." And Elizabeth lapsing back into a foggy dream-state. The sweet medicine was still affecting her. Or maybe it was Nigel himself, Nigel the mesmerist who had had her under a spell from the moment she met him.

"You hit me," she said.

"If I slapped you it was because you brought it on yourself. You shouldn't push me to such rash action. I'm not used to being contra-dicted. I am still very much the lord of the manor and my word is law. But you kept on about your mother after I said no, and I'm not used to that and I don't intend to get used to it."

Part of his anger stemmed from the fact that she had caused him to lose face. Even if it was only in front of her, it was shameful for a man to lose control and allow a weak side of himself to come out. Because that was what slapping her had been, a weakness. He despised men who hit women, and he'd done exactly that. She had brought it out of him.

"She tripped and fell," was what Doc Perry had said when Nigel returned from Indio to find Elizabeth in bed and the servants milling about as if their anthill had been kicked over. Nigel had seen Elizabeth fall against the chair but had thought nothing of it. He had come home expecting either a sulky or oversolicitous wife. He had not expected her to be in a sickbed with a gloomy doctor delivering bad news while the Norringtons and Elizabeth's lady's maid avoided looking at him.

However, the old Indian woman, he noticed, had skewered him with what he supposed was the Indian equivalent of the evil eye.

He didn't care. He had expected to come home and return to his maps and plans for irrigation. But now, with Elizabeth pretending to be an invalid and a pall of gloom hanging over the house, he was going to have to play a part everyone was expecting—the anxious husband—when his energies should go into building the plantation.

Why did there have to be so much drama in the world?

He needed to think about their situation. Nigel had always thought of other people in terms of how they could advance his own life. Any fellow he met, he would make an assessment to see if the man possessed anything of worth that would improve Nigel's lot—whether it was money or skills or knowledge or even just an amusing manner to while away an otherwise boring afternoon. With Elizabeth it had been easy—she had wealth, social standing, and beauty to make a fine contribution to his own image and ease of living. And the seduction had been blessedly simple and quick.

But now things had gotten complicated. She was showing a trait of contrariness and he wasn't pleased with that. She still had her poise and beauty and her own fat trust fund, and someday she would inherit the Van Linden fortune. But she had stepped out of bounds and now he had to push her back in.

Elizabeth's hair hung loose over her shoulders. Releasing her hand, Nigel reached up and stroked the long blond hair a few times, then he gathered a hank of it into his fingers and gave it a tug. "You will do as I say from now on. Do I make myself clear?"

When she didn't answer, he tugged again, harder, jerking her head to the side. "Do you understand?"

"I understand," she whispered.

"Nothing is going to hinder my plans to build my plantation. I have enough to deal with what with Indians and competitors and incompetent workers. I cannot have a headstrong wife foiling me at every turn. Do you understand?"

She didn't answer fast enough. He pulled her hair again and she winced. "Yes," she said. "I understand."

"Don't make me lose my temper again. It's your job to be vigilant and to obey. I want a son. I need an heir. Otherwise, what is the purpose of building an empire? So don't provoke me again, am I perfectly understood?"

She nodded woodenly.

Nigel thought for a moment, searching her face, her voice, her manner for signs of resistance. "I mean it, Elizabeth. I will not tolerate disrespect. Not from people, not from animals."

He fell silent to let his meaning sink in and, as it did, as Elizabeth saw the glacial patina come into his eyes and heard the coldness in his voice, she started to tremble. Her stomach grew tight and started to heave. But she hadn't eaten in three days. There was nothing to come up.

"Yes," he said. "I'm talking about Button. He ruined my slacks. Worse, he caused people to laugh. Our guests laughed at me, Elizabeth— me, Baron Stullwood. And then I was forced to laugh at myself, to show that I am a good sport. I couldn't tolerate such an animal in the house."

His voice went far away. How could he be talking like that, Elizabeth wondered, while just outside the window, ruby-throated humming-birds hovered among bright yellow jasmine?

"So you see, Elizabeth," Nigel said as he stroked her neck and pressed a finger to her throat, painfully, "I am a man of my word."

Elizabeth sat in motionless shock as the meaning of what he had said slowly sunk in. He spoke in such a matter-of-fact tone that, surely, he wasn't saying what it sounded like he was saying. She shivered and shivered. She wanted to scream. There was too much sunlight. Nightmares were always cast in darkness. She found her voice. "But . . ." she began, barely able to work her lips. "What did . . . where is he?"

"The dog?" Nigel shrugged. "Long gone from here, that's for sure."

The trembling grew stronger. Oh God, oh God!

Button!

He rose from the bed and said, "So keep that in mind should you decide to defy me again." He looked down at her for a moment and then suddenly, for good measure, grabbed her hair and kissed her so hard that she made a strangled sound in her throat. He forced her lips apart and thrust his tongue deeply into her mouth until she gagged. Then he roughly let go and said, "You taste awful."

At the doorway he paused and said, "I am going into Los Angeles tomorrow and when I return I want to see you out of this bed and in your proper role as my supportive and obedient wife. I think of myself as a fair-minded fellow, Elizabeth. But I have my limits. When someone crosses me, or underestimates me, well, that is a situation that needs to be corrected. I have to nip your disobedience in the bud because if it happens again, I can't predict how severely I might react."

* * *

The canary-yellow Stutz Bearcat ripped along the foothill road, sending up clouds of dust and dirt. It was impatience and annoyance that caused Nigel to speed.

He ran his fingers through his hair and tried not to think about Elizabeth, lying in her bed, weak and unattractive. She not only annoyed him, she caused him to be distracted, made him dissatisfied even. Nigel didn't like being at the mercy of his emotions. Emotions were a tool, to be used as needed, to be enjoyed, or to be dominated, as the situation called for it. But never to be a man's master.

Now that he thought about the whole incident, apart from the fact that the child might have been a son, Nigel was in a way glad it happened. It freed him from the pretense of being in love with her. He had needed the masquerade to pull off the seduction and then to win the father over with the aim to getting power of attorney over Elizabeth's trust fund. Nigel had that now. Still, he would proceed cautiously and not touch her money just yet, saving it for emergencies. Besides, he rather enjoyed the challenge of establishing the plantation entirely on his own, with his own cleverness and resources. A man living off his wife's money struck Nigel as somehow weak and effeminate.

He drove hatless, to feel the desert wind in his hair. Putting Elizabeth from his thoughts, he released a shout and divested himself of annoyance and impatience. He wouldn't let petty grievances spoil his fun. He had never felt so alive, so electrified. Twenty-five years old and on his way to owning this valley.

It was a great time to be alive! Post-war Americans were eagerly spending, and the economy was spiraling upward at a record clip. Production was up. New consumer goods, such as radios and electric refrigerators and faster cars, were driving corporate profits through the roof. He had read in the financial pages that his father-in-law's steel company was operating so efficiently that Van Linden had been able to reduce the workday from twelve hours to eight, to employ ten thousand additional workers, to raise wages, and still the company showed an increase in profits!

Everyone was enjoying a higher standard of living, thanks in large part to the new credit system of installment buying. Gone were the days of paying the entire price up front. Ordinary folks could now afford luxury goods by paying for them a little at a time—even if it did mean they were adding forty percent of the cost to the ticket. It was no wonder that with such prosperity, the stock market should be enjoying a soaring boom as thousands of "little people" now invested and earned overnight windfalls.

Nigel had no doubt that such a mushrooming economy would only continue to expand and spiral upward. Wall Street doomsayers who predicted that a big crash was coming were talking out of their arses. America was a nation of happy consumers, and with the new credit system—"Pay as you ride," the automakers declared—money was going to continue to move and flow and carry the country forward.

Which meant that with consumerism on the rise, people could afford to treat themselves to luxuries previously beyond their reach— exotic Arabian dates!

He laughed out loud to think that just one year ago he had been in rainy old Derbyshire receiving news that his father had robbed him of his birthright. At the time, it had been like a knife in the heart. But now, Nigel realized it was the best thing that could have happened to him. Otherwise, he never would have left and he would not now be carving a brand-new kingdom for himself.

As he raced up behind a one-horse wagon hauling tall milk cans, an elderly man at the reins, Nigel blasted his horn. The horse reared, nearly tipping the wagon and sending milk cans to topple and spill. Nigel swerved around the wagon and sped on ahead, sending grit and gravel into the old man's eyes.

Why stop at dates? Nigel thought as the wind whipped his hair. With the thousands of available acres and plentiful water runoff from the Santa Rosa and San Jacinto Mountains, there was no limit to his vision. Figs! Avocados! Apricots! Almonds! Spread the name of Stullwood Plantations across America. Fruits from his farms finding their way to millions of breakfast tables.

He laughed to think that he was managing it all on the meager inheritance from his father. He might have to go into the red and juggle a few loans and debts before his enterprises saw profits, but Nigel was determined to become that peculiarly American breed: the self-made man. And there was always his safety net should he need it, Elizabeth's trust fund.

A scarlet flash brought Nigel out of his thoughts. Squinting into the sun, he saw up on the right, on a plateau that overlooked the desert, just a few miles past the boundary of the Indian reservation, a long, sleek automobile parked in front of a construction project.

Nigel had passed the site before, on his way to and from Indio. Local gossip said that a house was being built on that spot, owned by rich movie people who were looking to get away from the Beverly Hills social scene—a "hideaway" mansion, as it were. Producer Jack Lamont and his movie actress wife, Zora DuBois.

Nigel had only ever seen Model-Ts, trucks, and work crews up there. But the striking red Cadillac limousine could only belong to the owners. Deciding to make the acquaintance of his new neighbors— and thanking God that people closer to his own kind were moving into a valley full of Indians and common white folks—he pulled off the main road, sped up the gravel drive, and came to a halt in front of the half-finished, three-story house that overlooked the Coachella Valley.

It was something out of antebellum South, a gothic wedding cake with Greek pillars and porticoes and balconies—a true plantation home, Nigel thought, a far sight more fitting to his personal purposes than the Spanish monstrosity that was La Alma. It occurred to him that part of the La Alma property encompassed a foothill plateau much like this one, rising behind the Spanish-style house, with a view that looked out over Palm Springs and the desert. He got out of his car and went up the marble steps without acknowledging the limousine driver who sat behind the wheel of the Cadillac, smoking a cigarette. As he felt the weight and grandeur of the big house settle around him, Nigel toyed with the idea of building such a home for himself.

He walked through the entry where there were as yet no doors and found himself beneath a rotunda that made his footsteps echo off the marble floor. Directly ahead, a grand staircase swept away to floors above. To his right, a room lined with shelves awaiting books and trophies. To his left, what could only be a ballroom awaiting glittering chandeliers and musicians on the far stage.

It was Sunday, so there was no work going on, but the air was filled with the smell of brick dust, mortar, and paint. As he strolled through empty rooms, some finished, some half done, opening doors, eyeing gold fixtures, admiring the quality craftsmanship, he came into an enormous kitchen, where a stocky little man was squinting over blueprints spread out over the counter.

He looked up. "Who the hell are you?"

Nigel held out his hand. "Nigel Barnstable, ninth Baron Stullwood."

"Jack Lamont." They shook. "Baron, huh? You some kind of English lord?"

"You might say that." Lamont was pudgy with ginger hair, a scrubby orange moustache, and thick, round eyeglasses. In England, Jack Lamont would be approaching Lord Stullwood with hat in hand, obsequious, eyes cast down, begging for an audience. But in the months that Nigel had been living in Southern California, he had found that a new kind of aristocracy ruled America. Britain might be bogged down with titles and leaky mansions and money that was so old it had disappeared, but Hollywood had spawned a whole new aristocracy based on wealth and fame and nothing at all to do with blood or lineage. A whole new breed the likes of which the world had never seen before, a breed not unlike himself.

"I live just a few miles west of here. In Palm Springs."

Lamont removed his glasses, inspected them, then replaced them on his nose. "Say, you the folks that bought that big Spanish-style house? Desert spirit or something?"

"The very one."

"Zora and I looked into buying that place, you know, to get away from the hectic life and rest up between pictures. But my wife wanted something that was all her own. I see you've planted some trees."

Nigel gave the man a look and thought: Let's see you call it "some trees" by the time I'm finished with this valley.

A woman materialized in the archway that led to the dining room. "Do I hear an English accent?" she said.

Nigel couldn't help but stare. He had never seen a woman in trousers before. It gave him a moment of shock, and then he decided he liked the look. She had slender legs that flared into a very fetching set of hips. The blouse that was tucked in at the waist strained over a bosom he tried not to linger over. And then he found himself caught by a dazzling smile with the deepest dimples he had ever seen on a pair of cheeks. She had the thinnest arching eyebrows he had ever seen, painted on most likely, but other than that, no makeup. Her skin was very white with a dusting of freckles over the nose. She had big eyes, wide and bold. Her reddish-gold hair stood out in frightful curls, as if something had scared her.

He returned to the smile that was fetching and flirtatious. "Yes," he said. "I'm English."

She came in, and he realized with a second shock that she was barefoot. There was a sauciness to her step that made him think of girls who teased but never delivered. He remembered that she was supposed to be a movie actress. But she didn't look familiar so he decided she couldn't be very famous.

"My wife," Lamont said. "Zora DuBois."

"How do you do?" Nigel said, receiving a handshake that was a little strong for a woman. Her eyes never left his face as she said, "Pleased to meet you, English."

He couldn't place her accent. Somewhere around New York City, he would guess.

"Excuse me a minute," Jack Lamont said. "I have to check on something." He gathered up the blueprints and left.

"Hey, English," Zora said as soon as her husband was gone. "Ever been to Brooklyn?" Her eyes flashing, pupils dilating.

He laughed. "Can't say as I have." He had met her type before. Got her kicks by knowing hubby was in the next room and could walk in on them any minute. He had to confess, it was a game he rather liked playing himself.

"Have you seen any of my movies?"

She seemed to be daring him. He wondered where this was leading. "I'm afraid I haven't."

To his surprise, she took no offense and, in fact, sent him a cryptic smile.

Before she could ask him something else, Nigel turned the tables and said, "Do you like riddles?"

"Depends." She leaned against the kitchen counter and folded her arms under her breasts, as if, Nigel couldn't help thinking, to make them look bigger.

He thought for a moment, tilting his head, then said, "It is greater than God and more evil than the devil. The poor have it, the rich need it, and if you eat it you'll die. What is it?"

She looked up at the ceiling, arching a creamy white neck, then came back to meet his eyes. He saw challenge there and a mind at work. She doesn't want people to think she's smart, Nigel thought, intrigued. She is putting on a façade. "I don't know," she said. "What is it?"

He debated withholding the answer, or giving the wrong one, to catch her at her game of deception. But they weren't alone. There was the husband in the next room, so he said, "Nothing."

She gave him a little-girl frown and formed her lips into a pout.

"That's no answer," she said.

He laughed. "Yes, it is. Nothing is greater than God, nothing is more evil than the devil, the poor have nothing, the rich need nothing, and if you eat nothing you'll die."

Their eyes locked again and just as he thought she was going to grow bored and quit the game, she surprised him by saying, "You're wrong. I happen to know I'm greater than God, and I've met men more evil than the devil. Who cares what the poor have? And the rich always need something. And if you have nothing to eat, then drink champagne. Marie Antoinette said that."

Nigel leveled his gaze at her, taking in the girl-next-door freckles, the lively green eyes, the eyebrows that he could almost swear were drawn on. Suddenly he wanted to stump her. "All right, then, answer me this: You walk at a pace of three miles an hour. You leave your house and walk for forty-five minutes, turn right and walk another half hour, you stop to rest for fifteen minutes, and finish your walk an hour later. How far have you traveled?"

Without a beat, she said, "To Macy's, for shopping."

He leaned back and, affecting a nonchalant air, tried to figure her out. Either she was very stupid or she was very clever. Nigel decided that he was going to find out, and have fun doing it.

Lamont came back into the kitchen. "Seeing as how we're about to be neighbors, you'll have to come to our housewarming party," he said as he took his wife's arm and they all walked out. "We expect to move in in a few months."

As he drove away, Nigel smiled to himself and amended his previous goal: Not only was he going to own this valley, he was going to have Zora DuBois as well.

*   *   *

"Is there any change?"

"None, Mr. McNeal, and we're all worried sick."

Cody knew that by "all," Miss Wilson meant the Norringtons and Doc Perry. Certainly not Nigel Barnstable. Cody had seen him drive off that morning in his flashy yellow car, no doubt racing to another meeting in Indio with date growers. Cody would wager that Barnstable hadn't even looked in on his ailing wife before he left.

"Her Ladyship won't eat. She won't leave her bed. And she's getting weaker by the day."

They were in the east wing, outside the master bedroom. "Mr. McNeal," Fiona said, "I understand that a miscarriage can be devastating. But I've known Her Ladyship for years. This is something more than depression. It's almost as if she blames herself for the accident. But it wasn't her fault. She tripped and fell. And . . ."

"And?"

She lowered her voice. "Whenever His Lordship visits her, Her Ladyship seems even sadder."

She didn't voice the rest. That she wondered what exactly had happened on that fateful afternoon when the staff were all enjoying their day off. Her Ladyship tripped and fell hard against the back of a chair, triggering the miscarriage. But why wasn't his Lordship showing more concern? Fiona would have expected him to be by his wife's side day and night. Instead, after brief visits with Elizabeth, he was out in his orchards, shouting orders, meeting with engineers, looking for places to drill wells, working himself ragged so that he came in late, ate a solitary supper, and went to bed. Did he blame himself for not being there when she fell?

"Dr. Perry was in just this morning, trying to coax her to drink one of his special tonics, but she won't. She says she just wants to be left alone."

"Well, that isn't an option," Cody said, turning to walk away.

"Where are you going?"

"To fix things."

* * *

Luisa was not surprised when Señor Cody came to her house with a request. She had been expecting it. He was a man who had lived with Indians; he knew about their special medicine.

"Will you do it, Mother?" he asked.

She saw the worry in his eyes, heard the concern in his voice. "It is not a sickness of the body, Señor, but of the spirit. White man's medicine will not help. She needs the spirits. Bring the Señora to us."

"Miss Wilson," Cody said when he returned to the bedroom. "I've arranged for the Indians to intervene. They have a treatment that will help your mistress."

"A treatment?" Fiona's eyes widened as she imagined barbaric Indian cures.

Cody went to the bedside where Elizabeth sat propped against satin pillows, a counterpane over her legs. She wore a white nightgown and her hair streamed in tangles over her shoulders. She was staring out the window, but she didn't appear to be looking at anything. Her eyes were blank. A sickness of the spirit, he thought. Her soul was in peril.

"Elizabeth," he said gently. "I'd like you to come somewhere with me."

"Not right now." She didn't look at him.

"Won't you trust me?"

She finally looked up, and he saw desolation in her eyes. "I trust you. I just don't want to go anywhere right now."

"Then it looks like I'm going to have to take you there."

Drawing back the counterpane, he slid an arm under her legs and behind her back and lifted her. "Please put me down," she said, but she didn't resist or struggle. She was shockingly weak.

He carried her through the house to the kitchen where Luisa Padilla was waiting. He turned to Fiona. "Miss Wilson, you have sat at your mistress's bedside for hours on end. You need your rest."

"But—"

"We will see to it that Mrs. Barnstable is made comfortable and is treated well."

Being used to taking orders, having followed orders all her life, Fiona Wilson said her first no. "I won't leave her Ladyship's side. She trusts in me. She relies on me. A poor companion I would be if I abandoned her in her most serious hour of need."

Cody glanced at Luisa Padilla, who gave a nod of consent.

"Everything will be all right," he said, and he walked out into the sunlight, Lady Elizabeth in his arms, Fiona immediately behind.

*　　*　　*

The women had prepared the pit by the time Cody arrived with Elizabeth.

Secluded among a cluster of mesquite trees on the reservation but away from the village, they had scooped and shaped a long hole in the ground, two feet deep and snug enough to hold Elizabeth's shape. A fire was going in a pit and when the coals died down, they were raked out and the hot sand beneath was poured into the bottom of the pit. The women then laid fragrant creosote branches and leaves over the hot sand. And then a blanket.

"Now you put the Señora in the pit," Luisa said.

Cody gently laid Elizabeth in it, and she sighed when she felt the warmth through the blanket. He positioned her head so that it was cushioned on the lip of the pit as if she were taking a leisurely bath. The women placed blankets over her, and more hot sand so that she was enveloped in a soothing heat.

"You go now," Luisa said to Cody, while the women arranged themselves in a circle around Elizabeth.

"I'm not leaving," he said.

"No, no! Forbidden for men to watch. You can stay," she said to Fiona. "But men cannot watch."

He sank to the ground next to Elizabeth and, crossing his legs, reached for her hand while Fiona took a seat next to him. "I'm staying right here," he said. "For as long as it takes."

Luisa exchanged a worried glance with the other women—would the medicine work if a man watched? It had never been done! Then she took her place in the circle and led the others in a chant. It was a soothing, pleasant chant, sung in the old Cahuilla tongue, sacred words that were spoken in this valley long before Spaniards brought the words of Spain and Mexico. Ancient words delivered in a lilting melody that almost seemed to make the overhead mesquite branches quiver.

When an hour had passed, Luisa went inside a nearby hut and emerged with a ceramic cup. Kneeling next to Elizabeth and sliding her arm under her neck, Luisa brought the cup to Elizabeth's lips. "Drink, Señora. This is healing medicine. Healing the spirit. The spirits will know you have this in you, and they will come to you and mend your soul."

"What is it?" Cody asked.

"It is *kikisulem* tea, made from the three end-leaves of a plant used only in women's medicine. We have surrounded her with good magic. She will dream now, and when she wakes up, she will begin to heal." She smiled. "You are a good man, Señor. You are forbidden to be here, but you stay."

He returned the smile but kept his eyes on Elizabeth. "How did you get to be so smart, old mother? At school?"

"I never went to school," she said, also watching Elizabeth. "A priest taught me to read and write Spanish. When I became old enough to think my own thoughts, I knew I had to learn English. That was hard."

Elizabeth moaned. "What is it, daughter?" Luisa asked.

"My baby . . ."

"Your child lives now in Telmikish. He is with good and kind spirits in a beautiful land in the east protected by golden mountains. You will seem him again someday. This life is but temporary. The future life, and your child, awaits you. Sleep now, daughter."

While Elizabeth slept and the women murmured a continuous, soft chant, the sun dipped behind the mountains and long shadows crept across the desert. Luisa studied the face of the man who sat with the Señora, a man not her husband, a man with his own troubled soul, whose ancestors lay far to the north among pines and snow. "There is nothing to fear, Señor," she said. "When we die we return to Mukat. We go to Telmikish where there is no sickness or sorrow. This world is just to raise children in. Telmikish, the next world, is the real world and it lasts forever."

"I hope you are right, Mother," he said.

"We are all brothers and sisters, Señor. We are all related. At the time the sun in the sky was created, people on earth were all the same color. But some people were afraid of the new sun so they ran away and they grew pale, and became white people. But the children of Mukat were not afraid of the sun and we stayed close, which is why we are brown."

As darkness fell, Cody frequently looked back at La Alma, its lights seen through Barnstable's date palms, half expecting the see the yellow car pull into the drive, expecting to see Nigel come striding across the plain to demand to know what the Indians were doing with his wife.

Luisa brought out more tea and this time handed it around. When she gave Fiona a tin cup of the brew, and she saw the Englishwoman's dubious expression, she smiled and said, "Lipton's tea. From Lardner's store."

Fiona and Cody consumed three sweetened cups of it while the women chanted into the night. Luisa brought blankets out and passed them around. "We sleep now while the Señora walks in the spirit world."

But Cody knew he couldn't sleep. While Luisa and the others wrapped themselves in their blankets and curled up on the ground, he continued to sit, holding Elizabeth's hand, with Fiona vigilant at his side.

As he watched her, he felt emotions tug at his heart, determined to make him feel. He was taken back to a Montana farm where he was in the stable, sitting up through the night with a sick colt. The small, fragile animal lay on its side, panting, while Cody sat on the hay, the colt's head in his lap. He was sixteen and crying, and afraid his father or one of the farm hands would come in and see him weeping like a girl. But Cody wasn't a man yet then, he hadn't yet left for Horsethief Creek in Colorado, where his youthful heart would learn hard lessons about life.

Elizabeth's hand lay in his, small and pale and defenseless, like a newborn creature. Never had Cody felt so violently protective of a life. And another, more turbulent emotion raged in his blood. The urge to kill the man who had done this to her. Uncertain that he could control himself, Cody had avoided crossing paths with Nigel Barnstable. Luckily, the man was preoccupied with a massive irrigation project that kept him either out on his many acres, or attending meetings in Indio and Riverside. But Cody, feeling the fury bubbling just below the surface, knew that it wouldn't take much for him to give Nigel the thrashing he deserved.

As Cody watched her eyelids flutter in a kikisulem dream, he wondered what wondrous landscapes filled her head.

Elizabeth was surrounded by heat, a warmth that enveloped her like a tender embrace. Fog, all around. Deep silence. But she wasn't afraid. Through the mist, a hand reached for her, hard and callused. She delivered herself into it, feeling safe, protected.

And then she was walking through a meadow surrounded by forest. Her heart was light, her spirits buoyant. She had let her hair down, to lift in the mountain breeze as she strolled among tall grasses and spring flowers. She felt deliciously warm and at peace, and a delightful fragrance filled her head. Although she was alone, she felt the hand holding hers. She didn't question it. The phantom hand made her feel secure. It was strong and rough, the hand of a man who roped cattle and broke horses and worked on ranges and built cabins out of logs. The hand of a cowboy, a drifter who looked for himself in ghost towns.

Suddenly, a hissing sound, like steam escaping from a broken pipe. Elizabeth stopped and looked around. A cloud sailed across the sun, darkening the day. The hissing grew louder. She turned in a slow circle until she saw—

Elizabeth gasped. Directly in her path lay a snake, coiled like a rope, its head standing on a tall neck, its tail rattling behind. A pattern of red diamonds decorated its fat body.

She slowly backed away. She turned and started to run when there it was again, in her path, coiled, ready to strike. She froze. The flat head, shaped like an arrowhead, was pointed straight at her, forked tongue licking in and out.

The hissing sound from the rattles grew louder until it was deafening. Her heart raced. She knew that if she turned, it would be there again. That no matter which way she turned, the deadly snake would be poised to strike, to kill her.

As cold panic gripped her, Elizabeth did not see the dark gray shape materialize at her side. *The large, muscular body, gray shaggy coat, the trembling haunches, the golden eyes and alert ears. It fixed on the snake, with Elizabeth in between.*

The wolf dropped down, eyes on the rattler, his ears flattened back, his brown muzzle wrinkled in a menacing snarl, fangs bared. The powerful body tensed up. Elizabeth couldn't move. And then he sprang. She screamed. The wolf's jaws clamped down on the snake, his growls loud and unearthly as he swung the snake this way and that, whipping it back and forth as it writhed in his mouth. The snake lashed out, striking, striking, trying to sink its fangs into the wolf. The wolf tossed his head violently from side to side, his muzzle dripping with blood as the rattler fought back.

Elizabeth held her breath as she watched the battle. She cried out when the snake struck the wolf on the forehead. But the wolf didn't stop. His forehead running red from two punctures, he continued to shake the rattler.

The snake repeatedly struck the wolf on the head, the neck, the shoulders. "Stop!" *she screamed, horrified at the sight of the blood streaming from the puncture wounds. But the wolf wouldn't let go.*

"You're killing him!" Elizabeth screamed.

"Get her out of there!" Cody shouted, getting onto his knees, yanking the blankets away. Taking her by the arms, he pulled her up from the pit, drew her into his arms and held her tight as she sobbed hysterically against his chest. "It was killing him!" she sobbed over and over.

"It was a dream," he said. "Just a dream, Elizabeth."

She grew quiet in his arms. Out on the desert, a coyote called to the moon while, overhead, three meteors, one after the other, traced silver streaks across the black sky.

Luisa said solemnly to Cody and Fiona, "She is not yet healed. But she knows now what has broken her spirit. With this knowledge, she must go to a beautiful place and stay there and pray to whatever Creator she worships. She must ask him for help. Speak her heart. Pour all her worries and sorrows into the Creator's ears, whether he is Mukat or Jesus, and he will listen and tell the Señora how to heal herself."

CHAPTER SEVENTEEN

HE WAS IN THE corral, saddling up his mare.

Dressed in the usual black shirt and black jeans, boots with spurs, sleeves rolled up to expose muscular forearms as he cinched the saddle. The other horse, Elizabeth noticed, was already saddled and tethered to a post. The spring air was lukewarm with a bite in the wind. The horses in the paddocks stood in what sunshine they could find while the morning peace was disturbed by the whine of the grindstone in the ramada where the ranch hands did harness and tack repair.

"Good morning, Mr. McNeal," she said as she approached him. "Are you ready?"

"I am. And please remember, I'm not an expert rider. Weekends in Central Park."

He led her to the other horse, a beautiful Appaloosa that was black with a "blanket" covering her hind quarters—white with black spots. "According to the ranch hands, Star belonged to the previous owner's daughter. So she's broke for a lady. She's easy to handle," Cody said. "Won't spook or bolt. And she's a good trail rider. Shall we go to the beautiful place Mrs. Padilla recommended?"

Elizabeth had been living inside herself ever since the Indian medicine had sent her the vision of the snake and the wolf. Outwardly, she went about life as if everything were normal, overseeing the seeding of a vegetable garden, talking to local women about organizing a lending library, making changes around the house to modernize it— mechanical activities to keep her body occupied while her mind worked to understand her new situation. Confining herself to her house, however, and working at mechanical tasks, pretending that nothing had happened, that everything was okay, wasn't working. Elizabeth felt the pain and despair festering inside herself as she and Nigel went about their daily routines in polite pretense. But he had instilled fear in her. He had killed her dog. He had threatened her with physical abuse. She could not go on like this.

So she had to get away—away from the walls and heavy furniture and pretense of normalcy, away especially from the fear that dogged her from morning until night. However, beyond the radius of a few miles from the house, Elizabeth was unfamiliar with her surroundings.

"You have suffered soul loss," Luisa had said. "Now you must go to a beautiful place and cry your heart out to your Creator. Pray to your God and then listen. That is the most important part. Once you have prayed, listen. Put all thoughts from your mind, and answers will come to you."

But where was a beautiful place? Elizabeth had been in Palm Springs six months now and knew little of the area beyond the town limits. "Ask Mr. McNeal," Fiona had suggested. "I understand he has been exploring the region extensively."

Elizabeth stroked the soft hair on the horse's neck, thinking of poor Button. It felt good to touch an animal again. "Let's go to the beautiful place," she said.

He helped her up. Elizabeth hooked her right leg around the saddle's horn so that she rode sidesaddle, and Cody handed her the reins.

Elizabeth wore a straw hat with a wide brim. Although the day was not hot, the desert sun was bright. She wore a white blouse and a long white skirt, and Wilson added a shawl, in case Her Ladyship caught a chill. The wind in the desert was never predictable and could blow hot or cold, especially in the spring.

They left the corral and followed the dirt track that ran alongside the fifty-tree grove where workers were high on ladders pollinating the female trees with white powdery pollen collected from the male date palm. Farther along lay the new irrigation canals Nigel had had dug from the Mesquite Canyon stream to his orchards, diverting water from the Indians' small gardens and crops.

They rode silently through the town, past shops and fields, and houses set back from the lane. At the edge of town they passed the one-room schoolhouse on Ocotillo Avenue. Next to it stood the small

Protestant chapel with a white steeple, large enough to hold twenty congregants. Across the street, on a dirt lot, the Catholic priest from Banning held Mass.

They passed a new building under construction. The sign said, Monte Vista Hotel. Farther down the road, another new guest establishment had just opened, Sunshine Court. More rooms to accommodate visitors to the desert.

Elizabeth watched Star's shiny head bob up and down. Up ahead, Cody rode his black mare. The day was perfect, the sky a deep blue, the breeze mild and refreshing. People in buggies and wagons, in the occasional motor car, and on horseback called out and waved. She and Cody waved back. But Elizabeth was apprehensive. That morning, Nigel had left for Indio but there was no predicting when he might return. Nevertheless, she had to get away from the confines of the house. Too many questions hounded her. The things Nigel had said to her three days after the tragedy, when he had pulled her hair and then violently kissed her. What should she do with this new turn in her life? How could she live with this knowledge, with this changed Nigel who was suddenly a stranger? Should she give up on the marriage or must she fight to save it? What did this mean for her wedding vows?

Luisa Padilla, who had lived here all her life, seemed to think the desert held the answers.

Presently they came through a grove of cottonwood trees and a broad vista opened before them.

Elizabeth gasped. The desert, normally a yellow gray, had suddenly been laid with carpets of dazzling purple-pink verbena. Pale yellow primroses by the hundreds opened their delicate petals to the sun. Clumps of ocotillo cactus, as far as the eye could see, displayed their blazing red "tongues."

Cody reined his horse at the base of Eagle Canyon from where Elizabeth saw that the mountain slopes, composed of granite, had by some magic blossomed with thousands of golden flowers of incense-bush and huge clusters of heavenly-scented purple and white heliotrope in heady numbers.

And the birds! They must be in the thousands, chirping, tweeting, calling out in their myriad songs. Elizabeth had heard that the Banning Pass was a channel for migratory birds that came to Palm Springs every year to feed off the desert flowers, but she had no idea they would be in such colorful profusion. Especially the precious, tiny humming-birds that stayed in constant motion in flashes of crimson and emerald.

Elizabeth's lips parted as she stared at the breathtaking landscape. The colors! The beauty. "I didn't know the desert could bloom like this."

"The desert is full of surprises," Cody said as they sat in their saddles. "Cahuilla territory has high mountains and wooded valleys, rocky canyons, wide stretches of desert, oases of palm trees and cotton-woods, rushing mountain streams and sky-blue pools. This country has many faces."

He turned to smile at her. "Do you want to hear an interesting legend about this valley? It's said that five hundred years ago a violent earthquake opened a rift from the Salton Sea to the Pacific Ocean, causing a massive tidal surge that filled the valley like a basin of water. The Cahuilla talk of their ancestors sighting a massive brown beast with white wings gliding on the water. Close in, they saw that it was a vessel of some kind, with spires and ropes and men hanging in the rigging. Supposedly the lost explorers of this galleon had sailed around the impromptu lake, searching for an exit, probably wondering if they had found an entrance to the new, mysterious continent. And then the tide had carried them back out, no doubt to return to Spain to report of their discovery of a new land, which the ship's captain christened California, a name derived from a fictional paradise peopled by black Amazonian women and recorded in a 1510 work entitled *The Adventures of Esplandián*. California was said to be a remote land inhabited by griffins and other strange beasts, and rich in gold. But later explorers claimed that California was unpredictable and shifted shapes and therefore could never be conquered."

Elizabeth tried to imagine the valley filled with water, turning it into a sea. "Could that possibly be true?"

He grinned. "That's the charm of legends, isn't it?" Cody dismounted first, then he came around to help Elizabeth to the ground. His hands on her waist, he took her weight as she slipped out of the saddle. She put her hands on his chest and they stood for a frozen instant, bodies touching, their faces inches apart.

The moment stretched as they looked into each other's eyes, then Elizabeth whispered, "You know the truth, don't you, about my accident? I had a suspicion that Luisa overheard what happened. And I believe she would have told you."

She waited. He said nothing. But she knew that Mr. McNeal knew her secret. She could see it in his eyes. But he was a gentleman and would never tell. Luisa also knew the truth, and she too would keep the secret, as would Doc Perry. But Fiona Wilson and the others believed Elizabeth's story that she had tripped on the living room steps and had fallen against a hard-backed chair.

She could never tell anyone what really happened. If the truth somehow reached her parents, it would devastate her mother. So it would remain a secret between Luisa, Mr. McNeal, and herself. A strange and terrible secret binding three strangers.

"I was hoping for a girl," she said now, bringing up the subject for the first time as they stood close together. "I had her all fleshed out in my mind. I knew her thoughts, her dreams. I was going to encourage her to grow up to be a unique individual, to follow whatever path she chose. I pictured her as a baby, then a child, then an adult. Losing her was like . . . losing a person I had known all my life."

She stepped back. There, it was out. Elizabeth had spoken her first words on the subject. Now she could begin the fight to reclaim her life.

Cody stayed silent for a while, then reached into a saddlebag and brought out a pair of binoculars. "Let me show you the flowers."

They walked along the crystal clear stream where fish swam in and out of river rocks, and cattails grew in profusion. As Elizabeth watched how the sunlight danced on the sparkling water, she thought of the man at her side, the ever-present black Stetson on his head. His long, black duster coat hooked behind his holstered six-shooter.

When Cody saw where her eyes were, he said, "Does my gun make you nervous?" He pulled his coat over the pistol to hide it.

"I'm not used to being around firearms."

"They're a necessity where I come from. Do you think you can find your way back by yourself?"

"I beg your pardon?"

"I'll take you to a beautiful place where you can explore it with these," he said, holding up the glasses. "And then I'll leave you alone, if you can get back all right."

"Leave me?" she said.

"I think these things are best done alone."

She felt a sudden, mild grip of panic. "I would prefer that you stayed, Mr. McNeal, if you don't mind."

He smiled. "Only if you call me Cody. I'm only twenty-eight, years away from being Mr. McNeal. All right, I'll stay. I can be quiet," he said, adding, "if I really try."

They arrived at a shady spot, and Cody took out a handkerchief to brush leaves off a large boulder for Elizabeth to sit on while he took himself a few strides away, pretending to interest himself in mushrooms growing beneath a green mesquite bush. It would give Elizabeth the space and silence that she needed.

There were three things she couldn't put from her mind. The first was Nigel striking her a second time. Not that the first time was pardonable or deserved, but anyone can commit a rash act in the heat of the moment. It was repeating it that she couldn't get over. The first time he slapped her, Nigel should have been shocked by his own actions and been immediately remorseful. Instead, he had done it again.

The second thing she couldn't let go of was that he had gotten into his car and driven off. She had fallen into the living room and slammed heavily against a chair and she had cried out. A loving Nigel, no matter how angry in the moment of the quarrel, would have rushed to her aid. Instead, he had walked out and driven off to his appointment in Indio. The key word, she knew, was "loving." But he wasn't a loving Nigel. A waiting hydrologist came first.

The third thought in her mind was barely tolerable, but she couldn't put it away, and even if she could, she would have felt as if she were betraying Button. So she had to dwell on his fate, as unpleasant as it was. Had Nigel truly done something to the little dog or was he just using the dog's disappearance as a chance to hurt her? No, she decided. That was wishful thinking. Nigel had done something to Button and Elizabeth couldn't bear to think what. They had searched for days after he vanished and found no trace. "Got eaten by coyotes," was the general consensus. Unless Nigel had killed Button first which, in a way, might have been a mercy instead of abandoning the little poodle out in the savage wilderness.

One of these three hauntings in her mind was burdensome enough, but all three kept her awake at night and drained her. It was like a shouting match up there, with each mindful thought insisting on being the worst. A woman should only be plagued by one worrisome thought at a time. Three at once made her feel, at times, as if she were being pulled apart.

The worst of it was she had no one to talk to about it. Certainly not about the things Nigel had said and the way he treated her the night he came into her bedroom and he told her he was going to turn her into an obedient wife. No one knew about that, and no one was going to. Nigel's treatment of her made her feel ashamed, even though she knew it shouldn't. But the shame was there, and there was nothing Elizabeth could do about it.

Her throat started to close up and tears stung her eyes. She didn't want to cry in front of Mr. McNeal, but she couldn't help herself. The crying came easily, like breathing, and it seemed to help a little. Elizabeth couldn't grasp the enormity of her loss. Not just the baby, but she had lost Nigel as well—it was as if he had walked out of her life, as if he had announced he didn't want her anymore and was leaving a stranger in his place to keep her in line. "I have to show you who's boss." This, from the man who, not long ago, had said, "You are my goddess. I worship at your feet."

So much loss was not to be measured or reckoned with but simply endured. Loss, by its nature, was permanent. It was never going to change, so why would the mourning of that loss change it? There was no mending it or making it right. Loss was so complete. A final thing, and it was hard to come up with a healing for something so final. It was like death.

Yes, she thought as she looked back down the way they had come. From her vantage point, she could see the desert stretching away to distant mountains. Something has died and will never come back. I am in deep, powerful mourning, not just for the almost-baby, but for the loss of a man I loved, the loss of a dream. Elizabeth knew beyond a doubt that Nigel as she had known and loved him was never coming back—if he had existed in the first place. It didn't matter. In her heart and mind, the loving Nigel had been real, her love for him had been real, and now he was gone; therefore, her grief was very real.

Elizabeth knew that others knew she was grieving over the loss of the child. They had no idea the depth and extent of her grief, that it involved a lost husband. At least widows got to mourn; they got sympathy and special considerations. She was a widow without those luxuries; she was a widow and no one knew it.

She turned into the wind that swept up from the desert and closed her eyes. The wind felt old, as if it had traveled thousands of years and over thousands of miles just to kiss her face.

She thought of the healing properties of the desert. People came out here to let the clear, dry air ease their lungs and the hot mineral springs restore their bodies. But the desert was panacea for the soul as well. Here was an uncluttered corner of the world where everything worked on a precise schedule at a preordained pace, in patterns and routines created back before time—a reassuring clockwork that reminded a person that, despite tragedy and loss, this faithful old world continued on in a predictable, comforting way.

She opened her eyes and looked out at the gray-yellow vista that some people thought of as a wilderness. The desert is prehistoric, she thought, and mankind was born in the vast spaces of East Africa, back when man was short and stooped and just learning the value of an opposable thumb. Back then, as now, an endless, flat, uncluttered wilderness allowed a man, or a woman, to find his thoughts, to spend time with them, to sort and analyze the myriad ideas, observations, and suppositions that percolated to the surface. In the desert, you could figure yourself out, figure others out, too, if you had a mind to. "I will have to show you who's boss." It became a refrain in her mind. It filled her head and she couldn't get it out. So as she mulled it over out here in the desert, those words Nigel had said as he towered over her, a revelation about herself made an entrance into her mind: I left the sphere of one controlling person and stepped into the sphere of another controlling person.

This thought threatened to close in on her. Suddenly she wanted to hear another voice, reassure herself that she was not alone here in the desert. Cody. She liked the sound of his voice. It was deep and mellow and made her think of men who sat on their horses through the night, watching over cattle to keep the herd quiet and calm. She wanted to hear about his life, about someone else's existence so that she could be reminded that there was a bigger world than the one that was Elizabeth Barnstable.

"How is it that you have no family, Mr. McNeal?" she asked now, recalling what he had told her of himself at the Christmas party.

He looked at her for a moment, trying to discern if she really wanted to hear about his life when she was supposed to be mending her own. But she had asked a question and it was polite to answer, so he said, "My father died ten years ago, and my mother died when I was a baby."

"Your father raised you alone?"

"He hired an Indian woman from the nearby reservation. She was a member of the Blackfeet tribe. She was my wet nurse for two years. She breast-fed me along with her infant son. She was the only mother I ever knew. Her name was Sinopa, which means Fox Kitten."

Cody's voice was deep and calming. His speech slow. He spoke like a man used to finding ways to fill his hours on the lonely prairie. He took a faded photograph out of his shirt pocket and came over to show it to her. "This is us."

Elizabeth saw a man and a boy standing in front of a farmhouse, grinning beneath the Montana sky. Standing slightly to one side, an Indian woman in fringed buckskins. In the distance, a paddock with cattle, a few horses, what looked like local Indians working as ranch hands. The picture gave the impression of days of hope and happiness, and a bright future.

She handed it back. "I'm sorry you lost your father. You must miss him and your home."

"That I do," he said softly, as he replaced the picture in his pocket.

Elizabeth suddenly didn't know what to say in response to such an unexpected baring of private sadness. So she said, "I love the story you gave me as a Christmas present. When did you start writing?"

Cody sat next to her on the boulder and looked at his hands. "My father taught me to read and write. I chafed at my lessons until one afternoon as I was practicing writing the alphabet, all of a sudden it made sense. I discovered that I could combine letters and make words. And then I discovered I could string words together and make sentences. I would sit by the fire in evenings and listen to my father's stories. When he was done, I always felt sad. The story was over. The words that floated on the air had vanished. It left me feeling empty. And then I started writing them down and I wasn't sad anymore because I still had the stories and could reread them."

Elizabeth saw the shadow of a red-tailed hawk swoop along the ground, startling a jackrabbit and sending it running for cover. It was a placid setting, private and sylvan, and far from the cares and woes of the real world. Elizabeth thought she could sit there forever.

"I was eleven when I wrote my first story," he said. "A local boy was killed in a farming accident and the grieving family sent away to Helena for a marble headstone. They wanted it engraved with the boy's name, dates, and a message that angels had come for him. But when the headstone arrived—I was visiting their farm with my father—the engraving read, 'In Memory of William McKinley. A Nation Mourns.' Naturally, the stunned family wrote to the headstone maker and he wrote back apologizing, saying that he had been about to carve their son's marker when he received the news that President McKinley had been assassinated. The shock had sent him into a strange confusion.

He offered to send a correct headstone, but they would have to pay for it, and as the family couldn't afford it, the marker dedicated to President McKinley was placed on the son's grave." Cody paused. "I don't know if it struck me funny or sad at the time, but I was glad that I had written it down, and I haven't stopped writing things since."

He pulled a piece of paper out of his shirt pocket and said, "I wrote this down this morning." And he handed it to her.

Elizabeth read: "In a logging camp in Oregon, I met up with a heavy gambler named Joe Dunkenfeld. So addicted to cards was he that he played until he was out of money and then put up his wife as a wager in two-handed euchre. Luckily, Dunkenfeld won and got his wife back. Later that night she stabbed him in the heart and took off with his winnings. She was a looker, too."

Elizabeth smiled and handed it back. He looked briefly at her smile, and then he looked away.

Finding her in the living room, collapsed on the floor. Carrying her to the bedroom, laying her on the bed.

He concentrated on an ancient pictograph carved into a rock. There were hundreds in these canyons. This one was a spiral with human figures standing on either side of it. Cody had no idea of its meaning. "There's a way of life that's vanishing and I want to keep it alive," he said to Elizabeth, "so folks won't forget the great events and courageous pioneers that forged this nation. In my travels, I passed deserted army forts that once dotted the West as a necessity to keep peace between the Indians and the white settlers. But the Indians lost the war, they're safely on reservations, and the cavalry is no longer needed.

"I was visiting the Rosebud Sioux reservation in South Dakota when the first automobile arrived. It was ten years ago. Former warriors, looking like chiefs in their full beaded buckskin regalia and eagle-feather war bonnets —six of them—all climbed into the car and smiled for a photographer. Maybe not smile," he added. "Maybe it was more like a grimace. They seemed either amused or frightened, I'm not sure. The other Indians gathered around were amused. I thought it was sad.

"With the buffalo gone and their beef delivered to them in tin cans, they seem lost. Still, I believe the missionaries, when they arrived with Bibles and plows, meant well. Their motto was 'Kill the Indian and save the man.' It's a pity they couldn't save both."

He noticed that a faraway look had come into Elizabeth's eyes. He didn't know if she was listening. It didn't matter. He knew she had come out here to find answers and to heal her soul. And sometimes, stories were a way of coming to terms with events in one's life. He knew she was thinking about her husband, the terrible thing he had done to her. While Cody spoke of Indians sitting in cars, Elizabeth's mind would be going over and over that day when Barnstable had shown his true nature. She would need to think of consequences now and arrive at conclusions. Not right now, not today, but she would be starting the process of taking stock of her life and her future.

She hadn't described her vision in the heat-pit to him; she had simply said, "It was horrible."

He picked up a twig and traced lines in the dirt. Nearby, a small brown lizard sunned himself on a rock. Elizabeth looked up, shading her eyes, and peered at San Jacinto's summit, majestic and jagged against the blue sky. She hadn't looked at it in weeks. But now she wanted to, needed to. There was still some snow up there. She wondered if people could reach that peak, or if it was unreachable, if perhaps no one had ever explored up there. Luisa once told her that the Mesquite believed that the gods dwelled up there, two miles above the desert.

She thought about Nigel. He didn't know the Indians had buried her in a hot pit and made her see the truth of her life. The Ebony Club came to mind, replaying Dixieland and the blues in her head, re-showing the dancers beneath the glittering ball moving to the madcap rhythm of the Charleston. It was a kaleidoscope. There was a message in it but she couldn't make sense of it.

She returned her attention to McNeal. He was wearing his usual Western shirt that was black with white piping and pearl buttons, black Levi's, black boots. She wondered if he owned any other clothes.

"Do you still own the ranch up in Montana?"

"No. We fell on hard times. When I heard of a gold strike in Colorado, I told my father I'd go and get rich and come back and save the ranch. I struck it rich, and then lost it, and then my father died and we lost the property. After that, I roamed the West making my living as a jack-of-all-trades. Wrangler, roper and brander, scout. Worked in logging towns up north. Worked as a trapper out of Whitehorse in the Yukon. Spent a stint on a salmon boat on the Kenai River in Alaska. I even lived for a while with the Sioux Indians up in the Dakotas."

Cody noticed that a few strands of blond hair had escaped the knot at the nape of her neck. They reminded him of a pleasant memory. "You've never seen anything like the wheat fields of Dakota. You can ride from sunrise to sunset and never get out of them. They sweep away like a golden sea as far as the eye can go."

Their eyes met and held for a long moment, then he said, "I want you to see something." Lifting the binoculars to his eyes, he scanned the mountain summits and said, "There." Handing her the glasses, he pointed her in the right direction, saying, "Just past the timberline, on that rocky ledge. Do you see it?"

She searched and then drew in her breath. "Why . . . it's an eagle! Sitting on a nest." Elizabeth saw the white head, the angry brow, the hooked beak.

"The hatchlings are going to be born soon," Cody said. "They lay two eggs, but the first chick to hatch frequently kills its younger sibling as it hatches. The dominant chick tends to be the female, as they are bigger than the male, and more aggressive."

Elizabeth couldn't take her eyes off the sight, as she held her breath and watched a miracle occurring nearly two miles above the desert floor.

As she handed the binoculars back, she said, "Mr. McNeal, may I ask you a personal question?"

"Any time."

"Why do you always wear black?"

He looked down at himself, as if surprised to see clothes on himself. "I hate to make decisions about what to wear, and black is practical. So I bought five of the same shirt and three of the same pants. I like to keep things simple. And you promised to call me Cody."

"Why is it, Cody, that you move from town to town and not put down roots?"

He rubbed his hands together. He opened his palms and stared at them, then he looked at Elizabeth and said, "I'm looking for someone."

She waited for him to elaborate, and when he didn't, she said, "You were leaving Palm Springs at Christmas. You went to Tylerville, and then you were going to look for another ghost town in the high desert, and you were moving on after that, you said. But you came back and took the job Nigel had offered you. What changed your mind?"

When he hesitated, she said, "You thought I wasn't safe around Nigel. You saw something in him . . ."

She looked into Cody's eyes and knew she could tell this man anything—this man who had sat with her through the night, holding her hand while she dreamed violently of a snake and a wolf, and had held her afterward, comforting her. "Pour your words into the Creator's ears," Luisa had said. But Elizabeth didn't want to talk to God; she wanted to talk to Cody.

She watched a brown and white roadrunner rush by. It stopped for a moment, cocking its head. Its tail went straight up and its crest rose up on its head. And then he was off, crest flattened, long tail stretched out behind. "I met Nigel a year ago onboard a ship crossing the Atlantic," she said quietly. "It was all so romantic . . . I look back now and see how vulnerable I was to the charms of a stranger. All my life, Mother selecting my clothes for me, ordering for me in restaurants, telling me not to slouch. And then a handsome stranger swept me off my feet with the promise of excitement and glamor. And most of all, freedom. I realize now that I knew absolutely nothing about Nigel Barnstable. I married a stranger."

She now knew what the Ebony Club had been trying to tell her, drinking champagne, feeling the rhythm of the hot jazz in her blood, dancing the wild, uninhibited Charleston—a woman on the brink of liberation. She had fallen in love with the fast life, with the excitement it delivered, with the promise of freedom and a life unshackled by doting parents.

"I think that I mistook the love of excitement and liberation of a courtship as love for Nigel. I fell in love with a man created from my imagination." A man, she realized now, who had only been interested in her money. As an heiress she had been brought up to be on the alert for such men, had developed a keen sense for fortune hunters. Yet she had not seen it in Nigel.

Elizabeth could not believe now how naïve she had been, thinking that by eloping with Nigel she was gaining her freedom. She hadn't gained freedom at all; she had simply changed jailers. She saw it now, the subtle manipulation, the control. Looking back at their courtship in New York, seeing as bright as day what she had been blind to at the time: Nigel ordering for her in restaurants, choosing the movies and plays they went to, saying, "Wear the blue dress tonight, darling, it so suits you."

Was it her fault? she wondered now in sudden fear of discovering a weakness in herself she hadn't known was there. Because of growing up under Mother's firm control, is there a need in me to be controlled still?

No, she refused to believe that. But if it were true, just in case, she was going to be vigilant in herself from now on, and about the people she gravitated toward. She must be the mistress in her life, no one else.

Elizabeth looked at Cody, then up at the alpine slopes of the mountain, and finally across the flat desert that seemed could do with a few caravans and Arabian tents. There was a spirit in this place, in its many faces—from desert to hot springs, to mountain streams and snow-capped peaks. A force that Elizabeth would never have sensed, would never have connected with had she not come out and sought it. The desert heals, but one must seek it out, ask for the healing, and then listen. It was the soul of the desert. Had the builders of her house sensed it, too? Was that why they had named their home La Alma del Desierto?

Elizabeth hadn't poured her sorrows out to God, as Luisa had instructed, she had instead talked to Cody. But perhaps God had been eavesdropping because she already felt strength returning, felt courage and determination filling her soul. I am going to regain my freedom and my independence. I will start the process of severing myself from Nigel. He thinks so little of me that it won't occur to him that I would launch a fight for my freedom. He thinks I will be his meek slave for as long as it pleases him. So I am going to take advantage of that arrogance and use it against him. I am going to turn the tables, and Nigel won't even know it. From now on, whatever happens in my life will be on *my* terms.

Freedom—she had to free her soul from Nigel. But she also had to learn to be free in practical ways. She needed to be an independent woman—emotionally and financially. She thought about this. Yes, it was time to do something new. She was going to stand up to men. She could not fight Nigel yet, but she could fight for her financial freedom. She would go back to New York and start there.

CHAPTER EIGHTEEN

"HELLO, MOTHER," ELIZABETH SAID as she came into the bedroom.

"Darling! I'm sorry I wasn't able to come to the station to meet you." Mrs. Van Linden was sitting up in bed, a shawl around her shoulders, satin pillows at her back. "Where's your father?"

"He had to go to the office. He said you and I can have the day together and we'll see him tonight."

"And Wilson?"

"She went straight downstairs."

Mrs. Van Linden smiled. "That will be a reunion. Please have her come up when she's settled. I would so love a visit."

Removing her hat, Elizabeth sat on the edge of her mother's bed. "How are you feeling? Daddy says the doctor has put you on a new medication."

"The man's a quack. He says I have cardiac insufficiency. I think it means I have a groggy heart. I'm just a little fatigued is all. You've gotten brown. You look like an Indian."

Elizabeth smiled. "You wouldn't say that if you ever saw a real Indian."

"Tell me about Palm Springs. Have you made friends out there yet? You don't mention any in your letters."

"I'm trying. But the ladies there don't quite know what to make of me."

"That's what I was worried about. There's no one of your own class out there."

She studied her daughter's face. Something seemed different but she couldn't pinpoint it. Gertrude was suddenly fretful with herself. A mother should be able to know immediately if something was wrong with her child. "Is everything all right with you and Nigel?"

"Nigel and I are fine. He's busy with the plantation. I wish you could see it, Mother. We're in the middle of thinning the crop. The fruit is now the size of a small olive and if all the dates that a palm produces are allowed to develop, the branches break and the crop is lost. So our Mexican workers are climbing ladders and chopping away, morning till night. But apparently," she added with a smile, "it's a process that calls for a lot of shouting and laughter and an occasional sudden, loud song."

Mrs. Van Linden gave her daughter a skeptical look. *I ask about her marriage and she answers with Mexicans.* "All right, darling, why are you here? You didn't come three thousand miles to talk about date farming. When we got your telegram, we were thrilled that you were coming for a visit. We planned shows and plays, dinner at the finest places. But I have a feeling those are not in your plans. Especially as you have come without your husband."

Elizabeth got up and walked around the room. It felt good to be home. It also felt strange. It seemed as if she had left only yesterday, and at the same time, as if she had been gone a lifetime.

She had been surprised when Nigel had readily permitted her to go to New York. She had thought she would need to invent an excuse, something to do with her parents so that Nigel couldn't refuse permission. She would have thought that forbidding her to come would be part of his control over her. And then she thought: No. He wants everything to appear normal, so that if I try to tell anyone the truth, no one will believe me. Nigel puts on an act of perfect husband. I will be seen as a spoiled, neurotic, and ungrateful wife.

He did, however, say two things: "Don't tell your parents about your mishap. We don't want them worrying about your clumsiness." But Elizabeth had no intention of telling them about the miscarriage. Keeping them happy and unaware of the ugly truth was paramount. The second thing was: "Tell your father I have some interesting and lucrative investment opportunities to offer him." She had no intention of telling her father that either.

Elizabeth realized something about Nigel: that selfishness was not living as one wished to live, but rather it was expecting others to live as one wished to live. Nigel possessed a deep need to control and dominate, to transform the environment to suit his needs, to manipulate people into living according to what suited him. As if the world and all its inhabitants had been created solely for the pleasure of Nigel Barnstable. She now saw Nigel's charming riddles and word games as a way of drawing all those around him into his sphere, snatching the spotlight from someone else who might already be the center of attention.

Although she had completely healed from the miscarriage—physically at any rate—and things appeared to have returned to normal at La Alma, it was only appearances. Behind the normalcy, Nigel worked his devilry. There was no further physical abuse, but he would drop reminders of his control: "You aren't going to wear that dress, are you?" An inconsequential daytime dress that he couldn't possibly care about, but that was the point, showing her that he controlled even things he didn't care about. Every aspect of her life was commented on, criticized, corrected, from, "You put too much sugar in your tea," to, "You shouldn't be reading James Joyce." Little daily torments intended to gradually wear her down, she knew, to break the backbone she had displayed on the day of the tragedy. She wasn't going to let him break her. But she also wasn't going to fight him in the way he clearly expected, by standing up to him so that he could strike her down again. To outwit Nigel, Elizabeth was going to use the strategy of the unexpected.

And that was why she had come home. To take that first strategic step.

"I'm here on business, Mother."

"Business! What sort of business?"

"I have come to arrange for my own finances. I want to control my own money."

"Not that old argument again," Mrs. Van Linden said, fussing with the lace on her bed jacket. "Why any woman would want to involve herself in finances, I don't know. Writing checks, balancing ledgers, conducting business in a bank. It's all very . . . mannish."

She watched her daughter stroll around the room, touching things. Elizabeth was different from the excited bride who left New York last year.

"Something has changed, Elizabeth. You're different. What happened out there? Are you sure everything is all right between you and Nigel? Your father and I had hoped there would be a baby on the way by now."

Elizabeth paused to inspect a painting. It was new. Impressionistic, or something. She didn't like to think about "that" aspect of her life, Nigel resuming his marital privilege. Elizabeth knew she couldn't refuse, and that to even attempt to might provoke violence. But he expected nothing of her, and so nothing she gave.

"Everything's fine, Mother," Elizabeth said. "The date farm is quite large and demanding of Nigel's time. Which is why I want to control my own money. I hate going to him every time I need something for the house."

"Your father won't allow it. You know that."

"We'll see about that. I'm afraid Daddy's going to have to adjust to a few things. I'm going to learn how to drive."

"What! You know what your father has to say about that. Women haven't the head for automobiles."

Tell that to the movie starlets with their sporty cars, Elizabeth thought. The magazines were full of pictures of them. Photographers followed them around and snapped photos of the chic young actresses getting in and out of their flashy roadsters. For those fast and daring flappers, the car was a status symbol.

For Elizabeth, it meant freedom.

She said, "Women managed to drive cars and trucks while the men were away at war, Mother. Being in a time of peace should be no different."

"War is one thing, but the world must now return to normal."

Elizabeth doubted that the world would ever be normal again. Too much had changed and was continuing to change. "There is an auto garage in town. The mechanic gives driving lessons. I am going to hire him."

Mrs. Van Linden frowned. "A young lady of your station should have a chauffeur."

Elizabeth smiled. "If you saw Palm Springs, Mother, you would see how ridiculous that was. We are very rural. As it is, I have a horse named Star. A beautiful Appaloosa."

"Well," Mrs. Van Linden said, drawing her bed jacket closer to her throat, "don't ask me to put in a good word with your father for you."

"I wasn't going to ask you, Mother. I'm going to talk directly with Daddy myself. I don't need a third party to intervene on my behalf. I want to learn to stand on my own two feet. I want to do something, Mother. I want to make a difference in the world, to leave my mark.

I don't want to pass through life as Mrs. So-and-So, and leave this earth with just my children as proof that I passed this way. Something outside myself. And the first step toward achieving that goal is to control my own money."

Mrs. Van Linden narrowed her eyes. It wasn't so much what Elizabeth was saying as what she *wasn't* saying.

"But you *are* going to give me grandchildren, aren't you?"

Elizabeth smiled. "I hope to . . . eventually." She came back to the bed and patted her mother's hand. "I've quite worn you out, haven't I, Mother? I'm sorry. I'll go freshen up, and I'll join you for lunch."

*   *   *

It felt good to be below stairs again. Sitting in a proper servants' hall, having tea at a long table, exchanging news and gossip and jokes without being in earshot of those upstairs. It felt good to look up at the windows set high in the wall and see the legs of pedestrians hurry by, dogs on leashes, automobile tires. Basement life, a whole other world from that above, with its own hierarchy, social structure, rules. A person knew his or her station here, what was expected of one, what one's duties were.

Yes, it felt good.

And yet . . .

As the butler, wearing a gray apron and gloves as he polished a silver soup tureen, intoned in a deep voice, "One would not think that a short, fat, ugly little man, a pitcher at that, would hit so many homeruns," and as Mrs. Van Linden's lady's maid repaired a hem on one of the Madame's skirts, and as the maids talked about the new delivery boy from Korbitski's Grocery, Fiona suddenly felt stifled. Buried. Not only below stairs but below ground.

She thought of spacious La Alma, spread out and wide open to admit golden sunlight, with tall windows that gave out onto vistas of desert and mountains.

Having helped Lady Elizabeth out of her traveling clothes, drawing her bath so she could wash away the grime of train travel, and laying out a nightgown for Elizabeth's afternoon nap, Fiona had come downstairs for a reunion. Her companions had been riveted by her description of her new home—the isolation of it, the rustic flavor of the village, the single-level house that continued to confound the staff (Mrs. Norrington saying, "Take this tray up to Her Ladyship," when there was no "up" at La Alma). And although Fiona had done her best to describe the local Indians, she knew her audience of six maids, the cook and assistant cook, four footmen, and the butler, pictured war bonnets, tepees, and arrows.

But now . . . in New York less than a day and Fiona felt strange yearnings creep into her heart. She missed Doc Perry. More than she had expected to. And the farther the train had sped from the West, the more he had filled her thoughts. They were enjoying a courtship of sorts that had so far gone no further than holding hands. But Fiona found herself wondering what it would be like to be intimate with him. She had witnessed the sex act when she was a child. Her father never cared who was watching when he came home drunk. But, with her parents it had seemed the act of animals, two brutes grunting. Fiona knew that it would be something wonderful with the right man.

When Her Ladyship had announced her intention to travel to New York and asked Fiona to accompany her, Fiona had seen it as an opportunity to obtain her freedom. When Mrs. Van Linden had exacted a promise of loyalty from Fiona, she had essentially locked her into servitude. And now, should Leland Perry ask her to marry him—and that was her dearest hope—how could Fiona say yes when she was bound by a promise to stay with Elizabeth?

The housekeeper came into the hall, clapping her hands and informing the maids that there was work to be done. She turned to Fiona. "Madame has asked that you go up and pay her a visit."

"Mrs. Van Linden?" Perfect. This was the chance to ask her to release Fiona from her promise.

*   *   *

Mrs. Van Linden brought the cup close to her chin and held the biscuit in the tea until it softened, then she sucked it up. It would never have occurred to Fiona before now that Mrs. Van Linden was enjoying a snack in the presence of a guest without offering anything.

But she wasn't a guest. She was a servant.

She thought of the twenty-one who dined below stairs and slept in attic rooms, a large domestic staff whose sole duty it was to see to the comfort of two. Back in Palm Springs no one had servants.

She looked around the opulent room decorated in French rococo, the enormous bed occupied by the middle-aged woman, with satin sheets and counterpane. Fiona thought of the small room that had been assigned to her during their stay on Park Avenue—up in the attic, small and cramped, with a single dresser and a hard cot. She pictured her room back at La Alma, originally designed for guests, with a large fireplace and glass-paned doors opening onto a patio riotous with red and pink bougainvillea, blue and orange bird of paradise, yellow roses. And more sunlight than ever saw the inside of the Van Linden mansion.

While Mrs. Van Linden brought Fiona up-to-date on Park Avenue news and gossip, Fiona thought of being turned out of her home when she was fourteen because her parents could no longer afford to feed her. Going into service as a scullery maid. But then, before the war, a girl like Fiona had no choices. But she lived in a different world now. She could choose to be doctor's wife. Perhaps help Leland with his patients, a nurse of sorts. After all, hadn't she been taking care of ladies for twenty-five years?

She thought: I don't want to be a maid anymore. I don't want to jump up at bells and whistles. I want to be a wife. I want my own home. I want a man who loves me. I want to be normal.

Fiona waited for an opening in order to lodge her request. Mrs. Van Linden would ask her how she was doing in the West, did she enjoy her life out there, was she adjusting, and then Fiona would say, "The truth is, Mrs. Van Linden, I have found a beau. We have been going out together. He is a professional man, well established and respected in the community. It is possible there will be a marriage proposal in the near future, and I would like your permission to leave my post as your daughter's lady's maid."

"I'm glad we have this chance for a visit," Mrs. Van Linden said now, setting her slushy tea aside. "I wanted to talk to you about Elizabeth."

"The thing is," Fiona began.

"You know, Wilson, I am so lucky to have you, a person I can trust to watch over my daughter. I suspect things are not altogether perfect with my daughter and her husband. She won't say, of course, but I sense something happened. I'm worried about her, Wilson. I want you to stick to your promise that you will stay with my daughter and make sure she's all right."

When Fiona hesitated, Mrs. Van Linden lowered her eyebrows in a way that was all too familiar to Fiona. It meant Madame was about to get her way, no matter what. "I hope you don't have any ideas about leaving our employ. Need I remind you," Gertrude Van Linden said, "that when the Countess turned you out with not a single reference and you had no place to go and were in a destitute circumstance, I took you in, gave you employment, saved you from the poorhouse or worse?"

"No, Madame, I don't need reminding. I am forever grateful for that."

"But I sense hesitancy on your part. Is there something you are not telling me?"

Where to begin? How to explain the desire to break away from servitude? How to make this privileged woman understand how Fiona had lived a life of missed opportunities and now that she had one, she needed to beg for her freedom?

Mrs. Van Linden continued to skewer her with her eyes. A clock on the mantelpiece chimed the hour, a dainty sound, but it made Fiona suddenly anxious and filled with urgency. She was suddenly uncomfortable in surroundings she had been comfortable in for years.

"You know," Mrs. Van Linden said, as she picked a piece of imaginary lint from her satin counterpane, "gratitude is a funny thing. It can be strong and powerful at the moment of its creation, such as when a servant is rescued from the brink of destitution. But gratitude is also a fragile thing because it seems to lose its strength over the years until there's nothing left of it. Is that what I am sensing here, Wilson?"

"Not at all," Fiona said, a touch too quickly. She suddenly felt very defensive.

"Then let me hear your promise again. Your promise to stand by my daughter no matter what, and I will take it as a sign of your continued gratitude." Before Fiona could open her mouth, Mrs. Van Linden added, "But if you would rather not, that is all right with me. But then I would have to let you go, you understand. I would have to free you from our family's employment and find another lady's maid to send back to Palm Springs."

Fiona stared at her, unable to believe her ears. The Madame was threatening to fire her! While release from her promise was what Fiona had come hoping for, she had not wanted to be released from her job. What if Leland didn't propose after all? She wasn't sure of his intentions, she was only hopeful and wishful and prayerful. But those didn't guarantee a marriage proposal.

If I am released from my service to Elizabeth, and Leland doesn't ask me to marry him . . .

The hope that had driven her for three thousand miles and had filled her for days now seemed to wither in the face of logic and reality. Fiona wondered if she had been born to live constantly on the edge of losing her employment. Hope turned to surrender. Mrs. Van Linden was right. Gratitude should not be a thing that died but should remain eternal. And a woman's word, especially a woman in Fiona's circumstance, was her most precious possession. "You have my word, Madame," she said while thinking, it's best that Leland doesn't ask me to marry him. That way, there will be no pain. "I promise I will not leave Lady Elizabeth's side."

*   *   *

Henry Van Linden was in his study going over the accounts of one of his many companies. Although he had a staff of accountants overseeing the finances of Van Linden's considerable holdings, Henry believed in being personally involved. He often declared that it was what got him where he was today.

He looked up from his work when Elizabeth presented herself in the open doorway. "Am I disturbing you, Daddy?"

"Not at all, pumpkin!" He hefted his bulk out of the chair and came around to take her hands. He wore a red satin smoking jacket, sashed at the waist, over black trousers. His slippers, Elizabeth noticed, were Persian-style, with the toes turned up and adorned with tassels. For his prosperous girth, the slippers seemed out of place. "My God, pumpkin, it's good to have you home. Your mother and I have missed you terribly."

"Daddy, I have something important to discuss with you. I've been putting it off until the right time."

His face suddenly lit up. "Have you come to bring us good news?" he said in a loud voice. "Something you felt a need to tell us in person?"

"What?" she said, confused by the joy that sparkled in his eyes. "Oh!" she said, suddenly understanding. "No, no news, Father. I just need to talk to you."

The light went out of his eyes and his smile fell. As he led her to upholstered chairs arranged in front of the fireplace where golden flames kept the evening chill out, he said, "I can guess what it is you wish to talk about, and I can tell you right now that you're wasting your time. I won't talk about what you've come for."

He took a seat and the chair groaned. "I'm not going to change the terms of your trust fund and that's that. The money remains in Nigel's control."

Elizabeth remained standing, warming herself at the fire. Behind her, a grand portrait of her mother rose from the fireplace mantle, a painting executed by a famous artist when Mrs. Van Linden was a bride. Henry could not deny the strong resemblance to Elizabeth, creating the effect that both mother and daughter were standing over him. He wasn't in the mood for a fight. He wanted this to be a pleasant reunion before she ran back to the desert.

Elizabeth saw this as something more than the issue of gaining control of her money. She saw this moment as a test—to see if she had the strength and conviction to stand up to her new resolve. It was one thing to declare that she was going to fight for herself, that her life was going to be lived by her own terms from now on, quite another to act on those words. If she could win this argument with her father, then she would know she had what it took to stand up to Nigel.

"Grandfather left that money to me," she said, and he knew by her tone that the fight was on. "It is mine, and I wish to have control of it."

"My father set up that trust fund with conditions, Elizabeth."

"Conditions that are outdated. When Grandfather established my trust fund, the world was very different. But the world has changed and so the conditions of my trust fund must change. I am adamant on this, Father. I will not back down."

He sighed. Elizabeth seemed to have grown a stubborn streak.

"I can be reasonable on this," she said. "A compromise. If you can't turn my trust fund over to me for legal reasons, then a new account, one that you establish out of your own money. A household account. Right now, Nigel pays the servants and the farm workers. I want more control over my own house."

"It's out of the question."

"Very well then, I'm not leaving until you agree to my terms."

He blinked, wrinkled his nose, frowned. "Eh? What do you mean, not leaving?"

"I plan to stay in this house until you give me my financial freedom."

He chuckled. "As much as I would love to have you here with us forever, you need to go back to your husband."

"Then agree to my terms."

"What's gotten into you? Is this what living in the West does to women?"

"Maybe. But if I am going to continue to live in the West, I want my own money. I mean it. If I have to handcuff myself to my bedpost, I will."

"But . . ." he sputtered. "You have to go back to your husband."

"Not until I have money of my own. I am adamant on this, Daddy."

"What does Nigel say?"

"He is not a party to this negotiation."

Van Linden rose from his chair and went to a window and looked out. He saw automobiles chugging down Park Avenue, spreading headlight beams in their path. Across the way, gaslights created a wonderland of Central Park.

"I mean it, Daddy. If you insist on treating me like a little girl who cannot even handle pocket money, then I will stay here under your roof where you can take care of me just like a child."

Van Linden mulled her words over, her tone, her new backbone. As he did so, he found his thoughts segueing from his daughter to the greater population at large.

The world had gone crazy. It was as if the war had knocked everyone senseless. People dancing the madcap Charleston, flappers raising their hemlines up to the knee, women smoking—and taking control of financial affairs, learning to write checks, standing in bank lines with men. And college students having contests about how many live goldfish they could swallow, how many kids they could pack into a car. Dance marathons that went on for days until couples collapsed and had to be taken away by ambulance. The country was in the grip of madness.

And the economy! It was getting out of control. With everyone buying on credit, there was no actual money circulating. Housewives buying shares in the stock market. Everyone spending, no one saving. The world was in the grip of materialism on a scale that had never before been seen. And the whole of it was like a balloon that kept expanding. Van Linden was terrified that soon it was going to burst and this economic paradise would collapse like a house of cards. Banks would fail, the stock market crash, men lose their jobs, money shrivel up, and everyone would be left with a mountain of debt and not a penny to their names.

His musing startled him because he suddenly found himself looking at his daughter in a different light. A thought occurred to him that had never occurred to him before: with the world gone crazy and the economy no longer predictable or stable, perhaps it was a good idea to arm his only child with defenses. Perhaps she *should* be schooled in basic finances, for her own survival. After all, how solid were Barnstable's finances? How would he do in an economic storm? What if he were one of those same ruined men Van Linden was worried about, and no longer able to take care of Elizabeth? He himself wasn't going to be around forever. Elizabeth was the most important thing in the world to him—then wasn't now the time to make sure she was armed for a possible coming calamity?

Amazed at this revelation, surprised by the conclusions a man can arrive at when he is forced to, he turned to her and said in a voice filled with wonder, "My regular doctor is retiring so he referred me to a specialist on Fifth Avenue. I waited in the exam room, and when this woman in a white coat came in, I thought she was the nurse until she introduced herself as Dr. Rogers. So help me God, I got up and walked out."

He chuckled and shook his head. "I've never been a man to fight progress. Progress is what made this nation mighty and strong. Someday there'll be women politicians. Maybe even president of the United States."

He looked at Elizabeth again and a smile crept to his face. "So you really mean to stay here if I don't give you an account of your own?" He chuckled again, feeling so much better now that he had decided to give his daughter some protection rather than fight with her. Her strategy impressed him. Rather than stamping her foot or whining or coaxing, she was using sound business tactics. She was a chip off the old block, that was for sure.

"You *will* be turning twenty-one this year. You should be allowed to govern your own money. But—" He held up a stubby finger. "First, a trial run. I will establish a checking account for you. We'll see how well you do, and then we can talk about something more substantial."

"Thank you, Daddy," she said as she gave him a tight hug. She had taken the first step. Next was going to be an even bigger, more challenging one. But she was going to face it, as the wolf had faced the rattlesnake.

CHAPTER NINETEEN

"BEFORE THERE WERE PEOPLE," Luisa Padilla said to the children sitting on the ground at her feet, "there were spirits. They lived every-where in this valley. Even after they went away, when the first people came, the spirits could still be seen.

"When you look out and see a mirage that looks like water or people or a village, those are the old spirits of the desert. The rainbow spirits lived here first. When the people came, the color-spirits went away to hide behind clouds. The colors-spirits come with the dawn and play games at sunset. The color-spirits shine with the moon and the stars at night so that we know they have never left us. They are with us always, just as the spirits of our ancestors are here with us now. Which is why, my sons and daughters, we must respect this place we are about to dwell in, for it belongs not to us but to the spirit world. We are their guests. If we treat them with respect, they will do us no harm."

It was the same story she told children every summer when the village broke up and moved to the higher camp in the mountains. The setting for the summer camp was filled with trees and grass and shaded by the tall mountain peaks. The air was cool. The stream ran with cold water. The people would live well for the next three months.

Mesquite pods were ripening. Soon, the whole community would take part in harvesting, after which the women would be busy drying the pods, then grinding them or roasting or boiling them. A little later, yucca and manzanita berries would be ripe for harvesting. Finally, acorns and pine nuts would be gathered.

Their main source of meat was deer, which the men hunted by the streams in the late afternoon, when the deer came out of the forest to drink. But the people also ate skunks, raccoons, squirrels, and rabbits, and certain birds, such as quail and ducks. Men with special skills found and killed rattlesnakes, whose meat and skins were highly prized. Women and children trapped and collected lizards. Tortoises, too, were prized for their meat, their shell being used for making household utensils and ritual rattles.

All the meat of an animal was used: it was roasted, boiled, or cut into strips to be dried as jerky. The jerky was either chewed directly or recooked in water to soften. Usually game was skinned before cooking, but sometimes not, because the fur and skin, acting as a protection against the heat of the coals, enabled the cooked meat to be lifted directly from the charred skin and eaten. Marrow was eaten by cracking the bones; the bones were crushed and ground into a powder which was mixed with other foods as a mush; the blood was cooked and stored in a leather pouch or in sections of gut. At every stage, the spirit of the animal was respected. The family thanked it for giving them sustenance and life.

They had also brought their pets with them. Children liked to keep small birds and reptiles, and they gave them names. Each family had a dog because when Mukat created the world, he created the dog to guard the home.

Dispersing the children Luisa stood up and looked around for her granddaughter, Gabriela. Isabella was here, helping her mother erect their summer hut. But Gabriela was nowhere to be seen.

As usual. Her head in the clouds again!

Maybe she was back at the big house. Luisa struck off down the mountain trail to the valley below.

*   *   *

Cody was overseeing the delivery of hay bales from an alfalfa farm outside of Banning. As the ranch hands hauled the bales from the six-horse wagon, Cody inspected each bale to make sure it wasn't clogged with weeds, making it unfit for horse feed. But he was having a hard time concentrating.

Cowboys don't like surprises.

Surprises can cause a horse to spook, to rear up and throw his rider. Spooked horses sometimes took off like a shot and could gallop for miles not knowing its rider's boot was caught in the stirrup and he was being dragged bloody. Surprises, like Indian raids, could even cause a cowboy to end up dead.

Such was Cody's frame of mind as he oversaw the delivery of the hay. He supposed the cowboy's dislike of surprises had to do with the environment he worked in, a place of unexpected rattlesnake nests and sudden storms and lightning and angry bears and quicksand and cattle stampedes and ambushes by outlaws that ended with a bullet in the back, life being the dangerous business that it was. Now that he really thought about it, most surprises that cowboys encountered could result in death.

He didn't think he was going far out on a limb to think that his own recent surprise could ultimately mean his death, because he knew two things about Nigel Barnstable—that he was capable of committing a cold-blooded killing, and that he was the kind of arrogant bastard whose jealousy knew no limits.

Cody was mulling all these thoughts because of a surprise that had jumped into his life and caught him so off guard that he felt as if his mare had gotten spooked and had bolted and now galloped across the desert with Cody helplessly caught in the stirrup.

Elizabeth. Her absence had had an unexpected effect on him—a powerful surprise that he had not seen coming.

He missed her.

Other than his father, Cody McNeal had never missed anyone before. That was one of the advantages of the drifter's life. You moved on before you could form any kind of bonds that would make you sharply feel someone's absence. And he felt Elizabeth's in a powerful way. He couldn't stop thinking about her. When he was shoeing or grooming or exercising the horses he would find himself glancing toward the house, expecting to see her there among the scarlet bougainvillea and shimmering green hummingbirds.

It troubled him. Should he even be thinking about a married woman?

Cowboys lived by simple rules. You never steal a horse. You always have your friend's back. You don't cheat at cards. Share your tobacco. And give your last strip of jerky to a hungry man. Not setting your eyes on another man's woman was at the top of the list.

Cody had the feeling he was slipping down a dangerous slope because his thoughts were forbidden and nothing good ever came from entertaining the forbidden. But he couldn't stop thinking about her. How do you stop thoughts from entering your head, he wondered. The very act of telling himself that he mustn't think about Elizabeth was itself thinking about Elizabeth!

In the past, he would just pack up, saddle up, and ride off. But he was stuck. He couldn't leave her—not with that unpredictable, volatile husband. But staying was a torment. A man should be able to control what he was thinking. What worried Cody was that if his thoughts continued as they were, he was going to fall into a moment of weakness and reveal his hand—which could lead to disastrous consequences, for himself or for them both.

And what was the point in thinking about her anyway? It wasn't as though their friendship could ever be anything more than just a friendship. Was he, by thinking about her, opening himself up for fresh pain? But there she was, walking through his mind as if she owned it . . .

Through the date palm grove, on the other side of the hundred trees, Cody saw Nigel Barnstable traipsing around the property with a visitor in a white suit. A hydro-engineer brought out from Los Angeles, Cody had heard, to search for places to drill for artesian water.

Cody hated Barnstable. And Cody hated the fact of hating a man. Hate was a powerful word and he had used it in only two instances that he could recall. Neither had to do with a man.

But the fact was there. Nigel Barnstable woke unpleasant emotions in Cody that he would rather not feel. The man did not deserve Elizabeth. And yet she was his, and there was nothing anyone, least of all Cody McNeal, could do about it.

He saw Luisa Padilla emerge from the hundred-tree grove and approach the house. As she walked past the paddock where hay was being unloaded, they acknowledged each other with a nod. Cody and the Indian woman had entered into a secret pact. When Elizabeth sent a telegram, announcing the day of her return to Palm Springs, Luisa would inform Señor Cody.

*   *   *

Luisa nodded toward Señor Cody, to let him know she had not forgotten. She would let him know when the Señora was to return.

Luisa was no longer suspicious or wary of the white man's wife, now that she knew that the Señora was as much a victim of him as Johnny Pinto had been. And now that the Señora had undergone one of the

Cahuilla's most secret and sacred rituals, the women's heat pit, she had become, to Luisa's thinking, an honorary member of the tribe. As such, she had earned the right to be protected by them.

When Luisa passed the date palm grove, she saw the irrigation canals the Señor had dug without the Indians' permission, diverting too much water from the stream to his new trees, more water than he had a right to. Chief Diego was not pleased and did not intend to let the Señor get away with it.

But that was men's business. Luisa shifted her thoughts to Gabriela. Where does her brain go? Luisa wondered. What was it about Gabriela that she could not hold a thought for longer than a minute? Not at all like her cousin Isabella who was obedient and stayed at a task.

Luisa loved Gabriela. Granddaughters were special. Her daughter's daughter, therefore, double the love. Luisa's people had a saying: "When a child is born, so is a grandmother." But sometimes, a granddaughter could be a handful.

Lifting her long skirt, Luisa stepped over the patio flagstones and walked to the house.

*   *   *

Gabriela liked working in the Señora's house. It was large and beautiful, and looked like the movies stars' homes she saw in magazines.

At fifteen, Gabriela Seco had seen little of the world beyond her reservation, where she shared an adobe house with her mother, father, and three siblings. She had always thought they were well off: there was plenty of food; Gabriela had three dresses and two pairs of sandals; she enjoyed the festivals when friends and relatives came visiting; she enjoyed traveling to other villages in the valley, for gossip and gifts. And she knew that someday soon her mother would be helping her to find a husband to begin a family of her own.

Gabriela had been content until her grandmother, Luisa Padilla, had taken a job at the big house called La Alma and had brought Gabriela and her cousin Isabella to come and work here, too. Suddenly, the girls were exposed to a whole new, wonderful world and Gabriela could not keep away. She knew she was supposed to be up in the canyon, helping with the summer camp, but this bedroom was something beyond anything Gabriela could have dreamed of.

With the Señora away, it was an opportunity to explore.

She lifted each crystal perfume bottle on the Señora's vanity table, held them up to the light, pulled up the stoppers, and sniffed the fragrances. She ran her hands over the Señora's gold hairbrush and comb. Filled her eyes with the dazzle of her jewelry. And fingered the delicate fabrics hanging in the cupboard. The Señora lived like a movie star!

When Gabriela came to a magazine lying open on the dressing table, she picked it up. It was one of the many magazines devoted to films and film stars. There was always a beautiful woman on the cover. This one had red-brown hair, short and curly. Her face wore a lot of makeup, with darkly rimmed eyes and bright red rouged lips. She was smiling, yet her eyes were sad. Gabriela had learned to read when missionaries came to the village one spring. She and her cousin Isabella had sat side by side and recited their ABCs. She sounded out the name beneath the photograph. Zora DuBois. Gabriela pronounced it "Duboys." The actress had very thin eyebrows. Gabriela ran a fingertip over her own eyebrows. They were thick. Zora's hair was very short, with deep waves. Gabriela fingered her long, straight braids. Zora was very pale. Gabriela was brown.

The photograph was mesmerizing. Gabriela was caught in the actress's dark, soulful eyes, as if the actress were trying to communicate directly with the young Indian girl.

Gabriela knew how the actress's voice would sound—soft and reassuring, like a breeze. A voice as beautiful as the actress herself. As she stared at the photograph, Gabriela almost expected to see the lips move. "Sister," the beautiful woman seemed to be saying, "you can be special. You can be different. Look at me. I am special."

For as long as Gabriela could remember, she wanted to be separate from her cousin Isabella. From early childhood they had always been paired together and referred to as "those girls."

"Which one are you?" Mrs. Norrington would ask. "Gabriela," the girl would reply, wondering why the housekeeper bothered asking because she never called Gabriela by name.

Gabriela tried not to dislike the lady or her job. It was nice to take money home to her mother every week. And the other girls in the village envied her. They all wanted to be maids at La Alma. But it was the confusion of her with Isabella that bothered her. "Are you twins?" strangers would ask. Isabella never seemed to mind that the cousins were mistaken for sisters. But Gabriela minded. She wanted to be noticed as an individual, not part of a set. True, she and Isabella had gone around together since they were toddlers. The families always gathered at one house or another, their mothers being sisters. So all the kids ran around together—the Secos and Padillas—and maybe that was why they all looked alike. They all grew up laughing the same way and talking the same way and walking and covering their mouths when they ate the same way.

But Gabriela didn't like being lumped as a pair with her cousin, like the silver candlesticks in the Señora's house. Isabella would displease Grandmother, and Grandmother would scold the two of them. Grandmother never saw the difference. The sameness to her cousin had bred in Gabriela a deep yearning to be different, and to be noticed for that difference.

But the actress on the magazine cover . . . was it Gabriela's imagination or had Zora's gaze shifted and now she looked directly at her? Hadn't she been looking off into the distance, sadly, while she smiled? A trick of the eye, Gabriela thought, while at the same time thinking, yes, she is looking at me and she is trying to tell me something . . .

The moment froze. Sounds that had been coming through the open window drifted away. Gabriela felt briefly disembodied, as if she had stepped outside herself and she sensed that this was a very special moment. What is it? she wanted to ask the beautiful actress. What are you trying to tell me?

Zora's lips seemed to part, and a breeze came to the girl's ears. She listened. She knew it was a very important message.

"Gabriela!"

She jumped, dropping the magazine. Grandmother was standing in the doorway, a sharp look on her face. "You do not belong in here," Luisa said. "Unless you are dusting or sweeping or making the Señora's bed. Come out now and help us with the camp."

Gabriela hurried out, saying she was sorry, while her grandmother gave a pull at one of her braids, saying, "You girls . . ."

*   *   *

"Artesian wells are common in the Salton trough and Borrego Desert, Mr. Barnstable," the young hydrologist said as they walked the property to the west of the hundred-tree grove. "They occur where hardpan underlays surface materials. This seals off an area so that water can't infiltrate the subsoil. Water pressure builds up and seeps through the surface. One way to find a deep well is to look for natural surface water. Another way is to find clumps of mesquite and other plants that have long taproots, so you know they've reached a water table below."

They paused at the base of a narrow ravine where tangled brush and inedible scrub grew on sandy soil. A pleasant wind blew, carrying the sounds of industry at Barnstable's plantation.

"Drilled wells," the hydrologist continued as he scanned the ground, "can be excavated by simple hand drilling methods—augering, for example, or sludging, jetting. Or we can try machine drilling rotary or percussion. The deeprock rotary drilling method is most common, and drilled wells can get water from a much deeper level than dug wells can—often up to several hundred meters."

They came upon Nigel's irrigation canals, which his workers had dug from the Mesquite Canyon stream, to skirt the back of the property and branch out to feed the hundred date palms. The canals were broken up, kicked in. Fresh, recent. The third time so far. "I keep digging them," Nigel said in frustration, "the Indians keep breaking them down."

"Then may I suggest you funnel your water from a source higher up, and by a more stable means? A flume, for example."

Nigel hadn't thought of that.

"Let's take a look up there," the hydrologist said. "I think we might do better with a chute rather than drilling."

They trudged up Mesquite Canyon, the engineer removing his white jacket as the day grew warm and the climb more strenuous. "This is as far as we can go," he said presently as he paused to consult his survey map of the canyon. "According to this, from this point on the water belongs completely to the Indians. But we can build a wooden canal from here, where you still own water rights."

Nigel thought about this. Here, on his own property, the stream was narrow and spilled lazily along its bed. But farther up the canyon, where the Indians had established their summer camp, the stream was wide and rushed with force.

Why, he wondered now, should he settle for less water when he could go up there and take as much as he needed?

*   *   *

"There you go, Lois," Doc Perry said as he handed Augie Lardner's wife his last bottle of insomnia medicine. His own homemade recipe of water, crushed juniper berries, and honey. And 25 percent alcohol.

She paid him, thanked him, and left. Perry watched Mrs. Lardner waddle down the street, her next thirty nights guaranteed of good sleep. But after that? He had nothing else to give her.

The same with Mr. Allenby's hand tremors, and Rev. White's nervous stomach—all the minor but inconvenient ailments that local folk brought to Doc Perry to be cured. They swore by his tonics and elixirs, nostrums and cures. He had kept folks happy and free from nervousness, insomnia, indigestion, backache, and arthritis pain for ten years.

But now his medicines were drying up. Without alcohol, all he had was colored water.

Turning away from the window, he noted the time. In five days Fiona and her mistress would be back in Palm Springs. Leland anticipated a delightful reunion with Miss Wilson at which they would consummate their courtship. He would suggest a buggy ride in the moonlight. He had even managed to find a pre-Prohibition bottle of red wine, purchased at a great price. A picnic beneath the stars, a blanket on the sand. And the delicate and willowy Fiona would be his.

*   *   *

Traffic was heavy in the streets of Hollywood, but Nigel wasn't in a hurry as he drove slowly down Hollywood Boulevard, looking for a defunct nightclub.

He had heard about it from the Lamonts when he had visited their construction site again. He had expressed boredom living in the desert and wondered where one went for nightlife.

Finally, there it was, the Pink Flamingo nightclub, where the shuttered front door and darkened neon lights testified to its having been closed down. A sign plastered on the entrance said, "Gone out of business." It was happening all over town, all over the country. Establishments that had relied on the liquor trade lost their customers and went broke overnight.

Nigel pulled into the parking lot next door and found a space between a Packard Runabout and a Lincoln Sports Phaeton, each of which he knew cost over a hundred thousand dollars—in a town where the average house sold for eight thousand and the average car went for three hundred! The sign of a wealthy patronage.

He walked down the dark alley to the rear entrance of the Pink Flamingo, where he knocked three times on a plain, unmarked door. A panel at eye level slid open. A man said, "Yeah?"

"Ali Baba sent me." And the door swung open onto a bright, noisy club scene.

Shedding his coat and handing it to the pretty hatcheck girl, Nigel straightened his tie, smoothed back his hair, and entered the dazzling crowd. The orchestra played "Ain't We Got Fun" while illegal booze, smuggled in from Canada and Mexico, or supplied by bootleggers, flowed. Like thousands of restaurants and clubs throughout the United States, the Pink Flamingo, instead of closing its doors, had become a speakeasy, so called because one must speak quietly about such a place so as not to alert the police to its existence.

The local cops knew about the Pink Flamingo, of course. Everyone knew that the chief of police was there every Saturday night with his mistress, enjoying French champagne.

As Nigel moved through the crowd, he recognized the nightclub's owner, a piggy-faced man named Tony Riccio. He wore a wide-brimmed white felt fedora, tipped at a rakish angle, and a white custom silk suit with gold buttons. Diamonds flashed on his fingers. He had recently come to Los Angeles from Chicago, where it was rumored he had ties to certain crime bosses. The word was, Chicago was getting too competitive, whereas Southern California was up for grabs.

Riccio picked his teeth with a solid gold toothpick as he greeted his guests.

Other mobsters had come to town and grabbed other clubs in the Los Angeles area. With Riccio they had formed a syndicate with an aim to having a monopoly on the lucrative illegal booze market in Southern California.

They were a new breed of gangster that had been spawned by the public's insatiable thirst for alcohol. With extremely limited avenues of supply for the average citizen, men like Tony Riccio saw profit in hiring rumrunners to smuggle in rum from the Caribbean or hijackers to steal whiskey from Canada. They also bought large quantities of liquor made in homemade stills and in moonshine operations out in the deserts.

Federal agents were supposedly responsible for raiding speakeasies, finding moonshine operations, and arresting gangsters, but many agents were under-qualified and underpaid, which led to a high rate of bribery. It was even rumored that men signed up as "Prohis" because it was an easy way to make money.

Nigel kept his eye out for Jack Lamont and his wife, his new neighbors in the Coachella Valley, wondering if they would be here tonight.

And there they were!

Well, Jack, at least, sitting with two men in tuxedoes, and a woman Nigel didn't know. Lamont's wife, Zora, was nowhere in sight. The booth was large and curved, upholstered in pink satin, and had room enough for ten people.

"Hello," he said as he approached. The table was spread with fine crystal and china. The meal consisted of filet mignon, twice-baked potatoes, and asparagus tips. The drinks, Nigel knew, were the best scotch, bourbon, brandy—no moonshine for these Hollywood hotshots. While the men tucked into their feast, the woman's went untouched. Champagne bubbled in her crystal stem glass.

She struck him as vaguely familiar. An actress. He might have seen a couple of her movies, but her name eluded him.

She wore a black cloche hat, so named for its bell shape, firmly fitted to her head, with just a hint of black hair showing under the brim. The hat sat low on her forehead, barely revealing her brows, but her eyes were exposed, blackened to emphasize their shape and size. Her lips were ruby red. She even rouged her cheeks, which one saw on only a few women. He knew the type of actress she was. She portrayed the "vamp," shorthand for "sexual vampire," a ruthless siren who seduced men for their money and left them shattered.

Vamps were extremely popular. Their sultry looks and plunging necklines sent the message that they were of loose morals. This actress's attitude now, Nigel saw, was one of disinterest and boredom. He assumed that the effect was to boil a man's blood, and on the movie screens apparently it did. A vamp's male fans were legion. They had female fans as well, who had started wearing cloche hats and blackening their eyes. On this actress, Nigel thought now, it was hot. On shopgirls, it was not.

"You were right about this place," Nigel said as he casually lit a Dunhill cigarette with his gold lighter. "Mind if I join you?"

"By all means! We're discussing business. Maybe you'll be interested." Ginger-haired Jack Lamont with his thick glasses snapped his fingers at a waiter and when the man came over, Nigel ordered a gin and tonic.

But as he sat down, Nigel received a shock.

When he glanced at the actress sitting next to Lamont, wondering where Zora was, wondering if she knew he was out with another woman, and he saw the quick flicker of a smile at the corners of her mouth—playful, teasing—Nigel's mouth fell open.

The woman was Lamont's wife. The vamp was Zora.

Good God, he thought, suddenly intrigued. He recalled how, when they had first met at her house in Palm Springs and he had confessed he'd never seen any of her films, she hadn't seemed to take offense. On the contrary, she had sent him a cryptic smile. Now he knew why. He had seen her movies. He just hadn't known that the lady with the mop of reddish curls was the sultry vamp in the films, and she had clearly enjoyed the subterfuge that day when they first met.

His interest piqued, he frankly assessed her now. Gone were the trousers accentuating flaring hips, the blouse straining over a generous bosom. Instead she wore a sleek black gown and her breasts seemed to have been flattened. As their gazes met, she sent him the barest of winks, and he thought: Bravo! Well played.

When his drink arrived, Nigel looked around at the crowd and recognized a few patrons as being in the movie industry. Although he had never had an interest in filmmaking, one couldn't avoid hearing all about it in Southern California. And what he had heard, and read in newspapers, made Nigel admire the men who worked in the industry. They were shrewd and clever, possessing keen business sense. A man had but to set up a studio, charge production companies to film there, then he distributed the finished product to movie theaters that his studio owned. Nigel applauded such crafty genius—creating a product that people craved, and then offering it through outlets that only he owned. Independent theaters hadn't a chance to screen popular names so they struggled and withered and died while audiences lined up at studio-owned box offices, cutting out the middleman, creating pure profit. It was brilliant entrepreneuring.

Such business acumen was starting to give him ideas for his own expansion plans. Chatting with these fellows, he knew, picking up tips, strategies, getting into their minds would provide revelations for the enlargement of Stullwood Farms—which he planned to turn into an industry.

Nigel listened with interest as Jack Lamont and the agent discussed Zora's new film, *Forbidden Flowers*. "I'm telling you, Jack, with the right backing, we could afford lavish sets, costumes stitched with real pearls and diamonds, authentic antiques shipped from Europe. No expense spared."

Lamont sipped his drink and said to Nigel, "Have you thought of investing in films?" Before Nigel could respond, Lamont went on.

"I tell you, the movies have never enjoyed a bigger boom than today. The United States produces an average of eight hundred feature films annually. That's 82 percent of the global total. Can you even imagine the revenue that generates? Whatever money you put in you'll get back a hundred times over."

Nigel said he'd give it some thought, but investing in movies wasn't his focus right now. He would borrow the movie industry's business model—maybe purchase a trucking line that would ship only his dates and no other grower's—but getting involved in movies he would leave to other speculators.

He couldn't take his eyes off Zora. The transformation astounded him. Not just the physical aspect, but she was playing out her vamp persona here in this crowded nightclub. People would stop by the table to say hello and congratulate her on her latest film and she would barely acknowledge them. Her blasé aspect was pure perfection. Zora languidly reached into her purse to bring out a cigarette and a long cigarette holder. When it was fixed in place, she propped her elbow on the table and waited while her three companions competed for the honor of lighting it. Intriguing performance, Nigel thought, sitting back to puff on his own cigarette, trying to reconcile the sparky Zora at her desert mansion, calling him "English" and engaging him in witty banter, with this sulky, jaded woman of the world.

As if she felt his gaze on her, Zora shifted her smoky eyes to him and *she* shot him a quick wink.

He grinned. The sparky Zora was still in there. His fascination grew.

"Listen, Barnstable," Lamont said when their plates held nothing but remnants of an expensive meal. "Come by the studio in the morning. I'll leave your name with the guard at the gate. I've got more to pitch to you. I can't let a friend miss out on a financial bonanza like I'm offering."

Nigel didn't respond. He noticed that Zora wasn't speaking much. She certainly didn't speak to those who stopped by her table. Nigel thought about it. And then it occurred to him that maybe the Brooklyn accent wouldn't go with the vamp image. The heavy consonants and brassy tones suited a bubbly girl with freckles and a mop of curly hair. But an immoral seductress would be expected to speak in low tones, possibly with a foreign accent, French perhaps. At least, that was what movie audiences would imagine as they saw her on the screen and read her dialogue on the intertitles.

Nigel wasn't too familiar with the townships that made up New York City, but during his brief stay while courting Elizabeth he had done some exploring. Brooklyn was a neighborhood of poor immigrants and the working class. Hardly an appropriate background for a glamorous seductress.

He found himself wanting to know more about her.

The band now played a tango and ladies in evening gowns were being swept, carried, and dipped around the dance floor. Nigel rose to his feet and held out his hand. Zora considered it and then, with the barest dimple making an appearance on her cheek, she slid her cool fingers into Nigel's hand, burned him with a smoldering look and rose with the grace of a swan. The black evening gown plunged even lower in the back, he noticed. The long string of pearls around her neck followed the V of her neckline. Nigel saw erect nipples beneath the silk.

She followed him onto the dance floor, where Nigel drew her into a seductive embrace, and as they launched themselves into the sexy dance, Nigel said, "Have you noticed we don't like to hear about what other people dream? I mean, any time someone says, 'I had the strangest dream last night,' we shut them out. Why is that?"

He didn't wait for a response. "I suppose it's because dreams aren't real. But if someone says, 'I did the strangest thing yesterday,' we would perk right up and listen. But dreams don't exist. Although," he said, looking into her smoky eyes, "I could be interested in your dreams. What strange meanderings, I wonder, does your sleeping mind engage in? What would they tell me about you? Which Zora would be in the dreams? The one I met in Palm Springs or the one I am dancing with tonight? Fancy that. I met a mystery woman and didn't even know it!"

Her eyelids gave a little flutter. He knew the other Zora was in there, looking out at him through fake-Zora's vampish eyes. Yes, he thought. A man who is interested in your sleeping mind . . .

As he spun her around the floor, Nigel marveled at how this chance encounter had turned out. He was used to being the center of things, the puppet master as it were, Nigel dazzling others. To his surprise, the tables had turned. Nigel Barnstable found himself suddenly the one being dazzled, and he decided he quite liked it.

Watching his wife with Nigel on the dance floor, Jack Lamont was neither jealous nor suspicious. In fact, he loved watching Zora dance with other men. They held her willowy form in their arms, they inhaled her perfume and looked into her eyes, they felt the *promise* of Zora against their body, but she would never be theirs. Men might try, but no man was going to take her from him. Jack knew that Zora was desperately devoted to him. He had rescued her! She came across flirty and maybe even available, and men told themselves she couldn't be that devoted to pudgy, middle-aged, ginger-haired Jack. And yet she was. She professed it to him as she lay in his arms at night, the darkness sharpening her insecurities as she clung tightly to him and whimpered, "Don't ever leave me."

Jack knew her story to the most minute detail. She had grown up Agnes Mulroney in a Brooklyn tenement among Jews, Italians, Irish. Her mother had cleaned offices at night, and her father was nowhere on the scene. Inquiries about him always earned Zora a vague response. And then one day when she was eleven, Zora saw that her mother's gold wedding band had turned her finger green. The next day, a nice new gold band was in its place and that was when Zora realized her mother had never had a real wedding ring but periodically bought one from a novelty store for a penny and wore it until it went green. So her mother wasn't married, Zora realized, which made Zora a you-know-what, as she thought it in her head.

But it wasn't the crushing poverty or the fact of being a bastard that made Agnes Mulroney run away at the age of fifteen with Jack Lamont. She could have toughed it out, stayed and helped her mother, maybe even could have gone to secretary school and worked at one of the offices her mother cleaned. But Mrs. Mulroney invited an "uncle" to stay in their two-room flat one summer and Zora learned of another type of man.

As for Zora's powerful insecurities that lay just below the surface so that she needed constant reassuring, Jack suspected she had inherited them from her mother, a highly nervous woman governed by deep insecurities. Every afternoon when she headed off for the office buildings where she emptied wastebaskets and scrubbed floors, she would look at her daughter and say, "Today is the day I lose my job. Tomorrow we will be evicted." Zora never knew why her mother always made this dire prediction, why she was so certain that she teetered eternally on the brink of joblessness, yet it was a notion so fixed in Mrs. Mulroney's mind that she warned her daughter on a daily basis that they were soon to be living in the street.

Zora got out before that happened. After making her first movie, and making a small name for herself, she went back to the old neighborhood.

Her mother wasn't there. The old apartment was occupied by a Jewish widower who had the saddest face and longest beard Zora had ever seen. Word in the neighborhood was that Bridget Mulroney had run off with one of her boyfriends. That had floored Zora. She hadn't known her mother had boyfriends, except for the one "uncle" who liked fifteen-year-old girls. She hadn't known much about her mother at all, Zora realized, and understood something about herself from that new fact: the reason she wanted to re-create herself was because she hadn't really been anybody to begin with. Too, the fact of her mother disappearing instilled in Zora a new insecurity, as if her mother, in leaving, had left her daughter the only legacy she could, her deep insecurities. After that one trip back home, Zora had plunged herself into the job of becoming a movie star, and the more her star rose, the deeper her insecurities became.

Jack remembered the day he discovered Zora, when he was still making movies in New York. She was Agnes then, and held her drawers up with safety pins. They had put out a casting call for a walk-on part and over a thousand girls had shown up. It was part of a promotion for a new movie coming out. Nothing drew in big box office more than hope. Every girl in line wanted to be the next Lillian Gish. They came fat and thin, tall and short, overdressed, dressed in rags, but all of them desperate to get away from whatever life they were stuck in. Jack had gone through the screen tests in rapid-fire fashion, the faces flashing on and off the screen as his boredom stretched. And then one face blazed on the screen and he sat up.

She was plain, wore no makeup, her long, curly hair drawn back in a bun. Not exactly a beauty, no, not that. Maybe not even really pretty. But something . . .

He had the projectionist play her quick test again, and then again, and then in slow motion, and then frame-by-frame until the projector's bulb burned a hole through the film. Jack had been transfixed, although he couldn't have given specific words. The girl simply had "something."

He found her application form and sent a car to her address in the slums. An hour later she was in his office in Manhattan, looking frightened and much younger than he had thought. She had listed her age as eighteen, but he suspected she was barely fifteen. But already womanly developed. He asked her a few questions, then got her in front of a camera again, this time in costume and makeup.

She dazzled.

She could never make it as a stage actress, he knew, not with that homely accent and even homelier voice. But up on the movie screen she was a goddess. He knew he had found a gold mine. He signed her on under one condition, that she marry him. He didn't want anyone else getting his hands on her. Jack was thirty-five years old, but Agnes didn't mind. She would do anything to get away from Brooklyn. And in time he became her entire life, choosing her movies, her parts, coaching her, creating her. Zora had gone from living with a nervous woman on the edge of constant panic to the sphere of a strong, secure man, and out of that an intense devotion had grown. In ways, she was still immature, still a skinny, frightened child, ashamed of her past, constantly worried that somehow it would catch up with her—the neighborhood of struggling immigrants crammed into brownstone houses that had been converted into flats, where people sat on fire escapes on hot summer days, and rubbish heaps in the streets attracted flies and ragged children. The men with the pushcarts, hawking their wares. The little cubbyhole shops that sold everything from thimbles to overcoats. The Orthodox Jews in the long black coats and wide-brimmed black hats that for some reason made little Zora girlishly uneasy. Zora hated being sent to the bakery for day-old bread. "If they have two-day old, all the better," her mother, weary from a night of scrubbing floors, would say. "And don't let that old crook haggle a single extra penny out of you." And the butcher, where little Zora was sent to buy soup bones that her mother would simmer all day until they had palatable broth to soak their two-day old bread in.

Jack knew every detail of her story, and out of that came a deep love for her. But his love was not in any straightforward way. Not like a paved highway that never veered from its intended direction. Jack's love for Zora was more like a meandering river that changed moods at each bend. Sometimes he lusted after Zora in a husbandly way, other times he cradled her protectively as a father would his little girl. That was because Zora herself was never one thing but always changing.

Jack sat back in the plush booth of the Pink Flamingo speakeasy, puffing on a Cuban cigar, and watched with contentment as a rich and handsome English lord guided his Zora around the dance floor and, despite the closeness of their embrace, the long look into each other's eyes, Jack Lamont knew beyond the faintest doubt that Zora wouldn't even think of betraying him with the man.

*　　*　　*

Standing outside the bunkhouse, Cody finished his cigarette in the quiet desert night.

Elizabeth was coming home in five days.

What was going to happen next? Was she going to fight for dissolution of her marriage, or had the visit with her parents changed her mind? Was she going to return with the decision to work on her marriage, would the Van Lindens have persuaded her that staying was the best? And would Elizabeth then spend every day putting up a cheerful face and pretending everything was all right?

Just like I did when I returned to Montana eleven years ago and told my father I had had a run of bad luck, that the gold had dried up before I could get my pan into the water, keeping the ugly truth buried deep in my heart until, six months later, I buried my father in the snow.

Cody turned his face to the northwest. A cold wind blew down from the Great Basin Desert, making him think of Tylerville. He felt the tug again, as if the ghosts of Tylerville were calling to him. But he would never go back.

He went inside the bunkhouse where the ranch hands were asleep, snoring, coughing. One was propped up on an elbow, reading a paperback novel by flashlight.

A small desk stood at the end of the long dormitory, next to Cody's bunk, with a kerosene lamp on it. He took a seat and, pushing aside the inventory list he had been working on, opened a leather-bound book with blank pages. He had purchased it at Lardner's.

Dipping his fountain pen in the ink bottle, Cody wrote, "Tylerville had six banks, seven gold assayers offices, nineteen saloons, and assorted shops. There was no school and no church, but the jail was the biggest I have ever seen."

He paused. Reaching for a silver flask, he uncorked it and took a bracing swig of bourbon. This would be the last of it. He wondered if he would get a taste for bootleg.

He thought of Belle and Peachy, and felt a sharp pain at their memory. *I don't want to think about you. I don't want to remember.*

But he had to remember. Cody had often found, when writing stories, that forgotten details suddenly presented themselves. Knowing that he would never find Peachy without remembering Peachy's last name, he had decided to take a crack at writing the Horsethief Creek incident. It might jog Peachy's last name loose and bring it to the front of Cody's mind.

Once he found Peachy, he would be able to move on. Go back to Montana, take up the cowboy life again, and get down to the business of forgetting a woman named Elizabeth Barnstable and the troublesome way she had of filling his thoughts.

Cody turned to a fresh page, hesitated, then wrote, "Belle's eyes were the blue of corn flowers, and her flaming hair put any Utah sunset to shame. Her looks were deceptive . . ."

CHAPTER TWENTY

AS THE TRAIN SLOWED AND PULLED into the Palm Springs depot, Elizabeth looked out and saw Cody on the platform, standing beneath a glowing lantern.

Although it was almost summer, desert nights were cold. Elizabeth donned her silver fox fur coat, picked up her heavy carpetbag, and left the stateroom. The train stopped, the conductor lowered the steps and offered her a hand as she climbed down.

Not many passengers disembarked because the *Sunset Limited* had just come from warm southern states. It was the trains that came from the north that brought the hordes and crowds to the desert, people from cold, snowy states seeking heat and sunshine.

She paused to look at Cody at the end of the platform. In Levi's, sheepskin jacket, and black Stetson, he was breathlessly handsome.

Upon receiving her own bank account, having the checkbook placed in her hand, like a golden key to a magical kingdom, Elizabeth had expected to feel different. Surely she, her circumstance, had changed. She no longer had to ask her father or Nigel for money. She had the power to write a check for anything she wanted.

She realized now that she *had* changed, she *did* feel different. But it had nothing to do with money.

To her surprise, the change had to do with Cody McNeal. She had known while she was in New York that she missed him. She had thought about him every day, had carried him around in her heart as she had revisited her favorite city places, silently pointing them out to him, sharing the skyscrapers and monuments and arches with the prairie cowboy.

But now that she saw him standing there alone on the platform, knowing he had come just for her, that he was here for no other purpose than to collect Elizabeth Barnstable, made her ache with both joy and desire—and also fear. She wasn't returning home to Cody but to Nigel, a man who five months ago had slapped her so hard she had lost her baby, a man who had blamed his horrific act on her. A man she could no longer live with but who had threatened to show her who was boss.

She felt as if she were returning home to a dangerous animal that must not be wakened.

Cody turned, and when he saw Elizabeth, he paused. The moment was just for them, no matter who else was on the platform or watching from the train. Their eyes met in lantern-glow as the engine took on water and porters unloaded luggage and the engineer had a talk with the conductor. Elizabeth and Cody looked at one another and then, removing his Stetson, Cody came toward her with a smile on his face. "Elizabeth," he said.

"Cody," she replied, caught in his eyes, realizing that, yes, he was the source of the change in her. She knew that now. It had nothing to do with finances or checkbooks or a small victory over her father. It was this man, tall and fine, who had carried her when she had fallen, who had sat with her during an Indian vision-ritual, who had taken her to see the wildflowers and had shown her an eagle's nest.

She had missed him so!

And then she realized in wonder that she was truly done grieving for her failed marriage, done blaming herself, done being a victim. And with these things decided, she realized she could finally admit to having feelings for Cody.

A carriage had come with the La Alma property, a stately landau that had been kept in excellent condition by the previous owners. While Fiona rode with the ranch hand up on the driver's seat, Cody and Elizabeth rode in the back with the convertible top raised as a buffer against the chill night wind. It formed an intimate shell-like enclosure so that, side by side, with the driver's and Fiona's backs to them, Cody and Elizabeth were afforded some privacy.

It didn't seem right to Cody, however, that Miss Wilson should ride on the driver's seat while he himself rode in cozy and protected comfort. Menfolk should be at the reins and out in the wind and elements, he thought, while the womenfolk were in the back, warm and safe. He knew it had something to do with servants and their masters and being in one's place, but a man should be up on the driver's seat and a lady riding in the back. Strangely, it was Miss Wilson herself who had insisted on the arrangement.

He shook his head. He didn't understand a hierarchical world, although he knew it existed. The cowboy life was an egalitarian one. Maybe the trail boss gave orders, but every man got the same plate of biscuits and beans.

The driver of this carriage was a gray-haired Mexican cowboy named Jesus. The old vaquero had been the ranch manager at La Alma before the Barnstables arrived, and he was a mighty competent man with horses and livestock. But his poor English, sparking the new owner's impatience, had gotten him demoted and now Cody was his boss. Old Jesus was driving the carriage in the cold desert night while the young usurper rode in the back like a king. It upset Cody's sense of fairness.

Cody knew that he was thinking all these unnecessary and irrelevant thoughts, as horses' hooves and creaking wheels made the only sounds in the silent desert night, because he needed to put off thinking about Elizabeth, sitting so closely next to him in the rocking carriage that their arms and shoulders were pressed together. He needed to fill his head with an inner discourse on the unfairness of a hierarchical world so he wouldn't have to think about Elizabeth.

But he couldn't think about anything else.

He was afraid to look at her. They were ensconced in a bubble-world that was populated by exactly the two of them. They had never been so intimate before. It felt close to marital. He both enjoyed it and feared it—feared mostly for himself as he summoned every ounce of willpower he could find to keep from taking hold of her gloved hand. His body wanted to betray him. His need to touch her was overwhelming. He'd broken horses up in Montana, riding broncos that had bucked until they had given up and Cody had stayed in the saddle. He needed that amount of strength right now to keep himself from reaching for Elizabeth's hand.

In the three days and nights on the train, two conflicting emotions had consumed Elizabeth: apprehension at seeing Nigel again and anticipation at seeing Cody. It was like feeling hot and cold at the same time, two extremes competing for space in her heart. But her mind was filled with unknowns. Of course, no one could predict the future, but one certainly could plan a course into it. And Elizabeth's course was to end her marriage and then see where she was to go from there. She prayed that her life as a free woman had Cody McNeal in it.

But it was one thing to make the decision, another to carry out the plan. Nigel would not grant her a divorce; she knew that beyond a doubt. So she would have to fight for one, and Nigel would fight back. There was already a battle of sorts waging between them, Nigel's determination to control and dominate her, Elizabeth's steadfast resistance to him. But a divorce proceeding would bring out the worst in them both, she feared. The war that lay before her was going to be unpleasant, she knew, and dangerous. But it was worth it if she could believe Cody would be her reward at the end.

She suspected he felt the same toward her, but she wasn't sure. There was a mysterious side to Cody that she knew nothing about. He had confessed to being a drifter, to needing to search for someone until he found him. What if he suddenly took off one day? What if he found that man and rode out of Palm Springs to continue on to his destiny? There was so much Elizabeth wanted to know about Cody, so much she needed to know about her place in his life.

But she did know one thing: she would not continue to live with Nigel Barnstable. And if she had not come to the decision in New York to dissolve her marriage to Nigel, she would have come to it tonight, for here was the final proof of the state of her relationship with the stranger she had married: she had sent a telegram to Nigel, informing him of the date and time of her arrival, but it was Cody who had met the train.

She looked up at the stars because she was afraid to look at Cody. If they looked at each other in this proximity, their noses might almost touch, and lips couldn't be far behind. And that was a dangerous line to cross. Just because she had decided she wanted to be free didn't mean she was free already. And the term "adultery" was particularly distasteful to her. When she had wrestled with the thorny dilemma of marriage vows, and how her feelings about Cody must violate those vows, she had solved the dilemma by reminding herself that she had spoken her vows to an impostor and so they were not binding. Still, she was perceived as being married by others. What, in fact, did Cody think? How could she find out without crossing a line?

There was something vaguely sinful about her thoughts. When she imagined herself kissing Cody, it felt like a transgression. And she didn't want their kisses to feel that way. They had to be glorious and God-sent and the most perfect thing in the world.

But she wanted him to kiss her.

Her heart was racing. It was Cody's nearness, the large manly shoulder pressing against hers. He sat with his legs apart, as men did, so that his knee touched hers. It was the most erotic sensation she had ever experienced. But then she realized her heart was racing for another reason: they were drawing near to town, near to her house where she would soon be face-to-face with Nigel, and she had no idea what to expect. Punishment for having gone away? Something small and cruel to detract from any happiness she might have gleaned from a visit with her parents? Perhaps a cold shoulder? Or sham charm? She never knew. And she knew Nigel did it on purpose to keep her on her toes and off-balance. Being unpredictable, she had learned, was one of his more insidious weapons.

As the carriage drew up into the drive, and Elizabeth saw the Norringtons standing in the glow of the open front door, she thought how much she loved this house, how she had grown to love Palm Springs and how eager she was to become part of the desert, with its scarlet sunsets and unexpected snows. But the divorce . . . what was that going to mean in terms of the house? Divorces meant a division of assets. Would Nigel keep the house? Where would she live if he did? And if she kept the house, would he even allow it? Nigel would be a man of cunning reprisals, she suspected. And she knew that from now on she must walk with caution.

She went straight to her bedroom. Shortly after the miscarriage, she had moved out of the master bedroom. No one questioned it, not even Nigel.

When she had left for New York, she had had no intention of passing Nigel's message of financial opportunities to her father. But then she had thought better of it. For her own sake, and for her plan to work, she had to appear to be compliant and obedient. So she had explained to her father about the date industry and Nigel's plans to monopolize production in the Coachella Valley. Her father had listened but had said nothing to her about his thoughts. But when he saw her off at Grand Central Station, he had handed her an envelope, which she now brought to Nigel.

She paused in the doorway to his office. Of course he had not come out to meet her when the carriage drove up. Still, in case Nigel was watching from a window, she had politely thanked "Mr. McNeal" for the ride from the depot and had left him and the driver to take the carriage around to the back.

She looked at Nigel now. He was handsome, broad-shouldered, like a magazine advertisement for expensive men's shirts. The charming came easily to him, and others were easily charmed, as she had been.

His desk was covered with books, magazines, pamphlets, newsletters, all with agrarian titles: *Arabian Desert Plants*, *Woody Plant Seed Manual*, *USDA FS Agriculture Handbook*, *Date Palm Cultivation*. His new obsession to turn the valley into Arabia. She wouldn't be surprised if he imported camels. A map was spread out and she saw, by place names, that it was the whole Coachella Valley. Palm Springs was circled in red. Then another, wider circle around that. And another and another, expanding outward like a bull's-eye, and each had a year written on it in Nigel's hand. She puzzled it out for a second and then realized that it was his plan for expansion. By 1930, Nigel's red circle would encompass the entire valley from Banning to Indio, Joshua Tree to Mount San Jacinto. And she wondered for one detached moment what it was that went through men's minds that made them act so crazy when they saw land.

Strangely, there was an issue of *Hollywood Reporter* on his desk. It seemed out of place.

He looked up. "Ah! I thought I heard you come in. What did your father say to my investment proposal?"

She handed him the sealed envelope. "This is his response. I don't know what it says."

He calmly slit the envelope open with an ivory and silver letter opener and read the letter inside, without so much as an inquiry into how her trip had gone, if her parents were in good health, or if she had brought news back. All he cared about was how others pertained to his own life. Even now, caring not a wit about her father but her father's money. It made her suddenly angry. It was one thing to disrespect her because maybe in his mind she deserved it. But it outraged her to see how he regarded her father, a powerful man in the world of industry and business, but to Nigel, just another person to be used.

She wanted to shout, throw things, strike him about the head with his books and maps, and tell him what she thought of him. But Elizabeth knew she could not afford such a luxury. She knew that to win her battle against Nigel, she must construct a clever strategy and proceed with her campaign without him knowing it. *I will slowly arm myself with pistols and sabers and bayonets, troops and machines of war, and he will not see them, will not see my army coming, so that by the time I sound the bugle for attack, he will be overwhelmed and defeated.*

Nigel finally looked up from the letter. He wasn't pleased. "He turned me down," he said. "The fool has the audacity to say there's no future in date growing." Anger flared in his eyes, and Elizabeth knew he had no one to direct it at but her. Not having her father here to argue with and "show who was boss," Nigel chose the next best thing.

Their eyes locked. She stood her ground although her heart was racing. She braced for the sudden lurch from his chair, the fist, the blow, the pain. She saw tides and eddies swirl in his dark eyes, a reflection of the turbulence in his mind? He seemed to be weighing things in his brain, although she could not guess what. His lower eyelids squinted up like a twitch. The way the dark eyes bore into her, she wondered if he could see through her own pupils and into her mind and see her plans for war, her secret gambits and weapons. And for an instant she thought she had lost before she had even begun.

Elizabeth had thought that having money of her own now, which meant a little more freedom and a bit of power of her own, would make her feel less fearful of Nigel. She had made the long journey back to New York, had stood up to her father and won a victory—a small victory to be sure, but a step toward greater victories to come.

And yet, standing here now, once again in Nigel's proximity, the object of his wrathful gaze, Elizabeth felt the fear rush back like a tidal wave. The day, five months ago, returned with full force and detail, as she lay in bed, hurting and helpless, Nigel making threats, telling her she must be obedient, that he was the boss. And it occurred to her for the first time that perhaps having her own money, her own bit of power and autonomy might not turn out to be the wonderful thing she had thought it would be. Mightn't Nigel see this slice of indepen-dence as a threat to his own control over her? Mightn't he take her bid for independence as an act of rebellion against him?

Is he going to punish me for what I have done?

For the first time, Elizabeth realized that, now more than ever, she was going to have to conduct her life under a cloak of secrecy. Nigel didn't know about her new bank account. There was no reason he should, as it was separate from her trust fund. When they had set it up with a national bank that had branches in Riverside and Los Angeles, only Elizabeth's name had gone on it, with her address here in Palm Springs. Now she realized she could not allow Nigel to see the bank statements, and any correspondence from the bank must be intercepted. She would have to go to Lardner's herself for their daily mail.

Only now did she realize that freedom came with a price. Secrecy and cunning must now become part of her life, which she had thus far lived honestly and openly.

"I'll speak to him myself," Nigel said at last, turning away from her, dismissively. "You no doubt failed to explain my venture to him the way I had instructed you to. I should have known better than to trust you to deliver a simple proposition. I'll write him a letter, and then he and I will talk on the telephone. He will come around to my way of thinking."

He returned to his map, picking up a pen and resuming the restructuring of the Coachella Valley.

Elizabeth left, filled with a new apprehension. She had thought that having money would make her feel secure—courageous, even. But now she saw the money from another side, as something Nigel would take as a threat to himself, or an offense, or even an act of war. She also had seen, in the flash in his eyes after reading her father's letter, that Nigel would extend his punishments to her, not simply for her own infractions, but for the infractions of others.

She went to the kitchen to fix herself a cup of oolong tea. Thankfully no one was there. The Norringtons had retired, and Wilson had been given the rest of the night off. Luisa and the granddaughters had gone back to their village. As Elizabeth filled the teakettle, she looked out the window and saw a pinprick of light among the hundred-tree grove. Flaring, then dying down, flaring again, dying down. Someone smoking a cigarette.

Retrieving a cardigan from a hook by the back door, she slipped it on and went out into the night where orange blossoms filled the air with sweet perfume.

Cody stood in the forest of date palms, their great canopy blotting out moon and stars. He could barely see, through the cluster of massive tree trunks, the lights of the big house. She had gone in there three hours ago. He hated to think of her in there with Barnstable. But it was none of his business.

Despite the cold night, Cody was hatless, the sheepskin jacket hanging open, his shirt unbuttoned at the throat. As he drew on his cigarette, savoring the flavor and heat of the Bull Durham tobacco, he kept his eyes on the big house.

She had been gone for two weeks. The longest two weeks of his life. What had changed in New York? Surely something had. Cody had never been to New York City, but he had seen pictures, movies. It was a place of massive buildings and many people. A place of power and decision-making. It was also Elizabeth's home. She had gone back to her roots to find a beginning and start over. What had she decided? What new path had she chosen, as surely she had not decided to stay in New York. No, that was an insupportable thought.

When he saw her, materializing from the thick, dark trees as if his imagination had decided to reward him, Cody threw down his cigarette and tamped it with his boot. "Elizabeth!" He was surprised to see her. It didn't strike him as wise for her to join him out here in the darkness. If Barnstable were to see them . . .

"I want to tell you something," she said softly, looking around. The Indian village was dark and deserted, as they had moved up the mountain for the summer. From the bunkhouses, men's voices, a guitar, a harmonica. The big house, no sign of Nigel. "I wanted to tell you right away."

Something urgent, Cody realized, to make her risk Barnstable's jealousy. Cody was suddenly apprehensive. *She's decided to move back to New York, and I'll never see her again.*

She came slowly toward him, walking in a way he had never seen before. Cody had thought he had identified all of Elizabeth's walking moods by now, when she was melancholy or deep in thought searching for a vegetable patch, or striding down the main street with energy in her step, when she had tramped through canyons calling out for Button. But this gait was shy, hesitant, as if a whole new way of thinking were impelling her.

She stopped a few feet away as nearby blossoming orange trees gave off their pungent scent that heralded the coming of a hot summer. Her eyes met Cody's in unspoken communication, feelings moving on the air as if demanding to be felt.

Cody wanted her, now, urgently. But he made no move. She was not free, and he would never take another man's woman. He had made promises to himself years ago when, in his grief and selfishness, he had stolen from another man, had taken what was not his.

She came to a standstill in the moonlight. They looked at each other across the small space between them, neither knowing what to do next, what was permitted. What did friends do when they were reunited? Friends hugged. A simple, friendly, welcome-home hug. So when Cody in fact said, "Welcome home," she took the bold step and when she reached him, his arms opened and went around her. They embraced. She felt her heart go to Cody's and join it. But she also felt a thousand eyes watching them—imagined, only, but frightening all the same. How could so wonderful and comforting and exciting an embrace seem so sinful? No, not sinful—forbidden. There was a difference.

His body felt so good. For one delirious moment he was hers. She dared to slip her hands under the jacket and feel the hard muscles of his back. She could smell him—tobacco and leather and shaving soap. He was warm and solid, and she never wanted to let go.

For Cody, it rocked him to his core to feel Elizabeth in his arms this way—not helpless as she had been twice before, but upright and holding him as a woman with her own mind should. She was both strong and delicate. He pressed his lips to her silken hair but allowed himself to go no further.

They stepped away at the same time, not wanting to, but aware that the night had eyes. "I need to tell you something," she said. She had practiced it on the train. Cody was going to be the first and only person she was going to say it to. What she had to tell him needed lead-up, preparation, a preamble to soften the jolt of her news. But words failed her now as she looked up into his eyes and still felt weak and melted from his embrace. The rational mind, it seemed, turned to jelly when the heart took over. So she said simply, "I'm getting a divorce."

There, she had said it. To say the word out loud made it real. So far it had only been a word inside her head. But spoken, as she had done it just now, gave solidity to the commitment she was making. Elizabeth was not naïve. Divorce was a drastic step, especially when instigated by the wife. This was a man's world. Divorce was not the luxury of women. As with winning the right to vote, divorce for a woman was a long and hard battle. Even after the win, Elizabeth knew, the divorcée was cast in questionable light. Men spoke a divorcée's name with a wink. She was a woman who had "been around." To other women, she was a woman who couldn't keep a man. It was why so many remained in unhappy marriages rather than take on the stigma of divorce.

"I'm going to hire a lawyer," she said, because Cody hadn't said anything; he just stared at her. "I have the money now. I can act on my own. I will seek advice and then start the proceedings."

Cody finally came to life. He himself didn't know why he froze at her news. Maybe it was because it was too good to be true. It was what he wanted, Elizabeth to be free. If you ask for the moon and someone gives it to you, you have to experience some kind of shock, don't you?

"Nigel cannot know," she added. "If he were to catch even a hint of what I'm planning—"

Cody held up a hand. "I won't say a word, Elizabeth. I promise. My God, divorce . . ." A look of admiration came into his face. Worry and concern as well—he knew what she was taking on. But then a wave of joy swept over him. She was going to be free! As his emotions fought for dominance, Cody felt a strange urgency come over him as a new truth presented itself, harsh and unavoidable. He had to tell Elizabeth the truth about himself, and he had to tell her now.

He was suddenly nervous. He had trailed a thousand head of cattle through rough country, encountering storms, flash floods, rising rivers, wolves, and cattle thieves. But all of that paled when compared to having to make this confession to Elizabeth. "I have to tell you something," he said.

She waited. She kept an eye out for anyone watching or walking nearby. When she heard a twig snap, she froze, looked around. Nigel, coming to inspect his grove? Then she saw the gray, shaggy shape of a coyote sneaking away through the trees.

Cody had never told anyone about Belle and Peachy and Horsethief Creek. How would Elizabeth judge him? We are creatures of judgment, he thought. Everyone judges everyone else. But if he was going to form any kind of bond with Elizabeth, if she was going to be free someday and he had a chance at being in her life, he wanted it to be on honest terms. He didn't want to offer himself piecemeal, showing her only the best parts while keeping the ugly truth hidden, because then it wouldn't really be Cody McNeal she was embracing, it would be an incomplete copy of himself, all spit-polish and shine. He wanted her to love him for all his facets, good and bad, because then it would mean it was true love.

And there was the fact that she had fallen in love once before with a man who charmed her with a façade, only to leave her devastated when she learned his true nature. Cody would not do the same.

He searched the grove for words, took a deep breath and said, "I was seventeen. We had just come through two bad winters up in Montana. My father couldn't pay the bank on our mortgage, and they were threatening to sell the ranch out from under us. I heard of a gold rush in Colorado. My father grubstaked me with the last of his money, plus an heirloom gold watch, my mother's wedding ring, and her cameo brooch. I went to Colorado promising him I would strike it rich. I staked my claim and broke my back panning for gold at Horsethief Creek. A year later, I was all of eighteen and a rich man. I stored my gold with one of the banks in town. And then a girl named Belle drifted into town with a hard-luck story and the biggest, bluest eyes I had ever seen."

He bent to pluck a blade of grass and shredded it as he said, "She caught the fancy of every man in town, but she chose me. She worked her magic and cast a spell on me." Cody shook his head at the memory. "We got married four weeks later. We stood before a justice of the peace, said our vows, he pronounced us husband and wife and gave us the certificate to prove it."

Cody's voice grew quiet. "I don't remember much about the wedding night. My friends threw a party in one of the saloons and I got drunk. Apparently they carried me up to a hotel room and Belle put me to bed. When I woke up the next morning, Belle was gone. And so, I discovered an hour later, was all my gold. She had taken the marriage certificate to the bank and cleared out my account. I never did know what happened to her after that."

Elizabeth didn't know what to say. "I am so sorry," she said.

"I told you that I'm looking for someone. His name was Peachy but I don't recall his last name. I do recall that Peachy stood up with us during the marriage ceremony, and I reckoned he would have signed the certificate as a witness. So I wrote to the Denver County records office and asked for a copy of our marriage license, hoping to get Peachy's last name. But they wrote back and said there is no record of a marriage at Horsethief Creek in 1910 between Cody McNeal and a woman named Belle. Maybe it wasn't even a real ceremony. Maybe Belle and the man who passed himself off as a justice of the peace traveled around faking marriage ceremonies to give her access to men's bank accounts."

Elizabeth couldn't take her eyes off Cody's face. She wanted to touch it. "But why are you looking for Peachy?"

Cody walked a couple of steps away, rested his hand on the rough trunk of a date palm. Then he said, "Peachy was a prospector on the claim next to mine. I nicknamed him Peachy because whenever I asked him how he was doing, he always said, 'Peachy!' A cute kid with freckles and hair the color of carrots. A bit simple-minded, I suspect, always good-natured, always buying drinks for everyone. He had a sweetheart back home, she was all he talked about, how he was going to set her up in a fine house and give her all the dresses and jewelry she wanted. Peachy was in love, no doubt about it.

"But when Belle left me and took my gold, I fell into the grip of a strange madness. I not only had a shattered heart, but I had let my father down—he was counting on me to save the ranch."

He paused again and Elizabeth saw the pain in his eyes, heard it in his tight voice. "Peachy didn't trust banks. He kept his gold with him at his small camp. I crept in one night and took Peachy's stash while he slept, and I ran away. When I got to Montana, I discovered I was too late. The bank had already sold the ranch. The new owners were living in the house my father had built with his own hands. They had kept him on as a worker, and he was living in the bunkhouse. I lied to him and told him the gold had run out before I got there. He said it was all right and we'd manage, but he died that winter. The doctor said it was pneumonia from going out into the snow to save the cattle. I think it was his spirit. After he lost the ranch, the soul just seemed to seep out of him. I couldn't stay so I took to drifting."

He squinted at the moon rising round and ivory over the mountains. "I thought about Peachy. I wondered what happened to him. Did disaster strike him, too, because of the loss of his gold? Was he able to get back home to his sweetheart?

"You see, Peachy was naïve. He didn't possess worldly smarts. He was gullible and trusting and without survival skills. I once had to show him how to start a fire without a match. A kid who, if he strayed three feet from his farm, would get lost. I took his gold and left him nothing but his pans and bedroll—and the devastating knowledge that a man he had called friend had taken everything from him.

"I returned to Horsethief Creek to find it a ghost town," he went on. "But there's more." He drew in a deep breath to brace himself. "I encountered a few old miners still panning the creek. They told me that there was a terrible riot there, around the time I left. According to the story, one of the miners accused another of taking his gold. A fight broke out. It spread through the camp and resulted in the deaths of four men."

He faced her squarely. "I caused that riot, Elizabeth. It was Peachy who accused another man of taking his gold."

"You don't know that—"

"Yes, I do. When I took Peachy's stash, I didn't think of consequences. I thought only of my shame and saving my father's ranch. I didn't think of what would happen after I left. Four men died because of me. And maybe Peachy was one of them. I visited the graveyard outside the ghost town. The markers had no names because no one knew who they were. What if Peachy lies in one of those graves?"

She didn't know what to say. What did you say to a story like that? She wanted to comfort him with words and touch, but neither was a luxury available to her, not here, not while still being Mrs. Barnstable with her husband in the house beyond the trees. "I am so sorry," she whispered, and she meant it with all her heart.

"You know what kills me more than anything?" Cody said, and Elizabeth saw dampness in his eyes. "It was so easy. Too easy. I remember thinking, as I slid my hand under Peachy's pillow, it's your own fault I'm doing this, Peachy, because you should've put your gold in the bank like everyone else. I can still feel the weight of Peachy's head as my hand felt underneath for the stash. His head let him down, Elizabeth. Peachy was relying on his head to be the alarm, like cowbells on a fence warning of a breech. But Peachy's head just slumbered on as my thieving fingers pulled out an old sock filled with nuggets. I blamed Peachy and Belle and Montana bankers—they had forced me to commit an unforgivable act. I ran off cowardly into the night."

Elizabeth looked up into the rugged, square-jawed face with scars and sun-weathered skin—looked at but saw only a scared eighteen-year-old boy as he stole from a friend, stole not only Peachy's gold but Peachy's security and maybe even Peachy's life. Cody was a man but Elizabeth saw a boy, callow and frightened and caught in a panic because a woman—his first—had crushed his heart, and he had made a promise to his father that he could no longer keep.

"So now you know, Elizabeth, I owe a debt and until I have paid it, I cannot rest."

Elizabeth tried to think of words of comfort, but none seemed adequate. His tale had moved her deeply. "What do you know about him?" she asked. It sounded feeble. She should be offering so much more. But, actually, knowing the facts of Peachy were what was going to lead Cody to finding him.

"After a back-breaking day of panning for gold, Peachy got drunk and told me all about himself. But I only half-listened, not knowing that someday finding him was going to be the sole and urgent focus of my life. I remember that his name sounded Irish and that he lived in a place that had 'ville' or 'city' in it. Maybe 'burg,' I don't know. But I do remember that Peachy had said if he didn't strike it rich in Colorado, he would keep trying and go wherever gold was found. And that is what I am doing. And I won't stop until I find him."

"So you're punishing yourself?"

Cody nodded. "I suppose I am."

"You were only eighteen." *Just as I was only nineteen when I fell in love with a man capable of sudden brutality.*

His eyes met hers. "The reason I'm a drifter, Elizabeth, is because a new town is temporary relief. I am so busy learning the new landscape, the people, the local gossip and news that it all crowds the old memories out. But as I become familiar with a town and its citizens, as my mind becomes less challenged, my guard drops and the memories, like hungry wolves, come rushing in. And so I have to move on, to run from the dark devils, to find the one town in all the world where I can finally leave the memories and the pain behind and lead a normal life."

He released a ragged sigh. "And, yes, I am driven by a guilty conscience. I can never allow myself to settle down into a comfortable life, I can never allow myself happiness—not until I know what happened to Peachy."

"But you've been in Palm Springs for a year."

"It's the longest I've ever stayed in one place."

Their eyes met again and the moment stretched until it grew uncomfortable and Cody felt himself slipping toward a deadly precipice. Needing to keep talking, needing words to pull him back from the abyss, he said, "But you know what? I've started writing the story of me and Belle and Peachy. I have a compulsion to go back into the past. Maybe it's because I need to change it. I know it can't be done," he said, tapping his head. "But the need is in here," he added, placing his hand over his heart.

He reached out and touched her hair. "I learned long ago that if you don't have friends, then there's no one to let you down. Or vice versa. If I don't have friends, I won't let anyone down, whether I mean to or not. Elizabeth, I've only ever missed one person in my life—my father. After I buried him I missed him so sorely that I couldn't sleep and I cried when I was sure no one could see. But when you boarded that train, Elizabeth, and it carried you out of this valley, I felt a hollowness inside me that was frightening. A part of me went away on that train, but now it's come back."

Through the trees, they suddenly heard a door open and slam. They stiffened, listening for footfall. When none came, Cody said, "You'd better go back in. Nigel will be wondering where you are."

But how could she, when Cody had just laid bare his soul?

He saw the hesitancy in her eyes, the frown. She was torn, he knew. Just as he was. He took a step back from her, to break invisible bonds they had had no right to create, giving her a chance to slip away. "I'll stay here while you go back to the house."

He watched her go. He had wanted to say more but didn't want to give her false hopes. As he was recording the events of eleven years ago at Horsethief Creek, Cody had found memories returning, people and incidents he had forgotten. It was as if the pen were setting his thoughts free. What other memories were going to be revealed? Peachy's last name? The town he had said he was from?

He didn't want to give Elizabeth hope that might not come to anything, but Cody couldn't help embracing that hope himself. That soon, they would both be free.

As the fragrance of orange blossoms filled his head and as he filled his mind with Elizabeth's beauty, he knew that from this moment forward, wherever life took him, even in distant future years, the scent of orange blossoms would make him think of Elizabeth.

And then he thought: No. I won't need orange blossoms. Wherever life takes me after this night, even into distant future years, I will *always* think of Elizabeth.

*　　*　　*

"My dear Fiona, forgive me for not meeting you at the train station, but when Mr. McNeal said he was picking you and Elizabeth Barnstable up, I decided that my presence might raise some eyebrows, and protecting your good reputation is my number one priority. Can you come see me Saturday evening? I have planned a special picnic, just the two of us. I missed you terribly. Yours, Leland."

Fiona had been overjoyed to find the envelope on her pillow when she and Her Ladyship returned from their New York trip. She had been disappointed that Leland hadn't come to the depot to meet them, and then Mrs. Norrington said he had come by and asked her to give Miss Wilson this note.

She had read the note a hundred times since, pressing it to her bosom where her heart raced with love. A special picnic. Just the two of us.

And then, in the next instant, her joy had collapsed into fear and dread.

Fiona had been in an emotional storm since the afternoon Mrs. Van Linden had exacted a verbal promise from her never to leave Elizabeth's side. Fiona had had no choice but to reiterate her promise as a sign of gratitude. She had also been forced into the promise by another simple fact: that she did not know what the future held. What if Leland didn't ask her to marry him and there she would be, out on her own once again, with no employment and no references and, worse, no husband? She couldn't take that gamble. So she had repromised Mrs. Van Linden, and Fiona had been miserable ever since as she both hoped for Leland's marriage proposal, and at the same time dreaded it, as she would have to turn him down!

So now this invitation to a special picnic, which could mean only one thing. And while Fiona should be walking on air for the sheer joy of it, she was walking with wooden feet as her emotions pulled her this way and that. Please, oh please, my dearest Leland, ask me to marry you. But I cannot, as I am not free, so don't ask me!

Taking the path to Leland's front door, she saw him standing on the step to greet her, as if he had been watching for her in the lane. The smile on his face, and the way his hair had been combed and pomaded, the obvious new suit, the shined shoes—he wanted to look his best for her. Just as she did for him, wearing a new dress purchased at Macy's in New York. The latest fashion, with a little cloche hat that matched her clutch bag.

She looked at the man on the step, attractive features glowing in the last of the sunlight. Leland was not film star handsome. No chiseled jaw or impressive nose or deep-set brooding eyes. There was a merriment about his face, even when he was serious, that made one think he was about to burst into jocularity. His face drew one to him, compelled one to want to know more about him. Fiona knew that Leland had known many ladies in his life. It did not make her jealous. If anything, she thought with pride, he chose me.

"There you are," he said with a smile that sent her heart soaring while also filling her with anxiety and apprehension.

Leland had decided against a buggy ride into the desert. The Santa Ana winds were kicking up, sending dust devils over the sand, uprooting cactus and small plants. His final seduction could just as easily be carried out in the small garden behind his house, where an arbor covered in brilliant bougainvillea provided shelter and romantic privacy.

He took her hands and held her with shining eyes. "You were gone for a lifetime," he murmured

He led her through the house and out into the garden, which was cast in shadow as the sun was setting and evening darkness was slithering across the valley. Overhead, three white owls chased one another in the dusk, flying in quick, intricate patterns, calling *nik-nik-nik*.

Leland had set lanterns out, glowing in the gathering gloom. A blanket lay spread on the floor of the arbor. Fiona saw the picnic basket, the loaf of bread, block of cheese, the wine. But she had no appetite. She was nervous, fearful, and yet hopeful as well. Never had she known such confusion!

Her body ached—sweetly, longingly. She wanted Leland to engulf her with his strength and maleness. She had never been so aware as she was in that moment the utter femininity of her life, serving ladies and matrons with the help of maids and housekeepers while butlers and footmen existed on the periphery. She wanted the attention of a man now. She wanted to be the center of a male world.

Beneath the arbor, Leland paused to look at her, then he bent to kiss her. They had kissed before, but this time his lips were parted. Fiona did the same and when his tongue touched hers, an electric jolt shot through her. She was suddenly on fire. And she thought: am I to give all this up for a promise exacted from me by blackmail? There had to be a way . . .

He helped her down to the blanket where she sat on one hip, her legs tucked modestly under her skirt. Leland knelt on one knee and poured two glasses of wine. Both went untouched as Leland reached over to stroke Fiona's cheek, hair, neck. She closed her eyes and moaned. He kissed her again and she met it with passion.

He eased her back so that she lay looking up at the leafy arbor. Bougainvillea petals danced around Leland's head. The wind howled out on the desert, but the house and citrus trees provided a windbreak. She welcomed his weight on her. Leland's hot breath on her neck. His hands exploring. It was heavenly, not at all the rutting of her childhood.

And then he slipped his hand under her skirt.

"Wait," she whispered. "Leland, there is something I have to tell you." And as soon as she said it, Fiona was filled with sudden hope. Leland was a clever man. He had survived by his wits for years. And now that he was clearly demonstrating that he wanted her, surely he would come up with a solution to her dilemma. Yes! Leland would know what to do about her promise to Mrs. Van Linden and how they could still get married.

She sat up to face him. "I made a promise to someone . . ." She tried to think of a way to explain it. "I promised Mrs. Van Linden that I would never leave her daughter's employ. It's a long story, Leland, and I will tell it to you. But, for now, you have to know that I must continue to live at La Alma."

He looked at her in confusion. "Okay," was all he said.

Now it was Fiona's turn for confusion. "Leland, what I am saying is that when we get married we will have to work out living arrangements. I can't go back on my word and leave Her Ladyship, I can't leave La Alma, but of course I want to be your wife."

He stared at her as if she had just suggested they spread their wings and fly.

"You do understand, don't you?" she said, mistaking his look for one of disappointment, expecting him to shout out his indignation over promises and Mrs. Van Linden and Fiona living at La Alma. Instead he said nothing, and the silence suddenly seemed ominous. And then a horrible revelation struck her. She looked at him in shock. "You *were* going to ask me to marry you, weren't you?"

He opened his mouth but nothing came out. And then she saw the look of a man caught in a trap.

She pressed her hand to her mouth, where moments before, Leland had kissed her with the passion of a man intent on marriage. Or so she had thought. Then she looked at the picnic basket, the bread and wine, the blanket spread on the grass. "Oh God," she said. She stumbled to her feet. "Oh God." She reached for one of the arbor posts to steady herself and a bougainvillea thorn stabbed her in the thumb. She snatched her hand back. "Oh God," she said again.

Leland stood up and frantically searched for something to say. What on earth had just happened? This was a disaster.

Leland felt the breath go out of him, as if someone had kicked him in the stomach. "My dear Fiona, I am so sorry you thought that.

If I misled you in any way, I apologize. It's just that . . . I'm not the marrying kind."

Tears rose in her eyes. "Well, I'm not the *other* kind." She pushed past him. "I'm going home."

"I'll walk with you."

"No!" she cried. And she fled down the garden path to disappear into the night while Leland stood there with his arms hanging down, feeling like the stupidest man on earth.

*   *   *

"Are you sure you don't want me to go with you?" Cody said.

They were standing on the railway platform while the *Sunset Limited* took on wood and water. "I prefer to go alone. I need to go alone."

It was vitally important to Elizabeth that she make the trip into Los Angeles, a hundred miles away, on her own. For the first time in her life, she was going somewhere without a companion. Even such mundane errands as shopping at Macy's had always been in the company of a footman or a maid. This was symbolic of her liberation. And it excited her.

"Remember what Augie Lardner said about the courthouse," Cody said. "That's where all the lawyers' offices are."

"I'll remember," she said with a smile. She knew he was going to worry about her. For this reason, she hadn't told Cody that she had altered her agenda, that she was also going to seek the services of a gynecologist. She knew that Nigel wanted an heir. Elizabeth needed to take steps to ensure that it never happened.

"All aboard!" the conductor called.

She extended her gloved hand and Cody took it. From now on, they must practice extreme caution. "I'll be back this evening, Mr. McNeal," she said in case anyone was watching from the depot office or the train.

"And I will be here to meet you."

She would be home before Nigel knew she was even gone. That morning, as Norrington dressed him, Nigel had informed the butler that he was driving into Indio to meet with a representative from a drilling company and would most likely be staying over at a hotel.

The conductor called, "All aboard!" a final time, and Elizabeth climbed the steps up to the railway car. Steam jets hissed from the giant iron wheels, the cars groaned and creaked, and the train slowly pulled away to continue its westward trek. Cody remained on the platform long after the train had vanished into the hills.

*   *   *

From the scorching desert the train headed into cooler air as it chugged westward, up through the Banning Pass and into greener country. The tracks ran through orange and lemon orchards, acres and acres as far as the eye could see. Elizabeth saw fruit stands along roadsides, where cars and horses were pulled up. She spotted the occasional gas station and motor court with cabins. And then the train entered more densely populated areas, towns that radiated out from Los Angeles.

Finally she arrived at Union Station, where she hired a taxi to take her to the courthouse. She rode through streets designed for horses and carriages but clogged now with a river of black automobiles, all belching smoke, all sounding their horns.

The courthouse stood on West First Street and Broadway, not far from downtown Los Angeles and, as she had been told, tall buildings stood like sentinels on the streets. Not exactly the skyscrapers of Manhattan, but impressive enough.

She paid the cab driver and entered a twelve-story glass and brick monolith with LEGAL BUILDING printed on its marquee. She had no idea how to go about choosing a lawyer, she would learn as she went. Someone, in all these offices, should be able to guide her.

Crossing the spacious lobby, noisy with foot traffic, she found the building's directory, and as she perused the long list of names, she saw specialties listed: criminal defense, personal injury, bankruptcy, real estate, probate. When she came upon "Family Law," she realized that must be the specialty she needed. One firm, listing twelve men, added as their specialty, "divorce and custody cases."

They were who she needed. But before she headed for the elevators, Elizabeth finished perusing the directory, just to be sure. A lone name jumped out. Mary Clark, Esq., Family Law.

A woman! Elizabeth stood for a moment in indecision. And then she thought: She will fight for me.

The office was on the third floor. This is it, Elizabeth thought, as she stood before the door with a milky glass pane and the words MARY CLARK, Esq. printed in gold. The biggest step of her life. Was this what it had felt like for the women who had chained themselves to the White House fence, demanding the vote?

Opening the door—so prosaic a gesture and yet she knew it would be crossing an invisible frontier—Elizabeth walked in and found in a small office, a woman sitting at a desk. "I'd like to see Mrs. Clark," Elizabeth said. "It's personal legal business."

The woman rose with a smile. "You're looking at her. And it's Miss. But I don't recall making an appointment for this hour."

"Do I need one?" Elizabeth looked around. She saw no other doors and realized that Miss Clark didn't seem to have a receptionist or secretary.

Miss Clark gave her a long look, then said in a kindly tone, "One doesn't just walk into an attorney's office and get seen right away."

She was around her mother's age, Elizabeth gauged, late forties, with graying brown hair drawn back in a bun. She had surprisingly pretty features, and then Elizabeth wondered why she would be surprised. What had she expected? Women who worked in a man's world must perforce be mannish. But Mary Clark was small and feminine. Even the tie at her throat, narrower and shorter than a man's, was ladylike.

Elizabeth looked at the shelves packed with books, the desk stacked with folders and letters and legal-looking documents, and felt an unexpected thrill go through her. How wonderful it must be to possess such an education, such knowledge and power.

"I'm sorry, I didn't know I was supposed to make an appointment." In all her twenty years, Elizabeth couldn't recall needing to have an appointment. Whenever she or her parents needed medical or dental help, or the last minute services of a seamstress or tailor, they simply showed up and were taken care of. "I've come all the way from Palm Springs. Can I make an appointment now and come back?"

Another long look and Miss Clark said, "I had planned on using this hour to write briefs, but I suppose they can wait. Please, have a seat Miss . . . ?"

"Mrs. Elizabeth Barnstable." They shook hands, and Elizabeth sat in a chair facing the desk.

"Before we begin, Mrs. Barnstable, let me assure you that I attended an excellent law school and graduated in the top fourth of my class. Those are my credentials there." She pointed to a wall of framed documents.

"You don't have to explain to me," Elizabeth said.

Miss Clark's mouth lifted in a faint smile. "Mrs. Barnstable, if I may give you some advice? Always check the credentials of any professional whom you hire. They won't be offended, and if they are, then you should not hire them."

"I will remember that."

Miss Clark folded her hands on the desk. "How can I help you?"

"I wish to obtain a divorce, and I need to know my rights and my chances."

"Very well, I'll take some information down first and then you can fill me in."

As Elizabeth told her story, Miss Clark took notes on a pad of lined paper, the gold pen making a scratching sound while through the open window, sounds from the street below drifted in—cars honking, trolley bells ringing, a policeman's whistle.

When she had Elizabeth's details and history down, Miss Clark sat back and, tapping the pen on her wrist, said, "I must warn you in advance that obtaining a divorce is not easy for a woman. Sometimes the fights get very nasty. There's a saying—truth is foreign to the divorce court. Mr. Barnstable could accuse you of infidelity, and even if you have never even thought such a thing, his lawyers could take innocent relationships and incidents in your life and twist them into something ugly. Does anyone else live with you?"

"No." Then: "Well, we have servants, do they count?"

"Definitely. In fact, they will be the ones your husband's lawyer, when it comes to it, will focus on because servants are privy to the secrets in your life. While you have to put on a good act for friends and neighbors, you have to put on a better act for servants. Your friends and neighbors will be called to testify. It is important that the only thing they can say is that your marriage appeared to be stable."

The irony of it struck Elizabeth, that Nigel's insistence that they put on the appearance of a normal and amiable marriage should now be used as a weapon in her own favor. "But is a court trial necessary, calling witnesses? Nigel assaulted me. He made me lose my baby. That should be enough for grounds."

"I know that, and I sympathize. But, Mrs. Barnstable, you didn't go to a hospital. And at the time of the incident, you told everyone that you tripped and fell against a chair. You can't now change your story. Your husband's lawyer will tear your testimony apart. We need an overt act of cruelty and abuse. With witnesses and proof. But don't provoke him into action. You survived the last assault, you might not be so lucky next time."

"He forces himself on me in the bedroom."

"That doesn't count. There is no rape in marriage. He would be exercising his conjugal rights." She leaned forward. "Mrs. Barnstable, as unpleasant as it might be, I suggest you continue to humor him for now. If you resist, or deny him his marital rights, it could end very badly for you. I've seen it before. From now on, you will have to lead an exemplary life."

When Elizabeth started to say, "There is a man," Miss Clark held up her hand. "Nip that in the bud right now. Any evidence that you are engaged in extramarital activities will ruin your chances forever of getting a divorce. It will be impossible, unless your husband turns around and sues for divorce. But if, as you say, you suspect he married you for your money, I'd say your chances of that are slim. So be on your best behavior from now on. In the meantime, I will put one of my investigators on the case to learn as much about your husband's activities outside the home as we can. It's important that we build a case of bad character against him. He will be followed, photographed, but discreetly. My man is very good at what he does. Is there a chance there are other women in your husband's life?"

"Would that be grounds for divorce?"

"I'm afraid adultery isn't enough in the man's case. While adultery on the part of the wife is enough for a man to divorce her, the same isn't true for the husband."

"That hardly seems fair."

"Current divorce laws aren't fair. They greatly favor the husband. We need something more. If he hits you again, go to a doctor at once and have pictures taken of the injury. Get as much documentation as you can." Miss Clark glanced at the small watch pinned to the lapel of her tweed jacket. "I'm afraid our time is up. You will need to pay me a retainer for my services. A hundred dollars will do."

Elizabeth drew the leather-bound checkbook out of her purse. Placed it on the desk. Opened it. Helped herself to one of the pens on the desk. Dipped it in the inkwell and slowly filled it out the way the new accounts manager at the bank in New York had shown her. She waved it to dry the ink, then handed it across. Never had putting pen to paper felt so liberating.

"How shall I contact you?" Miss Clark said, rising from her chair. "Is it safe for me to send correspondence to your home?"

Elizabeth had already thought of this. "You can contact me by telephoning Lardner's General Store in Palm Springs. My home is not yet on the telephone, but someone from the store will get a message to me. When you contact me, I will take the train in to Los Angeles."

Elizabeth had a feeling that hers was not the first highly sensitive and possibly dangerous case Miss Clark had handled. She would bet that, through word of mouth, Miss Clark found many such desperate women walking through her door.

"One last thing," Elizabeth said. "Could you recommend a woman doctor? A gynecologist."

Their eyes met. Miss Clark nodded in understanding and, opening a drawer, brought out a business card. "I frequently refer my female clients to this woman. In fact, I'll give her a call so her office will be expecting you. I'll ask if she can see you right away, considering you have come such a distance. Her name is Dr. Violet Greene." Mary Clark gave Elizabeth a direct stare and spoke pointedly as she said, "I understand that you are going to see Dr. Greene about a medical matter. If anything other than your health is discussed, I cannot know about it, do you understand?"

Elizabeth understood enough from what she had learned from Libby and the extremely controversial "birth control" movement in New York. Not only had doctors been arrested for breaking the federal anti-obscenity law by educating patients on the facts of preventing conception, as well as distributing contraceptive devices, patients themselves had been arrested and put in jail. Elizabeth knew to move with caution and to be circumspect in her approach for advice.

As she tucked the card into her purse, she had the curious sense of having stepped aboard an underground railroad of sorts, such as the secret network of routes and safe houses created by African slaves a hundred years ago while escaping to free states and Canada with the aid of sympathetic abolitionists. How many women, seeking asylum and liberation from nightmare marriages and desperate situations, were helped by women such as Mary Clark and Violet Greene?

"Remember, while I have my investigator looking into your husband," Miss Clark said, "you yourself must now lead an unimpeachable life. The slightest gesture could be misconstrued and used against you. Don't shake hands with men. No innocent pecks on the cheek. Like Caesar's wife, you have to be above reproach. When I have collected enough grounds, I will file the divorce papers. There will then be a hearing and witnesses will be called. We have to be sure no one can say they saw you in any compromising circumstances. Divorce cases are always harder on the woman. If the husband strays, judges tend to wink and look the other way. It's an old boys' club, and women are not allowed to join."

Another taxi ride took her to a medical building six blocks away, where a nurse admitted Elizabeth at once, despite patients in the waiting room.

Dr. Greene was in her sixties, white-haired, and didn't smile much. She wore a white doctor's coat over a skirt and blouse, and listened with a serious expression as Elizabeth repeated her story.

"I am starting my divorce case against Nigel, and although I was told I might not be able to have children again, there is still a chance that I can conceive. Nigel wants an heir, and I can't let it happen. If I do, I will never be free of him."

It was a story Violet Greene had heard time and again. She sympathized with such women and was a personal supporter of the new birth control movement.

But she had to be on her guard. The most frequent requests she received were for birth control advice and paraphernalia, both of which were illegal to disseminate, and prescriptions for medicinal alcohol, which was limited and regulated. She had heard of doctors getting caught by policewomen disguised as patients.

"You do know that what you are asking me to do is illegal?" Dr. Greene said, settling gray, somber eyes on Elizabeth, making Elizabeth wonder what strange and tragic sights they had witnessed. "Mrs. Barnstable, I believe women should have the right to control their own bodies. Unfortunately, the lawmakers and judges don't agree— that's because they are all men. Until we get women in Congress and the White House, we will be under their thumbs." She leaned forward, clasping her hands on the desk. "If this gets out, I will lose my medical license. And most likely we will both go to jail. Do you understand the severity of this situation?"

"I do."

Dr. Greene searched Elizabeth's face, studied her body language, reviewed the story of spousal abuse resulting in a miscarriage, and she arrived at a decision.

She got up and went to a locked drawer, and drew two items out of it. The first was a pamphlet. "This explains about human reproduction and the various home methods that have proven helpful in contraception. Don't let anyone see this, and never tell them were you got it from."

The second object came in a flat envelope. It was yellow and made of latex. "It's called a diaphragm. I will show you how to insert it and keep it in good condition, you must make sure there are no holes in it."

"Will my husband . . ."

"He will be unaware that it is in place. In addition," the doctor said, "there is new research being conducted on human ovulation. Do you know what that is?"

Elizabeth shook her head.

"It is when an egg is released and ready to be fertilized. Prior thinking was that a woman was at her most fertile phase just after or just prior to having her period and that the middle of her cycle made her safe from getting pregnant. Research now shows that we were wrong. It is in the middle of the cycle that you are most likely to get pregnant. If you use this diaphragm and persuade your husband to engage in intimacy in days closest to when you have your period, you should be relatively safe, although nothing is guaranteed. However," Dr. Violet Greene said, her manner softening, "I wish you good luck."

*   *   *

When she returned to Palm Springs, Elizabeth commenced the next phase of her road to liberation. Driving lessons first, she thought now, as she walked down the lane, and then the purchase of her very own automobile.

Sweeney's Auto Garage, half a mile from La Alma, was situated between Lardner's General Store and Allenby's Grocery. It stood on a dirt lot and consisted of a small office, a garage, and a gasoline pump. Tom Sweeney lived in a cabin in the back.

When young Mrs. Barnstable walked up, he looked at her in surprise. "How do you do, Mr. Sweeney," she said.

"Howdy."

"I understand you give driving lessons."

"That I do, ma'am," he said, wiping his greasy hands on a rag. "In my brand-new Model T, right over there," he said, pointing.

"When can we start? Would today suit you?"

His bushy eyebrows arched. "*You* want the lessons?" He shrugged. "Give me five minutes, and we'll get you on the road."

CHAPTER TWENTY-ONE

AFTER WEEKS OF LESSONS, this was Elizabeth's first time driving alone, and it was an amazing feeling. She had not expected it to be so heady. She laughed out loud.

As she raced along the foothill road beneath sun and sky, at the dizzying speed of forty miles an hour, the sense of liberation was immense. It wasn't just the motion or the speed, it was the possibilities. The automobile had no limits, unlike a horse that had to be fed and rested, needed to be brushed and groomed and shod and stabled with care. The car carried her along the dirt road in perfect comfort—no back-wrenching sidesaddle, no unladylike astride saddle. No jamming one's feet into the stirrups at a gallop. No sore derriere at the end of the day. No pain at all! Just sitting as if one were at a table, with hands comfortably resting on the wheel as the landscape rolled by.

When she had told Nigel she was going to take driving lessons, he had surprised her by saying he thought it was a good idea. He had further surprised her by ordering a car from a Riverside dealer and having it delivered to La Alma: a bright red 1922 four-seater coupe with a convertible top—perfect for the modern woman, he had declared, and the wheel spokes were red, too. It wouldn't have been her own choice, it seemed flashy, but she knew it had to do with Nigel's image and, after all, the car suited her needs.

Thinking of Nigel brought back unwanted memories of the bedroom.

He continued to visit her in her own separate bedroom to claim his conjugal rights. Elizabeth never resisted. She would lie in bed, waiting, and he would come in without knocking. She allowed him the illusion of being in control. And perhaps he had been, until now. Since her visit to Dr. Greene, Elizabeth now made sure the diaphragm was in place.

The first time, after that doctor visit, Nigel had come to her in the darkness, disrobing and slipping between the sheets. He didn't kiss her or caress her. Nothing was expected of her, simply to be a receptacle. He went about his business coldly and mechanically, as if he were pollinating one of his date palms. The only words he uttered were, "Don't give me a girl."

Finally it was over and he left. As Dr. Greene had promised, Nigel was unaware of the contraceptive device. Elizabeth lay still for a moment, then she got up and went into the bathroom, where she douched with an astringent wash. By such small but powerful strategies was she going to win her freedom from him.

Putting Nigel from her thoughts, she scanned the flat desert ringed by lavender mountains, a yellow-gray expanse broken by the occasional cactus and tree, with a few rolling dunes crowned with wild grass.

The July morning was already warm. Elizabeth knew they faced a hot summer. She did not mind the searing heat that penetrated skin and went right to bone, a baking heat that induced languor and an almost dream-like state. The constantly blowing wind evaporated perspiration so that, if such a thing were possible, it was a comfortable heat, unlike the humid dripping summers of the eastern seaboard.

She had been in Palm Springs for a while now, and she still couldn't get over the sky. It was a blue she had never seen before, a whole new shade of blue that she couldn't even name. It was clear and flawless and beautiful, and as it stood behind towering green palm trees, it was a blue that etched everything in startling detail. Sometimes, standing in Nigel's groves, looking up at the graceful spreading crowns, she could distinguish the sharp thorns that grew along the stems of the fronds, the detail was that sharp. The result was a curious three-dimensional effect that was exaggerated. Any landscape was three-dimensioned, but the blue of the desert sky seemed to magnify the effect, render trees, bushes, boulders—even houses and mountains—in deeper relief. As if the desert were larger than life, with a bigger soul than anywhere else.

And the sun, sparkling on the shiny green fronds, produced a gem-like effect, as if God had spilled a box of diamonds on His creation.

Elizabeth Barnstable was falling in love with the desert. In fact, she sometimes thought the desert was whispering to her, the same way she sometimes thought she heard the whispers of Mount San Jacinto. Ever since they first arrived, she had felt a strange connection to this place, even though it was very foreign and alien to her. The American Southwest could not be more different from New York.

As she smiled to herself now, thinking of the unlimited possibilities of automobile travel, the car let out a sudden bang. It shuddered. And then Elizabeth saw the steam rising from beneath the hood. Guiding the car into the shade of a cottonwood beside the road, she gave a little laugh and then a sigh, thinking of human hubris and the limits, after all, of woman and machine.

Parking and getting out—she would let the engine cool down and add water to the radiator from the canvas bag that hung from the front fender—Elizabeth stretched her legs. Then, slipping into heavy gloves, she unlatched one side of the hood, as Mr. Sweeney had taught her, and folded it back to expose the top of the radiator. Seizing the cap, and standing back, she unscrewed it to let a geyser of steam escape. Okay, she silently conceded. Maybe the automobile isn't a perfect replacement for the horse, but she would soon be on the road with her books again.

The books were a gift from her parents.

Mrs. Van Linden had gotten the notion that there were no books in the western states, that no one read, that it was all cowboys and Indians, gunfights and illiteracy. And so she had gone to a bookstore in midtown and ordered five hundred pounds of books, "a tasteful variety," she had told the clerk.

The crates had come out with the Barnstables last October, and Norrington had seen that they were shelved alphabetically in the library room of the house. Elizabeth was going to use them as the foundation of a lending library for Palm Springs. In the seven months since Elizabeth had visited the teachers, Misses March and Napier, she had hoped they would reach out to her with an interest to launch a literacy program in the valley, especially among the Indians. So far, they had remained as politely standoffish as the other women of Palm Springs.

An invisible wall seemed to stand between them. But Elizabeth was not going to give up. To get her embryonic project started, she had decided that an exchange program with the small library at Indio would be just the ticket—it would help to legitimize her own new town library that Mr. Lardner had generously offered to host in a corner of his store. And so she was on a day trip to meet with the librarian there, to donate new books that they badly needed, and to receive advice on how to get her own library up and running.

Waiting for the radiator to cool, she went through the books and selected a collection of poems by Tennyson. Settling herself in the shade of the cottonwood, wondering if any other motorists or folk on horseback would come her way, she read a few pages, but when she came to *The Lotos-Eaters* and read, "In the afternoon they came unto a land in which it seemed always afternoon," she paused and looked out at the golden desert. Yes, she thought. The land of the afternoon.

Setting the book aside, she went to check the radiator. It was sufficiently cooled to add water. After she emptied the canvas bag and hooked it onto the fender, she started to screw the cap onto the radiator but it slipped out of her hand and dropped into the nearby grass.

Elizabeth kicked this way and that with her shoe, searching for the cap, and when her toe struck something hard, she bent down to see what it was. Pushing the grass aside, she exposed a small boulder rising from the sand, no more than a foot high. But what caught her attention was the petroglyph carved onto its smooth surface—a spiral with human figures standing on either side of it. It looked familiar. Where had she seen it before?

She touched it. The sunlight around her seemed to soften. The drone of bees in a nearby patch of flowers intensified. Elizabeth felt briefly removed from the modern world as she asked herself: Who had painted this? When? Why? What did it mean? And she felt an intense curiosity sweep over her.

As she restored the radiator cap, started the car, and resumed her drive to Indio, she thought about the petroglyph, the desert heat, the color of the sky that needed a name other than "blue," and she was suddenly filled, for inexplicable reasons, with a sense of joy and eager anticipation.

*   *   *

Luisa watched Señor Barnstable saddle a horse and ride away from the property. She knew where he was going. Up the canyon to look at the water again.

She and her granddaughters were hanging clothes on the line, but her thoughts were about the growing tension between Chief Diego and the Señor. She had told Diego to let the Señor have water from the creek, that there was enough for all. But Diego said the Indian must make a stand. Soon, he said, that greedy white man was going to bring in more trees, and then he would steal all the water.

Luisa feared the anger and hostility would bring bad magic to her people, perhaps sickness or flood or famine. She listened to the spirits, she watched for signs. But there were no messages yet. On top of that, she still had no young apprentice to teach the secrets of spirit reading to.

She picked up her empty basket and returned to the house, where she informed Mrs. Norrington that she was going away and would not work for several days. The lady in the long black dress frowned, but no one could force Mrs. Padilla to come to work.

She had a more important job to do.

Returning to the deserted village—it felt empty and ghost-like, with not even a dog or a chicken because everyone was up in the canyon for the summer—she filled a basket with bread, nuts, deer jerky, and dried mesquite pods. She selected a blanket, filled a gourd with water, and took down her spare sandals. She would leave at once, following the tracks and trails that had crisscrossed the Coachella Valley since the beginning of time. She would travel every day, at dawn and after sunset, resting during the sweltering heat of the day.

She had to find the next spirit-reader before she died.

*　　*　　*

As the chestnut mare picked its way along the narrow trail that scaled Mesquite Canyon, Nigel kept his eye on the creek as it meandered to his left through cottonwoods, willows, and mesquite trees. Higher up, he knew that oaks grew in dense groves, and beyond, pines and cedars. His only concern was the water. That damn Diego kept sabotaging his irrigation canals. Very well, Nigel thought. If you can't share, I'll just take what I need.

An aqueduct, the hydro-engineer had suggested. Why spend so much money and effort and wasted time sending test drills down for artesian wells when all the water he needed was right here, tumbling down San Jacinto's rocky slopes? Yes, Nigel thought, as he rode his horse in and out of dappled sunlight, feeling the air grow crisper and cooler. We'll start somewhere up here. Build a diversion dam and sluice the run off down an indestructible concrete ditch.

Let's see the redskin bastards sabotage that.

He had come up here nearly every day since the first foray with the engineer. Nigel wanted to make his presence known to the Indians, whom he knew were nearby, watching. He had to find just the right spot for the diversion dam; he had to make sure that construction was possible, that there was room for the workers and a passable trail to bring up building materials. For Nigel, failure to get the water was not an option.

Chief Diego stood among the cottonwoods, watching the Señor. "He will steal our water," he said quietly to the man who stood next to him, José Seco, the medicine shaman. "This will anger Pa'akniwat, who lives in all ponds and streams and springs. That is why we pray to him and ask permission to take his water. The white man will not ask, he will take, and this will anger Pa'akniwat and in his anger he will withhold water from our people."

"But what can we do, brother?"

There was an office in a town called Washington, DC. The office was called Bureau of Indian Affairs, and the men there decided where the Indians would live. Diego had visited an office once. The Sheriff of Riverside County had one. Diego had his photograph taken there years ago, when a treaty was signed by the chiefs of all the Cahuilla bands. The treaty told them that their land was now called a reservation and if they wanted to receive free food from the Great Father they must stay on the reservation. If they leave, they are on their own.

But this Bureau also protected the Indians and made sure white men did not steal from them. There was an agent in Banning. Diego would send a telegram, and the agent would come out and stop the Señor's theft of Indian water.

If that didn't work, Chief Diego knew of other ways to stop the white man.

*   *   *

When a young man came to the back door, Fiona recognized him as the town's handyman. He also took care of Doc Perry's horse and buggy. He handed her an envelope. "From the Doc," he said.

She stared at it, afraid to open it. Fiona had been miserable for days—Leland making love to her, the setting so romantic and heavenly, Fiona blundering with the word "marriage" before Leland had spoken it himself.

The look on his face.

Fiona had never felt so mortified, so utterly ashamed of herself that she had wanted to run and hide. He had had no intention of proposing to her. He had thought he could use her, that she would give in, that she was a loose woman. Was that really how he saw her? A woman who traded her virtue for a glass of wine under an arbor?

As she had wept into her pillow, she had consoled herself by telling herself she had made the right decision back in New York when she had renewed her promise to Mrs. Van Linden and had kept her job. It was a pitifully small consolation for the pain in her heart, but it was consolation, at least.

But now he had sent a letter: "My dearest Fiona, I write to you from a realm of abject misery. I am so sorry for the pain I caused you. I did not mean to imply that I thought you were a woman of loose morals. I handled it all so badly that I would not blame you for never speaking to me again. But I have searched my soul until it is scrubbed raw, and all I can see is that I am but a poor shell of a man without you in my life. I am begging you to give me another chance."

She didn't have to think about it. She just ran to his house. And he flung open the front door and they fell into each other's arms, not caring who might be walking or riding by. They both spoke at once.

"I'm sorry!"

"I was stupid."

"Can you forgive me?"

"Jumped to foolish conclusions—"

"I love you."

They kissed for a long moment and then he stood back to hold her at arm's length. "Fiona, before we speak of anything else, there is something I have to tell you about myself. Let's go for a walk."

While Fiona, nervous and apprehensive, walked at his side, Leland fell into deep thought. In the months that he had gotten to know the lovely, gentle Englishwoman, he had discovered one fundamental characteristic of Fiona Wilson: her innate honesty. It was something she held dear above all other human traits. They had gone to see a movie in Riverside and the plot had involved deceit. Afterward, over dinner, Fiona had told him that she could tolerate any kind of a man's weakness, as long as he had integrity and told the truth.

Those words had made him sharply aware of the reality of his situation—a reality he had ignored for years. That Leland Perry, being neither a professor nor a doctor, was a fraud, a huckster who had spent a lifetime swindling gullible people out of their money. Even though, in later years, he had managed to establish himself as a respected medical man, the truth was he was a fake. Some might even call him a quack.

The day was hot; they walked slowly along the deserted lane. There were few houses nearby, dotting the flat tracts of undeveloped land. "Fiona," he said, stopping suddenly in the shade of a fig tree. "I need to tell you something that I should have told you months ago. And you'll probably want to have nothing to do with me after you hear what I have to say, but I have to say it."

She smiled up at him. "What could possibly make me want to have nothing to do with you?"

"It's about me, my life. A secret. Something that no one knows." He lifted his hat and ran his hand over his hair. He looked up through the leafy branches overhead. And then out to the desert that stretched away to purple mountains sharply etched against the sky. "I want to be completely honest with you about myself, but it means revealing something that will diminish me in your eyes, I fear."

She smiled and touched his arm with a gloved hand. "Leland, if it's about you not being a real medical doctor, I already know."

His eyes widened with shock. "You do?"

"Lois Lardner told me. And others know it, too. I'm afraid your secret isn't as secret as you think. What do I care that you didn't go to a proper medical school? Getting to know you, I have found a man of compassion and integrity. And what I have witnessed, and heard from others, is that people value you, Leland. You do have a lot of medical experience, even if you aren't formally trained. You can set bones, remove bullets, deliver babies. You're knowledgeable and self-educated. And you never promise to cure anyone, you always send them to specialists."

She smiled and took his hand between hers. "But more than anything, you lend a kind ear and a sympathetic shoulder, which often is all a person needs."

He looked down at his hand cradled between two white gloves. He couldn't speak. His heart tumbled about. And then he frowned. There was more. Yet another confession.

A breeze came up and rustled the overhead branches. He looked into her kind eyes, felt the patience in her soul. Leland had never entertained the notion of marriage. He was born for bachelorhood, or so he had always thought. Love 'em and leave 'em smiling had been his philosophy on the tracks and trails of the West. He had never thought he would be a one-woman man, but that was how it was turning out.

He realized that, for the first time in his itinerant life, he *wanted* to get married. He wanted it so badly it kept him awake at night. It wasn't just the lovemaking he yearned for, it was so much more—the companionship and sharing, sitting in the parlor by the fire and just knowing that the person next to him cared about him. It was a profound revelation. And now that it had struck him, he couldn't think of anything else.

The problem was, his lucrative business was about to dry up.

He couldn't get involved with moonshiners. It was too risky. But there was one solution. They could leave Palm Springs and go where the liquor was legal, Mexico or Canada, and live out their lives there. Would she go with him?

"My dear Fiona, I desperately want to ask you to marry me, but the harsh truth is that my livelihood has been drastically altered in the past year. The fact is, I need alcohol to make my medicines. It's how I make my living."

"I'm not against alcohol, Leland," she heard herself say while her heart raced and his words echoed in her ears: *I want to ask you to marry me . . .* "And a lot of medicinal recipes contain alcohol. Did you think I would disapprove?"

"My supply has been cut off. My not being a licensed doctor means I cannot resort to drugstore prescriptions. I have no way of making my medicines."

When she realized he had stopped speaking and was looking at her as if waiting for her to say something, she said, "Oh," while she continued to hold his hand between hers and what she really wanted to shout was, "Yes, I will marry you!"

"Fiona, there is a solution to my dilemma. I have been thinking of moving to Canada or Mexico where alcohol is legal. I am asking you to marry me, yet I can't promise you a home here, or even in America."

"Canada or Mexico?" She blinked at him. Why was he mentioning geography? Oh, the alcohol problem. And then she realized she hadn't been fully listening. And now that he was elucidating a little further, she realized he was talking about leaving the country!

"The choice of country is yours," Leland was saying with a smile, as if he were inviting her to pick out a new carpet. "I will be happy in either place as long as you are there with me."

"Go to Canada?" she said feebly, picturing the moon because that was what Canada meant to her.

His face fell. He had thought she would jump at it. And then he belatedly remembered: the promise to Mrs. Van Linden.

"Leland, you know I'm not free to leave the country. I'm not free to leave Palm Springs."

Leland made a sound of exasperation—at himself. He had been so pleased with arriving at a condition of wanting to get married that he had completely forgotten what she had told him a few days ago. "Can you state your case to Elizabeth?" he said. "Surely she will see the impossible position the promise has put you in and give you permission to leave. After all, it's about her, isn't it? It should be Elizabeth who lets you out of the promise."

"Part of my promise to Mrs. Van Linden was to not let Elizabeth know about the promise!"

"What!" The day was going from bad to worse. He wanted to go back to the house and start over. "Confound it, Fiona!"

"I'm sorry," she cried, apologizing for something that wasn't her fault. "Mrs. Van Linden said Elizabeth would be angry with her if she knew her mother was keeping an eye on her through me!"

He stared at her in utter disbelief. What was it with some people that they felt so free to manipulate other people's lives? "So you are bound by a promise to keep the other promise a secret? That is unreasonable!" he shouted, causing Fiona to quickly look up and down the shaded lane to see if anyone heard.

"How are you to live your life," Leland said in a raised voice, "bound by such an impossible promise? Surely you can explain to her—"

But Fiona thought of her drunken father who had broken promises all the time. Fiona would not be like him. "Leland, I have to keep my word. Why promise something only to break it later?"

"If it's an unreasonable promise," Leland said with a flash of anger. "It has to be explained to the woman that—"

"No, Leland," Fiona cried. "It is important to me that I keep my promise. What does a woman have, if not her word? Look at me. I have neither status nor wealth. I am a servant. But at least I can have my honor. If I break my promise to Mrs. Van Linden then what do I have left? How can you ever believe any promises I make to you?"

She saw the parade of emotions march across his face, the convoluted thinking going on behind his eyes, torn, like herself, wanting something so desperately yet needing to hold on to honor. "Can't you find a replacement for your position as Elizabeth's maid?" he said, casting about for simple solutions. "Would Mrs. Van Linden accept that as an honorable alternative?" Fiona heard desperation in his voice and a fretfulness she had never heard before. She suspected that, having been a con man for most of his life, Leland was used to getting his way. "And I don't see how Elizabeth needs looking after," he added a little petulantly. "She's a strong woman. Adversity can reveal our hidden strengths. It might take a while, but she will come to terms with what Nigel did and find a way to live with it."

The words hung in the air for a moment, and then Fiona said, "What do you mean? Live with what?"

"The miscarriage," he said without thinking, being so fretful about their own situation.

"Leland, what are you talking about? What did Nigel have to do with the miscarriage?"

He stared at her. "Oh my God . . ."

"Her Ladyship tripped and fell against the back of a chair. That's what she told me. Is that not true? Leland, tell me what happened. What did His Lordship have to do with it?"

He had never felt so miserable or regretful as he did in that moment, because the mood of the day had changed, he felt as if he were on the brink of an abyss and he was about to tumble in. Fiona didn't know the truth about the miscarriage. With this new information there was going to be no way to persuade her to leave La Alma. "When she told Nigel she was pregnant," he said miserably, but having no choice, "he became angry."

"Angry?"

"He . . . lashed out."

She gasped. "Do you mean he struck her? Did Her Ladyship tell you this?"

"Mrs. Padilla overheard a row. She heard him strike Elizabeth."

Fiona stared at him for a moment, then she turned away. Wringing her hands, she walked a few paces along the dirt lane, paused, turned around. He saw how white she had gone. Leland got a sinking feeling in his stomach. The look on Fiona's face, the tone in her voice—he suddenly wished he could grab his words back, make something up, tell her a mountain of lies just to get the two of them back to where they had been, on the brink of wedded bliss.

"His Lordship caused the miscarriage," she said slowly, a sick feeling growing inside her. His Lordship had used violence against his pregnant wife. "I had no idea," she said, pressing her fingers to her lips. "It explains so much. The silence in the house. They have barely spoken since the miscarriage. I thought His Lordship was blaming himself for losing the baby, for not being here. I thought their silence was shared grief when, in reality, it is something else altogether. And if Her Ladyship were to get pregnant again—" Her eyes widened in horror. "Leland, she must be protected. If he is so savage with her a second time, it could threaten her very life! Leland, I can't leave her! I can't run away to Canada.

"And so I can't marry you, Leland," she added unhappily. "I have to stay at La Alma and protect Her Ladyship. But Leland," she said, stepping close, "I want to be with you. I cannot marry you, but I will be with you in the way you want."

But he didn't want her that way, not anymore. Leland had undergone a vigorous soul search and had found himself deeply lacking in character and integrity. He wanted to change that. Along with his new honesty, he wanted a new morality for himself.

When he saw the tears streaming down her face, he pulled her into his arms and held her tight. "My sweet, sweet Fiona," he said. "I cannot believe we have come this far in our lives. I cannot believe I have finally found a woman whom I love with all my heart, only to arrive at an impossible place."

"Oh, Leland," she sobbed. "What are we going to do?"

He didn't know, but Leland Perry silently vowed to find a way.

*   *   *

Nigel was so absorbed in the topographical survey spread before him that he did not hear a distant door open and close, Mrs. Norrington say, "Good evening, My Lady," or Elizabeth's request for a cup of tea.

The hydrologist had advised an aqueduct. Yes, Nigel thought now, as he studied the map with its elevations marked off, the placements of creeks and streams, the flow of water from the San Jacinto snow pack. Somewhere up here, he thought, as he tapped his pencil on a point not far from where the current summer village of the Indians stood. First build a diversion dam, and then sluice the run off down a man-made flume, right into his date groves.

Dropping his pencil, he leaned back in his chair and stretched his arms over his head. He liked the way things were going for himself and his plantation. He enjoyed being the smartest man within miles as, so far, he had yet to meet a man who could outwit or out-strategize him in the date growing business—even the seasoned growers around Indio. He gave some credit to his new friends, the movie people, a particularly savvy bunch when it came to financial know-how. No wonder Hollywood was such a boomtown. Nigel was learning from them. They certainly didn't stop at cutthroat tactics to get what they wanted; why should he?

Nigel had gotten more involved with the Lamonts, although he had not as yet committed any money to them, still unsure of the wisdom of investing in movies when he had his own expansion plans to think about. He had learned that Zora DuBois's real name was Agnes Mulroney. It fascinated him, the ability of movie colony members to reshape their lives so perfectly. Not just physical appearance, but entire identities were remolded and reinvented into whatever one desired. Zora was a past master at it, because she moved between the two personae with ease, the girl next door among her friends, but out in public, in places like the Pink Flamingo, she stepped out as the untouchable vamp.

Bravo, he thought in admiration.

And wasn't that in fact what he himself was doing? Not to the extent of changing his name, but he had uprooted himself from British tradition and planted his boots on new soil with an aim to reinvent himself and this desert. He would wager that his life would make a terrific movie.

With Zora playing his leading lady, he thought. Maybe some steamy love scenes. Although she flirted with him when she was the country girl, and gave him the come-on when she was the vamp, it hadn't gone any further, and he wondered if it ever would. Zora was the first woman who had really gotten his blood high. She was, after all, the first one who seemed impervious to his charms—maybe it was because she had a number of charms herself.

Nigel's musings were interrupted by the sound of footsteps. He heard her come in. Heard her stand before his desk. He made her wait. "Mrs. Norrington said you wished to see me," Elizabeth said.

As he pretended to study his map, he strung the moment out, to let her wonder why he had summoned her, to give her a chance to fidget so he could interpret her body language or look for signs of guilt. Finally he said, "You were gone a long time."

"I was taking books to Indio. I told you that."

"I know how long those trips take." He finally looked up and settled his eyes on her for such a long time that Elizabeth wondered if she was supposed to say something more. And then Nigel surprised her by saying, "You wouldn't be seeing another man, would you?"

The question so caught her off guard that she found herself speaking too rapidly, defensively. "The car overheated. I had to pull over and wait."

He waved a hand. "I know you are not a terribly clever or imaginative woman, Elizabeth, but I doubt you are stupid enough to have an affair. And even if you did," he added casually, "it wouldn't last, I'd see to that."

He paused to let the clock over the mantel tick a few times, while an owl perched on one of their chimneys called, "*Hoo-hoo-hoo.*" Then, inspecting his fingernails, Nigel said, "Do you remember Richard Ostermond on the *Mauretania*? The fellow who couldn't stop talking about himself?"

Elizabeth blinked. And then she swallowed. The defensive reflexes of a woman fearing she was about to hear something very bad. "What about him?" she asked, feeling a cold presentiment steal over her. Dr. Ostermond had gone missing from the ship. "Misadventure," the authorities had said. But what kind of misadventure they had never been able to determine.

"He was showing you too much attention, and I had to stop him."

The clock kept ticking but the owl must have flown off because the rest of the night was silent. "Stop him?" Elizabeth said, thinking her words came out somewhat stupidly. Nigel was at one of his games, she realized, because his eyes were fixed on her as he studied her every reaction to his every word.

"You see, Elizabeth, you are mine. I own you. And I have rules when it comes to my possessions. They are off-limits to other men. Any man who looks at my automobile with a covetous eye, or my horse, or my wife will know what the words 'suffer the consequences' truly mean. Am I perfectly understood?"

She tried hard, but no words came from her mouth.

"It was a simple ruse," Nigel said with a shrug. "I knocked on Ostermond's stateroom door late one night and told him I'd been out on deck and had seen the most remarkable sea creature following the ship. And you know what? The fool believed me! He followed me out, and as I pointed down to the water, and the fool kept saying, 'Where is it?' I helped him over the side." Nigel gave a small laugh. "You should have seen the look on his face as he fell. Past all those portholes filled with lights, and he just plunged down with a look of such disbelief on his face that I had to laugh."

"So you see," Nigel added as he picked up his pencil and returned his attention to the topographical map on his desk, "any man who displays an interest in you won't do it a second time because the desert here is like the ocean. A man can be taken out there and left to die and never be found or heard from again."

Elizabeth stood numb and immobile for a long moment, trying to understand what she had just heard, if she had heard right, if Nigel had just said what he said. Because none of it could be true.

She opened her mouth to speak. She had no breath. She needed to leave this room, leave the house, leave the world, but how did one take one's leave after hearing such a thing? She felt as if she had been kicked in the stomach. Nigel had hit her again, and this was worse than the first time, because he had used words and a flip tone rather than his hand. She wanted to say something about her purse, leaving it in the car, needing to give him a reason for leaving, that she had to go out to the carriage house and get her purse. And then she realized he didn't care why she would leave the room, why she would do anything at all for that fact. So she left and made her way down the hall toward the kitchen, where a kettle was whistling for Elizabeth's evening tea.

"Would you like something to eat, My Lady?" Mrs. Norrington said as Elizabeth stumbled through.

"Left my purse," Elizabeth gasped as she headed for the back door. And then, amazingly, she was all of a sudden normal and was able to collect herself and say, "It's late, Mrs. Norrington. Why don't you and Norrington retire for the night? His Lordship and I can manage." She didn't know why she had said it. The Norringtons always seemed to know when to retire for the night, but Elizabeth felt a vague sense of ill ease knowing they were still up and about while Nigel had just confessed to murdering Dr. Ostermond.

*   *   *

In the bunkhouse, by the glow of a kerosene lamp, Cody was working on his book about Peachy and Belle and Horsethief Creek. He looked up and saw, through the window, Elizabeth emerge from the back of the house. He watched her for a moment. She seemed distraught. She didn't seem to know which way to turn as she started one way a few feet, then stopped and went another direction. She was wringing her hands, and he knew something was wrong.

He jumped up and hurried out. "Are you all right, Mrs. Barnstable?" he said, glancing at the kitchen window where he could see the Norringtons cleaning up for the night.

"Are you all right?" he repeated, his alarm growing.

When she saw the pen in his hand, she said, "How is your story coming along?" She said it to keep herself from blurting the terrible thing Nigel had just confessed to her.

He frowned. Her tone was strange. She seemed agitated. But as she apparently needed calming, he kept his manner amiable and his voice low-keyed as he said, "I am experiencing some revelations. I was writing about Peachy and all of a sudden his last name came back to me. Isn't that something?"

She stared at him, her lips parted.

When she didn't say anything he said, lamely, "It's O'Doule. Peachy O'Doule."

She glanced back toward the house, a quick, furtive gesture that made Cody think of a frightened deer. Something happened in there, he realized. Something involving Barnstable, he would wager. Fury started to rise in him. He wished it was in his power to storm that house and give the bastard a thrashing within an inch of his life.

"Are you all right?" he asked a third time, when clearly things were not all right.

Elizabeth looked at Cody and realized he had just told her something, good news that they should be celebrating, but it escaped her now. All she could think of was that Nigel had thrown Richard Ostermond off the deck of the *Mauretania*.

CHAPTER TWENTY-TWO

THEY WERE RIDING UP Chino Canyon, steeper and more rugged than Mesquite Canyon, two lone people in a virgin wilderness. Elizabeth kept her eyes on Cody's broad back as she followed his horse on her Appaloosa.

"There's an abandoned logging road," Cody had said when they left La Alma that morning. "Not many people know about it. I want to show you something."

And now they followed it, a narrow, rutted road that had been cut into the barren escarpments years ago by a timber company that went bankrupt. Here, California fan palms grew in such profusion that they created a curious jungle-like atmosphere in the desert setting. Ahead, the rocky walls of San Jacinto rose boldly to the sky. And the road gradually climbed to meet them.

Elizabeth never ceased to be amazed by the dramatic differences in elevation, temperature, and moisture that gave Palm Springs its diverse vegetation. Already she and Cody had gone from sand dunes and sand fields covered in chaparral and mesquite to a woodland of willow, cottonwood, oak, and pinyon pine, and from here they could travel to higher elevations where ponderosa pine and incense cedar grew in dense forests.

She and Cody rode past shimmering ribbons of water rushing between smooth, clean boulders, creating sky-blue pools and sparkling waterfalls. The air was crisp and filled with the sound of the mountain run off. It was September, officially fall. It had been weeks since Nigel's confession about Ostermond and his subsequent threat to mete out the same punishment to any man who showed interest in Elizabeth. While she was trying to figure out how to live with this new knowledge, her impulse was to go home to her parents. But that would solve nothing. How could she tell anyone what Nigel had admitted to doing? He would deny it, charm his way out of it, smilingly say his beloved wife had had a dream. No one would believe he was capable of such an atrocity. But then, did Elizabeth herself truly believe it? How could she know for sure he had done it? Nigel had lied to her before, why couldn't he be lying now? Use the fact of Ostermond's unsolved disappearance as yet another scare tactic to keep her in line.

Nigel hadn't brought it up again. He knew that what he had said was enough, Elizabeth was certain. He had planted the sickening seed and now it was quietly growing, a daily reminder of his power over her.

But there was one person who had to be told—Cody, for his own safety and survival. He had to know how dangerous the situation had become. She hadn't wanted to tell him, but she had finally come to the conclusion that Cody needed to be sharply aware that, from now on, he must be even more circumspect in his interaction with her. In the past weeks, Elizabeth had avoided contact with him as she feared that the most innocent friendly gesture could be interpreted wrongly by Nigel. And Nigel had been home all summer, with not even a visit to Indio, the construction of his new aqueduct the singular focus of his attention.

But now he was away in Arizona, and Elizabeth was seizing the opportunity to talk to Cody. As they rode up the canyon, gaining in elevation, Elizabeth looked back every now and then to see if anyone followed. But all she saw was a sleepy town that was barely more than a village, scattered houses, small farms green with orchards. Nigel's voice echoed in her mind: "You are mine, Elizabeth, I own you." He had made her paranoid, she realized, imagining his spies behind every rock and tree. Or maybe it was because she herself was spying on him.

Elizabeth doubted that Nigel knew he was being watched by a private investigator. She and Mary Clark were being very cautious. Since Elizabeth couldn't freely go into Los Angeles whenever she felt like it—Nigel would certainly be suspicious of such trips—she and her lawyer had devised a plan of communication. Miss Clark mailed ladies' magazines to Elizabeth in Palm Springs and secreted within them were her reports on progress the investigator was making. "Your husband was seen going into a speakeasy," Miss Clark had reported, "that is owned by a known gangster with ties to the Chicago underworld. We are exploring that arena, and other avenues. It looks promising for your case. Please continue to send me all the evidence you can find. It is extremely helpful."

Each time Nigel left the house, and Elizabeth saw that he was going to be engaged in his date palms, she quickly went through his clothes. Pants and coat pockets delivered up some interesting clues as to the nature of his occasional drive into Los Angeles: matchbooks from nightclubs, receipts from expensive restaurants, parking stubs, even a woman's monogrammed handkerchief—Z.D. Elizabeth packaged them up and shipped them to Mary Clark, who then handed the evidence over to her investigator. With such leads, she had assured Elizabeth, they would be able to construct Nigel's life outside of Palm Springs.

"We're almost there," Cody said, calling back over his shoulder.

In the past few weeks Elizabeth had been aloof, ever since the evening she had come home from Indio, pulling the new car into the old carriage house, laughing about the engine overheating and the discovery of a delightful petroglyph just like the one they had discovered back in March. And then she had gone into the house with a lively step—to come out an hour later looking distraught and lost.

And then, this morning, returning from the depot where she had taken Barnstable to catch the train to Arizona, she had solemnly asked Cody if he would accompany her in a search for petroglyphs, but he knew it was just an excuse.

Cody felt that Elizabeth was dreading what she was riding up here to tell him. He knew her well enough to sense that about her, the gravity of her mood, the lack of even the barest encouraging smile. Her husband had traveled three hundred miles away, and she still had to climb a mountain and enter a forest to whisper her terrible news.

For the first time, Cody had left the bunkhouse without his gun belt strapped around his waist. Twelve years ago, when he was a green seventeen-year-old and headed for the Colorado gold fields, he had strapped the Colt on for safety and survival—although there were fewer hostile Indians and outlaws in the West than in prior decades. But there were two things a cowboy never went without: his horse and his gun. But now he was gunless and it felt strange. The reason he had left his holster and cartridge belt on a hook, creating a feeling of ill ease and vulnerability in himself, was because of Elizabeth. He suspected she was uncomfortable around firearms. And since Elizabeth's ease of mind was a growing concern for him, he decided to sacrifice his own ease of mind for her.

Cody felt a change coming over him, stealthily, like an unknown enemy creeping up on him. He didn't know what was lying in wait up ahead or how he should prepare for it. He knew it had something to do with having stayed in one place for fifteen months, the longest he had stayed anywhere. It also had to do with the place itself, not just a sleepy little town but the ever-changing desert and the majestic mountains that stood sentinel around it. Cody was transitioning from cowboy into a man of letters. He wielded a pen more lately than he did a lariat. Not only was he in the grip of a compulsion to write about Belle and Peachy and himself at Horsethief Creek, he had started sketching the story of the gunfight in Tombstone, Arizona, that caused his father to flee to Montana.

The upward slope was leveling out, the trail growing easier. Willows, mesquite, and cottonwoods grew in profusion here, creating a sun-dappled wood with a gurgling stream. Elizabeth felt her thoughts drift to the man riding ahead of her.

When she had expressed an interest in reading some of Cody's story, he had given her one of the notebooks he was filling up with the colorful narrative of his life, which seemed a lot to Elizabeth, considering Cody was only twenty-nine years old. She kept the book hidden so that Nigel wouldn't find it, and she only read it when Nigel was out of the house.

They finally arrived at a place where the creek had spilled over its banks, flooding the road. "We'll leave the horses here," Cody said, lifting a lantern from the horn of his saddle. "There's an Indian trail that picks up on the other side. Be careful, these boulders are very slippery. Take my hand."

Cody went ahead, stepping onto a giant rock. He held out his arm and helped Elizabeth across. Then he stepped onto another, as water rushed beneath him. Elizabeth followed. She lost her footing, and he grabbed her. They held onto each other for a moment as she steadied herself.

She clung to him as the freezing water rushed below, sending up a fine spray, roaring in its mad dash to the desert sands far below, creating a moment of thrill and danger. Cody held her so tightly she felt his heart beat against her breast. His jaw brushed her forehead.

She wanted the moment to freeze in time, to hold them there as if by special cosmic dispensation while the rest of the world carried on its prosaic business.

But they had to move. Securing her hand in his, Cody advanced to the next boulder, and the next, Elizabeth trustingly planting her shoes where Cody's boots had stepped. They continued the perilous crossing until they were on the other side and on a foot trail. Following it through mesquite bushes and cottonwood trees, they presently came upon a cave. He went in first, Elizabeth followed. "When I first came to Palm Springs, I explored a lot of these caves," Cody said as he struck a match to light the lantern. "I couldn't believe it when I came upon this. I don't think any other white man has set foot in here."

Elizabeth stared with wide eyes, turning in a slow circle as the miracle of the cave gradually revealed itself to her.

The smooth walls were covered in hundreds of figures—some carved into the rock, others painted on with various pigments. As Elizabeth stared at them in wonder, turning slowly to sweep the walls and ceiling with her wide eyes, she realized that, although primitively executed with stick arms and legs, the human figures were visibly all female, with breasts and long hair and clearly defined vulvas, and they were all working at different tasks—nursing babies, grinding acorns, weaving baskets.

She leaned close to examine a figure at eye level: female, with a small figure between her legs, a wavy line connecting the two. "This one is giving birth," she murmured. She wished she had a camera.

Since discovering the petroglyph the day her car overheated, Elizabeth had started taking solitary walks in the countryside, in the mornings and evenings, as the days were too hot. In the heat of the day, false pools of water shimmered far out on the sand, mirages that trick the thirsty traveler into thinking that a refreshing drink lay just yards away. The heat rose up from the desert floor in waves, giving the landscape a "vibrational" look. No one ventured forth in these peak hours.

In her walks, during which she carried the weight of the memory of poor Richard Ostermond, Elizabeth had come upon many more petro-glyphs—hundreds of them all over the region, like signposts or terri-torial markers, or maybe they were warnings to others, or greetings, or maybe they commemorated special events. Through Lardner's catalogs she had been able to order books on Indian art peculiar to the Southwest, hoping to interpret the messages on the rocks. But it turned out that the interpretations by the specialists who wrote the books were all speculation. One expert claimed that a spiral symbolized a doorway while another said the spiral represented a dream.

Those ancient people, Elizabeth could not help thinking, had gone to a lot of trouble to carve, incise, and paint their symbols for others to read. It seemed a shame that their meanings were lost.

And as she thought of lost meanings, a curious irony occurred to her: that, in her hope to bring literacy to the valley, to share reading and knowledge, she had been sidetracked by a quirk peculiar to the desert—an overheated car—which had led her to finding a lost petroglyph, sparking her interest in rock art. The glyphs, she realized, were the "books" of the ancient Indians. They told stories and spread knowledge as her own books did, offered in a lending library. They were connected, her books and the rock art. And just as the skill of reading white man's books must never be lost, so should the skill of reading glyphs never be lost.

And yet it had. Not even Luisa's people could read the rock art anymore.

Cody said now, in the soft glow of the lantern, "In other caves nearby, the artwork depicts hunting parties in which there are only male figures. I've encountered other prehistoric caves in my travels. Near Green River, Utah, I found the same curious separation of the sexes." Elizabeth watched his handsome features, illuminated in the lantern's glow as he spoke.

"Maybe, thousands of years ago," Cody was saying, "men and women didn't live together, but in segregated groups, men doing men's things, women doing women's things. This cave would have been where the women lived, and the others were where the men lived, before they paired off in marriage."

Elizabeth gazed in wonder at the communal industry covering the walls and the ceiling, women helping one another, working together. "I envy them," she said.

"Why?"

In the lantern's intimate glow, Elizabeth noticed a small scar on his jaw. She wondered how he got it. "I am trying to make friends with the ladies of Palm Springs," she said. "I invite them to my house but they seem uncomfortable. And they don't invite me to their homes."

He smiled. "Maybe it's because you live in a palace compared to their houses. You're rich, they're not."

"I thought people in the West were all about equality."

"It only goes so far. People are still governed by human nature. They've never met anyone like you before." He added softly, "I know I sure haven't."

Cody liked the way the lantern's light shone on her hair. She stood so close to him that her arm brushed his. The air in the cave was close; he could smell Elizabeth's fragrance. It was a floral scent, delicate and pleasing, like the woman who wore it. He also sensed her tension and anxiety. She had waited for her husband to leave before daring to be seen in Cody's company. He sensed that she was putting off her bad news, or maybe she was still searching for the words. What was she bracing herself to tell him? That she was going back to New York and they would never see each other again?

I'll follow her, Cody decided now, influenced by the lantern's seductive glow and the shine of Elizabeth's hair. I will follow her to New York even if Peachy isn't there and I never find him. And I will stay there, to be with Elizabeth.

"I have something to tell you," Cody said now, on an impulse, wanting to give her more time to think her thoughts, and perhaps to temper her anxiety with good news—or maybe he just wanted to put off hearing her bad news. "I've never told anyone about Peachy before. But now, as I'm describing Peachy on paper and the things he told me about himself, I remember more details about him. He had told me the town he came from and all I remember is that it has 'ville' or 'town' in it, like Evansville or Georgetown."

"There must be a hundred or more such towns in America," Elizabeth said.

"But it's a start," Cody said. He had started writing letters seeking a lead on a man named O'Doule, "tall, long-limbed, carrot-colored hair, approximately aged thirty." He also remembered that Peachy had mentioned never being west of the Mississippi before, so his home must be to the east of that mighty river. He had also talked about buying a small tobacco farm with his gold. Tobacco narrowed the field further, but it still covered seven eastern and southern states that Cody could think of.

Targeting Kentucky, Virginia, North Carolina, Pennsylvania, Georgia, Alabama, and Tennessee, he had written to public records offices and newspapers because these places were repositories of town facts. He addressed letters to "Any Barber In Town" because all men needed haircuts and barbershops were hotbeds of gossip. But more than anything, he hung his hopes on local post offices because eventually everybody sent a letter to someone or came into the post office hoping to receive one.

The more letters he wrote, the higher his hopes rose, and the higher the hope, the more focused he became on his mission.

Cody set the lantern on the cave's floor, brushed off his hands, and said, "There's something you want to tell me, isn't there, Elizabeth? The reason we have come here, for privacy. It's about Nigel, I suspect. Something happened the night you came back from Indio."

Before speaking, she looked at Cody in gratitude. For a few moments she had forgotten her reason for being here. Cody had taken her out of her nightmare world and had given her paintings and ancient lore and a few words about Peachy O'Doule. And it had felt good. Now she said, "I've been debating telling you something, but all I can arrive at, Cody, is that you need to be told."

He listened as she described Nigel's visit to her room three days after the miscarriage. She spoke haltingly as the words caused physical pain, describing how he purposely prodded her swollen face, pulled her hair, told her how everything was all her fault and that she needed to learn who was boss.

And when she was finished and the last unpleasant word left the cave, she waited for Cody to say something. But he looked so stunned, so disbelieving that she grew anxious. What was he thinking? When he finally said, "I wish you had told me, Elizabeth," she heard such passion and anger in his voice, it made her weak with relief.

"I kept silent for several reasons," she said. "Mostly to protect you. I knew you would want to go after Nigel in retaliation."

"You were right, and I still do." He waited while the musty smell of the cave filled his head and hundreds of stick-figure people watched in silence, like an audience waiting to be entertained, and he thought distantly that this wasn't the first time this cave had heard a woman's painful admission of an unacceptable life. God, but he wanted to get out of there and run back down the mountain and deliver a message with his fists.

Elizabeth hadn't known what a burden her fear of Nigel had become until now, as she shifted some of the weight of that burden onto Cody's strong shoulders. He looked at her with shadowed eyes as the words tumbled from her mouth, and she realized that Cody now shared her secret. She was no longer alone.

"There's more," she said quietly, cautiously. This was a fragile moment. Cody seemed volatile now, his emotions on edge. Perhaps she should stop while she could. But then, reminding herself that he needed this knowledge for his own personal safety, she said, "It's the reason I'm telling you now about Nigel's visit to me after the miscarriage. I had to give this a lot of thought and I decided that, for your own safety, you needed to know." She paused. Was her story going to sound too bizarre and unbelievable? Or was it going to push Cody into a rash action that could have serious and unforeseen repercussions?

He listened grimly to a farfetched tale of one man throwing another man off an ocean liner. "Tell me honestly," she said at the end of it, "do you think Nigel is capable of killing someone?"

The memory of Johnny Pinto flashed in his mind. He knew very well what Nigel Barnstable was capable of. But Cody wanted Elizabeth to be able to hold on to the shred of hope that her husband wasn't a murderer. Cody wrestled with violent, unfamiliar emotions. They frightened him. Emotions, out of control, that could plunge them both into chaos and danger. "Elizabeth!" he said suddenly. "The bastard is terrorizing you. I can't stand by and do nothing!"

"Cody, wait!" Elizabeth grabbed his arm. "Don't make me regret telling you! Please! Listen to me," she said, trying to offer reason to a man who was boiling with fury. She felt the hard muscles beneath his sleeve, flexed and tense, ready to start the fight. "It would be foolhardy to underestimate the violence Nigel is capable of." She thought: we are all capable of violence, given the right circumstance. With Nigel, it seemed he didn't need much in the way of circumstance. "Cody, there is no telling what Nigel would do if you confronted him. I have managed through sheer will and wit these past months to keep him at bay, to fool him, and to keep you and me safe. We can't ruin it now!"

The unfamiliar emotions swept over him like a wave. How could he just stand there after hearing what he had heard, knowing what he knew now, that this damn fine woman, who deserved a hell of a lot more than Nigel Barnstable, who deserved a hell of a lot better than Cody McNeal, had been brutalized? What kind of man learned what he had just learned and didn't do something about it? How could powerful emotions render a man so powerless?

All Cody could think was that he was supposed to do something—but what? Elizabeth was another man's woman, plain and simple, and Cody had clear rules about that. But there was also the rule about coming to the rescue of the victimized. Why had she just told him these terrible things if not expecting him to act? Why was she now looking at him with eyes full of pleading if not expecting a reaction from him, a solution, a remedy? She would never come right out and say the words, "Help me." He suspected she was too proud to do that, or maybe she was too kind to put him on that spot. Or maybe she was afraid he wouldn't help after she asked. But her eyes were saying, "help me," and it made Cody feel weak and powerless.

And then, in a staggering revelation, he realized she wasn't saying, "help me"; she was saying, "take care of yourself." She had exposed the dark, shameful side of her life for his own sake, so that he could be on his guard, be extra cautious around Nigel, so that he knew now how tenuous life had become at La Alma.

And then the time for wrestling with emotions was over. He reached Elizabeth in two strides to pull her into his arms and kiss her hard on the mouth. Elizabeth delivered herself into his embrace. His body felt good, natural. She fell back against the wall, Cody pressing against her as the kiss grew more passionate. Suddenly they were filled with urgency. Elizabeth clung to him, feeling the heat of his body through his clothes. Cody cupped her breast and felt her heart throbbing under the silk blouse. He kissed her neck, her throat. She arched her back and held on to him. She breathlessly kissed him back, hooking her arms around his neck to pull him to her. His jaw, unshaven, was rough. She slipped her hands under his jacket to explore the hard muscles of his back. It was the desperate embrace of two desperate people, caught, trapped, not knowing the way out. An embrace that sprang from fear and desire and a tumultuous love that neither of them could define nor contain.

Abruptly, Cody drew back. It felt wrong. Stolen moments like this were not what he wanted with her. Looking over their shoulders, wondering if they would get caught.

"Elizabeth, listen to me," he said forcefully. "After I buried my father, I set my sights on only one goal, finding Peachy. Since then, I have not really lived. But I want to live, Elizabeth, I want to live life to its fullest, to explore all that this world has to offer, its ups and downs, its treasures and feasts. And I want to do it with you, Elizabeth. It's hard to see you every day, to be near you and not be able to touch you. But I will never jeopardize your future and your happiness. One reckless move on my part and any chance of divorcing Nigel could be destroyed forever."

He stepped back, shaking his head. No, it was all wrong. He wanted Elizabeth like he'd never wanted anything before. But he felt as if he were being manipulated into committing an act that went against his most basic moral and ethical code. Nigel, forcing them to hide in caves in order to express their feelings for each other. It wasn't right. He wasn't going to let Barnstable drive them into an act of deceit and self-shame.

He reached for the lantern. "People saw us leave town together. They might notice a lengthy absence." As much as it killed him to do so, he took Elizabeth by the hand and led her out from the dark cave into the bright light of day.

*   *   *

Nigel wondered if he was falling in love, because he found himself becoming attracted to Zora in a way that he had never felt before. He had supposed a grand romance would present itself to him someday, although it was something he would never actively pursue, mainly because being in love called for a surrender of oneself—at least giving a part of himself to another human being.

Or maybe he was just falling in love with the idea of her. Nigel was becoming more and more enamored of the West and this land of unceasing opportunities, where a man without two cents in his pocket could end up living in a mansion. Zora's rags-to-riches story, a girl from a poor neighborhood in Brooklyn to being one of the radiant stars of movie screens everywhere. It fascinated Nigel.

Zora personified the spirit of this country that allowed peasants to become kings, a place where people changed their names as the cavalier notion struck them. Jack Lamont and Zora DuBois, obscenely rich, shining symbols of this strange new world.

Nigel was also one of those shining symbols. He now fully under-stood who he was—a man who had had the courage to walk away from centuries of tradition and carve a whole new life for himself from scratch. The self-created man! He liked it. He loved it. And he couldn't wait to see where this Promethean evolution was going to take him.

Shifting his thoughts away from the seductive Zora, he addressed the job at hand. Standing in the shade of his date palms, he was giving instructions to a pack of tough-looking white men whom he had handpicked to do some ruthless work.

Nigel couldn't trust his Mexican workers as they tended to side with the Indians, so he had gone to Banning, where white men were looking for work. "You're going up there to oversee the work being done by the Mexicans," he explained to the leader of the five he had brought back with him. "That's what you tell anyone who asks what your job is here. Do you understand?"

They understood very well, and they also knew to keep their mouths shut. The Englishman was paying them top dollar to stand watch over construction work being done on a ditch high up in the canyon. Their secret orders were to keep an eye out for Indians.

Two months ago he had started work on the new concrete aqueduct. And in those two months, Chief Diego had launched attacks on the project, destroying equipment, slashing the bags of cement, breaking down the temporary diversion dam. Every morning, Nigel would ride up to see the previous day's work in ruins.

"Make a camp up there," he told the new men whose backgrounds and characters were unknown to him, as he had asked no questions. He didn't care if they were bank robbers on the lam—in fact, that might be a boon. He just made sure each man was armed with a pistol or a rifle and knew that if any Indians tried to interfere with the construction of his irrigation ditch, they were to shoot.

"I wouldn't say shoot to kill," he said now in a low voice as the men prepared to ride up the canyon with their pack mules. "Just shoot in the air. Send a message. If they don't heed it, then stop them by any means you can. I'm building that ditch on my land to carry my water to my trees. The law is on our side."

He watched them ride off, hard-bitten looking men who would see to it that Chief Diego remembered his place. Then Nigel turned back to the hundred-tree grove where a man from Los Angeles was waiting for him.

Nigel's dates had started to ripen. They were ripening at various intervals, some faster than others, so that full harvesting would commence in October and continue until Christmas. The man from Los Angeles was a produce buyer who distributed to hundreds of markets and fruit-packing plants in Southern California. He had come to sample the first fruits from Stullwood Plantation.

The workers had constructed ramadas around the perimeter of the groves, open shelters constructed of upright posts and roofs made of dried palm fronds. Beneath these shady shelters, the newly harvested dates would be rapidly inspected and classified on long tables. From there they would go into wooden packing crates filled with straw and the words "Stullwood Plantation" printed on the lid.

Having been handed the first, earliest fruits from the anticipated harvest, the produce distributor smacked his lips and said, "Sweet, moist, and meaty. What's your price, Mr. Barnstable?"

"Whatever the other growers in the valley are charging you, I will charge less. I will undercut any other farm."

The man's bushy eyebrows shot up. "You'll hardly clear a profit."

"Let me worry about that. Just think about your own profits if you go into business with me."

The distributor pursed his lips and rubbed his white beard. "At that price, I can guarantee pretty much the whole Los Angeles market."

"Excellent," Nigel said, thinking of the shipment of the additional hundred date palms that was on its way, at that moment, from Phoenix, Arizona, to be planted on the western side of the hundred-tree grove.

His plan to monopolize the Coachella date market was under way.

Nigel paused to shield his eyes from the bright desert sun and drew in a deep breath. He felt like shouting for joy.

He knew he had been born to be the master of this place—the yellow-gray sand sweeping away in improbable flatness to lavender mountains in the distance. Master of every grain of sand, every pebble and leaf and cactus spine and lizard and bird and tree—and even the people. Especially the people! Mexicans and Indians, easily subjugated, but the white people, too, trickling into the valley every day like columns of tiny ants, scuttling in with their store-bought belongings, erecting their wood-frame houses, and scratching out little vegetable plots. All subject to their new lord and master.

Nigel was going to make something of this place. Lift Palm Springs above its rustic beginnings, rescue it from its Indian roots and sleepy, indolent ways, and turn it into a paradise where people of quality would eagerly come to enjoy the sun, the fresh air, the freedom.

As he returned his attention to the distributor, he laughed softly at the secret he shared only with himself. This ramshackle community with stunning potential that ordinary men could not see was going to be famous someday, along with the names of Stullwood and Barnstable.

And then he was going to hand it to his son.

*   *   *

Elizabeth had never been inside a hair salon.

But she smiled as she stood in front of Decatur's Salon. She was smiling because the people of the caves had spoken to her. At last, the meanings of petroglyphs had come clear. And they had given her answers.

She had done everything she could to make friends in Palm Springs, had gone out of her way to invite people to her home, to chat with them in the grocery store or at Lardner's, waving and saying hello when she passed them on the street. She had attended services at the Protestant church. At every turn she had been met with friendly politeness.

As she had ridden back from her visit to the caves in Chino Canyon, Elizabeth had thought: I am not in New York anymore. She had been going about it all wrong. She had expected the ladies of Palm Springs to adjust to her, when it should have been the other way round.

Mr. and Mrs. Decatur, a barber and his hairdresser wife, had built a small business establishment on Palm Springs' main road, a simple wooden structure consisting of two large rooms separated by a wall, each side with its own entrance from the street. Each had a large plate glass window that allowed people to look in. Elizabeth looked in now and saw that there was but one chair in the barbershop, with extra chairs for customers who were waiting. On the women's side, the salon had three stations, each with a hairdresser and client. There was also a hair washing station, a curling station, a drying station, a manicurist's table, and three chairs for customers to wait in. The place was busy. All chairs were occupied.

In the barbershop window, next to a red-and-white barber pole, a sign said: "Men Only. We do not trim ladies' hair."

A sign in the salon window said: "Lady Hairdresser Trained in Barber School for Expert Ladies' Hair Cutting."

Few women had dared to cut their hair short until a story was published in the *Saturday Evening Post* by a writer named F. Scott Fitzgerald. Bernice *Bobs Her Hair*. Suddenly, women were lining up at barber shops all around the country, invading the men's domains, to sit in barber chairs asking to have their hair cut short.

As she looked at the two storefronts, the barbershop and salon, Elizabeth thought: Men's caves and women's caves.

She went inside, a bell tinkling above the door. She was immediately met by the pungent scents of shampoo, styling lotion, ammonia. The sounds of snipping and clipping filled the air, along with the deafening drone of ceiling fans going round and round, and the blasting of the hair-drying fish so that the hairdressers and customers had to shout to be heard. All the ladies were talking at once.

Mrs. Allenby sat beneath the hair curling apparatus while Lois Lardner sat in front of the hair dryer. Miss Ethel Kincaid, the town seamstress, sat in the middle chair, getting a trim from Mrs. Decatur, while the two school teachers, Miss March and Miss Napier, sat on either side of her, being taken care of by Mrs. Decatur's adult daughters. Women she had tried to get to know with little success.

She heard accents: Miss Marsh spoke with the genteel accent of the South while Miss Kincaid clearly hailed from the North, Wisconsin or Minnesota, saying, "Oh yah." Elizabeth thought: No one was born here. We all came from someplace else. We are all newcomers.

And a truth struck her: It isn't "them and me." It's *us.*

She let the door shut behind her as she waited to be noticed. And then, one by one, the voices fell silent.

Mrs. Decatur, recognizing the newcomer as the lady who lived in the big house that overlooked the town, said, "May I help you?"

"I would like a trim and a curl, please."

The ladies exchanged puzzled glances. Whenever they saw Mrs. Barnstable around town, she always had the perfect hairdo, upswept in Gibson Girl fashion, with never a strand out of place, even when she was seen riding out in the desert on her Appaloosa. In fact, the ladies thought collectively now, Elizabeth Barnstable was always perfect. In her expensive clothes, alligator shoes, matching handbag, and white gloves, she always looked as if she had just stepped down from a movie screen.

"If you'll take a seat," Mrs. Decatur said, indicating a chair that had just been vacated. "You said you wanted a trim?" she asked as she removed the pins to let Elizabeth's long hair drape down.

"Just an inch or two." Elizabeth would have loved to try for a bob, but she had no idea how Nigel would react to it. "And then some wave, please. My hair is hopelessly straight."

As Mrs. Decatur went about her work, Elizabeth relaxed and surrendered to the moment and listened to the chatter.

Their voices flowed over her like a warm, therapeutic bath. She filled her ears with words of triumph and complaint and expectation and doubt. They aired their woes like sheets on a clothesline, swapping intimate details and advice on wombs, breasts, bladders, sleepless nights, inattentive husbands. They talked about laundry soap, movie stars, books, and what a wonderful thing air mail was going to be when it came to Palm Springs.

Elizabeth just listened, learning everything she could about her neighbors as she watched the uneven ends of her long hair disappear. "I was wondering, Mrs. Decatur," she said. "If you could recommend a good night cream? My skin has been feeling tight lately."

"It's the desert air. I have just the ticket," the hairdresser said. "A lotion I will give you before you leave. And please call me Dorothy."

"It must be exciting to see your farm grow so," Miss March said, in the next chair. The teacher was having curlers removed from her shoulder length hair. "Your husband is very progressive, isn't he?"

"Yes, I suppose he is."

"Augie Lardner said he saw Mr. Barnstable chatting with the movie people who are having that big mansion built down the way."

Elizabeth had no idea what she was talking about, but as Miss Clark had reported on Nigel visiting a speakeasy in Hollywood, it wouldn't be hard to believe he had made friends with movie people.

"Have you met Zora DuBois?" asked Miss Napier, who was receiving a hair vitalizing treatment in the other chair.

Elizabeth turned to her. She saw excitement in the teacher's eyes. We are on common ground, Elizabeth thought. And we are entertaining a subject that isn't spouted from a soapbox. What a snob I must have looked to them! "I haven't met Miss DuBois personally, not yet."

Elizabeth watched as the hot curling tongs, heated over an open flame, came close to her head. But Mrs. Decatur protected Elizabeth's scalp with a thick towel. One wave, then another and a third, being hotly sculpted into her long hair and formed in place with a pleasantly scented pomade. As the hairdresser worked, she said, "These waves will stay in place until you wash your hair. I'll give you the pinch clips you'll need to wear at night to hold the wave."

When Miss March was finished and removing the rubber cape, Elizabeth said, "Your accent is intriguing. Are you from the South?"

The teacher broke into a broad smile. "Why, yes! Atlanta, Georgia. I've heard that you come from New York."

"I do. Did you attend teachers' college in Atlanta?"

A few minutes later, Miss March said, "You know, Mrs. Barnstable, we never did finish our conversation about establishing a lending library. I think it's a wonderful idea. We should ask townspeople to donate books. We could even give our group a name, like Ladies Library League, for example."

"That's a wonderful name," Elizabeth said. "And please call me Elizabeth."

She saw Ethel Kincaid rise from her seat by the magazines and come over to say, "You must join our weekly sewing circle. Bring your mending. We meet at my house. We all bring potluck. You'd be surprised how much fun we can have doing a dreary job." She patted Elizabeth's shoulder as she left the shop.

Elizabeth hadn't needed to come to the salon. Fiona Wilson always did a nice job of fixing her hair. But the idea had come to her in the Indian cave where women were depicted at communal chores, helping one another—the idea that she needed to meet women on their ground.

Elizabeth smiled at herself in the mirror. She had made friends at last with the ladies of Palm Springs.

CHAPTER TWENTY-THREE

AS CODY BRUSHED BACK his thick black hair, he scrutinized himself in the mirror. He had what he thought was an ordinary face. Back in Montana, folks had often remarked how strongly he resembled his father, and the ladies always turned to look when George McNeal had ridden into town. They said he was a handsome man. So maybe Cody was no judge of himself.

He had shaved and changed into fresh clothes, and then stopped himself when he automatically reached for his gun belt. Up north, no one thought twice about an armed man, but here in Southern California, the only men wearing firearms were in the movies.

But the Colt had been a necessity in the past.

Traveling through West Texas towns that had reminded him of home. Not the flatness, of course, he'd never seen flatter country. But the mood of the place had felt familiar. None of the hectic pace he'd found in cities where the modern age made a man hurry. In West Texas, the clocks were still set back twenty, thirty years.

In Odessa he'd worked for a while as a roughneck on oil rigs and, out in the west, he had seen lightning flashing on the plains. Great forks shooting down from the night sky, as if God were practicing smiting sinners. With each flash he could see the heavy clouds hanging low. It would be raining there and flash flooding somewhere else. After work, he and other roughnecks went into town to unwind. There were a lot of cowboys in the saloon, good old boys knocking back whiskey before it was illegal, and listening to honky-tonk on the piano. Those rowdies had necessitated a man carrying a gun.

As he turned away from the mirror, he looked at the small desk by his bunk.

The story now filled three notebooks. He had held nothing back. His callowness, his blindness to Belle's seduction. His theft of gold from an innocent youth. A bare bones, frank and honest study of what gold fever could do to people, and when you threw love and greed into the mix, how lethal it could be.

Elizabeth was reading parts of the story, and she had suggested that Cody send it to a publisher, to share it with the world. But Cody didn't know that anyone would be interested in another man's story. Besides, he had a whole lot of other things on his mind these days without worrying about a publisher.

Cody felt a new yearning starting to build in him, fresh and different and intangible. It was the yearning to stop drifting and settle down.

It all depended on Elizabeth. If she never gained her freedom, would he still be able to live here in Palm Springs, be near her, see her, talk to her and know he could never have her in the way he wanted? The old saying about not crossing a particular bridge until you came to it offered him not a lick of comfort. He needed to know his future now, not when he came upon it.

Vigilance could be exhausting, Cody thought. A man of easy manner and casual ways, he now needed to be constantly on the lookout for Nigel Barnstable, had to watch every step he took, every gesture he made, every word he uttered to make sure none of his actions toward Elizabeth could be misconstrued by Nigel. When he encountered her, he would touch the brim of his hat and say, "Ma'am." And then he would think, was it too much? Not enough? Would Barnstable pick up on the fact that they were avoiding being friendly? What was the norm in these cases? Where were the lines drawn? Could he say, "How are you doing today?" Too much? Or would Barnstable eye the two of them and think they were being too stiff and formal and suspect they were hiding something? After all, McNeal had been working here for a year now, shouldn't he be on more familiar terms with his employer's wife? Carrying around so many questions, not finding the answers, feeling as if his entire life were a constant dilemma, and feeling as if he walked on eggshells was a tiring job. Cody only relaxed and breathed a little more easily when Barnstable was out of town.

As he took a brush to his dusty Stetson, Cody thought about brains and minds and thinking, and how some men drove themselves crazy with their thoughts, especially men on their own, or sitting *their horse of a night on a cattle drive*, with just the million-star sky over them and the prairie stretching away into tomorrow. Thoughts could be deadly, he reckoned, so men ought to be careful in their manner of thinking.

For himself, he knew what drove him crazy, what thoughts he couldn't allow into his head. They all involved Elizabeth, which made it difficult because she was all he thought about and all he wanted to think about. But two thoughts in particular were more dangerous than others: his burning hatred of Nigel Barnstable, which he had to control no matter what, and reliving their kiss in the cave.

Their mouths together, Elizabeth's body pressed against his, was a line he should never have crossed.

He had broken one of the rules that he lived by and, to Cody's thinking, you break one rule, you've broken them all. A chain is only as strong as its weakest link, and so a set of rules is only as obeyed as a broken one. He felt as if his whole moral skeleton had fallen apart and he needed to build it back up.

Now here was the tricky part. He still wanted Elizabeth and found himself not regretting the kiss one bit. He also held a proprietary attitude toward her now, a possessiveness that the kiss had bestowed on him—especially as she had kissed him back and had been a mightily willing participant in the whole event.

Thinking of this brought him to the new thought that had entered his mind and wouldn't leave. The notion that Barnstable was visiting Elizabeth's bed.

Cody was certain it was happening. Not that he would ask Elizabeth—he would never put her in so insulting a position as to have to answer. But she and Nigel were husband and wife, and Barnstable was a man who would claim his rights. Cody didn't want to think about it, it killed him to think about it, but men's brains sometimes had minds of their own and, thoughts being what they were, had a way of making a man think them.

So he had plunged himself into his writing and taking care of La Alma's horses and livestock and holding himself in check and praying that Barnstable's path didn't cross his own at a moment when Cody wouldn't be able to account for his actions. He wished there were a swifter solution to their problem instead of lawyers and divorce courts and judges and papers. Like frontier justice, when horse thieves were hanged from the nearest tree the minute they were caught. A frontier divorce was what was called for now, if there was such a thing.

So, between his kiss-claim on her and Elizabeth's slow dissolution of the union, it seemed they had entered a gray area that had no rules or definition. But none of this reasoning helped. The hard fact was that neither of these conditions was known to Barnstable. He would consider himself as firmly married and the sole proprietor of Elizabeth.

Cody knew she wouldn't resist her husband's visits. But he vowed right now, once again to God, that if Elizabeth ever came to him for help, if she but said the word, Cody would rise up and Nigel Barnstable would never touch her again.

Hearing voices outside, Cody was reminded that it was time to put the muddle of his life from his mind and get going. Settling his Stetson on his head, he left the bunkhouse.

Out on the shaded lane, Cody joined other citizens as they headed toward an enormous tent that had been erected on the vacant land beyond the schoolhouse, surrounded by wagons and horses and a few automobiles. Folks had come from miles around, it seemed. Used to be, he thought, you saw a big tent going up outside of town, you knew it was going to be a Jesus revival, with lots of clapping and foot stamping and shouts of hallelujah. But this tent brought a religion of a different kind, a new religion.

The traveling cinema had come to town.

A young woman sat by the entrance, collecting money. People paid their ten cents and went inside to find rows of folding chairs. Cody saw Elizabeth a few rows ahead, sitting with the Norringtons. He decided to take a seat near the back.

It was a madhouse, noisy and exciting. No windows, just a string of overhead bulbs running off a belching generator. The Lardners were there, the Allenbys, the Decaturs, Fiona and Doc Perry. All the townsfolk it seemed, plus familiar faces from outlying farms and homesteads. A few Indians, too, had come to be entertained. Everyone eyed the enormous projector at the back of the tent, with its giant reels ready to transport them to another world.

When the piano lady appeared, everyone cheered and stamped their feet. Not because they were eager to hear her play but because it meant the program was about to begin. They heard the electric generator rev up, giving off a great hum, the door flaps were lowered, the lights turned off, creating darkness, and the projector sprang to life.

Words appeared on the screen: "LADIES PLEASE REMOVE YOUR HATS."

The screen then came to life with the image of President Warren G. Harding at his desk in the Oval Office, signing papers in the presence of smiling men while photographers took flash pictures of him. The intertitles read: "President Harding signs the Federal Highway Act of 1921, allocating over a hundred million dollars of federal funds for the improvement of America's highway system."

The next film clip showed the president riding in the back of a chauffeured convertible, the top down as he waved to crowds along the street. The intertitles read: "Harding declares that America is in the age of the 'motor car' and that the automobile reflects our standard of living and gauges the speed of our present-day life."

A shoe came suddenly hurtling through the air from the back of the tent, to sail over the audience's heads and land smack in the center of the screen. A drunken voice shouted in the darkness, "Show the galldurned movie already!"

Next on the newsreel was a view of a courthouse with a crowd gathered on the steps. The intertitle explained that the trial of Fatty Arbuckle had entered its tenth day.

Popular screen comedian Roscoe Arbuckle had been accused of killing a young actress while engaged in sex with her. Rumor had it that he had raped her with a wine bottle.

Another shoe hit the screen and rowdies in the audience started booing.

Finally the film began, a western filled with the usual characters playing out a familiar story.

Elizabeth was amazed at the pandemonium that ensued. Nothing like the polite audiences in the New York movie palaces, California desert folk expressed their enthusiasm with cheers and whistles and catcalls. They also brought snacks, so that the air was filled with the sounds of wax paper rustling, the munching of crispy chicken and crunchy corn. And people talked, about the movie or other things, while the pianist did her best to drum out the right music at the right time, banging on the keys when there was action on the screen, pressing the foot pedal to get it as loud as possible, softening it to syrupy melodies during romantic scenes, and babies howled and kids screamed and adults carried on conversations and folks read the intertitles out loud for those who couldn't read.

Outside, Nigel was debating going in. It was December and his big harvest was over and stacks of crates had been taken to the train to be shipped into Los Angeles. Everyone was saying his crop had been a good one and that his dates were of excellent quality. After weeks of hectic activities among his groves, Nigel found himself with a bit of leisure time on his hands.

The movie poster outside the tent said, "A photoplay of tempestuous love between a beautiful Indian princess and a wild Western outlaw!"

Nigel was there out of curiosity. Despite his proximity to Hollywood and his casual friendship with the Lamonts, he had seen few movies since arriving in Southern California. Films didn't really interest him.

But a movie had come to Palm Springs. And it cost ten cents. So he thought he'd go inside and get a feel for what audiences saw in such cheap entertainments.

There had been a lot of publicity about this controversial film. It was based on a best-selling novel that was being read by American women everywhere—about forbidden love with sexual and racial overtones. A love triangle that consisted of the hero, the Indian woman for whom he had a powerful lust, and the virginal rancher's daughter who pined for him.

As the house was packed with no vacant seats, Nigel stood at the back with other standees. The film took place in Texas but he recognized the background behind the actors on the screen. The scene on the "San Antonio River" had been filmed nearby at Two Bunch Palms. The riding scenes had been shot near Hot Springs. Mesquite Canyon was clearly identifiable in the "cattle ranch" scene. The entire movie, he realized, had been shot in and around Palm Springs by one of the many film companies that came through here.

What amazed him now, as he surveyed the audience who sat enthralled by the story unfolding on the screen, was that even though the movie had been filmed around their own neighborhood, these people—these residents of this area—were being taken away to a place over twelve hundred miles away! They weren't watching a movie of their own backyard, as it were, but were being drawn into a panorama they believed to be half a continent away.

The power of illusion. The power to persuade.

Nigel soon found himself not only getting caught up in the story and the action, but a new energy infused him as he listened to the roar of the audience, their applause, the whistles and hollers as they participated in the drama of "good" Jack Rollins and "bad" Sagebrush Sam and the exotic Princess Morning Sun and the pure and virginal Mary Cummings.

But not everyone there was swept up by the film. Sitting in the last row, just a few feet away from Nigel, Doc Perry wasn't paying attention, as his thoughts were focused on his personal dilemma—his finances and Fiona.

His income was shrinking. A few patients had remarked that his medicine no longer worked and so sales and therefore income were dropping—because he no longer added alcohol to his recipes! But, sitting in the dark with Fiona, sharing an experience with her was the most satisfying moment of his life. He didn't want it to end. He knew he could go up to Canada or down to Mexico, where alcohol was legal, and live comfortably there, but he wanted to be near Fiona.

As the cavalry chased a band of Indians across the screen, with much exchange of arrows and rifle fire, and cheers and catcalls from the audience, Leland drew in a deep sigh and his nostrils picked up a pungent aroma nearby. Glancing out the corner of his eye, he saw Mr. Sweeney, who owned the auto garage, swigging from a silver hip flask that he brought out now and then from his jacket pocket. There was no mistaking the smell of distilled spirits.

Pre-Prohibition or illegal? Perry wondered. The amendment had been in effect for two years now. It was doubtful anyone still had a private stash of legal liquor left. More and more citizens were turning to bootleg moonshine.

He had struggled with the dilemma for months but now, being no closer to a solution than before, and being on the brink of bankruptcy, Leland Perry realized that there was only one way he could continue to carry on his current lifestyle and still be close to Fiona.

He decided now that it was worth the risk, no matter how deadly. He had to seek out the unlawful services of a bootlegger.

A few seats down, Cody was watching the film in rising irritation. He couldn't begin to count the number of inaccuracies in it. It made him think of what Elizabeth had said about his book. "Cody, it made me laugh and cry. And I got angry, too. You bring those people to life. You make the reader want to know them—actually you make the reader feel she *does* know them. All the ups and downs, the triumphs and heartbreaks—Cody, it is a story told so well that you must share it with the world."

But he hadn't been sure he wanted to share his life with the world.

Now, however, as he watched in growing irritation an impossible tale unfold on the movie screen, with characters that verged on clownish, the costumes and sets all wrong, skewing the true West to give audiences a cheap thrill, he thought: Real cowboys don't wear sparkling white clothes and shirts with fringe. They don't kiss their horses or take ranchers' daughters for sunset rides. The life of a cowboy is rough and dirty and hard. And there's never a hero in a white hat to save the rancher's spread. There are worse villains than men in black hats—they're called bankers, with fat stomachs who threaten a man's way of life with a piece of paper called a mortgage, something way deadlier than a Colt six-shooter.

And American Indians sure as heck don't have princesses! The Indian concept of status and hierarchy and bloodline was vastly different from the white man's, but these moviemakers didn't care, or maybe they didn't know, but what got under Cody's skin now was that millions of people around the world were going to see this travesty about the West and take it for gospel!

Cody thought how good it had felt to record and preserve one of the last of the Western gold rushes and to tell the story of one of the West's many forgotten ghost towns. In a flash he realized that here was the way to preserve the West, in his stories. At least, to offer people a view that differed from what Hollywood was giving them.

Down in the front row, however, there was one member of the audience who was frozen with awe—Luisa's granddaughter, Gabriela, who gazed up at the screen with an expression that could almost be described as reverent.

Her head was filled with movie actresses. Ever since the one on the magazine cover that had almost spoken to her, seven months ago, the film star named Zora, Gabriela had been able to think of nothing else. Look at them, she thought when she saw their photos, their movies—special women. Each unique with her own style. No one would call them twins as she and her cousin were often called. They are not like a pair of candlesticks over a fireplace.

And Gabriela's yearning to be different and special grew.

When Nigel saw the words THE END come up, after Jack Rollins removed his white cowboy hat and finally kissed Mary Cummings on the lips, he heard a collective sigh from the women in the audience.

He looked around and thought: These women are aroused . . .

Nigel laughed. Look at them! Putty in the hands of a film director, a screenwriter, and most of all, the actor who played Jack Rollins. It was a power never before seen in the history of the world. Men with a genuine desire to please and transport an audience, to influence those sitting in the seats, to change people's lives and maybe even improve them—here was the real power, the real control over the public. It wasn't politicians or the men in Washington who governed the lives of the citizens, it was men with cameras and film and vision. The president of the United States hadn't one-half the power to influence as the men and women up on the movie screen did. When Zora DuBois raised her hemline, fifty million American women raised theirs.

The power of film to influence was astronomical. After all, wasn't he himself in this part of the world because a man with film and a camera had made a motion picture about ranchers, outlaws, and the hero who had saved the day? In his own case, it was what he had seen on the screen in the *Mauretania*'s theater, the beckoning vistas that no still photograph could depict. And suddenly Nigel's doubts about investing in movies were dispelled. He would telephone Lamont first thing in the morning.

*   *   *

The cluster of palms up ahead were in the area where Augie Lardner had said it was rumored a moonshine distiller was in operation.

Doc Perry slowed his buggy.

There wasn't a real driveway, just a two-rut track between trees and a fence with a sign that said, KEEP OUT. Perry cautiously guided his horse through the gate, recalling what Cody McNeal had told him about getting shot at by bootleggers up near Tylerville.

The smell of sour mash filled the air. Perry had learned a little about the liquor-making business. Corn or grain was used, with sugar and yeast, and distilled in an apparatus of fermenters, pots, copper tubing, pipes, and condensers. The resulting white lightning, which was 200-proof grain alcohol, was diluted with water, glycerin, and oil of juniper, and allowed to "age" for a few hours. Crushed juniper berries added to the liquor made for a fine gin, while caramel coloring, prune juice, and creosote oil turned the hooch into scotch. Honey, bitter almonds, sulfuric acid, and tincture of saffron flavored with oil of pears produced a popular peach brandy. All sold at high prices in speakeasies around the country.

Folks in the area suspected an illegal distillery operation in these parts when drunken ducks were spotted at a nearby stream, trying to fly only to crash down into the water. Farther up one of the canyons, someone had reported seeing deer reeling and falling down. One of the problems facing bootleggers was what to do with the used corn or grain mash after the alcohol had boiled off. Clearly someone had been dumping the stuff where there was wildlife.

Perry came upon a shack with distillery apparatus in the dusty yard. The moonshine still rattled and gave off foul steam. He brought his buggy to a halt and waited. He knew he was being watched. Presently, he heard someone shout, "I got my shotgun on you!"

"I am here to offer you a business transaction," Perry called out. "I assure you I am not the police. I am a customer." And he waited nervously, with sweat dripping between his shoulder blades, for the bootlegger to appear.

*   *   *

Back in town, Cody walked into Lardner's carrying a precious package. It weighed a pound and was wrapped in brown paper and string. The recipient was a New York publisher.

He couldn't believe how nervous he was handing the package over to Mrs. Lardner for postage, asking that it go out on the afternoon train. *I faced down a mountain lion outside of New Jordan, Wyoming. I came face-to-face with a stagecoach robber holding me up at gunpoint. I climbed one of the tallest oil rigs in the state of Texas. And none of those moments compares to the scariness of this.*

He knew it was because he was about to place his life—his heart, his secret pain, his dark devils—in the hands of strangers three thousand miles away. Cody decided it was the bravest thing he had ever done.

CHAPTER TWENTY-FOUR

FIONA SAT IN WINTER sunshine as she mended a hem on one of her Ladyship's riding skirts. Her mind was not on her work. She was thinking about Leland.

Since learning the truth about the miscarriage, Fiona had kept a careful watch on Her Ladyship. But at the same time, her love for Leland Perry had intensified to the point where it was unbearable to be out of his presence. She wanted to go home with him, sleep with him, be with him. She had thought their separations would be tolerable, after all he was only a short distance down the lane. But it might as well be a thousand miles for the way she ached for him in her bed, and couldn't sleep, and fantasized about him making love to her.

It couldn't be tolerated any longer. She deserved happiness. She deserved a chance to make Leland happy. He was right, it was unfair of Mrs. Van Linden to hold her to a promise that virtually enslaved her. Besides, the Norringtons were here, safe and loyal, so she wouldn't be abandoning Elizabeth. And to round things off, Fiona would only be just down the road, on hand should Elizabeth need her, thus keeping her promise after all.

A new year lay just days away—1922. It sounded so modern and so full of promise. She decided she was going to make a New Year's resolution: she was going to marry Leland Perry.

Having made the decision, and liking the sound of the word resolution, Fiona began to pack up her sewing things, humming happily to herself, when a grim-faced Mrs. Norrington came into the kitchen. "Miss Wilson," she said. "Might I have a word with you?"

*   *   *

Luisa knew where to find Diego.

It was where he was spending his days, instead of in the village weaving quail nets or fashioning spears for hunting. When the Señor had started taking water from the Mesquite Creek, Diego had turned all his thoughts to that one direction.

Luisa didn't want to get snared into Diego's war with the Señor, but she needed his permission for something. She found him far up the trail in Mesquite Canyon, with his shamans, spying on the Señor's Mexican workers as they slowly built a deep, wide ditch of bricks, covering it all with cement. There were more white men now, holding rifles and scanning the nearby woods for Indians.

"Diego, I need to find an apprentice. The spirits aren't speaking to me as much as they used to. I fear they will soon be silent, and then how will I teach the next spirit-reader? You must let me choose a child from our village."

The normally implacable chief gave Luisa such a startled look that it startled her in return. She knew she had overstepped bounds, both in her preposterous suggestion but also in speaking so boldly. But something had to be done.

The old man scowled as he said, "What was done for generations must continue to be done. Change is bad for the health of the tribe."

"But change is happening anyway," she said. "The band at Indio have bought a truck and now take their produce to other villages to make a profit. Our people speak of radios and telephones and moving pictures. Diego, change is happening. We will lose our culture entirely."

He held up a brown, weathered hand and said in an affronted tone, "We will speak of this no more, Luisa Padilla, in case we anger the spirits and bring bad magic upon our village. Say a prayer to Mukat and tell him you are sorry for your runaway words. He will understand. You are, after all, only a woman."

Luisa wanted to say more. She thought of the pile of gifts in one corner of her house—baskets and beaded jewelry and acorn cakes to be given to visitors who came for the annual winter ceremony honoring Mukat. But the fiesta had come and gone, and the gifts remained.

In her sixty-two years, this had never happened.

Fewer people had attended. And for the first time, even some of her own villagers had not attended. They went to Hot Springs to visit relatives who had a Victrola that played music. They were being lured away from the spiritual world by the material one. Perhaps next year, she thought ruefully, it will only be her and the chief and the shamans. There will be no one to play the sacred drums. No one to dance the sacred dances. Mukat will be forgotten.

She wanted to say to Diego, if the creator of the world dies, does the world die with him?

But she turned away to leave her husband to his men's game with the Señor.

*   *   *

"The liquor is so strong," Leland Perry was saying to Fiona over dinner, "one gallon will last me months. Mrs. Lardner will be able to sleep again and Mr. Allenby's hand tremors will subside, along with his wife's arthritis pain, and Reverend White's nervous stomach." Once he had flashed money at the old moonshiner out in the desert, Doc Perry had been able to make a deal with the man. Hard cash for a gallon of white lightning, with the promise of more as needed. "Watch out for federal agents," the old man had said as Doc Perry was pulling his buggy away from the shack. "They shoot first and then ask questions."

He looked at Fiona across the table. He could tell she was far away. "Am I boring you, my dear?"

She brought herself out of her thoughts. She was thinking of Mrs. Norrington's startling announcement that morning: that she and her husband had had enough of desert life and were going to give notice at the first of the year and move to Los Angeles. It had come as a terrible blow. How could Fiona leave Her Ladyship now? She had based her decision to marry Leland on the comforting fact that the Norringtons would be at La Alma. But now they were leaving, and Fiona's dream of marriage was shattered.

"Is it safe?" she said, as she picked at her food.

"Safe as houses," he said with a smile. "Federal agents can't be bothered with a man who buys a gallon of hooch. It's the truckloads they're interested in."

He had been reluctant to tell her at first that he was resorting to illegal liquor for his medicines. She knew he had been worried what she would think of him. But Fiona was proud of him. Prohibition was a ridiculous law, and if people found ways around it, more power to them.

Like Leland. She knew he had been scared to go to a gun-happy 'legger, but she knew he had done it to be able to stay in Palm Springs and be near her.

"Leland," she said, getting up from the table, going around to stand behind him. Wrapping her arms around his neck, she bent to kiss his ear. "I want to be with you. But I can't. So I will be content with this hour."

He got to his feet and, taking her by the arms, said solemnly, "Take heart, my dearest, a solution will come to us. For now, I have a Christmas present for you."

He left the dining room and returned with a large, flat box wrapped in colorful paper and ribbon. She opened it. She stared. Her eyes widened. "Oh, Leland . . ."

"I hope you like it, my love," he said, tears shimmering in his eyes.

*   *   *

The day before Christmas, and Cody felt a curious melancholy steal over him.

He was writing about the shoot-out in front of the O.K. Corral in Tombstone and his father's involvement as a witness. Thinking of his father took him back to Christmases in Montana, when the snow reached the eaves of the roof and the wind blew so fierce the snow fell sideways. There was snow here, in Palm Springs, but it was five thousand feet in the air and was observed through bright green palm fronds.

His musings were interrupted when one of the ranch hands came into the bunkhouse with the daily mail. As always, Cody rose expectantly, wondering if a barber in Virginia or a newspaper man in Tennessee remembered a boy named Peachy O'Doule.

Jorge handed him one piece of mail, an envelope bearing a return address in Kentucky. He stared at it for a long moment, his heart starting to race. After years of searching for Peachy, was the search about to come to an end?

*   *   *

Nigel whistled a tune as he tied his bowtie.

He was looking forward to the coming evening. A Christmas Eve party at the Lamonts' Palm Springs home. The cream of Hollywood would be there. It promised to be a sparkling affair. Lamont had hinted that he had something to show Nigel, leading Nigel to believe it must be a script or a book, a movie project of some kind, now that Nigel was amenable to investing in films.

Elizabeth came in, a pile of linens in her arms. "Really, Elizabeth," Nigel said with a frown. "We have maids to do that sort of thing."

She eyed the tuxedo. "Are you going somewhere?"

"I'm going to a Christmas party along the road."

The Lamonts, she assumed. As she started to put the linens away, Nigel said, "Elizabeth, I'm growing impatient for my son to be born. You should have gotten pregnant by now."

She looked at him, wondering how far she could go, if she might spark an outrage or if he was in one of his reasonable moods. She decided to try for the latter. "There is a possibility," she said cautiously, "that what you did to me might have rendered me incapable of having children."

No outrage was sparked. He simply said, "You mean what you did to yourself. Really, Elizabeth, when are you going to take responsibility for your actions? You can't blame me for the loss of the child. You are to go into Los Angeles and see a specialist. If there is something wrong with you, I want it fixed."

Elizabeth pressed her lips together as she set the linens on the bed. For seven months she had lived in fear, had gone through the moves and motions of an actress on a stage, following every word of advice from her lawyer, leading the exemplary life of a contented wife while being secretly in love, filling her lonely nights with the memory of a forbidden kiss, hating one man, yearning for another—meeting Mary Clark in the anonymity of the town of Indio, holding herself together, drawing strength and spiritual sustenance from ancient pictographs and arrowheads.

Now she suddenly wanted to scream. She wanted to toss her finely crafted plan to the wind and scream her anger and hatred and secrets at him, let him know what he had done, how she felt, and how she was going to get back at him. But in an instant of level-headedness, she told herself that Nigel would probably find it all amusing, and then her secret advantage would be lost.

In the end, it all boiled down to one thing. "Nigel, why do you want to stay with me? We are clearly not happy together. Why not divorce me and marry someone more suited to you?"

To her surprise, he accepted her question with equanimity. "People of our class do not divorce, and Stullwoods especially do not divorce. Now I want a son to inherit my empire. When your father dies, his entire fortune goes to you, but it will be under my stewardship. And someday that fortune will pass to my son."

He looked at her in the mirror. "I mean it, Elizabeth. You are my wife, and you will stay my wife. I will not court another woman. I want a son. Go see a specialist and get yourself checked out."

"And if I can't get pregnant?"

"That is not an option. You had better not let me down, Elizabeth."

She stared at him, the handsome advertisement for expensive men's shirts. Because that was what he was, unreal, not flesh and blood, a reflection in glass.

She released a long breath. The moment of anger and confrontation had passed. She had not blurted her secret strategy. She was in control of herself again. She turned and started to leave the bedroom. But when she reached the door, he said, "By the way, I'm glad you took my advice and learned to drive. A man of my position should only naturally have a wife who is progressive. And I'm glad you followed up on my idea about the lending library for the valley. We Stullwoods have always taken care of our people."

Elizabeth couldn't believe it. The free library had been her idea. By claiming the idea as his, he had taken it away from her. She saw the future—bit-by-bit Nigel was going to whittle her away until there was nothing left.

"By the way," he added, "don't think I don't know what's going on."

To her blank look, he said, "Your little band of followers. The Norringtons, Fiona Wilson, the Indian woman and her girls."

Elizabeth frowned. "What—"

He reached her in three strides and his arm shot out so swiftly she couldn't react. He seized her wrist in such a painful grip that she gave a cry. "You have them all eating out of your hand," he said, increasing the pressure of his grip so that she sank to her knees. He bent low to her face. "The way they watch you, hover around you. Like a little army. Well, they can't protect you. And it would be a shame to have them suffer the consequences of your disobedience."

"Nigel," she moaned, trying with her other hand to pry his fingers from her wrist. "You're hurting me."

He increased the pressure. And when he gave her arm a quick twist, tears sprang to her eyes.

"If you break my arm—" she began through clenched teeth.

"What? People will wonder? But everyone knows how clumsy you are. You simply fell again." He bent closer. "Now listen to me. I am going to have a son. And if I don't get him through you, there are other means. But you will be his mother. You will raise him and be a loving mother."

She winced and made a sound in her throat. "No one would believe it."

"Oh, yes, they would. I'll find a cooperative girl, offer her enough money, and then you and I announce that we're going on a cruise around the world. When we return to Palm Springs, we will be proudly carrying our newborn son. As far as everyone is concerned, he will be a Barnstable and a Van Linden. But I assume you would rather the child be your own. However, I am not a patient man, Elizabeth. I will give you one year, after which time I will resort to other means to father my son. And then we will be a perfect family."

He shoved her down, releasing her arm where red welts were already rising. "One year, Elizabeth. Don't let me down."

*   *   *

Nigel drove his Stutz Bearcat through the star-cast night, the cold wind whipping his hair and, as he began to meet up with other cars and traffic never seen in this peaceful valley, he realized they were guests from other towns and cities, arriving at the Lamonts' for the party.

The antebellum house on the plateau overlooking the desert was finished, and the Lamonts were throwing a fabulous Christmas party as a house warming.

Cars were jammed in the driveway with parking valets running to and fro, and chauffeurs jockeying for space. He was amazed that so many people had made the long drive from Los Angeles and Hollywood for a chance to glimpse the Lamonts' new getaway home. Nigel left his Stutz parked by a sand dune and climbed the stone steps to the entrance.

The entry was a giant marble rotunda that made one think of capitol buildings, with Greek and Roman statuary. A flying staircase swept dramatically to the second floor, and in the center of the round entry, an enormous glittering Christmas tree rose nearly to the ceiling, covered in twinkling electric lights.

Nigel moved through the upbeat party crowd with a martini. The atmosphere was charged with energy and the sound of a loud jazz band. He glimpsed people on a dance floor, flappers and dapper young men enjoying the hell out of themselves. We came through a devastating war, Nigel thought, and now we want to live. This new generation owned the world. It was great to be alive, to be in one's twenties and to know that the world was theirs.

As he threaded his way through evening gowns and dinner jackets, he felt eyes checking him out. Nigel had known from an early age that he was handsome. Women wanted him; men envied him. He walked with aplomb, the debonair leading man of motion pictures. His tuxedo, tailor-made, accentuated his broad shoulders and trim waist. Before he had stepped away from the mirror at home, he made sure that not a hair was out of place, not a fleck or speck marred his perfection.

He sauntered through rooms crammed with expensive statuary and tapestries, imported furniture, paintings, and the trimmings of new wealth. He perused the many trays that floated through the lively crowd on the uplifted hands of faceless waiters: foie gras on crackers, caviar on toast points, crab-stuffed mushroom caps, shrimp puffs, chicken livers wrapped in bacon. At the buffet, two chefs carved hams and haunches of roast beef. There were potatoes creamed with sharp cheese, buttered asparagus tips, mussels in white wine, coq au vin. For dessert: ice cream, tarts, crêpes, raspberry charlotte, crème brulée.

And suddenly Zora was there, materializing from out of the shimmering crowd, in her country-girl persona, with bouncing red-brown curls and dressed in a sleek white gossamer gown. She seized his wrist. Her eyes flashed brightly. "English! There you are! Jack has a surprise for us!"

He laughed. Nigel couldn't decide which of Zora's façades he preferred. Maybe it had to do with his mood at the time. Although Nigel rarely experienced boredom, if he should ever find himself in a stagnant moment, he would want country-girl Zora to snap him out of it. But when he was high on his own energy, Nigel fancied the dark, jaded vampire. Opposites, yes. When he was dark, she should be light, and vice versa. "What kind of surprise?" he said, allowing her to lead him through the crowd.

"I have no idea!" she cried. "But knowing my husband, it's going to be something so special, we shall have to take sedatives and lie down afterward."

He knew why she was country-girl at her parties. It was so she could talk to her guests and her Brooklyn accent wouldn't matter. When she was the sulky vamp, she had to stay silent.

Lamont's private office was upstairs in a quiet wing of the house, with a tall Negro guard at the door. When Zora led Nigel inside, he was surprised to find that they were the only ones there. He had somehow expected to find Lamont's office crammed with sycophants, deal makers, writers pitching ideas, actresses wanting screen tests. But the short, pudgy, ginger-haired movie director was alone in a spacious office appointed with expensive furniture littered with books, scripts, newspapers, magazines. On the walls, photos of Lamont with famous people, plus awards and certificates and documents.

"Barnstable!" the small man boomed, approaching with open arms and a smoking cigar. "Glad you could come. I've something very exciting to show you."

Nigel glanced at Zora, who shrugged and gave him a mystified look. But her eyes were shining, and he wondered if she had been indulging in something more than champagne. He knew she occasionally dabbled in cocaine, as most of her friends did.

Lamont spoke rapidly and with enthusiasm. "I'm sure you've heard, Barnstable, of the new deal between Warner Bros. and Vitaphone, a company that manufactures equipment for 'sound' films."

Nigel had indeed heard of it. The soundtrack apparently was printed on phonograph records, which were then played on a turntable coupled to the movie projector motor while the movie was being screened. It was a brilliant solution to the soundtrack problem, he thought. Films were always distributed with their musical score written on music sheets, to be given to the organist or pianist playing the accompaniment to the movie. But at some theaters, especially in small towns, musicians preferred to play their own music. The result was that audiences across the country did not have the same movie experience.

Lamont led his wife and Nigel to a curious apparatus in the center of the room. It was a movie projector of sorts, but with larger than normal reels, and a larger body as if to make room for more machinery. Nigel had never seen one like it before. Jack turned out the lights and started the projector. On a screen on the opposite wall his image appeared, sitting at his desk, smiling for the camera. He started to speak and it so startled Nigel and Zora that they jumped. They heard him. There were no intertitles. Jack's lips moved and his voice came out.

It was just a short piece, and when it was over, Jack turned the lights back on and beamed at his guest. "Well?"

Nigel looked around. "I don't see the record player. Where did the sound come from?"

"That's just it!" Lamont cried. "The problem with the projector-gramophone setup is that they have to be perfectly synchronous. If they aren't, lips and voice don't match and it's confusing to the audience, even comical. But this technique puts the sound directly on the film."

He paused to let Nigel spend a flabbergasted moment, then he went on, "They record the sound in a separate machine that is essentially a sound camera with the lenses and picture shutter missing. It's an optical tape recorder, if you will, that uses film rather than tape and is mechanically interlocked with the picture camera. No more silent movie. No more reading intertitles. The audience will hear the actors directly in their own voices."

"Think of it!" Lamont nearly shouted. "And you mark my words. Audiences will catch on to hearing the actors on the screen. Barnstable, my friend, this is an historic occasion, the very first time-frame-synchronous human voice is heard from a sound recording. Of course," he added, "it's an outrageously expensive process, but I guarantee you, Barnstable, that the men who get in on the ground floor of an investment like this will make millions!"

While Jack and Nigel talked excitedly of the financial possibilities of this new system, Zora stared at the blank screen and felt cold fear creep into her bones. A memory popped into her mind: last year, being interviewed by *Photoplay* magazine. Upon being introduced to the journalist, adding that she was flattered they wanted to do a story on her, Zora had caught a flicker of surprise in the woman's eyes. She had then commenced with the questions, and upon each of Zora's responses, that queer flicker occurred. And then a frown, and then an amused smile. Zora got the oddest feeling that the woman was trying not to laugh, yet Zora had not said anything funny. It wasn't until the article came out that Zora learned the truth: "One was surprised to hear Brooklyn, thick and comical, come out of that sultry mouth. While Miss DuBois possesses a provocative screen presence and undeniably enthralls both men and women, her manner of speech does not fit. This reporter was surprised to hear the legendary vamp speak in an accent that more suited the slums of New York than the glamour of Hollywood."

It had thrown Zora into a funk for weeks, but the article had not put a dent in her box office receipts, and the fan mail kept rolling in, so she had gotten over it and judged the reporter an idiot.

But now, in her husband's private office, with Jack and Nigel talking rapidly about patents and licenses and "the revolutionary effect of sound on the movies," a new reality dawned all over her so that she was instantly consumed with a terror greater than she had ever known.

Of course, Zora had heard talk of the coming "sound" revolution; it was the talk of Hollywood. She had heard about experiments being done in laboratories, the progress they were making, but she hadn't known they had come this far.

But they had come this far . . . and now it was here, in her home!

She felt her stomach turn into an icy knot, and she began to tremble as an unthinkable future began to form in her mind. As a child Zora had been invisible. A skinny little thing in old dresses that hung on her in the embarrassing way secondhand clothes did. At a shop counter, holding up her penny, little Zora eclipsed by the customers crowding for service. Bigger boys shoving her out of the way, sometimes snatching the precious penny and running off laughing. She'd go home empty-handed, crying, and no one in the busy street would bother to stop and ask a little girl why she was crying. Sometimes she was invisible at home, too, as her mother lay stretched out on the threadbare sofa, a wet cloth on her face. When Zora's tugs at her mother's skirt elicited silence, Zora would go to the mirror to make sure she wasn't really invisible.

So when she first saw herself on a movie screen, a remarkable transformation had taken place inside her. She had looked at her image, larger than real life, and had thought: there I am. Not invisible after all. And, over time, as she saw herself on the screen again and again, she began to think that her very soul was up there, the camera had captured her essence and projected it for the world to see.

But what if she stopped making movies? What would become of her essence? Would she lose her soul? Would she become invisible again?

And now the sharp panic began, like a physical thing coiled inside her abdomen, a small, growing parasite that fed on her fears and insecurities. It was because of her accent, the way she came down heavily on certain consonants. Jack often joked that when she spoke her last name, DuBois sounded like an expletive. She tried to keep herself from saying "terlet" instead of "toilet," and "boid" instead of "bird," but it was a difficult habit to break.

As she listened to Jack pitch the investment to Nigel, something new
began to dawn on her. She tried to grasp it, an intangible hobgoblin
dancing at the edge of her mind. And she suddenly realized in shock
that it wasn't just the technology that had her scared out of her wits.
What she was feeling now was completely different and new, and so
terrible that she thought she was going to be sick.

Jack, her hero, her rescuer, her comforter when the insecurities
got to be too much, was standing there smiling as he used words like
"revolutionary" and "future," unaware that each word, like his smile,
sliced into her heart. Jack was her rock, her stability, the one person
in all the world she knew she could rely on—and he was betraying her!

It was worse than if she had caught him in the arms of another
woman. This was Jack promoting the new monstrosity, persuading
people to invest in it, praising the delights and benefits of the beast
that was going to destroy her career. He had gone over to the enemy
camp. He had abandoned her. Instead of championing her cause by
fighting off men who would dare to bring sound into movie theaters,
he was joining their ranks—and smiling!

*   *   *

It was evening. Cody had seen Barnstable drive off earlier, dressed for
a party. The Norringtons had gone across the way for dinner in Mrs.
Henry's dining room, and Miss Wilson was with Doc Perry. So Cody
knew Elizabeth was alone.

After receiving the unexpected letter, Cody had saddled his mare
and gone for a run in the desert to clear his mind. But as he walked
toward the house, he wasn't clear minded at all. The letter had had
a startling effect on him and now he was filled with misgivings and
even fear.

He looked through the kitchen window, glowing with light,
and saw her at the stove. He gave the back door a quick knock and
stepped inside.

She turned. "Cody!"

"It's Christmas Eve, Elizabeth."

"So it is. I was just making myself a cup of tea." She had been
thinking about Cody for the past two hours, ever since Nigel's attack,
which had left her scared and on edge. Nigel had demonstrated that
he had no compunction against injuring her, to break a bone even.
Her wrist, hidden beneath a long sleeve, throbbed painfully. While

she planned to hide the injury from others, she wanted Cody to know what Nigel had done—she needed him to know.

She needed Cody's strength right now more than anything, needed him to comfort her and help her find a way out of this nightmare. Now, not only must she herself not get pregnant, she had to get away from Nigel before he brought a bastard son home. Elizabeth had no doubt there were girls desperate enough to sell a child. Nigel would just use his charm and his checkbook, and the son and heir would arrive, enslaving Elizabeth to Nigel forever.

Six months. It was all she had and now she felt a mild panic begin. But Cody would reassure her. He would listen and perhaps give advice. But mostly it was just unburdening herself of this secret to the man she loved—he would give her the strength and courage to see this through.

Cody strode across the kitchen to stand so near that she could detect the aroma of tobacco on him. He hadn't removed his hat. He was so terribly handsome. "I'm glad you came by," she said. "I have a Christmas present for you."

"And I have one for you. But as it is too large to wrap, I will have to take you to it. Why don't you change? We're going for a ride. Nigel will never know. We'll take the phaeton. I'll ride up on the driver's bench while you ride in the carriage. Should anyone see us, it will merely be La Alma's ranch manager taking his employer's wife for an evening ride."

Alone with Cody for an evening carriage ride . . . an opportunity to tell him what happened and Nigel's threat to father a child with another woman. Removing the kettle from the stove, she said, "I'll be ready in a minute."

Despite the arctic temperature, they drove through the deepening dusk with the folding top down. But Cody was warm in his sheepskin jacket, and Elizabeth was bundled up in a fox fur coat. For added warmth, she had tied a scarf over her hair and Cody's Stetson was set firmly on his head.

The millions of desert stars illuminated their way, creating towering monsters of palm trees and squat alien creatures of cacti and scrub. The winter mesquite was leafless and skeletal, yet possessed its own eerie beauty. As Cody guided the carriage up the old lumber road, Elizabeth looked at his broad back as he held the reins. Yes, she thought, as she cradled her injured wrist in her lap. I will tell Cody. He will take me into his arms and say that we will fight Nigel together.

With wheels creaking and the horse's hooves going clip-clop, they finally arrived at a valley, ghostly and silent.

"It's called Big Horn Valley," Cody said, as he brought the horse to a halt and they sat for a moment in the primeval splendor. The moon was unusually bright and seemed to hang close to the earth. Elizabeth savored the moment, her aloneness with the man she loved, wanting nothing more in life than this.

Then Cody stepped down from the driver's seat to stand next to Elizabeth, still ensconced in the carriage, then looked around cautiously. Although he supposed they were miles from the nearest human being, and certainly Barnstable was distracted by the amusements of his famous friends, caution was still part of Cody's daily makeup.

Elizabeth reached into her coat pocket. "Merry Christmas," she said, handing him a box wrapped in red tissue paper.

He opened it to find a gold pen and pencil set. "For future stories and books," Elizabeth said.

He turned the pen around and around in his fingers, feeling its heft and balance, thinking of the words that were going to come from it. Thinking how, every time he wrote with it, he would think of Elizabeth, and it would be like holding her in his hand. "Thank you," he said softly, knowing that if no one else in the world found merit in his writing, this woman did.

"And now for your gift." Cody held out his hand to help Elizabeth to the ground. "Cover your eyes."

She laughed, gloved hands on her face, feeling relaxed for the first time in months. Thinking that this moment was all the Christmas gift she needed.

Taking her by the shoulders, he turned her and said, "You can look now."

She dropped her hands and looked around. At first she saw only dark forest and a meadow illuminated by stars and moon, granite slopes covered in ghostly snow. And then, directly ahead, across the valley, a sheer wall face that had not been visible upon first entering the valley. It was a hundred feet tall, slate-gray and so flat that—

She gasped.

An ancient petroglyph had been carved into it—a giant bighorn sheep, heavy of body, with great curled horns, magnificent and grand. "It's beautiful," she whispered. She fixed her eyes on the carving, wondering how it had been done. The Indians would have had to construct scaffolding and then labored with stone axes to etch the enormous figure.

Drawing her gaze away, Elizabeth looked around at the grassy meadow ringed with pine trees and oaks. Now she saw, on other rocky walls and large, upthrusting boulders, more petroglyphs. "This valley is full of ancient carvings and rock paintings," Cody said. "There must be hundreds, maybe thousands of them. This was probably a sacred place at one time. Come, I'll show you."

They tramped over the grass, pausing to inspect symbols and mysterious figures in the moonlight. Some had been carved into the rock, others had been painted on with dyes that had withstood the ravages of weather and time.

They stood in silence for a while, respecting the grandeur of the valley, its moonlit silence. "Do you suppose they're watching us?" Cody said.

"Who?"

"The ancestors who dwell here."

When Elizabeth smiled and brought her fox fur collar up to her face, Cody said, "Did you know that the sun has given you freckles?" He touched her cheek. "You didn't have these when you first came to Palm Springs."

"I try to hide them."

"Don't." He bent his head and pressed his lips to the freckles. "I write words down every day," he said, taking her by the shoulders to face her in the ivory moonlight. Coyote yelps sounded in the distance. "I even wrote a book filled with words. But when I look at you, Elizabeth, every word I ever learned in my whole life leaves me. My head is exploding with things I want to say to you. But they aren't finding their way to my throat. You have a dangerous power over me, Elizabeth. You've done to me a thousand times more than what Belle ever did, and that was hard. It took me years to get over Belle."

He lifted her gloved hand, the uninjured one, and kissed the palm. "I'll never get over you. Not that I would want to."

Elizabeth watched the wind ripple Cody's hair. She saw starlight in his dark eyes. When and where did they first meet? Surely not here in the desert, and surely not in a time span that was measured in mere months. Their love spanned eons and continents. We first met millennia ago on a continent that no longer exists except in poetry and people's imaginations.

Should she bring Nigel up now? Or should she wait, rather than spoil this beautiful moment? Tomorrow would be soon enough to tell him what happened. Elizabeth just wanted to savor her closeness with this man in such a magical setting.

"I have to show you something, Elizabeth," he said, suddenly serious. "I've been wrestling with it, debating whether to show it to you. But now I know you have to see it. A letter came today . . ."

She waited, while coyotes talked to the moon and owls called out to mates. He reached inside his jacket and handed her an envelope. "You heard from someone!" she said, suddenly hopeful when she saw, by moonlight, the postmark—Kentucky. "Do they know Peachy?"

"Look at the return address. The name."

She read it. Connor O'Doule. A brother? she wondered. Father?

"Read it," Cody said.

The letter was from Peachy. She read it by moonlight.

"The feller at the post office showed me a letter from another feller who was looking for me, and that was you. Yeah, I remember you. You had the claim next to me on the creek. I remember that woman you took up with. We all said she was bad luck but you were smitten bad. And when she run away, taking your gold, I swear I'd never seen a man so broke up. I figured it was you that took my gold. And I hated you for a long time. I tried panning for more gold but then a riot broke out at the camp and some fellers got killt, so I gave up and left. It wasn't easy making my way back home, and then I had nothing to offer my sweetheart. But she stood by me and we managed and now we have our farm and we're struggling but we're okay. I can't say as I've ever totally forgiven you for what you done to me. There were other fellers you coulda stolen from. Why me? I never done any harm to you. But because of what you done, my Hannah and I are struggling to make our farm a go of it. If I'da had that gold, we'd be doing good right now. But we owe the bank a heap of money. Nearly five hundred dollars, to be precise. My gold would have gone a long way to pay that, yes sir. Anyway, that's not your problem, is it? Yours truly, Connor O'Doule."

Elizabeth stared at Peachy's signature for a long time. The cold penetrated her fox fur coat while, in the night sky, a falling star streaked from mountain peak to mountain peak, creating a silver rainbow.

Cody didn't know what he had expected when and if he ever heard from Peachy. Several scenarios had filled his mind in his years of searching. Foremost was finding out Peachy was dead, either in the

Horsethief Creek riot, or of appendicitis in a farmhouse somewhere. Or maybe he was running a fine tobacco farm just as he had said he would, with pretty Hannah raising a bunch of happy kids. But none of the scenarios had involved his own feelings and his reaction to finally learning the truth.

Strangely, a sense of loss stole over him. No one had died, but something had. His quest. His reason for living. The thing that had gotten him out of bed every morning for nearly twelve years—the need to find Peachy had died.

But there was something else, something more significant. "Elizabeth, I'm scared," he said suddenly.

"Scared? What could you possibly be scared of? You found Peachy."

He thought for a long moment. "Somehow, over the years, the search for Peachy became less about Peachy, less about the search, and more about a way to govern my life, to keep myself in check. Always, finding Peachy was the foremost thing in my life. I couldn't allow myself to do anything until I had closed that chapter." He paused, then said, "Do you know what snubbing a horse is?"

"No."

"It's part of their training. You tie them to a snubbing post—also called a patience pole—and leave them to stand for hours. They need to learn to stand tied up, to learn to wait when they don't want to, because a horse that won't do this is a danger to himself and others. I thought of Peachy as my snubbing post. My need to find him kept my emotions in check, kept me patient and focused. Whenever I felt that I might fly out of control, I would remember my goal—to find a particular man and settle a debt. I didn't have the luxury of giving in to my emotions, of venting my anger on someone. But now I do, Elizabeth. I'm free, and it frightens me. I cannot bear the thought of Nigel putting his hands on you, thinking he owns you, treating you the way he does. And now there's nothing to hold me back."

He took her by the shoulders and said with passion, "I have been at war with myself, Elizabeth. From the moment I picked you up off the living room floor and carried you into the bedroom, I have nurtured a fierce need to teach Nigel a brutal lesson. The anger has simmered inside me all these months, and I have barely been able to keep it in check. Now I am going to have to fight even harder. I hold myself in check, now, Elizabeth, for your sake alone. But I don't know how long I can hold back."

She stared at him, her gallant hero to whom she had expected to vent her newest fears, to tell him of Nigel's latest abuse, to show him her wrist so that he could give her words of comfort or a strong shoulder to cry on. But now she couldn't! She mustn't.

Laying her gloved hand over her throbbing wrist, she said, "You must go away, leave Palm Springs—"

"That is the last thing I would ever do!" he cried, his voice echoing off mountain summits, sending ghostly owls to flight. "My struggle is not so great that I would run from it. And I would never abandon you, Elizabeth. No matter at what cost to myself, I would never abandon you. This is something I will have to be vigilant about because there is nothing to stop me now from going after Nigel and delivering swift frontier justice. The quest is over; reparations will be made. I'll send Peachy the five hundred dollars I owe him, and then it will be just myself, Cody McNeal, all on his own with no duty to another man. I feel a danger within me, Elizabeth, a recklessness that frightens me."

She held her breath as she looked up into dark eyes burning with anger and anguish.

"I'm afraid that I'll do something that will hurt _you_, Elizabeth. Nigel—" He lowered his voice, reined himself in. "I despise the man you are married to, Elizabeth, and that's what scares me. I can't take things lying down. I am a man of action. All these months, knowing what he did to you, and I—" He turned away and slammed his fist into his hand. "I have done nothing about it! While he walks free! I know Nigel would retaliate by taking it out on you and that is the sole reason why I haven't already gone after him."

As she felt his tension, his power, heard both fear and anger in his voice, and knew that he spoke truthfully of himself, Elizabeth realized that she couldn't tell him about Nigel—not now, not ever.

"It's Christmas Eve," she said. "Merry Christmas, Cody."

He looked at her. Then he released a sigh and smiled. "Merry Christmas, my dear Elizabeth." He kissed her mouth. Her lips were very cold.

Then he helped her up into the carriage and returned to the driver's seat to take up the reins. As the carriage began to creak out of the valley, Elizabeth glanced back at the giant bighorn sheep petroglyph and felt as if she and Cody had just come to a frightening and dangerous crossroads, and they had no idea which way to go.

PART THREE
1922

CHAPTER TWENTY-FIVE

ELIZABETH FOUND FIONA IN the kitchen, clearing the breakfast dishes. Now that the Norringtons were gone, with just Mrs. Padilla and the girls helping at the house, Fiona took it upon herself to take care of small chores.

"Fiona, I'm going for a horseback ride. Would you please lay out my riding outfit?"

"Very good, Milady."

Elizabeth paused as she watched Fiona wipe her hands on a towel and remove her apron. Fiona had been on Elizabeth's mind lately. The others had left—Ethel, Mrs. Flannigan, the Norringtons—for various reasons. The West seemed to do that to people. Only Fiona had stayed, and it occurred to Elizabeth to wonder why. Elizabeth knew the surface details of Fiona's life, but nothing of what motivated her. How did one go about asking such a deeply personal thing?

She knew that Fiona was stepping out with Leland Perry. It seemed they had been seeing each other for about a year. Surely it was becoming serious. Why weren't they engaged to be married by now?

Whatever the reasons, Elizabeth was glad Fiona was there. She had come to regard her as more of a friend than a servant and had even stopped calling her Wilson, but the more familiar and friendlier, "Fiona."

Before she went to get dressed for her ride, Elizabeth made sure her writing desk was locked and that she took the only key with her. She drew open the center drawer and ran her finger over the large slender book inside. Her personal ledger. Filled with names, dates, numbers.

Elizabeth enjoyed receiving the monthly bank statements, checking for mistakes or accuracy, checking off columns, balancing the final total. She would make sure Nigel was out, busily inspecting his many trees, meeting with out-of-town growers and distributors, creating new business contracts, spreading the tentacles of Stullwood Plantation farther and farther from Palm Springs. Now he was contemplating the export business—shipping his different varieties of dates to Canada and Europe. It took up a great deal of his time, which gave Elizabeth opportunities to see to her own small financial endeavor and that brought her immense satisfaction. Sending away to Sears Catalog for things Lardner's did not carry. Sending away for more library books. Sending donations to the Salvation Army and the ASPCA. She was not totally autonomous, as her father kept an occasional eye on the account and made deposits as needed. But so far he was pleased with her handling of money.

Elizabeth wasn't sure if Nigel knew about her secret account. If he did, he didn't seem to care. Other than exercising his marital rights, Nigel hadn't touched her since Christmas Eve, although she knew the threat was always there. The wrist had healed, but the fear of it happening again had not.

Nor had Nigel brought up the subject of fathering a bastard son again, but like the physical threat, Elizabeth knew the threat was still there.

As Fiona selected Elizabeth's clothes, adding a jacket because the March day had a bite to it, and the wind was coming down from the nearby snowy peaks, she thought about her mistress's frequent solitary rides on the Appaloosa. Fiona had noticed, as she had noticed this morning, that whenever Elizabeth went riding, Mr. McNeal was always seen saddling his own mare at the stable and then riding away on his own. Elizabeth would leave about half an hour later. They would also return to La Alma at different times and from different directions. But Fiona knew what was going on.

And she was worried about these secret rendezvous with Mr. McNeal.

She didn't blame them for wanting to be together. Just look at her and Leland, seizing every chance they could. But Fiona and Leland were unattached and free to see each other. Elizabeth was not only married, but married to a controlling and jealous man. Fiona feared that Her Ladyship and Mr. McNeal were playing with fire. Who knew how His

Lordship would react if he found out? Leland had told here there were rumors that His Lordship was the one who killed Johnny Pinto, shot him in cold blood as the boy was surrendering. Fiona wasn't sure it was true, but Leland said it was the Sheriff himself who had disclosed the fact to someone, who had then passed it along until it was something that men murmured about wherever men were gathered.

And of course Fiona knew that His Lordship had caused the miscarriage, although Elizabeth didn't know that Fiona knew, and Fiona would never tell her.

But the fact remained that when it came to Mr. McNeal, Elizabeth needed to exercise extreme caution, although Fiona couldn't very well tell her to be careful because, first of all, it wasn't her place, but mostly because she would never be so unkind as to reveal to Elizabeth that she knew her secret. How shameful must it be for a woman to find out that others knew she was married to a cruel man and seeking solace outside of her marriage?

We are all trapped in a way, she thought. We all have our prisons. Whether we are held hostage by social status, lack of money, unfair promises, or a bad marriage. For some, the simple fact of being a woman is chains enough. The lucky ones might find a way out. Fiona prayed that she and Elizabeth were among the lucky ones, because until Elizabeth was free, Fiona would remain a prisoner.

But there was now a glimmer of hope. One day, while straightening up the sitting room adjacent to Elizabeth's bedroom, Fiona had seen the key in the writing desk. Elizabeth had taken to locking the desk and taking the key with her. Fiona had wondered why. Her Ladyship had gone to Indio for the day with a carton of books to exchange with the library there. Seeing the key in the brass lock, Fiona had been unable to resist. Under other circumstances, she would never have snooped, believing in respecting the privacy of others. But, these days, the circumstances were not normal. She herself was trapped in this house because of the circumstances of Elizabeth's life. Fiona felt a need to arm herself with as much information as possible. Or perhaps, because she was trapped here, she felt entitled to know all the facts.

She had opened the drawer.

An envelope with a recent postmark lay on top of what looked like a bookkeeping ledger. Fiona picked it up. The envelope was addressed to Elizabeth Barnstable, in care of General Delivery, Indio, California.

She was puzzled for a moment, wondering why Her Ladyship was receiving mail in a town over twenty miles away, but when she saw the return address, she froze. The letter was from a Mary Clark, Esq., in Los Angeles. What had made Fiona freeze were the two words under Mary Clark's name: Family Law.

Private correspondence with an attorney who specialized in family law, kept secret in a locked drawer—Fiona had stood immobilized for a protracted moment. What exactly was family law, and how did it pertain to Elizabeth?

She had debated for one brief moment and then, listening for the sound of an approaching car, but reassuring herself that Her Ladyship would not be back for another hour, Fiona had opened the envelope and drawn out the contents. It had turned out to be a bill for services rendered. Mostly it was fees for the attorney's hours, but one item had jumped out: a fee for filing preliminary documents with the divorce court.

Divorce!

At first Fiona had been hurt. Why hadn't Her Ladyship confided in her with such an enormous piece of news? But she had quickly realized that this was, in fact, very dangerous news. For Fiona's own sake, she realized, Elizabeth had not told her about this. Should His Lordship question Fiona about his wife's private doings, her own ignorance would save her.

The enormity of her discovery had hit Fiona as she realized that what she had just found was, in fact, a ray of hope! She wasn't stuck in this house after all. Elizabeth was working to secure her own freedom, which meant Fiona's freedom as well.

She had then glanced down at the ledger. She started to reach for it and stopped. It was one thing to read the lawyer's letter—Fiona had felt entitled to do so because Her Ladyship's status had a direct impact on her own—but snooping into someone else's private finances was crossing a line Fiona would not cross. Restoring the letter and closing the drawer, leaving it as she found it, Fiona had felt such a rush of hope that she couldn't wait to tell Leland.

And then she had realized she couldn't tell him. This was too volatile a secret to allow beyond this room. So secretive that Her Ladyship hadn't confided in her closest companion. While Fiona's feelings had been hurt at first, she now understood the enormous need to keep this information hidden. Not that Leland would purposely tell others, he was still a loquacious man, and the less he knew of this the better.

She wouldn't tell Her Ladyship that she knew. But it was hope now, and Fiona was going to cling to it.

*　　*　　*

Cody was already at the head of the trail in Chino Canyon, not far from Big Horn Valley. He was waiting for Elizabeth and, as he did so, kept an eye out for hikers and other people on the old logging road. They had a rule: if either of them saw someone else, they turned around and went back, the secret meeting abandoned. Even if the intruder were a stranger, a tourist, a mountaineer from another country, they couldn't risk word of them being seen together getting back to Nigel. So Cody checked his pocket watch. If Elizabeth wasn't here in another ten minutes, he knew she had run into someone and could not come.

Once again, as he sat on his horse and heard the cold wind whistle down from the mountain peaks, he thought of the curious twists and turns of life.

After receiving Peachy's letter three months ago, Cody had sent a letter of apology to Peachy, along with a check for a hundred dollars with the promise of more to come after his book was published. The response had come in a brief note: "I forgive you for what you done. Sincerely yours." That was when the focus of Cody's life had permanently shifted from what had happened at Horsethief Creek and his search for Peachy, to what was happening here in Palm Springs and his fear for Elizabeth and himself.

To his surprise, however, forgiveness from Peachy had presented a whole new, startling revelation to Cody.

Just as the search for Peachy had helped Cody keep his anger in check, helped him hold back from taking fists to Nigel Barnstable, Peachy had also stood between him and Elizabeth. Cody had known that he could never cross the forbidden line with Elizabeth as long as he had to find Peachy.

But now he was free, and just as he had discovered he now only had his own willpower to hold himself back from teaching Barnstable a brutal lesson, he had nothing but his own willpower to keep himself from crossing a dangerous line with Elizabeth. No excuses, no duties and obligations to stand between them, just their own moral standards—and Cody's human weakness and the overwhelming desire to make her his.

It scared the hell out of him.

Finally, there she was, on the mountain road riding toward him on her high-stepping Appaloosa.

They smiled wordlessly, with relief and joy, but with an underlying tension as well, and then they followed the old road to their favorite place, Big Horn Valley, the pristine wilderness that Cody had given to Elizabeth as a Christmas present.

Elizabeth never really relaxed when she met Cody in secret. She felt as if the mountain had a thousand eyes. Was Nigel's among them? Would he punish her with broken bones, with Cody retaliating in such a volatile way that it would end in tragedy? Knowing now about Cody's self-confessed fury that he was struggling to keep in check made Elizabeth all the more cautious on what she told him about Nigel. She felt as if they all sat on a powder keg and that one wrong word, from any of them, would set it off.

But the day was too beautiful for somber thoughts. The air crisp, the sky that same blue for which she had found no name. And the wind carried the occasional arctic sweep from the snows that loomed above them. Elizabeth refused to let Nigel's darkness spoil her few precious moments with the man she loved. She thought about the good things in their life. The New York publisher to whom Cody had sent his book had bought it. Cody was going to call it *The Last Gold Rush*, and was dedicating it to his father. There would be some editing and polishing, they had told him, and then it would go to press in late summer. And the first magazine to which he had sent his story, *Gunfight at the O.K. Corral*, had bought it. And when they sent him their letter of acceptance, they had included a check, along with an invitation to send more stories.

"I'm going to telephone Mother and have her order your book," Elizabeth said now, breaking the silence to invite Cody into her internal dialogue. La Alma had recently been connected to the Southwestern Telephone Company. Elizabeth was thrilled. It had to be a party line, but it made her feel less isolated.

Cody didn't understand the allure of telephones. He had talked on a telephone once. It didn't impress him. He didn't see why folks were in such a hurry to communicate. Letters worked perfectly well as far as he was concerned. The news got there just the same, only a few days later.

And now there was talk of Southern Sierra Power bringing electricity to the valley. Progress was slowly coming to Palm Springs. More people were discovering the desert. Two new hotels had been built, a guest ranch, more citrus and date farms.

Finally the road turned around a bend, and opening before them in the embrace of snow-capped mountain peaks was Big Horn Valley ringed with dense pine forests and a beautiful meadow in the center, lush and green and budding with early wildflowers. It was March, but at this height—3,000 feet above the desert floor—they were still below the snow line.

They reined their horses and looked in dismay at two motor cars racing through the meadow, tearing up grass and wildflowers. In shock, Elizabeth realized it was Nigel and his friends. She and Cody stayed back, unseen.

Miss Clark, Elizabeth's lawyer, had recently reported that her investigator had seen Nigel in the company of movie people, attending parties that were being covered in the gossip columns. So far, there was no solid evidence of adulterous activity, nothing incriminating, but the investigator was going to stay on it.

Elizabeth had told Miss Clark about Nigel's abuse on Christmas Eve, how he had almost broken her wrist, and his threat to father a son outside the marriage, and so new urgency had been added to the case and the need to move as swiftly with it as possible.

There was, however, one ominous cloud that could harm their careful plan. A doctor in Los Angeles had been arrested for disseminating "obscene materials" and fitting his patients with contraceptive devices. Mary Clark cautioned her, "Don't go back to Dr. Greene, Elizabeth. We suspect she will soon be under investigation." And Elizabeth's connection to Greene, no matter how tenuous, could hurt her divorce case.

Sitting on their horses in the protection of trees, hidden from those in the convertibles, Elizabeth and Cody saw Zora DuBois throw her head back and scream at the top of her lungs. Elizabeth recognized her from tabloid photographs. Next to her, at the wheel of a new Dodge Brothers sedan convertible, Nigel was laughing hysterically. The car flew over boulders, sending dirt and vegetation into the air, tires swerving on the uneven ground, threatening to careen out of control. In the back seat, a man Elizabeth recognized as Jack Lamont was holding onto his hat with one hand and the back of the front seat with the other. The pale-faced woman next to him, a known wealthy Hollywood socialite, likewise held on.

The second car was driven by a movie producer. Riding with him were his wife, and a screenwriter and his actress girlfriend. Elizabeth had seen their pictures in the newspapers. She knew they were celebrating the final wrap of Zora's latest movie, *The Modern Magdalene*, a project that, according to the tabloids, Nigel had invested heavily in.

The cars came to a halt. Nigel stood up and looked around. He was holding a rifle. Cody and Elizabeth stayed well hidden in the trees, watching, while their horses grazed.

"See anything?" Jack Lamont called out.

Zora said, "I need to stretch my legs," and stepped down to the grass. Her cloche hat was askew. As she re-fitted it to her head, bringing it low on her brow, she walked away while her companions searched the trees and meadow for movement. They appeared to be eager to pull triggers.

When Zora reached the second car, she turned and, lifting her arms above her head, arched her back and stretched. Elizabeth suspected it was for the movie producer's benefit. Elizabeth suspected that everything the actress did was calculated to catch a man's eye. Not that Zora needed to do anything to get a man's attention. According to the gossip columns, she was naturally beautiful and possessed an allure that could not be named. She was slender and yet, strangely voluptuous. Elizabeth noticed how the cashmere sweater-top she wore clung to her breasts like a second skin. Her long skirt was formfitting and showed the outline of her buttocks and thighs. Elizabeth saw no evidence of underwear.

This was the first time Elizabeth had seen Zora in person. Magazine photos, static and in black and white, were quite different from a flesh and blood woman, dressed in colors and moving her body in provocative ways. It occurred to Elizabeth for the first time to wonder if there was anything going on between Nigel and the actress. So far, Mary Clark's investigator had only ever seen Nigel in the company of the couple, and he had yet to see another woman in their company. They appeared to be just three friends seen in popular Hollywood haunts. But what if there was something more, something overlooked?

And then Zora did a strange thing.

Elizabeth and Cody, hidden among the trees, watched as Zora cast a furtive glance at her companions, then quickly drew up her skirt and reached up to her stocking garter to pull out something that flashed silver in the sun. She uncapped it, brought it to her lips, and tilted her head back in a long drink. She restored the flask to the garter and smoothed down her skirt before her companions saw it.

A secret drinker? Elizabeth wondered, as Zora returned to her car.

She looked at Nigel, standing up in his car, handsomely dressed in a white tennis sweater and white flannels. He leaned on the windshield as he looked for game. He didn't seem to be paying Zora any attention. But then, when Elizabeth and Cody were in the presence of others, they did not pay any attention to each other either.

Elizabeth wondered if Nigel was going to see any return on his movie investment. She knew the plantation was doing well and that he could afford the gamble. But because she wanted the divorce to go smoothly and quickly, when the time came, she would not fight for any of Nigel's money—not from the plantation or from his Hollywood investments. She didn't want any of it.

There had been a private screening of the movie before its release. Elizabeth had read one of the reviews. *The Modern Magdalene*'s tagline was: "She went from good to worse." It was touted as a "moral message" movie—a supposedly educational eye-opener for parents and a warning to young people about the dangers of drugs. In the film, Zora DuBois went from an innocent young woman on the verge of entering a convent to a debauched drug addict turning tricks to support her addiction.

At Elizabeth's side, Cody watched the scene with a wary eye. He couldn't decide if he and Elizabeth should try quietly leaving—and risk one of their mounts snorting and giving their presence away—or stay and hope Barnstable and his friends would just drive away. But then that risked spooking the horses.

"There!" Lamont shouted suddenly, pointing to ponderosa pines.

Everyone turned and saw, standing in a pool of sunlight, a large bighorn sheep, brown with a white muzzle, its magnificent horns like two haloes embracing its head. "You drive!" Nigel snapped at Lamont as he got out of the car and climbed into the back seat. "Hurry!"

Elizabeth watched in horror as the sheep stood frozen in the sunlight while the motors rushed toward it, and then suddenly it turned and bolted. But instead of plunging into the safety of the trees, the animal veered to the right and darted across the open meadow. Lamont stepped on the accelerator and followed the zigzagging animal, Nigel standing up in the back seat with his rifle aimed.

In the second car, the movie producer stood up and fired. He missed. The screenwriter took a turn firing. He also missed.

The terrified animal ran this way and that, the cars veering left and right, but gaining ground as birds flew up out of the grass and rabbits darted from underbrush. The peaceful valley was suddenly filled with the roar of engines, gunfire, men whooping and hollering with excitement.

Elizabeth watched, trying to control her suddenly skittish Appaloosa, as Nigel finally took aim and caught the ram in the head. It went down. Everyone cheered.

Satisfied that the animal was dead, Nigel signaled to Lamont to turn the car around. Cody and Elizabeth watched as the two cars drove off, to disappear through the other end of the valley.

"I can't believe he did that!" Elizabeth cried. "He just killed it and left. It was just target practice to him."

Recalling Johnny Pinto, Cody said grimly, "I reckon we'd better leave while we can." He looked up at the snow-covered mountains, the pine forests, the deep blue sky. He heard, in the far distance, a rifle shot ring out, and a familiar murderous thought entered his mind.

They turned their horses and rode through the high grass on the perimeter of the meadow, watchful for the return of the cars. Elizabeth was dismayed to find modern graffiti carved over the ancient images, names and dates left by more recent visitors. They came upon an empty bottle of bootlegged liquor. They saw cigarette butts in the grass. Tire tracks crisscrossing the meadow. The rotting carcass of a rabbit that hadn't gotten out of the way in time.

Elizabeth paused at a gray boulder about a foot tall. She bent to examine, in the sunshine, a scene carved into the rock—bighorn sheep, leaping, running, standing side by side. There must have been hundreds of them, painstakingly carved into the rock by a skilled hand.

And engraved over the sheep: Daniel Reeves, Virginia, Setember 1880.

He spelled the month wrong, Elizabeth thought. What right did Daniel Reeves of Virginia have to desecrate this artwork? What right does Nigel have to race through this peaceful valley in his noisy, smoking automobile and destroy everything in his path?

Elizabeth surveyed the beautiful wilderness around her, felt the crisp sylvan breeze on her face, and took herself back two years. If only she could truly go back in time with the clear vision she had today and see Nigel for what he was. Go back and change the past. But that was impossible. She tried not to dwell on her horrendous mistake, but every morning she woke up to find Nigel in her mind, crowding out all the other thoughts she was supposed to be thinking, making her gnaw on this mistake she had made that got her trapped where she was today. The only thing that gave her relief from mulling over her mistake was to think of Cody. But there, too, was no clear answer or path. He had his own past mistakes to wrangle with, his own current non-freedom—because of her. How do we get ourselves stuck in these briar patches, she wondered.

"Elizabeth," Cody said, shielding his eyes as he pointed, "who are those men?"

She squinted across the valley where two men stood near a parked vehicle. "Let's find out."

They returned to the dirt road, watchful and cautious—but they had heard more rifle shots, farther away, as Nigel's hunting party moved on—and they followed it until they reached the parked car. Now they saw the surveying equipment, the map spread out on the car hood with rocks anchoring it.

"Howdy!" Cody called as they got close to the surveyors. The men turned, smiled.

"Hi there," they called back.

Cody looked around from atop his horse. "Looks like you boys are taking the lay of the land."

They were an older man and a younger man, dressed in black suits with straw hats on their heads. While the younger man concentrated on calibrating a complex-looking instrument set on a tripod, the older man said, "A hotel outfit bought this valley. Going to build a resort on this spot."

"A resort?" Cody said. "All the way up here? That old logging road won't accommodate much traffic."

"Naw, folks'll be coming up from the back way, from Idyllwild on the other side of the mountain. Better roads there. One of them is even paved."

"What kind of resort?" Elizabeth asked, looking out across the grassy meadow, the wildflowers, the dense forests of pine and oak. And among it all, hundreds of boulders carved with ancient petroglyphs.

"They tell me there's gonna be a two-hundred room hotel, with a swimming pool, tennis courts, and a nine-hole golf course."

Elizabeth stared at him. "But the meadow isn't large enough for all that."

"Oh, they'll be cutting down all those trees and razing all the rocks and things, level it out. This high up, it'll be cool in the summer. Tourists will flock here in the thousands."

"But . . . where will the animals go?"

He tipped his hat back and squinted. "Animals?"

"The animals that live in this valley. The bighorn sheep, the deer, the coyotes, the rabbits. Where will they go?"

He shrugged. "Dunno. Just go someplace else I reckon."

"You can't be serious!"

He shrugged. "Look, it's not my idea, lady. I was just hired to survey the property." He turned away and said something to the younger man.

Elizabeth stared at them for a moment longer, at the surveying equipment, the map, then she looked around the valley again and felt the cold mountain air sweep down from the top of San Jacinto and blow through her soul.

She closed her eyes and pictured Nigel again, standing up in his new car, god-like, shooting at anything that moved. Racing across the pristine meadow as if it were his private playground. That's how it was at Stullwood, she thought. A thousand acres owned by one man, to do with as he pleased.

It isn't right.

"Cody, this valley was once a sacred place to the Indians. They had gatherings here, maybe to pray for rain, perhaps to commune with their ancestors. Now it's home to animals that live wild and free." Her voice grew tight. "It isn't right that . . . someone should be allowed to destroy all this history, this beauty." Daniel Reeves and Nigel and others like them.

Cody heard the anger in her voice, saw how her eyes flashed like blue ice. He wanted to offer magic words, a spell, an incantation that would make everything all right: Nigel, the dead ram, the movie people, the surveyors, the resort builder, this valley. He wanted to be wearing armor and riding a war-horse and slay all who would bring tears to those beautiful eyes. But he was just a man—a man with his own fights and foibles.

"Men like Nigel," Elizabeth said in a tone of constrained fury, "cruel and selfish, should not be allowed to slaughter innocent creatures. This valley should be protected."

She lifted her eyes to the giant bighorn sheep petroglyph standing big and bold on the cliff wall across the valley. Simple, striking, magnificent. And in imminent danger of being destroyed.

And a revelation came to her in that moment. She had come to Palm Springs searching for her purpose in life, her calling. She knew she would find herself out here. But she had to begin somewhere. She couldn't just sit and wait for a "call." The idea for a library had been a good place to start, and she looked back now and saw the clear path that had brought her here, although she hadn't seen it at the time. The idea for a library, and then learning to drive so that she could carry the books up and down the valley, which in turn led her to discovering the desert's many diverse and wondrous petroglyphs and Indian art. All leading to this moment . . .

Nothing happens by chance, she thought now, feeling suddenly very excited. In the desert, one sees patterns everywhere—in the sand, the sky, on the backs of lizards, in the tracks of mountain lions—even in the manmade patterns of ancient petroglyphs. Elizabeth looked back and saw the pattern of her life that brought her to this point. And Nigel, though he seemed like a mistake, was a vital part of that pattern because he had brought her to this place, a place she was meant to be.

Suddenly, Elizabeth knew what she was meant to do. No matter what it took, no matter to what extremes she must go, she vowed she was not going to let this valley be destroyed.

CHAPTER TWENTY-SIX

LUISA PADILLA!

She was kneeling in front of her hut, grinding acorns in her metate. She looked around to see who had spoken. But there was no one nearby. She rested back on her heels and squinted in the early morning sunshine. The valley lay before her, a golden desert broken only by trees and scrub and, now, more houses. "Who is speaking to me?"

It is I of the sacred waters. Hear me!

Luisa closed her eyes. She recognized the voice as the spirit of Sechi, which meant "boiling water." "I hear," she said.

It is urgent that you take your granddaughters to the sacred water.

She sucked in her breath. It had been a long time since she had visited the sacred hot springs eastward of her village. "When must I go?"

At once! This morning! Go and collect them! Go now!

"Yes," she said, rising to her feet. She looked around the village where men and women were at their early morning labors. Where were Isabella and Gabriela?

Luisa hadn't planned to travel today. The Señora had asked that the silver be polished and the linens ironed. But Luisa would not think of disobeying a spirit.

She found the girls sitting under a mesquite tree, looking at a movie magazine. She watched them for a moment. Beautiful girls, taking after their mothers, Luisa's granddaughters. Sixteen years old now, soon to turn seventeen and ready for marriage. But what man would have them? Their heads were in the clouds. They lived on soda pop and daydreams. They wanted things they could not have. They were not satisfied with the Indian life.

Yes, Luisa thought now. Sechi had spoken wisely. A ritual visit to the sacred hot springs will save those two girls.

The farms and gardens and oases of the valley were watered by subterranean springs beneath the desert. Some of the springs came out of the ground hot and steamy and filled with powerful medicine that white men called "minerals." The Indians drank the sacred water; they also bathed in it. Long ago, a local clan had built a small wooden shack over the hot springs for the purposes of sacred cleansing, physically and spiritually. It was also a time to connect with one's people, past, and culture. When Luisa had first sat in the little hut, inhaling the steam, visions had come to her, spirits of ancestors long dead had spoken to her. She envied her granddaughters now for what they were going to experience. She was also happy for them. It was going to be a memory that would stay with them for the rest of their lives.

Calling out to the girls, who immediately tried to hide the magazine, Luisa announced their unplanned trip. They must set off at once, with a stop at La Alma to apologize to the Señora for not coming to work today.

The Cahuilla tribe was scattered throughout the Coachella Valley in villages that ranged from Banning to Indio. They were connected by a complex pattern of trails, tracks, roads, and sometimes just broad expanses of sand and cactus. The individual bands were never still, they did not remain solely in their villages because they had a tradition of visiting that went back generations—traveling to other villages for sacred and political rituals, bringing tribute on ceremonial days, attending weddings and births, arranging marriages, taking care of the sick, and reinforcing familial ties.

After receiving permission to take the day off, with the Señora saying, "By all means, you must go," the three walked down the tree-lined road that was the town's main street, passing the general store and drugstore where Isabella and Gabriela were well known. They passed new shops and the auto garage and the church and the small white house where Doctor Perry dispensed his medicines.

They followed the road with the foothills rising to mountains on their right, scattered buildings on their left, behind which barren desert swept away to the mountains in the distance. Many ancient trails crisscrossed the valley, some for trade, some for hunting. The one Luisa and her girls followed was called a "friendship trail" because it was used for visiting.

The sun climbed high, the day grew warm. They passed the villages of other clans, waving to them and calling out greetings. They entered cool oases where palm trees grew in bunches and mesquite trees offered shade. A red-tailed hawk followed their progress for a while and then, with a cry, flew out to the desert. Luisa paused to look up at a rocky precipice and saw a handsome bighorn ram with a smaller horned ewe. She took it as a good sign.

They passed another canyon and another. The day grew hot. They stopped at an oasis to drink from a stream and to eat their date cakes.

Afternoon created long shadows cast by San Jacinto's two-mile-high peaks. Luisa knew that the sacred hot springs lay just ahead. She had brought gifts for the chief and shaman of the local village. She and her granddaughters would be given sleeping accommodations.

She frowned as they drew near to the hot water oasis. There were automobiles parked there. When she had last been here, there were no cars. And then she saw white people getting out of them, or driving away. And then she saw the painted sign: "Healthy Springs, twenty-five cents an hour."

"Grandmother?" Isabella said. "Who are those people?"

As they neared the steaming pools embraced within smooth boulders, they saw white people in skimpy clothes, sitting in the hot water. They were laughing and talking and drinking out of tall glasses. The door of the steam hut opened and two white men came out, towels wrapped around their waists. Seated at the door was Fernando Seco, Luisa's cousin. He was taking money from the white people and handing them towels.

Luisa stopped in her tracks. What was this? Allowing outsiders into their sacred places! And taking money for it! Great Mukat, is it the end of the world?

And then the true significance of Sechi's message hit her. This visit had nothing to do with her granddaughters but rather with the whole tribe. The spirit had wanted Luisa to see with her own eyes what was happening at the sacred springs and do something about it.

But what? What can I do?

*   *   *

Two weeks had passed, and she had no solution for what was happening at the hot springs. Nor did Chief Diego.

He was growing increasingly worried about the ditch the Señor was building. Great concrete reservoirs had been constructed at the back of the white man's property, with large valves and spigots. The canyon stream, once diverted from its natural path, would run into these tanks, to be controlled as the Señor wished.

It isn't right, Luisa thought. Nature knew where to send water and how much. It was not up to men to control water, to change the desert.

But that, too, was not her concern. Once again, she was searching for Gabriela.

Just yesterday, she had gone searching for the girl and had found her in La Alma's rear garden, squatting on her haunches and watching something with intense focus. Six fat little birds with comical topknots on their heads, pecking in the dirt for insects and seeds.

"Granddaughter," Luisa had said, and the birds bolted, running single-file behind the larger male, until they disappeared under a bush.

The girl had looked up, a moment of confusion on her face, and then she broke into a smile. "Aii, Mukat," Luisa whispered. "Go to the village. It is the agave harvest. Hurry."

"Yes, Grandmother," Gabriela said, and she had run off.

Once again, the lazy girls were avoiding their chores. But Luisa had an idea where to find them.

Luisa went first to Lardner's General Store, her granddaughters' favorite place. But they were not there. Luisa continued on. She came to the hairdressing salon where she stopped to look in. The place was busy. All chairs were occupied. She went inside, a bell tinkling above the door. She let the door shut behind her as she stood immobilized. Luisa could neither speak nor move. She heard the blood pounding in her ears. She couldn't breathe. *Aii, Mukat! The world is coming to an end . . .*

For there, in a hairdresser's chair, sat Gabriela, her long hair chopped off.

Luisa felt the world swim around her. She thought she was going to faint. But she held herself together and waited, trembling with rage and fear and sudden sickness in her belly.

Isabella stood next to her cousin, giggling. When they became aware of someone standing behind them, the girls turned and saw their grandmother. They froze wide-eyed.

Stiffly, with dignity, Luisa turned and exited the shop to stand outside and wait.

The girls came meekly out. "Grandmother," Gabriela said. "I just wanted to know what it was like. It will grow back."

Luisa held up a hand and began to walk. The girls followed. Across the street, past the boundary of the reservation, and onto the dry alluvial plain. She entered the village, Gabriela and Isabella close on her heels. They began to cry.

"Aii, Mukat!" Gabriela's mother cried when she came out of her hut. "Have you gone *loca*? Have you no shame?"

As Gabriela sobbed and tried to talk, Isabella ran to her mother's hut, crying, while Luisa left them. She continued through the camp where everyone now stared in astonishment at Gabriela's short hair.

Luisa approached the ceremonial house with respect. Diego sat beneath a ramada, deep in conference with the elderly shamans. Luisa knew they were talking about the stolen water. It was all they talked about. "I wish to speak," she said.

He invited her to sit.

She sat, crossing her legs. Wind rustled the overhead cottonwood branches. Luisa listened. She heard no voices. "Diego, I am afraid."

"Of what?"

"Do you see Gabriela's hair?"

"Women's concern, not men's."

The girls cutting their hair had shocked Luisa into an emotion she could not name. It was a sick anger that was unfamiliar to her. But there was more. The anger was laced with a terrible fear for which she had no words.

I did not see this coming. For a girl to cut off her hair—Luisa closed her eyes. It was an unthinkable calamity. The worst of omens. The spirits had not warned her.

Were they talking to someone else? She was sixty-two years old by white man's reckoning. She should have started the training by now. "I did not see this," she said to Chief Diego. "The spirits did not warn me. We need a new spirit-reader. I am old. Our people will perish without the help of the spirits."

Luisa's visions had always helped the clan. One year, when she "saw" a flash flood destroying the village, she warned them. The people gathered all their things, animals, food, and moved to higher ground. The flood came, but the people were saved.

"I must find the child before I die, Diego."

Diego turned his thoughts away from the white man and the stone ditch he was building, sifted through his many thoughts, then said solemnly, "From forever, always the child who is chosen tells his parents, and they bring the child to the spirit-reader to be taught how to use his gifts. So it was with you, Luisa. So it was with the spirit-reader who taught you, and the one before that who taught him, all the way back to the beginning of the earth. We cannot change it."

"We must, Diego. The child must be trained. It takes months and years. Diego, I must select a child myself and teach him."

He shook his head. "This is very serious. We cannot break tradition."

Luisa thought for a moment. In all her life she had never acted without instructions from the men in her tribe or from the spirits. Like all the women of her clan, Luisa had been raised to be obedient and submissive, never to speak out of turn or to act on her own. Yet she must. "I wonder, Diego, if in order to preserve something that has always been done, we must do something that has never been done."

Diego's thoughts tumbled in his brain. The Señor's concrete ditch was getting nearer the valley floor. All Diego's attempts to stop it had failed. Neither the sheriff nor the Indian Bureau was helping. When the ditch opened, the white man would take even the Indians' share of the water. The clan would need to know when that was going to happen. They would need the counsel of the spirits.

"Very well, wife. Call upon the spirits to name your successor."

*   *   *

"Spirits of this place, in all humbleness and humility, I call upon you."

Luisa knelt at the circular hearth in her small house, sprinkling fragrant herbs onto the hot coals, a gift to the gods. She waved her hands in the sacred smoke that rose from the burning mesquite wood and drifted up through the hole in the roof.

She shook a sacred tortoise-shell rattle while the smoke from the burning mesquite filled her head. She chanted: "Beings of the spirit world, send your new messenger to me. Send the child who will be your conduit to this world after I am gone. Seek him or her out . . . speak to him, speak to her. Tell the little one to come to the house of Luisa Padilla . . ."

"Grandmother?"

Luisa's eyes snapped open.

"Grandmother, are you home?"

Luisa blinked in the smoky darkness. "I am in here, child."

The curtain over the doorway moved aside, sunlight poured in, a silhouette blocking the light. "I have been looking for you, Grandmother."

"Why?"

"I . . . I don't know," the girl said, coming all the way in. "I was going to La Alma to help the Señora when I suddenly thought I needed to see you. Do you need me, Grandmother?"

With effort, Luisa rose to her feet and struggled to compose herself. This could not be right. The spirits were playing a trick on her. Why did they send her most disobedient, most incorrigible granddaughter? Gabriela! She has no discipline, no respect for the old ways. She cut off her hair.

They chose her and that is that. You must accept their wish, Luisa Padilla.

"Come in, Gabriela," Luisa said finally. "I have something to tell you . . ."

CHAPTER TWENTY-SEVEN

"I SURE ENJOYED THAT story about the shoot-out in Tombstone, Cody," Augie Lardner said as he reached for a can of boot polish. "You write a good yarn."

When he had decided to write his father's story, Cody had written to the Tombstone newspaper for information about the forty-one-year-old incident, and had been able to piece together facts from eyewitness accounts, statements made at the hearing, and his father's own telling of the story. Cody had then dramatized the piece with action, dialogue, and the characters' inner thoughts and feelings.

A simple story, really, but one driven by passion and the thirst for revenge. The *Sunday National Reader* had invited Cody to submit more stories. He had sent two: *Calamity Jane* and *The Last of the Blackfeet*. The magazine bought both.

"It was so realistic," Augie said, as he placed Cody's purchases in a sack. "I was on the edge of my seat, wondering what was going to happen next. Imagine a lawman acting like that, turning outlaw himself for revenge. I don't blame George McNeal for getting out of town like that."

Cody smiled as he picked up his purchases—tobacco, cigarette papers, boot polish, shaving cream—and said, "Thanks."

He paused. Lined up on the counter were large glass jars filled with sweets and candies. Cody noticed a new variety—the pieces were small, flat-bottomed, and cone-shaped, and wrapped in silver foil. "What are these?"

"Just got them in. They come all the way from Pennsylvania. They're solid chocolate and they're called Hershey's Kisses."

Cody pulled out a coin. "I'll take five." He would find a safe moment to give them to Elizabeth. She loved chocolate, and he knew that Nigel never gave her presents.

As Mr. Lardner wrapped the pieces in a square of tissue paper, Cody looked through the store window from where, down the street, he could see the driveway leading up to La Alma. Because of his duties around the property, taking care of the livestock, overseeing the ranch hands, his path frequently crossed Elizabeth's as she worked in her garden, went for walks, or took her Appaloosa out for exercise. Cody and Elizabeth were always polite and friendly, but formal—the lady of the house and the ranch manager—unable to find stolen moments alone together so that his yearning for her became almost unbearable.

And her private life had become a mystery.

Since their last intimate encounter, up in Big Horn Valley weeks ago, they had not been alone. When they did meet, in the open, in the sunlight, with witnesses around, Elizabeth rarely mentioned Nigel. Cody sensed she was keeping something from him. If Nigel harmed her physically in any way, would she tell him? *She knows what I would do . . .*

"So what do you make of that?" Lardner asked, as he jerked his head toward the shop's large window. "Think the new ditch is going to be a boon to the town?"

"Water's always a good thing," Cody said, thanking Augie as he left. He kept the rest of his words silent—that he thought Barnstable's new concrete ditch, being put into operation today, was going to slice open a whole new bag of troubles for Palm Springs.

He stepped into the sunshine and paused to watch townspeople starting to gather at the back of Barnstable's property. Indians, too, and a few date growers from around the valley. Quite a crowd just to watch some mountain water come tumbling down. Maybe, Cody thought, some had come in the hope of witnessing a rousing good fight between Chief Diego and the white man. Problem was, the Indians had knives and spears, the white men had rifles. Cody wondered if he should get his gun, just in case.

*   *   *

As Elizabeth finished combing her hair, fixing the deep waves with stiffening lotion, she looked at the time. Nigel had announced to everyone that he was officially opening the new aqueduct at noon. She knew he wanted to make a grand, dramatic gesture of it. There was bound to be a crowd, with people coming from as far away as Banning and Indio and Twentynine Palms, to witness either his triumph or failure. Some were even hoping for failure, Elizabeth knew. The Indians and the other date growers were not pleased, and it created a tension that polarized the valley.

Elizabeth had learned to do her own hair since Fiona had taken on other duties around the house. In fact, Elizabeth required less and less from her lady's maid, arriving at a point where she could select her own clothes, dress herself, fasten her own necklaces. In the few weeks since learning that a big developer was going to build a resort at Big Horn Valley, Elizabeth's resolve to stop the project had grown, and as she had begun her campaign—mostly research and a few letters at this point—she decided that a woman who was going to spearhead a movement against a major corporation to stop them from doing what they wanted should be able to dress herself.

The surveyors in Big Horn Valley had said the valley was going to be developed by a company called Quinlan Resorts, that they had "a string of ritzy-titzy places all across the Southwest like a diamond and turquoise necklace. Resorts for rich folk." Rich folk like Nigel, she thought now, as she checked the clock again. And the more she thought about it, the more it worked its way under her skin, like a splinter that couldn't be gotten to. Festering. Making her think of camels with straw on their backs. There might be other arenas where Nigel had the advantage and she had to fight tooth and nail to win, like the divorce court, but here was one rich man's playground she could put a stop to. Blocking Quinlan's development of Big Horn Valley into a snooty resort for people like Nigel had become, in Elizabeth's mind, a blow against Nigel Barnstable himself.

Much of her inspiration had come from John Muir, the Scottish preservationist who founded the Sierra Club twenty years prior, and who had fought to create Yosemite National Park, finally succeeding in 1890. She bought his book, *The Mountains of California*, and read passages that transported her. "Now you cross a wild garden, now a meadow; and ever and anon you emerge from all the groves and flowers upon some granite pavement or high, bare ridge commanding superb views above the waving sea of evergreens . . ."

He could have been describing Big Horn Valley and the San Jacinto Mountains. Elizabeth knew that John Muir had visited Palm Springs in 1905, so perhaps he had gone up the trails of San Jacinto and included Elizabeth's mountain in his sweeping description.

She wasn't sure yet of her plan of attack. She needed information. Her preliminary work was gathering data—on the company, on its plans for Big Horn Valley. It also occurred to Elizabeth to look into the legality of such development. Weren't these mountains protected? Wasn't there a bureau of wilderness conservation or something? Once armed with the facts, she would launch a letter writing campaign—to politicians, to concerned groups, to newspapers, and anyone who would listen.

So far she had learned that while there had been public interest in creating a protected park system since the mid-1800s, the decision to set these special places aside was not an obvious, or easy, one. No road map existed for the journey that created the national parks because no places quite like them existed anywhere else in the world.

But public outcry against unrestricted logging in the Northern California forests, irresponsible mining of their minerals, and unregulated damming of rivers finally got the government's attention. Responding to such calls, Congress and President Abraham Lincoln put Yosemite National Park under the protection of California during the Civil War, and in 1872, President Ulysses S. Grant made Yellowstone in Wyoming America's—and the world's—first truly national park. The National Park Service was then created in 1916, just six years ago, with a mandate to protect the parks for the enjoyment of future generations and to promote their use by all people.

Elizabeth had so far sent letters to the Department of the Interior, the Bureau of Land Management, the California Department of Fish and Game, as well as to private groups such as the Audubon Society and the Sierra Club. These people who had fought to save Yosemite Park and who were now fighting to save Sequoia National Park wrote back, inspiring her, giving advice, and encouraging her to act.

She wondered if she would have to try some way to keep this a secret from Nigel. Would he disapprove? Would he try to sabotage her effort? Or, as he had done in the case of the lending library, would he claim credit for coming up with the idea himself?

She had been back to Big Horn Valley several times since the day she and Cody had met the surveyors. Because Nigel insisted on it, Elizabeth rode up the canyon accompanied by Mexican ranch hands.

Occasionally, Cody was in the group. Although she doubted any of the Mexicans reported to Nigel, as their English was poor, she and Cody made sure their behavior together was nothing less than polite and professional—"Mrs. Barnstable" and "Mr. McNeal."

But the yearning was always there and sometimes so intense—as Elizabeth watched Cody ride up ahead on his mare and her body ached for him—that she wondered if their sexual desire was palpable in the air. And as they loped through the meadow's tall grass, and Cody's eyes met hers, her heart would leap and a flush would warm her face— surely they were giving themselves away!

But Nigel was busy with his aqueduct and orchards, and had given no sign that anyone had reported to him that something was going on between the Señora and Mr. McNeal. Still, they could not let their guard down, and as intensely as they desired to be together, since their one stolen kiss at Christmas, there had not been another.

She looked at the clock. Noon. Time to join the crowd and witness her husband's victory over the desert.

*   *   *

As Doc Perry waited with Fiona Wilson, anticipating the dramatic arrival of the water, he watched the Indians. They were giving the white folks the stink eye. Tension clogged the air. He wondered if the Sheriff should be called. Where was old Diego? Up at the top, he supposed, to stop Barnstable from setting the water free. Was this going to end in a bloody mess?

Doc Perry was glad the project was over. The slaves of Egypt when they built the Pyramids had it better than those poor Mexicans who were driven hard by Barnstable's gang of white-men overseers. Over the months, Leland had been called up the canyon to repair an alphabet of wounds and injuries, as haste was urged upon the laborers, who in turn lost fingers and toes in the hurry. Hauling bricks broke men's backs. Fights broke out, too, so Leland had gone up the canyon with his black-eye salves, along with sutures and antiseptics and gauze.

Say something for the Indians though, he thought, they had a right to defend and keep what was theirs and make sure Barnstable didn't steal water that belonged to them. Not that Doc Perry was a friend of the Indians—not since Chief Diego banished Leland from the reservation ten years ago, threatening a sickly curse on him if Perry should set one toe on Indian land ever again—but he halfway admired the old chief's restraint in this whole water affair. Sabotaging the cement equipment, stealing tools, causing as much damage as he could, Diego drew the line at inflicting physical harm on a person. Leland figured it was because the Indians had an affinity for the Mexicans. They were all Indians under the skin, he supposed, the Mexicans descending from Aztecs and all.

What was the old boy going to do now? It was one thing to kick over irrigation canals dug in dirt, or to take axes to the temporary flume that had been made of wood. But, like in *The Three Little Pigs*, old Diego wasn't going to be able to huff and puff and blow a concrete aqueduct down.

*   *   *

Luisa stood beneath a cottonwood tree on the edge of the reservation, her mind walking two paths: the stealing of Indian water with no one stopping the thief, and how much she had learned in these past days of tutoring Gabriela.

She remembered when her own teacher, Juan Rivera, had said, "There comes a day when the teacher becomes the student." And so it was. But Gabriela was turning out to be a difficult pupil. Luisa would say, "Close your eyes and open your heart to let the spirits in." And she would catch Gabriela staring up at a red-tailed hawk circling the sky in search of prey.

Was I ever that disobedient? Luisa wondered. Did Juan Rivera have to strike me with a reed to bring my itinerant mind back to the lesson?

Yes, she admitted to herself, recalling the day when she was so bored, feeling the hot sun bake her skin, back before the railroad came through the valley, back before white people came and it was just Indians and Mexicans living here, and Juan Rivera goaded her, prodded her, calling her a mule and a donkey, saying, "Listen to the water in the creek. Listen to the wind. What are they telling you?"

But all Luisa, twelve years old and restless, heard was water and wind.

And then one day as she was humming to herself and practicing twining pa'ul fibers together to make a basket, she suddenly heard a voice, "Luisa Seco." This was before she was Luisa Padilla. But she didn't really *hear* it. Her ears had nothing to do with the voice. Nor did her brain. It was more like a feeling, as if something were being poured over her. She froze. She listened. More words had poured over her, except they weren't normal words, they were pictures and concepts and intangible ideas.

The manner of communication didn't matter. She shot to her feet and ran to the village warning the elders that a pale-skinned man was coming and that he was going to offer to buy all the food they had and pay them handsomely for it. "But he will go away, promising to return with the money, and we will never see him again, and we will have no food for the hot summer."

And so when the stranger came—it was a group of strangers, and they said they represented something called the Southern Pacific Railroad—and they wanted food—Chief Francisco insisted on seeing their gold coins first and then he parted with only half of the acorns and berries and deer jerky.

Juan Rivera died two years later after a proud and distinguished career of saving his people from catastrophe. He died content in the knowledge that his people were safely in the hands of a very good spirit-reader.

Luisa now prayed that her death would be as contented. But from what she was seeing in her scatterbrained granddaughter, she feared that was not going to be so.

Setting Gabriela aside, Luisa turned her mind toward the canyon and the place where a showdown was taking place. Two men fighting over water.

*   *   *

Halfway up the canyon, at the base of the main waterfall from which the heavy snow run off tumbled and churned, the workers had constructed a large round reservoir that then emptied into the new ditch. A temporary wooden gate had been built over it to guide the collected water toward the wooden ditch. Now the Mexicans stood ready to break the wooden gate at the Señor's command.

Diego and his shamans stood on the other side of the creek, stone-faced and tense. Within a day, he knew, once that gate was broken down, the Indians' stream would dry up while all the Mesquite Canyon water rushed down to the white man's reservoirs and irrigation ditches. And no one had come to stop him.

The reservoir had been dry while under construction, with diverted water running down the temporary flume. Nigel now strode along the concrete lip of the new flume, swinging a mighty ax, and, ordering the Mexicans to step aside, heaved the heavy tool over his head and slammed it down on the rope that kept the gate closed.

Nigel felt powerful, confident, and more in control than ever. His financial empire was growing. Using the marketing model of his movie industry friends, he first created a craving for his product—by having the produce markets offer free samples of his dates, and then selling the first box at a discount price. Next, he followed the example of the movie theater chains by allowing his dates to be distributed only to the large market chains, squeezing the mom-and-pop groceries out of the loop. It was a lucrative deal for all concerned, as the markets that carried the in-demand fruit marked their prices up and sent a kickback to Nigel. Thus the public, wanting sweet and luscious Stullwood Plantation dates, were forced to go to the big markets and pay higher prices. Just like the movie theater chains.

Soon Nigel was going to expand into worldwide distribution.

The gate swung open and all the water that had been backed up behind it burst out, tumbling down into the concrete reservoir, quickly filling it. And then it gushed over and continued its frothy journey down the brand new ditch. As the rushing water started rolling down the artificial channel with a roar, Nigel jumped onto his horse and spurred it into a gallop, his white overseers riding behind him as they flew down the beaten path that had been created during the channel's construction, whooping and hollering as they chased the water down the mountain to the flat land below.

Nigel felt like Napoleon crossing the Alps on his courageous war-horse, Marengo, the magnificent gray Arabian famous for carrying the Emperor safely through battle. The painting by Jacques-Louis David filled Nigel's mind as his horse raced alongside the newly released water—the violence of the image, with the ferocious alpine wind at Bonaparte's back, Marengo's long tail and voluminous mane flying in the wind, the stallion's eyes wild with terror as it rears up on hind legs, Napoleon's red cloak snapping all about.

It was exactly how Nigel saw himself, and he knew it was how others saw him at that moment, the Indians and the villagers, watching awestruck as the new master of Coachella Valley crossed his own violent and treacherous Alps.

Even better, this was how his son was going to see him, proudly watching Father race the water gushing down the new flume, the boy wishing he could ride with him, telling himself that he was going to be just like his father someday.

When the roaring water reached the valley, the townsfolk cheered. The water roiled and boiled and sent up a welcome spray. The sight lifted everyone's spirits. Bringing water to the valley was a symbol of promised prosperity to the arid desert. The Allenbys and Lardners, Miss March and Miss Napier, folks from all around clapped and whistled and made their approval known. When they looked at the churning water racing past them, hurtling toward Barnstable's newest orchard, they saw not water but fields of clover and alfalfa, groves of oranges and lemons, orchards filled with apricots and almonds, soil so fertile anything could grow in it. More than anything, they saw expansion. With water, more tourists would come, more people to build homes and businesses.

But the visiting date growers did not cheer, their faces showing every reaction, from being impressed with Barnstable's feat of engineering, to fear and outright worry. It was like watching a sleeping giant start to wake up. Collectively, they thought: there will be no stopping this man.

On the other side of the plain, at the edge of the reservation, the Indians stood in watchful silence. Already, in the first minutes of the opening of the Mesquite Canyon ditch, the natural stream that had spilled down from San Jacinto's summits for thousands of years, was shrinking to a trickle.

CHAPTER TWENTY-EIGHT

THE TWO FEDERAL AGENTS watching the moonshiner's lair weren't interested in the old 'legger himself. He was a small fish. The feds had received a tip that infamous gangster Tony Riccio, who ran speakeasies in the Los Angeles area, was sending some men out to the Palm Springs area to pick up a large shipment of illegal hooch.

They sat in the cover of dense mesquite trees, in a government-issued Model T Ford, passing a silver hip flask back and forth to keep warm against the cold desert night. They were family men, grateful to have jobs, and not giving a damn if they caught Riccio or anybody else for that fact. They would either drag some miscreants back to headquarters in Los Angeles tonight, or they would shoot them here and save themselves a lot of trouble. Shoot first and blame the gangsters, an idea that grew increasingly appealing as the warm bourbon (gotten from a pharmacy with a doctor's prescription) went down.

*　　*　　*

Doc Perry guided his new Model T along the rutted track. It was six months since he had visited the bootlegger's secret lair, and he did not relish coming back. But the gallon of white lightning had run out, and he needed more.

He didn't know if it was a good thing or not. Leland's medicines were selling better than ever, which was why he had been able to trade in his horse and buggy for a motor car. His patients, which were pretty much everyone within a radius of twenty miles, claimed his new generation of recipes worked even better on their jitters and nerves and insomnia and aches and pains than the previous lot. But he didn't like making the late-night drive to a hideaway occupied by a half-drunk, trigger-happy moonshiner.

He saw a light up ahead. It swayed beyond the trees like a lantern. Leland slowed the car, his stomach rising to his throat. In all his travels all over the West, he had managed to avoid outlaws, gunfights, lynchings, all the fracases that marked frontier life. And now here he was, in modern 1922, driving an automobile, living in respectable Palm Springs, about to defy a constitutional amendment. Federal law. Which meant steep fines and even prison, if caught.

This was going to be the last time. After this, he was going to find a way to go legitimate. No more underhanded dealings for Leland Perry. Fiona deserved better.

*   *   *

Inside the shack, the bootlegger's pimply buttocks went up and down, making the cot springs squeak. The woman who lay beneath him had come out to Hollywood hoping to get in the movies but couldn't compete with the thousands of others who streamed into California from Idaho and Kansas and Virginia. Unable to find a job, she hooked up with a gold prospector who brought her out to the desert, and when he didn't find gold, he abandoned her. There was only one way to survive, and if she didn't think about it or pay too much attention to the men she serviced, she made a good living for herself.

Mary Lou came once a week to the moonshiner's shack hidden in a remote date grove, and their sweaty copulating was now disturbed by the sudden sounding of a horn. The light from automobile headlamps swept the rickety walls. "Jesus!" he said, pushing himself up. "What time is it?" The honking got louder. He knew it was Archie the Aspirin, one of Tony Riccio's lieutenants, so-named because he had a way of making his boss's headaches disappear.

"Crap, I'm not ready. You have to go!"

"Hey," she said, covering her nakedness. "Where's my money?"

"I didn't finish."

"That's not my fault."

He got up, buttoning his pants. He reached for his shotgun, hinged it to insert a shell into the barrel, snapped the gun back closed, and flipped the safety off.

*   *   *

"There they are," the federal agents said in unison, seeing headlights, blinded momentarily so they couldn't see who was in the car tilting along the rutted track. They reached for their rifles and stepped out into the cold night.

Bringing his car to a halt, but leaving the motor running, Leland got out and called through the darkness, "It's just me, Homer. I need another gallon—"

Two deafening cracks tore the night. From the corner of his eye, on the other side of a formidable barrel cactus, he saw two explosions of light. Then he felt something sharp and burning rip through his body. He fell against his car. He grabbed himself and felt a warm wetness cover his hand.

Someone shouted, "Federal agents! Put your hands in the air!"

A volley of gunfire erupted in the night. Leland heard bullets pinging off metal and rocks. He kept his head down and his hand on his stomach. And then, his hand soaked in blood, he went very light-headed and slumped to the ground.

*   *   *

Fiona stirred in fitful sleep. She was dreaming about a woodpecker, drilling away at a tree in the garden. She opened her eyes. It wasn't a dream. Something was tapping at her patio door.

She parted the curtain. "Leland!" He was leaning against the glass, clutching himself around the middle. When she opened the door, he fell in. She barely caught him. He stumbled to the bed and fell on it. "I've been shot," he gasped.

Fiona lit a lamp and pulled his jacket and shirt open. When she saw the blood she cried out. She ran barefoot through the house and when she reached the other wing, she moved silently and tapped as softly as she could on Elizabeth's door so that His Lordship, sleeping in the bedroom opposite, wouldn't hear.

The bedroom door opened. "What? What is it?"

"It's Leland. He's been shot."

They ran back through the house to Fiona's bedroom, where Elizabeth saw Doc Perry sprawled across the bed, panting, the white sheet running red with blood.

"I'll go fetch Mr. McNeal," she said, thinking that Cody must have had some experience with gunshot wounds.

"No!" Leland said suddenly. "Don't get him. Don't get anyone . . ."

"You need help," Fiona cried.

He grabbed her wrist, bloodying the cuff of her nightgown. "There were federal agents there. And the bootlegger was shooting. If one of those agents got killed . . ." He struggled for breath. "They saw me. Fiona. They saw my car. I might get accused of being involved. I might go to prison. I'm a fugitive from justice. Anyone who helps me is breaking the law." He grimaced. "I shouldn't have come here. I should have just kept on driving."

"Nonsense," Elizabeth said. "We're going to take care of you. Fiona, please fetch the emergency kit from the kitchen."

As Elizabeth helped him out of his jacket, Leland winced and said, "I don't think the bullet hit any major organs. My bag . . . in my car . . . forceps, sutures."

She dashed outside, running barefoot over gravel and weeds, and saw the Model T by one of the corrals. Headlights on, motor still running. Turning it off, seeing the blood on the front seat, she searched in back and found his medical bag. Elizabeth hurried back to Fiona's bedroom, closing the patio door and drawing the curtains.

Removing his shirt, the two women laid Perry back on pillows. He was shockingly white and sweating profusely. "Fiona, go and look out. I might have been followed . . ."

Elizabeth sponged the bloody abdomen until she got a better look at the wound, a few inches to the right of his navel. She had never seen a bullet hole before. It looked so small and innocent, yet so destructive.

"There's no one out there," Fiona said, coming back in and closing the door. "No cars coming down the road."

"I don't know how I got out of there," he gasped. "I fell to the ground; next thing, I'm driving away as fast as I can. I'm sorry, dearest," he said to Fiona. "I know you didn't want me to go back to the moonshiner, but I had run out . . ."

Giving her maid and the doctor a curious glance, Elizabeth went into the adjoining bathroom and returned with clean towels. "Tell us what to do," she said.

"You'll need to widen the wound. Cut an inch slice through the center of the hole. And . . . hand me a probe."

Telling herself that it was no different from punching holes in a piecrust, Elizabeth made an incision through the wound.

"Iodine," he gasped. "Pour it in . . . generously. Give me a towel to bite on. I might scream, and we can't risk your husband—"

But Elizabeth was slipping out of the room and when she returned, was holding a bottle of brandy. "Nigel won't notice it missing for at least a year. I took it from the back of his supply. Drink up as much as you can, then tell us what to do."

Leland used the probe on himself. Numbed with expensive Napoleon brandy, he slid the metal instrument slowly into the bullet wound, through skin, fat, fascia, and muscle—thankfully between vital organs—until he felt it touch something solid. "There it is," he whispered. "The long narrow forceps . . . no, not those. *Tissue* forceps . . . like long tweezers. Yes, those . . ." He guided the forceps into the wound and then his hand fell away. "I fear I am going to faint . . ."

Fiona grasped the instrument, closed her eyes, and felt around. Elizabeth watched anxiously, her eyes flickering from the oozing wound, red with iodine, to Leland's gray, perspiring face to the closed bedroom door.

"I have it," Fiona said. Tucking in the corners of her mouth, she concentrated on drawing the bullet back out through muscle and fat, fearful of losing it in the mysterious hinterland she imagined the human abdomen to be, and finally brought it to light.

"He's fallen asleep," Elizabeth said, as she dried Leland's forehead. "Would you rather I stitched him up? I do need the practice," she added with a faint smile.

"I'll do it," Fiona said somberly, the full significance of what had happened hitting her only now. She began to shake. "He could have been killed. I might be a widow right now . . ."

"*I'll* do the sewing," Elizabeth said, as she sorted through curved needles, silk thread, and scissors. "If it isn't good, Doc Perry can re-do it himself tomorrow. In the meantime, we shall let him stay here."

Ten minutes later they were in the kitchen, two women in bathrobes at midnight in a silent house, making themselves a cup of tea, each privately pondering the unexpected adventures of desert life.

Widow? Elizabeth thought as she sat at the kitchen table that had once sufficed as a servants' hall for a domestic staff. She was keeping alert for any noise outside . . . a car motor, tires on the gravel, men's voices in authoritative tones. Had Leland been followed? Would the agents be able to identify him?

Is a federal agent lying dead in the desert?

The police might come to Palm Springs searching for Doc Perry's car. At the least, he was a witness to the shoot-out. At the worst, the feds might think he was in collusion with the bootlegger, which he was! Only as a small-time customer, but criminally involved all the same.

Elizabeth decided she would hide the car in the barn, tuck a blanket over the bloody seat. At that point, Cody would need to be brought in on the secret. There was no avoiding it. But Elizabeth found a strange relief in knowing that Cody would be part of it. Knowing that Cody was always nearby was a constant comfort. Although Nigel had not physically abused her in six months, nonetheless his unpredictability kept her on edge. And when, at times, she sensed tension in him, when he withdrew into cold silences and she feared he could suddenly lash out at her, she drew great comfort from the knowledge that Cody was in the bunkhouse on the other side of the corrals, that he would be able to hear her should she cry out for help and come at once.

"Fiona, listen to me. If lawmen come around, asking questions, we will say that Doc Perry was with us the whole evening. Agreed?"

"Oh, yes, My Lady. Thank you."

Elizabeth thought for a long moment, pondering a night of federal agents and bootleggers and gunshot wounds. She thought Fiona looked drawn and anxious. She had just referred to herself as an almost-widow. Was it possible she was keeping a very enormous secret from everyone? Elizabeth felt a little hurt, and a little confused, wondering why Fiona hadn't confided in her about a secret marriage? For what else could the word "widow" refer to? Trying to figure out how to most tactfully ask the question, Elizabeth finally just said, "Do you want to tell me about you and Leland?"

Fiona turned the cup around and around in its saucer. Her facial expression went by turns from worry to nostalgic, to fear and then to joy. "We got married at Christmas," she said, feeling so bone-weary that she thought she would fall asleep right there at the table and stay asleep until the wood absorbed her completely.

"But why the secrecy? And why don't you live together?"

Fiona smiled as she thought of Leland's special surprise Christmas gift six months ago: she had unwrapped the large flat box to find that it contained a white satin headband such as flappers wore, with a modest wedding veil attached. A box with a diamond ring in it. And an application for a marriage license, all filled out and waiting for her signature. On New Year's Day they had gone to the justice of the peace in Indio and quietly gotten married.

"I didn't want to leave you, Milady. Alone in this house, I mean." She spoke haltingly, tracing the wood grain of the tabletop with her fingertip. "I didn't want you to know that I knew about His Lordship's assault on you." She looked up and met Elizabeth's eyes.

"I see," Elizabeth said.

"Leland told me. Please don't be angry with him," Fiona added hastily. "He let it slip because he thought I already knew."

"I'm not mad at anyone," Elizabeth said wearily—*except for the man who caused all this need for secrecy and fear and subterfuge.*

"I knew you were keeping it very private, Milady. But at the same time, I needed to stay near you in case His Lordship tried it again. But I couldn't let you know that I knew the truth, so Leland and I decided to keep our marriage a secret for now and live in separate homes."

Now came the hard part, to decide whether or not to divulge the fact of Fiona's promise to Mrs. Van Linden. If she told Elizabeth, could she word it in such a way that Elizabeth's mother wouldn't come out looking despotic? The promise hadn't been voluntary on Fiona's part. Mrs. Van Linden had demanded it of her.

Fiona paused, centered her attention on her teacup, then said quietly, "And I promised your mother I would watch over you."

Elizabeth frowned. "I beg your pardon?"

"Your mother was worried, and so I said I would stay with you."

Elizabeth sat back in her chair and rubbed her neck. The adrenalin of finding a wounded Leland in Fiona's room was receding, and in its place a powerful fatigue rushed in. Her mother. Of course. Even three thousand miles away, Mrs. Van Linden couldn't let go.

Perhaps that was how it was with mothers and one should simply accept that fact. Hadn't Elizabeth herself, when she had found out she was pregnant, been swept up in a most powerful feeling of protectiveness toward her child, her head already spinning plans for his or her life without yet consulting the baby itself? "I appreciate it," she said. "I would imagine my mother asked you to stay with me but that she worded it in stronger tones. She shouldn't have done that to you, Fiona. Yes, she gave you a job when you most needed one, but that didn't mean you were to be enslaved to her until the day you die. Consider the promise fulfilled."

"Thank you, Milady," Fiona said in a tight voice. As it was a time for confessions and revelations, Fiona knew she had to divulge one last secret. She drew in a breath and said, "And you should know that I know about Mary Clark."

At Elizabeth's sudden startled look, she quickly added, "No one else knows! I found out entirely on my own. I saw an envelope, the return address . . ."

"Oh," was all Elizabeth could say.

"If there is anything Leland and I can do to help . . ."

"I don't want to get you involved."

Fiona smiled. "I am already involved, Milady."

Elizabeth listened to the night and thought of relationships and how things are never what they seem and rarely go how you want. "Please call me Elizabeth. I stopped being Her Ladyship long ago."

Fiona felt the weight of the world lift off her shoulders and waited for exuberance to rush in. It didn't. She knew she would need to live with this conversation for a while before she settled down to enjoying her own happiness. "We engaged in quite the debate, you know," she said, marveling at the new status she now suddenly held. No longer a servant but her Ladyship's friend and confidante. "I told Leland I had to live at La Alma and be on call for when you needed me. What kind of a marriage would it be for us, I wanted to know." She smiled. "Do you know what Leland said? He said, it would be him and me and that the living arrangement didn't matter. He just wanted me to be his wife."

"Of course you must live with your husband," Elizabeth said. "You can still come to work here during the day. After all, Mrs. Padilla and the girls don't sleep at La Alma. And you will continue to draw your salary."

Fiona's eyes widened. "Thank you, Milady—Elizabeth!" she quickly amended, intense relief washing over her. The money had been one of her worries. With Leland's income being dependent on so unstable a commodity as alcohol, they relied on Fiona's wages to supplement his income from sales of his medicines.

"Now," Elizabeth said, rising. "I have to go and hide that motor car, and you need to go look in on your husband."

Fiona found Leland sitting up in bed, inspecting his wound. "Not bad," he said with a wan smile. "Oh, Fee, I've made a muddle of things, haven't I? On top of all this, I didn't get any alcohol!"

Fiona searched his face. The paleness was subsiding. He had

taken a few more sips of the brandy, now his cheeks were pinking. A thought seemed to be trying to form in her mind, to get her attention. Taking his glass into the bathroom, she rinsed it and brought back fresh water. Handing him the glass, she sat on the bed again and said slowly, "Leland . . . is there possibly a way to make your medicines without alcohol?"

"What? Without alcohol? They would just be colored water with sugar added."

"But you do add some herbal ingredients, don't you?"

Suddenly Fiona was thinking of the creosote tea that Luisa had given to Elizabeth for menstrual cramps and which Elizabeth in turn had passed on to Fiona for a backache. "Leland, the Indians in this valley possess a wealth of knowledge on the medicinal values of local plants and herbs."

He patted the gauze dressing back into place and sank into the pillows. "Chief Diego is also the medicine man. I doubt he'll give me any handy hints."

Fiona fussed over the pillows and pulled the comforter up to his chin. Kissing his forehead, she said, "Why ever not?"

"When I first came to this valley with my medicine wagon, with an eye to settle down, I went onto the reservation in the hope of selling my wares to the Cahuilla. But the old man demanded I give him one of my bottles, and I did. He took a taste, spat it out, and threw the bottle to the ground. He accused me of selling alcohol to his people, which is illegal. I tried to explain that alcohol is a time-honored medicine dating back to Moses and the pharaohs, but he wouldn't listen. He said if I came onto the reservation again, he would report me to the Indian Bureau and have me arrested. There's been bad blood between us since."

"Then I wonder," she said, the new idea blossoming fully in her mind so that she smiled, "if it is time to mend a few fences . . ."

*   *   *

"It's my duty to inform you, Mr. Barnstable," the federal agent said, "that this is a serious complaint, and I have to look into it and report it as thoroughly as I can."

Chief Diego had lodged a complaint with the Indian Bureau in Banning and the agent had come out to inspect the new concrete ditch. Then he had sought out the party involved, finding Nigel at work in his newest date grove, supervising the thinning of the budding fruit bunches.

Nigel didn't respond as he strode from tree to tree, stopping to look up and watch the workers high up on ladders, cutting out the center clusters and dropping them to the ground.

"Mr. Barnstable," the agent said, "I have no choice but to file Diego's complaint and inform the Bureau in Washington. Have you nothing to say to this?"

"Don't stop there!" Nigel shouted up at the workers, cupping his hands. "Take another center!" He shook his head. "If they leave too much behind, the branch breaks and then we've lost the whole cluster."

"Listen, my friend," the Indian agent said, tilting his hat back. The day was hot and dry, winds minimum. Sometimes he hated his job. "You and I are white men, and we prefer white people and all that, but I am working for the government and for the interest of these Indians, and I must insist on a strict compliance with the provision of the contract with the Indians concerning water rights."

Nigel finally looked at the agent, leveling his eyes at the man who was bald and pink and sweating. He thought for a long moment, guessing at the cost of the man's cheap suit, imagining the demanding wife and kids. "As you say, friend, you work for the government, and we all know how slowly the wheels of bureaucracy can sometimes turn. We all know how paperwork can sometimes get lost." Nigel pulled out his wallet. "What will it take to slow the clock?"

The agent tried to look shocked and offended. But the truth was, his wasn't the most thankful job. Sometimes, the Indians cast him as a villain, as if it were his fault their government rations had been cut back. So a man had to seize perquisites where he could. Even so, accepting bribes was a serious charge.

"How about a hundred to start?" Nigel said.

The man's eyes widened. "To start?" It amounted to half his monthly wage.

"Let's just say you are unofficially on the Stullwood Plantation's payroll."

The agent put his pudgy hand out and said, "For that amount of money I'll strap Chief Diego's complaint to the back of a tortoise and point it in the direction of Washington, DC."

*　　*　　*

Luisa scanned the grass huts in the embrace of oaks and cottonwoods. Higher up the slope, stately pines and cedars grew.

She lifted her gaze and saw, deep in the piney boughs of an ancient fir tree, an owl sleeping the day away. After nightfall he would be seen wheeling against the stars in search of rodents. It was a good sign. Owls were the reincarnated spirits of ancestors, especially those who had been brave and wise.

Keep watch over us, Old One, Luisa said to him silently.

Then she saw a familiar white man trudging up the trail. He was limping. This is not good, she thought. Diego will not be pleased to see this white man.

"Greetings, *Mother*," Doc Perry said as he drew near. He had been told at the village that Chief Diego had established a camp at this higher elevation, to be closer to the headwaters of the white man's new ditch. He looked around at the cluster of crude huts, the few men sitting in the shade, the handful of women to take care of them.

When he saw Chief Diego, sitting alone with his eyes set toward the creek, no doubt to make sure Barnstable didn't draw off the rest of the water and leave the Indians bone dry, Leland presented himself to the old Chief.

Doc Perry had brought a brand-new Turkish meerschaum pipe given to him long ago by a grateful patient, the bowl carved into the likeness of a growling lion. He brought it out now as he sat beneath the ramada and packed it with tobacco. Striking a match, he lit it, took a few puffs, then handed it to Chief Diego.

The old man stared at it, working his lips in and out over his few remaining teeth. "Is it a pipe of peace?" he finally asked.

"I come humbly to beg your forgiveness for my offense years ago. I was not the same man then that I am today," Perry said, holding the pipe out, seeing the interest in the old man's eyes. Used to smoking plain clay pipes, Diego must find the carved meerschaum alluring and possibly full of magic. "I wish us to be friends," Leland added.

The Chief took the pipe, inspected it, then placed the stem between his lips, closed his eyes, and puffed vigorously. Tangy, fragrant smoke filled the air.

As they shared the pipe, handing it back and forth, a phrase sailed through Perry's mind: The passing of an age.

He hadn't given it any thought until now. In all his travels throughout the West, he had looked at Indians as part of the landscape, like antelope and cottonwoods, colorful props in a stage play. They might differ from tribe to tribe (aggressive buffalo hunters on the Plains, peaceful agrarians in the Southwest), and their costumes varied, their dialects regional, but they were ubiquitous, from ocean to ocean, red, brown, copper-skinned people with faintly Oriental features, living close to the earth, simple and primitive.

He couldn't imagine what it was like to see a new race suddenly appear, planting their boots in soil that for millennia had belonged to the Indian—a race with pale skin and strange customs, squatting on the prairies in log cabins, slaughtering the buffalo, spreading a new faith with new gods—an unstoppable tide of men and women in wagons, cutting a wide swath through sacred hunting grounds, relentlessly pushing the Indian out of the way. Bloody battles ending in tragic massacres—Sand River, Little Bighorn, Wounded Knee. Until the red man waved the flag of truce and retreated to government reservations.

Perry felt the peace of the moment settle over him. He had never thought about the peace pipe ritual before, its purpose, its rewards. Now he saw it as the red man's equivalent of breaking bread. It connected the parties in an unspoken treaty that said, now that you have sat at my table and eaten my bread, we are no longer strangers, no longer enemies.

He suddenly wanted to know more about the old shaman, his thoughts and fears, the details of his boyhood. We come and live among them, Perry thought, foist our values and culture on them, yet we know nothing about the people we subjugate. "I'll bet you have some stories to tell," he said, knowing that all men had stories to tell and wanted them to be heard.

Chief Diego closed his eyes and puffed on the white man's peace pipe. He tasted the smoke in his mouth, warm and woody, filling his thoughts with memories. The tobacco lifted him up and carried him back over the seasons, back through mesquite harvests, antelope hunts, the risings and fallings of the stars, back to a summer long ago when he was a boy and white men came through the valley, stopping to visit with the Indians in their mountain camp. They brought gifts to trade for skins and hides—glass beads, paint, calico cloth, and a dangerous water called whiskey.

Diego opened his eyes and handed the pipe to his visitor. "Yes, I have stories to tell. In the long-ago," he said softly, "white men sought peace with the Cahuilla. They gave us gifts. They gave us a special water to drink.

"At first the water burned like fire and our men spit it out. But they saw the boastful white men drinking the water and laughing. Our men did not like that. They were strong and brave hunters. They could drink the white man's firewater. So they drank it to prove their strength. After a while, our men liked what they were drinking. It no longer burned. It made them feel different. Braver, stronger. They started to dance. They chanted up to the sky. They started to walk funny. And they kept drinking.

"Their speech changed and soon they became angry. Our men quarreled among themselves, fighting over the jugs of firewater while the white men laughed. Our women became frightened. They gathered up the children and babies and ran into the woods to hide. From behind the trees they watched their fathers and husbands and uncles and sons begin to fight among themselves.

"An old grandmother tried to stop them. They knocked her down. Other women ran in to stop their men from going crazy. They received blows from husbands and sons. They retreated to the trees, their scalps bleeding. A young wife ran into the crazed men carrying her baby, pleading with the crazed men to stop their madness. She thought the baby would bring them to their senses. They knocked her down. The women in the woods wailed up to the sky, begging the gods to come down and stop the craziness.

"Our men danced around the fire and yelped and howled and fought with their fists among themselves while the white men laughed. And then our men began to fall to the ground. They passed out. Soon the camp was quiet but the women were too afraid to return.

"At dawn, the white men were gone and our men were waking up. They vomited. They felt sick. Their heads held great pain. They were covered in wounds as if they had gone to war. The old grandmother was dead, the young wife and her baby were dead. The women wailed up to the sky. There was great shame in the village that day and for all the days after. Our men were not strong and brave hunters. They drank the firewater and became devils. The women were angry for many days and would not forgive the men. When white men came again, they were told to go away and not give whiskey to the Indian anymore."

Leland Perry stared at the wrinkled copper face for a long moment, then he said, "And I came along and tried to sell alcohol to your people."

"A small boy cried beside the body of the young wife," Diego said. "I was that boy."

Diego squinted at the white man in the shiny waistcoat and tall top hat. And he pondered the strange turns of life. His people had perfected all manners of reading omens and signs and messages, had honed the practices of predicting the future—his wife the spirit-reader, himself the star-reader, his fourth son's eldest son a cloud-reader. All these people reading the signs all around them, and still surprises popped up like squirrels out of their holes. It occurred to him now that maybe not everything should be known, that maybe there was a reason the gods kept surprising humans.

He said, "It is not good for us to remain enemies. Friends are too few." He handed the pipe back and Perry took a puff. They shared the pipe for a long, silent spell until it was time to knock the ash on a rock and refill it. When the bowl was packed again, Leland handed the tin of tobacco to Diego, and the old man took it without a word, slipping it into his shirt pocket. "You have come to ask me something," he said. "I will listen."

"The Cahuilla are known for their good health and their medicines. And you, old father, besides being a star-reader, are known for being the best medicine man in the valley. I would like to learn from you, if I may humbly ask."

Puff, puff. Closed eyes. Wrinkled bronzed cheeks going in and then out. Leland noticed that the shamans had come to sit with them, while Luisa Padilla stood a short distance away. He sensed a lessening in the tension, and a growing curiosity in the air.

"What you ask for, my friend," Diego said at last, "plants that we use for medicine, how we prepare them and use them, we call this *Temalpakh*, which is the Cahuilla word for 'from the earth.' I will tell you what you need to know."

CHAPTER TWENTY-NINE

"SEÑOR BARNSTABLE," PEDRO GONZALEZ said, "if you undercut us like this, we cannot afford to operate our farms. While we are all competitors for the date market, we have also formed a cooperative. We have agreed to sell for the same price, and that way no one is outbid. But if you do this, some of us will go bankrupt."

Nigel had had a small working office built in the heart of the hundred-tree grove—a wood frame shack from which Nigel ran his sprawling plantation that now covered many acres. Here, his Mexican foremen came for their daily orders, as did the hired guards supervised by mean-faced Yancy, who loved keeping the Indians in check.

And it was in this office that Nigel now held audience with a very worried man, Pedro Gonzalez.

Gonzalez looked around at the orchard he had helped plant two years ago. Gonzalez himself had brokered these trees, going around to farms near Indio, getting good deals for the English newcomer, arranging for the tractor-drays to haul the massive date palms, and the truck rigged with a crane to maneuver them into place, even providing the manual labor. Gonzalez had thought at the time that Barnstable's prosperity would mean prosperity for all the growers in the valley as the wholesale distributors would switch from the Florida and Arizona date producers and look to the Coachella Valley as their sole source.

But apparently the Englishman had plans of his own.

"I never signed any agreement," Nigel said, "and I don't join cooperatives."

"But after all the help I gave you—"

"I can go elsewhere now," Nigel said, cutting him off as he walked out of the shack, forcing the other man to follow. "The broker in Phoenix is happy to take over supplying me with trees and labor." Nigel had also made the acquaintance of a tree broker in Mexico who claimed he could deliver mature date palms, ready to produce fruit, at half the cost of the Phoenix growers. If such an arrangement panned out, Nigel could lower his prices even more and cut the Indio growers out of the market altogether. When bankruptcy came, he would buy their farms at ten cents on the dollar.

"But, Señor, you would put me out of business."

Nigel turned, hands on his hips, and faced him. "I'll be happy to buy your farm right now, Gonzalez."

The man stared at him. Was that his plan? To bankrupt them all and then buy their farms at a fraction of what they were worth?

Nigel strolled away, and Gonzalez watched him go, a tall, arrogant young man in expensively tailored clothes. What was Pedro going to tell the others? They were all just simple farmers, struggling to make an honest living through cooperation. But this white man was gobbling up all the land and all the profits. Soon, the distributors would go only to him.

And where will *we* go?

The thought grew in his mind as he marched away from Barnstable's groves, as he climbed into his truck and drove off, growing in his mind, swelling with anger and resentment. He had seen it before, rich farmers forcing the poor ones out.

There was only one answer. Nigel Barnstable had to be stopped.

As Gonzalez drove past the reservation, glimpsing the rustic houses, the poverty-level way of life, the struggling little gardens, the withering orchards—he saw, on the side of the road, a wooden sign that said, *Indian Cemetery*, and when he saw a lone figure standing at one of the graves, an idea came to him.

Pulling his truck into the shade of a cluster of cottonwoods, Gonzalez got out and walked among the crosses and headstones. Chief Diego was standing at Johnny Pinto's grave.

"It isn't fair, my friend," Pedro Gonzalez said. "First he takes your grandson from you, and now he is taking the water from your children's mouths."

"Not so easy," Diego said, "to break cement with Indian axes."

"Who says you have to break the ditch? Perhaps a bag of cement placed just right . . ."

*   *   *

Doc Perry kept looking out his kitchen window as he boiled leaves in a small pan. Fiona was due back any minute with the last of her things. She was moving in with him today.

In a curious turning of tables, Elizabeth was helping Fiona to make the move, assisting her in packing, loading the bags into her car, driving Fiona to his house. After years of waiting on ladies, Fiona had a lady waiting on her. And Leland couldn't be happier. She had asked if she could change the living room curtains and he had cried, "You can change the whole house!" Confirmed bachelor Leland Perry, settling down with the one true love of his life.

And now, he was embarking on a new, honest career.

The leaves nicely done, he added a teaspoon of sugar to disguise the bitterness, then he poured the tea into a clean bottle with a label that said, Doc Perry's Cough Cure. He had bottled ten so far and expected to bottle another twenty.

The Indians called the plant *tanwivel*, but Leland's botanical encyclopedia identified the plant as *Eriodictyon trichocalyx*, which regular folk called Yerba Santa. The Cahuilla had been harvesting the medicinal plant for centuries. It grew up to eight thousand feet on rocky slopes and was proven to alleviate rheumatism, sore throats, and asthma. It was Doc Perry's first foray into the manufacture of herbal remedies based on lore he had learned from Chief Diego.

After this, his next recipe consisted of the stems and leaves of *Larrea divaricata*, known to the Cahuilla as *atukul*, more commonly known as the creosote bush.

There were many more steps to these concoctions than in his previous remedies, when all he had to do was add alcohol to colored sugar water. But he found an unexpected satisfaction in his labor, feeling very hands-on, much as a chemist might experience in the back of his shop. The creosote, for example, could be made into a tea, an ointment, an antiseptic powder, and an inhalant—to cure colds, poisons, infections, poor circulation.

He whistled while he ground creosote leaves with a pestle.

There was nothing like a brush with death to give one a new zest for life.

The shooting incident at the bootlegger's lair hadn't gotten a mention in the press. No one had come around looking for the driver of the Model T. And apparently, no one had gotten killed in the shoot-out. Leland kept his ear out for gossip and had learned that the feds arrested the 'legger and took him away. If these medicines worked as successfully as the Indians claimed, Leland would have no more need for alcohol. Even better, the ingredients were out in the desert and mountains, free for the plucking, which meant pure profit!

However, success was going to depend on how his patients reacted to the new cures.

Nigel was in the shed in his hundred-tree grove, scowling at a news item in a Hollywood industry magazine: the box office figures for Zora's latest movie, *Forbidden Flowers*. It was a disaster. Last year's Modern *Magdalene* had done so well that Zora's ambitions for her next picture had been extravagant and unrealistic, turning the production into a money pit. And now no one was lining up at the box office to see the movie. Word was, Lamont was going to take a bath on this one. But Nigel was thinking of his own investment, down the drain.

Nigel was losing money. On top of that, the shine had worn off Zora DuBois. Whereas he had once thought she was clever and a genius at shifting so easily from guise to guise, her recent actions disappointed him. She had taken to drinking heavily, and he supposed it was fear of the coming sound revolution. But, instead of facing it head on, taking on the challenge, the way she had invented the Vamp, she had turned to drink. She sought solace in vodka, and Nigel's prior admiration for her had dropped dramatically.

He heard footsteps outside and looked up to see one of his foremen walking up.

The man went by the name of Yancy, and he kept the Mexican workers in line.

"The tanks are dry again, sir."

Nigel swore under his breath. The fourth time in two weeks. Diego had his men watching the ditch and when Nigel's armed guards weren't looking, the Indians crept in on silent sandals to clog the ditch with rocks and stones and dead wood. No amount of threats from the Sheriff or Indian agent, or from Nigel himself, had slowed the old bastard in his determination to sabotage the new ditch.

"Take five men and ride up the canyon. Find the old chief. Make him understand that I won't tolerate these acts of sabotage. I don't care what you have to do, get it done."

"Yes, sir, Mr. Barnstable, sir."

"And Yancy, take rifles."

*   *   *

Gabriela and her grandmother sat in the shade, a few yards away from the small camp up the canyon, created by Chief Diego as a place where he could keep watch on the new ditch and make sure it didn't carry water.

"You are trying too hard, granddaughter," Luisa said. "You cannot squeeze your prayers to the spirits."

Gabriela twisted her fingers in rising panic. Last week, Grandmother had said she wasn't trying hard enough! She desperately wanted the lessons to work. She silently begged the spirits to speak to her.

Gabriela had thought it would be wonderful to be a clan shaman, for then she would be special. For a long time she had dreamed of being different, of not being one of a pair of candlesticks. When Grandmother Luisa had told her that the spirits had selected her to be the next spirit-reader, Gabriela had been overjoyed. She would be respected and revered, and hold a special place during fiestas. Perhaps she would even marry a chief! But, after six months of instruction with Grandmother, the spirits weren't speaking to her.

And now Grandmother was looking disappointed—doubtful, even, and it threw the girl into a panic. For months she had boasted to her friends about her new status, and she had seen the change in their attitude toward her. But Grandmother was growing impatient, starting to question if she had interpreted the spirits' intentions correctly. What if Grandmother decided she had been wrong and looked elsewhere for the apprentice? Gabriela did not want to lose her new position.

Luisa tried to think of another way to train the girl. The lessons were about patience and silence, stillness of the spirit and acceptance of all things. In frustration, Luisa thought: the mind of a child is open. It is still receptive to the spirit world the child lived in before he was born. But Gabriela is seventeen and her mind is cluttered with thoughts of boys and babies. How can the spirits make themselves heard?

And why had they chosen her?

Luisa knew that Gabriela was prideful. She had been boasting to friends about her new status. This was no way to begin life as a shaman. "Clear your mind, child," Luisa said again. "Speak in the silence of your head. Call to the spirits. Tell them you wish to hear their messages . . ."

*   *   *

Yancy followed the trail up the canyon beneath the noon sun, six white men scrapping for a fight. There was only a small camp up there. Diego and his shamans, a few women and children. Camped there to keep an eye on the concrete ditch and make life miserable for Mr. Barnstable. Yancy liked his job. It paid well, left him leeway to do pretty much as he wanted, and kept him out of the crosshairs of the law.

"Okay boys!" he shouted when he sighted the huts, and they broke into a gallop, bursting into the camp with rifles blazing. The startled Indians jumped up from the cookfires. As the riders raced their horses through the camp, sending women and children running and screaming, they trampled gardens and knocked over poles where jerky was drying.

Yancy's men dashed this way and that, shouting, "Yeehaw!" as they fired into the air, making their horses rear up and bring hooves down on ceramic ollas, smashing them, trampling the stored acorns and beans. The men drew out their lariats, twirling them over their heads as they chased down men and women, to let the looped ropes fly and catch the Indians around the shoulders, yanking them off their feet and dragging them to the ground.

They let out larger loops and sent them flying to catch the huts, toppling them, while Indians huddled inside. They dragged the huts away, demolishing them, and steered their horses to the frightened people, their violent hooves dangerously close.

Luisa and Gabriela jumped to their feet and ran to the camp, to help those who had fallen, to snatch children out of the way. One of the riders galloped after Gabriela and leaned from the saddle to knock the butt of his rifle against her head. She dropped to the ground. Luisa ran to her, falling to her knees.

And then Chief Diego appeared, standing still and silent in the middle of it all.

Drawing their horses back, to sit in saddles while the animals pranced in place, snorting and nickering, Yancy and his men leveled rifles at the unarmed Indians. "Mr. Barnstable don't like you messing around with his new ditch. He wants you to stop blocking the water. Now get to work. Pull every rock and stone out of that ditch. Now!"

When none of them moved, he leveled his firearm at Luisa and fired. The shot missed her by inches, to ricochet off a nearby boulder. The deafening ring sent Diego's men running to the ditch, to begin frantically removing the debris. Yancy and his men laughed as they watched, firing off a round every now and then to keep the Indians on their toes.

Once the water was flowing again, the white men rode off, leaving the Indians to nurse wounds and collect scattered possessions. While Gabriela sat with a wet cloth on her head, looking dazed, Luisa tended a wound on Diego's hand, where he had cut it pulling a sharp rock out of the ditch. "Husband, we need to tell the Sheriff."

"The Sheriff will not help. He did not help Johnny Pinto. He will not help us now." Diego clamped his jaw firmly.

"Then report it to the Indian agent in Banning. This is our land. That is our water. The Señor can be legally stopped." But when she saw the stubborn set of her husband's chin, the look of hatred in his deep-set eyes, Luisa said, "If you fight him, it will end in bloodshed."

But Chief Diego said nothing. He knew the Indian agent. He was not to be trusted. In a dispute, Diego knew the agent would side with the white man.

"The people of Palm Springs will help when they hear of this," Luisa said, trying another tack. "Mr. Lardner. Mr. Allenby. They have been our neighbors for years."

Diego held his head high as he said, "They will not help. No one helps the Indian. You saw how they cheered when the stolen water came down the mountain and flooded the Señor's groves. We are enemies," Diego said grimly. "The white man and Indian will always be enemies from now on and forever."

"Then we will die without water," she said bitterly. Luisa wanted to tell the white people what had happened, tell them about the stolen water. But what would that lead to? Would they stand up to the Señor? Would they help the Indians?

What if they did not?

* * *

As Cody knocked at the back door, he made sure he was under the cover of night and that no one saw him. Elizabeth answered. "Cody!" She quickly looked around, searched the darkness behind him.

"Don't worry," he said, stepping inside, closing the door. "Nigel is back at the orchard, working. I just left him there. Elizabeth, I've been fired."

"What!"

"Nigel sent one of his men for me. I had no idea why I had been summoned. And then he said my services as ranch manager were no longer needed and that I was to clear out at once."

"Oh God . . ." She clutched her stomach. "Why?"

"I don't know. Your husband never explains his actions."

"Do you think he suspects us? We've been so careful." But they both knew that all the precautions in the world couldn't dampen their yearning for each other. Without knowing it, lovers could give themselves away with a glance, a word, a moment that went on too long . . .

Cody looked down at her, saw the fear in her eyes. He wished he could do something to allay that fear, wished he could hold her, stay with her through the night. But he knew he couldn't linger another moment. It was too dangerous. "I'm going to get a room at Mrs. Henry's. It's just down the road. If you need me, telephone or send Mrs. Padilla." He paused in the small space between the garden door and the kitchen. "I love you, Elizabeth," he whispered.

"And I, you."

He pulled her into his arms to draw her hard against him and kiss her deeply and for a recklessly long moment. And then he was gone.

She waited by the door while he was in the bunkhouse, packing. She shivered with the cold and with fear. It scared her that Cody was no longer going to be just a hundred yards from the house. It had brought her great comfort to know, on late nights when her fears peaked, when Nigel came to her bed and reminded her of the deadline to give him a son—now only three months away—that Cody was nearby. But somewhere else in town? A phone call away? It was unthinkable.

Did Nigel suspect? Was that why he had let Cody go, so abruptly, with no notice? But if he had found out about them, how was he going to react?

She watched Cody ride off on his horse, the man she loved, the man whose mere presence brought intense comfort—riding off into the night to leave her suddenly alone.

CHAPTER THIRTY

WHEN THE TELEPHONE RANG, Elizabeth ran to the kitchen praying it wasn't Cody, canceling their dinner tonight. Nigel had taken the train into Mexico, to meet with a date palm broker there and wouldn't be back for a few days, and so they were going to enjoy a few stolen hours together.

But the caller was Mary Clark, her lawyer. The conversation was brief. "I received your Christmas gift and wanted to thank you for it. I will be in Indio tomorrow if you would like to get together for lunch." Elizabeth didn't know if Lois Lardner, the postmistress of Palm Springs and the town's telephone operator, listened in on conversations or paid attention to addresses on envelopes. But Elizabeth couldn't take chances. Nigel did business with Augie. A slip of Lois's tongue to her husband, and then Augie making a casual remark to Nigel . . .

And so Elizabeth and Miss Clark had devised a code. From what Mary had just said, Elizabeth knew that the lawyer had received the latest package Elizabeth had sent to her, evidence she hoped would incriminate Nigel in extramarital activities, and that she would pass it along to her private investigator. Additionally, Miss Clark had sent Elizabeth a written report and mailed it to her in care of General Delivery at the Indio post office.

Nigel had made no more mention of finding a girl willing to give him a son, but that didn't mean anything. The deadline he had placed on her a year ago was up. Perhaps he was already looking for a girl, entering into a strange contract, and Elizabeth would only know about it nine months from now.

Thanking Miss Clark and wishing her a Merry Christmas, Elizabeth hung up and returned to getting ready for the evening. Cody was joining her for dinner, and Elizabeth was so electrified with anticipation she could hardly breathe.

Cody had expressed doubt about the plan, but Elizabeth was adamant. Nigel controlled every other aspect of her life; she was not going to let him ruin Christmas Eve for her, to control her even in his absence. But they would exercise caution. Cody knew how to enter the house unseen, and Mrs. Padilla, who had prepared the dinner for them, could be trusted not to say anything.

Elizabeth no longer thought Nigel had fired Cody because of suspicions. If Nigel did suspect something going on between them, he would have revealed his hand by now. She decided the dismissal had less to do with Cody than with Nigel promoting the foreman of his security guards. From the way Cody's replacement was acting, lording it over the Mexicans, the swagger in his walk, she suspected he might have asked Nigel for the job, and it was nothing more than that. Still, she and Cody had grown extra cautious.

They had also devised a way of seeing one another on a near daily basis. Seemingly random encounters—at Lardner's, at Allenby's, even the corner church on Sundays—carefully orchestrated to appear to be the chance encounters one found in small communities.

But tonight they were to be alone for the first time, and Elizabeth was weak with anticipation.

*   *   *

There was plenty of room inside the ceremonial house now. Not like the old days, Luisa thought, when everyone stood shoulder to shoulder, jammed in for the winter fiesta honoring Mukat. No crowding today.

It frightened her. Cousins in Hot Springs had not come. Nieces and nephews in Indio had not come. Aunts and uncles in Whitewater had not come. They had other places to be. "Christmas," they said.

Bad magic had come to the valley. The Señor and his men riding their horses through the camp, firing rifles, terrorizing Luisa's people. Now there were white men with rifles patrolling the canyon, up and down, all the time, watching the new concrete stream, protecting the stolen water. Luisa's heart cried for her husband. She knew that Diego felt defeated. How could he fight such power? Diego was too proud to ask for help and therefore the Señora's evil husband had won. Did Diego not see that pride and defeat went hand in hand?

Now we will dig wells and maybe the evil Señor will steal that water, too.

* * *

As Cody tied his Western-style string necktie, making sure the two narrow panels were of equal length, he thought about his coming evening with Elizabeth.

It was an untenable situation. They had progressed beyond friendship. They were in love. It was getting harder and harder to be alone with her and not take her in his arms, make love to her. But he couldn't stay away. He couldn't leave her alone in that big house on Christmas night. But there were no crutches or barriers, like his quest for Peachy had been. Now it was just Cody McNeal and his willpower, and he was not sure which would win.

He left the boardinghouse and stepped into the freezing night. He had heard that the snow level was unusually low this year. There was a dusting of white powder in Big Horn Valley and the pools higher up in Mesquite Canyon were iced over. Turning his collar up against the cold, he looked around to see if anyone was about—but folks were inside, gathered at their fireplaces—and headed down the deserted road toward La Alma del Desierto with a broad stride.

* * *

Elizabeth put the finishing touches to her wardrobe. She had struggled all day, deciding what to wear. She had always liked dressing for Christmas, but it was going to be only the two of them as Fiona, Mrs. Padilla, and the two girls had gone home early. She had finally settled on a pink silk blouse with a long white skirt belted at the waist. Her hands shook as she pinned a brooch to her collar. She was excited at the thought of being with Cody tonight. She was also nervous.

When he was near, a heavy ache filled her chest so that she could barely breathe. She wanted him to make love to her. But Elizabeth would not become an adulteress. And she knew that Cody also lived by a personal code of honor, never touching another man's woman.

But how long would they be able to keep up the pretense? How much longer could they be strong?

She paused to inspect herself in the mirror. She wore her blond hair casually now, long and drawn back in a clip at the nape of her neck, in waves as Mrs. Decatur at the salon had taught her. Elizabeth had been in Palm Springs over two years now, and the prospect of the approaching new year—1923—excited her.

Upon the advice of newly made acquaintances at the Sierra Club and other groups concerned with environmental protection, Elizabeth had slowly, through the summer and fall, formed her own group, stemming from her Ladies Library League, which she had founded with the teachers, Miss Napier and Miss March, Mrs. Allenby, Mrs. Lardner, and Miss Kincaid, the seamstress. They called their new group Citizens for Wilderness Preservation and were proud to be part of a growing movement in America to preserve the nation's natural beauty.

They had spent the past months engaged in a letter writing campaign to bring attention to the fact of the destruction of an undisturbed valley filled with rare flora, vanishing wildlife, and precious Indian artifacts. Letters had gone out by the dozens, not only to senators and congressmen, insisting that the legality of the sale of Big Horn Valley to a privately held corporation be examined and questioned, but to newspapers nationwide, bringing to the public's attention the fact that the population of the bighorn sheep in the San Jacinto Mountains was shrinking (and that the local antelope had already been hunted to extinction), as well as the fact that certain rare plants that grew only in Big Horn Valley would be eradicated by the construction of a resort there.

Elizabeth had made it her personal task to write to universities and museums, bringing to their attention the hundreds of examples of unique rock art in Big Horn Valley and that their destruction would be tantamount to the burning of books.

The response had been encouraging. Individual citizens and groups had written back in support, asking how they could help, even donating money. The only quarter Elizabeth had not heard from was the Quinlan Corporation itself, to whom she had written numerous letters expressing her dismay over their planned destruction of a wildlife refuge and the desecration of sacred land.

However, despite public support and promises from government officials and agencies, the rescue of a wilderness, it seemed, was a slow and cumbersome process, involving many opinions and personalities, not to mention a clunky government bureaucracy whose mentality was "we'll get to it eventually."

But now Quinlan Resorts had announced the groundbreaking, which would take place in the spring, and Elizabeth's group, boasting now a membership of over fifty, had only a short time in which to stop them.

Strangely, there was no support from Luisa's people. Chief Diego was remaining adamantly silent on the issue of Big Horn Valley and its petroglyphs, and Elizabeth suspected it was because she was heading the campaign, and she was the wife of his most hated enemy.

As for Nigel, he too remained strangely non-vocal on Elizabeth's new project. She had tried to keep it a secret but with the local citizens getting involved, asking tourists and visitors to sign petitions and to boycott Quinlan hotels to show their disapproval of the planned resort, Nigel was bound to find out.

Elizabeth had expected him to sabotage the whole thing, possibly by openly voicing his support of the new construction, and yet he had surprised her by saying nothing. She wondered if he saw her mission as doomed to failure and therefore not worthy of one minute of his attention. Elizabeth didn't know if she should be relieved or nervous about Nigel's attitude. Could it be that he was, in fact, planning something that was going to end up in disaster for her wilderness group?

He had purchased more land in the Coachella Valley and had ordered mature almond trees to be shipped in by train. On top of that, Elizabeth had been startled to see Nigel mentioned in the *Los Angeles Times* as a "local investor who was throwing his hat into the ring of sound motion pictures." The article carried a photo of Nigel signing a contract, along with other smiling men. In the picture, Elizabeth recognized Jack Lamont and his wife, Zora, who was not smiling. The story had gone on to explain that, although reliable sound technology was still a few years away, there was no doubt that sound was going to revolutionize motion pictures and change the movie-going public's experience in ways not yet imagined.

Elizabeth could see why, compared to his financial adventures and involvement with modern progress, Nigel might find her wilderness movement as quaint, possibly even trivial, and therefore beneath his notice. She prayed it was so, and that it was not just naïve wishful thinking on her part.

She checked the time. Cody should be arriving any minute. It would just be the two of them tonight. The ranch hands were celebrating in the bunkhouse, playing guitars and singing Mexican songs. The foreman, Yancy, and his white security guards had saddled up earlier and ridden out of town, most likely heading to the new roadhouse that had opened up ten miles down the road, offering billiards and cards, a dance floor with musicians, and no doubt female companionship.

When she heard the firm knock at the back door, her heart jumped. Cody!

He wore a heavy sheepskin jacket with the fleece turned inward. The sight of him made her heart rise to her throat. "Merry Christmas, Elizabeth," he said, handing her a thin, flat gift wrapped in green tissue paper and tied with red yarn. She closed the door and took his coat. He followed her through to the living room. She had placed a silver teapot and cups on the coffee table in front of the fire, and as she poured now, she wondered if she should put a record on the Victrola. Classical or jazz? Something romantic, or as far from romantic as possible?

She watched Cody's profile as he added wood to the fire in the fireplace—fragrant mesquite. The glow illuminated his rugged features and the shining highlights of his wavy black hair. How many nights had he sat at alone at a campfire under the stars, exploring his innermost thoughts, looking just like that?

When he stood up and turned to face her, her heart leapt. Now, she said silently. Take me now . . .

He joined her on the sofa and looked at her in wordless wonder. He couldn't escape the hard truth that he was in another man's house, with overwhelming physical desire for another man's woman.

But he treats her cruelly and she is leaving him and Barnstable doesn't love her. But I love her and cherish her and want to lay all the world's riches at her feet.

So how did the rules apply to all of that? Nothing was ever black and white. There were too many shady areas, undefined and out of focus.

You make your own rules, he thought, as he tried to think of something to say, now that they were alone and sitting close together in front of a blazing fire while cold winter wind blew across the desert.

Their eyes met. Neither could speak. They both felt the tension of the moment. "Open your present," he whispered.

Gently pulling away paper and yarn, Elizabeth's eyes widened. The photograph was ten inches by eight, and set into a matted frame seventeen inches by fourteen. "Oh, my," she whispered. "It's beautiful."

It had been a year since Cody had taken her up to Big Horn Valley—his Christmas gift to her—and she had seen the elegant pictograph. Since then, the valley had become the focus of her life. And now here it was, in all its perfection, Big Horn Valley—the towering pines against a clear sky, the meadow looking like snow as it lay in the bright sunlight, and in the center, the granite wall displaying the pictograph of a bighorn sheep carved into the rock more years ago than anyone could remember, and by artists whose names were long forgotten. "Cody, how did you do this?"

"I went into Riverside and found a professional photographer willing to take wilderness pictures. We drove to Big Horn Valley and spent the whole day at it."

"But . . . this must have been expensive!"

He smiled. "My book is starting to earn royalties, and I've sold a few more stories."

She gave him a long look, then she glanced at his Stetson where he had placed it on a chair. "Where's the rattlesnake?"

"I sold it." He shrugged. "It was just a hatband."

She brought her eyes back to the framed photograph. It was so . . . perfect. The play of shadow and light, the sharpness of form, the clarity of details. If it hadn't been in black and white, Elizabeth could almost believe she was standing in Big Horn Valley. "It's to help you remember," Cody said. "To keep your passion stoked."

"As it so happens," she said, rising. "I had remembrance in mind, too." From the sideboard in the dining room she brought out a small box tied with silver ribbon. "Merry Christmas, Cody."

He opened the box. "A bolo tie!"

"I had it custom made. I thought it would look good on you."

The bolo was comprised of a black leather cord, the two ends fixed with gold tips. The slide was a purple turquoise cabochon set in gold. "Custom made?" he said. "By someone here in Palm Springs?"

"I found a custom jeweler in Los Angeles."

"That's a hundred miles! Just for a bolo tie?"

Seeing his reaction, his joy, the marveling look in his eye, made her heart soar. "It's no ordinary bolo. I went first to jewelers in Riverside, but they didn't have the capacity to fill my request. They suggested I try the jewelry district in downtown Los Angeles, where I might find someone with wider connections."

"Wider connections? I don't follow."

"The purple turquoise is local, from the Mojave. But the gold that it is set into is from Montana."

He brought the bolo out of the box, to turn it this way and that in the light, momentarily overcome. "Montana . . . how on earth did you manage that?"

"The jeweler in Los Angeles wrote to a company in Helena called Western Gold Mining. Correspondence went back and forth, I told the jeweler what I wanted, he purchased gold from Western Gold and made that slide for me. The back is engraved."

He turned it over. *To CM from EB, with love.*

"Let's see how it looks." They rose from the sofa, and Elizabeth stood before him and unknotted the string necktie, sliding it out from under his shirt collar. She stood so close he could detect the fragrance of her bath soap. He saw dark flecks in her blue eyes. Elizabeth brought the black cord over his head, tucked it up under the collar, then pushed the slide up to his throat and secured it there. She stepped back. "Very handsome," she declared.

A large antique mirror in an ornate gilt frame hung on the wall in the front entry. Cody went to it and stared at his reflection in speechless wonder. "It comes with a certified letter of authenticity," Elizabeth said with a smile. "You can be assured that wherever you go, you will always have a piece of home with you."

He saw her in the mirror, standing behind him. You are my home, he thought.

Their eyes met in the glass. Elizabeth's moist lips parted. Cody turned and, pulling her into his arms, kissed her hard on the mouth.

She melted against him, her arms around his neck, her body molding to his. The kiss held for a long moment and then, with a soft moan, he drew back and, cupping her face with his hands, said, "As God is my witness, I have never loved a woman as I love you."

She struggled for breath. "And I love you, Cody."

They held on to each other as wind rattled the windows, bringing with it distant strains of music and laughter from the Lardners' place, where a Christmas party was under way.

Elizabeth didn't want to leave Cody's embrace. She wanted to stay exactly as they were for eternity.

Cody stepped away long enough to remove the sheepskin coat and let it drop to the floor. Then he had Elizabeth in his arms again, kissing her, drawing her so tightly to him that she was breathless.

He bent and, sliding his arm under her thighs, swept her up and carried her back down into the sunken living room, kissing her the whole time.

Gently laying her on the shaggy bearskin rug in front of the fire, he held himself up on one elbow and looked down at her. He stroked her hair, traced the lines of her face, ran a fingertip over her lips. Then he kissed her again, softly this time, slowly. Their tongues met and Elizabeth arched her back to press against him.

This is right, this is not wrong, he thought. We belong together, Elizabeth and I.

He ran his hand up her smooth thigh. She felt the rough skin, reminding her of his cowboy days. Cody kissed her neck, her throat. He unclasped the brooch at her throat, undid the buttons of her blouse, sliding the sleeves down her arms. Elizabeth drove her hands under his shirt, pulling it up to rake her nails over tight sinew.

"Hurry," she whispered, but he moved slowly.

Their clothes came off and they felt the hot flames on their bare skin. Outside on the desert, the temperature fell and the stars shone like ice. But Cody and Elizabeth were aware only of heat and each other.

The feel of Cody came as a surprise. She had made love with only one other man in her life—Nigel, who had soft skin and narrow bones. Cody was built of solid, compact muscles, his skin rough and scarred in places. Her Montana cowboy.

Nigel had been raised in a pampered, gentrified world, but Cody had been hammered out on the forge of perilous cattle drives and harsh plains winters. His body told his history. The puckered scar on his thigh was the result of an attack by a wild bull. The pebbled skin on his upper arm where he had scorched himself rescuing a family from a burning farmhouse. The extra bony knob on his right wrist was testimony to the day he had been breaking in a wild mustang and got thrown, fracturing his wrist.

It excited her, drove her out of her mind, to be in the arms of this rugged drifter, man of a vanishing West who now drove himself deep into her and touched a place Elizabeth hadn't known existed. The living room spun. The flames in the fireplace flared. She thought she would explode with pleasure.

And then she did. The orgasm took her by surprise. She cried out as she rode the wave of pleasure to its end, when she exhaled with deep joy. She had not known that women climaxed, had not known that women could enjoy sex as much as men did . . .

Cody thought he'd never felt anything so soft as her silky hair, nor seen a color so suggestive of angels. Her skin was like cream. He tasted every part of her. Explored her mysteries. When he possessed her, and she trembled and moaned, he knew that he had come as close to pure bliss as any man could.

He had never loved so deeply as he did in that moment, and he knew that he would never love again as he loved Elizabeth.

PART FOUR
1923

CHAPTER THIRTY-ONE

"A ROAD IS UNDER construction on the other side of the mountain," Elizabeth was saying, "and it will bring thousands of year-round tourists to Big Horn Valley."

Her group, Citizens for Wilderness Preservation, was crowded into her living room, sitting on every available space, some even sitting on the tiled floor. They had initially met at the schoolhouse, but as their numbers had grown, Elizabeth had looked around for more accommodating space. La Alma was the logical choice, and so she had waited until what she hoped was one of Nigel's amenable moods and had asked if they could hold meetings here. He had said yes. Sometimes, when things were going particularly well for Nigel, he could be generous.

But of course she still questioned his motives, she was still always on her guard. Perhaps, because men had joined the club, he wanted to keep an eye on things, as he occasionally came through the house during one of their meetings. Or perhaps it was so he could have one more thing to hold over her and use to control her—"Do this or I will forbid your group to meet here again." But another, chilling motive occurred to her and struck terror in her. What if he had seen one of Mary Clark's letters? Fiona had, when Elizabeth had carelessly left the key in the desk drawer. She had been religious about keeping the key since, but what if there was one day before that, maybe even the same day Fiona found the letter from Mary Clark, and Nigel saw it and knew she was planning on filing for divorce? What if he was putting on an act so that when time came for taking depositions from people who knew the Barnstables, no one could say a bad word against him? And Elizabeth would never win her freedom.

Was that possible? Could Nigel have such knowledge and not react with violence? Did he possess that much restraint?

Nigel had also said nothing about finding a girl to father his son. The deadline had come and gone. Was he still going to carry out his threat? Was he already carrying it out?

Mary Clark's investigator was turning in fewer reports on Nigel's social activities, as he seemed to be meeting more with businessmen and less with the Hollywood people. In fact, Nigel hadn't been seen with Jack and Zora in a while, and Elizabeth now wondered if it, too, was part of his carefully constructed "perfect husband" act. She never knew what to expect of Nigel, how to gauge his mood, how to guess what he was thinking.

Besides the members of the Ladies Library League, the Allenbys were there for the meeting, Doc Perry and Fiona, the Bledsoes, the Thornhills, and the Reeds, local families. Mrs. Decatur from the hair salon. Joe Waldinger, who recently opened a hardware store in town. Reverend Scott, who recently married. Andie Kuhn, who owned the local poultry farm. And Fred Schipley, a veterinarian who had moved to Palm Springs three months prior.

Cody was not a member. While he would have liked to officially add his name to the roster, which was public record, and while Elizabeth thought that, with *Goldrush* being on the best-seller list, his name would lend an air of celebrity and weight to the group, they had decided that the less they were seen together, the better. However, Cody had joined the letter writing campaign, reminding people that just as America's Western history should not be forgotten, neither should land in the West be allowed to vanish beneath concrete.

Elizabeth's group was starting to have an impact.

She had organized a motor trip up to Big Horn Valley, where she had shown them the pictographs. They had seen graffiti, trash, evidence of partying. Worse, the preliminary groundwork for construction had already begun. Elizabeth and the club's members had gone about and plucked up all the surveyor's sticks, erasing the chalk lines where trenching was going in. They had sent letters to the Quinlan Hotels and Resorts Corporation asking them to withdraw from Big Horn Valley. They had received no response. So they went up weekly to sabotage the project until Elizabeth had finally gotten a letter from the company insisting she and her group cease their illegal trespass on private property. Elizabeth had even retained an attorney in San Diego, an advocate for citizens' rights, referred to her by Mary Clark. Elizabeth and her group were challenging the validity of the land sale to Quinlan Resorts Inc.

The living room windows were open to admit spring sunshine and breezes. The day was cool but in a month the desert would start to turn hot. Some of these people, Elizabeth knew, would leave the valley for a cooler summer residence. She would not. Despite searing temperatures during the day, the nights were balmy and sometimes even chilly. Elizabeth would stay and fight the Quinlan Corporation, who had announced the commencement of trenching in four weeks. She was determined to see that it did not happen.

But, despite her determination, her thoughts drifted.

Did it show, she wondered? Could her friends tell that she and Cody had made love, were officially lovers even though it had only been the one time at Christmas? Did she still glow three months later? It was agony to be away from him. Just as painful to be near him. She was amazed at how dramatically the physical world had changed. Overnight, God had repainted the flowers, giving them deeper hues, sharper outlines, greener greens and redder reds. Even the homely ocotillo cactus, for much of the year just an ugly arrangement of large spiny dead sticks, became the desert's crowning glory, making Elizabeth think enormous pots of these would have graced Solomon's majestic temple. Everything became better, larger, taller, hotter, colder. Her nerves had been tuned up. Songs were prettier, noises spoke to her, even margarine tasted good. Life vibrated all around her as she wanted to shout out that she was in love with the most amazing man in the world.

Elizabeth was proud of Cody. His autobiographical novel, The *Last Gold Rush*, had come out to great critical acclaim. He had sold more short stories, and the *Sunday National Reader* was asking for yet more. He was driven to set the Old West down on paper. When he wasn't in his room at the boardinghouse, putting pen to paper, he could be seen around town, at an outdoor table, or in the shade of a mesquite tree, spinning his tales of gunslingers, ranchers, roughnecks, gamblers, homesteaders, preachers, and saloon girls.

Elizabeth loved watching him when he didn't know he was being watched. Rolling a cigarette—the paper in one hand, the small pouch of tobacco in the other, tapping out a portion, pulling the purse string with his strong white teeth, rolling the smoke, licking the edge of the paper, sealing it, putting it in his mouth, striking the match on the sole of his cowboy boot. The simple, elegant action of a man in no hurry to keep up with the world's hectic pace. A man who kept his own hours, lived by a basic, honest set of rules, avoided conflict but stood his ground when the time was right.

Watching him climb up onto a saddle swept her away to other places, other times where she pictured longhorn cattle and prairie nights beneath a million stars. And on hot days, when he wore his sleeves rolled up on his muscular arms and the top buttons of his shirt undone to reveal sweat-glistened chest hairs—when he removed his Stetson to wipe the inside with a handkerchief, it made her throat go so tight she could not, for that burning, magical moment, breathe.

They had not dared make love since their one time. The risk was too great. But the longing was even greater. Sometimes late at night, the silence of the desert pressed down on her as she lay alone in her bed, wondering if she were the only person on earth, her sexual longing would grow intense, unbearable. She would run her hands down her body and imagine they were Cody's hands. She would close her eyes and moan with sweet, aching desire. He was not far away, just down the road in Mrs. Henry's boardinghouse, alone in his own bed. She would wonder if he was thinking of her in that same moment, if somehow their mutual yearning for each other drifted out into the night to join somewhere among the palms and dunes in a spectral embrace.

Do Cody and I make love while we sleep? Do our souls, unconstrained as we of the flesh must be, meet secretly in the desert canyons to satisfy passions that must remain suppressed in the corporeal world?

Elizabeth sighed. It was a nice thought. But even if it were true, it didn't sate her craving for him. A craving that grew with each passing day.

"Upon the advice of our attorney," Elizabeth said now, bringing herself back to the business at hand, "we have filed for a preliminary injunction challenging the legality of the sale of public land to private interests, a sale which was conducted without public disclosure, discussion, or vote. The motion will seek to immediately halt the commencement of construction in Big Horn Valley."

Mrs. Lardner raised her hand. "What if Quinlan Corporation wins?"

"We will simply escalate our efforts, both in the courts and on the disputed site. But we have to get our voices heard. We have to gain additional public and institutional support. Which is why I called this meeting."

The dining table was covered with papers, envelopes, pages of stamps, and other supplies. Elizabeth handed out sheets to everyone. "I applaud all of you for what you have done so far, writing letters, spreading the word. I have obtained additional addresses. The US Forestry Service. The Department of the Interior. The Bureau of Indian Affairs. The Society for the Prevention of Cruelty to Animals. State senators and congressmen, as well as the office of the governor. I would like all of you to write one letter to each address, copying the letter that I have written on the back of this sheet. I would then ask you to include a flyer with each."

Besides weekly trips to sabotage the surveyors' work in Big Horn Valley, Elizabeth's group collected signatures on petitions and sent them to the state capitol in Sacramento, as well as to government representatives in Washington, DC. And with the number of visitors to the Coachella Valley increasing daily, they took turns going to the train station to hand out flyers to disembarking passengers.

Elizabeth could not get the Indians to participate in the protest. Nigel was Chief Diego's enemy. Why would he lift even a finger in support of his enemy's wife?

The meeting concluded with Elizabeth informing everyone of the court date for the preliminary hearing at the county courthouse in Riverside to request an injunction to stop work. "I urge as many of you to attend as you are able. I ask that those of you with automobiles give rides to those without transportation."

Everyone filed out, each with his or her assigned task, and Elizabeth smiled at the last man to leave. "Thank you for coming, Mr. Welner."

They shook hands. "Thank you for inviting me. Your talk was most enlightening, Mrs. Barnstable. I am impressed with your club's goals and efforts."

He was the manager of the Mirage Hotel, the valley's newest resort. It boasted seventy rooms, a restaurant, and a nine-hole golf course. The Quinlan Corporation was planning something bigger, much fancier and more exclusive. Quinlan's resort in Big Horn Valley would cut into the Mirage's profits.

"I shall be sure to pass this along to the managers of the other hotels and guest ranches, Mrs. Barnstable. We all have an interest in preserving San Jacinto's wilderness."

She handed him a stack of flyers, "Could I prevail upon you to put these out at your check-in desk?"

Elizabeth and her group had come upon the carcass of a bighorn ram that had been shot by a hunter and left to die. Under the photo Elizabeth had composed a caption: "The population of the bighorn sheep is shrinking. If we don't protect our wildlife, there will soon be none left. Say no to the Quinlan Resort Project in Big Horn Valley."

As Elizabeth cleared the dining room table, collecting all the material, Luisa came into the room. "Pardon, Señora. There are some men wishing to see you."

Elizabeth went to the front door to find three men in business suits standing there. "Mrs. Barnstable? I'm John Lydon of Lydon and Gardell, attorneys at law. This is my associate, Mr. Gardell. We are here to represent the interests of our client, Mr. Jay Thomas Quinlan." And he pointed to the third man.

*   *   *

"Have you heard?" Augie Lardner said, as he handed Cody his mail. "Someone bought the parcel between the schoolhouse and the church. Word is, there's going to be a motor court built there."

"Ought to be good for business," Cody murmured as he sifted through his mail. The "motel" was the latest innovation in hospitality and inn keeping—a curious phenomenon springing from the auto industry and America's new love for the road. A hotel where the guests drive up and park outside their own door.

"Some fellas from the highway department have been here," Augie said. Nothing went on in Palm Springs that slipped past the observant and nosy ape-faced Augie Lardner. "They say the road from Banning to Palm Springs is going to be paved with asphalt. They're going to call it Palm Canyon Drive, and you mark my words, that's going to attract more shops and business."

The community was mushrooming. Wealthy Hollywood movie people, following the Lamonts' example and attracted by the hot, dry, sunny weather and seclusion, were starting to build private homes and estates. Palm Springs was being touted as a "playground" for the rich and adventurous.

And tourists were finally discovering the desert. Families on car trips stopped in Palm Springs on their way from somewhere to somewhere.

The "new nomads," motoring in twenty million cars on roads built for horses and wagons, demanding more pavement, more speed.

Cody added a newspaper to his purchases. The front page was still carrying the story about the discovery, back in November, of a tomb in Egypt, said to be untouched for over three thousand years. America was in the grip of Egyptian fever. Every day, newspapers across the country printed pictures of the latest treasures being brought out of King Tut's tomb. He knew Elizabeth was following the story. The newspaper was for her.

Thanking Mr. Lardner, Cody stepped out into the spring sunshine and thought again of Elizabeth—she occupied his every waking moment.

He couldn't pinpoint the exact moment he had fallen in love with her. It had been a succession of moments, small, sharp instants that weren't recognized for what they were at the time. The way she tucked her lace handkerchief in the sleeve of her sweater. The way she laughed. The directness of her gaze. The flicker of her tongue on her lips when a word eluded her. Ordinary bits and pieces, but when gathered to form a whole, created a woman like none he had ever known.

As he neared Mrs. Henry's boardinghouse, he saw an unfamiliar motor car in the driveway of La Alma and three strangers in business suits stood at Elizabeth's front door. Without hesitating—he had seen Barnstable's horse tethered outside the shack in the orchard that served as Nigel's office—Cody picked up his pace, hurried around back, and let himself in through the kitchen door.

"Who are those men, Luisa?" he asked.

She paused with a rolling pin in her hand, and shrugged. "I do not know, Señor, but I think the Señora is worried."

*   *   *

Elizabeth eyed the third man in the group. Quinlan was not at all how she had imagined him from his letters, politely requesting that she cease trespassing on his land and to stop publicly maligning his corporation. She had pictured a pale office-type with eyeglasses and smooth skin. But Jay Thomas Quinlan had the husky build and ruddy complexion of an outdoorsman. She would have thought that he would be on her side, protecting the wilderness, instead of destroying it.

"May we come in?" Lydon said.

Elizabeth eyed the briefcases, the expensive suits, the slicked-back hair and smiles that looked as if they'd been practiced in a mirror. She thought of the flyers and papers and picket signs and lists of names spread out on the dining room table—her entire strategy for fighting Quinlan—and she said, "We are meeting next week in court. We can talk then. And I want my lawyer present."

"We haven't come about your injunction. We have come to serve you papers." Lydon reached into his briefcase and produced a document. "This is a court order barring you or any member of your group to set foot on Quinlan land, and that includes Big Horn Valley. If you do, you will be arrested and put in jail."

She scanned the document—injunction power, trespass to land, criminal and civil penalties—then said, "Gentlemen, not only do I plan to set foot in Big Horn Valley whenever I wish, I am going to see to it that every citizen will be free to do so, as long as the historical relics and the animals are protected."

Quinlan spoke up, offering a smug smile as he tugged on his French cuffs with diamond cufflinks. With the look of the lumberjack about him, the fancy clothes seemed ill suited. "I must say, little lady, you come as a mighty big surprise. I pictured you older, matronly. A woman whose kids have moved out and now needs something to fill her time. You know, rescuing cats and the like. I sure wasn't expecting a looker like you."

"I believe our business here is done," Elizabeth said crisply and stepped back to close the door.

"Look, little lady," Quinlan said, placing a paw-like hand on the door jamb, "I'm sure you mean well. You and your housewife friends taking up little causes here and there. But you don't know what you're doing. And you are certainly in way over your head. You're dealing with the big boys here. I would be happy to explain it to your husband, if he's around." Quinlan looked pointedly at Cody, who had come to quietly stand behind her.

"My husband is not at home. You can speak to me."

Quinlan lifted his eyebrows and, giving Cody another pointed look, said, "Okay, Elizabeth, it's like this—"

"*Mister* Quinlan, you may address me as Mrs. Barnstable or Lady Elizabeth."

He shared a chuckle with his companions. "This is how it's going to go, little lady. I own that land and you have been trespassing. It's that simple. Next time, I have you arrested. Is that simple enough for you?"

"As a citizen I have the right to object to the sale of public lands to private interests. And I intend to continue to exercise that right."

The three exchanged the withering look of men forced to suffer fools, then Mr. Gardell, the tallest of them with a bowler hat on his head, said, "We are also here to give you fair warning that you are coming very close to slandering our client in press interviews and letters to newspapers. If need be, we can get another court order, one that forbids you to make any mention of Mr. Quinlan or his corporation in any public forum. We are prepared to take this as far as necessary, Mrs. Barnstable. We have the resources and the manpower."

Quinlan interjected with, "We certainly don't need housewives stuffing envelopes." The three shared a laugh, then they said a cordial "Good day," and left the front steps.

As they climbed back into their convertible and drove off, Elizabeth closed the door and heaved a heavy sigh. The visitors had unnerved her, with their unexpected arrival and their important papers and their threats. The lawyers looked expensive and high-powered, and Elizabeth knew only too well the vast resources at Quinlan's disposal. She thought of her group's attorney, a citizens' rights advocate who was not wealthy and who was known for taking on underdog causes, and a woman lawyer at that! Was she going to be a match for those men when it came to trial?

"They saw you," she said to Cody, with worry in her eyes. "I told them my husband wasn't home and they looked at you and exchanged a glance. What do you think it means?"

"It means," he said as casually as he could although he felt the same wariness, "that I am a family friend. A cousin. A handyman who dropped by to fix a faucet. It's none of their concern who you have in your home." But as he said it, hoping to reassure her, Cody went to the front window to look out and saw, in alarm, that Quinlan's car had turned off the main road and was following the track toward Nigel's office in the orchard.

*   *   *

"Pull off here, Tom," Quinlan said as he rode in the passenger seat, with Tom Gardell driving and John Lydon in the back seat. He had glimpsed the Stullwood Plantation sign on their way into town, an arching wooden sign supported on two posts that now gave him an idea. He knew enough about Elizabeth Barnstable to know she was married to a date grower here in Palm Springs, and since she had said her husband wasn't home, it would seem that the man would most likely be found at work.

Inside the small wooden building, with the two windows and door open to admit sunlight and spring breezes, Nigel was going over the latest agriculture reports from the federal government. And there was a new conundrum that had been giving him grief for the past few weeks—the matter of how to get an edge on the date market.

As self-confident as he had been at the start, that his plantation was going to be a smashing success, that same confidence was now being put to the test. It was becoming obvious that sheer numbers of acres and trees wasn't going to lift him to the dominant position in the date market as he had expected. While Gonzalez had protested that Nigel's underbidding with the distributors was going to bankrupt the other growers, they all still seemed to be doing well. The past Christmas season had been a bonanza for them all. And it rankled Nigel to no end.

"Advertise," Jack Lamont had said when Nigel had voiced the problem. "Those growers have been in this valley for years. Their names and reputations are well established. You're the new kid in town. You have to make your mark, get folks to notice you. I can give you the name of a good ad man. It's the only way you'll gain the advantage."

"You need an edge over the other growers in the valley," the advertising agent had said when Nigel had driven into Los Angeles to meet with him. "I suggest you first of all set up a fruit stand on the road. That highway is going to be paved in the next couple of years, connecting Los Angeles to Phoenix, Arizona. Build a proper store. Hire someone to write a cookbook filled with date recipes."

"Date recipes?" Nigel had said, finding the man's suggestions common and unappealing. Nigel Barnstable, ninth Baron Stullwood, a shopkeeper!

"Sure, why not? The other growers offer milkshakes made from dates for motorists who stop. Stullwood Plantations needs to offer more."

"What kind of recipes?" Nigel had asked, not liking this new territory. He had come to Palm Springs to create a paradise, not write a cookbook.

"How the hell should I know? Make them up. Desserts, of course. But get creative. People like that. Make the book flashy, with a little history of the date, the different kinds. Folks like to read things that make them look smart to their friends. Hey, we're in the Southwest, so why not tamales and tacos filled with dates? No one has to actually eat the stuff. It's just one thing more that Stullwood offers that other farms don't. Get a camel, tie it up outside your store, and give kiddies free rides. You need to turn your place into an attraction. That's the key word, *attraction*, something that attracts customers."

Nigel wasn't sure he liked the idea. It didn't sound dignified or suited to his personal vision of Stullwood Plantation.

"Now, for ad copy that's going into nationwide magazines, you need something more than what the other growers have. They all claim to have the sweetest, most luscious dates in the world. Hell, all dates are sweet and luscious, so what else is new? Stullwood has to make a grander claim, something new and innovative."

This was what Nigel had been chewing on for the past few days without any brilliant ideas coming to him.

"Hello there!"

The sunlight streaming through the open doorway was suddenly blocked. Nigel looked up to see a stranger standing there, grinning. "Hello!" the man said again. "Would you happen to be Nigel Barnstable?"

"I am," Nigel said warily. The only visitors he ever received in his orchard office were his workers. No one in a suit and tie and shiny shoes had ever come in here before.

The stranger offered his hand. "Jay Thomas Quinlan, at your service."

Nigel stared at the hand.

"I was just up the mountain," Quinlan said, withdrawing his hand, and wondering if the husband was going to be as big a pain in the ass as the wife. "Inspecting my property up there. Your wife and her group have been mighty busy giving me grief. I have to get the surveyors up there again. If this keeps up, I'll have to fence it off and put armed security guards in place. A man has a right to protect what's his, I reckon."

He looked around the rustic shack. "Nice little operation you have going here. Don't care for dates myself." He made a face. "Too sweet."

Quinlan suspected Barnstable had no involvement with his wife's protest group, as his name was not on the membership roster. Nor had Quinlan's lawyers found Barnstable's signature on any of the petitions his wife had filed with the court and various government agencies. "I'm sure she means well, but the little lady is in way over her head."

Nigel stared at the visitor, a man in an expensive suit, late thirties, smiling a little too easily. Nigel said, archly: "The 'little lady' you are referring to is my wife, Lady Barnstable, Baroness Stullwood, and you will accord her that respect."

Nigel conducted a rapid and negative assessment of his visitor. When two gentlemen meet to discuss business, there was protocol to follow. It must first be determined on whose territory they were to meet, who had called the meeting, the nature of the topic to be discussed, the outcome each party hoped for, concessions each was willing to make—a whole list of unwritten, unspoken rules for the gentlemen businessmen.

But Quinlan had elected to flout every single one.

It automatically put Nigel in a bad temper and on his guard, with an instant determination not to be open-minded and certainly in no mood to make concessions.

Quinlan's smile remained fixed as he said, "You're a businessman, Mr. Barnstable. You know how a company relies on its good name. Your wife and her little group are besmirching Quinlan Hotels in letters to newspapers."

Once in a while, Nigel wished there were men he could admire for a sustained time. For a short while he had admired Jack Lamont. The ingenuity and creativeness of filmmakers had impressed him. But only for a short while. It was because it had been new and different, and Nigel had thought: Bravo. But once he had learned from them, discovered their tricks, and applied their business model to his own, they were no longer new and different, and he had no more use for them.

Because of Elizabeth's group's involvement with Quinlan Hotels, Nigel had looked into the corporation and knew they owned a chain of hotels that catered to an upscale clientele and profited in the millions. If this was a man Nigel could admire and learn from, there was no chance of it now. Not only was his manner and approach inappropriate, Quinlan clearly had a problem with Elizabeth, a woman, and he had come to the husband for a solution!

Maybe what annoyed Nigel about him most was that he had walked in assuming that Nigel would side with him against his own wife. Nigel didn't like men who made assumptions about him, as it called for judging him before they knew anything about him. You don't know anything about me, he thought now. Yet you walk in here and assume I will not only grasp your attitude toward my wife and her plan to impede the construction of your resort, but that I will side with you on the matter.

Making assumptions was the mark of either a lazy man or a hopelessly unimaginative man—traits that tried Nigel's patience. To keep an eye on Elizabeth, to keep track of what her group was getting into, Nigel had discovered that the local conflict was part of a greater, and increasing, movement in America—the popular trend to set aside wilderness areas and protect them for public enjoyment. In a way, he realized now for the first time, that he and Elizabeth were not working at cross-purposes. While Nigel was creating a new wilderness by planting trees where none had been before, Elizabeth wanted to protect trees that were already there.

It was a curious revelation and one that might deserve further pondering. At the moment, however, all Nigel was thinking about was that in the news articles he had read, he had learned that Quinlan had inherited his hotel chain, founded forty years ago by his grandfather. Quinlan was not a self-made man, making him yet smaller in Nigel's eyes. He also didn't like Quinlan's liberal use of the word "little."

"Your wife needs to learn the meanings of libel and slander and the significance of repercussions," Quinlan said, the fixed smile turning hard, threatening.

A wasp flew into the shed, creating a racket as it flew about looking for a way out. Nigel stared at Quinlan. The man was actually standing there insulting his wife. What is there in my stance or manner, Nigel wanted to ask, what shows on my face or what is it that I have said that has led you to believe you can come in here and insult my wife?

This was a new thought for Nigel Barnstable. Whenever he thought of Elizabeth and other men, it was always from the vantage point of the jealous husband. Nigel couldn't abide other men even looking at Elizabeth, let alone talking to her, passing the time of day with her, asking her for directions to Indio. He knew she was beautiful, and he knew men were bound to look at her. But he didn't have to like it.

Quinlan, on the other hand, was coming from a place that Nigel had not even considered: a man who was insulting her!

Nigel felt his hackles rise. Criticism of Elizabeth was criticism of Nigel Barnstable! Did the idiot think I would marry a stupid woman? Nigel suddenly took Quinlan's words personally. His defenses rose, not in Elizabeth's honor, but for his own, and he suddenly wanted to teach the arrogant rogue a lesson.

Nigel's tone was icily cool as he said, "You dare to come on to my property and insult my wife, and think you can get away with it?"

Quinlan's manner remained nonchalant, showing that he could not be intimidated. "She trespassed on my property and she insults me in the press. I say turnaround is fair play."

Nigel mulled this over for a long, dangerous moment, curling his fingers into fists, then he stepped close to Quinlan, menacingly, their faces inches apart. "Do you really want to do this—here, now? Because we can."

The air was suddenly charged as the two men, equally matched, looked at each other, all pretense of civility gone. Quinlan realized he'd made an error in judgment, something he wasn't used to doing. Progressive groups run by women, he had found, often involved husbands who were happy to be excluded. He had assumed Barnstable would be one such husband, and as a man of commerce, inclined to listen to reason and maybe rein the wife in a little. Instead, he was a young, foreign upstart, in Quinlan the Texan's eyes.

Quinlan sized up the situation and arrived at the conclusion that it wasn't Barnstable who wore the pants in his family. Quinlan came close to voicing this but stopped himself. As it turned out, Jay Thomas Quinlan did know the rules regarding gentlemen and business dealings. And a prime rule was you didn't walk into a man's office and cast his manhood into question. Quinlan thought of the Mexican workers outside, a small army of them, and he'd seen a couple of white men with rifles.

He stepped back, popped the smile back into place, and said, "I just dropped by for a neighborly visit, considering we are going to be neighbors very soon. You have a good day now, y'hear?"

After Quinlan left, Nigel stood rooted in the little wooden shed from where he ran his empire. He wondered what had just happened. A stranger had materialized, and they had nearly come to fisticuffs. Nigel needed to think. He sensed that his mind was trying to tell him something . . .

Nigel hadn't given Elizabeth's project much consideration, as he didn't think she had a chance at succeeding. It was just something to occupy her until she got pregnant, or until he procured a son. Once she had a child to take care of, her interest in the valley would wane. But Quinlan's unexpected visit, with a show of being totally unthreatened by Elizabeth, made Nigel think now that Quinlan felt very threatened indeed. Nigel gave this some thought. Apparently Elizabeth was putting up a bigger fight than he had thought, raising the issue to the level of getting attention from some powerful arenas. Quinlan was certainly worried.

Nigel had no doubt that the Texan's big corporation would steamroller activists like the simple folk of Palm Springs. So what was Quinlan worried about?

And then something the Texan said, a simple phrase, nothing out of the ordinary, sounded in Nigel's head: "*You know how a company relies on its good name.*" That was what Quinlan was worried about. His company's reputation.

And suddenly the most astonishing notion entered Nigel's mind, so swiftly and so completely formed that it momentarily took him aback. For weeks he had been wrestling with a dilemma peculiar to his position as a new date grower in the valley: how to rise to the top of the market. "You need to advertise," the ad agent had pressed, while Quinlan had said, "A company relies on its good name."

Nigel seized the ledger that was lying open on his desk, grabbed the pen in the inkwell, and hastily wrote in an excited hand: "At Stullwood Plantation, we not only grow the best dates, but we are a family-oriented farm that cares about our community. Stullwood Plantation established the first traveling library in the Coachella Valley and now Stullwood Plantation is fighting to preserve our local mountain wilderness by campaigning to keep big developers out. Join us in our fight to stop big building in our pristine wilderness. Come to the Stullwood Plantation in Palm Springs, visit with us, and let us tell you what you can do to join in this noble effort to save the environment and wildlife. And while you are here, enjoy free samples of our delicious fruit."

When he was done, feeling elated, weightless, and as if he had run ten miles, Nigel laughed out loud, marveling at the twists and turns of life. This was going to give him the edge over the others growers who could only advertise that they'd been in the Coachella Valley for a long time and that their dates were sweet. But could they claim to be community activists? Could they claim to be part of an extremely popular and growing national movement to preserve the forests and mountains and lakes and wildlife? No! But Stullwood Farms could! My company will not only have a good name, it will have an excellent name, a name which shoppers in a grocery market will equate with conservation and noble endeavors. They will see the Stullwood name and think of protected pine trees and majestic bighorn sheep thriving

in a special preserve, they will think of hiking in preserved wilder-
nesses and camping beside protected lakes and will think that the
folks at Stullwood Plantation made this possible.

The irony of it! His own wife and her adversary had, through
their conflict, unwittingly given Nigel the solution to his problem.

CHAPTER THIRTY-TWO

"YOU HAVE TO DO something! You can't let this happen to me. "Oh God!" Zora bawled. "I'll die if this happens to me!"

They were in their Palm Springs mansion overlooking a desert laid with carpets of blinding purple and red and yellow and blue wildflowers. "Jack," Zora was saying as she paced back and forth in his den, a high flush to her cheeks. "I need you to do something."

She was wearing her "country" slacks, custom-made ladies' trousers that she only wore at home but which daring young women across the country were starting to adopt. But her fans would have been shocked to see her hair in such disarray, and the paleness of a face without makeup.

Jack gently took her by the shoulders and said, "Baby, I've told you, the technology is coming, there is no stopping it. Thomas Edison tried to stop the phonograph record, claiming the cylinder was better. But the tide was too strong until he gave in and joined the disc revolution. It's the same for sound films. They're coming and it's too strong a tide to stop."

"But you don't have to help it!" she cried. "You don't have to feed the monster with our money!"

He didn't know what to say that would mollify her. He blamed himself. Ever since he had demonstrated his new sound projector to Nigel Barnstable, Zora had spiraled out of control. "I've told you, we can work around the sound problem, baby. We can re-record your lines during post-production, using another actress. We can give you fewer lines. You can play women who don't talk much."

She stared at him. Another actress? Fewer lines? *Women who don't talk much?* The panic bubbled higher. It clogged her throat. "Is that it? You're already grooming another actress to replace me? Someone who talks like the Queen of England. Who is she? I demand to know. I'll scratch her eyes out!" She pounded small fists on his barrel chest. "Jack!" she screamed. "Don't make me hate you!"

He stepped back in shock. "What? Hate me? Zora, you are making way too much of this. Pull yourself together." He didn't like it when she got this way, the insecurity that no amount of reassuring, no special words, no gestures could assuage. But he softened. It wasn't all that long ago that she lived in a slum with her mother, at the mercy of bosses and landlords who could put them out on the street with a snap of the fingers. "Why don't you go to that new spa in Indio and have a relaxing soak in the hot mineral springs, maybe get a massage?"

"Indio?" she shrieked. "Massage? Yes! That is what I will do!"

She ran out and Jack started to go after her, but he caught himself. Bringing her back would do no good; he knew that from before. Maybe he should find a hospital, a sanatorium where she could rest for a while under a doctor's care. She was only twenty-three. A rich future lay before her. Jack was going to see to it.

When he heard a car start up, he went to the window and saw her shiny roadster spin off down the dirt road, kicking up clouds of dust. He briefly thought of going after her, and then decided that she needed to get the panic and anger out of her system. She had done this before, whenever they had an argument, got in her car and drove off, to either come back filled with apologies, or to be found stranded and out of gas. Jack wasn't in the mood to play the game today. And there was no traffic out there, nothing more hazardous to the occasional motorist than a slow desert tortoise. Deciding he would give her an hour, and if she didn't come back by then, he'd go out looking, he returned to his desk that was littered with plays, manuscripts, scripts, letters, and contracts and got back to work.

Zora sped a few miles down the unpaved road and came to a stop in the shade of a flowering jacaranda. As delicate purple flowers dropped down onto her car, and into the car as she had the top down, Zora cried softly into her hands. She couldn't remember the last time she had been happy. She couldn't remember much of anything really— she had taken up the habit of using cocaine along with the vodka. Jack knew she was drinking, he just didn't know how much. It was a secret she had learned from another actress who used cocaine to stay slim—sniffing cocaine while drinking alcohol kept one from getting drunk. She also hadn't slept for days, but Jack didn't know that either, being embroiled at the moment with shooting a movie in a studio in Los Angeles.

The shock of the sound projector nearly a year ago, seeing Jack on a screen, his lips moving, his voice filling the room, had plunged her into a rare despair. Vodka had numbed it a little, but the fear was never far. Even when she slept, she dreamed fear-filled dreams. And then one day, when she hadn't even had the will to get out of bed and Jack worried over her, he had suggested she pay a visit to Bernie Mayfield, Hollywood's renowned acting coach. "He's a master at diction. If anyone can get the Brooklyn out of you, it's Mayfield."

Sixty-five-year-old Bernie Mayfield had run a successful acting studio in New York until arthritis compelled him to relocate to the warm, dry climate of Southern California, where he opened a studio that catered to film actors. Lately, Mayfield's clients had expanded to famous actors coming to him in a panic, fearful of the coming sound era. It was predicted that many careers were going to crash on the rocks. Rudolph Valentino, the highest paid actor in Hollywood, wasn't going to make it with his heavy Italian accent. John Gilbert, Hollywood's leading villain, didn't have the voice to match his masculine, tough-guy image.

And so Zora had gone to Mayfield, and he had given her exercises to do, sending her home with a phonograph record of an English actress reciting lines from Shakespeare. Zora had listened and repeated what she heard over and over, remolding words in her mouth, making her tongue and lips work in a way they weren't used to. But it had worked! She could tell. She could hear it. She could feel it in her mouth. Mayfield had then taken her to a recording studio on Hollywood Boulevard, where an excited Zora had read Shakespeare into a microphone. The technicians had imprinted the recording onto a phonograph record and Mayfield had played it for her in his studio.

Zora closed her eyes at the memory: sitting comfortably in the big leather easy chair, smiling as he started the record going, the hissy sound emerging from the Victrola's trumpet, and a thin voice riding on the hiss: *Shall I compare thee to a summer's day? Thou art more lovely and more temperate.* Zora listening, her smile remaining in place. *Sometime too hot the eye of heaven shines,*

And often is his gold complexion dimm'd. "Zora suddenly frowning, looking at Mayfield to say, "Who's that?"

"It's you. You're listening to yourself recite a sonnet."

The sudden realization that it was her, that he hadn't put on another actress's recording by mistake, recognizing the new way she pronounced certain words—yes, it was her, Zora DuBois, but . . .

She had stared at the revolving record, the arm undulating as the stylus rode the grooves, and a stranger's voice emerged from the trumpet, a homely, nasal voice belonging, surely, to a woman who was fat and frumpy and not at all glamorous or desired by millions of men: *When in eternal lines to time thou growest: So long as men can breathe or eyes can see . . .*

Zora whispering, "That can't be me," even though the truth was already stealing through her blood and bone. The look on Bernie Mayfield's face. The pity . . .

Her accent was perfect, if a bit strained and forced, but perfect. She wasn't from Brooklyn anymore. Exercises and practice could improve any accent or speech impediment. But there was nothing that could be done about the voice.

Zora DuBois talked through her nose.

She recalled little of the session after that, while the fat nasal woman on the record droned on in a very uninspired reading, and Zora heard words come from Mayfield's mouth: voice coach, singing lessons, breathing lessons. *Nasal surgery.*

Zora had been a natural. That was what Jack and the other movie men back in New York had said seven years ago. "A screen natural." She hadn't had to work at it. She just walked in front of the camera and the film did the rest.

But now . . .

Mayfield had said: Lessons, training, working, re-working, exercises, re-training, practice, practice, practice. Words that were not in Zora's lexicon. She didn't even know *how* to train and practice. Except for the past couple of weeks talking like the Queen of England, Zora had never worked at her craft. She hadn't even *had* a craft. She was just herself.

The world had done a crazy spin and Zora thought she was going to fall over. She barely remembered running out of the studio and onto the crowded sidewalk, where tourists with Brownie cameras searched for movie stars to photograph. They hadn't given the slender girl, weeping into a handkerchief and running as fast as her narrow skirt would allow, a second look.

Now, beneath the flowering jacaranda, she reached into her purse for a small packet, sprinkled white powder on the back of her hand, and inhaled it sharply up her nose. She followed it with a swig of vodka from the bottle she kept hidden beneath the car seat. She sat and stewed for a moment, her mind filled with confusion and self-pity. Hadn't her mother said something a long time ago about how men will always let you down? Mother, wearing a pretend wedding band that turned her skin green. Zora started the car and sped down the dirt road and out toward the open expanse of desert, visions and memories filling her head.

When the wheels of her car became mired in sand—she had been unaware of leaving the graded road—and stalled and got stuck and the motor died, Zora looked around and thought the place was familiar— the boulders and dunes and spreading mesquite trees. She recognized it as a place just outside of Palm Springs where Babylon and Nazareth and Texas and Algeria had all been filmed—a place of chariot races and crucifixions and cowboy shoot-outs because the sunlight was so perfect and the weather so stable that they couldn't be filmed anywhere else.

In shock she realized that here was also where she had filmed her first movie, *Salome*. Here, at barely sixteen, Zora had danced on the hot desert sand in front of a fake Jerusalem Temple. While a small orchestra seated in folding chairs had played an exotic melody beneath palm trees and blue sky, with an audience of cameramen and crew, jackrabbits and red-tailed hawks, Zora had swirled her seven veils in an unchoreographed dance that came from her soul, with a freedom and bliss that had been captured on film. Audiences had wept to see her slender form and sorrowful face. Meant to portray an evil seduc-tress, Zora had transformed John the Baptist's executioner into a sympathetic woman trapped in her own vices, trying through the grace of God to escape her own depravity and fleshly torments. It was the performance of a lifetime. People had lined up at the box office again and again, skyrocketing young Agnes Mulroney to fame and wealth. A glittering future had stretched before her.

But now that future was growing increasingly more tarnished with each utterance of the word "sound."

Zora sprinkled more cocaine on her hand and followed it with a long drink of vodka. She looked around at the yellow-gray expanse beneath a sky that didn't seem anchored to the earth. She didn't understand the allure of the desert. Well, she could understand why so many movies were filmed here, but to live here? Why had she and Jack built a house in this wasteland anyway? She couldn't remember just now. Strangely, where she wanted to be at that moment was back home in Brooklyn, where no one thought she talked funny because she talked just like them. She wanted to be back in the shabby apartment where she and her mother had played a game of pretend with hot water and stale bread, describing food for each other and pretending that was what they were eating. She thought vaguely of the lobster and caviar back in her house where she lived with Jack, all the French cheeses and German sausages and Swiss chocolates, and none of it compared to sharing a heel of stale bread and hot water with her mother.

Why had she left? I could have been a secretary by now, or be working in a clean shop waiting on clean people, and I would walk proudly into Drucker's bakery, where old man Abe would address me as Miss Maloney as I set down my dime and ask for his absolutely freshest loaf of pumpernickel.

She was falling asleep and didn't want to, now that she was enjoying her thoughts. So she carelessly sprinkled more powder on the back of her hand and inhaled it deeply into her nose. Then she closed her eyes and waited for the jolt that would bring her back to full wakefulness. And while she waited, she felt other memories come rushing back. She found herself thinking: it wasn't all shabby. There had been good moments. Agnes and her mother taking walks in the park on Sunday. Watching other people eat ice cream and cotton candy and convincing themselves they were too full to add dessert. Making fun of animals in the zoo. Finding a bag of peanuts, half full, and sitting on the grass to savor them. Her mother telling funny stories about a grandpa Zora never knew. ("He would walk all over the house looking for his glasses while they were on his forehead.")

Good times. When it was just Zora and her mother against the world, spinning dreams and tomorrows and futures together. How had she forgotten them?

Resting her head back, feeling the warm sun on her face, Zora decided she was going to go home, back to Brooklyn, and ask the Jewish man with the saddest face and longest beard she had ever seen if he knew where the previous tenant had moved to, Mrs. Mulroney. She hadn't asked at the last visit. But now she wanted to find her mother and ask her so many things. And reminisce, too. Reminiscing would be nice, Zora decided now, as languor stole through her bones and sinew.

We will eat, too, she thought happily. All those years of hunger, Momma and I pretending to eat. But now that I am a famous actress and I have to keep my figure, I still can't eat. I so badly want to eat. I will take Momma out to the best restaurants, and we will gorge on filet mignon, and mashed potatoes with gravy, and strawberry tarts with whipped cream.

As her soul drifted pleasantly on the desert air, she heard a voice from long ago, her mother leaving for her job of scrubbing floors, saying, "Today's the day I lose my job."

Yes, Momma, Zora silently replied, as the sun warmed her body and she grew lethargic and wonderfully sleepy. Yes, Momma, she thought, today is the day I lose my job . . .

A mile away, Gabriela was searching through a broad patch of evening primrose that lined a depression between two sand dunes. The white flowers were closed at the moment, but they would open at sunset and fill the air with a sweet scent. She was searching for sphinx moth caterpillars, a favorite food of her people. As she added new ones to her basket, thinking how good they were going to taste after they were dried in the sun, she thought of her continued lessons with Grandmother Luisa and how she was failing miserably at reaching the spirit world. How long was Grandmother going to be patient before she finally gave up and found another apprentice?

Gabriela now took her lessons seriously. The day the white men galloped into the camp, lassoing men and women, dragging them to the ground—Gabriela herself getting rifle-butted on the head—she had realized the need for the clan to have a spirit-reader. Grandmother was getting old, her senses were growing dulled, fewer messages were coming through her. No longer boastful, no longer seeing her status as a shaman as making her special and privileged, Gabriela had realized how serious her position was, how vital she was going to be to the safety of the clan.

"Spirits do not have voices like we do," Grandmother said in her instruction. "They speak to us on the wind, in running water, the rustling grass. They leave messages in the sand and up in the clouds." But Gabriela was beginning to despair. As she plucked a white flower and opened its petals to inhale its sweet fragrance she thought: I cannot let my people down.

"Gabriela Seco!"

Startled, she straightened and looked around. Who had spoken? She was all alone out on the sand, not far from the edge of the reservation. "Gabriela, help!" Where was the cry coming from? Finally she saw, a short distance away, an automobile stuck in the sand. "Help!" someone cried.

And then she saw the birds in the sky. Turkey vultures. Circling, circling. Coming lower and lower.

Gabriela lifted her skirts and broke into a run.

As she drew near to the car mired in the sand, she waved her arms to keep the birds away. She approached slowly, wondering if the driver was asleep. She was startled to see a young woman behind the wheel. She came around cautiously and stared at the pale, unmoving face. In shock, she recognized the famous movie star, a woman Gabriela had watched in envy on theater screens, whose social life and fashion trends she had followed in movie magazines. Zora DuBois, an actress whom Gabriela wished to emulate.

She frowned. The woman didn't seem to be breathing. Gingerly, she placed her hand on Zora's chest and felt for the heartbeat. There was none. This gave the seventeen-year-old pause. Zora looked so much younger, sitting here in perfect death. On the screen, committing her sins, she had seemed so much older. But here, pale and childlike, she was closer in age to Gabriela than Gabriela had guessed. And it startled her.

Why was she here? Why had she died?

Gabriela saw the half-empty vodka bottle on the car seat, and the white powder spilled here and there and sprinkled, too, on Zora's pert little nose. Gabriela had heard of such things going on in Hollywood, and hadn't Grandmother Luisa warned her about the dangers of being among movie people?

A heavy sadness swept over the young Indian girl. She was sad down to her toes, and she just wanted to stand there for a very long time and let the sadness engulf her. She laid her hand on the young woman's shoulder and whispered, "Go to Jesus, go to Mukat."

The shadows of the vultures fell over her as they circled above, gliding with magnificent outspread wings on the desert thermals. They were waiting for her to leave. They wanted to come down and—

Gabriela must run to the village and tell Grandmother about the dead film star. The Sheriff had to be told. People must come and take her away.

But as she started to leave, Gabriela paused and, looking up at the gliding silhouettes, said in her mind, "Please stay away, Grandfathers. This one is not for you. She is not one of us. She belongs someplace else."

She turned to go, and then stopped. In a lightning-quick moment, a sudden understanding so struck her that she had to reach out for the car door to steady herself.

The vultures had spoken to her. They had called her here. And she had heard them.

And I spoke back!

She began to tremble as the staggering revelation swept over her. The birds had called her to this place—and she had spoken to them without thinking! She had spoken to them as naturally as she spoke to Grandmother.

I have never spoken to birds before; why did I speak now?

And then she thought: Because I can hear them.

"Please stay away, Grandfathers," she said out loud, and then she ran back to the village in case their hunger was greater than their compassion.

*   *   *

"I need to speak with Doc Perry right away," Mrs. Decatur, the hairdresser, said when Fiona answered her knock at the front door.

Fiona stepped aside to let her in. "He's with a patient. Is there something I can do for you?"

Mrs. Decatur gripped the handle of her purse and tipped her chin. "I prefer to speak to him in person. It's about the new medicine he gave me . . ."

Fiona's life had been one of blissful happiness since moving in with her secret husband, nine months ago. At forty-five years of age and having served mistresses all her life, she had slipped into the role of wife and being mistress of her own home with the ease of slipping into shoes.

And Leland was the most loving, kind, and attentive husband a woman could ask for. She knew that she was in the middle of living happily ever after. And yet . . . at the back of her mind there had been a shadowy unease these past months. It drove her to hesitate when the phone rang; it sent her to the window to frequently look out for strange automobiles. His wound had healed nicely, yet that night of the shooting at the bootlegger's place had left her with a sense of waiting for the second shoe to drop. He had, after all, been involved in an altercation with federal agents.

And then there was the business with Leland's new Indian medicines, which he was mixing himself. His first recipes were tentative and needed testing, most of which Fiona tried for herself, mainly to watch for adverse affects. The few that affected her negatively weren't serious. Leland adjusted the recipe until he found the right formula and was ready to start dispensing. That was six months ago. He had received a few complaints, mostly that the medicine didn't seem to be working anymore and "could I take a double dose?"

While most of the Indian remedies worked, those that were intended for insomnia, pain, and anxiety had little effect. That was where the alcohol was so important. So Leland had gone back to Chief Diego and, explaining his problem to the old man, had learned of an additive that aided in these ailments. "But you must take care," the medicine man had said. "Too much is dangerous, too little will not work. We use it sparingly."

Leland had acquired the additive (which could only be purchased in bulk at a Los Angeles market), and now here was Mrs. Decatur perched in a chair, giving Fiona the dread feeling that a nasty chicken had come to roost.

*   *   *

The mesquite was leafing out. Soon the long green pods would appear. Come July, they would turn a thick brown, and Luisa's people would harvest them.

She noted the position of the sun. Gabriela was late again for her daily lesson in spirit-reading.

Luisa looked up and down the path that connected her house to the rest of the village. The hour was growing late. Tired of waiting, she left her hut and marched out of the village. When she reached the edge of the reservation, she waited for a car to pass, then she went across. She went first to inquire at Decatur's and then the drug store and finally the beauty parlor.

No one had seen Gabriela.

Luisa had been praying over the problem for the past few months—it had been a year since the spirits had revealed that Gabriela was to be the next spirit-reader. But Luisa was having serious doubts. Gabriela should be receiving messages by now. Perhaps when Gabriela came to her grandmother's house, saying she had a feeling her grandmother needed her—perhaps that was just a coincidence. If so, then Luisa had wasted a whole year of her life.

She went back through the village, inquiring after Gabriela, and it was a young man named Tomás Seco, one of the village's finest hunters, who said, "I saw Gabriela. She went up the canyon." He pointed westward into the rocky ravine where majestic palms marched like soldiers on the banks of the gushing stream.

Thanking him, Luisa struck off on the trail that ran parallel to the stream that should have been roaring with snowmelt and cascading in misty waterfalls over giant boulders, but instead only trickled because the water was rushing down the white man's concrete ditch. As she climbed in elevation, she came to meadows and groves of oaks and manzanita trees. Wondering if perhaps young Tomás had been mistaken—why on earth would Gabriela come here?—Luisa stopped and listened.

She heard something that did not belong in the sylvan wilderness. High and melodic and pleasant.

Someone was singing.

Luisa proceeded cautiously through the trees until she saw, up ahead in a small clearing, a shaft of sunlight illuminating a solitary figure.

Gabriela! She was looking up, as if at something high in tree branches, and she was singing to it in the Cahuilla tongue.

Luisa stood transfixed. She had not known Gabriela possessed such a beautiful voice. Gabriela herself was very comely. Her cotton skirt reached her ankles and her blouse was long-sleeved. A modest Indian girl. Luisa was pleased with what she saw. But who or what was she singing to?

Suddenly Gabriela stopped and turned to look in her grand-mother's direction. "Come," she said, "let me show you something."

Luisa came out of hiding—how had the girl known she was there?—and went to stand next to her.

"There," Gabriela said, pointing to a branch high up in the oak tree. "Do you see him?"

Luisa had to search, but eventually found the unmistakable shape of an owl. They spent their days in the protective camouflage of leafy trees. If Gabriela had not pointed right to him, Luisa would never have found him.

"He brought me here," Gabriela said with a smile.

Luisa frowned. "What do you mean?"

"I was fetching water at the creek. He was perched on an ocotillo cactus, and he told me to follow him. He flew off and brought me here. I have been singing him to sleep."

Luisa didn't know what to say. To observe an owl in flight during the day was a rare thing and a very good omen. But why had he brought Gabriela to this place? She looked around the clearing and recognized it as the place Chief Diego had chosen for their summer camp. In a few weeks, the villagers would be packing up their goods, their babies and animals, and trekking up to this protected valley, where they would live until summer went away and autumn was here.

But as she looked around, Luisa saw something that surely Chief Diego had not seen when he came before. "Aii, Mukat," she whispered in alarm. The manzanita bushes that grew in profusion in this place, providing edible berries and leaves that the people would rely on for subsistence, were all brown and brittle. Luisa bent close to inspect the bushes. There was a blight on the bark. And there were no early berries. The leaves were brittle and turned to dust upon her touch.

This is a bad luck place, she thought. If Diego brought the villagers here, something terrible would happen to them. He must find a new place.

She looked at Gabriela in amazement. The owl had brought her here to tell her this.

Gabriela smiled as she saw the look on her grandmother's face. Gabriela hadn't told her about the vultures because Gabriela was herself uncertain exactly what had happened when she found the dead actress. She had needed to think about it, and to see if the experience would be repeated. She didn't know why the vultures had chosen to speak to her when they had, or why, after months of lessons, the spirit-messages had finally started to come to her. All she knew was that she was indeed a spirit-reader.

"You do not need to worry anymore, Grandmother. I have seen the world of the white man. I am now ready to follow the Indian path." She knew that the vultures had called her to Zora's car on purpose so that she could see for herself the path she must choose. Gabriela had prayed for Zora DuBois and had burnt sacred mesquite wood for the safe journey of her soul to whatever afterlife Zora believed in.

"I did not understand, but now I do." She laid a gentle hand on her grandmother's arm and said with a smile, "I am ready for my lessons now."

* * *

"Leland, Mrs. Decatur is here, and I don't think she's very happy."

When Doc Perry had voiced his predicament to Chief Diego, that certain complaints were not being relieved by the local herbs—namely, sleeplessness, pain, and anxiety—the chief had told him what the Cahuilla turned to for sedatives and mild pain relief. The poppy seed. But since many had to be used in a recipe, and Leland couldn't roam the valley plucking California red and orange poppies for their few seeds, he had found a supplier in Los Angeles.

It was simple to do. He would pour a pound of black poppy seeds into a bowl, add two quarts of hot water and half a cup of lemon juice. Stir and let sit. After an hour, he would strain the water through a cheesecloth into a bottle. He tested it on himself first and found that several cups of the tea soon put him in a mood of utter contentment and relaxation. A few more cups and he was ready for a nap. Mrs. Decatur was one of the first patients to receive the new formula.

Going out to the parlor to face her, Leland put on his best sympathetic smile and said, "My wife says you wished to speak to me?"

"It's about that new medicine," the hairdresser said. As plump as a partridge, she flexed her chubby fingers and said, "I have never had better relief from my rheumatism, and I wanted to tell you in person. As an added bonus, I have been sleeping very well. I just wanted to let you know how grateful I am, Doctor, and that I am going to recommend your tea to my friends and customers."

Perry almost cried. For the first time in his life of carrying the false title of "Doctor," of hiding behind a fake medical school diploma, of dispensing colored water as medicine—for the first time in a life of false promises and flim-flam and hucksterism, Leland Perry was a true healer at last.

CHAPTER THIRTY-THREE

"YOU OUGHTA TRY SOME," Augie Lardner said when he saw how Cody McNeal was eyeing the display of bottles on the store counter. Variously colored and sized, and variously labeled, they all appeared to be the manufacture and proprietary products of the town's own Doc Perry. "That tonic there makes me feel ten years younger. And Lois swears by his insomnia cure. Says it's all pure ingredients and they're all herbal cures that he learned from the Indians."

He had heard about Leland Perry's change in the way he concocted medicines. Indian cures were famous for being better than anything laced with alcohol.

"Trenching begins in two weeks," Lardner said. "You going to be there, Mr. McNeal, up in the valley, protesting with the rest of us?"

"I wouldn't miss it."

So far, Elizabeth's group had been unsuccessful in gaining an injunction to keep Quinlan from breaking ground. Citizens for Wilderness Preservation had gone to court in their first case of Citizens vs. Quinlan Corporation. The outcome was still pending. The trial judge had taken testimony from the plaintiff and the defendant, while the smug Quinlan had sat on one side of the courtroom with a team of five attorneys and expert witnesses and Elizabeth had sat alone with her group's citizens' rights attorney. It boiled down to who had the best lawyers.

But Elizabeth was determined to win.

As he paid for his purchases, he looked across the street at La Alma. Elizabeth was there. He wished he could march across and just walk in and be with her. It was a powerful pull, and a mighty big test of his willpower. But there was no predicting where Barnstable would be on a given day. Since the launch of a massive advertising campaign to thrust Stullwood Plantation into prominence, he could be seen anywhere in the area, with his advertising agent and photographers in tow. He had commissioned an enormous roadside sign, called a billboard, to be erected at the bottom of the Banning Pass—the western entrance into the Coachella Valley—advertising Stullwood Plantation in Palm Springs, inviting motorists to stop in for refreshing milkshakes and free samples. At the bottom of the billboard was the bold announcement: "Stullwood Plantation, proud founder and supporter of the Citizens for Wilderness Preservation group. Join us in the fight to preserve America's natural beauty and wildlife!"

Nigel's claim for credit annoyed Cody, but Elizabeth said that as long as it was helping their cause, she didn't mind what Nigel claimed. And Cody had to admit, motorists were indeed stopping to visit the new roadside fruit stands Nigel had constructed, while the foundation for a proper store was being laid, and visitors were dropping their coins and bills in the jars labeled "Save Big Horn Valley."

But Cody didn't trust Barnstable's motives. He seemed to be polishing his own personal image, and Cody suspected why. Elizabeth herself had voiced the suspicion that Nigel might know about Mary Clark and Elizabeth's plan to file for divorce. Was it possible? Did Barnstable really have that much restraint, to know about Elizabeth's secret plans to leave him and yet not go into a show of volatile temper? Cody burned so badly for Elizabeth, especially at night alone in his bed, reliving their one time together at Christmas, that he had a few times jumped up and gotten dressed to cast all caution to the wind and race over to La Alma to carry Elizabeth away on his horse. But of course he never got as far as his door. How much more restraint would Barnstable need, with his cruelty just beneath the skin, to keep from lashing out at the woman who would dare to leave him?

Or maybe Barnstable didn't know about Elizabeth's plans at all and things were exactly what they appeared to be: Nigel jumping on a popular, activist bandwagon for the aggrandizement of his date farms. It was impossible to guess what went on inside Nigel Barnstable's dangerous mind.

*   *   *

Elizabeth consulted her calendar where she had marked days with cryptic little symbols. Counting back, and then calculating in Nigel's overnight absences, she estimated that tonight he would be demanding sex. He had become very predictable, a trait Elizabeth used to her benefit.

If not tonight, then the next or the next. So she would be prepared. It had worked for nearly two years. "Don't refuse him," her lawyer had advised. "The judge will throw this in your face if you do. As long as you can tolerate it, let him have his way. You will be free of him soon enough."

Tolerate it, Elizabeth thought, as she prepared for bed. It sounded easy. Just lie back and wait for him to finish. It was what prostitutes did, wasn't it? But it wasn't just the physical part; it was the dehumanizing way he went about it. No lust, no desire, but soullessly and mechanically.

Bathed and in her nightgown, she proceeded with the blessed protection. But when she opened the small, gold powder box, long emptied of its dusting powder, she found it empty.

She frowned. Surely she had restored the diaphragm, washed and dried, to its hiding place. She checked other places—drawers, boxes, linen bags. It was nowhere to be found. What could have happened to it?

She sat at her vanity table and, staring at her reflection, went back in her mind to the last time Nigel had visited her bed. She recalled him leaving, closing the door behind himself without a word. Elizabeth staying in bed for a short while, just in case, and then getting up, going into her private bathroom, washing, using the douche prescribed by Dr. Greene. Cleaning and drying the diaphragm and carefully putting it in the box, placing the box in plain sight on her vanity table.

But now it wasn't there. Surely Luisa wouldn't have touched it.

And then a chill shot through her. *Nigel.*

It was the only explanation.

He must have gotten suspicious. Sending her to the doctor to get checked out, making sure she was capable of getting pregnant. And still nothing had happened. And so he had gone snooping? And had found the instrument of her deceit.

Oh God! Oh God, oh God, oh God . . .

Her heart started to jump around in her chest. A cold sweat broke out over her body. She felt sick, faint. She rose from the chair and reached for the wall. She stumbled along, clutching her stomach as if Nigel had already delivered the first punishing blow. When did he find it? How long has he known? How is he going to punish me?

Elizabeth couldn't think straight. Should she run? Stay and fight? Scream for help?

Telephone Cody.

No, don't draw him into this. Nigel owns a gun . . .

As she tried to think of what to do, how to prepare, find a way out, Elizabeth told herself she should have already thought of these things. Nigel wanted an heir, he had made that clear enough. The sex wasn't about love or intimacy or being a couple; it was pollination, plain and simple. And he was an impatient man.

When Nigel had permitted her to hold her group meetings at La Alma, Elizabeth had at first thought he wanted to keep tabs on her around the men, maybe to see who was paying her particular attention. But then when he started acting so amenable when the group was at the house, the terrible notion that he had found out about Mary Clark had hit her like a hammer—he must be building his defense against her divorce claims. He was on his best behavior so that Mary Clark wouldn't be able to get a single person to say a negative word against Nigel Barnstable.

But even so, she hadn't been sure, as he had showed no actual signs of knowing her secret plans, that maybe it was all in her imagination generated by fear.

But this . . . in her gut, in her most primal instincts, she knew that Nigel had found the diaphragm, he knew she was keeping from him his most cherished desire. Worse, she was subverting his plans and sabotaging his dream.

Retribution was going to be swift and violent.

She looked around for something to defend herself with. He was going to punish her, and she was going to fight back. And now that she thought about it, as she considered arming herself with a letter opener or a fireplace poker, this was a moment that was a long time coming and fated to happen. Nigel was going to beat her senseless and then tell her it was her fault, tell her in his cold, ugly way that she alone was to blame if he beat her black and blue, and maybe even lecture her afterward, as she lay in bed recovering from her injuries and shattered self-esteem, how she had driven him to do what he had done and no wife should treat her husband so.

These thoughts flew through her head as she frantically searched through her vanity table, picking up metal nail files, manicure scissors, rat-tail combs, anything for defense against the wrath that she knew was about to come. She thought of running. Going to the Indian village and seeking refuge with Luisa's people.

And again, full circle, telephoning Cody for help. But she mustn't let Cody know—he would fly into a rage and go after Nigel, and who knew what the terrible consequences would be?

"Are you looking for this?"

She spun around. Nigel stood there in his dressing gown, holding the diaphragm between thumb and forefinger, pinching just the edge of it as if he had just found a decomposing rat.

"I got suspicious," he said, as he tossed the offending object down. Elizabeth saw that a hole had been torn in it. "You're not every imaginative when it comes to hiding things. That powder box was the first place I looked."

When he had told her to see a specialist, she had visited a Dr. Greene in Los Angeles. He wasn't sure about the reliability of a woman doctor, but then had decided that perhaps a woman would know more about these things than a trained medical man. Dr. Greene had put Elizabeth through a series of tests and had sent a report home with her, stating that Elizabeth was in excellent health and should in no way have trouble getting pregnant. "Sometimes," she had added at the bottom, "these things just take time."

But it had been months, and Nigel's impatience was skyrocketing— *Why* hadn't Elizabeth gotten pregnant by now?

And then came an answer that had never occurred to him, mainly because it was crafty and of a deceitful nature: Elizabeth herself impeding her own impregnation.

She had gone to a woman doctor. Women doctors were notoriously sympathetic to the new birth control movement, and once he thought about it, Elizabeth was showing surprising fortitude and resourcefulness in her campaign against Quinlan. Couldn't that same fortitude and resourcefulness be called upon in her secret rebellion against him?

He had no illusions about their marriage. From the day the baby was lost, so was Elizabeth's love for Nigel. He didn't delude himself— Elizabeth most likely hated him. But that didn't interfere with his plans for a perfect life. What did interfere was the possibility that Elizabeth was using secret birth control. And so he had gone in search and had found it in the powder box.

He knew he should be angry and punish her but that would be a waste of time and effort. He simply wanted to get on with seeing his ambitions realized. "Lie back," he said, untying the sash of his robe. "Make this easy on yourself."

She tipped her chin. Part of her wished he would hit her, wished they could get into a violent, physical fight. But the repercussions could be disastrous. She needed to stay in control. "A year ago you gave me a deadline, what happened to it? What happened to paying a girl?" she added bitterly.

"I changed my mind. Paying a girl to breed with me would leave too many loose ends. And I wouldn't know what sort of mongrel background my son would be coming from. I would prefer the child came from you. But if it still doesn't work, yes, there is that plan to fall back on. Don't fight me, Elizabeth, and we can be civilized. If you do fight me, remember that I am stronger than you and once threw a rather heavy man off a swiftly moving ocean liner."

*   *   *

"It's called an inter-uterine device," Dr. Greene said two days later when Elizabeth could get an appointment. As she lay in the stirrups, feeling vulnerable and angry, but more determined than ever to win her emancipation, it occurred to her that her doctor, Violet Greene, was named for two colors, and she wondered in detachment if the woman's parents had done it on purpose.

Elizabeth had not made the decision to come here today lightly. Mary Clark had cautioned her not to go back to Dr. Greene. More doctors were coming under federal scrutiny for disseminating contraceptive information and devices; there was a high probability that Dr. Greene was falling under that scrutiny. But Elizabeth had to go back. She knew she had no choice but to risk getting arrested. The alternative was to continue to have unprotected sex with Nigel and risk getting pregnant.

"Science doesn't really know how it works," Dr. Greene said as she commenced the illegal procedure, "but once the small spring is inserted into the womb, the chances for conception drop to a mere two percent. You leave it in place—we will change it in six months. It will not interfere with your period, you will still be able to conceive after it is later removed, and your husband will not detect its presence. Do you wish me to go ahead?"

Dr. Greene paused. She wished there were some way she could allay Elizabeth's fears, but there wasn't. Her hands were tied. "I have to caution you, Elizabeth. I don't know how much longer I can help you. And I don't know another doctor I can refer you to if you need further help. Do you still wish me to continue?"

"Yes," Elizabeth said, and a tear, for reasons she didn't know, rolled from the corner of her eye.

When had the world become so unbalanced? Why did men have all the power? Back in history, when power was being handed out, were the women standing behind a door? When the full realization of inequality in the world struck her, it was like a blow. She winced and said, "Ouch." But it was Dr. Greene's instrument, pinching.

CHAPTER THIRTY-FOUR

"COUSIN URSULA HAS KNITTED another sweater for you. Can you meet me at her place tomorrow at noon?"

"Ursula" was the code word for urgent. And Ursula's place was a restaurant in Indio where Elizabeth and Mary Clark met to discuss her ongoing divorce case.

"Thank you for driving out to meet me," Mary said as she rose from the table to shake Elizabeth's hand. "I had business in the area and thought it a good opportunity to bring you up-to-date on things. Something serious has come up."

The small restaurant had outdoor patio seating, and the table Mary had selected was tucked away in a corner, out of the earshot of other patrons.

"I was happy to come," Elizabeth said, seeing the strain on Miss Clark's face, shadows under her eyes.

"I've taken the liberty of ordering tea and salads." The outdoor café had a Spanish name and sported Mexican décor, with a menu offering tacos, enchiladas, carne asada. Lighter fare was offered for the less adventurous.

"That's fine," Elizabeth said, as she sat down and removed her white gloves. The spring day was warm. Despite snow on the mountain peaks, afternoons at this time of the year could reach into the nineties. "What is it you wanted to talk with me about?"

Mary Clark looked around at the few other patrons seated at the small tables, then she leaned forward and said quietly, "Elizabeth, you know that I truly want to stand up to Quinlan with you at the Big Horn Valley protest. But now I can't go. Something has happened. I couldn't risk telling you by phone call or telegram. Elizabeth," she said in a strained voice that startled Elizabeth—Mary Clark being normally even-keeled and collected. "Elizabeth," Mary said again, "Dr. Greene has been arrested."

Elizabeth sat back in her chair. "What!"

"Someone informed on her. She has been arrested for distributing birth control material, and her patient files have been confiscated. Birth control is a violation of federal anti-obscenity laws," Mary Clark added, lowering her voice and looking around, as if waitresses could be spies for the federal government. "There was a court ruling in 1918 that exempted physicians from the law that prohibited the distribution of contraceptive information to women—provided it was prescribed for medical reasons. And those medical reasons have to be very specific, such as pregnancy directly putting a woman's life at risk. Not for the simple reason of limiting the size of a family. There is a chance, Elizabeth, that arrest warrants will be issued for patients who asked for or received birth control advice, printed matter, or devices without legitimate health reasons."

"Dear God," Elizabeth whispered. She had known that going to Dr. Greene was a risk, but she certainly had not foreseen *this*.

She shivered, despite the desert warmth. When black, menacing shadows suddenly swept over the patio, briefly darkening the day, she looked up and saw flocks of birds flying eastward, wings desperately flapping as if they were fleeing for their lives. Swallows, she realized in surprise. Migratory birds that annually flew up each spring from Argentina to nest in the ruins of an old Spanish mission a hundred miles west of Palm Springs, on the Pacific Coast. The swallows stayed in San Juan Capistrano until the fall. Why would they be flying eastward now?

She looked to the west and saw a clear sky. But the air felt charged. Her skin prickled as if there were an electric source nearby. She almost felt as if her hair would rise up and stand on end.

Or was it just her imagination, the shock of hearing about Dr. Greene?

"I am telling you this to warn you, Elizabeth. A lot of people want to get a look at Violet's files. Tabloid newspapers will pay a lot to get ahold of the names."

"But aren't those files confidential?" Her own file! Elizabeth suddenly felt sick. In the hands of Nigel's lawyer, the file would shatter any chance or hope of obtaining the divorce, would shackle her to Nigel forever, and deny her the chance to be with Cody! If it comes to that, she thought, we will run away. If I am never to gain my freedom then I will risk anything and everything to be with Cody.

And then Elizabeth thought, as her mind raced while flocks of swallows raced across the sky: what if Dr. Greene had written something else? "Patient says husband is abusive, caused a miscarriage and fears he will cause another." Mightn't such a file work in Elizabeth's favor? But the sad fact was, she had no idea what Dr. Greene had written in her file.

Mary reached out and touched Elizabeth's arm. "You need to know that I, too, am in real danger of getting arrested because of my association with Violet, as I have referred quite a few clients to her. But be assured, Elizabeth, that I will never divulge your name or anything we discussed in private. However, I cannot speak for Violet. She has her family to think of. If prosecutors offer her a deal . . ."

Elizabeth rubbed her arms and felt even colder. Tea and salads arrived. Neither was touched.

"What can I do to help?" Elizabeth asked.

Mary held up a hand. "Don't volunteer to get involved right now. Mary has a lot of support, from family and friends and pro-contraception groups, women's rights organizations. But there is a chance you will be called to testify. In which case, I will prepare you for testimony."

An hour later, as she drove the twenty-three miles back to Palm Springs—worried about kindly Violet Greene, a compassionate woman who didn't deserve prison, and worried about Mary Clark who fought for women's rights—Elizabeth peered through the windshield and saw dark clouds gathering behind the mountains. The valley was sun-lit, the sky a flawless blue. But over there, behind San Jacinto, black, wrathful-looking clouds were building.

Elizabeth realized she was scared, an emotional state she was finding herself in all too frequently of late. She hadn't told Cody about Nigel finding the diaphragm and how he had reminded her of what he claimed to have done to Richard Ostermond, a scare tactic to keep her in line. It could be the last straw that sent Cody over the edge. Did Nigel even suspect he had such a volatile opponent in his former ranch manager? Cody wasn't a violent man, but Elizabeth knew that Nigel's treatment of her was the one thing that could send him on a vengeful, possibly deadly mission.

As the wind picked up, she recalled horror stories the locals had told about Pacific storms that rolled swiftly in from the ocean to slam against the Santa Rosas and San Jacintos, dropping torrential rains on the western slopes without shedding a drop on this side of the mountains—but then furious runoff appeared minutes later, flash floods roaring down ravines and gullies and canyons, sweeping away everything in their path. "Whole wagons and horse teams," Augie Lardner had said. "Gone just like that," with a snapping of his fingers.

Gripping the steering wheel, Elizabeth tried to keep her eye on the road as well as on the black menace rising up behind the mountain. When a sudden wind picked up, sending a tumbleweed in her path, she leaned forward and mentally urged the car to go faster, faster . . .

*   *   *

When Cody heard his window rattle, he looked up from his writing and noticed that the day had gone suddenly dark. He got up to look out and saw Mrs. Lardner, behind her store, frantically retrieving laundry from a line, the clothes flapping and churning. The morning had been calm and peaceful. But something was coming up, fast and furious.

Craning his neck, Cody peered up at the mountain's peak and, with a shock, saw nasty black clouds billowing up from nowhere, threatening to engulf the day. He had seen flash floods in his travels, whole communities carried off, caught unaware by great walls of water tumbling down the Rocky Mountains.

"Dear God," he murmured as he watched the clouds engulf San Jacinto's summit and then . . . roll right over it. The mountain couldn't hold the storm back. It was coming this way, and it was big.

There was a sharp knock at his door. "Mr. McNeal? Are you in there, dear?"

He opened it to find a flustered Mrs. Henry, his landlady, in the hallway. "Augie Lardner just telephoned. He said a big storm is coming and I should bring my patio furniture inside. Would you be so kind as to help me?"

Five miles away, Nigel was too busy inspecting his newest grove to notice the day abruptly change. Sunlight to dark, just like that.

Having purchased twenty acres of Southern Pacific Railroad land—not contiguous with his plantation but down the road a spell—and planting them with an additional hundred trees, he now rode his horse along the columns of date palms, his thoughts embroiled in empire building.

His first billboard, the one erected by the main road coming down from Banning, was diverting motorists to Stullwood Plantation, where they enjoyed cold shakes and cookies and candy and cakes all made from dates, plus the dates themselves, and enjoyed them all so much that by the time they arrived at Indio and saw signs for Gonzalez Date Farm and others, the motorists were too full of dates and sweetness to stop so they kept on going to Yuma, Phoenix, Albuquerque, El Paso. Nigel got it into his head to erect a duplicate billboard eastward of Indio and, amazingly, the offer of free samples, plus the idea of buying products from a company that was fighting to save America's wilderness inspired folks to drive right past Gonzalez Date Farm and the others and go the few extra miles to Stullwood. And once the new store was open, Nigel intended to offer date ice cream and free camel rides.

All thanks, ironically, to Jay Thomas Quinlan. Nigel was finding that the world of commerce was a great deal more intriguing and full of surprises than he would have thought three years ago when his father's will was read and Nigel decided to go out into the world and make something of himself. Even adversaries like Quinlan had something to offer if you just listened.

As a wind picked up and the brim of his hat fluttered, Nigel saw one of his Mexican foremen come running up. "Señor! Señor! Look!" The man pointed, his eyes popping out.

Nigel turned and saw, hanging over the mountain, a mass of clouds so black and menacing that he was for a moment speechless.

"Una tormenta, Señor! Big storm! And it comes this way!"

"My God," he said, feeling the wind increase against his face. He had never seen anything like it. "It looks like a squall line. And it's moving fast!"

The crop! A young, budding crop at this time of the year, the fruit no bigger than berries, fragile and vulnerable, hanging in new clusters. "When the rain season comes," Gonzalez had told him months ago, "you have to cover every bunch with waterproof covers. Heavy waxed paper is best."

But it rarely rained in the Coachella Valley in April. And never storm-strength.

Wheeling his horse around, he galloped back to the hundred-tree grove where the Mexican ladies who ran his fruit stand were frantically trying to cover the countertops with canvas tarps. Nigel galloped by, past the new store almost finished, and by the time he reached the grove, fronds were being whipped into a frenzy. The workers were running this way and that, searching for cover. "Get up those ladders!" Nigel shouted. But his orders went unheard.

Jumping down from his horse, he grabbed the men, seizing them by their shirts and arms, shouting at them to get up and cover the dates. They started up the ladders, but as soon as his back was turned, they climbed back down and ran off.

The fronds, heavy and covered in sharp thorns, thrashed about overhead. And then a few began to come apart from the crowns, threatening to crash down to the ground. Nigel stared up in horror. The massive fronds, clashing against one another, created a blood-chilling sound—an unearthly hissing roar that made him think the world was coming to an end. The wind rushed among the trees, abruptly shifting directions, causing the massive trunks to vibrate and shudder. Nigel was transfixed. Surely a storm couldn't topple these mighty giants!

*   *   *

After Mrs. Henry's furniture was secured, Cody went out to the main street to see debris being furiously whipped up. Augie Lardner's outdoor newspaper rack flew over, sending the *Los Angeles Times* and the *Riverside Press* flapping away down the street. Avulsed tree branches flew through the air. Papers and trash kicked up and carried along, spinning in the air.

Holding his hat to his head, he looked across the way at the Indian village. They had not yet gone up to their summer camp in the mountains and they all stood now, looking up at the black clouds, their clothes and hair whipped about. Then, in horror, Cody saw the water rising in Barnstable's concrete ditch. A flash flood had already begun.

He ran.

"Get out!" he shouted as he plunged into the village. Dried palm fronds were flying off the tops of ramadas. Grass roofs were stripped away. Women frantically searched for children while the men struggled with large ollas filled with nuts, berries, acorns, beans.

And then the rain began. Big, fat, cold drops. The level of Barnstable's ditch rose and spilled over the edges. The alluvial plain between La Alma and the village was suddenly turning into a lake, the water foaming and swirling in an unstoppable tide with debris being tossed about on the churning surface.

From behind closed windows, the townsfolk watched in fear. No one ventured out into the violent weather. Those few who had been caught out in it ran for shelter, slamming doors behind themselves to listen to an unearthly howl as the wind rushed down the main street, stripping siding from walls, yanking lanterns from doorways, sending projectiles into windows with terrifying sounds of glass splintering and shattering. In the livery stable, John Wheeler and his sons struggled to calm the horses, while at La Alma the ranch hands tried to round up what stock they could—horses, goats, chickens—and get them into the barn. The roof of the tack room tore away with a frightening groaning sound and sailed away on the wind.

*   *   *

In the date grove, Nigel screamed at the Mexicans, striking them with his riding crop, cursing them, raining blows on them as they covered their heads with their arms. But they ran and disappeared through the trees. Fronds fell with great snapping sounds, landing on the ground with heavy thuds. Running into a supply shed, he came out with a roll of wax paper. Tucking it under his arm, he tried to climb one of the ladders but lost his footing.

He fell, landing on his back. But he got right up, reached for the ladder, and climbed, the wax paper roll clutched in one hand. He kept his eye on the berry clusters, shivering and trembling beneath the protective canopies. How secure were they? Could the wind tear them away, even before the rain got to them? As Nigel climbed, he felt the first wet drops on his arms and face, his hands and feet slipped on the rungs of the ladder. The berries, small and orange and clustered tightly together, looked fragile and vulnerable. He had to protect them, keep them safe from the storm. But when he neared the top, a strong gust slammed into the tree. The trunk shuddered violently, Nigel's feet flew out from under him and down he went, thudding onto the wet ground, the wind knocked out of him.

He lay stupefied for a moment as the storm raged and the crashing fronds created an eerie, hissing roar overhead. Rain pelted his face. He struggled back to his feet, and as he reached for the ladder again, a large green frond, ripped from the crown, came thundering down, sharp thorns slicing Nigel's arm. He cried out and fell back. He dropped the roll of wax paper and grabbed his wound, where he felt warm blood

seep through his sleeve. He cried out again in pain—part of the thorn
had broken off and was lodged deep in his bicep.

And then the water came.

Nigel saw the ditch and concrete reservoirs start to overflow, cascades
of water pouring over the sides and spreading over the ground, the
water rapidly seeping into the dry sand, filling the shallow depressions
around the bases of the trees, filling up like bowls and then sinking down
into the sand to dampen the soil around the trees' delicate root balls.

Nigel thought in shock: *the trees will be destabilized.*

*   *   *

Elizabeth gripped her steering wheel as the wind buffeted her car. She
kept an eye out to her left, where arroyos and gullies emptied onto the
valley floor—dry now but soon to be boiling over with rushing water. She
tried to go faster but the wind pushed her back. Leaning forward, she
peered up through the windshield and saw the black clouds swallow San
Jacinto's two-mile-high peaks. The storm would soon slam the valley.

She couldn't get caught in it!

And then the rain hit. Hard and drenching so that she couldn't
see through her windshield. The road quickly ran to mud, with
ribbons of water causing her tires to hydroplane. She wrestled with the
steering wheel and then she was blinded by a rain so drenching that the
windshield wipers couldn't keep up. She rolled her window down and
stuck her head out, receiving a blast of cold rain in her face. Through
the downpour she saw the edge of town—the blacksmith, the church,
Sweeney's auto garage. But the street was flooded.

She stopped the car at the edge of the flood. Getting out, barely
able to see, Elizabeth ran the rest of the way and came upon a chaotic
scene. Upturned wagons, horses galloping into the storm. Through
the pouring rain she saw a man lying in the mud, a bleeding gash on
his head. It was Joe Waldinger, who owned the new hardware store.
Doc Perry was seeing to him. "Is he all right?" she shouted.

Perry nodded, ribbons of water running from the rim of his hat
that had somehow managed to stay on his head.

"Have you seen Cody?"

"Not since the thing began!" he shouted. Leland Perry was drenched
through and through. And now, so was Elizabeth.

She saw Fiona running toward them, Perry's medical bag in her
hand. The three managed to get Joe to cover, then Elizabeth delivered

herself back into the maelstrom in search of Cody. In horror, she saw the water from the overflowing ditch rushing toward the Indian village where people ran to and fro, yelling and shouting in an effort to save what they could.

Where was Cody?

*　　*　　*

Cody had ducked into a hut to sweep a crying child off his feet and hoist him up onto his back. Locking the child's arms around his neck, Cody shouted, "Hold on tight!" Then he scooped up two more toddlers and ran from the village as the houses came apart, boards and logs and tree limbs flying.

Elizabeth finally saw him, running up onto the plateau where Indians were trying to protect the children, huddled and shivering in the wind and rain. She was about to call out to him when, before her horrified eyes, part of the plateau started to break away, the dry soil having become saturated too quickly. People tumbled into the water below.

She ran to them. Above, Cody and the others scrambled to help everyone to higher ground. More of the rocky shelf fell, trapping people below. Elizabeth couldn't see through the rain, couldn't see Cody.

*　　*　　*

When Augie Lardner looked out his store window and saw Cody grab a child and run with it, taking it to higher ground—and then saw Elizabeth run down the street, drenched, running straight for the beleaguered Indian village—Augie conducted the most rapid thinking of his life. Big bodied with an ape-like face, here he was hiding in his store, afraid of a little gusty wind, while out there, Elizabeth Barnstable, slender and willowy and who looked as if she could be carried away on a sneeze, was braving the violent elements.

He was suddenly filled with shame, and then with pride, and then with nothing at all as he darted from the safety of his shop and plunged into the ferocious wind, battling it, nearly getting blown off his feet until he reached the village and laid hands to anything he could. Having witnessed this brave act, Allenby joined him, and Sweeney the mechanic, seizing children and food stores to hurry them to safety.

Indian women were running about, holding up their skirts, tripping and falling as more people from the town now threw themselves on the mercy of the storm and ran to the Indians' aid. They plunged in—dainty Mrs. Henry and petite Miss March and gimpy Mr. Marden—grabbing what they could, knowing that the Indians' entire food supply was stored in these flimsy huts and ramadas.

With the huts breaking up and so much debris flying through the air, the water now swirling around her ankles, Elizabeth ran after Luisa and together they scrambled up to the remaining ledge where everyone stood. But as soon as they arrived, Cody shouted, "Look!"

And they saw, down in the village, Chief Diego, whipped by wind and rain, battling his way toward the ceremonial house. His bandana had come off, his white hair flew ghost-like about his head. "What is he doing?" Cody shouted.

"He is saving the maiswat!" Luisa cried.

Cody knew she was referring to the sacred medicine bundle that was guarded by the clan's chief shaman. It consisted of an enormous reed mat with ceremonial objects enclosed inside, all vital to their sacred rituals. "The house is going to collapse!" Cody shouted. And in that moment, after Diego slipped inside, the wind caught an old cottonwood tree, its roots dead and rotted, and sent it crashing down onto the house.

Cody ran down the hill and plunged into the knee-high water that was still rising. He slogged through the swirling eddies as more structures crashed around him, trees toppled, blankets and clothes floated on the water, harder objects banged against his legs. On the plateau, holding on to one another, Diego's people watched in terror.

Having left Fiona to take care of Joe Waldinger, Leland Perry arrived at the village as Cody was struggling in the downpour to reach the collapsed ceremonial house. Perry joined him, as did Augie Lardner. "My God!" Augie cried, pointing. The two men turned to see a wall of water, ten feet high and boiling with mud and logs and rocks, racing down the canyon toward them.

Together with Cody they frantically tore apart the roof of the house and Cody fell in, to disappear beneath branches and fronds and rising water. Elizabeth looked back and saw the flood coming. Those on the plateau were safe, but the village lay in its violent and destructive path and everything was going to be swept away.

"Cody!" she screamed.

She watched Augie and Leland work frantically to clear the collapsed house, the water now at their waists.

The people on the bluff held their breath. And then two heads appeared, bobbing on the water, as Cody swam out, holding the unconscious chief's head above water.

In horror, everyone watched helplessly as the rushing wall of water slammed into the village, like a giant burst dam, swallowing everything, including the men, who disappeared under the churning current.

In his orchard, Nigel watched helplessly as fronds came crashing down around him and clusters of baby dates were ripped from the trees and carried away. But the trees did not topple. Nigel had thought they would have been destabilized by the water seeping into the sand, but they held as they were slammed and pummeled by the merciless storm, their thick trunks trembling and shimmying—but not coming down.

"Yes!" he shouted in the middle of his grove, his first one, planted by a crane and the blood and sweat of men. Now he watched the fruits of that vision and labor stand firm against a storm that had carried off his wooden shed where Quinlan had visited, that had torn parts of the newly constructed shop away, that was stripping the landscape of brush and trees—but Nigel Barnstable's sentinels stood strong.

And then—

He saw the wall of water rushing down the canyon toward him, the same wall that was heading for the Indian village. The flash flood was ten feet high and churning with branches and rocks and dead animals, and it was headed for the Indian village—and Nigel's grove.

"No!" he cried, the wind snatching his voice away.

He stood immobilized as he watched the water tumble toward him. He stood and watched as it slammed into the first trees. He saw the brown water churning around their bases as if determined to dig them up. In horror, he saw the first trees sway precariously, whipped by the wind, assaulted by the flood . . . and then he saw the first one fall, crashing down like a felled Goliath, to splash thunderously into the water, sending up a high spray.

"No!" he shouted again.

And then the next one swayed, toppled, and fell so majestically that Nigel stood in awe of what he was witnessing.

When the water reached him, he looked down in surprise, wondering what was tugging so violently at his legs. He stared for a moment, at the churning water, then he felt his footing give way, his balance start to go, and he realized in a moment of clarity that he was about to be swept away by the flash flood.

Pulling his feet up out of the mud they had been sinking into, Nigel backed away from the advancing tide, his eyes on his swaying trees as they fell, exposing their sodden root balls. He stumbled backward, not watching behind himself, pulling himself away from the scene of horrific destruction. He kept going until he felt firmer footing and kept staggering backward until he reached the wooden sidewalk in front of Decatur's Beauty salon, where the wind still raged but beyond the reach of the water, and Nigel watched in frozen dread as his trees fell like Roman columns, like an empire coming down.

*   *   *

Just as quickly as it had come, the squall line moved on, the rain passed by, the wind died down. But people were still screaming and shouting, the village was all but gone, the ditch continued to spill into the newly formed lake that was now flooding the central street of Palm Springs. But the flash flood that had tumbled down the canyon had spent itself.

The clouds passed and humid sunlight came out as Elizabeth clambered down from the plateau, snagging her clothes on uprooted trees, her face smeared with mud. She had to find Cody.

Others were now down in the flooded village searching for loved ones. Everyone was soaked to the skin, clothes dragging, mud-covered.

She found him, leaning against a tree while Leland Perry examined the dazed chief, the floodwaters receding, dissolving into the sand.

Elizabeth ran into Cody's arms. "I thought I had lost you!"

Luisa also came running, holding her skirt above the receding flood. She had wondered, when the storm first struck, why the spirits had not warned her or Gabriela. But she knew now that this flood was punishment from Pa'akniwat, guardian of all waters. We are the People of the Water; we have protected streams and ponds and hot springs for generations. But we have let the white man steal our water and Pa'akniwat is angry. And so the spirits had withheld their warning.

She knelt in the muddy water and laid her hand on her husband's face. Diego's eyes fluttered open. He smiled.

"He'll be all right," Doc Perry said, surveying the scene of destruction, the bedraggled, woebegone people. "Just a few bumps and scrapes," he added and, cold and wet through, struck off toward the others, to search for injuries that needed tending.

*   *   *

Mindlessly gripping his upper arm where the thorn of a date palm frond was still lodged, Nigel surveyed his devastated orchard. Most of the trees had fallen, and all the fruit had been ripped from the crowns. The crop was ruined.

It was no longer a hundred-tree grove. Nigel counted twelve still standing. But they had no berries. Several hundred pounds of dates had been lost to the storm. Nigel walked among the fallen trees, stepping around root balls almost as tall as himself, and he felt a profound sadness come over him.

He came to a standstill between two toppled giants that only that morning had stood as titans in the valley. Now they lay in such forlorn dejection that Nigel wanted to cry. He felt he had let them down. He turned in a slow circle, counting the trees that still stood among their fallen brothers, and a queer kind of fear suddenly gripped him.

He had never felt so vulnerable. It was frightening what nature could do. It was also humbling—a state of mind Nigel had never experienced before.

The Mexican workers emerged from their hiding places, sheepishly, looking as if they didn't want to get punished. But how could they have stopped the storm from doing this? Nigel was unaware of them as he grieved for his fallen trees and felt fear grip him most powerfully.

And then, as he stood there feeling pain throb in his arm, the warm sun starting to evaporate the pools and puddles of rainwater, creating a steam-bath atmosphere, the wailing sounds starting up in the Indian village, a new emotion swept into Nigel's heart, like his own private, dark storm, to push fear and sadness aside.

Raging anger boiled up inside him in a flash of self-righteous indignation. Nature had no right to do this to a man. It wasn't fair and it wasn't right.

He turned his face westward toward La Alma where, on the far side of the property, his larger orchard stood, and he wondered how much had been destroyed. And the newest grove, on Union Pacific land—was it, too, devastated, or had it been spared?

While the men around town inspected damage and asked after one another's shop or home, genuinely caring about their neighbors' good luck or bad luck, Nigel thought only of Nigel and how he was going to rebuild his empire.

And build it he would—rescuing these fallen trees, replanting them in sturdier soil, sturdier holes, packing them with good solid earth that wouldn't wobble under the first bit of water. Nigel pictured dams and ditches and channels to impede and divert future floods. He would keep himself better apprised of the weather—surely *someone* had seen signs of this storm coming.

Yes, he thought, starting to feel better, discovering that making plans helped a man allay his fears, that filling his head with plans made him forget his sadness and anger and the urge to curse his fate. A man had only to be informed and vigilant and he would not be vanquished next time. Nigel did not like feeling humbled. It was new to him. He didn't like it and he didn't intend to feel that way ever again.

He looked for his Mexican foremen—they would get started on the cleanup at once. The piles of fronds needed to be cleared and hauled away. The trees would need to be inspected for damage and their viability determined. Then he would arrange for the crane—when the ground was thoroughly dry again and could withstand the weight—and replant his orchards.

In fact, Nigel started to feel invigorated as he barked orders at his Mexicans, and they nodded vigorously, eager to show that they were still good workers despite what had happened. They all had families back in Mexico and desperately wanted to keep their jobs at Stullwood Plantation.

Nigel didn't look for Elizabeth or for anyone else. He was aware of people milling around, scratching their heads, going through debris, and the Indians wailing in their village, but he wasn't worried about Elizabeth. She was bound to be around somewhere. When Elizabeth did come into his thoughts at this moment, it was only in connection to her trust fund, which he was now going to help himself to. And he congratulated himself on the wisdom of not dipping into the fund before now.

With her large fortune, there was no limit to what Nigel Barnstable, ninth Baron Stullwood, could do.

CHAPTER THIRTY-FIVE

"I DON'T THINK ANYONE else is coming," Cody said. They had already delayed their departure by one hour. They had to get going. "It looks like we're it."

He was referring to the members of Citizens for Wilderness Preservation, who were joining in the effort to stop the groundbreaking ceremony in Big Horn Valley. They had exhausted all legal channels. The final court ruling was in favor of Quinlan, who had been given the go-ahead to commence building his resort.

Because the storm had also impacted Big Horn Valley, the ground-breaking ceremony had been postponed to give the sodden ground time to dry out so that trenching could begin. In the meantime, the residents of Palm Springs had banded together to clean up the town, repair and repaint buildings, all citizens pitching in whether they had suffered destruction or not. Those most severely affected were the small farmers, whose crops had been destroyed.

But the beautiful, perfect desert weather had returned, and optimism was high.

Everyone agreed things could have been worse. To see Mr. Barnstable's flattened groves, mighty trees felled by wind and rain, made folks think that their own little houses and shops could have just as easily been leveled, and yet they hadn't. The event reminded people how powerful nature could be, how nature had to be respected, and how fragile the environment was.

Walking through Barnstable's destroyed orchards, where Mexicans with ropes and chains hauled away trees that could not be saved, folks, thoughts went to Big Horn Valley, where the rocks and trees and wildlife were facing a different kind of destruction. If the people of the Coachella Valley had been keen on saving Big Horn Valley before the storm, they were now feeling protective of every single rock and stone and blade of grass in Big Horn Valley.

So a great convoy of cars and wagons and horses had been agreed upon and arranged, and the day was at hand.

"I don't understand," Elizabeth said, looking up and down the road. "I made sure everyone knew the date and the time, and absolutely everyone said they would participate." They stood anxiously beneath the blue May sky—Cody and Elizabeth and those who had come to La Alma, waiting in front of Elizabeth's house for the rest to show up. She had expected over a hundred people to stage the protest at noon. Only seven had come.

Elizabeth had also informed the editors-in-chief of major newspapers, as well as newsreel companies. She hoped they were already there, in Big Horn Valley. Quinlan would have photographers and reporters on hand as well, she knew, to commemorate the event. It would be a grand ceremony, with Quinlan digging the first shovelful of dirt before the work crew got started.

Elizabeth intended to stop him from digging the second shovelful.

Miss March, one of the teachers, said now, "Perhaps the others misunderstood and thought we were to gather at the foot of Chino Canyon."

Elizabeth rubbed her neck in frustration. She hadn't slept. She was nervous, anxious, even a little fearful. It had been a year since she first encountered the surveyors in Big Horn Valley and she had realized she must fight to preserve the wilderness—twelve months of hard work, campaigning, writing letters, talking to the press, talking to anyone who would listen, arguing in courtrooms, putting up posters, handing out flyers, Quinlan himself showing up at her house to harass and intimidate.

And now the moment of truth had arrived. All avenues exhausted, Elizabeth and her group now needed to get physical. However, once Quinlan dug that first ceremonial shovelful of dirt, Elizabeth knew, it was going to be next to impossible to stop the new resort hotel from going in.

It had to be today. Now.

Was Miss March right? Was it possible the others were already at Chino Canyon, waiting for her? Or were they simply staying away because the shock and fear were wearing off? Now that recovery from the violence was under way, crops getting replanted, roofs being repaired—had an old complacency come back and settled in? "I hope you're right," she said. "Let's go!"

"Wait," Cody said. "Someone's coming."

They watched as a chic little roadster sped up the dusty road from the west. And when it came to a halt at the base of La Alma's driveway, they watched a petite woman wearing a long skirt, blouse, and cardigan sweater step out. She held her hat to her head as she approached. "Am I too late? I had to stop and repair a tire." Mary Clark looked around. "Or am I too early? Where is everyone?"

Elizabeth ran down to give her a hug. "We think they're all at the canyon. Mary, you said you couldn't come!"

Clark spoke in a low voice. "In anticipation of possible arrest because of my association with Dr. Greene, I began putting my office and files in order. And I came across a newsletter published nine years ago by Margaret Sanger, promoting contraception using the slogan No Gods, No Masters. When I saw that slogan I was reminded that I am an advocate not only for women's rights but for the rights of anyone who is treated unfairly under the law, anyone who is exploited—or any place that is exploited." She smiled. "I might be in jail tomorrow, Elizabeth, but today I am going to add my voice to yours and tell the world that Big Horn Valley will have no gods or masters."

They went in three cars, heading west on Palm Canyon Drive. The Santa Anas were howling down from Utah and Nevada to screech across the Sahara-like dunes that stretched from Banning to Hot Springs. Cody had to fight to control the car as sand blasted the windshield and at times brought visibility to zero.

When they arrived at Chino Canyon in the shelter of foothills, they found no cars waiting. "Do you suppose they've already gone up to the valley?" Elizabeth asked. So many promises, the utter relief and gratitude for having survived the storm—where were they all?

"We have to hope so," Cody said. "We're running out of time."

They went slowly up the old logging road, Cody and Elizabeth and the two teachers in the lead car, the other two cars following. When they rounded a bend, Cody had to quickly slam on his breaks.

"What on earth!" Elizabeth cried.

The way before them was blocked by a pile of rocks and boulders and mountain debris.

"Was it an avalanche?" Ethel Kincaid asked, as they all got out to look.

Cody surveyed the blockage, scanned the mountain wall that rose on their left, saw boot prints in the dirt. "This is no natural avalanche. This was manmade. We won't be able to get around this roadblock in time. I'm sorry, Elizabeth, we can't get up to the valley before the groundbreaking ceremony."

* * *

Nigel watched impatiently as the sparkling water from Mesquite Creek trickled down his concrete ditch, into his cement reservoirs and then into the irrigation canals. This was completely unsatisfactory!

Despite the recent storm and flood, the desert was dry again, and with summer almost upon them, Nigel needed to get water to his new trees. He had purchased them from a broker in Mexico, who had shipped them across the border, female date palms with big clusters of orange berries hanging from their crowns. The crane had been brought out again, and another feat of planting, and the orchard was restored. But it needed water, and the engineer he had hired to repair the ditch was doing a miserable job of it.

Nigel thought briefly of the groundbreaking at Big Horn Valley and his chance at grabbing some good publicity for Stullwood Plantation. But this was more important. He had to go see what the fellow was doing up there now that the water wasn't running full force again.

Calling for his horse to be saddled, Nigel was soon galloping up Mesquite Canyon.

He reached the top end of his concrete ditch, where his foreman, Yancy, was sitting guard, a rifle lazily across his knees. He stood up when Nigel drew near.

Nigel eyed the small waterfall tumbling into the reservoir, a pale blue pool with an opalescent surface glinting in the sunlight, a delicate spray surrounding the fall, filling the air with a delightful mist. From here the water continued its journey down to the valley, but it wasn't enough. This waterfall should be thundering, foaming, sending up a drenching spray. Why was there still such a meager amount?

He looked around. "Where's Parsons?" he asked of Yancy.

"Lunch," Yancy grunted.

"Lunch! Well, when he gets back, you can tell him he's fired! I'm going up ahead to see what the problem is." From here down to the valley, the concrete ditch was in good shape and seemed to have no blockage. So clearly the problem lay farther upstream.

"Yessir," Yancy growled, and something occurred to him—that a man had a right to leave his job for a lunch break. A man working hard to fix a troubling ditch for a farm owner who never did have the courtesy of a please or thank you, denied the simple human right of lunch.

Unable to take his horse any farther, Nigel dismounted and took to the trail on foot. "You might not want to do that, sir," squint-eyed Yancy called out, half hoping Barnstable broke his fool neck but feeling the need to shout the warning anyway. "The run off is something fierce up there!"

But Nigel ignored him, setting his boots firmly on an ancient dirt path that had been trodden flat by generations of sandaled Indians.

The canyon grew narrow, the granite walls straight and shear, the water meandering along at his right. Here, occasional outcroppings of determined shrubbery dotted the stony walls—yellow and orange poppies, scarlet Indian paintbrush—and shaggy fan palms here and there.

The main falls stood just below the snow line, where he expected to find great foaming sheets of water thundering down, sending up an icy spray that pricked the face. Whatever was keeping the water from reaching his ditch, it lay just ahead.

*　　*　　*

Cody tried to budge the rocks and boulders that blocked the road. "I don't think the others are already up in the valley, Elizabeth. This avalanche was created during the night. Quinlan isn't taking any chances."

Then where was everyone? "Cody, go back into town. Find out why the others didn't show up."

He stood back, brushing off his hands. "I'm going up to the valley with you, Elizabeth. We can climb over this."

"Please, Cody. We don't have time to argue. The others and I can climb over this rubble and hurry to the building site." They had to get there before Quinlan drove his shovel into the dirt. That was the whole point to being there today. Otherwise, his triumphant picture would appear in the newspaper and they would give it a headline like, Quinlan Starts His Resort Without the Interference of Protestors. And then Elizabeth would be back to square one and have to start all over again and from a much weaker position. "Go, please."

He had to think about it. Cody wasn't a man to leave a group of helpless ladies stranded in the wilderness. "Let me help you over this roadblock," he said and held out his hand.

The women tackled the rocks and boulders, with Cody's help and by helping each other, pulling and pushing with great effort, slipping, snagging their stockings, but making it to the other side where they straightened their clothes and hurried along the old dirt road while they heard Cody start a car and go back down the canyon.

Elizabeth led the group across the grassy meadow to where Quinlan already stood at the building site with men in suits carrying briefcases, and men in overalls holding picks and shovels. There were flatbed trucks loaded with lumber and pipes, and large tractors waiting to start leveling the ground.

There were also policemen with paddy wagons.

The peaks of San Jacinto were still covered with snow, but the snows at this lower elevation had melted, to dissolve into powerful streams and run offs. The alpine air was brisk, causing people to shiver inside jackets and cardigans, but the profusion of rainbow-colored wildflowers gave promise of the summer soon to arrive.

Quinlan stood under an ancient oak tree that Elizabeth knew was scheduled to be cut down, the stump uprooted because it stood where the hotel's lobby was going to go. Surveyors' stakes with orange string tied to them marked where the cornerstone of the building was to be laid. Quinlan stood ready with a brand-new shovel, a big satin bow tied around the handle. A few feet away, a photographer adjusted his camera on a tripod, flash powder ready.

"Here they come!" one of Quinlan's companions said.

When Elizabeth and her friends arrived at the oak tree, a little out of breath and flushed in the cheeks, Quinlan grinned. "Is this it? Your big protest group? Seven women? Well, girlie," he said in amusement. "You're just in time for your arrest." He chuckled when he saw the big purse she carried. "Never know when you'll need a hankie, I guess," he said to his companions. They laughed.

"Okay, ladies," Elizabeth called out. "Now!" She pulled a long chain out of her large handbag, flung it around the trunk of the tree and twice around her waist, and before Quinlan could blink, produced a padlock and secured the chain. At the same instant, the women locked arms and formed a human barrier, blocking Quinlan from the patch of ground marked by orange stakes.

He turned and shouted at the police, "Get these women out of here!"

One policeman tried to ax the chain off the tree while other officers approached the women warily, and the photographer's flash powder exploded in a bright light, filling the air with the smell of magnesium. Quinlan snapped, "Don't take pictures of *this*, you idiot! And *you*!" Quinlan shouted at the reporter who was scribbling on a notepad. "Don't write any of this down."

"Yes!" Elizabeth cried. "Write it! Tell your readers that Jay Thomas Quinlan has no right to destroy a wilderness that belongs to the people!"

"For God's sake, woman, I'm going to create a paradise for people to come to."

"And you'll charge them money. I say people should be allowed to come to this valley for *free*!"

Quinlan kept his smile fixed as he said, "I'm not spoiling anything, just making it accessible for folks to come and stay awhile. You've been harping about making Big Horn Valley available to all citizens. That's exactly what I'm aiming to do."

"But with a big hotel? Swimming pools? Golf courses? That sounds like ruination to me. As long as I draw breath," Elizabeth added, "there will be no resort built in this valley."

She pointed to the cameras being hand-cranked by cameramen. "How do you think movie audiences will react to the brutal arrest of peaceful people who are simply trying to save a forest? You can have the police manhandle us and take us away in handcuffs, but it won't be in secret. You can't do this hidden behind doors anymore."

Quinlan looked at the film cameras. He knew what they would capture: a slender, blond-haired young woman wearing a flowing white dress as if she were a goddess—or a movie star—chained to a tree and standing defiantly before a man twice her age and a hundred pounds heavier.

"And I can promise you, Mr. Quinlan," Elizabeth said, her voice growing stronger, "we will be back and in greater numbers."

Quinlan shrugged. "Then you'll see more of the inside of a jail than you will of this valley. And while you're dining on bread and water, trying to remember what the sun looked like, I'll be building my hotel on this spot."

She tipped her chin. "Then I suggest you hire a large security staff for round-the-clock protection, because you can't keep the entire population of the Coachella Valley in jail. We'll keep coming, Mr. Quinlan, until you leave this valley once and for all."

Quinlan shrugged. "Fine. I can afford as large a security staff as I need. I can also fence this entire meadow if I have to. And yes, I will put everyone in jail."

The reporter wrote down every word.

Leaning close, Quinlan said in a quiet voice, "You don't want a war with me, girlie. Trust me, it will only end badly for you."

Her eyes met his and she read the unmistakable message in them: No woman was going to get the better of Jay Thomas Quinlan.

"Sergeant," Quinlan said, "Start with that one," and he pointed to Miss Napier, the last in the human chain and the smaller of the two teachers. "Arrest her!"

*   *   *

Reaching the topmost thundering waterfall, Nigel turned and looked down. He frowned. So far, whatever was blocking the water between here and the beginning of his aqueduct was eluding him.

He was above the crests of the fan palms, where he could see all the way into the valley. At the base of the canyon, a few thousand feet down, the land was flat, expansive. He could see the patchwork quilt of Stullwood Plantation, green squares interrupted by yellow stretches. The view was blocked by rocky outcroppings and the shaggy tops of palms. If he stepped out onto the boulders, he would be able to see all of the valley and into Arizona.

As he secured his footing, planting his feet firmly on the first boulder with the water foaming and roaring, Nigel felt as conquerors before him must have felt—God-powerful, invincible. If only Grandmother and brother Rupert could see him now, as they sat on the green lawns that were planted by others, as they walked through forests grown generations ago—Grandmother and Rupert themselves contributing nothing, creating nothing, changing nothing.

He drank in the breathtaking view of desert and mountains then turned to get back to solid ground. But as he started back across the slippery boulders, he saw, on the bank of the churning stream, a red diamond rattlesnake, as big as a python, coiled, its rattle held high, its head swaying on a long neck, forked tongue flicking in and out. He looked to his left. The boulders were too wet and too far apart for him to reach the other bank. He had to go back the way he came.

He looked at the snake, its menacing eyes fixed on him.

*   *   *

A burly policeman in a long black tunic coat ran up and placed meaty hands on Miss Napier. Grabbing the teacher by the waist he pulled her away from Miss March but their arms remained steadfastly locked. As the cameras rolled and magnesium exploded in photographers' hods, as the other cops snickered and the workmen laughed, enjoying a day of feminine hijinks instead of having to work, Miss Napier gave out a shriek. The officer pulled at her, yanking her off her feet so that her legs shot up in the air, kicking, and her skirt flew up.

"Hang on, Millie!" Miss March cried. "I've got you!"

With her free arm, Miss Napier lashed out and knocked the cop's helmet off. The construction workers and truck drivers burst out laughing. When Miss Napier clouted the officer in the face, they cheered. Other policemen rushed forward, reaching for the women, the officers' faces boiling with indignation.

Struggling to keep her lock-hold on Mary Clark's arm, Elizabeth watched Miss Napier in fascination. The prim and petite schoolteacher had turned into a feisty wildcat as she flailed and kicked and twisted her body this way and that as now three policemen tried to harness her.

And the surprising Mrs. Kincaid, a sedentary widow whose life was concerned with needles and threads, buttonholes and seams, now digging her heels staunchly into the soil of Big Horn Valley.

Battle brings out our hidden strengths, Elizabeth thought in amazement, as the eight women, locked in a line like a chain, anchored to the massive oak tree, struggled to keep their balance as, at one end Miss Napier fought the good fight with three annoyed and bewildered policemen, while at the other Elizabeth held on to the chain around the tree trunk and Mary Clark's elbow.

Mary Clark, linked to Elizabeth's right arm, was hoping they got arrested. What a forum it would be for human rights. "Those are city police!" she yelled to the reporters. "They are out of their jurisdiction. And we have a right to be here."

"This is private property, little girl," Quinlan said smugly.

"We do not recognize the legitimacy of the sale of state land to private citizens," Mary shot back. "And city police have no authority here."

"They're here to evict trespassers from private property."

"Then show us your warrant."

"What do you know about warrants?" Quinlan said.

"I'm a lawyer," she said, as she struggled to remain upright, the battle at the end of the line was so fierce.

"Lawyer!" Quinlan barked. He looked Clark up and down. "Are you really a lawyer?"

"Yes, I am."

He laughed and his companions chuckled. "Well, little girl," he said, folding his arms, "I'd say you need to grow a few inches and wait a few years. And then I suggest you get yourself a pecker." Turning to Elizabeth, he said, "And to you, little lady, I recommend you ask your lawyer here how much jail time you can expect for this trespass. I'm going to tell you just one time, little lady," Quinlan said. "Step aside and allow us to proceed."

"We are not budging."

Quinlan squinted up at the sky, the alpine breeze ruffling his perfect haircut. He tugged at his shirt cuffs, causing diamond cufflinks to wink with sunlight. He seemed to roll a few things around in his mind. Then he turned, placed two fingers in his mouth and let loose a whistle so sharp that it hurt everyone's ears. In unison, the tractor operators brought their great motors to life, smoke belched from exhaust pipes, and giant rubber tires began to roll.

Six behemoths, as if awakened from a prehistoric hibernation, began to trundle forward, causing the ground to tremble. The engine roar was like thunder. The smell of fumes stung the pristine air. And they came steadily forward, the faces of the operators grim with duty.

* * *

Nigel was trapped.

He couldn't cross to the other bank, and the rattlesnake guarded the way he had come.

And then Nigel saw, in a clump of stunted trees, a shadowy watcher, standing, staring. "For God's sake, man," Nigel called. "Kill the damn snake!"

The man didn't move. Nigel narrowed his eyes. It wasn't Yancy, but the fellow looked somehow familiar. He was a young Indian, and he wore a midnight-blue shirt with white buttons, a bright yellow kerchief tied around his neck.

No! It couldn't be—*Johnny Pinto is dead* . . .

Realizing the snake wasn't going to move, Nigel turned carefully to his left and stepped out, his foot reaching for the boulder. Arms out for balance, he touched his toes to the rock.

As he conquered the boulder, he suddenly felt his feet fly out from under him. Over he went. Pain shot through his skull where it struck a boulder. And the water was so cold it felt like shards of glass . . .

* * *

As the tractors rolled menacingly toward the vulnerable women, Elizabeth glanced at Mary Clark. Certainly Quinlan would not go that far?

"Even if you push us aside with machinery," she said, "we will keep coming back. Even after your hotel is built, we will block the roads and put up protest signs." But as she spoke these brave words, she felt a quick, cold moment of self-doubt. Was she doing the right thing? Or was she acting impulsively and putting her friends in harm's way? A hobgoblin whispered in her mind: *Back down. Run away to safety.*

And suddenly the word "foolhardy" jumped into her brain.

Yes, she thought in a flood of last-minute timidity. This is reckless. I don't know what I'm doing. Best to give in for now and regroup to fight another day.

But then Quinlan didn't respond to her threat. Didn't even bother with a word or acknowledgment that she had spoken. With his eyes on the tractors, he flicked his hand at her, a fly-swatting gesture.

The fear stopped in her throat as she stared at him. She had seen that gesture before—many times in the past months. And a strange truth dawned on her—that she wasn't so much in this valley to stop the stacking of bricks and mortar as to stand up to Nigel.

Elizabeth turned and looked at the giant bighorn petroglyph on the mountain's face, the sun shining directly on the figure like a spotlight, and Elizabeth felt everything change—the world, herself, anything that had meaning. Suddenly she knew, in a bright, sharp revelation, that everything that had happened up until this moment was not about saving the valley, not saving the sheep or the petroglyphs. It hadn't been about them, or even Nigel and Quinlan. It had all been about her.

In that instant, something broke free inside her. A sudden courage she had never felt before, had not even known she possessed. Suddenly she wasn't afraid anymore. Not of Quinlan. Not of Nigel.

She measured the arrogant pose of Jay Thomas Quinlan, looked at the policemen and burly construction workers lined up behind him and the tractors coming steadily toward her and her group, and she thought: No. You don't get your way. My life as a victim—of my husband, of my father, of a society that says women have to be controlled—ends here.

"Hold the line, ladies!" she cried out. "Don't let the bullies weaken our resolve."

"Oh, dear," Mary Clark murmured as the tractors came closer, grew larger in her sight, mean-eyed men at the controls.

The ground shook. Movie cameras rolled. "Keep coming!" Quinlan shouted, waving his arms to direct the machines to where he stood. "We are going to break ground, and we are not going to let anyone stand in our way."

The stench from the gasoline fumes was sickening. The roar of the motors was deafening. But the eight women held steadfast as the giant, stinking beasts drew down upon them.

"Hey!" one of the policemen shouted, pointing. "Who the hell are *they*?"

Quinlan turned. The policemen turned, everyone turned to look back at the entrance to the valley. Even the tractor drivers, turning off their motors just feet from their human targets, rose from their seats to stare.

"What the hell?" Quinlan murmured.

Wagons and cars and riders on horseback were coming across the wilderness from the old logging road—the Perrys and the Allenbys, the Decaturs and Schipleys—everyone from Palm Springs and beyond.

And behind the townsfolk, hundreds more people—on foot, in cars, riding horses and wagons. Men, women, and children. Their skin variously hued from light to dark bronze, but all black-haired, wearing straw hats or shawls, long skirts and baggy trousers, the women in braids, the men with short-hair and bandanas.

Indians. Elizabeth recognized Luisa and Diego at the head of the astounding throng. But they were far more numerous than those who lived at Palm Springs. She realized that they were members from other bands—Morongo, Soboba, Santa Rosa. Luisa must have sent out the call to all the Cahuilla in the Coachella Valley, and now here they were!

To arrive silently and en masse, to stand shoulder to shoulder with Elizabeth and the citizens of Palm Springs. A formidable showing of Cahuilla unity and dedication. She also realized in a moment of curious irony that these would be the same ones Nigel had hired to work his first orchard, but Chief Diego sent them away, forbidding them to work for the white man.

And now they had come to stand with the white man.

"Christ Almighty!" Quinlan shouted, putting his hands on his hips as the horde made up of white people and Indians advanced toward him. "What is this? The frigging cavalry?"

Cody's car came to a halt in a cloud of dust and gravel; he jumped out. "Are we too late?" He looked at Quinlan, the shiny shovel, the untouched ground. "I guess we came just in time," he said with a grin.

The newly arrived women climbed down from cars and wagons and went to link arms with those chained to the tree, creating a formidable line, while the men walked around them and planted themselves in front of the human chain, facing down the policemen with batons who threatened their wives and sisters and daughters.

"Sergeant!" Quinlan shouted. "Arrest these people!"

The officer frowned. "I can't arrest the lot of them, sir. I haven't the manpower."

As Cody went to stand with Elizabeth, he kept a close eye on the truck drivers and construction workers, whose fists held hammers and shovels and axes. If a brouhaha were to break out, Cody thought, his senses sharp and alert, would the police have enough manpower to protect the citizens?

Quinlan surveyed the line of men and said with a sneer, "Do you fellas always let your women do your talking for you?"

With that, Cody removed his jacket, folded it, and draped it on a nearby bush. "Well, friend," he said as he slowly unbuttoned his cuffs and rolled up his shirtsleeves. "Where I come from there's talking and there's *talking*, if you get my drift."

Quinlan snorted. "Is that supposed to be some sort of cowboy challenge?"

"Take it however you want. But we don't want you here in this valley."

As if on cue, the valley grew still. A hawk cried overhead but received no reply. As the gathered men and women stood statue-like in a curious standoff that a passerby would puzzle over, Elizabeth looked from Cody to Quinlan and deemed them physically an even match. But she wagered that Cody would win if it came to blows.

*　　*　　*

Nigel gasped, surfaced from the churning water, and tried to get a handhold. But the current carried him down the stream, where he tumbled, was thrown this way and that. He felt the pebbles of the creek bed beneath his boots. He was carried past jutting rocks and rotted logs. He struggled for air as the current pulled him under, tossed him around, and allowed him to come up again, choking and coughing.

Quickly he went, going by so rapidly that he couldn't distinguish landmarks on the banks. Where were his guards? Couldn't they hear his shouts?

Faster he fell, tumbling end over end, hitting large rocks, tearing his flesh on outcropping plants. He heard a leg bone snap, felt pain shoot through him.

And then he was in free fall, dropping down a waterfall to land with a thud on the lip of his concrete reservoir. He was at the headwater of his ditch! But now the water was running with force, as if the blockage had been cleared. He cried out for help. Yancy was here, the others. And then he saw them. Standing on the bank, unmoving, offering not a hand or a branch for rescue. Their faces impassive as they watched the waters of San Jacinto vent their wrath on him.

Another snapping sound, another searing pain. Water filled his lungs. He went under and came back up. He was riding a water slide now, on his back, his arms and legs in the air. He could see the valley rushing up to meet him. Blood streamed down from his scalp. His other arm caught on something and wrenched his shoulder from its socket. He screamed in pain.

Down he went, unable to catch himself, unable to stop. The force too strong for one man. Leaving Yancy and the guards far behind. Leaving Nigel to the mercy of the mountain's secret and ancient forces.

And then he was floating, and everything slowed down. It gave him time to consider Yancy and the guards, watching him with such dispassion that they reminded him of himself on the day his father's will was read and Nigel, in pain and fury, had vowed to start over and make something of himself.

It was funny, this business of being crushed by water. It was as if time had slowed. He was aware of every gurgle, every ripple, every shining droplet that frothed up. Slowly, the minutes stretching like rubber so that the downward plunge, brutal and swift, felt like a leisurely glide. Maybe God wanted him to experience his death for a long time because that was how it seemed to the ninth Baron Stullwood. A lazy, dawdling tumble down a gentle cascade. Rationally, he knew it was an illusion, that the knock to his head had ricocheted his brain off his skull, causing all sorts of crazy notions to float through his mind as he raced to his doom.

Freezing water filled his mouth and nostrils and roared in his ears. He didn't know if he was upright or upside down. Slowly he tumbled, although to an observer, his descent was swift and savage. Faces floated before his eyes, like grotesque balloons, mocking him: Grandmother, Rupert, Richard Ostermond. And then a pretty face framed in sunlight-colored hair. Her name occurred to him: Elizabeth. It felt strange to think about her, he had gotten so out of the habit.

The water rushed and churned and his right shoulder came loose, shooting him through with agony. He could have sworn his concrete ditch was only two thousand feet long, so why did it seem as if he were being swept for miles?

He saw the final reservoirs coming, big cement tanks greedily awaiting the canyon's water. He tried to stop himself. But his one good leg snapped and sent him in a spin. When he fell toward the reservoir it was headfirst.

As his skull connected with the concrete lip of the tank, Nigel heard a voice in his head, loud and almost shouting, the voice of a little solicitor named Radcliffe, who cleared his throat too often, shouting, "You are ambitious. You were ambitious as a boy and grew to be an overly ambitious man. With this fierce ambition comes impatience and poor planning. Impatience leads to failure." Radcliffe's voice but his father's words in his final letter to his eldest son. Predicting his eldest son's fate.

As the icy waters closed over his eyes and face and filled his lungs, he silently cried: Take me back, Father, take me back! I want to start again . . .

*　　*　　*

Although Cody and Quinlan were squared off, it was Chief Diego who spoke. Everyone heard him as he said in a loud, dignified voice, "This is sacred land. You cannot have it. You cannot change it. You cannot build on it. Our ancestors live here. We cannot let you disturb them."

Silence fell over the valley as the two groups eyed each other, and hostility charged the air. The workmen in overalls shifted nervously as they gripped their shovels and pickaxes, and the policemen fingered their billy clubs. The movie cameramen stood ready to film today's event for newsreels to be shown in theaters across the country.

"What the hell are they doing here?" Quinlan growled to his lawyers. He had been assured that the local natives had relinquished all interest in this valley long ago. His legal team merely shrugged.

He turned back to Elizabeth and looked at her anew. Convincing the townspeople to join her fight was one thing, convincing an entire Indian tribe—the very race that claimed to be the original owners of this whole region—was another. He had underestimated her. He had made the crucial mistake of underestimating his opponent. Because she was a woman. This was something new: women who had to be reckoned with.

It wouldn't happen again. If this was going to be something new in the business world—his glance flickered to the woman lawyer at Elizabeth Barnstable's side—then Quinlan was going to adjust. He might even be the first man to adjust and, therefore, get an edge on his competition.

Without a word, he turned on his heel and marched back to the line of cars, his lawyers scurrying after him. The policemen, looking at each other, returned to the paddy wagons. The construction workers, likewise exchanging confused looks, turned and climbed aboard flatbed trucks. The drivers, who had watched the whole thing from their vehicles, started their engines. The operators of the behemoth tractors brought their beasts to life and after a moment, the stately parade of cars, trucks, tractors, and police wagons headed back to the paved road.

The townspeople filled the valley with cheers and catcalls, while the Indians smiled and quietly congratulated themselves.

Elizabeth went up to Luisa and Chief Diego. "I never thought you would join us. What changed your mind?"

With the late afternoon breeze rippling his shoulder-length white hair, Chief Diego said, "We thought we Indians were alone. The Señor has been stealing water from us, and we thought no one cared. We thought white men were our enemy. And then you and your friends helped us when the storm came. You saved our babies and our children." He turned to Cody, standing next to Elizabeth. "You saved my life, Señor. You put yourselves in danger. I asked the spirits: can Diego Padilla do no less?"

The Indians climbed back into their trucks and wagons and horses, or walked on foot, while the townsfolk returned to their cars.

When Cody came up with a key for the padlock, Elizabeth said, "Cody, where was everyone? Why did they come so late?"

"They thought today's protest had been cancelled."

The chain fell from her waist. "Cancelled!"

Reverend Scott stepped forward. "Mrs. Lardner telephoned me and said the event had been cancelled."

"Me too," Mr. Marden, the druggist, said.

"It was Augie Lardner who told me," said another. "Came to my house last night to say you had cancelled the protest."

It was finally sorted out that Lois Lardner had received a phone call from a man identifying himself as a colleague of Mary Clark, calling to inform everyone that the protest had been called off and asking her to please inform as many residents as she could. While Lois had called those who were on the telephone, Augie and Mr. Allenby had driven around town and to outlying residences to tell everyone it had been cancelled. The few who did show up hadn't been home to receive the word.

"And when we all arrived at the foot of Chino Canyon," Cody said, "there was Diego with his people. So we came up together. You did it, Elizabeth. You stood up to a powerful corporation and you won."

"It isn't over yet."

"It will be. Quinlan will find a way to make it look like pulling out of Big Horn Valley was his idea. Take the credit, Elizabeth."

"But I wasn't alone. I had help."

He shook his head. "Without you, Elizabeth, these people would not have come here to stop Quinlan."

The sun dipped behind the mountain, and San Jacinto cast its elegant shadow over the valley. The air grew chill. Elizabeth looked at the towering petroglyph, listened to the silence. She didn't know if they had seen the last of Quinlan or not. She didn't know if the fight had ended today or if it would go on for years. But she did know one thing: her campaign hadn't been about Quinlan. It had been about standing up to all men like Quinlan and Nigel who believed themselves to be entitled and privileged, who ran over people like a steamroller, who took whatever they wanted without asking.

She wondered what Nigel was going to say when he heard about what happened today. No doubt he would manage to place himself here at the event, in a letter to an editor, or in advertising copy, and claim all credit for Stullwood Plantation.

Elizabeth stared at the giant bighorn petroglyph on the mountain's face, looking otherworldly in the sunless twilight. She imagined the ancient artists up there on ladders with wooden hammers and stone chisels to patiently chip away the representation of a giant bighorn sheep. It could not have been an easy endeavor. Their message, though lost, must have been important. No single man, Quinlan or Nigel, had the right to destroy it. Nigel was wrong. This was not a land to conquer and change. It was a land to embrace and protect.

Elizabeth thought of New York and her path from a society girl to a woman of the West. She felt the desert and its mountain wilderness settle into her soul, as if to say: You have come home.

CHAPTER THIRTY-SIX

The string quartet played "Clair de Lune" in the shade of the towering date palms. A space had been cleared between two orchards, creating an area for the minister and the bridal party, and for a hundred chairs for the wedding guests. They were slowly filling up as the Lardners and Allenbys and other citizens of Palm Springs, as well as friends who traveled out from New York, came to celebrate the union of Elizabeth Van Linden and Cody McNeal—a garden of silks and chiffons, whites and pastels, ladies in extravagant hats and fluttering skirts, men in white flannels and straw boater hats. A welcome occasion to dress up in the desert and look forward to an afternoon of feasting, drinking, and dancing.

The lawyer, Mary Clark, was among the guests, as well as Dr. Violet Greene, whose legal case was gaining such national attention and sympathy that the attorney general, behind closed doors, was secretly working to drop the whole matter. Times were changing, as was the political climate. It was predicted that certain federal laws, argued to be unconstitutional, such as the prohibition of alcohol and the criminalizing of birth control, were soon going to be repealed.

The talk among the guests, as they spoke quietly while they awaited the entrance of the bride, was of the Quinlan Hotels and Resorts Corporation, headquartered in Dallas, Texas, withdrawing plans to develop Big Horn Valley. Jay Thomas Quinlan, CEO of the corporation, had told the press that he had backed out of the project because the conservationists had convinced him it was the right thing to do.

Claiming now to embrace and support such a worthy cause, Quinlan let it be known that his company was donating huge amounts to the Sierra Club and other environmental organizations. He sold the valley back to the State of California, making it public lands again. Then he had purchased a hundred acres in Palm Springs to develop into a world-class resort with a two-hundred-room hotel, swimming pools, tennis courts, and a golf course. His new resort, Quinlan added, was going to offer guided hiking and horse riding tours through the protected wilderness that was maintained through Quinlan funding.

The rest of the talk was about work that had begun on paving the main road, now called Palm Canyon Drive, linking Banning to Indio, making travel to the desert faster and easier. And once Sierra Power brought electricity to the valley, Palm Springs was going to enjoy a boom.

Indians had been invited to the wedding as well, but they preferred to stand along the sides and at the back of the seated white people, as they were unaccustomed to sitting in chairs.

Luisa, standing with Diego, looked back to the day, a year ago, when the Cahuilla bands had joined together in one cause at Big Horn Valley. All the cousins and uncles and aunts standing together as Indians.

We are not losing our Indian selves, she thought now, as she listened to the strange but pleasant music played on mystifying instruments. We are evolving, we are moving with the times, but we remain at heart Iviatim. Perhaps we can celebrate both Mukat and Christmas. Many years ago, we did not give gifts of cloth and bread because the Indian did not have cloth and bread. And then the white man brought them and we made gifts of them. Now we have phonograph records and hairbrushes. What is the difference? Cloth and records. We can still make gifts of them.

Looking back also on that day in Mesquite Canyon four years ago when the red diamond rattlesnake had spoken to her, she recalled also the first message from the spirits—the vision of a sunrise. She had thought it portended disaster. But now she realized that the dawn symbolized the future. That was the meaning of the message from the brown-and-yellow bird. That her people were to take heart and embrace the future.

We will be modern Indians. We will not be left behind, and we will not be forgotten.

Up at the big house, a catering service worked in the kitchen to create a feast that was to be enjoyed out on the patio, where long tables were being laid with white table cloths, china and silver, and floral arrangements. In the bunkhouse, mariachi musicians with their trumpets, guitars, and violins, and very wide sombreros, were getting into their black and silver charro outfits for the wedding reception. An area of the patio had been cleared for dancing.

In her bedroom, Elizabeth put the final touches to her bridal ensemble with help from her mother, Libby, and Fiona. The long chiffon veil flowed from a Juliet cap tightly hugging her blond hair. The dress, drop-waisted with narrow shoulder straps and reaching the ankles, was made of silk jersey with a top layer of sparkly tulle. Her bouquet was made up of stunning white roses and white calla lilies.

Elizabeth had thought that, due to her previous marital status, she should not wear white, but Mrs. Van Linden would not be cheated out of her big wedding at last.

It had been a year since Nigel's death.

The Mexican workers had retrieved Nigel's body from the ditch where he died. Yancy had told the Sheriff that he had followed his boss up the trail and had seen him standing on boulders at the waterfall. "I called out to him, but he didn't hear me. He was talking to someone in the trees, shouting at him to shoot the rattlesnake. But, for the life of me, Sheriff, I didn't see no snake and I didn't see no one in the trees. He musta been imagining it. And that's when he fell. Me 'n my boys we ran down after him and tried to catch him but the water was too swift."

Elizabeth had hated Nigel and had been trying to leave him, but when she saw his shocking, broken body, she had cried. She had arranged through the mortuary in Indio to have the casket sealed and Nigel's body shipped back to England, where he was laid to rest in the Stullwood family crypt. She had received a gracious letter on elegant stationery from Nigel's grandmother, the Dowager Baroness, and one from his brother Rupert, to whom Nigel's title had passed. They had politely invited her to come to England for a visit, but she would never go.

She and Cody had waited a respectable twelve months before setting a date. And now the day had arrived, and Elizabeth was so buoyant with joy, she felt luminous. In a few minutes, she was going to be Mrs. Cody McNeal. She had never thought such happiness was possible. Their future together dazzled.

Elizabeth was going to continue to run the plantation, now called McNeal Farms. She had met with Pedro Gonzalez and other growers, joining their cooperative and assuring them that her prices would reflect the going rate established by the cooperative. She took down the billboard outside of Indio, but left the one near Banning, with only a change of names—the association with wilderness protection remained. She also now hired Chief Diego's people to work in her orchards and paid them good wages, as well as paying for water from the Mesquite stream, with Chief Diego regulating the flow at the top of the ditch. Together, the plantation and the Indians would prosper.

Cody, in the meantime, was making a name for himself as a Western writer. He had published a second book, an account of life on a Montana ranch during the last years of the American frontier, peopling it with legends whose paths he had crossed—Wild Bill Hickok, Calamity Jane, Annie Oakley, Chief Sitting Bull, Jesse James. Next, he planned to write about the Cahuilla Indians, through interviews with Chief Diego and Luisa, their heads a treasure house of Indian lore, culture, myths, and legends.

Elizabeth looked through her bedroom window at the mountain towering over her property and thought of the fight she was going to continue—to have this wilderness legally protected and declared a state or national reserve. *I will invite scholars to Big Horn Valley—naturalists, anthropologists, Indian ethnographers—to sketch and photograph the artwork, perhaps to unravel the mystery of the pictographs . . .*

Emancipation, she knew now, did not lie in voting, or driving a car, or bobbing one's hair. Emancipation meant finding one's place in the world, one's purpose. She would keep the date plantation going, but her heart lay in this desert and these mountains, in their preservation and protection. With help from her friends, the Cahuilla, and with the man she loved at her side.

"We're done!" Mrs. Van Linden declared, admiring her daughter with tears in her eyes. "I'll go down and tell them to begin. Your father is just outside."

Mrs. Van Linden and Libby hurried down from the house, while Elizabeth and Fiona took their places at the head of the stone steps leading from the patio down to the orchard. Elizabeth took her father's arm, while Fiona was to be accompanied by Doc Perry.

The quartet switched to Bach's "Jesu, Joy of Man's Desiring," the minister stood beneath a rose bower, with Cody waiting for his bride. His black tuxedo was tailored in Western style, with charcoal floral embroidery on the jacket yokes, charcoal piping on the scalloped cuffs and pockets. Underneath, a black satin vest, a white shirt, and the Montana-gold bolo tie at the collar. His cowboy boots were polished, minus the spurs. For the occasion, a brand-new, black, tall-crowned, wide-brimmed Stetson on his head.

Fiona and Leland reached the rose bower and separated, with Fiona standing to the left, Leland to the right as Cody's best man. Elizabeth stood at the end of the aisle on her father's arm. Mr. Van Linden gave her hand a squeeze, his eyes filled with pride and admiration and love.

The string quartet struck up "Here Comes the Bride," the guests all rose, and with her eyes on Cody, Elizabeth began her walk down the aisle.

Cody watched her glide toward him, unable to believe his eyes, to believe his luck. All the miles he had covered, beneath prairie skies, in the shadow of majestic mountains, through deep snow and searing heat, in what he had thought was a search for a man but which had turned out to be a search for his heart's longing. He hoped someday to understand how it was that he deserved such a reward from such an unremarkable life, for certainly greater men than he deserved this great prize. Maybe in distant years, with the wisdom of age, the answer would come to him. For now, however, he could only stare at her and marvel that such an angel had come into this life, that she was his.

She came to a stop at his side and handed her bouquet to Fiona while her father went to join Mrs. Van Linden in the front row.

The minister began the service. As bees droned in the air, Cody and Elizabeth heard little of what the minister said, aware only of each other, swimming in each other's eyes, thinking the million thoughts that come to people on such a day.

They emerged from the wonder of each other long enough to recite vows they had prepared, Cody's from Shoshone Indian tradition, Elizabeth's from the Bible.

Cody took Elizabeth's hands and said, "Fair is the white star of twilight, and the sky clearer at the day's end; but Elizabeth is fairer, and she is dearer. Elizabeth, my heart's friend. Fair is the white star of twilight, and the moon roving to the sky's end; but Elizabeth is fairer, better worth loving. She, my heart's friend—to whom I pledge my life, my soul, my love."

Elizabeth looked up into his eyes and said, "Dearest Cody, entreat me not to leave you, or to return from following after you, for where you go I will go, and where you stay I will stay. Your people will be my people, and your God will be my God. And where you die, I will die and there I will be buried. May the Lord do with me and more if anything but death parts you from me."

Wind rustled the crowns of the date palms, dappling the gathered guests in pools of sunlight and shadow. A red-tailed hawk wheeled gracefully overhead, carving a sacred circle against the blue sky. In the distance, the train whistle of the Southern Pacific's *Sunset Limited* sounded.

In this sylvan retreat, among friends and flora, the air pure and perfect, Elizabeth and Cody lost themselves in each other as they spoke, "I do," and placed rings on each other's fingers.

The minister said, "By the authority vested in me by the State of California, I now pronounce you husband and wife. You may kiss the bride."

Cody bent his head and removed his Stetson—the only time in a cowboy's life when he removed his hat and kissed Elizabeth on the lips. The guests erupted in cheers while the quartet started Mendelssohn's "Wedding March," and out on the patio caterers waited with champagne and caviar, and the mariachi band got ready to strike up the first lively dance of the day.

As Elizabeth and Cody parted long enough to hold hands and start their retreat down the aisle, Elizabeth called to mind a line from Tennyson's *The Lotos-Eaters*: "In the afternoon they came unto a land/ In which it seemed always afternoon." Adding the closing line of the poem: "We will no longer roam."